Ah, Sweet Life

E. Adrian Dzahn

For permissions contact the author at eadzahn@comcast.net.

ISBN: 1507633092
ISBN 13: 9781507633090
Library of Congress Control Number: 2015900894
CreateSpace Independent Publishing Platform
North Charleston, South Carolina
First published in 2015

To Dave

In Memory of S.E.B.

Overture

ANCIENT HISTORY, PRIMORDIAL history—volcanic eruptions, glaciers moving and melting, ocean channels formed fifty million years ago—are recorded in these cliffs and all along the Washington coast. From up north near the Quileute Indian Reservation to down past the Queets and Quinault Rivers, the shoreline varies from sandy and stone beaches to low and easily flooded grassland to high, hard bluffs like the one behind me. In this particular spot, the Pacific has carved out a cove tranquil enough for small fish to survive. The unusual calm must be owing to the wide boulders curving around the cove's inner rim and the tall basalt rocks near the entrance, aligned like so many gravestones.

When we were here in August, harbor seals basked on the wider boulders. After the children's noises frightened them off, we went down the trail by the beach homes and climbed around the cliff into the cove. While she scanned the horizon with her binoculars, I poked at driftwood on the crescent of sand. "Come, look," she'd shouted, motioning quickly with her free hand. I had hurried over and stood where the boulder sloped up several inches, so our shoulders were even. She had on my cap almost to her eyebrows to keep the bangs still. At the party, with both in their navy blue, you could see right away they were mother and son.

Peering through the binoculars, I was stunned. Gray whales, too many to count, emerged under the rising mist, gliding with the slow, majestic dignity of a coronation. Arched gray block after arched gray block, another and another and another, the ocean's waves and currents no more of an impediment than air. "Must be fifteen, twenty," I'd said.

"Their flotillas can be in the hundreds, but this is really late for their migration. Boy, he's going to be jealous." Bring him next summer, I'd told her, but his crazy mutt will bark himself hoarse. Would he still be into whales anyway? The teenage years weren't just about physical changes.

That day we saw cormorants, gunnels, sea stars, snails, and all colors of seaweed. Today, the only signs of life, besides the keening gull overhead, are a few stalwart perch.

The book on marine animals has a chapter on how fish care for their young. In most species, the mother does the heavy hauling, but in a few, the male broods the eggs. In the gafftopsail catfish, the father carries the fertilized eggs in his mouth for weeks. When they hatch, he releases them into the water, but his paternal duties don't end: for an additional month he remains nearby so the babies can rush to his mouth for safety. How is that unconscious impulse handed down from generation to generation? Carried in genes on a strand of DNA? Imprinted after birth? And has Nature instilled any plan for when offspring cannot be protected?

Of course, no catfish—gafftopsail or other kind—can live this far north. The Pacific here never warms, not like the Gulf, not even like the Atlantic, where I was hatched and brooded into girlhood. A three-thousand-mile odyssey, though not across sea.

Overhead, clouds convene. The waves are breaking hard; this is April, after all, not August. Whitecaps dot the ocean where the whales had floated. The tall basalt rocks protect me from the wind's brunt. The seals have gone elsewhere this most un-pacific day. Spray hits the crescent of sand, and I retreat, my jeans speckled dark. I glance at the rolled-up sleeping bag and tarp.

Unanswered questions return, questions that have followed me these three thousand miles. *Had* he been told? Had he known decades earlier, while she was in the institution? Were there moments when he thought of calling? If I had gone to his apartment, would I have found a letter?

I look for the high-tide mark and unroll the tarp.

Book One

Chapter 1

"THAT'S THE LOOP." Keeping the motor running, he pointed to the tall buildings.

I climbed down from the cab, slung the knapsack over my shoulder, and thanked him. He was the best of the bunch, picking me up near Toledo and driving all night. Sure beat the joker in Hershey who'd asked if I was a boy or a girl. "Yeah," I'd said. Or the first ride, which got me out of Brackton, asking if I was albino. "No, Gemini."

The street was deserted like in some *Twilight Zone* episode. It wasn't quite dawn, but for a Friday morning, at least *some* folks should've been heading to work. The factories in the distance belching puffs of smoke were the only signs of human activity. I hit the gas station kitty-corner, bought a pack of cigarettes, and sprung for a map of the *Greater Chicago Area 1968*. How many streets could've changed in one year? The El people could tell me where to transfer, the cashier said, and which bus went to the college, and yes, the ladies' room was around back.

The full-length mirror was pretty brutal. Rumpled flannel shirt, T-shirt frayed at the collar, faded jeans torn at the knees and dotted with ketchup, mustard, and soda. I took off my Phillies cap. The hair wasn't too bad because it fell only to the earlobes and had none of Mathilde's waves, so gravity was enough to draw it back into place. Albino, my ass. My eyes were shaped more like Dean's but didn't have the merry wrinkles at the corners—his "smiling eyes," she used to call them. I'd inherited his forehead, not hers. I was skinny enough but at five-five too tall to pass for a jockey.

I grabbed the knapsack, left the gas station, and headed north. Keeping the skyscrapers in my sights, I reached the mastodon rust-iron pillars supporting the El tracks. Most of the stores looked closed, but a coffee shop was open. I bought a doughnut and joe to-go and went towards the lake. A park ran alongside it, and I found a bench facing east and watched the sun rise. Sailboats bobbed on the complacent blue. The faintest odor of fish wafted my way, but it wasn't overpowering, not like the time at the shore after the hurricane.

Certain memories stick with you like they'd happened yesterday, and the treasure trove on the beach that day was one. Among the strewn branches and debris we'd found a hip-high boot, an inside-out striped umbrella, a screen door that must've blown off its hinges but with the mesh amazingly intact, and an outfielder's glove—which neither of us could use, being southpaws. "Hey, Andy," Dean had shouted, waving a long white scarf in the air. I'd run over as fast as I could. "It's a wedding veil. Sure hope the honeymoon went smoother." Matt had had a fit at the stuff we'd brought home; I rued having to leave the rest behind.

As the sun inched higher, my mood rose too. The first bunch of hours on the open road had felt exhilarating, leaving South Jersey for Philly and nabbing a ride to Hershey. But then tedium had built upon tedium. And once it'd gotten dark, I worried about getting robbed, stabbed, and shoved out onto the shoulder. Yet now, farther west than I'd ever been, I actually felt primed for exploring. A good thing, since she was probably asleep, and you could really ruin a reunion by waking her.

Returning to Wabash, I looked for an El entrance and waited on the corner for the light to change. The second it turned green, a horn blared. Like a switch had been hit, like the horn had woken the entire city, Chicago came to life. Traffic popped up everywhere: cars, taxis, trucks, delivery vans, even bikes. People poured out of buses, sprang from doorways, teemed along the sidewalks like there was no tomorrow, halting at corners, charging when the light changed, jostling, checking their watches. A cop blew a whistle, raised an arm to halt a limo. *Thud*—a bundle of newspapers landed almost on top of me. *Chicago Sun-Times*. A jackhammer blasted, and a siren wailed.

The racket wasn't harsh; the noises had a harmony—a harmony of activity. Everybody had a part to play in this city drama. Energized, animated, they charged into the day and future. And having been cooped up in cars and semi cabs or stuck by the side of the road for so long, I welcomed the hustle and bustle. And the walking.

I crossed some river and continued north through a mix of neighborhoods, some with bars and restaurants and pizza places, some residential, some nicer, some shabbier. According to the map, which jibed with my meanderings, Chicago was charted like graph paper, most streets running straight north-south or east-west, except for Clark and Lincoln. But the city didn't seem sharp or precise like in some futuristic science fiction movie. I trekked through rough-and-tumble neighborhoods you could imagine dating back to the slaughterhouse era, neighborhoods of broad shoulders. Dirty brown and ash-gray buildings crouched like old codgers on a stoop.

Finally I hit another El station and asked the guy in the booth about getting to the college. He told me which train and bus to take and gave me a transfer. I clambered up the steps two-at-a-time, surprised by my wind.

Holy moly! The view from the platform was wild. Lake Michigan to the east, of course, but it was the city that grabbed you. Chicago sprawled away from the lake in all directions as far as the eye could see. Maybe it stopped somewhere, but I couldn't find a boundary. Low buildings and occasional tall ones and church spires and apartments and houses and houses and houses extended into the horizon. The vastness was glorious. *This land is your land, this land is my land.* Maybe Woody Guthrie meant natural beauty, forests and farmland and mountains, but there was beauty in man-made vastness too.

Philly and New York knew they'd have to make do with boundaries. If they wanted to keep growing, it had to be vertically. But surrounded by hundreds of miles of open space, no rivers or mountains or other barriers to pen it in, Chicago could spread outwards without limit. Even the blue sky was limitless, as limitless as my own possibilities. For at seventeen, I wasn't keen on remaining with Mathilde, having to explain crawling home at three in the morning, something Roy'd never had to do. And I wanted out of Brackton, the ugliest dead-end city in South Jersey. I'd toyed briefly with New York after hearing about the Stonewall riots, but Chicago was the obvious destination. Though we'd never used the actual word, the more I thought about it since Nina had left, the more it seemed to me we were in love.

The day after the phone call, I'd begun filching from GG's to pay Matt back for the theoretical bus ticket, since she was living pretty much hand-to-mouth after returning to the diner. I smuggled home just about everything the storeroom had to offer: rolls of foil, coffee, sugar. She appreciated it, not knowing it was stolen and not being one to look a gift horse in the mouth. GG's suspected me—they kept an eye on inventory like it was gold bullion—but they had nothing to go on besides motive. The worst they could do was fire me, which they did.

The train screeched into the station, and I boarded. How hard would it be to find prep work in Nina's neck of the woods? College students, *rich* college students, had to like eating out. Or I could wait tables.

Dean had once said that of all the kinds of jobs—and he'd had no small number—waiting tables was the most unpredictable, money-wise. Bartenders usually got a better hourly, and they didn't have to let somebody run a tab if they didn't trust him. *Even driving a cab, you have some choice. You don't have to stop for a stumbling drunk who looks like he slept in his clothes.* In a restaurant, though, once somebody was seated, you had to take their order and do all the running around they demanded, even if you were damn sure they'd stiff you.

Drake's, of course, was different; Drake's was classy. Dean wore a starched shirt, and they used linen tablecloths and napkins. *Now Mr. Smith, you like your prime rib medium-rare, isn't that right? And Mrs. Jones, you prefer the dressing on the side?* They loved the pampering, and he was happy to oblige; lighthearted conversation flowed from him like beer through an open tap.

Is that your daughter, Mr. Gabe?

Yes, that's my Andy. The bus drops her here when her mother's at work.

Always her nose in a book. Can't all be homework. What grade is she in, second?

She's in fourth this year. Time is flying right by us. Shall I bring you another Scotch?

Dean had done plenty of other restaurant work and tended bar in just about every lounge on the Millville road. He'd also held a handful of store jobs. Not knowing that our family wasn't normal,

I thought it was cool that one month he'd knead pies at the bakery and another, wait tables. Besides, wherever he worked, he brought home something different that they let him buy at discount or take for free, like half a cream pie or dinner rolls. Once a whole lobster: the tank was due to be cleaned, and Red Ruthie had no place to wait. I whined about the bib till Matt, he, and Roy put them on too. *That's how it's done, Andy.*

Even better than food or candies, he brought home stories. The bar ones were the best. I knew the regulars by name and would hang on the edge of my seat, watching him double up his fists like one of the Linehans. The Clambake had once had a real brawl, with chairs and tables getting knocked over and everything.

Tending bar was still years away for me; prep or waiting tables would have to do. And with any luck, I'd be able to hang out in the dorm while figuring out where to live. Smuggling food from the cafeteria was just the kind of prank Nina would warm to. The face in the window grinned as I imagined her surprise.

The campus was another world—a world of trimmed grass, groomed shrubs, nice flagstone paths, and ivy creeping up the brick walls. Everybody looked dressed for church, practically, the girls in wool skirts or slacks and matching sweaters, the guys in cords or khakis or jeans that looked brand new. It truly was a toss-up which was more manicured, the students or the lawns. Nina had to be suffocating in all the snootiness.

"Sorry, you need a student ID to get in." The guard at the desk was nice enough about it. I offered him a cigarette, not as a bribe but just to pass the time till I figured out Plan B. He shook his head, saying he couldn't smoke on the job. "You can call her."

I fumbled in my pants pockets. "Don't know where I put her number."

"What's her name?"

"Nina Delucci."

He scanned a list, picked up the phone on his desk, and dialed. I took the receiver and moved as far away as the cord allowed. *Beep, beep, beep, beep.* "Hey, it's me, Andy." More *beeps.* "Yeah, I'm downstairs." More *beeps.* "Okay, gimme a minute to finish my cigarette." Holding the ear piece down, I handed the receiver back, and he hung it up. "Shoot, I forgot to ask her her room number."

"312."

"Thanks."

Luckily, nobody else got off the elevator on three. I knocked on 312. Nothing. I knocked again, louder. Still nothing. I tried the door; it was locked. I didn't want to loiter in the hall and look suspicious, yet I didn't want to go back down and have to deal with the guard again. Maybe I could hide out in the can, if shimming didn't work.

I'd learned to shim your basic pin-tumbler by the time I was seven. We'd accidentally gotten locked out of the house, and Dean had taken a stiff laminated card from his wallet, slipped it between the back door and the jamb, and made me watch how he pressed the card while turning the knob and pushing with his shoulder. Once the door opened, he went in and grabbed his keys and then had me practice till I got pretty smooth. Of course I practiced a zillion times afterwards. In high school, I found the perfect shim card of my own, the *John Q. Public* credit card they handed out on Career Day. Shimming didn't work with all pin tumblers, but dormitories were a pretty safe bet; any place that had to install hundreds of locks was likely to do it on the cheap.

Some girl headed my direction, so I knocked again. Right before she came even, I said, "Yes, I can wait." She walked past and went around the corner. I slipped John Q. Public into the space between the jamb and door and turned the knob and pressed my shoulder against the wood. Presto!

The window let in a fair amount of light. Matching beech furniture ran along the right and left walls—bureaus, bookcases, desks, and beds—and gave the place a weird mirror-image feel. It took all of one second to figure out which side was Nina's—not the one with the photos on the desk but the one with an open soda can. The can was empty.

I put my knapsack down and lay on her bed, propping my head up on the pillow so I could see her face the instant she came in, the instant she saw me. Emotions didn't lie hidden with her; she'd never make a killing at poker. *Andy*, she'd squeal, that lovely squeal. She'd run and throw herself on top of me. Maybe she'd let me up for air in an hour. Of course I had a contingency plan if her roommate showed first. But it was the image of Nina arriving that played over and over in my mind, carting me off to sleep.

Either the giggling or door opening woke me. The ceiling lamp from the corridor shone on her like a spotlight in the now-dim room. Nina came towards me, flicking a switch that turned on the overhead. The pale gray sweater accentuated her dark hair. I was right about the squeal. Except that it sounded less like a kid at Christmas and more like a hyena stuck with a spear. Making an about-face, she rushed back and slammed the door, opened it an inch, closed it gently, and threw the bolt.

"What are you doing here?" she practically screamed.

"Not a whole helluva lot. Can't even find a beer in these digs." That didn't strike her as funny. She looked great, a bit femmed-up, but she always liked to dress nice. "Hey, hon, feels like a zillion years." I stood and took a step her direction, no longer able to contain my smile.

Instead of embracing me, she used both hands to shove me back down on the bed. So much for foreplay. But she didn't throw herself on top of me. She put her hands on her hips. Her pelvic bones for some reason reminded me of battleship prows. "What are you doing here?"

Again I stood. "Hey, it's not like you have somewhere else to wait. Anyway, what's the big deal? Nobody saw me, not even your roommate—"

"*I* see you!"

The seconds ticked by in our staring stalemate. An urge to laugh tickled up my esophagus. Maybe memories of staring contests with my cousins got jiggled loose, or else being on the road twenty-four hours and landing in a totally new city and not having grabbed enough winks—all that weirdness combined with the uppers and stuffy campus and Nina acting like the time her mother tossed her candle collection in the garbage just to be a bitch. Whatever the reasons, hilarity rose and pressed against my chest and throat till I couldn't keep it down. I laughed. I gazed expectantly, affectionately, for her to join in. Her pupils glowed blacker. This cracked me up totally. I had to turn away because every time I thought I was getting a handle on it, her expression set me off. Arms crossed now, she said nothing, absolutely nothing. Eventually my sounds ebbed into half-whimpers and subsided altogether.

Her voice was so quiet I had to strain to hear it. "If you don't get out of here immediately, I'll call security." Quiet but lethal. Her hands returned to the prows.

Damn my mouth. "Hey, he's all right. It's a shame they don't let those guys smoke on the job."

Nina's mother had once said their family came from Northern Italy, but temperamentally, Nina was pure Vesuvius. I watched her furiously battle the rising lava. Abruptly, her expression changed.

Her tone became matter-of-fact. "I'm sorry I didn't call and tell you, but I had no idea you were planning to visit."

Visit? She thought I was going to turn around and go back? "Tell me what?"

"How long did GG's give you? I thought they lied about vacation time."

"They did lie about vacation time. So I said screw them, and they fired me."

"I'm … my life is on a different track now. I should have told you."

I lit a cigarette and handed it to her. She paused but took it. I lit one for myself. "Hey, I can appreciate that. It's great you're at college. And I'm not a total idiot. I planned to tell your roommate you dated Roy and I just dropped by to say hi because I moved to Chicago." She faced away and watched the wall, letting the cigarette burn and not saying anything. "And if it's too risky for me even to come here, we can just hang out at my place, once I find something. I'm cool with that." How would I find a place?

"There is no we," she said. "That's over."

I sat on the edge of the bed and smoked. My voice came out pretty nonchalant. "If that's what you want."

"It is."

Though we'd been through this scene a dozen times, I didn't feel like playing it anymore. Should I tell her she acted more like a straight girl than she realized? But Vesuvius had buried Pompeii. Instead I gave the usual, "You know I can't resist you."

Nina dropped her half-smoked cigarette into the soda can. "You'll have to. The past is the past."

This part of the script was new. I leaned and grabbed my knapsack. When she said nothing else, I lifted it onto my shoulder and

/alked slowly towards the door, pausing to drop my cigarette in the can too.

"Wait." She was fumbling with her purse. Realizing the charade had gone on long enough? She came over and, seeing my hand fall from the knob, reached and opened the door herself. I had no choice but to shuffle into the corridor. A stereo nearby warbled *oh-yay-yay-yaaaay-yeah*. Who the hell listened to Roy Orbison these days? She pressed a piece of paper in my palm. I looked down and saw it was a twenty. "I know the travel must've cost you something, but it's all I have. My spending money for the week."

She wasn't lying. Without landing some big scholarship, she never would've been able to come here. And Mrs. Delucci wouldn't send her one red cent. My fingers straightened out the bill, my eyes sizing up ole Andrew Jackson. What a homely dude. Why did his name have to be Andy?

Should I give it back? On the one hand, Nina hadn't invited me to Illinois. It was my own stupid move. And she had a lot less money than all the bratty coeds she had to live around, which would grate on her. Besides, if I took the money, it was like being paid off. Nobody likes charity. Especially from somebody giving you the boot. Chicago was a big city, and jobs were to be had. Maybe other lesbians. Did she take me for desperate? On the other hand, twenty dollars was twenty dollars. I gave those dark eyes one last look and headed for the Exit sign, shoving the president's face in my pocket.

Chapter 2

I RETRACED MY path to the bus and El and headed south. The evening rush hour seemed to be in full gear; the platforms were crowded. You could tell it was a Friday from the excitement in people's faces.

"Wrigley Field," the conductor announced. Could I bring myself to root for a Chicago team? Not the White Sox, no—I could never warm to the American League. But to root for another National League team would be treason. Your hometown team was like family; you couldn't just switch to another.

Neon lights brightened the street below, so I rose and exited at the next stop. This neighborhood was hopping with bars and restaurants. Were any of the bars gay? I'd learned the term hiding on the stairs during one of Roy's poker games. Dennis or somebody said the bar near the junkyard was for homosexuals, which started them throwing around *fairy*, *fag*, *fruit*, *queer*, *queen*—probably the most synonyms they knew for any word. Then one guy said, "The queers call themselves *gay*."

The Friday after Nina had left for college, I tried getting past the bouncer as Violet George, but he wasn't buying it. After some beating around the bush, he did tell me the names of a few gay bars in Greenwich Village and about the Stonewall riots.

The bars I was passing now had both men and women. I bopped into a used bookstore to ask about a Y. While the clerk was helping customers, I loitered by the movie posters. One theatre was showing a bunch of Hitchcocks. Hell, I was ready to check into the Bates Motel—at least I'd get a roof over my head. Another, at Julesman University, advertised *The Nasty Children Film Festival*. If the festival ran movies back-to-back like the little theatre Edward took me to in Vineland when Matt worked weekends, I could get enough sleep to stay awake till morning, saving on one night at the Y. The poster listed *The Bad Seed*, *The Children's Hour*, and *Village of the Damned*. Shoot, they weren't back-to-back. But tonight was *The Children's Hour*, the only one I hadn't seen, so maybe the Fates were trying to tell me something.

I asked the clerk where Julesman University was, and he said to take a bus to the "IC," which was some train in the Loop, and get off on Fifty-Seventh Street in "Hyde Park." Was that a suburb? No, a neighborhood on the South Side.

The students wandering around Julesman looked as different from the scrubbed brats at Nina's school as Tramp was from some Fifi poodle—if anybody was dressed better than me, it wasn't by much. And they were helpful directing me "across the quads" to the building showing the movie.

A handful of people were already waiting by the door with the *Children's Hour* poster. Setting my knapsack on the floor, and seeing other folks smoking, I took out a cigarette. Where the hell were my matches?

"Need a light?" A small flame burst in my face, reflected in a pair of glasses.

"Yeah, thanks." I leaned forward and drew in. After straightening, I had a better look. She was nobody you'd notice, a few inches shorter than me and hiding a slightly stocky build under a loose navy sweater and jeans. Her hair was medium brown and medium length.

"My name's Stacy." She let go a short smile, maybe shy.

"Mine's Andy."

"Live in the dorms? Off campus?"

"Actually, I don't live anywhere at the moment. Just arrived this morning from South Jersey."

She gaped for about a month. "Just to see the movie?"

I could tell she was playing dumb. "Yeah, they ran an ad in the *Brackton Gazette*, my hometown paper. Thought I'd take in the show. Think it's worth it? Maybe I should just go back."

"Michael," she called over to a reddish-haired guy reading some leaflet, "this woman came all the way from New Jersey just to see the movie."

It felt weird to be called a woman when I was only seventeen, but I couldn't say it felt bad. Shoot, I'd left home, so I had to be an adult, right? Not that I'd put it up for a vote.

"Hope she likes it," Michael said, joining us. Were they a couple? Was she the Third Lesbian of Illinois? Maybe make that Second.

They didn't push for details on why I was in Chicago, and I didn't offer any. Stacy said she'd seen *The Children's Hour* a long time ago but wanted to see it again and also wanted Michael to.

Once the lights went off, I popped the last of Dennis's uppers. I probably didn't need it since the plot involved boarding-school girls spreading a rumor that their headmistresses were homosexual. I felt more wired when the movie was over than I had going in.

While we stood outside fishing for our cigarettes, nobody spoke. Was the silence a sign we were all gay? Wouldn't straight folks have had no qualms about plunging into conversation? The thing was: I didn't want to say anything, because if they weren't gay and I said I was, they might be disgusted, and that would deep-six any hope of crashing at their place. Even if they weren't disgusted—if the movie had made them sympathetic—they might take my confession as implying I thought *they* were gay, which could make them feel royally insulted, like I was saying Stacy wasn't feminine and Michael wasn't masculine. I remembered the kid in junior high they called Faggy Jake—till he hanged himself in his bedroom.

Michael suggested we go for a drink, and we headed across the campus. Lamplight made the buildings look like medieval castles and old mansions. We hit residential streets, a mix of houses and apartments, maybe some dorms. All the foot traffic at night was cool—our neighborhood in Brackton was a cemetery after eight. Still nobody spoke. Had the movie led them to figure me out, and now they were looking for a graceful way to split? Were there any Ys or other cheap places to get a room in this area?

After a minute or two, Stacy asked, "Was the movie worth the trip from New Jersey?"

"Definitely. It's the first I've seen Maverick without his boots."

"You never saw *The Great Escape*?"

"Hey, I'm *still* trying to pickpocket that good." We got into talking movies big-time, about *The Magnificent Seven* and *High Noon* and *Casablanca* and some Bette Davis flicks. Heck, even if Stacy wasn't a lesbian, at least she was a fellow movie addict.

"By the way," I said, "in case I get carded, my name is Violet George, and I live in Wilmington, Delaware."

"Didn't think you looked twenty-one," Michael said. "Stacy is the old fart here, almost twenty-two."

"Is Violet your sister?" she asked.

"No. Worked with a guy who used to fish driver's licenses out of the trash at the Motor Vehicles place. Guess a lot of folks who move across the bay toss their old ones. Anyway, Violet George was blond and not much older than me, and her name reminded me of *It's a Wonderful Life*."

"I *love* that film," Stacy said, which almost started us on a whole new slew of movie reminiscences—except we arrived at the bar.

The Hangman Tavern was a hole-in-the-wall, dimly lit, with a wood floor and wood tables. The bartender motioned to me and examined Violet George's ID. Michael ordered the pitcher, Stacy hit the can, and I brought three glasses to the table.

The surroundings eased some of my uneasiness at being in a strange city with strangers and no place to stay. I'd hung out in bars since I was six—the Saturdays Dean would open, he'd bring me along while Matt did the grocery shopping. I loved how the light streamed in the windows and made the brass taps shine and the dark wood counter gleam and the rows of liqueurs look like stained glass. I'd learned to read by sounding out *rum* and *Cutty Sark*. Walk, Johnny Walker. No Brackton cop would bust a neighborhood joint at one in the afternoon because the bartender's kid sat with *Dick and Jane* in her lap.

Stacy returned from the can, and Michael brought over the pitcher and poured. He raised his glass in toast. "To the drop-out."

"I just left graduate school," Stacy said after we'd all chugged our glasses half empty. She told Michael, "I don't know when I'll summon the courage to call Dad. *He'll* be bad enough, but he'll call Pamela, and she'll go on and on about my abandoning education. But I'm not. I *do* want to learn, just not mathematics."

Should I just ask if they knew somewhere I could crash for the night? Dennis's pill wouldn't keep me going, not with all this beer on top of it.

Stacy's voice got louder, but at least the tables near us were empty. "Hastings is all-white, middle- and upper-middle class. Everyone lives in a nice house—"

"Mansion," Michael said.

"Even the ordinary houses are nice. Nice schools, nice everything. I tried explaining—you remember, when they came in June—that I wanted to understand other people's *experiences*. If I were an anthropology student studying Americans, I said, my thesis committee would never award me a Ph.D. based solely on library research. I would have to do fieldwork, live among the people I was studying. And that would include not just white, well-off Americans but those from different races, religions, backgrounds."

"Is that what prompted Pamela's glorified-slumming speech?"

"Yes. She doesn't understand I have a different *yardstick* for success. A degree after my name, big salary, prestigious job—or being married to someone with that and having his children—that's not how I measure it. *My* yardstick has to do with knowledge about other people and self-knowledge."

Stacy turned to me like I should say something. I excused myself and went to the can.

The weird thing was, though she was in a different league, I sort of understood what she was getting at. Wanting to break out of whatever was penning you in. Hadn't I just uprooted and journeyed almost 1,000 miles? Sure, it was to be with Nina, but deep down I knew that if Nina had stayed in South Jersey, maybe I would have hung around longer, or gone some place other than Chicago, but I'd have gotten out eventually.

When I returned to the table, they hushed. Michael refilled our glasses, and his glance darted my direction for a second before he whispered, "I'll try your line of argument on my parents and say I'm switching my major to anthropology. My thesis topic is 'modern urban deviants,' and my faculty advisor *insists* I do fieldwork in the bars."

Before my mind could stop it, my big trap blurted out, "Say you're studying royalty and have to get to know some queens." Both of them laughed, and I laughed too. "Guess we had each other pegged."

I ended up telling them about Nina, and we traded stories about how and when we'd come out, me winning the Oscar for Youngest. I had put two-and-two together and come up with three in ninth grade, after the school librarian had pushed me to read *The Well of Loneliness*. Michael had come out to himself in tenth grade when he'd "finally chucked the Catholic Church," but not to anybody else till Stacy in college. She had come out soon after.

"It was the first I realized there were other options," she said. "I hadn't come across the idea in a book, and *The Children's Hour* treated it as sick." She explained how Michael had gone to some gay parties in Hyde Park and through the friends he'd made was able to introduce Stacy to a bunch of women. She'd had a brief relationship with some dermatologist "who unfortunately wanted to settle down, and I was just finding myself."

"You were finding *others*," Michael corrected.

"Yes, I wanted to sow some wild oats. Not that I ever *did*. But I wanted to get to know a lot of different people, to date, if you know what I mean?"

"Heck, I would've played the field in Jersey," I said, "if I could've found one."

They got to talking about some Gay Liberation group that had just started, folks organizing like they were doing in New York. A meeting was planned for Sunday.

When the pitcher was empty, Michael asked where I was headed next, and I said I didn't know. Stacy said I could crash at her apartment for the night; she had a sofa-bed in the living room. I said I might just take her up on it.

Chapter 3

I DIDN'T AWAKEN till afternoon. Scouting the apartment, I discovered a note on the kitchen table.

Andy, I hope to be back by 2:30. There's a little food in the refrigerator and cabinets, coffee on the stove. Help yourself to whatever you find. And you're free to stay here until you figure out your next step. Stacy.

She was right about the "little food," but I never got hungry till my third cup of joe anyway. I folded up the bed, grabbed some coffee, and returned to the living room.

Where did Nina think I was? Did she waste even ten seconds wondering? One brain lobe wanted me to call and gloat: *I found a couple of nice gay folks who befriended me.* The other lobe wanted her to think I'd been murdered.

It was actually easier thinking about Nina than about being homeless and jobless. I did believe Stacy's offer to crash was genuine, yet something bugged me. Was it the suspicion her generosity had strings attached? One string: I was supposed to become her lover. She didn't turn me on, not one whit. I could tell her it was too soon after Nina for another relationship—that kind of rejection shouldn't feel personal. What *should* I do next? Keep heading west, to San Francisco, wear flowers in my hair?

I strolled around the room. Bookcases crammed with books covered three of the walls. The fourth, by the window, had a stereo plus a zillion records. Right above one of the speakers was a bulletin board. The left side, a mix of newspaper articles and pictures, showed photos of four little black girls under the headline *Birmingham Church Bombed.* Another headline said *Bodies Unearthed Near Philadelphia, Mississippi May Be Schwerner, Goodman, Chaney.* I didn't know another state had a Philadelphia. Brotherly love, my ass.

The right side of the board contained poems. I recognized "The Road Not Taken" and the Wordsworth, but only one of the Dylan Thomas, "Do Not Go Gentle."

A key turned in the lock, and Stacy came in with an armful of groceries. "You're awake," she said, smiling.

"I'm standing and drinking coffee, but not sure I'm awake."

She set down the bags and took off her coat. "Do you need to call anyone, let them know you're here?"

"I'll wait till I figure out where I'm headed next. Can I pay for some of that?" Nina's hush money in my hand, I gestured at the groceries.

Stacy shook her head and asked if I was hungry—she planned to make spaghetti. I said I'd probably get an appetite at some point. "But I was wondering if I could use your shower? My arms are threatening to break off if they've got to stay near the pits much longer."

Maybe in self-defense, she said yes.

An hour later, washed and dressed, I sat down with her to a meal of over-boiled spaghetti noodles and sauce from a can. While we ate I kept the conversation going with questions about the city. I learned that Mayor Daley ruled Chicago like a fiefdom; that the notoriety from the convention riots had done nothing to tame the cops; that

Hyde Park was one of the few integrated neighborhoods and South Shore, a little farther south, another; and that in most areas, you took your life in your hands if your skin color didn't match that of the locals. A lid of weed cost ten dollars.

When we moved into the living room with our beers, Stacy put on Leonard Cohen, and I rolled a couple of joints from her stash. Before the first was smoked too far down, I rummaged through my knapsack for my roach clip, emptying half its contents on the floor.

"What's that?" she asked.

"You mean my journal?"

"You write!"

"Not if I don't have to." I found the clip and took the joint from her and inserted it in the little teeth. She shook her head when I offered it back.

"I write poetry," she said. "It's terrible, but someday I may get better."

"That's cool."

"Pamela and my dad don't think so. It's not a *worthwhile* pursuit."

"Hey, they teach it in college, don't they?"

"It can't be turned into a career. I understand where my father is coming from; he's a much older generation. I was a surprise baby. My brothers and sister, Pamela, are all in their thirties."

"What does *she* do that's so special, besides give you a hard time?"

Stacy crossed her legs and bounced an ankle. "I forget her title, but she works for GE." The ankle stopped. "Our mother died when I was eight. Pamela and Jim were away at college, and David was a senior in high school. Pamela moved back after graduation for a few years to help out. We have a housekeeper, so she really came back to help raise me. In tenth grade, she sent me to a shrink because I was coming home right after school and going directly to bed."

"The shrink any good?"

"He pestered me with questions about sex. I wasn't feeling sexual about *any*one—male *or* female. He theorized I was still grieving for my mother." Stacy smiled her brief smile. "No doubt. Anyway, that could be why I'm gay. I don't know what crossed the wires, but that's the way they are. So there's my boring history. Tell me yours, which I doubt is boring." She reached for the second joint and lit it while I swigged my beer. "You said all your crushes were on girls. Did that strike you as odd?"

"Everything struck me as odd." I told her how things had been fine till I was ten and Dean and Matt split up. Maybe it was the way Stacy acted interested without saying much, or the weird state my brain was in from too little sleep followed by too much, or just the beer and pot. But once I'd started talking, I couldn't seem to stop, telling her things I'd never told *any*body, not even Nina. Like how after Dean moved out, and Mathilde was working at the glass factory, Roy started raping me. Stacy's jaw dropped a good fifty feet, so I quickly added that he didn't use a knife or anything. "Which was good, because he's not that coordinated. As it was, he needed both hands just to get my panties down." That didn't cheer her any, so I tried, "Look, each time only took a couple of minutes. And when I was eleven and a half, he enlisted and was gone. Though the only fighting he saw was in bars—probably the army wasn't going to trust him with a gun. By the time he was discharged, he'd changed. Plus, I was in high school, so if he'd tried anything, I probably would've fought back."

"Your own brother!"

"*Half*-brother. Roy's father croaked when he was a baby. The guy must have known he'd planted the original Bad Seed. Matt married Dean a few years later."

"You didn't tell anyone about it?"

"Hell, no. I was hoping nobody'd find out."

"Not even your mother?"

I lit a cigarette and shook out the match. "She was going through enough heavy-duty stuff on account of Dean leaving. Even when she went back to waiting tables, she had to put up with insane hours and lousy pay. Plus Roy was always a handful. He'd kick over a chair for no reason. She looked so damn tired all the time. Heck, she *was* tired all the time."

"You didn't want to tell Dean?"

"Didn't see him that much after they split up. Don't think I knew where he was. Not till seventh grade." I remembered his surprised smile, how he came right over. "Our class was going to some museum in Philly, and when we got off the bus, he was by the newsstand reading the racing form. We saw each other at the same time. 'Hey, Andy, what are you doing? On a field trip?' Something like that. He looked at all the other kids and rumpled my hair—and the teacher, she comes flying over like a bat out of hell. Dean's all surprised and says, 'I'm her dad,' and she looks at me, and I tell her, 'Yeah.' 'Well, you've still got to stay with the class,' she says, 'and we're going to the museum.'"

"So you only saw him for a minute?"

I laughed. "Longer than that. Nobody budged because he starts telling me about his job as a cook on a cruise ship. 'You wouldn't believe all the ports we visited—in France, Spain'—he listed a bunch. Said he'd lived like a sailor, rarely going ashore, and there were storms, and one passenger actually fell over, but they rescued him. The teacher had a fit, with the whole class hanging on every word. *Eventually* she shoo-shoo-ed us to the museum."

Stacy said nothing for a minute. Then she asked, "No one else you could talk to? A friend or relative?"

"All my friends were boys. So were my cousins. Aunt Lorraine—Mathilde's sister—I was afraid of her. She barked at everybody; Roy, me, we were to blame if Matt wasn't feeling great."

After Stacy was silent a while, I told her I rarely thought about it. Not *never*, but not that much. What was the point? My brain had only yay much space; I needed to save room for the good stuff. "Anyway, maybe Roy's the reason *I'm* gay. Like you said, what difference does it make how the wires got crossed if there's no electrician in fifty miles to *un*cross 'em.'"

When did I start keeping a journal, she wanted to know. Senior year—the English teacher made us. "Hey, if it'll cheer you up," I said, "but *only* if you cheer up, I'll let you read some. Don't expect juicy stuff; I never wrote anything I wouldn't want the teacher to see. Or Mathilde, not that she was ever nosy."

I showed Stacy the pages about taking Nina to the track—using Nick for Nina—and it did make her smile. "This is wonderful," she said. "Your metaphors are amazing. I'm envious."

"You mean stoned."

"Okay, don't take me seriously, but you obviously took *this* seriously."

"I didn't want to get thrown out of the class—Nina was in it."

"And that explains why you say *whom*."

"No, the creative writing teacher, Miss Z, drilled 'who' and 'whom' into us. Wouldn't let us get creative with grammar. Not that much of it stuck."

"You took *creative writing*?" Stacy's voice shot up a zillion octaves. "You want to be a *writer*?"

I was sorry to have to level with her. "Only so they'd have to put me in shop instead of home ec for my occupational credits."

"Still, you liked creative writing?"

"Not the writing part. Had to read a lot too—novels, mythology, Shakespeare—which was okay, except for all the poems, no offense. But it was my best grade in high school and got me put in college-level English, which was where I met Nina. We glommed onto each other right away. Nobody else was from the wrong side of the tracks or had divorced parents. Hey, I let you see my journal. How about letting me see your poems?"

Stacy gave her shy grin. "They're slop compared to your journal." She rose and lifted a loose-leaf notebook off a shelf and opened it to some page.

Your face, averted, shoots anger
Straight like an arrow at my heart.
Bull's-eye.
Your ice cold shoulder cannot conceal
The stoked coals of your wrath.
No, you do not deceive me,
I, who have deceived you.
Betraying your trust, I betrayed myself,
Averting you forever.

Handing the notebook back, I said it was cool.

"That's my *best*."

For some minutes, neither of us spoke. The silence started making me uncomfortable, so I got up and moseyed to a shelf with photos. "Who are these folks?"

Immediately Stacy was right beside me. "That's David, that's Jim, Pamela." Pamela was almost movie-star glamorous.

"This your house? Michael's right—it is a mansion. What's that, the Tower of London?" At one end was a medieval-looking cylinder with a turret.

"My bedroom. I moved up there when I was sixteen. Pamela had a fit because of the isolation, but Jim and David took my side, so she gave in. Perhaps she was worried I would jump—the windows open wide. But I was never suicidal."

I showed her the scars on my wrist. "Tried once but chickened out. Matt was so surprised I'd scrubbed the tub. Hey, got any pictures of your mother?"

She smiled in this wry way she had and pointed to another shelf. Must have been twenty photos, mostly black-and-whites.

Then, as if on cue, we dropped all mention of our families. There was only so much you could wallow in past shit. We talked about books and movies and traded toasts, like prost and slancha, and she did here's-looking-at-you-kid, and I did mud-in-your-eye, and she did à-votre-santé, and I asked if she meant sanity.

She threw a small cushion at my knees. "French for 'To your health.' You knew that—you said you took French."

I reached down and grabbed the cushion, pretending to examine the design. "What's this, some kind of Indian god?"

She leaned forward to see, and I flung it at her forehead. She sprang up shouting, "Asshole."

"You started it!" I readied my arms for the return toss, but instead she dropped the cushion and grabbed my wrist, yanking me to the floor. I rolled onto my back, hoping the momentum would break her grip, but holding my wrist firm, she squatted and straddled me. While she groped at my free hand, I alternately shoved it out of reach and used it to try to free the trapped one. We remained in this pitched battle till seeming to freeze, two statues, one above the other. Years passed. The unspoken question hovered: would she lean down and kiss me?

The loosened grip on my wrist answered. She stood up, directing her gaze towards the window. "Look," she said, "you're the first person in a very long time I've felt close to. I barely know you, yet I feel we're on parallel wavelengths. I'm afraid to mess it up."

I too rose, bending to smooth my jeans legs at the knees and trying to find just the right words, but before I could, she asked, "Are you upset?" Her hands clasped together, the fingers nervously conferring.

"No. Louie, I think this is the beginning of a beautiful friendship."

Chapter 4

THE DAY WAS gorgeous. A spotless robin's-egg blue sky stretched forever, the sun showered everything benevolently in shine, and cool and crisp early-fall air tingled the lungs. Along the sidewalks, maples burnt red and orange; farther down, birch leaves melted gold. A banjo twanged, and a squirrel watched suspiciously from under a bush. Neither Stacy nor I had opened the Sunday paper to the job listings, and the single item on our schedule was the late-afternoon Gay Liberation meeting. We had hours of uncharted time to waste and wasted no time in getting to it.

Fifty-Third Street, Hyde Park's main drag, was bustling. We ambled past clothing stores, a deli, mom-and-pop grocery, fried chicken to-go, a few bars and restaurants, and an assortment of apartment buildings not tall enough to cast a shadow. Students, families, old folks dressed for church—everybody was infected by the sunshine, their conversations animated, their smiles seeming genuine. Hung-over winos crowded a stoop, and a drunk slept in a doorway under unfolded newspapers. A Chihuahua piddled the fire hydrant. A Sunday symphony of sights and sounds on a sunny city street not selling seashells by the seashore.

Stacy's excited voice drew the glare of a woman pushing a stroller. "Awake for two days, having hitched almost a thousand miles, knowing only a single person in the entire state, and she kicks you out, and with no place to stay, you go see a movie. Yes, that's crazy. Didn't you worry where you'd spend the night?"

"If I was going to worry, I should have done it before leaving Brackton. About following Nina, for starters. About *seeing* Nina, for starters. About some of the guys who gave me rides. My brain must be missing the worry lobe." A bottle cap appeared in my path, and I gave it a kick, sending it into a double-flip down the pavement. "Actually, seems to me I do better with*out* worrying. I did find a place to stay, didn't I? Even got my beer paid for. Why are you shaking your head?"

"Either you're incredibly lucky or I'm an incredible sucker." When we came even with the cap, Stacy kicked it a few feet further, saying, "I like how you look at your surroundings. Most women watch the ground when they walk."

"Maybe I wouldn't trip so much if I did too." I gave the cap a field-goal kick.

"It's because they're self-conscious. They're thinking about their appearance. We're brought up to care how we're perceived: are we pretty to men, how do we rank compared with other women. Instead of examining the world, we think about being examined ourselves." She reached the cap and kicked it hard. It rolled into the gutter. "Gay women get to break free of that self-consciousness." She went on about Eleanor Roosevelt and Simone de Somebody.

We stopped at the Hangman for a burger and beer and talked about feeling isolated and weird. I said how *The Well of Loneliness* clued me in there were other gay women *some*where but maybe only a couple in each state. The thing with Nina got started almost by accident, the two of us stoned and listening to records on her bed while her mother was at work. Stacy said she hadn't met more than five or six others. She and her ex had gone to a women's bar on the

Far North Side to meet more, but it was run by the Mafia or some other goons and pretty empty.

"The men's bars get literally *hundreds* of guys," she said. Her shy smile broadened a tad. "They've been spreading the word about the meeting for several weeks, and a lot of guys know gay women, so I bet we'll meet some this afternoon."

"I'll drink to that."

Before heading to the Gay Liberation meeting, we stopped at the university employment office—Stacy was hoping they would post their hours on the door. Sure enough: Monday through Friday, 8:30 to 5:00. She scanned the job postings taped to the side window, muttering that they didn't list much.

"Doesn't your Sunday paper have ads?" I asked.

"It does?"

"Usually. Since I'm not going back to Jersey, I was figuring on checking them out."

That made her grin. "If we both get jobs, we can get a two-bedroom."

The meeting was in an apartment belonging to a Larry and Charles. Stacy knew which buzzer to press. The guy opening the door said, "Welcome to the Palace." If it was a palace, I was a pope.

Easily forty other subjects had already arrived, sitting on chairs and couches or on the floor. The living room and dining room merged together so the space was large if not palatial. We tiptoed through the bodies and sat near Michael.

I scoped out the crowd. It was entirely male. Only a handful were obviously gay, like the guy in a white sweater wearing a bright orange boa. Five or six were black, and two were Chinese or Japanese. Despite there being no women, it was cool seeing so many gay folk. And with so many, I wouldn't be expected to say anything. Most of the guys smiled if our eyes met, though plenty stared nervously at the walls.

After a bunch more had arrived—all male—somebody said, "Charles, why don't you assume the role of chairman."

"Please, Mary, let's can the Robert's Rules of Order."

A guy introduced himself as Charles and said, "This turnout is several orders of magnitude more than we had anticipated." Loud applause. "And I half-hope no one else arrives. I don't know where we would put them."

"Not in the closet," somebody shouted. Another round of applause.

"The reason for this meeting is to create a Gay Liberation organization. The Stonewall riots taught us not to passively accept persecution anymore. Groups are forming in New York, San Francisco, Boston—"

"Do you envision an NAACP-type, where we go to the courts and sue for our rights?"

"That takes forever. We *still* don't have desegregated schools, and Brown versus the Board of Education was decided fifteen years ago."

"It's still our best chance. Equal protection under the laws, right?"

"In the meantime, we're getting thrown out of jobs, schools, our apartments—"

"Out of families."

Comments shot from port and starboard, bow and stern, giving me whiplash.

"People mug us with impunity; the cops do nothing."

"Sure they do—they bust you for looking at them funny."

"Our only hope of changing laws is through changing attitudes."

"Attitudes won't change, not in our lifetime. My parents are still anti-*Catholic*, for Pete's sake."

"You mean Martin Luther's sake."

"All the court cases in the world don't amount to diddly-squat without social acceptance. Homicide laws didn't stop lynchings in the South."

"Exactly! We need *social* acceptance."

The guy with the boa, who was standing against a wall, shouted, "I don't give two testicles about straights accepting me! I *do* care about them telling me I can't dance with my boyfriend in a gay bar. I *do* care about being arrested for holding hands. I want laws passed against arresting gay people for things that are legal for straight people."

"Right on! If straight people don't like it, don't like us, that's *their* problem."

"But they have the power. Unless their attitudes change, they'll still oppress us."

"Yes, that little thing called power."

"We're asking for a big change in people's way of thinking."

"Big? Try *seismic*."

"Isn't this a question of priorities? Changing society's views should be *a* goal but not our *first* goal. Our first goal should be ministering to our own community."

"Which community? Those out of the closet or still in it?"

"Who isn't still in it?"

"We need a crisis line."

"*I'm* still in the closet. I'll come to a meeting of all gay people and go to the bars but not tell my co-workers."

"I'll never tell my parents, not even after they're dead."

I wondered if it was okay to smoke. I didn't see any ashtrays, and nobody else was lighting up, so probably not.

"People aren't going to come out unless the repercussions are removed."

"Which means changing laws."

"Which means changing attitudes."

"They're part-and-parcel of the same thing, and both begin with showing the general public we're just like them. We hold down jobs, attend school—"

"No, let us *flaunt* who we are. Faggots have been at the vanguard of every great idea and artistic movement in history. Socrates, Michelangelo, Shakespeare, Milton, Oscar Wilde—"

"Shakespeare was gay?"

"Milton was blind, not gay."

"Are they mutually exclusive?"

"He means Milton Berle."

"Milton Berle's not blind."

Everybody was talking at once. Charles, waving his arms, yelled, "Quiet, everyone, please. Obviously our organization can go in a number of different directions, and there's no reason why we can't work towards the same goal of equality in different ways simultaneously. Let's divide into smaller—"

Boa clapped his hands loudly and shouted in falsetto, "Dancers, dancers, I want all the girls in Scene II."

"Some of you are focused on political change, so why don't we get a count. Raise your hand if political change is your primary interest."

"Political change from *within* the system or political acts *against* the system?"

"Those who want to work within the system—changing laws, working with legislators or on court cases—take the dining room. Those who want to talk about protest take this side of the living room."

"What about those who don't care about politics? I want *personal* liberation. I want to be with people who've had enough of hiding themselves."

"Those who want to talk about the personal side of liberation, take the kitchen. Those interested in public education, changing attitudes, take the den. And those interested in setting up a phone line for people at the end of their rope—several of you asked me about that—use this side of the living room."

"Is anyone else interested in working with their church?"

Only one hand shot up.

I was guessing most gay people gave up believing in God, either because He didn't answer their prayers to change them or else wasn't too pleased with their shenanigans. I myself had serious doubts. No, I didn't doubt—I'd stopped believing. When? Must have happened on the sly; I didn't remember a conscious decision. We had never been regular churchgoers anyway. In second grade, Gary Mueller had bragged his family were Lutherans because they followed Martin Luther, and I'd repeated his boast to Dean and asked if we were Lutherans too. No, he'd said, we were Lukewarms, which I'd taken to mean we followed St. Luke. But even after we stopped going to church, I must have still believed in God because when Roy started on me, I prayed like crazy. Fat lot of good it did.

Stacy said she was going to the den, the educating-the-public group, and Michael was joining one of the political-change groups. I said I was ordering the dinner sampler and would wander around.

Chapter 5

IT TURNED OUT there *was* a God—some dude showed up with several cases of beer. Like the other takers, I fished in my pockets for a contribution. Then I hit the kitchen, drawing stares. "Sorry if I'm interrupting. I lost track of what group is what."

"No, come on in. We were wondering where all the women are."

"Hey, if you find any, let me know."

"Do you go to the Day's End?"

I asked what that was, and he said a women's bar in the Near North, around Erie and Dearborn.

"Thanks, I'll check it out. Is this the bar contingent?"

"Our mission is broader. We're the 'personal liberation' contingent."

"Personal *expression*."

"Personal liberation *through* personal expression."

"Back to the point: we pay ridiculous prices and for what?"

I listened a while to them trashing the bar scene: not being allowed to dance; being charged a cover and steep prices for watered-down drinks; folks just standing around in silence, too scared to converse—"the bars are just meat-racks," somebody said.

After a bit, I wandered down the hall, where folks were talking about marching as a group in the upcoming anti-war demonstration. Protests were planned all over the country, evidently. A guy with a ponytail suggested they carry a banner saying "Gay people against the war."

"But the war and homosexuality have nothing to do with each other."

"They have *everything* to do with each other. It's the white, heterosexist, imperialist military-industrial-complex that got us into the war. All oppressed people are part of the same revolution."

"Besides, a lot of people march under banners: blacks, veterans, Quakers."

"No one knows what 'gay' means. They'll think we're *happy* protesters."

"And how many of us are actually willing to march in public?"

I moseyed on to the next doorway. This had to be the den. Stacy sat in an armchair listening to the guy on her left and didn't see me. "She's right," he was saying. "Even the radio interviewers are pros, so we need to have our positions well thought-out in advance."

"And consistent. They'd love to trip us up."

"One question they kept asking in New York was: isn't being gay 'abnormal' according to the Psychiatric Association?"

"Psychiatry is no more a science than phrenology."

"They don't know the difference between a statistical aberration and a disease. So what that there are fewer gays than straights? There are fewer left-handed people. Does that make left-handedness a disease?"

He had a point. And some of the greatest pitchers were south-paws: Whitey Ford, Sandy Koufax. Hitters too. So just because you were in the minority didn't mean that was bad. Cool!

"Other mammals—penguins and deer, I believe—engage in homosexual behavior. That proves it's normal for the animal kingdom."

"No—they'll say that just proves other species have perverts too."

"So there should be penguin psychiatrists?"

"Larry's right. The fact that homosexuality appears in many species means, ergo, it's adaptive—there's an evolutionary *advantage* to homosexuality."

"Like what?"

Larry removed his glasses and wiped them carefully with his sweater. "Homosexuality in other species means it's caused by something biological, perhaps even genetic, and not a psychological problem."

Did the Day's End have a pool table? Stacy had said her brothers had taught her to play. How hard would it be to get there?

"And if it's genetic, they can't argue we should change. You can't change your skin and eye color."

"Just because something is genetic doesn't mean it's good. Huntington's is genetic."

"What's Huntington's?"

"A fatal neurological disease. It starts with losing control of your arms and legs. You move bizarrely, like you're drunk or dancing. Eventually you lose control of other muscles and your mind and wind up institutionalized. Woody Guthrie had it."

"But homosexuality isn't fatal."

"It is if people kill you for it."

"This is all beside the point, which is: we are hard-working citizens who pay taxes and are entitled to liberty and equality."

"*Two* people in New York were asked by interviewers why being gay isn't an illness, and they looked bad because they had no decent answer."

"We just say it's a biological inclination throughout the animal kingdom and therefore natural and move onto something else."

Everybody nodding gave Stacy a chance to get a word in edgewise. "The problem with that answer is that the Women's Movement is trying to make the *opposite* point—that biology *shouldn't* dictate how we live our lives. Just because a person is born with two X chromosomes, not an X and a Y, and is *capable* of pregnancy, that doesn't mean her life's purpose should be having and raising children. She should be free to choose any lifestyle she wants."

"She's right. Their slogan is 'Biology is not destiny.'"

"But if being gay is a *choice*, doesn't that mean we could *choose* to be straight?"

"Who wouldn't if they could? Who loves persecution and discrimination?"

"Is that a rhetorical question?"

"Is that?"

Somebody down the hall called out, "They want us to wrap it up. We'll meet again in two weeks. And if anyone wants to march under a Gay Liberation banner at the demonstration next weekend, leave your phone number on the sign-up sheet."

Stacy yakked excitedly the whole way back to the apartment. "Homosexuality might be genetic, as fixed as eye color! I never thought of that. It could be in our DNA; it could have nothing to do with crossed wires. We're back to the old nature-versus-nurture debate." *Eventually* she paused long enough for me to ask if she felt like checking out the women's bar near Erie. "Not tonight. I want to iron some blouses and get my clothes ready so I can be at the university employment office first thing in the morning."

When we reached her apartment, she did agree to a joint. First I riffled through her record collection. It was terrific—Dylan, Stones, Simon and Garfunkel, Joni Mitchell, a zillion others. "You have everything," I told her.

"Not everything, but it suffices."

"*Suffices*? Jeez, I don't know where to start."

She took the ironing board out of the closet. "They're in alphabetical order by artist."

"I'm partial to the letter A. Is Jefferson Airplane under J or A?"

We smoked a joint, and while Stacy ironed, I sat listening to Grace Slick. Yeah, I wanted somebody to love, but I didn't *need* somebody to love. A few days ago my answer would have been different, but a seismic change had occurred. The shift in geography—from Brackton to Hyde Park—was smaller than the shift in my way of thinking.

For starters, nobody I knew growing up talked about *how* to live life. Stacy's determination to learn certain things about people and the world would strike my kith and kin as crazy. Sure, you could choose between restaurant and bar jobs, factory work and clerical shit. If you were ambitious, like one of my cousins, you might go to community college to become a bookkeeper. Actually, Dean's cousin Edward had gone to a four-year on the GI bill. Still, nobody talked about a philosophy of life. They were pro-union, of course, and would sooner drive off a cliff than cross a picket line, but that was simply doing your duty, like following the Ten Commandments, or most of them.

Did Dean have a philosophy? If *enjoying* life could be called a philosophy. No, he *did* have one, even if it was never spelled out. His good humor might have been innate, but he was careful not to use it to hurt people. If he wasn't a totally reliable provider, if sometimes fun got in the way of so-called responsibilities, it could be that an easy nature required elbow room. He enjoyed a good laugh, yes, but what he enjoyed more was making *other* people laugh. He wanted to infect the whole universe with his own lightheartedness. Wasn't that a philosophy?

One afternoon at the track—I must've been eight or nine— while Matt and I watched him carry over our ice cream cones, easily half-a-dozen women called out hello. "It's not just his looks," Matt had whispered. "He's handsome enough, but other men are too. It's his love of being alive. That's what sets him apart."

"Don't *you* love being alive?" I'd asked.

"Nobody does like him."

Even after he'd moved out, she'd never spoken of Dean with bitterness. It was a practical decision, a realization that a leopard can't change his spots. Maybe lightheartedness was a family trait, since Edward was easygoing, if not as outgoing. Being homosexual—I now realized Edward was—might have quieted him some. Would it do the same to me? The world could only hope.

I said, "That shirt number four? How many you planning on wearing tomorrow?"

"Three are for actual interviews, not the employment office. If I'm lucky, I may get some interviews Tuesday, Wednesday. Do you need to borrow clothes? Are jeans all you have?"

"Hey, don't worry about me."

She glanced up from the ironing board. "I could lend you money to buy—"

"I've got enough. I might not get out as early as you, but I'll get out. I'm just not into planning."

Her brows briefly furrowed. Then she mumbled to herself, "Do I have everything? Blouse, skirt, slip, pantyhose, shoes, purse—"

"Hope I'm awake early enough to see you in this get-up."

"Hope you're not. It's torture."

Chapter 6

"Have you ever done kitchen work?"

"Yes, ma'am. Prep of all kinds."

"What do you mean 'all kinds'?" She eyed me skeptically.

"Salads, sandwiches, potatoes—baked, mashed, fries, hash brown—"

"When could you start?"

"First thing tomorrow."

"I need somebody for dinner prep today. Four to eight."

Stacy was at the kitchen table, wearing jeans and a sweatshirt. "Sorry I missed the costume," I said, setting down my pack of cigarettes. "Any luck?"

"I filled out an application, which they'll send to different departments that are hiring. Now I just wait and see who calls for an interview. How about you? Did you find anything to wear?"

"Other than this? No."

She shifted uneasily in her chair.

"Hey, if I'm just going to work in the kitchen, I can wear jeans."

"But for an interview, won't they expect you to dress nicely?"

"Don't know what they expect." I sat across from her and lit a cigarette, exhaling at the ceiling.

She shifted again. After about a minute, she quietly asked, "Where are you planning to try?"

"Interviewing? Nowhere." When the cigarette was down to the filter, I pressed it into the metal ashtray. "Guess I should fix myself something to eat before I leave."

"Where are you going?"

I didn't answer till opening the fridge. "You know Portia's Pantry?"

"On Fifty-Seventh? Do they have an opening?"

I grabbed the milk carton. "Not that I know of."

"You'll fill out an application just in case?"

"No." I poured a glass and returned the carton to the shelf.

"Why are you going there?"

I opened a cupboard and took out the peanut butter, then grabbed a plate from the dish rack and lackadaisically removed a knife from the silverware drawer. "Where do you keep the bread?"

"Behind the toaster."

I made a sandwich and managed a poker face when bringing it and the milk to the table. Stacy repeated, "Why are you going to Portia's?"

I sat and said, "They want me to start at four. Kitchen prep. Mondays through Fridays, four to eight." I took a huge bite of the sandwich.

For a zillion minutes, Stacy's mandible or maxilla—I never could keep them straight—hung like a broken drawbridge. I was tempted to aim a crumb and toss it in.

"They *hired* you?" she practically gasped. "*Already*? Didn't they want references? Is that how you dressed?"

"Hey, this T-shirt's clean."

"You got a job? Sonofabitch!"

I grabbed a napkin and ever-so-daintily dabbed at my mouth. Stacy rose and shouted loud enough to wake the Far East. "I go to the trouble of washing and ironing this miserable outfit and put on pantyhose and shoes with heels, I give myself blisters on the way to the employment office, fill out their forms, and all I get for my efforts is a we'll-call-you. You do absolutely nothing except haul your rear-end out of bed and walk six blocks, and you have a job!"

"It's a cute rear-end, I've been told."

"Sonofabitch."

"Relax. Ten minutes before I showed, the prep guy's sister phones saying he got two weeks in the slammer. Portia—if that's really her name—hadn't even gotten around to putting up a help-wanted sign."

"You just went in and asked if there were any openings?"

"Why not? Timing is everything."

"Lucky stiff."

I shrugged. "Hey, some folks got brains; some, beauty; some, luck. Me, I got all three."

Prep at Portia's wasn't the greatest job in the world, and there were days I envied the guy in jail. But it paid. Not well, but it paid. And I was sure the cook and I'd have become best buddies if he'd spoken English. Julio would point to the remaining slices of tomatoes and grunt, "Mas." Or through the glass door at the salads in the pantry cooler. "Mas, mas." He did a pretty good job of divining what we'd need mas of, based on time of day or whatever he used—tea leaves, phrenology.

Despite all her worrying, Stacy got a job too— "particle tracking" in some physics lab. She was so pleased, she didn't complain about my quick promotion to the eight a.m. to four shift.

I hadn't had much of an opinion on Vietnam one way or the other till Roy had said we should bomb the dirty gooks all to hell, at which point the whole enterprise became suspect. The only argument in favor I'd heard was my Uncle Anthony's about the Domino Effect. At the Palace, I heard plenty of opposing: the U.S. was being imperialist and racist, and the Vietcong just wanted their independence. Heck, we didn't like being European colonies either.

The day of the demonstrations, Stacy and I met up with Michael and his buddies on the IC platform. They opened their black plastic bags to show us their signs, *Gay People Against the War* and *Equal Rights for Gay Soldiers*. To let people know, the guy with the soldiers sign said, that gay people were risking their lives to serve their country.

The Loop was like a Cecil B. De Mille casting call, thousands of people pouring into the streets. The mood was part-gleeful, part-earnest. I was surprised at the number of ordinary-looking folks, though there were enough guys with ponytails or wild curly hair to suds my Aunt Lorraine into a lather—especially the ones in camouflage jackets. I liked the bandanas worn Apache-style across the forehead and shirts with pictures of Che and Castro and Jim Morrison. Folks wore pins saying *Make Love, Not War* and *End the Draft* and *Sisterhood is Powerful*, and Stacy and I weren't the only bra-less sisters.

Yes, the times, they were a-changin'. The variety in the way people dressed and wore their hair, the colorfulness, the breaking of taboos energized me. The air itself seemed to champion freedom and a new way of being. Chuck society's old, staid rules of so-called normality and conformity—embrace the exuberant and joyful. I vaguely remembered some poem about drinking life to the lees—Stacy would know the name. The point was that life shouldn't be war and materialism and discrimination; it should be peaceful and fun.

The police weren't having fun. They stood shoulder-to-shoulder at the gaps in the barricades, clasping billy clubs, their faces beneath the riot helmets looking grim and resolute. With the overtime they were drawing, the grimness might've been an act. Still, you knew not to mess with them, not after the convention bullshit.

Michael's buddies kept their signs under wraps, but we had plenty of others to read: *Stop the Bombing, Vietnam Vets Against the War, Impeach Nixon, Bring the Troops Home.* Eventually the march began inching along State Street. "Hell, no, we won't go," we chanted, and "Pow-er to the people." The spectators, squeezed between the storefronts and barricades, cheered and waved. Folks sang "We Shall Overcome" and made fist salutes and hollered, "Free the Chicago Seven" and "Free Bobby Seale," and I did my own, "Free beer."

Finally our guys raised their signs, and we started chanting, "What do we want? Equality! When do we want it? Now!"

"Hold your own march," somebody yelled.

"It's all the same fight," Michael yelled back. "Liberation is liberation is liberation."

"You're fucked up."

"We're not fucked enough."

It seemed to me our signs were no more irrelevant than, say, *Support Migrant Farm Workers, Boycott Lettuce!* Who cared if it wasn't all one revolution? The more, the merrier.

"Pow-er to the people! Pow-er to the people!"

Several hours later, tired and hoarse, we called it a day. Somebody said we *should* hold our own demonstration, and somebody else said let's wait till the organization got more people because a poor turnout could do more harm than good. Michael argued that the only bad publicity was no publicity. I was a Lukewarm happy to go along on any Crusade.

The guys headed back to the IC station at Randolph. Stacy and I headed to Erie and Dearborn.

Chapter 7

THE *DAZE END* sign and door were down an alley. A short-haired woman in her forties shone a flashlight beam and studied our IDs before letting us enter. When my eyes adjusted to the dark, I could make out several tables occupied by women. *Only* by women. *Gay* women!

We got a pitcher, and Stacy poured, and we toasted Sisterhood. The other customers plus her and me and the bartender and bouncer made fourteen lesbians in Chicago alone. Here I'd gone through high school feeling like I was one of fourteen on the entire planet. True, the quick look-over everybody gave us and equally quick resumption of what they'd been doing wasn't a warm welcome, but we were the new kids on the block. I felt a little like we *were* kids; the others looked older.

Unfortunately, the atmosphere on the block didn't improve. Women walking past us never glanced our way. When I went up to grab some matches, neither the bartender nor woman paying for her drink—a James Dean look-alike—made eye contact. Twelve gloomy lesbians. When I returned to the table, Stacy pushed her glasses farther up her nose and asked if I thought it was the age difference—why they were so unfriendly.

"Beats me. Maybe you should become an anthropologist and study urban deviants."

We got up to study the jukebox instead. "The top row's a 1950s time warp," I said.

"The second row has a few Beatles, but they're not really danceable."

"Do you think 'Come Together' is more accurate for gay people or straight? And I'm not knocking Percy Sledge, but why put 'When a Man Loves a Woman' in a gay bar?"

"This one's ambiguous: 'I Never Loved a Man the Way I Loved You.'"

We did find some danceable tunes. When "Rescue Me" hit the turntable, I asked Stace if she wanted to dance, figuring with a little coaxing, she would overcome her shyness. Coaxing proved unnecessary—she was one maid-a-leaping, her lack of self-consciousness a wonder to behold. I kept my focus on her grin or the walls; if other folks thought her rough-and-tumble dance style wasn't exactly Ginger Rogers, I didn't need to know.

Nobody else danced, or threw a smile our way, or made eye contact. We agreed the place wasn't worth the price of a second pitcher, so we left, our hopes of finding friendly female co-deviants dashed, our egos dazed.

Nor did female co-deviants show up at the Palace, although more and more men were coming out of the closet to help the cause. Committees were formed and extra phone lines put in, actually listed in the directory under "Gay Liberation." I was impressed at the way Charles and Larry donated the Palace to the people.

Stacy and I staffed the phones two evenings a week, which consisted mostly of reassuring nervous guys they could be as anonymous as they wanted at meetings and should come and get to know other gay folks. We got plenty of crank calls too, but we always had a laugh over each other's smart aleck responses. Plus, the gay people calling sounded so grateful to have another gay person to talk to. It was hard not to feel good about yourself at the end of a shift.

And once the date was fixed, we told callers about the planned demonstration at the Civic Center. Easily two dozen people *I'd* spoken to sounded enthusiastic; Stacy counted at least that many; and the folks handling the phones the other nights probably counted even more. Whoever applied for the permit told the authorities we expected between fifty and two hundred demonstrators. Michael alerted newspapers and radio and TV stations.

On a cold, windy, bleak afternoon, seven guys and Stacy and I marched in a circle downtown near Picasso's deviant horse sculpture. Our signs said *Out of the Closets and Into the Streets, Equal Rights for Gay People,* and *End Discrimination.* We chanted, "Say it now, say it loud, we are gay, we are proud!" and the catchy "Two, four, six, eight, gay is just as good as straight."

Most passersby smiled, and the initial group of twelve cops dwindled to a pathetic two, who took turns fetching coffee in styrofoam cups. No TV cameras showed and only a couple of reporters. For fun, we sang songs from musicals, slipping in the occasional obscene lyric.

The entire news coverage was a small paragraph buried on page eleven of one daily saying *seven men and three women supporting 'gay liberation,' the right to practice homosexuality, walked in a small circle at the Civic Center yesterday, their message puzzling shoppers and tourists alike.* The assholes couldn't even count.

But we did start winning battles, or at least skirmishes. Michael and some other guys gave great radio interviews, which led to more phone calls to the Palace and more guys coming to meetings and coming out publicly. The times were a-changin', just slowly.

On the home front, the landlord let us move across the hall into a two-bedroom. The living room had this neat offshoot, an alcove of sorts that could work as a guest room. The little card in the mailbox slot with *Gabe and Grunner* sounded like a front for a bookie operation.

The bookies' first phone call was Michael asking if we'd heard about the Mark Clark and Fred Hampton assassinations. I had no clue who they were till Stacy said Black Panthers. Why were she and Michael on their side, I wondered. Wasn't their slogan "The only good honky is a dead honky"? Sure made "Biology is not destiny" look tame.

The racial tension all over Chicago had taken me by surprise. Sure, blacks and whites on the East Coast weren't exactly buddy-buddy, especially in parts of Philly. But here the hostility was thicker than frozen bratwurst. I had to chalk one up for Brackton: if they had *one-tenth* the racial animosity as here, I missed it. Sure, everybody hung out with their own group. The Italian boys—the greasers— hung out with the Italian girls, and the rich white kids whose mothers had never worked a day in their lives stuck with other rich kids. The two dozen blacks sticking together just seemed part of some species teen cliquishness, not racism or discrimination or anything important.

Aunt Lorraine was another story. She wasn't prejudiced against Italians, of course, but was always trashing blacks, Puerto Ricans, and Jews—except Jews were good doctors. Matt had thought the world of Opal, her old co-worker at the diner, and Dean was equally friendly to everybody. Once when we were leaving the track, he stopped a black guy in the parking lot and handed him some money, saying, "Thanks, Henry." Nobody could accuse Dean of being racist. He was an equal opportunity borrower if ever there were one.

Christmas Day, I phoned Mathilde, telling her I'd gotten a job doing prep and was sharing an apartment with one of the waitresses. "That was quick," Stacy said when I hung up.

"Caught them sitting down to eat. When she or my aunt work a holiday, they eat late. That's assuming they don't get an afternoon shift, in which case they have to postpone the whole shebang to the next day."

"They have to work on Christmas?"

"Matt's diner gets a lot of cops and firemen, so they stay open, and my aunt works at St. Joseph's Hospital and sometimes has to fill in. Besides, you were on long enough for the both of us."

Her smile signaled her call went well. "Dad has finally accepted my decision, and with Pamela I used a lot of jargon like nano and picoseconds, so she thinks my job is a high-level position requiring math."

Christmas at Matt's was easy to picture. Aunt Lorraine and Uncle Anthony would have carried in a case of beer and some side dishes. Anthony Junior and his brothers—Anthony Junior was a little older than me, and the twins were a couple of years younger—would have carried in the presents. Edward would hand out crisp five-dollar bills to my cousins and liquor to everybody else.

Even after Matt and Dean's divorce, Edward continued to come for the holidays. The time he left before the poker game, one of the twins asked how he was related to everybody, and my aunt explained that Edward's mother and Dean's mother were sisters, which made Edward and Dean first cousins.

"Why doesn't Edward go to Uncle Dean's for Christmas?" the kid had asked.

"Uncle Dean spends the day helping out at the state hospital, to cheer up the patients."

That had been news to me. I was glad the questions kept coming.

"Where *you* work?"

"No, not St. Joe's," my aunt had said. "State is a different kind of hospital. People go there to live if they can't take care of themselves. Uncle Dean's mother, Andy's Grandma Margaret, she lived there till she died."

Roy must have been home on leave because he butted in with something like, "They're all crazy and don't even know it *is* Christmas." Which was the first and only time I heard my aunt come to Dean's defense. "He's giving kindness to souls that need it. And when better than the Lord's birthday?"

Of course Roy had proceeded to make demented faces, crossing his eyes, drooling. Lorraine had looked ready to whack him, but my uncle whispered, "He's amusing the kids; let him be."

I didn't care. Secretly, I was proud. It was easy to imagine Dean's happy-go-lucky smile while he pushed a food cart into a room of wheelchair-bound folks. "Hey, Bessie, we've got some yummy gravy. Jack, my good buddy, you've got to down your vegetables if you want that apple pie." Maybe they wouldn't get his jokes, but they had to know somebody was trying to shed kindness on them, like my aunt had said. And I didn't want to picture him sitting home alone on Christmas. Maybe he had had girlfriends he could have celebrated with, but I didn't want to picture that either.

Somehow the state hospital had come up again just this past summer, when Matt, Lorraine, and I were bullshitting around the kitchen table. Matt had mentioned that Dean was pretty upset when the place first got affiliated with St. Joe's, and Lorraine said, "But it's much nicer now, Sissy, everybody says. And more residents want to train at St. Joe's because they can go to State for their psychiatry and neurology rotations."

Matt had just gazed sadly out the window. "I remember how upset he was at the changes. His mother wasn't helped by them."

"Nothing was going to help her, Sissy, not then."

Grandma Margaret had passed away when I was in junior high. I didn't go to the funeral—maybe it was on a school day. I'd never known her anyway; the dementia had gotten bad enough, she was moved to State when I was a baby. Roy claimed that during one of her visits before I was born, she'd thrown a glass at him, which Matt pooh-poohed. I could imagine Roy provoking somebody enough to throw just about *any*thing at him. If my grandmother had really done it, she couldn't have been all that demented.

Chapter 8

STACY CLAIMED THAT time slowed down only near the speed of light, but chopping onions and garlic and celery at Portia's slowed it down too. And chopping carrots and cucumbers and radishes and potatoes. And opening cans of baked beans and green beans and red beans and navy beans and lentils and tuna and soup and chowder and olives and sauces and pie fillings. All of it becoming mas and mas of a drag.

What made time slow down even more was relativity: the Palace was getting tons of new faces, even an occasional woman's. The Gay Liberation group had gotten good press, leading to more radio and TV interviews, leading to more people coming out. The liberation-through-personal-expression committee pressured the men's bars to allow dancing, which didn't seem like a big deal to some, but Michael argued that dancing made people feel good about themselves, which led to more closet doors opening, and it was proving true. If the price of drinks had gone up, well, like the Stones sang, you got what you needed.

The card tables at the Palace became so weighted with paper you were afraid of knocking into them. Some stacks contained position statements on civil rights, sodomy laws, discrimination. Others had speeches by gay folks in New York and San Francisco and brochures with catchy titles like *Know Your Miranda* and *The Signs and Symptoms of Venereal Disease.* Magazine and newspaper articles were xeroxed from local publications and *Newsweek* and even the *New York Times.* Somebody drew up a list of works by famous gay authors: Walt Whitman, Oscar Wilde, James Baldwin, Allen Ginsberg, Sappho, and Virginia Woolf, though I didn't see anything by Milton Berle.

And there were other lists: of senators and congressmen and aldermen to badger; laws in the works to support or oppose; newspaper and radio and TV employees and their phone numbers if, say, you wanted to comment on a show or get publicity for a protest. There were lists of government agencies and charitable organizations that might help if you lost your lease and needed temporary shelter, or got fired for being gay and needed to file for unemployment, or were kicked out of the army or even wanted to get *in* the army. A blackboard contained the when-where-and-what of meetings; you needed a scorecard to know who the players were. There were *standing* committees and *ad hoc* committees and *sub*-committees and maybe even *sub-sub*-committees.

I skipped most of the meetings but continued to do phone detail—Charles and Larry had installed *another* new phone line—and I'd tag along with Stacy to post signs on campus where, if nothing else, we could usually work in a game of pool or some burgers and beer. On the occasional occasions Michael and everybody headed out to a demonstration, we were happy to go along and get our fair share of abuse. It didn't matter if the cause was anti-war, anti-racism, anti-sexism, or antidisestablishmentarianism; I liked the camaraderie and whole idea of causing trouble. Plus, previous generations had put in their time for the right to organize and go on strike, so now it was our turn.

By summer, several areas of Chicago felt like home, and Lake Shore Drive was as familiar as a route to school. The huge Donnelley sign sat atop the printing-press factory, a massive structure of red-brick pillars and turquoise-rimmed windows. McCormick Place was even bigger. Just past the Field Museum, which looked like a baby Art Institute, the lawns of Grant Park spread, bordered by the Connie Hilton and papa Art Institute.

I knew Hyde Park like the back of my hand: the decent pizza place, the Rikki Tikki Tavern with its fake Polynesian décor, and the nearby Raven if you wanted to drink somewhere quiet. I checked out the tourist sights like the tidy, squat, Frank Lloyd Wright house and tall, imposing Rockefeller Chapel with its carillon. I visited the Museum of Science and Industry to watch chickens hatch, and Stace and I liked to walk to the Point, a small park-like area on the lake where students hung out in decent weather. Michael threw a Fourth of July picnic there; so did a million other people. If the grass got too crowded, you could wander down on the rocks; some folks even swam.

Portia canned me for showing up late three days in a row, but Stacy didn't have time to worry; I got a job waiting tables at a greasy spoon on Fifty-Third the same day. It being my first waiting gig, I had a lot to learn, and mostly what I learned was that waiting meant not only taking and serving orders but continually putting on fresh pots of coffee and refilling the containers of mustard, ketchup, sugar, sugar sub, salt, pepper, tea bags, syrups, and cream, plus scooting into the kitchen for new bottles of Tabasco and Worcestershire.

Yet it was kind of cool having some regulars, like the nurse who was a rabid Cubs fan and the mailman from Virginia Beach who liked to reminisce about his childhood. Once, at the ocean, his father had told him that if he squinted hard enough, he could see Europe. I laughed and said we'd done the same thing in Jersey. I must have been four or five. I remembered how Dean held me against his warm chest, the waves breaking all around, and I could taste the salt on the water splashing my face. *Yes, I could, I could, I could see Spain.*

By the end of summer, women too had come out in large numbers. Several new women's bars opened in the Near North, including Vicki's and Chez Shay, so playing the field supplanted fieldwork. Rhea actually fell for the line, "You really know how to turn up the heat." Others didn't seem to need a line, like the masseuse who gave terrific back massages and, as I told Stacy, "fronts too." A fine-arts major with some mighty fine hashish brought me to the Art Institute to see the point of *American Gothic* and points of *Sunday Afternoon on the Island of La Grande Jatte.* I understood *Nighthawks* without any help, felt like I'd been there. That fall might have been the first time I paid no attention to the standings, pennants, or even World Series.

The nights we hit the bars, Stacy was a good sport about going home alone, not that she didn't give me a hard time. "If all these women are so *cool,*" she said, "how come they're just one-night stands?"

"That's all they can stand me."

"You're usually the one who ends it. The Peace Corps woman was crazy about you."

"Yeah, but war broke out over my drinking."

"And the 'gorgeous' Tarot reader?"

"It wasn't in the cards. Hey, I lasted a week with the one you called 'Fuckin' A, man.'"

"That's all she ever said! Where did I work? A lab. 'Fuckin' A, man.' Where did I grow up? A suburb of New York City. 'Fuckin' A, man.'"

"I was the A."

Though Vicki's had the bigger dance floor, we preferred Shay's because it was more laid back. Plus, we became persona non grata at Vicki's the night her girlfriend tried to get me to dance with her. "A Bad Moon Arisin'" was playing, not the most danceable tune. Still, I tried some little two-step. Right at *I hear hurricanes a-blowing* Vicki grabs my arm and growls that I'd better do my drinking in some other bar. I say no thanks—Stace had just sprung for a whole pitcher.

"That's a shame, honey, because you're leaving anyway."

In certain times and places, *honey* sounds a lot like *fuckhead*. I say, "I ain't your honey, and I want my money back."

The girlfriend looks like she's trying to tell me something, but all I hear is *I fear rivers overflowing*. The next thing I know, Vicki has me up against the wall. "I said you better do your drinking elsewhere."

Don't go around tonight.

I squawk, "I want my money back," wishing the words had come out in a self-assured, John Wayne sort of way. They came out instead like Wayne Newton because Vicki's fists were pressing against my voice-box. Suddenly Stacy is dumping the pitcher over the boss's head. Vicki lets go of me and whirls around, and Stace might have lost some teeth if all hell hadn't broken loose.

Folks yelled and shoved and knocked over tables; somebody hurled a chair over the bar at the liquor bottles—you could hear glass breaking and screams. The lamp hanging over the pool table became a pendulum. I watched one woman swing a cue stick like a baseball bat.

We split before you could say Doc Holliday, laughing all the way to the IC station and agreeing that a pitcher was a small price to pay to see Vicki's joint get trashed. To commemorate the occasion, we sat in the photo-booth for one of those four-shot black-and-whites, both of us looking drunk as skunks.

At the next Fourth of July picnic at the Point we had everybody laughing at the story. It was a hot day, and we gorged on hot dogs and chips and slaw and watermelon. While Michael and his buddies went swimming, Stacy and I lingered on the warm grass with our cold beers, reminiscing about all the fun times we'd had together. The traffic noises subsided, and a hush came over everything, broken only by a child's happy shout. A flower-scented breeze kept us fanned and the tree-shadows hopping, and a flock of tiny birds swooped down from one branch to alight on another. Stacy belched and emitted a contented *Ah*.

"Ever feel you fret too much over stuff that doesn't matter?" I asked her. "Things that get me bent out-of-shape, like catcalls or somebody leaving a lousy tip or cutting in line—deep down, none of it really matters."

She nodded sleepily. "Sometimes the world forces our nose to the grindstone, but often it's our own selves. Work ethic, a sense that life is only about *doing*, not also feeling, seeing, thinking. *Appreciating* life is what's important. We're too easily sidetracked from appreciating."

"Make you a deal—you keep reminding me to focus on the good stuff in the present, and I'll do the same for you."

"Deal."

In the distance, whitecaps glittered. "And though I wish the Roy shit had never happened," I said, "I'm glad for the role I think it played in who I am. I like the part of me that roots for the underdog. I mean, I wouldn't want to *be* Roy—I'd rather be me. Why are you grinning?"

"If you only knew how similar . . . There's a fantasy I've been constructing—never mind, it's too beautiful a day. Let's enjoy the present, like you said."

It wasn't a hard row to hoe. The green-leaved trees and lake breeze, the blue-blue sky, the flowery scents all seemed heaven-bent on melting body and soul alike into a luxurious languid lethargy. Time stretched and yawned, letting Stace drift off into a reverie and leaving me to gaze stupidly from her to the water to the trees. I raised my bottle in toast. "To la dolce vita."

She raised hers. "To la dolce vita. La vie douce."

"You mean la vie ace." A lone, tardy bird came down from its loft and out into the light, perching with the others. A breeze rustled the leaves shading my face, and I closed my eyes against the bright sunshine. "Ah, sweet life."

For the next umpteen months, with some years thrown in, Stacy and my parallel lives continued on with only minor ups and downs. She quit particle tracking at the physics lab and got a job at a bookstore—and interviewed without pantyhose and shoes with heels and the rest of the old get-up. I quit lots of jobs and got lots of new ones, usually waiting tables or doing prep. Now and then she dated somebody; I dated lots of bodies. I rarely hit the Palace; she chaired the position-papers sub-committee of the public education committee, or the public-education sub-committee of the position-papers committee, or the party of the first part and the party of the second part. Eventually she left the Palace committees to become active in some lesbian writers group.

Whenever she gave me a hard time about not being political, I said I was my own liberation-through-personal-seduction committee. When she took a course to brush up on her French and began calling the women I dated my *femmes de semaine* and even *femmes du jour*— reminding me of the soup specials at Ellen's Deli where I was working counter—I pointed out *I* was learning a foreign language too, words like *tsuris*, *dreck*, and other *mishegoss*.

Grunner flew back to Hastings-on-Hudson a bunch of times, but Gabe left Chicago only twice. The first was when we hitched down to New Orleans for Mardi Gras. We crashed with a bunch of other gay folks, hit the parades and bars and parties nonstop, even drank on the trolley. On the return trip, I pulled a hamstring running from the Southern Illinois cops trying to bust us for hitching. The other mementoes we brought home were a sore throat (Stacy's), two purple beaded necklaces dangling a plastic decal of Bacchus (one apiece), and a hickey the size of Rhode Island (mine).

The second trip was to a women-only music festival in Michigan. The temperature got so hot, folks began peeling off their shirts and then everything else. After hours of beer and pot and listening to great music in the raw, I ribbed Stace, "Would you say this just *suffices*?"

As if on cue, the band broke into a funky version of "Get Back," and when the lead belted, "Get back, Loretta; your mommy's waiting for you, wearin' her high heel shoes and her low neck sweater," the drummer put down her sticks and stripped too.

Now and then I mused about going to Jersey and showing Stacy Brackton. Edward might know if Dean was around, and the four of us could go out for drinks. Stacy and Edward would talk movies non-stop, and Dean and I, if we didn't manage to catch up on everything, would share some laughs. But Stacy called it quits on hitching when our last ride back from Michigan did eighty-five with bald tires. Quitting jobs frequently, I never managed to save enough dough to afford the bus, and Grunner got pissed whenever I mentioned hitching by myself.

Chapter 9

AFTER THE MICHIGAN sunburns healed and the weather cooled, we hit Maxwell Street, a flea market in a grungy area of empty lots and old factories south of the Loop. Whatever commerce occurred weekdays, on Sundays Maxwell Street drew folks wanting to buy or sell used goods. Clothes and toys and household junk of every kind were displayed in every way imaginable: coats and dresses were draped across the tops and hoods of cars; shoes and umbrellas were crammed in open trunks; board games and LPs and toothpaste tubes and flashlights and yoyos cluttered up tables, carts, orange crates—you name it.

Such a Deal! a poster taped to a card table said and, in smaller letters, *All prices subject to negotiation.* I couldn't imagine much negotiating over plastic bowls, AA batteries, light bulbs, and boxes of Bic pens, not to mention crayons, Chinese handcuffs, sunglasses, steering wheel covers, and Christmas ornaments. A metal table on wobbly legs held a mishmash of cufflinks, earrings, handbags, flannel shirts, and mittens. Somebody was hawking London Fog raincoats off a wheeled rack; somebody else was practically giving away jigsaw puzzles.

A lot of things were hot, as everybody knew. Hyde Parkers were burglarized on a regular basis, yet they'd cruise Maxwell Street and return home bragging about the radio or amp they'd bought for a song. Probably half the time they were buying each other's stuff. Maybe the poster should have read *Such a Steal!* Some guy actually pulled up his sleeve with the B-movie line, "Wanna buy a watch?" The cops on foot patrol seemed bored.

After browsing for maybe an hour, we decided to walk north to grab a bite to eat before hitting some bar with a drag show Michael had recommended. Waiting by an empty lot for the light to change, we heard loud voices to our right. A large group of blacks were crowded in a cul-de-sac beside an old warehouse. They seemed to be listening to a white man in a suit and tie who stood alone on a platform. Whatever possessed her, Stacy headed towards the crowd.

I followed and joined her behind the last row of listeners. There had to be fifty, sixty people standing there, and a few more sat on the loading dock dangling their legs. An older guy sat up there too in a rocking chair, smoking a pipe. Except for the speaker, all the listeners I could see were black. They were also male. None wore a suit and tie like the white guy.

He looked thirty, tops. The oversized suit jacket drooped over his portly body, and his pants bagged. For somebody easily five-ten and 200 pounds, he had a high-pitched voice, an alto almost. Something about Martin Luther King was all I caught.

After a minute, a guy with a large afro shouted, "Who the hell *you* to be tellin' *us* what Du Boyze says?"

"Bet he ain't even *read* Du Boyze."

The preacher barely paused. "Du Boyze talks about the white and black races as *cultural* groups, not *biological*. There are no black souls; souls are colorless."

Stacy nodded.

"Who's Du Boyze?" I whispered.

"A black writer," she whispered back. "Spelled D-U, B-O-I-S but pronounced like he's saying—du-boyze."

Blanche would've had a fit, I wanted to say—if the guy next to me hadn't made me jump by yelling, "How can you be knowin' 'bout black souls when you so pearly white, motherfucker?"

The preacher kept right on preaching. "Our skin is merely a covering, like clothing, not integral to who we—"

"Bullshit!"

"Where does he say that?" This challenger held aloft a small book. As people craned their necks to see, he rotated the cover. Some squinted and nodded. He lowered the book and began to read. "'The American black man'—I'm quoting now—'would *not* bleach his Negro soul in a flood of white Americanism, for he knows that Negro blood has a message for the world.'" He looked up. "You still say Du Bois doesn't think we have different souls?"

The preacher shook his head as if he'd heard the objection a million times before. "Different by *experience*, by *culture*. He would not Africanize America—America has virtues the world should emulate: a culture of democracy, of equality, justice—"

"Equality?" Some of the men laughed.

"What America you talking about?"

"Justice for all *whites*."

"He's a comedian. Go on that *All the Family*, mister."

Two white gay women and a white suicidal missionary: which of us would they string up first? The blond? Surely there were whites near enough to hear if we screamed. Would they be afraid to come to our aid? Where were the cops when you needed them? The older guy in the rocker puffed his pipe contentedly. He'd tamp down any would-be rioters, wouldn't he? And what was Stacy thinking, standing with her mouth half-open?

The fellow with the Du Bois book approached the preacher and engaged him quietly one-on-one while the crowd bandied about *honky* and *motherfucker* and *white-ass*. I lit a cigarette and tried avoiding eye contact and smelling my own sweat. For whatever reason, nobody hassled us. The white fool paged through the book and held his hand up as if he would quiet the mob. Amazingly, he did.

"'Work, culture, liberty,'" he read, "'all these we need, not singly but together, not successively but together, each growing and aiding each, and all striving toward that vaster ideal that swims before the Negro people, the ideal of *human* brotherhood.'"

There was a moment of silence. The old man in the rocker asked, "Why you care so much about the black race?"

"We're the human race, sir."

"You, Mister White Skin, what's your name?"

"Tommy."

"Is that Tom capital-E?"

The preacher spelled out T-O-M-M-Y.

"The reason I'm a-askin' is I'm a-wonderin' if yo' might be related to my Uncle Tom." The guy made weird guffawing noises, thrilled by his own wit.

"Wouldn't you know it," somebody said, "*Uncle Tom* is white. *Everybody* famous. Next we be hearing Uncle Remus white too."

"Sonny Liston."

"Martin Luther King."

"Black Beauty."

The guy in front of us laughed so hard, he cradled his belly like it might spill bullets. Tommy descended the platform steps and approached the loading dock. Had he heard the "Uncle Tom might wanna get his white ass outta here"? Not that the loading dock was the way out.

I whispered to Stacy, "Let's split."

She smiled insanely and whispered back, "I'll give you ten dollars if I'm wrong."

"Wrong about what? Wrong we're not going to get killed? Fat lot of—"

"I'll give you ten dollars if Tommy's a man."

"*What?*"

She nodded.

I examined White Ass Idiot as he talked to the men on the loading dock. Sure, he was smooth-faced, but maybe he'd recently shaved. And some guys didn't have heavy beards. His bulk alone, and the large belly, made him more a candidate for male than female. The suit hung loosely, granted. But wasn't he crazy enough being a white *man* lecturing a crowd of blacks about race? How much crazier would he have to be to be a white *woman*, a white woman in drag?

He began to speak again, his voice not obviously male or female. "It's the content of our character that matters. Dr. King wanted race, skin color, religion, ethnic background, these auxiliaries of the soul to lose importance."

Stacy shook her head *no* and murmured, "King was against religious *discrimination* but not religion. He was a minister." Luckily, nobody but me heard her, though a couple of guys were giving us the up-and-down. Daylight was diminishing by the second.

"King was talking about the *future*," somebody yelled, "not the now."

"He was dreamin'!"

People laughed. Two cops walked over—I was glad one was black. A moment later, a patrol car crept into the cul-de-sac.

"Let's break it up," the black cop called out. "Time for everyone to go home."

The guy in the rocker, holding his pipe, smiled genially. "This is home."

"Hello, Joe," the black cop said.

The crowd slowly dispersed. Tommy strolled to a large, old Buick, got in, started the ignition, and fiddled with the rearview mirror. The headlights went on, the turn signal blinked, and the car carefully drifted into the street.

"Don't know about you," I said, "but I could sure use a drink."

We hit the bar with the drag show and stayed for two performances. Marjorie Morning Star was the spitting image of Diana Ross, or at least the wig was the same, and she mimed the words to "Where Did Our Love Go." Louisiana Lil was Rita Hayworth and Gypsy Rose Lee rolled into one, singing "Put the Blame on Mame, Boys" and stripping down to little more than a bra and jockstrap.

"You really think Suicidal Sermonizer was female?" I asked as we headed home.

"No prominent Adam's apple."

"He had on a tie."

"No beard—"

"No breasts," I said.

"The suit jacket was loose," she said. "Maybe if we can't get a heckuva whore to speak—"

"A heckuva whore?"

Stacy burst out laughing and took forever to stop. Then she slowly spelled H-E-C-A-T-E and H-O-R-E. "Not her real name. She was a New York journalist who now writes about feminism. She just published a book about starting some kind of women-only colony—the blurb says it's 'revolutionary.' The Lesbian Writers Conference has asked her to be the keynote speaker. But this Tommy would be great too."

"If he's a she."

Chapter 10

I WAS WAITING tables at the Grand Restaurant and Lounge in the Near North. Being under age, I got assigned the front room, which had some booths and tables plus the counter. My co-worker most days was Bertha, a gray-haired woman with a lumbering gait, maybe on account of the huge varicose veins in her calves. According to Libby, who worked the lounge, Bertha's husband was in a wheel-chair and "on disability," which might've added to Bertha's sadness.

Libby and the other gals working the lounge wore a ton of make-up—Troy, the manager, must have decided that any custom-ers wanting waitresses with sex appeal should have to sit where they would be tempted by the drinks menu. Our uniforms were these cutesy blue-striped blouses and navy blue skirts or navy blue pants. I wouldn't have taken the job without the pants option. Troy himself wore starched blue shirts and pressed slacks and never had a slicked hair out of place. He still looked twenty-two.

A metal counter in the kitchen stretched from the griddle al-most to the swinging doors. Whenever the chef or sous was done with an order, he would place it to his right on the counter, and a prep guy would add fries, lettuce, tomato, cups or bowls of soup—whatever else the order needed—and push the plate to the pick-up end. You got pretty good at guessing whether an order was ready just by where the plate sat, though of course the slip told you, but coming in through the swinging doors, you could eyeball a ham on kaiser, say, and from its position know whether it was your customer's, who had ordered a side salad, or somebody else's, whose order was complete.

The clientele was pretty decent; the worst we got in the front room were guys calling us *sweetheart* and *doll*. Some were old enough to be my grandfather. Maybe I had a soft spot for grandfathers because I'd never known my own—or grandmothers either, for that matter. Both of Mathilde's parents had died in a huge pile-up outside Vineland when she was in high school, Grandma Margaret had gotten dementia, and Pat, Dean's father, had died at forty from emphysema or some disease that hit working-class stiffs.

Maybe Matt's parents dying when she was fifteen led to her marrying old man Nash. She had had to move in with Lorraine and Anthony to finish out high school, and Lorraine no doubt became mother, father, chaperone, and drill sergeant all rolled into one, even though she was only three years older. And if all that wasn't punishment enough, Matt gave birth to Roy and then had her husband up and die, leaving her to raise the original Bad Seed by herself.

Yet even as a kid I thought that marrying Dean was the best thing to have happened to her—he was handsome, happy, and obviously crazy about her. From my now more-jaded perspective, he still seemed an improvement over the hands she'd been dealt. Granted, his frittering away paychecks at the track before she had laid eyes on them couldn't have been easy, but he gave her plenty of laughs and good times she otherwise wouldn't have known.

Troy expected us to hustle, but before too long I had acquired Mathilde's habit of never crossing the room empty-handed. If I didn't have dishes, I'd bring the coffee pot or water pitcher and do refills en route. Asking the customer how they wanted their steak cooked was a reflex, and I never bothered asking about condiments, just brought them all. I could rattle off the specials in my sleep and probably did. I acquired some regulars, folks asking to be seated in my booths, like the gay guys who worked in boutiques on Michigan and the straight guys I needled about the Sox. Troy knew, and knew I knew he knew, that I did a good enough job to be worth keeping, despite our mutual dislike. He was too self-important for my tastes, and I was probably too unimportant for his.

Usually when lunch wound down, Libby, Bertha, and I ducked out the kitchen door into the alley for a smoke. We'd BS about obnoxious customers, the slower prep guy, why did *we* have to refill the syrups—typical restaurant bull. Even days like today, where the temperature was below twenty-five and the wind speed above, and the alley one big sheet of ice, we slipped out, if only for a minute.

"My legs is freezing," Bertha said, huddling close to the wall.

"Why don't you wear pants?" Libby asked.

"Won't let me."

"*Who* won't let you?"

"Troy. Say I'm too fat. Make me look like a cleaning lady."

"He's an asshole," I said.

Libby tapped on her cigarette. "He can do what he wants because we're not union."

Bertha shifted her weight briefly to her bad leg. "No restaurants is union."

"That's because we're too easy to replace," I said. "If we went on strike, Troy could hire a whole new staff in less time than it takes to say 'scab.' Where I grew up, the glass factory employed two *hundred* on the plant floor, and when they called a strike, the owner knew there was no way he could find enough replacements, even for the unskilled jobs."

"We got skills," Bertha grumbled.

"How long did they go out for?" Libby asked.

"They never actually *had* to," I said. "The owner caved."

Libby told Bertha, "She's right; anyone can learn to wait tables."

"Bertha's right too; it's skilled. A lot of folks can do it but not well."

"I hate scabs," Bertha said bitterly. "Don't think of nobody else." She dropped her half-smoked cigarette on the ground and went inside.

After a few seconds, Libby said, smirking, "No one's going to look at her legs. He just doesn't like her."

"Doesn't like me either."

"But you work fast."

"I won't at her age."

She exhaled. "He'll try to get you to quit then."

"Hey, if I'm still working here in thirty years, he may as well put me out of my misery."

In February, Troy switched me to a breakfast-lunch shift. At first I was bummed at losing the bigger tips and having to get up so early. Yet joining the rush-hour swarms turned out to be a kick. Some mornings Lake Michigan was covered in fog, and the sky was an endless gray blanket. Others, Sol speared so many rays into the water you had to squint. Cars would line up at the traffic light; lamps would pop on in apartments; the IC would choo-choo past; and some tardy commuter would almost get himself killed rushing across the intersection. When the bus came, all us vacant-faced zombies would mutate into a civilized group by the doors.

Usually I got a seat, which was important when you were about to spend eight hours walking or running. I'd aim for one on the right so when we got on Lake Shore Drive, I could watch the waves breaking along the rocks. If the sun hit the windows at McCormick Place just right, they turned pink or gold.

In the Loop, I merged with the throngs and waited for a local north. The El clanging overhead woke me fully, made me almost feel lively, excited, full of purpose, like we were all part of some huge, intricate theatre production. The feeling lasted clear through arriving at the Grand, hanging up my parka, putting on my apron, saying hi to anybody I felt like greeting, being told which tables and counter spots were mine, and maybe serving the first few customers. The rest of the day would be typical bull, but the steady income was nice, and once baseball season started, I was home before the games came on.

Resetting Booth three, I pondered when to take my week of accrued vacation. According to Troy, it would "vest" next Friday. Hard to believe I'd lasted at the Grand six months—probably it was only the thought of a trip to Jersey that got me out of bed those mornings my hangover begged for more sleep. I'd already saved enough for the round-trip bus fare. Should I go in May? I wanted to be back in Chicago by mid-June when I turned twenty-one to start looking for a bartending gig. Stacy had teased me for planning ahead, but I said it wasn't planning; bartending was in my genes. "It's my biology destiny, my manifest destiny, and my rendezvous with destiny."

"If he tries that again, can't say what I'll do." Bertha's eyes widened in panic.

"Who, what?"

"First table in the lounge."

"Guy with the moustache?"

"Opposite him. Called me Granny. Tried to touch my bottom."

"Jeez, let me take over. Tries that, I'll pour coffee so he'll never spawn."

"You got customers." She tipped her head towards the guy at the counter, who was waving.

"I mean it: let me know if he tries that again."

Bertha was helping cover for one of the lounge waitresses who had called in sick, and I was handling all the front-room booths. Craning my neck, I peered around for Troy; he'd deal with the jerk more pleasantly than I would. No sign of the blue starched shirt, the slick, immaculate hair.

I dropped off the check, did some coffee refills, handled the register, then pushed through the swinging doors to see if Booth four's order was ready. Bertha stood at the far end of the kitchen by the back door, one arm in her old lilac raincoat, looking at me in sheer horror. Libby nudged me aside and hurried to her. The open turkey and mashed with gravy had a tomato soup beside it. I picked up the slip but went over and asked what was going on.

"She dumped a Hungry-Guy on a customer," Libby said.

"Au jus and all? Hope it was hot."

Trembling, Bertha said, "I'm fired."

Libby shook her head. "He said that for the customer. He won't really fire you."

"What did the guy do?" I hoped my question didn't sound like I was afraid Bertha overreacted, but if you waited tables, you had to expect some obnoxiousness.

"Put his hand up my skirt."

"What!"

Libby nodded emphatically. "I saw it and told Troy."

"Put it way up." Bertha began to cry.

My fists clenched, the order slip crunching into a ball. I dropped it in my apron pocket.

Troy barged through both swinging doors, keeping his hands high in the air. The crimson color in his face was every bit as vivid as the blue of his shirt. For some reason he shouted at *me*. "Don't you have customers waiting?" I started towards the counter as he stormed towards Bertha. She finished pulling on her raincoat, looking like a dog bracing for a kick. "What the fuck were you doing?" he screamed.

I couldn't hear Bertha's reply but did hear Libby. "I *told* you. He put—"

"I don't care *what* he did—he's a *customer*!" Troy lowered his voice. "Go find out what he wants, what it will cost to clean his clothes. She's off my premises."

Libby's jaw hung open a second, but she hurried past Troy and me and through the swinging doors. I picked up the tomato soup. "Get out of here!" Troy screeched in Bertha's face. She opened the alley door and left. He turned and strode towards me, shouting, "What are you waiting for?"

The bowls they used weren't big. I was holding the porcelain at the base, kind of like a shortstop who had fielded a grounder, taken the ball from his glove, and was about to do a quick underhand to second. With one jerk, I thrust my arm up, holding the bowl firmly and sending the scarlet liquid into Troy's face. He raised his hands as though I might do it again, but I quickly put the empty bowl down on the counter. He reached for the wall roll of paper towels with one hand, using the other to push the soup from his eyes. I used both hands to grab the open-faced turkey with mashed potatoes drenched in gravy, this time utilizing more of a lateral stroke, like a batter connecting with a slider that hangs too long over the plate. The meat, gravy, and potatoes scored a triple. Handing the gaping sous the empty platter, I shouted at Troy, "Fuck you," yanked off my apron, threw it on the floor, grabbed my jacket from the hook, and marched out.

Bertha was nowhere to be seen—not in the alley or at the bus stop. I scanned the intersection—no luck. I walked clear down to the Loop, muttering *fuck* a million times.

Stacy listened sympathetically, but her anxiety was obvious.

"Hey, don't worry; I'll find something else. You know I always do."

"But you were just about to accrue a week's paid vacation."

"Well fuck him for that too. My only regret is I didn't go into the dining room and deck the sonofabitch who'd groped her."

I grabbed a bottle of beer from the fridge and went to my room to sulk. So much for the bus ticket—I'd need the money for rent. Maybe the owner would fire Troy. Maybe pigs would fly. Why was the customer always right? The sonofabitch groper knew Bertha was justified. Troy didn't need his business, and who wanted him coming back anyway? Her husband had to have had the news by now. How much rage was racing through *his* veins? Being wheelchair bound could only have made it worse. Would she be able to get another job? Not any place they expected you to look sexy to straight men. Why did straight men get to determine who got hired? Plenty of customers were straight women or gay men. Why didn't places hire sexy *guys*, for *their* benefit? Not that it would help Bertha. But hey, plenty of us liked to get meals served by folks who were just ordinary, nice human beings. Why didn't *we* count—we who looked for our sex jollies in places other than restaurants? If we'd had a union, Troy wouldn't have dared fire her. Not that unions were always so terrific. Uncle Anthony's had fought letting blacks in. *You'd think they carry the plague.* Aunt Lorraine thought they did.

Chapter 11

THOUGH I NEEDED the money, I didn't have it in me to look for another restaurant job, knowing I'd be looking for a bartending gig come June. I asked Stace how she would feel about us getting another roommate and splitting the rent three ways. The alcove was kind of wasted, I said, and I could fit my bed and bureau in and hang a door.

She was fine with the idea. Michael had a straight friend looking for a place, a graduate student in Russian literature. No, Bess wouldn't be freaked out by our being gay, he said; she hung out with theatre people.

Bess freaked *me* out. She had carrot-red hair and wore pink sweaters and pink socks and pink nail polish. She painted the room pink and filled her shelves with pink stuffed animals. After she made some comment about the poor Russian people suffering first under the czars and then the communists, I said I was surprised she didn't like the communists since they were called pinkos. But for intelligent conversation, she had Stacy.

In fact, one evening they got into a marathon discussion about "Ivan's dream," which sounded more like some religious-philosophical fantasy than an actual dream. Stacy said she was constructing something similar, and Bess said her thesis topic was

Dostoyevsky's welten-something, which Stacy wrote out for me, *Weltanschauung*.

"Roughly translated, means 'world view.' One's philosophy of life, more or less."

"So why are you constructing a weltanschauung?" I asked. "Thought you wanted to experience life like us natives."

Two weeks after I turned twenty-one, a small bar near the Loop took me on as an assistant bartender for the weekday eleven to four. Stacy almost went into shock seeing me pore over a cocktails book before my first day. "You think I know how to make everything?" I asked, probably rhetorically. "What goes in a sidecar or how much Rose's in a gimlet?"

Luckily, my Aunt Lorraine had gone through a grasshopper, pink lady, and Singapore sling phase, so I knew those. And my co-bartender was patient. By August I could make manhattans and martinis and highballs with my eyes half-closed, and in September, they had me open by myself twice a week.

I liked opening. No customers showed for the first umpteen minutes, so you didn't have to hurry with the prep. The manager came in only to unlock the door and safe and give me a hundred for the till, usually while I was busy putting the chairs on the floor and wiping the tables. Then I'd fill the ice wells, check the front fridge was stocked with mixers, sodas, and anything else needing to be chilled, and bring out a portion of the garnishes. The evening kitchen help—what some folks called a "barback"—was pretty reliable; I didn't need to worry about things like the simple syrup fermenting. The old towels were in the laundry, the new were clean and stacked, and the glassware, ready to go.

Having the place to myself till the day barback came on, and the jukebox free till noon, I'd pick songs to sing along to while slicing up extra lemons, limes, oranges, and cukes, maybe cleaning extra celery for the bloody Marys and the mint sprigs for the mai tais and zombies.

I would have stayed there longer if I hadn't seen a *Help Wanted* sign in Murray's window. Dean had always said that even a scruffy steak-and-lobster pretty much guaranteed good tips—the guys who patronized them couldn't afford a nice meal out often, so when they did decide to splurge, they wanted *to feel like big spenders, men out-on-the-town. If they're treated right, they'll return the favor.* Murray's got hospital staff, police, firefighters, other folks with days off midweek, so even working the Monday-through-Friday, I was making enough to save some of it.

Maybe not Ivan's or Martin Luther King's, but Stacy's dream came true: Hecate Hore was coming to speak at the Lesbian Writers Conference. I couldn't help laughing when she told me they'd rented some huge hall in the Near North that could hold over a thousand. "Where you going to find a thousand lesbian writers? There can't be that many on the planet, much less Chicago. Not even if you went back in time to Sappho."

"It's not just for writers. Women want to meet authors, buy books, take workshops. And we set up areas to sell handcrafted jewelry, tie-dyed T-shirts, that sort of thing."

Her dream of owning a car also came true. Michael let us use his beater to practice driving and take the test, which I passed only because I had a joint on me when the examiner, a laidback black dude, asked if I had "anything good" to smoke. Stace bought an old four-door Chrysler with a huge backseat and trunk.

We used the car to schlep folding chairs to the holds-a-thousand hall, and in return for my hard labor and agreeing to attend the conference, Grunner agreed to accompany Gabe to Shay's when the conference ended. "Only for an hour, though," she warned, since she was among the select few taking Hecate Hore to dinner in the evening. That was okay—I could finish the pitcher myself and probably work in a game or two of pool with the regulars.

The conference place was a cross between a gymnasium and a warehouse, with concrete walls and a worn-down wooden floor. Arts-and-crafts booths were set up near the entrance, and a huge poster of Hecate Hore, a striking woman with long, reddish hair, looked down from a tall jury-rigged easel. Beside it was a table holding stacks of her book, *Hippolyta Nation*. The stage, at the opposite end of the hall, held a lectern and five or six chairs.

"Testing one, two, three. Testing one, two—" The woman at the mike patted it a couple of times, frying our eardrums with static. But it was cool that everybody hauling cartons, futzing with electrical cords, straightening chair rows, hanging signs and banners, barking orders, or taking orders was a gay woman. Stacy was in some kind of hyper-hysteria: excited about the "keynote speech," scared Hecate wouldn't get a decent turnout, and entertaining the possibility—I got her to admit—that with a large group of women interested in writing, she might find somebody with the "magic." I myself had long given up on finding any magic; in fact, I hadn't dated anybody since femme-de-Novembre had given me crabs.

Shortly after the front doors were opened, Stacy stopped worrying about the turnout—easily two hundred women swarmed through. What a contrast from when I'd arrived in '69 thinking I was The Lone Lesbian of Illinois. And it was a cool mix: what looked like college students, PE teachers, librarians, truck drivers, retirees going bowling. Several women had come all the way from Berkeley—they belonged to some writing collective. The one with cool turquoise earrings said, "We give voice to writers who aren't American or European dead white males."

When the keynote speech was due to start, I stood behind the last row of seats. Stacy said she'd be right back and went up the aisle to talk to the Berkeley lady. Six or seven black women congregated nearby, and a tall, thin one tossed me a grin. "Girl, they come any whiter than you?"

"Hey, when I bathe, it's even worse."

A younger one, her hair matted under a red kerchief, smiled shyly. She was cute, with big brown eyes and deep dimples.

I pointed to her wrist. "Neat bracelet."

Her full smile was huge. "This? It's just braided."

"It's neat, though, the different colors."

"If we black folk know anythin'," the tall one said, "it's braidin'. You watch out for us black ladies, now, you hear? We eat up blond folks like we wuz sharks comin' on a school o' guppies."

The cute one gasped in embarrassment. "We do not!"

"Not as bad as the bruddas, but we do it jest the same. S'like driving a Cad-ee-lac, havin' a white gal on yo arm."

"Stop talking ghetto," a third woman said. Her hair was straightened, something you didn't see much of nowadays. She told me, "Josephine's jive is fake."

"You spoil my fun," Josephine said, crossing her arms and turning to talk with the other women in their group.

"By the way, name's Andy."

The cute one said, "I'm Lish. This is Eleanor."

The woman with the straightened hair nodded and asked if I lived in Chicago. "Yeah," I said, "Hyde Park."

"Really?" Lish said. "We live in South Shore."

"Do you go to Julesman?" Eleanor asked.

"No. My roommate Stacy did. That's her, standing, the blue sweater."

"Is she your girlfriend?" Lish's dimples were *huge*.

"No, don't have one. Nobody can put up with me for long."

"Eleanor goes to the law school."

The mike made static, and we turned towards the stage. An older woman behind the lectern gushed, "Welcome, women, lesbians, writers! Are we *thrilled* to be here?"

Stacy squatted where she was in the aisle. The lectern woman went through a long series of thank-you's to this person and that for this and that and helping "to make this conference a reality again!" Somebody handed her a note. "If anybody owns a white Impala, license plate—"

"That must be Hecate." Eleanor pointed to a gangly woman in faded jeans and a pale blue work-shirt standing by the stage steps. She definitely resembled the woman in the poster. I put her age at about thirty, thirty-five—young enough to be a revolutionary, old enough to know what she was talking about.

When the lectern woman said, "Hecate Hore!" the gangly woman strode up the stairs and directly to the mike.

"Lesbian revolution now," she hollered. "We've waited long enough!" If she'd wanted our attention, she got it.

Chapter 12

WE HELD OUR breath some moments while Hecate surveyed us in silence. When she spoke again, her voice was softer. "We gather here as lesbians, as women loving women. I hear people say we're basically no different from everyone else, from heterosexual women, from straight and gay men."

"Right on, sister!"

Raising her arms, Hecate thundered, "We *are* different!"

You could feel an electric charge run through the audience. Nobody made a sound. Again her voice got lower. "The patriarchal cultures, including the United States of Oppression, have brainwashed us not to see this. We are different—we are *better*!"

Shouts and clapping pounded the room like a zillion monkeys on kettle drums. Lish smiled when I put my pinkies in the corners of my mouth and whistled.

Hecate was unmoved. "We are better, we are superior. I can't list all the ways—it would take weeks. Let me talk about the most obvious: our superiority in the act of sex itself. Yes, the act of sex. Male-female intercourse by *definition* is male arousal ending in *male ejaculation* inside woman. That is how society has always defined it: the sex act is complete when a man's penis has infiltrated a woman's vagina and deposited semen. *His* semen." She paused as if expecting disagreement. "Where is the culture that has defined the sexual act as *woman's* pleasure, *woman's* fulfillment? Yet lesbian love is just that. The purpose of lesbian sex is *giving mutual love*. Not taking and using but *giving*! And giving *pleasure*, not one's chromosomes!"

She unhooked the mike from its holder and stepped away from the lectern. "Let me tell you some other ways our loving is superior. Lesbians do not seek to deform each other, to pervert each other's bodies away from Nature. We don't want our lover to wear shoes that warp and hurt her feet. We don't want her to disguise and disfigure her face with make-up. We don't want her risking death under the surgeon's knife, as though her natural self is inadequate. There are women undergoing operations—*risky* operations—to make their breasts bigger or stomachs smaller. Women are dieting themselves to *death*. But we lesbians love women as we are."

The audience was hypnotized. I glanced over at Lish and Eleanor to see what they thought. Lish seemed attentive; Eleanor was harder to read. Were they lovers or just friends?

"How many centuries have women been taught to subordinate their own needs and desires to men's? Look at the Old Testament rapes. Look at the Chinese binding little girls' feet. The Indian widows tossed on funeral pyres. Whatever civilization you examine, if man is present, so is his inhumanity to woman."

Stacy rose from her squat and hurried back to stand beside me.

"People ask, *why do you call yourself Hecate Hore?* And I tell them, *to symbolize what I believe*. Hecate was a witch, and a witch is a woman with *power* and *will*. The negative connotations of witch were made by men, *man*-ufactured, in order to enslave women. Women were burned alive for their power and will. Joan of Arc, the Salem witches. And what is a whore but a man-word for the woman who does not follow the man-rule of complete subservience, a woman who demands payment for what she knows is man-domination and not love?"

Now Hecate paced briskly, her words matching the tempo of her feet. "It is time for history, *his* story, to be discarded. It is time for *our* story, *her*-story, to be written. We shall create the nation of Hippolyta." She pronounced it hip-*pall*-it-a. "Hippolyta was the Queen of the Amazon Warriors; she shall be our inspiration. We shall found a nation where we can choose love *and* freedom, sex *and* tenderness. Imagine not having to decide between them! We don't—lesbians don't have to pick between them!"

The crowd roared, revival-style, "We don't have to pick between them!"

"Men are constructed to subjugate, enslave, deform us," Hecate shouted. "We don't have to pick them. We don't have to pick the prick!"

Along with the exuberant crowd, I hollered, "Don't pick the prick!" Stacy wrinkled her nose. "Hey, not everybody's a crack poet. And it *does* rhyme."

"Hippolyta will be a nation of lesbians living peacefully and creatively, nurturing each other. Where we don't have to pick between relationships and equality—we can have both. Where we don't have to pick between being beautiful and being our natural selves—we can be both. Where we don't have to pick between being strong and being loved—we can be both. Where we don't have to pick!"

"We don't have to pick!" we echoed.

"Can this woman-nation be here?" Hecate asked. "Sadly, no. Men will never rest until we are subjugated, enslaved, subservient to their will. That is why the Amazon Nation turned to warfare and eventually perished: they could never rest from fighting off aggressor male armies. Man is born to want to dominate. But we do not need domination, do we?"

"No," everybody yelled.

"Do we need *enslavement*?"

"No!"

"We shall begin the search for an island for Hippolyta Nation."

Lish and her friends huddled. Were they annoyed Hecate wasn't mentioning racism?

Somebody in the audience called out, "How will we reproduce?"

"By artificial insemination," Hecate said.

Stacy moved down the aisle towards the stage. Lish tapped me on the shoulder and whispered, "We're leaving. It's not what we thought."

"Sorry."

"We want to go dancing. Do you know any women's bars?"

"Shay's is the closest."

"Can you come too?"

"Sure. Just have to let Stacy know."

I went down the aisle and whispered to Stace I was going to show some women where Shay's was and to meet us there. Trying to catch the back-and-forth between Hecate and somebody in the audience, she looked like she didn't hear me.

Hecate said, "She wants to know if gay men can be part of Hippolyta Nation. No. Gay men will not try to dominate us sexually, but they will try to dominate us in other ways. We think of them as our brothers, but our fight is not theirs. No, there is no room in Hippolyta for gay men."

Another hand went up, and Hecate went over and squatted, then stood again and spoke into the mike. "She asked if women can bring their sons. No, they'll have to wait until their sons are grown and join us without them."

"What about the baby boys," somebody shouted, "the boys born from artificial insemination?"

"As I said, we cannot admit them into our society because of their innate aggressiveness, their violent urges and need to dominate. We'll deport them."

Lish and the others were near the arts-and-crafts booths putting on their coats. I held up an index finger to signal one minute.

"Can't we bring them up with feminist values?" somebody asked. "Teach them about nurturing and sensitivity?"

"Wishful thinking," Hecate said. "It is in the male's genetic make-up to want to subjugate women. As he grows from childhood to adolescence to adulthood, he is destined to try to dominate every woman he encounters: mother, sister, wife, mistress, daughter. We can't pretend it isn't true; it is written in our herstory."

Stacy shyly raised her hand, which surprised me; she *hated* public speaking. Hecate looked like she was about to call on her but ended up bringing the mike to somebody else.

"At what age would we send the baby boys back to patriarchal society?"

"Soon after birth. Assuming we could maintain our separate nation near enough to a male-dominated country to have that kind of contact, which may not be possible. Any neighboring patriarchy would embody the male imperialist urge and try to subjugate us. Like the Amazons, we would always have to fight off invaders. Hippolyta will have to be far from any coast."

Hecate pivoted our direction, looking for the hand that had been raised before, but Stacy had lowered it.

"What will we do with the baby boys then?" somebody asked.

Hecate returned to the center of the stage and repeated the question so everybody could hear. "If our nation is on an island far from any coast, sending the newborn boys away will be impractical. We may use infanticide. Our capitalistic, materialistic, colonialistic way of life is not used to it, but infanticide has a long and necessary herstory. You see it not only in the animal queendom but in cultures without abundant food, cultures where people live in harmony with the earth, planting only what is needed. When a society has limited its resources to be in harmony with the earth, it has an obligation not to waste them. Sickly newborns drain precious resources without contributing, and in such societies, they have been dashed to death on rocks or thrown into the ocean. Quick and painless and therefore merciful."

Stacy's hand slowly rose. This time Hecate saw her, strode over, squatted, and tipped the microphone her direction. I cringed, afraid Stace would embarrass herself, not realize she was coming across too intellectual, too earnest, too *something*. She said a little timidly, "If we murder innocent children, aren't we worse than the men we're criticizing?"

Hecate stood abruptly and strode to the far end of the stage, gracefully sidestepping the cord. "Innocent? Innocent only until adolescence." She surveyed the entire audience, taking in the folks in the back, up front, on the sides—if her eyes skirted anybody, it was Grunner. "The catcalls, the groping and grabbing, are those innocent? Is rape innocent? Is throwing widows on funeral pyres innocent? Is forcing women into back-alley abortions where they die from infections and hemorrhage innocent? Tell me, is it?"

"No," the crowd bellowed.

"Is wife-beating innocent?"

"No!"

"Do we say never again to wife-beating?"

"Yes!"

"Never again to rape?"

"Yes!"

"Never again to patriarchy?"

"Yes!"

You would've thought she was handing out hundred dollar bills, the way people waved and shouted, clapped and made fist salutes. Stace came up the aisle, her lips quivering. I put my arm around her shoulders. "Hey, lady, let's get a drink at Shay's."

Lish and her friends stood by the doors. You couldn't hear much from there besides the bellowing. I dropped my arm.

Shay's wasn't packed but wasn't empty either. We found a couple of tables in the back we pushed together.

"I like going out with white women," Josephine said, slinging her jacket on a chair near the end. "The bouncer doesn't spend an hour reading our IDs."

Stacy sat at the very end, beside what was fast becoming the coat chair. I took the seat beside her and opposite the coats. Lish sat beside me, and Eleanor sat across from Lish. I was tempted to tell Stacy to switch with the coat chair so she could be next to Eleanor and join the conversation better, but she was staring at the wall. She hadn't said a word since her question to Hecate.

I bought a pitcher for the four of us—Josephine and the rest were getting cocktails. Lish and Eleanor asked me about the other North Side women's bars, and I could tell they wondered how welcome blacks were. I couldn't figure out a smooth way to mention that the two black women up front were regulars and that black women had been coming to the bars and parties since way back in '70—not without maybe putting my foot in my mouth. At least Shay's jukebox had plenty of Stevie Wonder, Aretha, Marvin Gaye.

When Eleanor went to the can and Lish was helping the woman on her other side dab up a spill, Stacy finally spoke. "What did you think of Hecate?"

"Knows how to not trip over a microphone cord," I said.

"Why did everyone applaud killing babies?"

"I'm guessing they just came to cheer her on, have some fun. That's your problem: you expected something intelligent."

She took a long swig of beer. "My problem is wanting to believe in someone. I need to grow up."

"Hey, don't do that. Who will I have to play with? Look, you were great, saying what you did. Took guts."

When Eleanor returned, Stacy went to the can. I refilled everybody's glasses and explained how she'd gotten shot down by Hecate and was still reacting to it, so they shouldn't think she was being unfriendly. After I described the whole baby-boys-off-a-cliff bit, Lish looked disgusted and said that was sick. Eleanor said she had no patience with people who used the word "enslaved" for something other than true slavery.

Stace returned to the table but made no effort to make eye contact with anybody. Eleanor meanwhile got absorbed in a conversation with Josephine. "Superstition" came on the jukebox, and my face must have lit up, because Lish asked if I wanted to dance.

"Sure. Just don't expect me to be any good." Damn, Foot Number One.

Lish did dance great. It didn't hurt that she was cute as a button, with large brown eyes and long lashes and dimples. If she thought I danced like a clumsy honky, she didn't let on. Then Aretha hit the turntable.

Looking out on the morning rain
I used to feel uninspired.

Lish rested her hand on my shoulder, and I put one hand on her waist. She drew me close and swayed to the music. Okay, she and Eleanor *weren't* a couple. When her cheek pressed into mine, all sorts of nerve impulses shot south.

We continued dancing to whatever came on, fast song or slow, and by the time Stacy tapped me on the shoulder and said she wanted to go soon, I could repeat what Lish had told me earlier—that Eleanor had room for me in her car. I felt guilty letting Stace go home alone after the big letdown but not guilty enough to go with her.

Chapter 13

WE DROPPED JOSEPHINE and her friend just south of the Midway on a block of tenements and burned-out buildings. Several men leaned against a car, and Eleanor waited with the engine running till the women were safely inside. The rest of the ride, I listened in on her and Lish's conversation in the front seat, but all I really gleaned was that they rarely hung out with "Josephine and her crowd."

Lish's building wasn't all that different from ours, at least at midnight. Again Eleanor waited with the engine running. Lish had her keys out and quickly opened the downstairs door. We walked up a short flight of stairs.

Lish lived with her mother—Mrs. Cornelius, according to the envelope on the hall table. Except for the hall lamp, no lights were on in the apartment. Lish quietly hung our coats in the closet. I followed her into the kitchen, where she put on the overhead. Filling the kettle, she asked if I wanted tea or something to eat. "I need to have something before I go to bed," she said.

I was nervous enough being in a black neighborhood where any white woman walking down the street could expect to be raped and killed, but to make matters worse, Lish wasn't following the usual script. The *last* thing some femme du soir and I did when we got to her house was emerge from inebriation. If we didn't make love the moment we walked in the door, we smoked a joint and drank and *then* did it. Once that was over, you could think about food.

A sound in the doorway made me jump about a mile.

"Hi, Mama. Did we wake you?"

A short, wide figure in a pale pink terrycloth robe waddled in. Maybe it was the thick lenses in her glasses that made her seem more like a grandmother. Her skin was the same color as Lish's, midway between dark oak and mahogany, and her mouth fell into the exact same mile-wide smile.

"No, sweetie. You know me an' ole Mother Nature."

"This is Andy."

"Nice to meet you." She continued beaming. No dismay at my color. Or sex.

"Mama, if I'm not awake in time, I can go later."

"That's fine. I know you girls like to stay up an' talk." Mrs. Cornelius beamed again and waddled out. Was she *used to* Lish bringing strange women home in the middle of the night?

Lish dropped a tea bag in a cup, asking what was wrong.

"Nothing. Just wondering what your mother's thinking."

"About you?"

I laughed nervously. "Well, yeah."

"Most my friends, we work three-to-eleven at the hospital—at Julesman—the afternoon-evening shift. This is our social time."

I sat and put my cigarettes on the table, glancing around for an ashtray. "What do you do there?"

"Central Records. Where they keep the patient files when they're not at the clinics." She poured the kettle, the steam rising from the spout. "My friends Verlene and Joy are nurses' aides, and Eva, she cleans for people but doesn't have to work in the morning. You sure you don't want something?"

"Got anything cold to drink?"

"Cola?"

"Sounds good."

Lish took a can from the fridge and, seeing my cigarettes, got an ashtray from a drawer. She made herself toast and me, a grape-jelly sandwich.

We talked about a bunch of stuff. I learned she was an only child, and her mother was a cook at a carry-out. Mrs. Cornelius left for work early in the morning and got home around two, right before Lish left for the hospital. Lish said nothing about her father.

When we finished eating, she excused herself to go to the bathroom. She returned barefoot and wearing a yellow robe. I used the can too and then went in the direction of the only light.

Her room was large, and the bed, where she sat with her legs pulled up under the robe, was a double. The glow of the lamp behind her threw her face in shadow.

I closed the door. "What will your mother think about my staying over?"

"My friends stay over sometimes."

I sat on the mattress and untied my laces. Before I'd gotten one sneaker off, she was caressing me. "What if she hears—"

"She won't, not if we're quiet." Her hands stopped touching me only long enough to turn off the lamp. "Your hair's so soft," she murmured.

"Not as soft as you."

Sunlight woke me. Lish wasn't in the room. I quickly dressed and went into the hall. Mrs. Cornelius's voice caromed from the kitchen. "He didn't talk for so long this time."

"Was the choir good?"

"Oh, yes."

As I sauntered in, Lish made no effort to conceal her delight. I apologized for sleeping so late. Her mother was wearing a dark dress patterned with little pink and white flowers, and again she peered kindly at me through the thick lenses. "You young need your sleep."

"Would you like coffee?" Lish asked.

"I can make it," I said, "if you tell me where everything is."

"It's already made."

Lish's mother slowly rose, leaning on the table for support. "I best be changing and getting myself down to Lonnie's." Lish asked if she wanted a ride, because Eleanor might be dropping by and could take her, and Mrs. Cornelius said, "No, no. I be needing the exercise. If I can't walk three blocks, I better say 'Take me now, Lord.'" She smiled as though it were our own private joke.

The moment her mother left the room, Lish asked if I could stay.

"Hey, I wasn't going to go till you kicked me out. But I'm gonna need some clean clothes."

She looked about to speak when the doorbell rang. She tightened her robe belt and left the room. I heard lots of voices, and Lish returned with four other women, all of them black, all talking at once. They made fleeting eye contact with me and definitely looked surprised.

"This is Andy, from ecumenical. She needs somewhere to stay while they re-paper her apartment. This is Joy, Eva, her baby sister Jerilyn, and Verlene."

"They're putting in wallpaper?" one of them asked. "How long will that take?"

I tried to sound casual. "And some bathroom stuff. Not exactly sure."

"Where do you live?"

"Is the landlord paying you? They can't just make you move out—"

"She lives in Hyde Park," Lish said.

They nodded as though that explained something. I gestured stupidly with my hands. "It's a long story. The landlord, he's not charging me rent in the meantime—"

The taller one turned to Lish. "It must help your mama, the extra cash."

Poised and smiling, Lish nodded. The others nodded too, approvingly.

"We tried reaching you last night, Lishie. We went bowling."

"I had dinner with Eleanor."

The group of them exchanged raised eyebrows. "How is she?"

"Fine." Lish's *fine* hung in the air.

"Always so tough."

"Not like gang girls—we don't mean that."

"She dresses feminine but doesn't move feminine."

Except for the refrigerator humming, the kitchen went silent. I managed to cross my legs and stick out my pinkie on the hand holding the coffee cup.

"She's *got* to act tough," Lish said. "They're training her to, at the law school."

"She always like that, Lishie. Remember how she dressed at college?" The one who asked was examining her long, bright red nails. "People saying she might be, you know, queer that way."

"I don't know who's spreading rumors," Lish snapped. "She happens to be engaged."

"We know him?"

Crossing her arms and keeping her eyes on the linoleum, Lish replied testily, "It's not official. And she's not sure what you'll say. Once you learn he's white."

My eyes hit the linoleum.

"Eva dated a white," somebody said.

I looked up in time to see the one with red nails flip her wrist. "That's what Eleanor remembers. You all stopped talking to me."

"We did not!"

"I don't mind you snubbed me. I'm just saying I understand Eleanor feeling like she does."

"Does he go to the law school?"

Lish's tone remained testy. "He goes to one in Connecticut. I'm not saying another word. I've already broken my promise. Don't you ever say a *thing*."

"We won't, honey, not if you give us breakfast."

They all laughed.

A couple of the women joined Lish at the counter and began taking out pots and dishes; the other two sat. "You want me to do anything?" I asked.

"No, we've got it."

In no time a feast of eggs, fried onions, sausage, and toast was on the table. The conversation flitted to a thousand different subjects, and when it landed on the hospital, I was able to toss in one of Lorraine's stories about a surgery mistake. When somebody complained about the cops stopping and frisking her boyfriend and somebody else said they'd done worse, I threw in, "Like to Mark Clark and Fred Hampton," which drew nods all-round. From then on, when they griped about whites, I felt they'd accepted me as an exception.

When we were done eating, on the pretext of having to give me a spare set of keys, Lish got me to follow her out. The second I closed the bedroom door behind me, she whispered, "Can you come back for dinner?"

"What time?"

"We eat at six. Come at five; I'll be done cleaning and have the roast in."

"Who all will be here?"

"Just me and Mama, maybe Eleanor."

The South Shore IC stop was just a few blocks from Lish's apartment, so I took the train home. Stacy wasn't around; through Bess's closed door, I could hear *The Nutcracker Suite* blaring. I showered and put on my work slacks and shoes in a feeble effort to look presentable. The idea of sitting down to dinner with just Lish and her mother scared me. I'd have to come up with fake answers to all sorts of questions and monitor my speech for damns, Chrissakes, and worse. I smoked a joint before leaving.

Eleanor sitting in the living room was a welcome sight; I wouldn't be the only guest. We had barely traded hellos when Mrs. Cornelius came in.

"So nice of you both to join us. Eleanor, it was so nice to see you at Easter."

Eleanor stood and hugged Lish's mom. "I would visit more if I didn't have so much studying."

Mrs. Cornelius beamed at me. "It must be worrying for you, having to move out of your apartment so sudden."

"Yeah, yes, and I really appreciate you—"

"Lish said you were one of the girls painting the church last summer. That was hard work. She came home so tired."

"Yes."

"Go sit down," Lish called from the kitchen.

The dining room table was covered with a white lace cloth, and the window curtains were a translucent white, giving the room an airy feel. The plates were real china with a floral design that reminded me of Lorraine and Anthony's holiday set. I couldn't remember Matt owning a nice set of dishes—or nice anything, for that matter. Roy would have broken it if she had.

Lish's mother bowed her head. "Be present at our table, Lord. Be here and everywhere adored. Thy creatures bless, and grant that we may feast in paradise with thee."

I joined the general *amen.* Lish stood and carved. "How's your family?" Mrs. Cornelius asked Eleanor. "Are they making friends?"

"Dad is." For my benefit, Eleanor explained her family had moved to Skokie so her little brothers could grow up away from the gangs. "Dad thinks Jewish people are just as racist, Mrs. C, but they don't want to be, because of the concentration camps."

"But your mama?"

"She's glad for my brothers, especially Aaron."

Dinner passed without my feet getting *too* far in my mouth. It helped that Eleanor did a lot of the talking. After Mrs. Cornelius went to her room and Eleanor and I washed the dishes, we settled in the living room, Lish taking the rocker. She filled Eleanor in on some of the conversation when Joy and Eva and everybody had been over, including the bit about the engagement to a white guy.

Eleanor plucked a piece of lint off her slacks. "And you wonder why I prefer hanging out with Josephine's crowd."

Lish began to rock. "I don't think they meant it unkind. More like protective."

"Ha!" Eleanor said. "And all that beeswax at Easter. I thought it was *good* of me to go."

The rocker halted. "Why *did* you?"

"So they would call and say—" Eleanor altered her voice to a sing-song, "'Yes, Charlotte, we saw Eleanor at Easter services, and she looked very nice.'"

"No one wants you to burn in hell fires."

"*You* don't seem concerned."

Lish rocked slowly but steadily. "I have a different picture of Jesus's love. But you can't fault them, because that's how we're taught."

Eleanor shook her head. "For black people to discriminate against other people is hypocritical. What happened to the idea of universal brotherhood?"

"It's a *goal*, Ellie. But we have slavery and lynching in our history. We feel strength in numbers. Being different feels to them like you're leaving the community."

"Which is also a sin, as my parents found out."

The rocker pace picked up. "Mama and me, we explain. Everyone knows what Aaron went through. They're just working it out inside." Lish tapped her sternum.

"It's all dishonesty and hypocrisy, yours as much as theirs."

Lish looked surprised. "Mine?"

"You bring home a white woman while saying it's a black woman's duty to marry a black man and raise a family."

Lish halted the rocker to stare at Eleanor. It was a pretty mean thing to blurt out in front of me. Lish's voice became quiet but intense. "I will not break Mama's heart. Hope, faith, and charity, and the greatest of these is charity."

Eleanor rose and snatched her sweater off the chair back. "I'm not going to argue about your mama or religion. But you won't recognize how you play along with the bigots in our own community. You don't *try* to enlighten them."

"They're my *friends*, El. I don't go to the law school every day like you. Maybe the people there are bigger-minded."

"Are you being true to *yourself*? Where's Lish in all this?"

"God gave me love for my people." For the first time Lish glanced my way, if briefly. "He also gave me a heart big enough to feel for others who aren't like me." Keeping the rocker motionless, she watched Eleanor put an arm in the sweater sleeve. "You know I fought a long time about these feelings."

"I have to go; I have an exam tomorrow."

We both walked Eleanor to the door. Lish looked sad. "Well, I covered for you."

"Thanks." Eleanor tried to smile. "Give my love again to your mama."

We spent the rest of the evening listening to the radio in Lish's bedroom while I helped her find places to stow my stuff. When a danceable tune came on, we'd stop what we were doing and boogie.

Many moons had passed since I'd spent the night at somebody's house, and many *more* moons had passed since I'd spent the night at somebody's house without feeling the urge to bolt the next day. I wasn't at ease with Lish, no, not by a long shot, but why should I be? We'd known each other barely thirty hours. On the other hand, in the past, claustrophobia had reared its ugly head in less time. Yes, we'd known each other barely.

After her mother was asleep we made love and then talked for a long time. She'd had one relationship before me, a woman "also struggling to understand God's will" who had decided He wanted her to go straight. Lish didn't say if the woman was white. I suggested fixing Stacy and Eleanor up, thinking they might hit it off, only to learn that Eleanor had a girlfriend at Yale.

"So the bit about her being in a relationship wasn't a complete lie," I said.

"Isn't that what you all call a *white* lie?"

"Hey, don't blame me; I didn't invent it."

Our schedules were about as unsynchronized as you could get. When I was arriving at the steak-and-lobster, Lish was just waking up. When I got off, she was just a few hours into her shift. So I'd grab a bite to eat and shoot some pool at Melissa's, a new women's bar near Old Town, then head down to the University hospital to meet up with Lish and her friends for the carpool home.

To explain my continued presence, we told them that the construction workers had accidentally blasted through a water main and one whole side of my building had had to vacate. Lish also said that her mother had bought a new vacuum cleaner with the rent money I'd given her. I *had* been giving Lish money to cover my share of the food and utilities, and Mrs. C *had* used some of it for a new vacuum, so that part of the story wasn't a lie of any color.

Lish's friends seemed to get used to me, maybe because I rarely said more than two sentences the whole ride home. Having just gotten off of work, they were champing at the bit to chatter about this -osis and that -itis, and nurses who were assholes, and doctors who were bigger assholes, and technicians and orderlies who were "real good-looking." One intern—a black guy—began hitting the vending machines the same time Lish took her break, which started Joy and Verlene chanting, "Lish's gonna marry a doctor, Lish's gonna marry a doctor." She smiled coyly, which only fanned their gossipitis.

Weekends were a mixed bag. Some days, I'd help with the cleaning and one time even let Lish drag me to church to help move pews. They were heavy sons-of-bitches; we could've used a little of the Lord's resurrection powers. We hit Shay's now and again for dancing since Melissa's jukebox was only so-so, but whenever Eleanor had to study, we stayed at Mrs. C's and either watched TV or did jigsaw puzzles—Lish refused to take public transportation after dark. I hadn't realized that black muggers and rapists preyed on black women even more than on white; I *was* a dumb honky, after all.

"Would you have liked me if I was white?" Lish once asked out of the blue.

"You mean you're not?"

"Ha ha."

"Hey, I don't analyze why I like somebody. Either I do or I don't."

The answer seemed to satisfy her. And it was true; I didn't analyze it. Obviously *some* combination of traits made her cute to me. If race played a role, was that bad? Was that worse than liking other women who were different from me in *other* ways? Hell, Delucci was about as different a *personality* as you could get. And what about Lish liking me being blond: wasn't *that* racist? Was it more racist if white men liked white women than if black men liked black women? Was white men liking black women more or less racist than black men liking white women? Who's on first? I-don't-know was on all three bases. And say our being different races was a turn-on for both of us: so what? Society was always touting *vive la différence*; opposites were *supposed* to attract. Wasn't that heterosexuality's big selling point? Maybe our mutual attraction was just a variation on the theme.

Already it was mid-June. Stacy and Bess invited me out for pizza the Saturday before my birthday, and though Lish had been invited too, she was helping with a church potluck. Arriving at the apartment in Hyde Park, I saw I'd gotten a card from Mathilde.

I gave her a call to thank her. Roy was there and wanted to say hi, so she put him on.

"Andy? Still in Chicago? What's going on?"

"Not much. What's up with you?"

"Cleaning out the gutters. Just a sec—oh, yeah, Happy Birthday."

"Same to you five or six months early. Thought she did the gutters in the fall?"

"Just had a storm—load of shit fell. When you gonna visit?"

"Not sure. Don't get vacation for a while."

"Remember Dennis? He's working in this bar in Vineland, and Dean came in. Dennis said he was acting weird and spilled—"

"Andy?" Matt said into the phone. Her voice then got faint. I could just make out "into bags. She's paying for the call." Loud again, "Are you working?"

"Yeah, at a steak-and-lobster—"

"Really? That's wonderful." Her voice got faint again. "I'll tell you later. Please, bag all that before the wind scatters it." Loud, "I don't want to keep you. It's your birthday; you shouldn't be paying—"

"That's okay. Roy living there?"

"Till August. Got a deposit on a place. The new restaurant in the mall, he knows the manager. It's not easy, finding a job that pays decent. Not in this area. Maybe Chicago's better. Oh, he's using the wrong bags. Take care, honey, and Happy Birthday."

Bess was still in the shower, so Stacy and I smoked a joint and shot the bull. She'd been promoted to assistant manager at the bookstore and really liked some poetry class she was taking. And Michael had invited some woman she might mesh with to the Fourth of July picnic at the Point.

"How are *you*?" she asked. "You've been together—what is it—over two months? This is serious."

"It is, and it isn't. We don't see all that much of each other, being on different work schedules. And some of the weekend is spent doing chores and being around her mother. But we have a blast when we go dancing. She hassles me a little about drinking, but I figure that's a staple of most relationships."

"Can you change your shift to be more in sync?"

"No, but Melissa's might hire me—one of the bartenders is leaving at the end of summer. Well, if it isn't the pink czarina!"

Bess sashayed into the living room wearing a pink smock and pink flip-flops.

Over pizza they filled me in on juicy tidbits from the Watergate hearings. Stacy said she had remade her bulletin board into a target with a picture of Nixon at the center and pictures of Mitchell, Haldeman, Ehrlichman, and other creeps filling in the concentric circles. Bess had dubbed them Rasput-ixon, G-Gordon-the-Terrible, John Dean Bad-enough, and Sonofabitch-John Mitchellovitch.

The night of my actual birthday—the start of my "twenty-third year to heaven," according to Grunner—Lish gave me two packages wrapped in flowery paper. She said I might not like one of them, at least right away.

"Will I guess which?" I asked. The first contained a brand new work shirt; all my old ones had air-conditioned elbows. The black vinyl cover on the second, a book, was a dead giveaway. *The Holy Bible.* "Hey, thanks, you never know."

"In unhappy moments, it's worth turning to."

"With you I don't have unhappy moments."

Chapter 14

LISH MADE SOME excuse to Verlene and Joy about why she couldn't come to their Fourth of July barbecue, and along with Eleanor we joined Josephine and her friends at Grant Park. The lake was a blue ten shades deeper than the sky and covered with a zillion sailboats. On land, a sea of half-naked bodies lolled on the grass or basked in lounge chairs. The smell of pot wafted by from time to time, and bongo drums bongo-ed in the distance.

I expected Lish to be in a good mood, since this morning I'd used the L-O-V-E word—she herself hadn't gone that far. But when I grabbed a beer from the cooler, she snapped I could start with juice. Moments later, she stalked off to the restrooms, prompting Eleanor to ask if we were squabbling.

"Not sure," I said. "Does her getting on my case about drinking count? Or my not wanting to go to church?"

"Are all your arguments about *your* bad habits and not hers?"

"Hey, who says—"

"*Alleged* bad habits," Eleanor corrected.

"The thing is, I never pretended to be any different than I am. She knew what she was getting into."

"Lish and her moral battles."

Feeling a tad guilty for griping to her best friend, I said, "That's to her credit, that she has moral battles. Take Nixon—too bad he doesn't."

Eleanor nodded. "And she wouldn't be in a battle if the relationship was just to pass the time."

"Hey, it's not that for me, either."

"I didn't mean to imply it was. Yet it puzzles me: she hasn't pretended her duty is anything other than marrying a black man. Doesn't that bother you?"

"I figure she'll get around to changing her mind. She's not the first person to struggle with being gay."

Eleanor looked thoughtful. "No, she's not. That must be the happy ending she subconsciously hopes for—that she'll change her mind."

I lit a cigarette and watched some frisbee tossers. "You don't have to answer this if you don't want to," I said, "but this struggle between the relationship with me and her so-called duties—who do *you* hope wins? Me or the black community?"

"It depends."

I laughed. "She's right—you already talk like a lawyer."

Eleanor didn't laugh. Instead, she weighed every word. "I hope *Lish* wins. I hope she finds a woman—and I'm not saying it isn't you—a woman who can give her the kind of loving relationship that would justify—for *her*, for *Lish*—abandoning her 'duties.' And it goes without saying—or should—her mother growing to accept it. No rift between them."

"I'll second that motion."

Lish returned in the same mood, so after a bit I joined a water balloon free-for-all and got really good at zapping them with my butt. Fortunately, the air was hot enough to dry my cut-offs in no time.

Among Lish's friends, Eleanor was the only one expressing pleasure when Nixon resigned. Eva, Joy, even Josephine's crowd seemed resigned themselves—resigned to Ford being just a watered-down version of Tricky Dick. I repeated Stacy's comment that maybe the country's disgust with Ford's pardon meant we would get a Democratic president the next go-round, and Eleanor said, "Lincoln and LBJ are the only presidents people admire."

One Saturday morning, I awoke from a sound sleep to see Lish looming over the bed. "Stacy's on the phone."

"What time is it?"

"Noon. Mama's not here, so you can go out like that."

I went down the hall and picked up the receiver. "Melissa called," Stacy said. "She's hoping to get hold of you today."

"Guess what!" I said when I came back in the bedroom. "Melissa offered me a job. The hours are great; our schedules will be almost the same."

Lish folded her arms and stared at the floor. I ran my hand along her cheek; she brusquely turned away. If this was what Jesus had in mind, I'd stick with the Old Testament.

"You'll start drinking even earlier," she said.

"Not on the job, no way." Shoot, if Ford could pardon Nixon after all the stuff *he'd* done, Lish could pardon me for the stuff I *hadn't* done.

I phoned Murray with a song-and-dance about having to go East for a funeral and not knowing how long it would take to wrap things up. Essentially I forced him to lay me off. "No hard feelings," I said, and he could just mail me my last paycheck.

Monday I began at Melissa's. Though the commute was longer and the pay smaller, tending in a gay women's bar was Andy's dream.

And the familiar tavern smells, the banter and jukebox and sound of billiard balls cracking together made it feel like old-home-week. Lish would get over being upset once she saw what a better mood I was in.

To speed up the process, I persuaded Eleanor to bring her in on Columbus Day to see firsthand that work was work. It took all of three minutes for them to start arguing.

As I set her soda down on the coaster, Lish was saying, "We're *all* sinners, El."

I threw Eleanor a look of apology, mumbling, "Drinks on the house."

Allegedly to retrieve my parka and gloves but probably to get out of housework, I hit Hyde Park the following Saturday afternoon. At least Eleanor would be coming for dinner at Lish's, and the three of us would hit Shay's afterwards. I hoped Stacy would be home now so I could corral her into joining us.

The apartment was empty. I peeked in on my alcove, then wandered aimlessly through the empty rooms. The solitude was actually nice. Till I realized it was still bugging me, the way on my birthday Matt had cut Roy off. So what if Dean had spilled a drink—or a whole pitcher, even? No, that couldn't have been it; she wanted to get Roy off the phone for some other reason. And not the leaves blowing away. Did Dean have somebody *with* him in the bar? Had he remarried? That made sense—Matt figuring I wouldn't want to know. Yet it would be *good* if he did, if they *both* did—got a fresh start with somebody new. Have a companion to grow old with. Would he tell me? No, that wasn't his thing, writing or phoning. Like *I* could complain? Pot calling the kettle—jeez, there I was being racist again.

A fifth of vodka sat on the kitchen counter. Was Bess drinking White or Black Russians these days? White versus black, everywhere you looked. I poured a shot's worth and drank it. Not bad, but could use a beer chaser.

"Oh, I thought it was Mama." Lish held the door open. "Are you drunk?"

Was it that obvious? I peered in the hall mirror. My eyes weren't bloodshot, and there were only two. "Need any help with dinner?"

"You can peel the potatoes, but the roast won't be out until eight." She headed towards the kitchen. "I thought you were getting your parka."

"Oops. Forgot." After hanging up my jeans jacket, I said, "Suppose it wouldn't be so bad, hitting Shay's at ten-thirty, eleven."

"Couldn't we skip one night?"

"*One* night? Saturday's the only time we go." I lingered in the doorway. It wasn't like the potatoes would roll away.

Lish put on the kettle. "You're at the bar after work Monday through Friday."

"That's just for one game of pool—doesn't count. And it's not with you."

"Don't you get tired of drinking? I like going out my Saturdays, but *you* party all the other days. Even the *Lord* rested on the seventh day."

"Who's He got to party with, the Holy Ghost?" My own mouth stunned me. And continued to. "Better yet, the Virgin Mary. She must be a barrel of laughs with a couple of martinis under her belt."

Lish's eyes filled with tears.

"Look," I said apologetically, "I just want you to get off my case."

She threw her hands in the air. "How am I supposed to save you?"

"Who asked you to?" I stormed out of the kitchen and into her room and began stuffing my clothes in my pack. She didn't follow. In the hall, I heard the kettle shriek and go silent. Very quietly I took my jacket from the hall closet, placed the keys on the mail table, and split.

It felt great to be home, even those days when Stacy was at her poetry class and Bess, out with friends. I toyed with the idea of buying some boards and making a bedside table, but getting high and listening to records or watching idiocy on TV filled the time adequately. Sufficed.

Grunner went to Hastings-on-Hudson for the holidays. Bess was supposed to go away but caught a bad cold, so at least I had the sounds of her coughing to keep me company.

Christmas Day I phoned Mathilde. She sounded cheerful. "How are you doing? Still at the steak-and-lobster?"

"Actually, I quit. Am working at a bar—"

"You quit? Those aren't easy to come by."

"I know. But the hours he was—"

"Don't let your brother hear—just a minute. Sissy, *I'll* get it."

"Sounds like a lot of commotion."

"Lorraine is trying to make the gravy using—"

"I'll let you go. Just wanted to wish everybody a Merry Christmas. Hey, Edward there this year?"

"He will be. Dean's car's in the shop, and he asked Edward for a ride to the Lion's Club. You know, for the blind? He helps there now instead of the institution. Sissy, I said I'll get it—"

"I'll let you go."

I caught Bess's cold and ended up calling in sick New Year's Eve, losing a great night for tips. I didn't even stay awake to watch the ball drop on TV. Happy New Year, my ass. And if January and February were any indication, all of '75 was going to suck.

March came in like a club of lions and was leaving like one. I wanted to hunker down, but Stacy nagged me to go with to some party. "It's near the Loop," she said, "so if you get bored, you can walk to the IC."

"And get frostbite."

"It's almost *sixty* out. The party's all women. And Bess is in Milwaukee for the weekend."

"More reason to stay home; I'll have the TV to myself."

But Good-Sport Andy went along for the ride. The apartment wasn't *that* near the Loop, but the night *was* really warm. The crowd was decent, and I didn't spot any exes, with or without axes.

Stacy and I stood watching the dancing. The combination of beer, music, and spring-like air coming through the open windows began to mellow me.

Rock me gently, rock me slowly.

Take it easy, don't you know

Stacy leaned over, whispering, "The woman in the corner keeps looking at you."

I knew which one she meant. Despite the dyke uniform of loose flannel shirt and jeans, the pixie conveyed something young, vulnerable. Was she even old enough to drink?

I have never been in love like this before.

"The two by the hanging plant come into Melissa's," I said. Stacy kept bobbing her head, almost to the beat.

A large young man in a suit stepped into the lit front entry, smiling and nodding. I gestured with my bottle. "Somebody can't take a hint." He stood talking to one of the hostesses like he had all the time in the world.

Stacy squinted and then stared. Though he couldn't see us—being in the light and us being where it was darker—it still seemed rude. And what was the big deal—folks wandered into the wrong apartment all the time. Her stare morphed into a gleeful grin. Maybe her beer had something in it mine didn't.

"Maxwell Street," she said. "The guy talking about du Bois."

Now *I* squinted. It *was* the crazy white orator who came yay close to sparking a race riot. The fellow—or maybe-fellow—squeezed through the crowd of dancers, smiling apologetically till he met up with the second hostess just a few feet away. Tieless and with the top button on his shirt undone, he-she offered a clear view of his-her Adam's apple. A barely detectable Adam's apple. An Eve's apple. Doggone it, Stacy was right. I'd be hearing about it for weeks.

"Guess you know how to call 'em," I said, starting towards the kitchen. "Want another beer?"

Her eyes remained on him/her. "Tommy, wasn't that it?"

The kitchen was mobbed, and it took forever to reach the fridge. When I began the return round of excuse-me's, I had to pause at the doorway to let a group through.

"Were you at Grant Park on the Fourth of July?" It was the pixie asking. Beautiful deep-brown eyes and long, dark lashes. Soft dark hair caressing her face. "They were tossing water balloons, and—" she made a charming giggle—"you stuck out your butt to break them."

"Actually, it was my evil twin. Except I don't have a twin. Good thing—the planet couldn't take two of us."

Her eyes shone. "You don't remember me, but I was helping fill the balloons."

"It's not that I don't remember you; I never *saw* you. 'Cause those dark eyes are not something I'd ever forget."

She blushed twenty shades of red. "My name's Laurie." Her lashes closed a little when she smiled, but you could still see the dark-pool eyes. Could still swim in the dark-pool eyes.

"Mine's Andy."

"I don't know anyone here except Darlene and Faye, my roommates."

"I only know Stacy, one of my roommates. She knows the hostesses. *They* sure know a lot of women." I rested Stacy's bottle on the counter behind me and twisted the cap off mine.

With sudden energy Laurie said, "Sometimes I wish the world was *only* women. Not really—I have friends who are guys. And my dad and brothers. But it feels so liberating to be around only women."

"I'll drink to that. You live near here?"

"No, Elgin. It's about fifty miles away."

"That where you grew up?"

"I grew up in Idaho. I'm not used to a big city. Darlene knows someone on an all-women farm in Wisconsin—"

Laurie and I talked through at least two beers, neither of us making any effort to find a chair or more space. She laughed at my jokes and gushed "I know what you mean" the few times I said something serious. After the blows my ego had taken with Lish, it appreciated a little appreciation.

An arm wrapped around my neck. The face that went with it was Stacy's, and it grinned. "Do you have any money on you?"

"Not that I'd fork over. Why?"

"Enough for IC fare? If not, I'll give you some. Tommy and I are going out for a drink someplace we can hear each other."

"Find out why she was trying to get herself killed at Maxwell Street, will you?"

Laurie and I continued talking till her roommates were leaving. She looked sorry to go. When I went into the room with the dancing, Sly was belting *I can take you higher*, and I began a two-step with my beer. "I can take you *high*-er!" I scoured the room for a familiar face, but in vain. A slow song came on, and those dancing sure didn't look like they would welcome an interruption. Everybody else seemed engrossed in private conversation. The grumpiness that had escorted me to the party was now stepping forward to escort me home. I found my coat, noticing nobody noticing, and left.

Chapter 15

When I awoke, Stacy's room was the way she'd left it. I put on coffee and took in the Sunday paper and sat in the living room watching the rain. The clouds spat viciously on everything animal, mineral, and vegetable. To think that yesterday had felt like spring.

Grunner spent forever fiddling with her key, but I remained on the couch, not wanting to look glad to see her. Or curious. If her evening had ended in the sack, what was it like? Did Tommy pretend to be a guy? Visions of dildos danced in my head.

The creature coming in the door wasn't animal, mineral, *or* vegetable. Her jacket was soaking wet; the jeans, plastered to her legs; the hair, looking like it had gotten raked, frozen, and mated with a porcupine. Worst of all, the instant Stacy saw me, she broke into the most repulsive shit-eating grin. "How's it going?" she practically squealed.

"How's it going with *you*?"

She tilted her head back and made gargling noises and gasped, "I'm in love."

"Is that what you call it? Looking like a hyena in rigor mortis?"

"Hungry? I haven't had breakfast. Tommy hates to cook, so he doesn't have much food around."

"*He*? Thought you were right about him being a *she*?"

"He wants to be called a he. Calling him a she in public could be dangerous."

I followed her to the kitchen. "His apartment is a studio," she said. "Everything all in one room. *Hundreds* of books. *And* his painting stuff. And he doesn't close the Murphy bed."

"A Murphy bed could be dangerous."

"Maybe with lightweight people like you. He says he's at paint-by-numbers, but it's not true. He *is* still learning skills, verisimilitude." She took out the eggs and milk.

"Vera who?"

"*Sor-ry*, I forgot you have a limited vocabulary."

"Hey, I really don't know that one."

"Means realistic, not stylized or impressionistic. Like Norman Rockwell, not Monet or Picasso." She said they had talked half the night, about their lives, philosophy, existentialism, who the hell knew what.

The rain had stopped by the time we finished eating so we walked to the Point. Clouds still blanketed the sky; the water was an ugly gray. Standing on one of the large rocks, arms akimbo football-coach style, Stacy looked out towards the horizon. "He grew up on a farm in Minnesota, an only child. As long ago as he can remember, he was convinced that his body was a mistake, like a clubfoot, and he was supposed to have been male. By sixth grade, he had decided he wasn't meant to live on a farm. The day after high school graduation, his parents drove him to the bus stop, and he boarded a bus for St. Paul, where a cousin had lined up a job interview for him at a shoe store."

A gull swirled overhead, eyeing something in the water. Any fish that would come near the surface on a day like this had to have brain disease. I scouted the ground for flat stones to skim, but the ones I picked up were more like pebbles.

"In Minneapolis, he had what he calls his epiphany: he could partially rectify God's mistakes. He phoned his cousin and said he had accepted a job offer in Wichita and would be going straight through. But instead, he bought men's clothes, found an empty restroom and put them on, and cut off his braid." Stacy broke into her idiotic smile. "That was his Saul conversion, he says, going from Terry to Tommy. He had his epiphany in Minneapolis so he didn't need to see St. Paul."

"Figures you'd like somebody with a dumb sense of humor." I tossed a pebble at the waves. "But he could have stuck with Terry."

"That's what *I* said! But he needed to train himself not to turn around if he hears Terry, in case he runs into someone from home. Hopefully they would just think it's one of those uncanny resemblances. Anyway, he came down to Chicago and took some night courses and got hired as a research assistant for a sociology professor." Stacy bent and scooped up some pebbles of her own and threw one into the lake. She had a lousy arm. "Unfortunately, the professor applied for a position at the University of Hawaii, and if he gets it, Tommy will have to find another job."

"The professor know he's female?"

"No. He legally changed his name. His driver's license, everything has him as male."

"What does he do when he visits his parents?"

"Doesn't. Told them he works for a newspaper that sends him all over the world."

"He's never going to see them again?"

"Someday. When he does, he'll say he has gone undercover for crime reporting—or else that he is in a witness protection program." She threw another pebble. "He was badly beaten once—three broken ribs. Had gotten careless."

"Didn't seem so careful at Maxwell Street."

Again she smiled. "He calls that his secular-evangelism phase."

I tossed a couple of pebbles at the water. "So when do I get to meet him?"

"Maybe next weekend. If you think *I'm* bad about using obscure words—"

"Hey, I don't mind asking if he knows Vera Similitude."

Eleven thirty on a Sunday morning was earlier than I liked to be sociable, but for weeks Stacy had been trying to get us to meet. Tommy's and my work schedules hadn't jibed until now, so I surrendered to the nagging and hauled my tired butt out of bed and followed her to the IC. She was galloping, but nothing I could say or do would stop that. Having to rush didn't make me any more kindly disposed towards the day ahead.

When we got off the train at Randolph, Tommy was sitting on a bench reading a newspaper. Stacy gushed, "Andy, Tommy; Tommy, Andy. Were you waiting long?"

Rising, he held out his hand, and we shook. In loose chinos and a light blue man's button-down shirt, Tommy looked unambiguously male, despite the smooth face and arms. Either he was naturally flat-chested or wore something underneath that did a good camouflage, because even the side without the pen protector in the pocket showed merely the outline of an undershirt. His height and overall bulk helped, as did the crew cut.

The two of them huddled but didn't kiss or touch, which was ironic since they would have looked like a boring straight couple. "He has to pick something up for his boss at a used bookstore," Stacy said. "Then we can grab lunch."

"Lunch? I ain't even had a second cup of joe."

"The bookstore has free coffee," Tommy said.

Not many folks were out, it being a grayish, muggy Sunday and the area one of warehouses and bars. The silence hanging over the streets and the Chicago River hung over the three of us. Tommy's pace was lumbering; if ever *I*'d tried walking that slowly, Stacy would have gone nuts. But her—*his*—bulk and the easy, smiling way he had of taking in the sights made it clear that this was the fastest gear on the bus.

The table with the free coffee was tucked in a little corner by the Medicine section, so I stood there scanning the titles. *Mendelian Genetics*. I remembered Mrs. H making us color in a chart with three generations of Fra Gregor's peas. Though she explained that Mother and Father each donated one-half their genes to make little Johnny, she omitted *how* the donation was made.

Tommy came over and began browsing through the medical books too. I tossed my cup in the trash and said I was going outside for a cigarette. Stacy joined me, and we watched through the store window as Tommy paid. The young woman at the register—pretty, with long hair and eyeliner around the eyes—laughed at something he said, having no idea he was female.

The second he came outside he began walking, and Stacy scurried beside him. Obviously they had picked a place to eat without asking me. I followed, remaining two steps behind. Stacy made some comment about the clouds, and Tommy said, "Fair is foul, and foul is fair."

Stacy scrunched her face into such an adoring look I wanted to puke. "We just memorized parts of *Macbeth* in my poetry class. 'Will all great Neptune's ocean wash this blood clean from my hand? No. This my hand will rather the multitudinous seas incarnadine, making the green one red.'"

"Incarnadine taste anything like grenadine?" I asked.

"I have often wondered," Tommy mused, "whether words like incarnadine and multitudinous were part of the vernacular in Shakespeare's day. Vernacular itself is an amusing word, an example of anti-onomatopoeia."

"What do you mean?" the happy spaniel arfed.

"As you well know," he said, "onomatopoeia refers to a word that sounds like its meaning. The *whiz* of an arrow shooting through the air. Anti-onomatopoeia should refer to a word that sounds the *opposite* of its meaning."

Eager puppy nodded over and over. Throw the ball, throw the ball!

"If you apply the concept in an abstract sense," he continued, "the word vernacular is, in contemporary American speech, the *opposite* of its meaning since it is *not* part of the vernacular."

At least I could see why they meshed; Stacy had to be the first person not to find him totally obnoxious.

The restaurant they chose was just some basic-American-fare place. Stacy and I shared one side of the booth, and while I actually studied the menu, they traded lines across the table.

"Sore labor's bath."

"Balm of hurt minds."

"Great nature's second course."

"Chief nourisher in life's feast!"

As if I'd asked, Stacy explained they were quoting from a passage in *Macbeth* about sleep. "Macbeth is listing all its virtues: sore labor's bath, balm of hurt minds, great nature's second course."

I was tempted to say I wouldn't have minded getting some more sleep myself but was a good little girl, instead asking, "Great nature's *second* course? What's the first, soup or salad?"

"Sleep is the second," Stacy said, "so being awake—consciousness—is the first."

Fortunately, everybody was too hungry to talk much when the food arrived. Once Tommy finished eating, he pulled one of his books from the bag. Stacy leaned forward, and he held the spine so we could read *Physician Ethics and Informed Consent*.

"For you or your boss?" she asked.

"Me. I'm curious what they have to say about the Tuskegee experiments."

"What are they?" puppy wanted to know.

"In 1932, our enlightened Public Health Service decided to study how syphilis wreaks its destruction on the body, including the brain. Insanity is one of the later symptoms. Sound noble? Doctors, nurses, scientists pursuing knowledge for the public welfare?"

He leaned back, jostling the booth so much that the lady on the other side, her back to him, hurled a harpoon glance over her shoulder. Tommy didn't notice. "They ran an experiment out of Tuskegee, Alabama, where a sizable percentage of the population had syphilis. The men they chose to study were black and poor. At the time, there was a somewhat reliable treatment for syphilis if you caught it early enough. However, instead of treating the infected men, the researchers simply observed how their symptoms progressed."

He smiled cryptically. This wasn't the earnest preacher at Maxwell Street but some cross between Perry Mason and Hercule Poirot. "By 1947," Hercule continued, "they had not just *a* treatment but a *very effective* treatment: penicillin. Did they give the black men in Tuskegee penicillin? No. Not in '47, not in '57, not in '67." He took the pen out of his shirt pocket and wrote on his placemat, large enough to be read upside down, the dates 1972 and 1932 and a minus sign in between. "For *forty years*, physicians under the auspices of the

Public Health Service deliberately withheld treatment from infected people so their suffering and death could be described. Although most of the physicians were white, some were black. Black or white, however, these weren't *sadistic* individuals. They considered themselves professionals and followed scientific protocols, using control groups and so forth, and thought the knowledge gained would help people in the future, including black people. But they watched hundreds of men get sicker and sicker and die—unnecessarily."

"No one objected?" Stacy asked.

"No one outside the study knew until 1972, when one tortured soul made it public." Tommy put the pen back in his pocket protector. "Don't forget, we had been through the Nuremberg Trials. How could their moral compasses go so awry?"

After that cheerful little lunch, I didn't see Tommy for several weeks because I landed a new job that had me working crazy hours. Two middle-aged women, Ginnie and Martha, had come into Melissa's during the Cinco de Mayo insanity and ended up offering me a position as the supervising bartender at their place southwest of the Loop. They paid me a dollar more an hour, seeing me as "an investment" because my personality gave the place atmosphere. Talk about insanity.

Actually, I almost didn't accept their offer, despite the hourly, because I was skeptical gay women would truck to that part of town. But Ginnie said their business plan didn't require a huge crowd because the bar was straight during the day, catering to the Hispanics who worked in the neighborhood. They closed at five, and now they would reopen at six as a women's bar.

I also was concerned about transportation. The streets surrounding GinMar's were a mix of factories, warehouses, and stores—some going concerns, some gone. And the buses to and from Hyde Park passed through ghetto. However, Stacy thought it was a great deal and insisted I use her car. The few times she needed wheels, she said, she would borrow Tommy's. And it turned out that Hallie, one of the other bartenders, lived in South Shore, so the nights we both closed we could offer each other rides home if one or the other of us had had to truck in that day by bus.

As a measure of how desperate folks were for a new place to party, word-of-mouth alone brought in scores of women the night we opened and all the weekends after. Folks *were* willing to travel a bit south, at least for reasonably priced drinks, a great jukebox, nice dance floor, and a pool table away from the foot traffic.

Being a supervisor didn't feel half bad. Not that I viewed my position as a license to be a jerk. *A good manager, like a good officer, takes care of his people*, Dean used to say. My perspective definitely broadened. When summer hit full force, Ginnie and Martha had a spat about when to run the air-conditioner, the walls being paper-thin, and I brokered a compromise: we would put up some cheap insulation and keep the thermostat a tad higher when the bar was relatively empty and nobody was dancing. I also pasted a sign on the bathroom door reminding folks to switch off the light when they left.

On the home front, Bess practically lived at the library, hell-bent on finishing her thesis and getting her degree next June. Tommy sometimes escaped his small, clammy apartment for our larger, clammy apartment, and I wondered if he would move into ours when Bess left. We got along fine now—he didn't care if my mind wandered while he acted his "semantic pedantic self," though when he too started throwing nanos and picos around, I finally asked what they actually meant.

Coming into the living room right at that moment, Stacy said gleefully, "Nano means one billionth, and pico, one trillionth."

"So what's the prefix for zillionth?" I asked.

"Zillionth," Tommy said, stroking his chin, "is essentially a closing-in on infinity, so it should be called a *zeno*."

Stacy acted like it was the funniest thing since Chaplin ate his boot. "He's making a joke about Zeno's Paradox," she told me. "Zeno was a Greek philosopher who said that logically speaking, a person should never be able to travel from Point A to Point B. In order to reach Point B, first you have to go *half* the distance, but in order to go half the distance, you first have to go half the *half*-the-distance—a fourth the distance—but before you can go a fourth-the-distance, you have to go *half* the fourth-the-distance, et cetera. In other words, with an infinity of half-distances to travel, you can never in finite time—"

"I get the point, or at least half of it." I did *not* get what was so hilariously funny.

Fall arrived before you knew it. The air-conditioner spat at GinMar's segued into a furnace spat, and again I brokered a compromise: the more bodies, the lower the thermostat. Some nights we had such a big crowd, I was tempted to turn the air-conditioner back on.

This particular night looked like a possibility; the nanosecond I walked in the door, Hallie shouted, "It's a birthday party." Mayhem and bedlam was more accurate. A banner saying *Happy 30th, Darlene!* had been hung over the jukebox, and the dance floor was filled to the max.

Ever since I met ya,
Seems I can't forget ya,
The thought of you
Keeps running through

It was okay hitting the ground running. Commotion sparked an adrenaline rush, and when your arms and legs were having a

coordinated day, juggling twenty things at once was fun: resting a
pitcher under the tap, tossing ice in glasses, stepping back and forth
to the fridge for the tomato juice and seltzer, banging the register
with an elbow, making change and hearing it clank in the tips jar.

"Hi!"

I turned back to the counter. Dark eyes, shy smile. "Hey, stranger. What can I get you?"

"You don't remember me?"

"I told you before: who's going to forget those eyes? Laurie.
Here for the birthday gig?"

"Darlene's one of my roommates. Ex-roommates, really."

"What'll you be drinking?"

"Whatever's on tap. Just a glass."

As she reached into her jeans pocket, her dark hair fell forward.
It had outgrown its pixie cut and tickled her neck. With her sweater
tied around her waist, I got a better view of her figure. Her breasts,
braless, were not too big and not too small; Goldilocks found them
just right. "Hey, this one's on me," I said when she held out a five.

"Two pitchers," Hallie yelled.

Laurie stuffed the bill in the tips jar, took her glass, and headed
towards the birthday crowd. By the time I'd poured the orders and
taken care of the counter refills, I'd lost sight of her. She could see I
was busy, couldn't she?

For the next zillion hours, Hallie and I and the part-time worked
like headless chickens. Stacy showed up at one point, sliding onto a
stool, saying Tommy had dropped her off because he had a meeting
early in the morning. "His boss got the job in Hawaii, so he has to
start looking for something."

"Shoot."

Hallie yelled over the din, "Jack Daniels rocks, Bloody M, shot
Schnapps."

"Hey, Hal, do me a favor—step back here just for a sec?"

I hurried to the pool area, pretty certain I'd spotted Laurie. "Look, I've got to work till closing, but maybe some night we can go out—"

"I'm moving to Wisconsin," she said. "To a farm that's all women."

"Cool. When?"

"Monday."

"Jeez."

"You could come too—there's room."

I cocked my head like I was considering it. "Can't imagine finding a women's bar to work in up there."

"Some of the women pay their room and board by doing chores. Planting, harvesting. You might not need a job off-farm."

I told her I'd think on it. Back behind the counter, I took over from Hallie, too busy even to chat with Stace. Laurie came up later to say goodbye and handed me a matchbook. "I wrote the phone number of the farm on the inside."

"Thanks. I'm going to put it in a safe place." I went to the coat hooks and tucked the matchbook in the jeans jacket pocket I never used.

Bad news came in threes. Ginnie announced we were closing the week before Christmas so the owner could install new insulation, and we wouldn't reopen till January. She would keep the paychecks coming, but for jobs that relied on tips, that wasn't much of a consolation. When I told Stacy, she acted sympathetic for a whole thirty seconds before getting distracted.

The following evening, I saw Hallie serve a table and dump all the bills in the tips jar. I pretended not to notice. So much for being management.

When I got home, the living room lights were on. Stacy and Tommy sat at opposite ends of the couch, a map spread out between them. "You wonder why we're awake at two-thirty in the morning?" Tommy asked. "Why is this night different from all other nights?"

"We have a proposition," Stacy said.

"Sorry, ain't into threesomes."

"Since Tommy's between jobs, and you won't have to be back at GinMar's until January, and I've got vacation time, how about driving East? We could visit with my dad for Christmas, take the train into the city a few times—see museums, the women's bars—and drive down to Brackton for New Year's?"

"Whoa." I took off my jacket and hung it on the stand. "This could be worse than a threesome."

"You don't need to bring us along," Tommy said. "We could drive there with you and stay at a motel, explore the area. It must have something 'worth a detour' in the *Michelin Guide*."

"Brackton ain't worth a blown-out Michelin tire."

"Doesn't Roy have his own apartment?" Stacy asked.

Roy wasn't the problem, I said. Hell, he could even be good for some laughs around the poker table. It was Mathilde. "She makes me feel guilty for rarely calling and never visiting. I know, I know: that's all the *more* reason to visit. Did I say it was logical?"

I ended up pulling a Zeno and agreeing to half the trip, the Hastings-on-Hudson/New York City half. Once we were there, I would decide if I wanted to go all the way to Point B.

Early December was crazy, with me trying to shore up extra hours at GinMar's while helping Tommy move all his stuff into a storage locker so his landlady could repaint his apartment. Plus, we were down to one car because he sold his to have extra cash for the trip.

As the day for departure grew closer, I was actually getting excited. Tommy and I talked about a bunch of things we wanted to see—Greenwich Village and museums and maybe the Stonewall and Times Square. He had never been to New York, and I hadn't since the *Nutcracker* field trip in eighth grade. Dean had taken us a few times before that—I still remembered the huge *T. rex* skeleton.

Stacy-the-Instigator, meanwhile, became a certifiable basket case. She kept insisting her father would never accept her being gay—it would practically kill him—so we had to be extra extra careful not to say or do anything to clue him in. We wouldn't be the only visitors either—Pamela and her fiancé, Charlie, would come up from the city, and Aunt Cherise would come down from Rochester. Aunt Cherise was even more judgmental than Pamela, but Charlie was "a really nice guy." At least Cherise would leave a day or two after Christmas on a cruise with her old Vassar buddies.

Wisely, in my mind, Stacy decided not to tell her father Tommy was her boyfriend, for that would guarantee scrutiny of his every move. The line about Brackton she used—since I refused to say for certain I would go—was that we might visit Mathilde for a few days between Christmas and New Year's if her vacation trip to Disneyland got cancelled.

"*Disneyland?*" I said, hearing what she had told her dad. "Matt's in her mid-forties."

"I was nervous—it was the first thing that popped into my head." She frowned. "I *really* want this visit to go well. My dad isn't young."

Chapter 16

INDIANA WAS VAST flat stretches upon vast flat stretches of straw-colored frozen sheen. A lone tree or house or silo in the distance was about all that broke up the sameness. I took the first shift at the wheel, and Tommy sprawled in the back. Stacy sat up front half-turned towards me so she could converse with him too.

Bicker was more like it. Now their topic was genetics, and after my feeble attempt to inject some levity by singing "Gary Indiana Gary Indiana Gary," I tuned them out. Unfortunately, that became hard when they started saying "sex." More unfortunately, they weren't discussing the act itself but "the male sex" and "the female sex," and the XY chromosome and the XX.

"Mitosis precedes meiosis," Stacy insisted. "It's *meiosis* when the chromosome pairs separate."

"*Regardless*," Tommy said, "each egg has a 50 percent chance of being fertilized by a sperm with the gene mutation."

His tone had a 99 percent chance of casting a pall, so I sang, "Mei*os*is sup*pos*es mi*tos*is is *ros*es, but *Mos*es sup*pos*es erroneously."

He muttered, "And you have psychoses." Stacy groaned happily; all was right with the world.

We stopped for supper in Western Pennsylvania but had barely been seated when they got into *another* argument, this one over whether you could prove that God didn't exist. Stacy said you couldn't prove a negative, and Tommy said you could, and I wanted to say, Jesus! Wasn't the whole point of this trip to enjoy hanging loose together? At least they didn't argue while eating.

Of course the second the waitress was done clearing, Stacy started up. "Just because we haven't *found* Him—or Her or It—doesn't rule out that He/She/It exists somewhere."

"We can prove it by examining religion *scientifically*," Tommy said. He moved his water glass aside, took the pen from his shirt pocket, and began to draw on the placemat. The slow, painstaking effort he put into whatever he was drawing had you wondering if he was replicating the Sistine Chapel. Actually, I wasn't far off: you could make out the boot of Italy.

"It's a map; we get it," Stacy said. She consulted her watch. "Can you hurry?"

Nope. His hand didn't accelerate one picosecond. Slowly and methodically he drew the outline of Turkey, descended to Egypt, drew Africa, looped east to hit Saudi Arabia, India, Southeast Asia, China and Japan, down to Australia. Waltzing Mathilda, waltzing Mathilda. Should I waltz in on Mathilde?

"What's your point?" Stacy said.

"Patience, my dear Watson, patience." He added North and South America and began drawing country boundaries. Without having to look sideways, I knew Stacy was a pressure cooker at a zillion millimeters of mercury. Then he added little crosses and crescents, a Star of David on the east coast of the Mediterranean, some symbols I didn't recognize.

About a year later, he swiveled the placemat 180 degrees and pointed with the pen nib. "This is a rough attempt to chart the distribution of the world's major religions. Buddhism across East Asia, blended here and there with Islam, a little Christianity. India is largely Hindu, although with a sizeable Muslim population. Pakistan, the Middle East, mostly Muslim. In Europe and the Americas: Christianity. I made no attempt to distinguish between the Church of Rome, the Russian and Greek Orthodox, or the Protestant denominations. And for brevity's sake, I omitted non-Islamic Africa."

At the word brevity, Stacy almost lunged across the table.

"Hey, what about us pagans?"

"Sadly, Andy, you're a dying breed." He looked again at Stacy. "The interesting thing is: I could have drawn this map a generation ago, or ten or a hundred. Since the spread of Christianity in Europe, and Islam in Asia and Africa, little has changed. The same with the Americas once the Europeans arrived." Leaning back in the booth, he encompassed us both in his gaze. "Obviously there are local variations, conversions on a small scale, like American blacks adopting Islam, but I'm talking about *large*-scale demographics."

Stacy's lips were pressed together, her eyes on the map.

"Now to the science," Tommy said. "A scientific theory must permit prediction, you agree? For example, do Newton's laws allow us to predict where a ball will land when propelled at such-and-such an angle with such-and-such a force? Can we predict how a population with syphilis will fare on penicillin? If a theory makes accurate predictions, then it's scientifically proven. You agree with that?"

Except for her mouth, Stacy's face didn't twitch a muscle. "So far."

"When it comes to why people believe in God, there are two possible hypotheses. The first is that people believe in God because there *is* a God, an entity somewhere in the universe. The second hypothesis is that people believe in God for reasons having nothing to do with an entity actually existing but because of something going on inside their own minds."

All Stace said was, "Continue."

"My theory follows the second hypothesis and postulates that people believe in God because they are indoctrinated as children, taught as children that God exists, *not* because a God exists in the external world. Now, let's test it. Can you predict a person's religion only by knowing the religion his parents taught him? Yes."

He rested the nib on India. "The subcontinent provides the clearest example. Here we have neighbors living side by side for generations, Hindus and Muslims. They share the same climate, the same topography, eat similar foods, drink the same water, breathe the same air, work at the same jobs, and engage in the same activities. They get the same diseases and so forth. Yet the Muslims believe in a single God and the Koran. The Hindus believe in a number of Gods and different sacred texts. They have *widely* divergent views on eternity and reincarnation."

He leaned his forearms against the table, his eyes pinning Stacy. "Why? Why the difference? Anything in their *external* world to warrant it? No—we've controlled for that, as I have described. The *only* difference in their lives is the religion they've been taught. And how else can you explain the virtually perfect alignment of beliefs between parent and child down through successive generations, Muslim in one house, Hindu in the next? Wouldn't you expect that if God were something *observable* like rain or flowers or animals, Hindu and Muslim neighbors would have *common* perceptions of the deity? Isn't it actually a *startling* coincidence that in all these places"—the pen jumped around the placemat—"everyone's beliefs coincide *exactly* with their parents' beliefs and not their neighbors'?"

As if she were still thinking it through, Stacy said slowly, "What if all religious people share the same *perception* of God but give it a different *name*? And different origin. They could perceive the same entity in the external, physical world, but the differences—the Bible versus Koran or Bhagavad Gita—they could be the bath water, not the baby."

Unfazed, Tommy pocketed his pen. "I agree that all religious people may share similar internal *feelings*. Homo sapiens is a single species. But religions posit very specific sets of *external* facts, facts about Nature and the soul and the creation of the universe."

Stacy didn't give up, which puzzled me since she'd always claimed to be an atheist. Maybe she felt in some sort of foxhole. "But if virtually all people perceive *something*," she said, "even if they interpret it differently, couldn't the something still be out there?"

"What kind of something?" Tommy said. "Where's the evidence?"

She reached for the check. "Do we pay the waitress?"

We grabbed some winks at a small motel and got an early start the following morning, taking the Tappan Zee Bridge across the Hudson just after noon. Traffic was light, maybe because it was Christmas Eve. Stacy was at the wheel and brought us through a bunch of picturesque residential neighborhoods, finally pulling to the curb on a quiet street. The half-dozen houses on the block were large and far apart and had trimmed lawns and bushes.

Her house—mansion, almost—was recognizable from the photos. The front yard sloped gently up to steps bordered by large shrubs. Most of the two-story extended to the left—I'd guess a good eighty feet—ending in what looked like a greenhouse. Shrubs also hugged the rounded tower to the right of the front door, but these had lost their leaves. So this was how the other half lived.

While Grunner unlocked the trunk, Gabe took a closer look at the tower, a brown stucco cylinder that contained Grunner's bedroom. Each of the two windows up high was large enough for Rapunzel's suitor. Between the top of the window frames and the parapet roof, a hideous gargoyle with foot-long fangs sneered down on us, its eyes reminding me of Peter Lorre's. A wrought-iron balcony curved around beneath the windows but was way too narrow for standing on and was just decoration. And it had no real railing, just an ankle-high wrought-iron strip.

Following Stacy up the path, I could see the strip was actually a row of daggers pointing skyward. Obviously Rapunzel's suitors would be better off using the front door. And it hit me that Big-Sister Pamela might have meant well when she'd argued against Stacy moving up there in high school. In a fire, you would have to choose among burning, getting impaled on the daggers just outside the window, or plunging to your death.

Stace rang the bell, and the front door was opened by a gray-haired man who gave one of those great involuntary smiles. The two of them hugged, and he even smiled at me, not minding what the cat had dragged in.

"Hi, Dad. Hope we didn't arrive at an inconvenient time."

"No, no, we've been waiting for you."

The front hallway was cavernous enough to hold Mathilde's dining and living rooms together. Several archways branched to several staircases and corridors. To my immediate right was a spiral staircase to the tower.

"This is Andrea. Andrea, this is my father."

"How do you do," he said, shaking my hand.

"And that's Tom." Stacy pointed to where Tommy stood at the rear of the car among the backpacks and suitcases. "Andrea's boyfriend."

What the—and thanks for the warning, Judas!

I said I'd help with the bags and hurried down the path. She had better not be expecting me and Tommy to hold hands and cuddle. I broke it to him that he was to pretend to be my boyfriend, and he smiled like the Cheshire Cat. We lugged the luggage to the house slowly.

After "Tom" got introduced, Mr. Grunner led us towards the sunroom, saying Tom could have David's room, and Cherise wanted to put me in Jim's room. Stacy said she wanted me to stay upstairs with her. He was fine with that.

"Chesterton!"

A big old St. Bernard hobbled towards us. After Stacy stroked his back, he sniffed his way to me. We passed a room with glass-enclosed bookcases and one with a shiny grand piano and an artificial Christmas tree. Mr. Grunner said tomorrow Pamela would be coming up alone; Charles was going to Boston because his mother was "quite ill."

"She didn't go with him?" Stacy asked.

"No, she wants to see *you*."

Halting, Stacy turned to me, her eyeballs bulging worse than the gargoyle's. She whispered, "Tell Tommy you're his girlfriend."

"Already did," I whispered back. "Says he likes me better anyway."

The sunroom had a long teak table and beyond it, the greenhouse I had seen from the street, containing all sorts of plants. To be polite, I said the tall woven screens were nice. What was even nicer, I thought, was the table having an ashtray.

"In winter," Mr. Grunner said, "we use the screens in the afternoon to block off the windows and keep the heat at this end." He pointed to another screen off to the side. "That hides an old sofa I wanted to get rid of ages ago, but no one will let me."

Stacy smiled affectionately. "It's the perfect napping sofa, Dad."

"That's what you all say. Before I forget, the Michaelsons invited us to dinner tonight."

Her smile shortened. "To be honest, we've been on the road for two days and were hoping for a quiet evening here."

"Let them stay, Alvin." The voice clattering in perfect time to the clattering high heels came from a sharply dressed lady in her sixties. Her hair was cemented in a "do," as Nina's mother would say, a platinum-blond mold. Oddly, the bright red lipstick and black eyelash goo, which you could see from twenty feet, made her look not cheap but rich as Croesus. Maybe it was the heavy gold bracelet or gold jacket and skirt, but I had the urge to shield my eyes from the glare.

Stacy gravitated towards it. "Cherise." They hugged.

"You look like you've lost weight," her aunt said.

"Looks are deceiving." Stacy introduced us, and Tommy extended his hand. Cherise took it uncertainly but gave a smile. I decided to go the femme route and smiled obsequiously.

"The Michaelsons will understand," Cherise said. "Stacy and her friends may need to catch up on sleep."

Mr. Grunner motioned for us to sit, which I did, and said he and Cherise had already eaten lunch, but Rosa had assembled some cold cuts for us before she went home for the holidays. Stacy went with her father to the kitchen to get them, and Cherise pulled out a chair near mine and sat, crossing her nylon-stockinged legs. They weren't varicose-veined.

"You are Stacy's roommate?" she asked.

"One of them. There's also Bess. She's working on her Ph.D. in Russian literature."

"Are you in school too?"

"Right now, right now I'm just working in a cocktail lounge till I figure out when to go back." The lady made me nervous. Would she ask what school? Tommy was no help, standing yards away reading a newspaper.

Cherise herself took me off the hook. "I wish Stacy would go back to school. So much potential. The one with the brains in the family." She waved her hand dismissively. "None of them are stupid. Pamela, if she keeps going, could wind up in the CEO's seat. Why she would *want* to, I don't know. She and Charles should be getting married and starting a family. I suppose having to be a mother to her brothers and sister when she was barely out of college has dampened her desire for children. What do *you* do, Tom?"

"I'm an Associate Professor of Sociology at Columbia."

I choked on the inhale and must've coughed for a good five minutes. Cherise seemed genuinely concerned, asking repeatedly if I was all right. I nodded, unable to speak. Was I supposed to jump up and alert Stacy to Tom's new career? And spend the entire visit shuttling back and forth to clue each in on the other's lies and alibis? Shoot, even if I'd wanted to, there was no way I could track Stacy down in this maze.

"You're awfully young to be an associate professor," Cherise said.

"I'm older than I might look."

Great, Tom, get her focusing on your body to guess your age.

Cherise looked again at me. "When you *do* go back, what will you study?"

I tapped the ash into the tray. "Haven't decided yet, between—"

"She *has* decided," Tommy said, "but is worried about her LSAT score."

Cherise raised an eyebrow, impressed. "You are going to law school?"

Stacy carried in a tray. "What about law school?" She was smiling, her father's obvious pleasure at seeing her having finally sunk in.

Tommy wisely waited till she had set the tray down on the table. "Andrea will apply once she accepts the fact that her LSAT score isn't as poor as she pretends."

In less than a nanosecond, Stacy's smile shriveled out of existence. She had the sense not to meet anybody's gaze; wordlessly she distributed the plates, silverware, glasses, and napkins. "Dad will be bringing in the cold cuts. There's also lettuce, tomato, and cheese, Andrea." She told her aunt, "Andrea's a vegetarian."

Cherise didn't seem to care; she rose and said she was going to call the Michaelsons. As soon as she left, I asked Stacy why was I a vegetarian.

"Rosa ordered the prime rib before she knew we were coming. The butcher gets it special. Even with Charlie not here, there won't be enough. Dad was offering to go without, but I said I didn't care—that you were a vegetarian, and I had gotten used to eating less meat."

"That's great for *you*," I said. "I *love* prime rib!"

Stace gave her hangdog look. "I'm just so nervous, I say the first thing that pops into my head."

"Well plug up all the damn holes so nothing else will. You know the last time I had prime rib?"

"You can have mine," Tommy said.

I crushed the cigarette into the tray. "No, I can't; I'm a vegetarian!"

Stacy looked damn miserable. And well she should have. Here I'd be sitting at a table smelling the roast and watching everybody else digging in and eating it, and my plate would contain nothing but a bunch of *god damn* vegetables. She picked at her cuticles. It killed me, but eventually I mumbled, "It's okay. You just owe me one, that's all. No— two or three or four." I turned on Tommy.

"And if you expect me to sound like somebody going to law school, you got another thing coming." But I didn't need to rake him over the coals—Stacy would.

Amazingly, we ate lunch in peace. Cherise went out to buy a gift for the Michaelsons, and Mr. Grunner, saying he was like a little child, went upstairs to take a nap. I put three slices of ham on my sandwich.

The grand tour included the library, piano room, and billiards room, which was in a side wing and a mess because raccoons had gotten in and destroyed the felt. Tommy took forever inspecting the guest cottage, which wasn't a cottage but its own wing with its own bathroom, kitchen, bedrooms, and outside entrance. Circling back through the sunroom, I had to admit that the couch Stacy and her siblings wouldn't let Mr. Grunner throw out, hidden behind one of the screens, did look comfortable. Plus it had pillows and a knitted afghan.

We returned to the front hall and went up the non-spiral staircase to the East Wing. Tommy's bedroom was two doors down from Cherise's, and they shared a bathroom. He set out a man's razor and shaving cream on the bathroom counter—I was impressed at his foresight.

Back downstairs, Stacy hit a switch to light the spiral staircase, and we began the climb to the tower. "You sure these steps are safe?" I asked. "They're pretty creaky."

"The creaks are a blessing in disguise. I can always tell who's coming; everyone makes a different sound. And be forewarned, the former owners got carried away with the nautical motif, and we never changed it."

She wasn't kidding. Except for the furniture, you would think you were on a ship. The walls were a pale blue, the porcelain knobs on the closet door were painted with seagulls, and the beige molding running around both the ceiling and floor resembled thick woven rope. The window-seat cushions had a sailboat design. It was the coolest room I'd ever seen, and I said I was surprised her brothers hadn't vied for it, but Stacy pointed out you had to go downstairs to use the bathroom. Even the inside door knob was cool: a fake compass, the needle serving as a bolt that rotated clockwise into a metal latch.

Tommy knelt on the window-seat cushions and pushed open a pane.

"What are you doing?" Stacy said. "It's freezing."

"I thought they were just for show." He swung the window closed.

Crik crik crik. Crik crik crik. Somebody was coming upstairs.

"That's my aunt."

Rat-tat-tat.

"Come in," Stacy called out.

The compass needle turned from east to due north, and the door opened. Cherise said from the threshold, "We'll be leaving shortly for the Michaelsons'. Your father is having coffee in the library. I thought you might want to visit with him."

Stacy took the hint and followed her aunt downstairs. Tommy grabbed *Candide* off a shelf and settled back on the window seat. I found a well-worn *Catcher in the Rye* and lay on the bed.

Stacy was right about the distinctive sound; her step had a multisyllabic *cre-aaa-aak*, *cre-aaa-aak*, *cre-aaa-aak*, worlds away from Cherise's *crik, crik, crik*.

After the Michaelsons' contingent left, we drove to a nearby town and ate supper at a Chinese restaurant that did not, I pointed out, serve prime rib. Stacy gave a rundown of the Christmas Day agenda:

Pamela would drive up from the city late morning; we would eat dinner around five, doing a gift exchange right before; and the following morning, Friday, Pamela would drive back down to the city with Cherise.

Stacy didn't want us all to leave Hastings the same day because her father might feel deserted, but what if we went to Brackton on Saturday, Sunday, or even Monday? That way, we would save the best part of the vacation—going into Manhattan—for last. I said I hadn't decided yet whether to go down to Jersey at all.

On the way back to the house, we stopped at a store for beer. Tommy bought a fifth of single-malt Scotch, and Stace grabbed a bunch of one-shot bottles for me and him to give her family during the gift exchange. She took a Michelin-detour route the rest of the way home, zigzagging down a hill and turning every possible direction, pointing out local shops and things. Tommy asked a zillion questions, especially about the trains. Did they go only to New York or also to Albany, Boston, D.C.? Did they arrive at Penn Station or Grand Central? I pitied the ship crew if he ever took a cruise.

Cherise and Mr. Grunner hadn't returned by the time we did, so after unloading the beers in the fridge, we were able to escape to Stacy's room to drink. We all crashed early, exhausted by the stress of being on our best behavior.

Chapter 17

ATHOS, ARAMIS, AND Porthos were lazing in the sunroom reading the paper, sipping coffee, and picking at muffins. All of a sudden somebody strode in with an enthusiastic "Merry Christmas!" She looked about thirty-five and wore a dark green sweater and matching slacks. Her features and chestnut hair were Hollywood-actress perfect. She embraced Stacy, who did the introductions. Pamela shook our hands like she really *was* pleased to meet us.

I volunteered to get her a cup of coffee from the kitchen, and she thanked me like it was a ten-mile hike. When I returned, Cherise had come in, and the three obvious females sat at one end of the teak table looking very serious. Again Tommy stood off by himself, again engrossed in a newspaper.

"So it wasn't *technically* a stroke," Cherise told Stacy.

Pamela gave me a thank-you smile and pushed out the adjacent chair, adding, "It can *lead* to a stroke."

"What are they doing for it?" Stacy asked.

"He's taking medication."

Cherise fiddled with her ring, its diamond the size of my kneecap. "He'll have a lifelong susceptibility. Which is why we need to spare him unnecessary stress."

From Mr. Grunner's health, the conversation moved to Charlie's mother's illness to Cherise's upcoming trip to the Bahamas. When Pamela said she wanted to bring her suitcases upstairs and unpack, Tommy volunteered to help.

The second they left the room, Cherise turned to me like I was a tarantula. "I want to have a private talk with Stacy." I mumbled that I'd get more coffee and scurried my hairy legs out.

After pouring myself a fresh cup and gazing out the kitchen window a few minutes, I tiptoed towards the sunroom. But before going in, I lingered just beyond the doorway.

"You can't wait for good things to happen," Cherise was saying. "You have to *pursue* them."

"I'm not waiting. I *am* pursuing—I'm doing what I want to be doing."

"A dead-end job? On the bottom rung of a ladder to nowhere? With all your *education*, your *abilities*. I remember when you used to play the piano—"

Stacy laughed. "I haven't played the piano for ten years. And I was never very—"

"You had ability. You didn't practice enough, that's all. And employers are *looking* for women who are good at mathematics."

"Dad accepted my decision a long time ago."

Hearing a chair squeak, I backed up a few feet.

"I have said all I have to say. You are aware of your father's health. It is time to grow up. And if this is your idea of growing up, if this is the best you can aspire to, that is—I will tell you what that is. That would be a huge disappointment to your mother."

Without planning to, I rushed forward, almost colliding with Cherise, who all but ignored me as she went past. I said to Stace, "Don't go buying that …"

She managed a half-hearted smile. "An amazing instinct for the jugular, hasn't she? But I'm not worried about my mother. If she still exists somewhere and can see what I've been up to, she's fine. I just don't want Cherise carping at Dad."

We did our own gift exchange in the tower, mostly books, except Stacy also gave me a red Phillies cap to replace the one I'd left at some femme de semaine's. And I promised them each stocking stuffers from the magic store in Brackton *if* I decided to go.

Actually, unbeknownst to them, I *had* decided to go. Mr. Grunner's pleasure at seeing Stacy had plucked one guilt chord, and his quasi-stroke had plucked another. In October, Dean had turned forty-six—he used to joke that his birth in '29 had started the Great Depression. And Matt was only a year younger. You never knew when somebody's time would be up. Dean's father had died in middle-age, and his mother couldn't have been much past sixty. Plus, she'd gone crazy years before. Of course, that was from drinking morning, noon, and night. Dean and I had always had the good sense to wait till we got off work. Shoot—when I closed at GinMar's, I didn't open my first beer till after 2:30 a.m., which should have earned me some kind of medal.

The rest of the afternoon, I hung out in Stacy's room while she and Tommy came and went. Christmas dinner would be enough socializing for me—Christmas dinner watching *other* people eating prime rib.

Now it was Tommy's *cru-uck, cru-uck, cru-uck* on the stairs. The compass needle went from three o'clock to twelve. He came in and sat on the window seat, asking if I'd decided which day to go down to Brackton.

"You mean *if* I decide."

He fanned the pages of *Candide*. "What if you'd be doing us a favor?"

"Who's us?"

"Stacy may have told you I'm someone who is accustomed to, who *needs* a certain amount of solitude. If I don't get it, I become irritable. It occurred to me that if you two were to go to Brackton for a few days, it would provide just the break I need. When you return, I will be eager for company and a more pleasant companion on the excursions into Manhattan and the trip home."

I pretended to deliberate. "Assuming I agree—and I'm not saying I do—you going to fill me in ahead of time on the story you'll give her father as to why you're not coming with?"

"He won't know."

"You'll stay in the city?"

"No, I'll stay in the guest cottage."

I squinted like he was nuts. "How's he not going to know?"

"I won't leave it. Has a kitchen, bathroom. I'll bring down some books, stock the refrigerator. In the unlikely event he comes in, I will say I wasn't feeling well and didn't want to put anyone to any trouble. But from what I hear from Stacy and Pamela, no one goes back there."

I made an elaborate show of hemming and hawing. "Okay, I'll go to Brackton. But you'll owe me too. Maybe a second prime rib."

"Let's see what Stacy thinks." He rose and went out.

My surprise quickly wore off. Tommy had been living alone till his landlady had started the repainting, and he had grown up as an only child on a farm out in nowhere, so he probably did get used to a certain amount of solitude. Heck, there were times even *I* wanted some.

And there was no denying the advantages to his remaining behind. They wouldn't be sniping at each other, for starters. And when I imagined, say, going out for drinks with Dean and Edward, Tommy was never part of the picture. Plus, he was so damn unpredictable. I wasn't paranoid like Stacy that folks would figure out his sex, but his unpredictability made *her* unpredictable. Pal-ling around with just Grunner would make *Gabe* more pleasant.

Stacy's *cre-aaa-aaks* sounded, the compass-needle went from three back to noon, and in she came, carrying a bag of ribbons and roll of Scotch tape. "I had a nice talk with Dad and Pamela." She took the little liquor bottles from the bag and began to tape on the ribbons. "Tommy said you decided to go to Brackton?"

"Figured as long as I'm this close."

"Do you mind if he stays here and just I go with you?" She repeated Tommy's spiel about needing time alone and how he would hide out in the guest cottage. I pretended to mull it over and said it was fine, as long as I didn't have to go by myself.

Right before dinner, we assembled in the room with the artificial tree. Its little bulbs reflected red, gold, and green off the shiny piano. Everybody had donned fancier duds: Mr. Grunner wore a necktie and navy sports coat, Pamela wore a red dress, and Cherise wore a blue dress. We had been forewarned, so I was in my black chinos and a turquoise crewneck Stacy'd swiped from Jim's room. She wore cords and a cardigan, and Tommy put on a suit and tie.

The gift exchange went without fanfare. Cherise gave Pamela and Stacy sweaters; Stacy gave her father leather gloves and Pamela and Cherise, silk scarves. Pamela gave Stacy a collection of Elizabeth Barrett Browning poems, apologizing if she already had them. Tommy and I gave out the miniature bottles of liquor, receiving in return, in a sort of combined family gift, toiletry sets. His said *Aftershave*; mine said *Chanel*. Now at least I had something to give Mathilde.

At dinner I quickly tanked up on wine since Stacy had begged me to sit beside Cherise to increase the distance between her aunt and Tommy, and nobody was drinking beer. The roast smelled excruciatingly good, and I glared at Stacy whenever she looked my way. Pamela and Tommy conversed quietly at their end, and I pretended to be listening in so I wouldn't get stuck talking to Cherise, who mostly listened in on Stacy's conversation with Mr. Grunner at the opposite end, though occasionally Cherise darted a glance at Tommy. When he got up and opened a third bottle of wine, Cherise asked Pamela what was so funny.

"It's not important," Pamela said. "Just that *'Il faut cultiver notre jardin.'*" Her dad looked puzzled, so she explained, "It's from Voltaire and translates into 'we must cultivate our garden.' Voltaire's philosophy is that we shouldn't despair at the world's unfixable problems and instead pay attention to our own lives, families, personal obligations." She quickly added, her eyes hopping to Stacy, "Of course, scholars may interpret it differently."

Stace started to say something but Cherise interrupted by asking, "Doesn't *your* generation want to *change the whole world*? You have the Women's Libbers, and now what—the *gays*, they call themselves. I never hear people your age mention more *modest* goals."

Poor Stace: she managed to choke on Yorkshire pudding. Luckily, Tommy changed the subject. "Voltaire is often called the Father of Atheism," he said. "Paradoxically, people think atheism spells the *end* of morality, but I maintain atheism is the *beginning* of morality."

While he poured Pamela more wine, she asked why, not realizing he was going to tell us anyway. "The Judeo-Christian religions advocate moral behavior as the means of going to heaven and avoiding hell," he said. "The imperative to be good, for the pious, originates in pleasing God and reaping His rewards."

"Religion is a great comfort," Cherise told him.

Who called it "the opium of the masses"? Somebody famous.

"Take the story of Abraham and Isaac," Tommy said. "We all believe that any *human being* commanding a father to murder his own son would be horribly cruel. Yet Abraham doesn't argue with God. Why? Because God is *almighty*. So Abraham follows God's commands. In other words, might makes right."

"So following God's commandments," Pamela said, tilting her head to one side and smiling, "out of fear of punishment isn't being moral?"

Cherise glared at her, then at me. What did *I* do?

"It's expediency," Tommy said. "Truly being moral is doing good deeds *regardless* of any benefit to oneself. And only atheists act without expectation of a benefit in the afterlife."

I couldn't tell if Mr. Grunner or Cherise were offended, though it seemed to me that questioning God's morality during His son's birthday dinner might not be the wisest move. Stacy apparently agreed because apropos of nothing, she told her father that I gave Tom a book of Shakespeare's sonnets for Christmas. Like hell. But that started everybody talking about "the Bard."

When we finished eating and Pamela asked how many wanted coffee, Cherise was the only taker. Mr. Grunner said he was like Winston Churchill and liked to take a short nap to feel refreshed. I couldn't wait to get back to the tower and hit the single malt. Pamela suggested to Cherise that they drink in the sunroom.

Stacy remained in the dining room to finish clearing while Pamela and I got the clean-up operation in gear in the kitchen, me scraping and her filling the dishwasher.

"I noticed you put butter on your roll," she said. "So you eat dairy?"

"Yeah. It's more a thing of losing the taste for meat than some huge principle."

"Is it difficult dating someone who *does* eat meat?"

"Not really. He puts up with my smoking." Jeez, I wanted that Scotch.

"My, we picked that roast clean—no leftovers."

Stacy came in the kitchen wearing her I-might-puke expression. Pausing in the far doorway with a tray of cups and saucers, Pamela asked, "Are you sure you won't join Cherise and me for coffee?" We were sure.

As soon as she left, Stacy said, "Cherise was staring *right* at his Adam's apple. Then his hands—"

"Relax. She can't be sure—not with his tie on."

"She doesn't like him, and the only reason I can think of—"

"I can think of *plenty*."

She didn't seem to hear. "I don't want her voicing suspicions to Dad."

"Did you leave her and Tommy in there together?"

"No, she went to the bathroom."

"Keep them apart till she leaves tomorrow morning. Take him to *your* room so she can't get him alone. I'll finish the cleaning with Pamela. Just save me some of the single malt. A *lot* of the single malt. Go!" Stacy scrammed into the dining room just as Pamela returned through the far door. I murmured "Bathroom," and scooted out.

The sunroom was empty, and the tray with the cups and saucers sat in the middle of the teak table. There was ample space for me to hide behind the screens amid the rows of plants in the greenhouse area. But what about the favorite couch? The one con was I'd be out in the open if anybody decided to poke their head around the screen. Yet there were several pros. First, I'd have a comfortable place to stretch out instead of crouching on the floor. Second, I'd be closer to the table and could hear better. And third, I'd have an alibi if discovered—I was pulling a Churchill.

Footsteps approached. I quickly scooted behind the screen and lay down on the couch, pulling the afghan over my face.

"It's not too cold in here, is it?" Pamela asked.

"It's fine," Cherise said.

"Here's cream and sugar. I'll check on the coffee."

The footsteps grew faint. I was alone with Cherise. Was she at the table? Sitting or standing? How long did it take for coffee to percolate? Ninety-nine bottles of beer on the wall, ninety-nine bottles of beer; if one of those bottles should happen to fall, ninety-eight bottles of beer on the wall. Ninety-eight bottles of beer—

Footsteps approaching along the hall. "The coffee's almost done," Pamela said. "What are you looking at?"

"The screen has a crack in it."

Again, Pamela's footsteps faded.

A squeaking sound. Scraping. Cherise sitting and pulling the chair closer to the table? Damn—a fart was building. Ninety-six bottles of beer on the wall, ninety-six bottles of beer. If one of those bottles—

Footsteps again. Cups rattling in saucers. Pamela's voice. "So you need to go to Bergdorf's?"

"Bloomingdale's. I didn't have time to try it on. It was similar to the style I bought two years ago. You know, with the belt."

"What's wrong—the fit?"

"I think it's *supposed* to fit that way, but I'm not going to parade around with so much exposed. In front *and* in back. Not a bathing suit for an old lady."

"Cherise, you're not old!"

"I'm *sixty*-three, not *twenty*-three."

"You look much younger. It will be *years* before anyone thinks of you as old."

"In this youth culture? I'm practically dead. You know, I had a talk with Stacy. I told her in no uncertain terms to find a direction in life. She cannot continue being a burden—"

"Dad said she was supporting herself."

"I mean an *emotional* burden. Without direction, without a serious career like you have or any indication of settling down and raising a family."

The fart was moving to the exit. Please, God, let it be silent.

"A bookstore fits her," Pamela said. "It may not be the most challenging job, but it's giving her experience."

"*Incarceration* gives experience! Chesterton, what are you doing?"

"And she's still so interested in poetry. We can't shrug it off as a phase." Pamela's voice grew soft. "Falling in love: who can predict that? Or make it happen?"

"You can set the stage so it *might* happen. Look how she dresses. Look at her friends!"

My fart had had enough incarceration. God saw that it was silent. Would the odor travel their direction?

"*Now* where's he going?" Cherise said.

Through the afghan I could see Chesterton sniffing the air by my feet.

"What's wrong with her friends?" Pamela asked. "Andrea is quiet, so it's hard to get a sense of her. Tom is *very* well educated—quite erudite, in fact."

"I just don't know. Something's not quite right. I can't put my finger on it."

Chesterton wandered away. So my farts weren't up to snuff? Or sniff?

Cherise again: "I have a difficult time picturing them as boyfriend and girlfriend. I will grant you Tom is educated, so what on earth does he see in *her*? She's—"

"She's cute, in a waifish, tomboy way. Some men like—"

"I don't see anything cute. Not the way she dresses, in pants and—"

"A lot of young people dress that way."

"A lot of young people going nowhere. *You* never dressed that way."

"I'm from a different generation."

"I don't accept all this *different generation* nonsense. We had our youthful rebellion, but through all that, even through the Depression, for heaven's sake, when so many people had *nothing*, absolutely *nothing*, they still took care to be as clean and neat—"

"I have never seen Stacy so *content*." There was something familial, Stacy-like, in the way Pamela spoke, as if talking out loud to herself. "She even seems *happy*, when she's not on her guard."

"What does she have to be on guard against?" Cherise squawked.

"To see her smile, to see the affection she shows Dad, I'm happy for that. Give her time for the other things. She's finding her way."

The gas began to build again. Cherise said, "I can't help wondering if there's not some wool being pulled over our eyes."

"In what way? You don't think Stacy's on drugs?"

"I don't know. I just don't know."

When they finally left, my abdomen quieted. I lay still a few minutes before getting up and peeking out from behind the screen. Chesterton was lying by the table, his eyes mournful. I dashed to the door and down the hall and took the spiral steps two at a time.

Stacy sat cross-legged on the bed; Tommy was on the window seat. They watched me pant and eventually catch my breath. "Here's the scoop," I said. "Nobody thinks—"

Stacy's eyebrows merged. "Where were you?"

"In the sunroom. With Pamela and Cherise. And Colonel Mustard and the rope. They didn't know I was there, except Colonel Mustard. I hid behind the screen, on the couch."

"You *what?*" Stacy's jaw almost fell off.

"Lucky you didn't get stabbed," Tommy said. "How now? A rat?"

"You *hid?*" Stacy sputtered.

"They were going to the sunroom for their coffee, so I figured if they were gonna talk about us, that'd be when. Here's the scoop. Your aunt thinks something's—"

"Rotten in the State of Denmark," Tommy said.

"Shush," Stacy snapped.

"Pamela thinks you're *erudite,*" I said in an aside to Tommy. "It's your aunt," I told Stacy. "She has a feeling that the wool is being pulled over their eyes."

"*Why?*"

"I don't know. *She* didn't know. Pamela asked if she suspected you were on drugs. By the way, Pamela thinks you're doing fine."

The sister's sisterliness didn't calm Stacy one nanowhit. Tommy rose from the window seat, saying, "Cherise threatened to come up to say goodnight, so this might be the optimal time for my post-prandial constitutional."

"Leave the front door unlocked so you don't need to ring to get in," Stacy called after him.

Despite being in high-anxiety mode, or maybe to pull some more wool, Stacy decided to go downstairs to visit with everybody.

Meanwhile I helped myself liberally to the single-malt. After *cre-aaa-aak*-ing back upstairs, Stace sat on the bed and leafed through the Munch book Tommy had given her. I stared through the large tower windows at the night sky.

Suddenly she straightened. I cocked my head. Yes, the stairs were creaking, a *cru-uck, cru-uck, cru-uck*. Tommy. The compass needle went counterclockwise from three to twelve, the door opened, and in he came. Soaking wet.

Stace was on her feet instantly. "What *happened?*"

Tommy closed the door and removed his jacket and laid it on the corner of the rug. Then he walked to the window seat and unzipped his pants and began peeling them off, sitting on the sailboat cushions to finish the job.

"Your neighbor has a little pond in the back. It looked frozen over."

I couldn't help laughing. "And you figured, hey, why not go ice-skating?"

"I was pressing it with my toe to test the thickness. I lost my balance."

Stacy meanwhile had grabbed towels from the closet and handed them to him. She picked up the wet clothes and stuck them in the hamper. I turned away as Tommy continued stripping. By sitting on the window seat, he was visible to anybody in the street below, but we were pretty high up, and nobody was likely to be out, much less looking. When I'd last peered down, the neighboring houses had drawn their curtains.

"Why didn't you go to *your* room?" Stacy asked, sounding annoyed.

"And risk running into your sweet-tempered aunt? Andy, why don't you pour me some Scotch while I finish changing." By now, he was down to just his white boxer shorts. He wasn't entirely

flat-chested, and his smooth belly and curved rear each alone removed all doubt as to his sex. He knelt on the window seat and
opened a pane. "It's carolers."

"Get away from there," Stacy hissed.

The singing drifted up.

"O come let us adore Him,

"O come let us adore Him,

"Chri-ist, the Lord."

The carolers stopped, and all was still. Cold air swept in the
wide-open window. Tommy reached to close it. I set his glass and
the bottle on the bureau. Nobody spoke—the quiet seemed to ex-
pand. Stacy stood with her lips slightly parted, intent, like she was
listening to a faraway carol. I listened too. From the other side of the
room came noises, faint at first, then louder. *Crik, crik, crik. Crik,
crik, crik. Rat-tat-tat.* The compass-needle went from three to noon.
High noon. Do not forsake me, oh, my darling.

Chapter 18

NOT EVERYBODY THINKS clearly in a crisis.

My first impulse was to barricade the door. I actually lunged that direction with arms extended. But my shoe hit a wet spot, and I slipped. Cherise pushed the door open, wanting to know why the staircase had water on it. Confronted by my stumbling body, she was at least momentarily distracted. I ended up careening into the jamb, getting the full impact in my shoulder, and bouncing back onto the corner of the bed, grasping in vain at the blankets before sliding onto the floor. She looked down at me and up at Stacy, then at the window. Why was it wide open, she demanded to know?

I turned. Where Tommy had been—where Tommy no longer was—was a dark void. Stacy brushed past her aunt and out the door.

"Good King Wenceslas looked out

"On the feast of Ste-phen."

"We're listening to the carols," I mumbled, getting up.

Cherise marched over and yanked the window shut. "Can't you listen outside?"

"That's a great idea," I said, running from the room and trying not to slip on the stairs.

With Tommy having fallen or leapt from the window, I was torn between grabbing the hall phone to call an ambulance and following Stace—she'd left the front door open—to minister either to an injured him or grieving her. Damn, I should have brought a blanket. Already my legs were taking me down the front steps and onto the lawn.

"Where and what his dwelling?" The carolers remained intent on their books.

Part way around the tower, Stace stood staring at the ground. I reached her and stared too, at the spot where Tommy would have landed, *should* have landed. With the foliage gone, the bushes offered a clear view of their skinny trunks. No Tommy. Could he have survived the fall, gotten up, and run? In only his boxer shorts?

"Right against the forest fence

"By St. Agnes' fou-oun-tain."

Bundled in heavy coats, scarves, and hats, the singers kept on as if nothing unusual had happened. The frost on the grass glistened.

"Where is he?" I panted, seeing my breath.

"I don't know."

In another of our cosmic synchronies, Grunner and Gabe looked up at the heavens. Just to the side of the windows, jaybird-naked except for his ballooning white boxer shorts, Tommy stood on the narrow railing facing the stucco. He must have been on the balls of his feet, his heels braced against the inverted daggers—his back arched as though his belly wanted to press itself into the curved wall. But it couldn't reach, not with his arms raised over his head and extended slightly back. Maybe he had teetered a moment, but he had managed to grasp the protruding lower jaw of the livid gargoyle. Any second, it seemed, the beast's fangs would bite down hard and sever his fingers.

The carolers went silent.

I turned to see their reaction. Oblivious, they paged through their books. The drapes of the house opposite remained drawn.

"Hark the herald angels sing,

"Glory to the newborn King."

I was yay close to laughing, either from relief that Tommy wasn't dead or that the carolers hadn't noticed him or maybe from the sight of him hanging from the gargoyle's jaw in only his boxers. But Stacy's look of transcendent horror stopped me. Had he fallen? Worse. Cherise stood on the front stoop.

"What's going on?" she called over, clasping her arms to her chest.

". . . and mer-cy mi-ild . . ."

"*Do* something!" Stacy whisper-hissed. "Don't let her see."

I did something. I bellowed, "God and sin-ners rec-on-ciled. Joyful all ye—"

The look of transcendent horror leapt from Stacy's face to Cherise's. Stacy ran past her aunt and inside. I kept bellowing, "Nations ri-ise. Join the triumph of the ski-ies!" Cherise came at me, yelling something I couldn't hear through my own angelic "host proclaim," but I ran forward and wrapped my arms around her in a bear hug. "Merry Christmas, Cherise, Merry Christmas."

"Let go of me!"

"Merry Christmas," I shouted as she struggled.

"What's wrong with you? Stop this!"

"Isn't whiskey good? I *love* it!"

She wriggled and writhed, but I didn't loosen my clutch, no way, not till after Tommy's shadow had passed over us and disappeared. The moment I released her, she hurried to the front door. It must have been locked because she began to press the bell and even pound. I looked up; Tommy wasn't in sight. Finally the door opened, and Pamela let her aunt in.

I was cold but not ready for the hell fires that surely were ablaze within. I waited outside another full minute before trying the knob. The carolers moved on, singing "Si-i-lent night."

The door was unlocked. Voices carried from the direction of the library. "She's drunk, that's all," Pamela said. "Come, I'll put on tea."

"How many neighbors must have seen—and the carolers! Your father—"

"Cherise, please, let's just forget about it. You look freezing."

"I *am* freezing!"

"Sit by the heat."

I raced up the spiral stairs. The room was empty. I hurried back down, almost colliding with Stacy at the bottom. "Is he okay?" I asked.

"Yes. He came in as soon as I opened the window. I'd locked the front door, so he had time to throw on something and get to his room." She took a deep breath. "We were lucky Pamela didn't answer the bell right away. She and Dad were having some serious discussion and thought we would answer it."

"Well while you were nice and cozy *in*side, I was *out*side. Hugging your aunt!"

"You hugged her so she couldn't come in?"

"*Ten* prime ribs!"

Stacy was the only one awake besides her father to see Pamela and Cherise off Friday morning. She said nobody mentioned the scene on the lawn to him. "And Pamela wasn't upset. In fact, she wanted me to apologize to you for her. For quote *flirting with Tom during dinner*." Stacy smiled but only for a second. "Charlie left her. He was carrying on with his secretary."

"Jeez."

"She didn't want to ruin everyone's Christmas, so she didn't say anything. Last night she told Dad they had broken up, pretending it was mutual. Anyway, getting drunk and flirting was a much-needed ego boost, but she said she had no business doing it at your expense and is sorry."

"After what Tommy put us through, she can have him."

Stacy cocked her head. "How about if we go to Brackton tomorrow?"

"Can't we go somewhere else? Tommy can still have time alone."

"Brackton can't be any worse than last night."

"Wanna bet?"

She hit my arm playfully. "Mathilde will be thrilled. You'll see—old frictions will fall by the wayside. You can use the phone in the library."

"What for?"

"To call and see if tomorrow is okay with her."

"We can just show up."

"What if she's not home?"

"I'm never that lucky. Besides, if I call, she'll say something to change my mind. I'll call when we're an hour away."

The three musketeers did a shopping trip to stock up on groceries for Tommy, smuggling the bags into the guest cottage. Supper was short and sweet, me sneaking bits of stew meat under the vegetables and Stacy soaking up the growing rapport between Tommy and her father.

Saturday morning, after promising Mr. Grunner she would phone once we knew when we would be heading back to Hastings, Stacy drove us around the corner and pulled even with the guest cottage. The street was deserted, but even if somebody had been looking, all they would have seen was a large fellow with a suitcase get out of the car, go in the side door of the house, and the car drive off.

Over the river and through the woods to grandmother's house we went. I found a decent radio station, and the rhythms of the music and highway quickly sent Stacy and me into our separate reveries. Mine of course were about arriving in Brackton, and surprisingly, optimism reigned. One version of the Prodigal Daughter's return had Mathilde answering the front door and fighting back tears. Another had her sitting at the kitchen table with Aunt Lorraine and thinking the rapping on the back door was Uncle Anthony or Roy. She calls *Come in*, and in I walk to their astonishment and joy. In the background, the band plays "For She's a Jolly Good Fellow." What if Mathilde wasn't around? But she'd never been big on traveling, not after the divorce—for her, vacation meant relaxing at home.

"I want to kick myself for being insensitive," Stacy said out of the blue. "I was so focused on my *own* anxieties—about Dad, Cherise—I ignored what *he* was going through. Being out of work weighs on him. He's also trying to decide whether to go back to school. Northwestern has a good journalism program." She hushed as abruptly as she'd begun.

Scene II: He's working at Drake's. Standing by the entry, he sees the door open. Almost does a double take, thinking *Her hair's as light as Andy's*. His hand automatically reaches for the black leather folders containing the menus and daily-specials sheets. He sees it *is* me and grins. *Andy! What brings you here? I'll give you ladies the best table in the house. I get off at midnight; where will you be?*

Or he was working elsewhere, and Edward arranged for me to surprise him at Drake's. *They hired you right out from under their competitor's nose? That's a big feather in your cap.* Even if his hair had grayed and thinned by now, he'd still have his open face, smiling eyes, athlete's easy gait.

The next time Stacy spoke it was to ask if we'd see Roy. "If he's moved back in at Matt's," I said.

"I don't want to be rude, but I don't know how I can be friendly to him."

"He was okay when I was in high school. We even shared some laughs—around the poker table, watching baseball."

"I suppose if *you* can forgive him, I should."

"*Forgetting* is more like it. And he can still be an asshole, just a regular one." We switched drivers, and I got us past Philly and the exit to the local roads. Stacy kept bugging me to phone, but I refused till my stomach had some beer in it.

Barren field after barren field passed by, parcels of no more than a dozen acres, some divided with chicken wire. Subsistence farming, if that. Probably by the same folks who ran the nearby gas stations and shabby stores. *Live Bait, Checks Cashed.*

We stopped at a 24-hour for sandwiches and a case, then Stacy took over, following my directions. The Animals came on. *I'm just a soul whose intentions are good. Oh Lord, please don't let me be misunderstood.* Tell me about it. I opened a can of beer.

"Will you get in touch with Dean?" she asked.

"Not sure if he's around. Hang a left at the used-truck place."

"Can you find out?"

"Edward would probably know. Mathilde might, if Edward mentioned it."

"You'd feel okay asking her?"

"Sure."

"Was she the one wanting the divorce?"

"Assume so."

"You don't *know*?" Stacy sounded surprised.

"Not really. One day she said he'd taken a job in Gouldtown and needed to live there because of when his shift started. Had to have been at least a year later that she mentioned the divorce."

"And he didn't say anything?"

"I didn't really see him again till seventh grade. The Roy shit had started, and I retreated from everybody. Plus the whole *block* was going to hell in a handbasket. Gary Mueller's mom died of pneumonia, and Marybeth Wesley's father beat up her mother pretty bad. I just assumed Mathilde had gotten tired of arguing about money. Never thought he'd cheated on her. Guess it *could* have been that. Nah, my Aunt Lorraine would've acted super-pissed at him, but she never did."

Just past the *Brackton 10 mi* sign, we stopped at a red light by a wide driveway entrance framed by two pillars. The placard on one said *St. Joseph's Hospital and Medical Center, Brackton State Campus.* "That's the institution where my grandmother lived." Beyond the chain-link fence a gray concrete hulk rose up, the architecture style part-Soviet and part-Dallas Book Depository. The windows were small and recessed.

"Anyway, I can't see Dean cheating," I said. "And not on principle. It's that the last thing he wants is to get tangled up in some complicated love triangle. Having to think up alibis and excuses and making sure they mesh: that's too much work. He loves the worry-free life—*that*'s his mistress."

"There's a phone at that gas station. Should I pull in?"

"Might as well. So much for *my* worry-free life."

I let it ring ten times, but nobody answered. "Guess we'll just have to show up," I told her when I got back in the car.

At Old Country Road, I said, "If you went right, after some miles you'd get to a housing development all by itself in the middle of nowhere. They promised the road would be widened to four lanes, they'd build a mall, and the whole area would get incorporated. But they never did jack-shit. The bus service stinks—maybe twice a day. So the folks who moved into the development are stranded. The Linehans, this family Dean's known since he was a kid, live there."

Once we hit the old neighborhood, the movie scripts shifted genre. Matt answering the rap on the kitchen door. *Andy, what are you doing here? Couldn't you have called?* Or, *Why did you pick now to visit?* And, *You stay out of touch and then think you can march right in any old time?* Or nobody answers the knock, and I go around front to ring the bell. Mathilde hastily closes her robe. An unshaven man, also in a robe, descends the stairs behind her. Maybe he answers the door. *You must be Andy. I can tell by the pictures on Mattie's bureau.* I hear myself say, *Nobody calls her Mattie.*

If she'd remarried, she'd have told me, invited me to the wedding, but what if it wasn't official—just a shacking-up? Usually folks didn't send out announcements for that. Would I mind? Not necessarily. Just wanted some warning—didn't want it sprung on me the second I arrived. *Whose fault is that,* Jiminy Cricket asked, *your arriving without warning?*

Before you knew it, we were on our block. "The corner house on the left, that's it." The wooden two-story, once upon a time white but now a dirt-speckled gray, looked unchanged. The small yard was no worse than it'd ever been. "Don't park on the street; too many teenagers rip on through. The driveway's on the far side of the house, see, almost to the corner."

Stacy turned left into the rutted driveway that paralleled Twelfth, and I told her to pull in next to Mathilde's car on the strip of yard between the driveway and sidewalk that had been worn down by a second set of tire tracks. I explained how when Matt had lots of company, some folks used the outer lane, and that way they didn't all have to move their cars if the first to arrive wanted to leave early. Roy liked to park in the outer lane so he could drive over the sidewalk and curb onto Twelfth instead of backing up. The garage itself had no room for a car, stuffed as it was with old lawn mowers, tires, broken appliances. Matt had used to ask Dean why we liked to visit the junkyard when we had our very own.

The kitchen light was on—a good sign. Maybe she was working graveyard and had just awoken. I rapped on the back door, the door where I'd learned to shim locks. After half a minute, I tried the handle. It gave in that old, familiar way you didn't realize you remembered. I brushed off my boots on the little rug and opened the inner door, calling, "Anybody home? Matt?" I stepped into the kitchen, leaving both doors ajar for Stacy.

Chapter 19

M ATHILDE APPROACHED THROUGH the dining room doorway, her narrow shoulders bulked out by a loose gray cardigan. She looked pleased. "Andy, what a surprise."

"I tried calling—"

"I just got back from the grocery."

We hugged. My height and a little heavier, she nonetheless felt fragile. When we stepped apart, I could see better. Her hair was too light to show much gray; the main difference six-plus years had made was now she looked her age. When I'd left in '69, she could've passed for thirty.

I introduced Stacy, and Mathilde said, "You'll stay overnight, won't you? You're welcome as long as you like. Sissy and everybody are coming for poker. She had to work Christmas, so we didn't eat till late. We're off tomorrow."

Gesturing for us to sit at the kitchen table, she asked if we wanted coffee. We both said yes and sat; I took out my cigarettes. While rinsing out the pot Matt told Stacy, "My sister Lorraine works in Admitting at St. Joe's—St. Joseph's Hospital—and sometimes has to work the holidays. You ever have to go there, don't expect the whole world won't know. How those gals gossip."

"It's like a soap opera," I said. "Real small-town." Suddenly it hit me. "Hey, is that why Dean went to Vineland for his vasectomy?"

Matt turned from the sink, surprised. "Who told you about that?"

"Overheard you telling Lorraine—maybe in junior high. I had to look it up in the dictionary. You told her it was because Vineland did it cheaper."

"You're probably right, that it was because he didn't want the whole world to know."

When the coffee was done perking and Mathilde joined us at the table, we gave a short description of the drive out but omitting Tommy. Then we traded stories about our jobs, and I quizzed her about the neighbors. Mrs. Schwenker still had a fender-bender every month; they couldn't get collision insurance anymore. The Wilson boy had gotten arrested for a string of burglaries, and the Quinlan boy was at Rutgers—hard to believe they'd been best friends all those years. No, she'd never heard a word about the Muellers since they'd left. The Wesleys? Moved away too, before the father had gotten paroled.

While we chatted, I took silent inventory of the changes. The appliances were a little the worse for wear. The plastic salt-and-pepper set, the toaster, the hot plates hadn't changed. The mugs were different, and the drooping plant on the windowsill was new. Did the glass jar with the wooden spoons always have that crack in it?

I asked who all was coming for poker besides Lorraine and Anthony, and Mathilde said Anthony Junior and Sharon. "They have twin boys now."

"Hey, I don't mind sitting out if there's too many."

"You don't need to. Sharon hates to play." Matt turned to Stacy. "The men call seven-card stud and draw, nothing wild. Except Edward might call deuces and one-eyed jacks. We tease him, call him 'One-eyed Jack,' because he had to wear an eye-patch. Some infection won't go away."

"Is he coming?" I asked.

"Wasn't planning to," Mathilde said, rising. "I'll call him. Roy might stop by. He's working at Torelli's. Quit the Cyclone because they passed him over for assistant manager." She shook her head sadly. "Experience doesn't count anymore. Two tours in the army, and they want him to answer to somebody younger. Isn't that the way of the world?"

"Torelli's the place in the mall?"

"Yes. Let me tell you something: don't bring up Women's Lib. The young gals wear the short skirts, get the men to order more. So they're given the best shifts. Never demand a decent hourly."

She went to the wall phone and dialed. "It's me, Matt. ... You have to come back for poker. Andy's here. ... Yes, with a friend. Yes, a surprise. ... Seven." Hanging up, she said she knew Edward would want to see me, telling Stacy, "There's only three left on their side—Edward, Andy's dad, and her."

I refilled everybody's coffee while Mathilde described the changes downtown, which included renovations on Main past the banks, the movie theatre adding a second screen, and new restaurants opening just off Bristol. "And they put in an escalator at the train station."

"Dang," I said, "I used to like counting all the steps."

"You still can on the station side."

"So what did they tear down on Main?"

"That whole block with the pawnbroker and bars."

"What about Louie's Magic Box?"

"That too."

"Louie's had great stuff," I told Stacy. "Plastic vomit, fake ice cubes with bugs in them."

The phone rang, and Matt patted my hand as she rose to answer it. "Good to see you again, Andy. Hi. ... Yes. ... I thought his wrist was broken? ... But you need it to steady the ball, don't you?" She smiled at the linoleum. "Don't get too drunk. I've got a surprise card shark here, two card sharks. ... No, I'm not saying. You'll have to see for yourself."

Mathilde continued smiling even after she returned to the table. "They're going bowling, Roy and his crowd. Dennis broke his wrist falling off his motorcycle."

When I toted the backpacks in from the car, Mathilde and Stacy were sitting side-by-side on the couch, their heads bent over a large book. "Uh-oh," I said, "the photo album."

Matt glanced at her watch. "Goodness, I better go up and get ready."

I took her spot on the couch. Stacy said, "We got to when you were nine or ten."

"That's pretty much it. Dean left the camera, but nobody learned how to load film before Roy got around to busting it."

I flipped to the front. Either Mathilde had removed most of the photos from their dating or Dean had taken them—the pages between her childhood pictures and the wedding party photo were blank. The wedding photo had been shot in some park. Matt wore a pale dress, and Dean looked proud and happy. Lorraine and Anthony stood on Matt's side, and Edward, on Dean's. Grandma Margaret sat beside them all on a bench, distracted by something on the ground.

"Money was tight," I told Stacy, "so this is the only wedding shot. Either that or Roy making faces ruined the others."

"She said he wasn't at the wedding. That four was a rough age, much rougher than the terrible twos, at least for boys."

"So was five and all the others. He never liked Dean, even when he was older. Dean taught him how to throw a baseball and football, deal off the bottom of a deck, all sorts of things, but it never made a difference."

"Do any of Roy's father's family live nearby?"

"Not that I ever heard. Nash was in his forties when he married Mathilde, and she was barely out of high school. If any of his relations are still around, they've lain low. Can't say as I blame them."

"Was this taken in Atlantic City?"

"Yeah, the Boardwalk. I remember that holster set!"

"You have Dean's mouth. The forehead too, and eyes a little."

"Not the wrinkles at the corners."

Matt came down the stairs. "You girls can use Roy's room. It's got the double-bed he bought last year. His new place, they sold him their waterbed."

"What happened to *my* bed?"

"The twin? He took it for his guest room. The double wouldn't fit."

The idea that Roy had my bed—my erstwhile sanctuary—pissed me off, but the idea of having to sleep in his room was worse. The first time, I'd barely gotten home from day camp. He'd yanked me by the arm, saying he had to show me something. His room didn't look any different except for the towel on the bed. Shoved, I was *on* the towel. On top of me, his weight pressing the air from my lungs. I tried to tell him I couldn't breathe. His hands startled me, under my shorts, pulling on my panties. I had *no* idea, *no* understanding of what he'd intended—it didn't make sense. Panting, grunting, animal noises. Searing pain. When he got up, I was stunned to see his pants around his ankles, his penis hanging. I knew what it was—when I was little, I'd walked in on Dean in the bathroom. But Roy's was hideous.

After that, I'd had the choice of going to his room willingly or getting my arm bruised. I'd been in Roy's room a million times in high school—Matt would store extra rolls of paper towels and other things she bought in bulk in there—but I'd never had to get *near* the bed, much less lie on it.

Chapter 20

"It's a ghost!"

"Hey, I'm not that pale!" I hugged Lorraine back. Her hair, darker than Matt's, showed the gray more, but her round face hadn't aged much. Her nostrils flared when she was either pleased or pissed, and I was hoping I'd gotten the lady, not the tiger.

Burly Uncle Anthony tucked the case of beer under one arm and put his other around me. "Look who's back."

"Like a bad penny," I said. "My friend Stacy and I, we wanted to scare you at Halloween but couldn't get the time off, so we're doing it now."

The corners of Lorraine's mouth curved up. "Scares like this are good. When did you get in? Is this a surprise for Sissy, or she been in on it?"

"Heck, if she'd known ahead of time, she might've skipped town. Can I get you something to drink?"

"I'll take a beer," Anthony said, resting the case on the counter. "Me too."

I handed out chilled cans from the fridge and squatted to stash the ones my uncle had brought. Mathilde came in the kitchen saying, "Shoo, Andy, I'll do that. You visit."

We went into the dining room, and I introduced Stacy. My aunt fired off a zillion questions: What was Chicago like? Was I working? How was the pay? How long were we staying?

Another car moved slowly past the windows. Doors opened and slammed. A baby howled. Lorraine jumped up and ran out. Anthony smiled. "Grandma to the rescue."

There was enough commotion in the kitchen that I decided to stay put. Anthony Junior came in holding a round, pink-faced no-neck in a blue snowsuit. I got up and hugged my cousin as best I could without squishing his kid. "How are you?"

"Good. I didn't know you were visiting."

"We didn't either. This is my friend Stacy. Anthony Junior. Who's this?"

"Jake. The quiet one."

Sharon brought in red-faced Joey, a bottle in his mouth. She smiled hello, as though speaking might un-pop the cork. I'd seen her a few times when they had first started dating and hadn't sensed much in common, but now we were family.

Lorraine ordered my uncle to get the playpen, and he hauled it in and set it up in the living room. Anthony Junior rocked Jake, ignoring Lorraine's endless advice. Sharon and Joey did this routine where he'd let go of the bottle nipple and howl, she'd shove it back in his mouth, and he'd swallow furiously till he felt like spitting it out again. Matt brought in bowls of chips and pretzels, napkins, ashtrays, books of matches. I dangled some plastic keys in front of Jake, which didn't interest him. Lorraine took a pacifier and a green teething ring into the kitchen to rinse them.

In the midst of this chaos, Edward arrived. He set a paper bag on the dining room table, and we hugged. His camel's-hair coat was a nice, thick wool. My cousin never flaunted his money, but if you wore anything nice at our house, by definition it was flaunting.

Now, though, I realized he was just middle class, several place-digits shy of Stacy's father.

Edward had aged some. What was he now, fifty-six? The flesh on his cheeks sagged, and his hair, grayer, had thinned. His coloring was the same as Dean's, the same light complexion and blue eyes. I introduced him to Stacy, and they shook hands. He withdrew a bottle of brandy from the bag. "Your visit calls for a celebration. I was afraid the Chicago winds had swept you into Lake Michigan."

While he went to hang up his coat, I asked if anybody else wanted brandy. Stace was the only taker, so I grabbed three tumblers.

Edward toasted our visit. "I hear the theatre is excellent. Especially comedy. Now what was the name?"

"Second City?" Stacy asked.

"Yes, that's it." In no time he and she were off-and-running about comedies and actors and what-not. They might've continued till the cows came home except that Lorraine announced it was time to ante.

"People are going to be coming and going, so everybody antes for themselves," she said. "Seven card stud, nothing wild."

I filled Stacy in on the house rules while Lorraine fired cards around the table. Within the next minute, folks brought their drinks to the table, took out their coins, and tossed their nickels into the pot. Sharon said she'd sit out till Joey fell asleep.

"King high checks."

"Check."

"See your check and raise you a check."

"I bet a nickel."

"Spoiler."

"Everybody in?" Lorraine dealt a second card up. A few of us checked.

"Nickel."

"What you sittin' on, two more hearts?"

"He's sittin' on a bluff."

"Watch you don't fall off."

"See your nickel and raise you a dime."

"What do *you* have?"

"Pay to find out."

"A three-suit flush, maybe."

"See your dime and raise a nickel."

"She's bluffing."

"So call her."

"*You* call her."

"With a six-three?"

"Pretend you have two aces in the hole."

"Holding out for an inside straight?"

"You play your hand; I'll play mine."

"I'll keep her honest."

"Too late for that."

"See the nickel and raise a nickel."

"Too rich for my blood; I fold."

"Andy?"

"Go fish."

We played some of the crazy games, like Woolworth's and baseball, and when Edward called nothing-wild, I got everybody to fold with an ace-king-queen showing but jack-shit underneath. Nobody bet much, lost much, or raked in much. When we weren't complaining about our cards, Lorraine told stories about the hospital: drunks in the ER, hanky-panky in the interns' lounge, the Mayor's hernia. Uncle Anthony told a slew of mostly ridiculous jokes, though one about a pigeon cracked us all up.

Eventually we took a break, and Stacy and I ended up with Edward by the dining room windows. I asked him if he'd seen Dean lately.

"Not since summer. Didn't appear to be doing too well. Nothing serious—don't be alarmed. I just mean staying sober."

I laughed. "And I was just telling Stacy I never saw him act even a little bit tipsy."

"That's what's odd," Edward said. "He's acting it."

"How bad? Like falling-off-of-bar-stools bad?"

"He had come by to return my pruning shears. Wasn't steady on his feet. Eleven in the morning."

I reached for my cigarettes, hearing Edward tell Stacy, "Our family, Andy's and mine, has had its share of alcoholism. Her father and I are first cousins—our mothers were sisters—and their parents, Andy's great-grandparents, were both alcoholics. In such bad condition that Nancy and Margaret—Nancy was my mother, Margaret, Dean's—were sent to live with relatives when they were still quite young."

"On a farm, right?" I said.

"Near Altoona. An aunt and uncle with children of their own. But I suppose on a farm you can always use more hands. Nancy and Margaret never saw their parents again."

"Jeez."

"As soon as Margaret reached majority—she was the younger—the sisters moved to Vineland and married." Edward peered down at his brandy. "My mother always felt that if her parents hadn't been addicted to 'the sauce,' as she called it, they would have been able to support the two daughters and keep the family together."

"I never heard that part."

He shrugged. "Who knows? My mother didn't know why Margaret drank the way she did, in light of what they had been through. Perhaps it was the miscarriages before your father was born. My mother was angry the first time she smelled alcohol on *me*. Eventually she accepted that I'd have a drink now and again with friends, but it took a long time for her to get over her fear I would wind up like her parents and sister. It's a mystery why some people can drink in moderation their entire lives and others can't. Margaret's husband, your Grandfather Pat, drank only occasionally."

"Matt said she never met him."

"Pat died right after the war. I was living in Philly then. The times I came down to Vineland, Margaret was always three-sheets-to-the-wind. Dean graduated high school and moved to Philly too and worked in one of the hotels until he was drafted—just before Korea, I believe. I'm sure he came down to visit his mother during that period and has memories he wishes he didn't. Which may be why he finds drunken behavior so distasteful. Oh, don't misunderstand me—he was very, very fond of her, so she must have been a devoted mother. He visited regularly at the institution even when she no longer recognized him. In fact, he continued volunteering there at Christmas for a number of years after she passed away. It's only recently that he's gone to the Lion's Club, which is in town."

"I remember him going to the institution when I was a kid, but that was while my grandmother was still alive."

Dean must have typically visited in the afternoon because the one time he didn't get back for supper made a huge impression on me. It was only days before my tenth birthday, and he hadn't come home even when I'd gone up to bed. I was having trouble falling asleep, too excited about the baseball glove I might be getting for a present. Was he out shopping for it? Did the stores only have right-handers' and he was still looking?

Then I heard his footsteps on the stairs. I called out, and he came in my room. Sitting on my bed like always, he stroked my back. At one point I rolled over, expecting the smile he always had for me. He was looking at the floor, and his hand fell away. I reached and squeezed it, smiling and staring to compel him to return the smile. After a moment he noticed and did. Then his hand broke free and rumpled my hair. Rising, he gave his usual "Sleep tight, and don't let the bed bugs bite," but his tone made me think I wasn't getting the glove after all.

". . . too far gone to have a conversation," Edward was telling Stacy. "Confined to a wheelchair, had to be fed, everything done for her. In her late fifties, if I'm not mistaken."

"But she couldn't have been drinking in the institution?" Stacy said.

"The damage was already done." Edward turned to me. "Do you plan to see him?"

"Is he in Brackton?"

"Has a place in the Cooper Apartments, over on Washburn. Does some of the grounds upkeep, and they take something off the rent. Would do him good. I wish I had his telephone number, but when I tried at Christmas, it had been disconnected."

"Guess I shouldn't stay out of touch so long."

"We have our own lives to lead. Especially when we're young."

"Hey, I know this may be a long shot, but could Dean have had the DTs when you saw him? Did you smell any liquor?"

Edward sipped his brandy before answering. "I don't remember. It was the unsteadiness I noticed."

"Just trying to make sense of it."

"You may be right. Let's hope it was a sign of a change for the better." He reflected a moment. "I would like to think he'd confide in me if there's some problem, but I don't know. We've enjoyed an odd relationship over the years. We don't talk often, but he's always been there. Especially when we were younger, when I was in a pinch of some kind, he'd lend a hand. I did the same for him. I've always felt we share a sense of family. Perhaps because our family is so small."

"Come sit down, everybody," Lorraine said. "Sissy, your deal."

Chapter 21

We BARELY GOT in another round before a loud rumbling in the driveway started one of the twins screaming. "Who drives a Sherman tank?" my uncle asked.

"It's Roy," Matt said. "His muffler fell off."

The other twin started screaming too, and Anthony Junior and Sharon hurried to the living room. The engine noises stopped; a car door slammed. A figure in an open leather jacket appeared in the kitchen doorway. The instant he saw me, Roy grinned. "Andy. When did you get here?"

I didn't have a chance to answer because the twins Mayhem and Bedlam took over. Anthony Junior said they were leaving because Joey had thrown up, Lorraine barked at my uncle to take down the playpen, Matt asked Roy if he'd parked behind them and he said yes, so he had to go move his car, and Lorraine ran hither and yon gathering baby stuff—diaper bags, pacifiers, teething rings. Matt got Anthony Junior's and Sharon's coats, the crying no-necks were bundled into their blue snowsuits, and everybody said goodbyes, Grandma and Grandpa ushering their offspring and offspring's offspring out to the car.

Roy came back in and, shooting half a glance at Stacy, said, "Ma, you know she was coming?"

"No," I said. "This is Stacy; Stacy, Roy." They traded curt nods.

"She surprised me," Matt said. "Take off your coat. What do you want to drink?"

"Beer." He dumped a bunch of coins on the table and took out his cigarettes, slung his coat on the back of Matt's chair, and sat, pushing her cigarettes out of the way. "How you been? Working? Still see that gal—what's her name, Nora?"

"Haven't seen Nora for eons. Must have graduated and gone forth to conquer the world."

He laughed; he was in a good mood. For all his faults—and they were many—Roy brought some energy with him. "Hear I'm working at Torelli's?"

"Matt was saying."

"How long you here for?"

"Not as long as I'd like. Got to be back at work next week, and Stacy's boyfriend won't put up with her being gone too many days. Heard you found a nice apartment."

"Had to get out of here; they were always on my case." Roy jerked his elbow towards my aunt and uncle, who'd come back in. "Acted like I was this big burden. Who do you think she calls to put up the storm windows?"

"Anthony can't lift things like that anymore," Matt said, handing him a beer. "You're still young."

He gave a bark-laugh. "What about when the pipes leak? Or the car doesn't start?"

Matt beamed like he was heaping on praise.

We all sat, and Anthony began dealing. "Nothing wild."

"You like Chicago?" Roy asked, glancing at his down cards.

I glanced at mine. Three of clubs and eight of spades. "Yeah. Pretty cool city."

"Where you working?"

"This little bar—"

"Ha! Ma was telling somebody a steak-and-lobster. How much they paying?"

When I said, Roy scoffed. "Must be hard up for bartenders."

"They think they are."

"Ace bets a nickel," my aunt said.

"See your nickel and raise a nickel," Roy said.

"I see your nickel, and it makes me fold."

"Ditto."

"You working tomorrow?" Mathilde asked.

Roy turned to me with an I-told-you-so smirk. "What now? Something Andy can do?"

"Lorr's giving me her old coffee table."

"I'm working," he said. "She remembers where they live."

"But can't you get it in the morning?"

"Hey, Stacy and I can get it. No big deal."

"You don't need another coffee table," Roy said. "I don't want to have to deal with a lot of junk when you croak."

Matt feigned indignation. "Who says *I'm* going first?"

"Yeah," I told Roy, "you get on enough people's nerves, and you'll be pushing up daisies before the rest of us."

He laughed. "Just telling Dennis, he'll probably push up weed."

"Does Dennis smoke *marijuana*?" Mathilde looked genuinely shocked.

"Jeez, Ma, halfa Brackton smokes marijuana."

She gave him an I-knew-you-were-joking smile.

Each time Roy got the deal, Mathilde sat out so he could call draw. As the evening wore on, he bet quarters more and more and raised up to the limit, getting the cards to usually scare the rest of us into folding. At least I derived satisfaction from Stacy seeing I hadn't exaggerated: he was still an asshole. I was sorry he left the big winner but not nearly as sorry as I was to hear Edward say he was going to D.C. tomorrow. I promised to stay in touch and visit more often.

Falling asleep in Roy's room turned out to be no big deal. The double bed abutted a different wall, Stacy was in it, and I'd had enough alcohol and stress for the conscious mind to quit on me in a nanosecond.

Chapter 22

DAYLIGHT SLIPPED ALONG the sides of the shade. Stacy snored the snores of the innocent, but otherwise the house was still. I pulled on my jeans and sweatshirt and tiptoed out.

My room looked smaller than I'd remembered, despite the bed being gone. The ironing board, empty laundry baskets, some cartons, and two standing lamps—probably broken—left little floor space. The shelves contained boxes of tissues and light bulbs Mathilde must've bought on sale, my few belongings relegated to a bottom shelf. I tried getting on my baseball glove, but it was too tight. The wooden box I'd made in shop opened easily on its hinges. I felt a pang of familiarity seeing the shells and shiny stones inside, the miniature cars and foreign coins, the movie ticket stubs.

The downstairs was just beginning to get the morning light. I put on coffee and washed the glasses and dishes we'd used at poker. While wiping off the dining room table, a sad spotted wood, I thought about the conversation with Edward. Yes, he and Dean would have helped each other out when they were young, even with a ten-year age difference. Dean was no dummy—he would have guessed his cousin was gay back when the tag "faggot" could've landed you in jail. Did he supply Edward with alibis, maybe a date for a friend's wedding? No doubt Edward had supplied Dean with cash.

Yet there was more to their bond than common chromosomes and watching each other's backs. They shared a perspective. What was Bess's word? *Weltanschauung.* A weltanschauung that said when life dumped shit on you, you might as well laugh while you washed it off. If alcohol was our family Achilles heel, a sense of humor had to be the Hercules bicep.

If it wasn't the DTs—if Dean *was* drinking heavily—maybe he was in an emotional trough. When he got it together again, when his natural resilience kicked in, he'd be his old self. Maybe, like Edward thought, a visit from me would do him good, be just the lift he needed.

After breakfast, Stacy and I drove to my aunt's for the coffee table. Amazingly, we managed to maneuver the thing in and out of the trunk and inside Matt's house without damaging it or us or the doorjambs. I hauled the old coffee table to the garage and then offered to give Stace the Grand Brackton Tour.

Despite the long drive the day before, it felt good to be on the road. I pointed out Matt's diner and Drake's Restaurant and the shabbier end of downtown near Front Street and the bus station. I had Stacy follow Main to the nicer end, which had banks and office buildings and stores.

"When do you want to visit Dean?" she asked.

"Tomorrow's the best bet, while Mathilde's at work. Mid-morning is the most likely time to catch him home and awake. Except when he worked at the bakery, he's never had a job that started real early. Why—you impatient to get back to Hastings?"

"Not at all. Do you want me to go with you when you visit him?"

"Why wouldn't I?"

We tooled past where GG's and Louie's Magic Box had been, and like Matt had said, the movie theatre had grown a twin. I had Stacy circle back and go across the Bristol Street overpass.

"Is that a river underneath?" she asked.

"No, train tracks. Make a left at the end of the bridge, and I'll show you the station, which is actually kind of cool."

She drove slowly down the steep hill. The steps on this side of the tracks were unchanged; the escalator must've been put in on the other. At the bottom, I said to just park in the cul-de-sac since train service on Sundays was spotty at best and nobody'd care.

In fact, nobody was around. We walked over the cobblestones to the stationhouse, a small brick building that dated back to the 1800s. The roof was gray tiles, and the windows were cemented over—maybe since it was built. I tried the iron handle, but the door was locked. Stacy perused the big chart on the stationhouse wall, and I strolled in the direction of Bristol.

The overpass had been built like a truss bridge, the foundation's large iron pillars now a rusty brown. Probably in later years, when it had had to support more than horse-drawn carriages, the bridge was shored up with cement. Some of the gravel between the ties looked new; so did some of the creosote. I paused briefly at the bottom of the steep staircase up to the street, then strolled back and joined Stacy.

She was looking at the *West Jersey and Seashore Railroad* chart and the series of maps illustrating various local lines and their charter and service dates. The Camden and Atlantic began running trains way back in June 1852, a hundred years before I was born, almost to the week. As a child, I'd been fascinated by the idea that folks alive in 1861, say, had seen the same steel rails and spikes and wood ties, that their eyes had taken in the same brick station, the same heavy door, the yellowed-glass transom with the iron-sculpted vine border, maybe the same black-rimmed clock, whose hands still moved. Of course to them it had all looked new, modern. I liked to imagine some kid back then wondering if the station would last so long that somebody in 1961 would be standing in the same spot wondering about them.

We drove back up the steep hill to Bristol. Sure, another escalator on this side could be handy—footy?—but I remembered liking counting the steps. Over a hundred—I used to know the exact number.

We hit a grocery, and for supper I threw together spaghetti using fresh onions, garlic, peppers, and mushrooms. Afterwards, Stacy, Mathilde, and I watched sitcoms and shared some laughs. I'd never admit it, but Grunner was right: old frictions were falling by the wayside. Of course, the visit wasn't over.

Monday morning was cold, and frozen dew dotted the ground, but Sol was blinding bright. Tooling along a tree-lined street, Stacy half-sang, "Glory be to God for dappled things. For skies of couple-color as a brinded cow." She'd pretty much quit reciting poetry around Tommy since it seemed to annoy him, but the worst she'd get from me was a who's-the-author-*this*-time? The patterns the sunlight made along the road through the bare branches *were* pretty glorious. "Gerard Manley Hopkins," she said.

The Cooper Apartments, a three-story brick, lay at the older end of Washburn. The entryway was stuffy, with us in our parkas and the sun streaming through the windows. Half a dozen metal mailboxes ran along the lobby wall. Dean's name wasn't on any. Should I ring a random bell and ask if they knew which apartment was his?

The room darkened. A shape loomed outside, blocking the sun. The door opened, and a large man came in.

"Can I help you?"

"Hope so. We're looking for Dean Gabe."

He studied us a moment. "He owe you?"

I couldn't keep from laughing. "No. I'm his daughter."

He nodded. "I can see it. Didn't know he had family in these parts."

"Actually, I live in Chicago."

"Ah." He nodded again. "Moved a few months ago. Sorry he did. The new guy, he doesn't take good care. Don't think he's even *touched* the rake. Your dad, he had the early ones bundled in no time. And just beer cans in the trash, not like Jones, if that's his real name. Two fifths a week. Rot-gut stuff. Reminds me, I better check if the Mrs. put the kitchen trash out." He held open the door for us; the cold air felt good.

"Happen to know where he moved?" I asked. "Or if he mentioned working somewheres?"

"Can't say as I do. We were in the Poconos." He walked to a line of garbage cans, and we followed. "Hold on a minute," he said, halting. "The mailman said he'd moved some place on Emerson. You know where Emerson is? Eight or ten blocks other side of the old Post Office." He shook his head. "Sorry he moved. Everybody here's sorry." He lifted up a garbage can lid and quickly replaced it.

Back in the car, I resumed my role as navigator to Stacy's chauffeur, and we both played Sherlock. "Doesn't sound like he was drinking a whole helluva lot," I said. "But doesn't sound like the DTs either. Maybe he was drinking early on and only went cold turkey right before seeing Edward."

"Wasn't that in August?"

"Maybe he went on the wagon and off. Gave it a shot, and had a shot."

Emerson was treeless, and fewer bushes separated the buildings. Stacy parked behind an old station wagon that had duct tape around the door. The first lobby we checked was littered with advertising circulars. The mailboxes had no Gabe. The next had a Gable—Paul, not Clark. The third had no Gs but lots of cigarette butts in the corner. The fourth entrance had a Garcia. We checked the buildings across the street. Two had no Gs; the third had a Garbey. On the next block, Gomez and Grady were the runners-up for garbled Gabes. A man about Dean's age walked by opposite us but was too short. A guy driving through the intersection had a thick dark beard. Was Dean wearing a disguise?

Across Wilson, the apartments got even dingier, and half the mailboxes were broken and nameless. I began asking the occasional pedestrian if he or she knew a Dean Gabe. The old woman in a kerchief didn't seem to know English; the boy with the dog shook his head; the two men with paper bags said no; and the man with his hands in his pockets said no and did we have any weed.

"Let's find a phone book and see if he's listed," Stacy said.

"But if he just moved—"

"The book could be new." We went to a phone booth outside a gas station, but the White Pages listed the Washburn address. Stacy said I should try the number anyway. I did and got a recording saying it had been disconnected. She tried Information, also with no luck.

"So much for finding him," I said. "Hey, nobody can say I didn't try."

"You're not giving up? You've come this far. It would be a shame—"

"The Fates may be trying to tell me something. Besides, why should we run ourselves ragged? He could've tried contacting *me*."

She used her annoying singsong voice. "Not long ago, in Chicago, someone who looked a lot like you said that people can feel *so* guilty about not keeping in touch with family that they refrain from contacting them even when they'd like to. She said it wasn't logical but still true." She dropped the singsong voice. "Tommy calls it 'the potential energy barrier.' Any time you want to make a dramatic change, do something you're nervous about, the most difficult part is the very first step. If you can just *broach* a subject, *dial* the phone, the subsequent steps, in comparison, feel like coasting downhill. Hence, change actually requires summoning up only the energy for that single, initial step, not the whole process."

Tommy said a lot of things.

Stacy started driving without waiting for directions. I smoked and watched the buildings and houses go past. It seemed like every funky little store had become part of a chain, either fast-food or national restaurant or car repair franchise. Lazy Susan's was now a McDonald's. Mama's, an Arby's. Perry's Donut Hole, a cheap oil change.

"Hey, what are you doing? Is it open?"

She had pulled into Drake's parking lot. The sign on the door gave the hours; on Mondays they opened at four. Which didn't stop Grunner from trying the door. It was unlocked.

Whatever else had changed, Drake's hadn't. Of course it had seemed immense when I was young, and now it was merely a decent-sized establishment, but the linen was still blue, the brass chandeliers gleamed, the dark wood floor shone. We stood by the rostrum watching two young men in starched white shirts moving briskly, fetching linen napkins and silverware. If they saw us, they didn't let on.

An impeccably groomed middle-aged guy emerged through the double doors in the back. Seeing us, he hurried over. "May I help you?"

I chickened out. "Was wondering if Willard still works here. Wanted to say hi real quick while we're passing through. Haven't seen him for—"

"Willard will be here until Kingdom come. I'll get him." The guy made an about-face and strode to the kitchen.

I could feel myself grin when Old Willard shuffled through the double doors. His silvery hair hung in a fringe from the bald spot, which had expanded to most of his head. He wore a white bib apron with large pockets, one no doubt holding his Luckies. I sprang forward to save him the trouble of coming all the way over. I would have offered my hand except he had a peeler in his.

"Hey, you probably don't remember me. I'm Andy, Dean Gabe's daughter."

"Dean's girl. Why yes, I do." His smile had as many gaps as teeth. "Haven't seen you since you were this high. Used to help me fill the salt shakers. Stand by that table. We had 'em all lined up—"

"The salt was in this huge canister. I was afraid of dropping it."

"That's right. Say, how many years was that?"

"About a million. I moved to Chicago in '69."

"Chicago? Big city. Those Bulls are a team to reckon with."

"The Cubs sure ain't. Say, Dean moved in the last few months, and I don't have his new address. Would you happen to know where he's living or working?"

Old Willard stroked his chin. "Don't think I've seen him since ... before Thanksgiving. That's right, him and a lady, couple of kids. Table in the corner."

"He mention where he was working?"

"No. Told the waiter to tell me Top O' the Morning was going to shine. It's our joke. We once put a couple of bucks on a filly called Top O' the Morning, and she paid thirty-to-one. So I came out to say hello."

Not wanting to keep Willard from his work, I only chitchatted a minute longer. Back in the car, Stacy said, "What about the Lion's Club? Wasn't Edward saying he goes at Christmas? He would have been there just a few days ago."

"Guess it wouldn't hurt to call." Were the kids girls? Did they wear dresses?

Stacy pulled into another gas station with a phone booth, but nobody answered at the Lion's Club.

We headed back to Mathilde's. Every quarter mile, it seemed, some truck farm or building was dug up but nothing put in its place. The story of Brackton. All sorts of great ideas and a bunch of people going to the trouble of making changes, of hoisting themselves over the potential energy barrier, as Tommy would say, but the project would die. It would be one thing if the project just stayed on paper, with nobody strung along, but that wasn't the Brackton *m.o.* Get folks to uproot—

"Go left at the light!" I shouted. "Why didn't I think of it before? If *anybody* knows where Dean is, it's the Linehans."

Chapter 23

OLD COUNTRY ROAD strayed past a stretch of small farms into un-incorporated, undeveloped county land. The Meadows, a cluster of ranch-style houses, sat alone in the middle of this nowhere like some scrap of watermelon rind picnickers had forgotten to toss. Jimmy Linehan—probably all the men who'd moved to the Meadows—had worked at the mill a few miles away. He died of emphysema when I was in junior high, but I hadn't visited since Dean had left, which was shortly after they'd moved from town.

From my child's perspective, the Meadows was a great place to live: several dozen houses with plenty of kids, fields for ball games and exploring, wide-open vistas. When I was older, I learned they had to pay an arm and a leg for garbage pick-up, sewer, and drainage, and they had no stores, schools, or much of anything nearby.

I directed Stacy to a small shunt of sidewalk-less road that snaked among the flat houses. "I'm pretty sure that's it, or used to be." The Linehans' house—if they still lived here—had a two-door sedan in the driveway. A bicycle lay on its side in the pockmarked yard.

The door was opened by a freckle-faced woman in her late thirties. The red hair, loosely clasped at the nape of her neck like yesterday's ponytail, boosted my hopes—all the Linehans had red hair. She smiled as though we'd interrupted a joke. "Can I help you?"

"Hope so, but I'm not sure. My name's Andy Gabe. I'm looking for Dean Gabe. If this is the Linehan house—"

"Who is it, Sherry?" an old woman called from another room.

"Come on in. I remember you." Sherry smiled like the joke got better. "We thought you was in Chicago."

Stacy and I followed her into one of those sprawling spaces that starts as a living room and seamlessly becomes the dining room and then kitchen. I recognized Mrs. Linehan, a round old woman sitting in an upholstered chair near the kitchen. On our way over, we circumvented a table with a glass ashtray containing diaper pins, a laundry basket with unfolded clothes, a tot-sized plastic tricycle, and a coloring book surrounded by crayons. The heavy old TV, encased in a large mahogany box, was tuned to some game show. Mrs. Linehan peered intently as I approached, her gray hair pulled into some kind of bun. She wore a loose brown housedress and stockings rolled up mid-shin and slip-on pink slippers. The ear I could see had a hearing aid.

Sherry turned off the TV and said, "She's looking for Dean."

The Linehans were almost family, and I'd been to their old house in town a zillion times. There were seven kids altogether, probably ranging in age from about ten years older than me— Sherry might've been the youngest—up to Dean's age or a tad older. Their house was always rollicking.

"You might not remember me," I said to Mrs. Linehan.

She shouted loud enough to give me a heart attack. "Course I remember you! A little squirt, you was. Says you moved to Chicago. What'd he say, Sherry? You was working in a fancy steaks-and-lobster?"

I knew I had a stupid grin but couldn't help it. "I'm working elsewhere now, tending bar, but it pays just as good. This is my friend Stacy. We're both on vacation, and we hit her father's place up in New York and drove on down here. Stacy, this is Mrs. Linehan, an old friend of Dean's mother."

"*Best* friend," Mrs. Linehan shouted.

"Thick as thieves, you mean." Sherry turned to us. "Have a seat. Can I get you sodas or something?"

"No, thanks." I sat in the chair beside Mrs. Linehan. Stacy sat on a hassock.

"You been at your ma's?" Mrs. Linehan asked, her voice not as loud. "She still over on—?"

"Yeah, same place. Dean, he must've moved a thousand times."

Almost cackling, Mrs. Linehan said, "Don't stay put long."

"That's one of the reasons I stopped by," I said, hoping it didn't come out rude. "The last address I have for him, on Washburn, the Cooper Apartments, they said he moved. Thought maybe somewhere on Emerson?"

"Emerson?" Mrs. Linehan gave Sherry a puzzled look.

"Yeah, Ma, Carmella's place." Sherry turned to me. "You know her?"

"No. Haven't talked to Dean in a while, actually. It's my fault as much as anybody's; I'm really hard to get ahold—"

The old woman let out another cackle. "He's impossible."

"Carmella's his lady friend," Sherry said. "He moved into her place back around October, wasn't it? But they've gone down to Florida."

"Daytona," Mrs. Linehan said loudly.

"No, Ma, they're just *stopping* in Daytona." Sherry turned back to me. "She's a very nice person, Carmella. We wondered at first—"

"Works at the Lotus," Mrs. Linehan said.

Sherry rolled her eyes. "She's the hostess, *not* a dancer. Dresses very respectable." She lowered her voice. "She's a hardworking gal trying to support two kids after her husband cheat on her. Ma met her a couple times, and I met her once. Dean wouldn't date her if she was trash. You know where they met? At the semi-finals. The Badgers, they went to the Championship play-offs."

I told Stacy, "That's the Brackton High basketball team."

"You know the last year we went to the semi-finals?" Sherry asked.

"No."

"What?" Mrs. Linehan said.

"I asked if she knows the last year the Badgers went to the semi-finals."

"Fifty-four, that's when," Mrs. Linehan said. "What about trash?"

"Ma, I just told them Carmella isn't trash, that Dean wouldn't—"

"Nice gal," she shouted. "Two teenagers. Good-looking. Staying with their father while they gone down to Daytona."

Sherry rolled her eyes again but kept smiling. "I think they were going to the Keys. Spending a day in Daytona, that's all."

"When is he, are they due back?" I asked.

"Not till middle of January, isn't it, Ma?" Sherry raised her voice. "Ma, when's Dean due back?"

"Second week January."

"Shoot. We've got to head back to Chicago before then."

Sherry made a sympathetic frown. "What a shame."

"You wouldn't happen to know Carmella's phone number or address?" I said. "Or her last name?"

"I got the phone number. You stuck it on the fridge, didn't you, Ma?" Sherry ducked into the kitchen and returned a minute later.

"Here, I copied it. Don't know the address, but I think Emerson is right."

"Thanks," I said. "Was wondering, how's he doing? I'm lousy at keeping in touch, and—"

"The last he stopped by," Sherry said, "I wasn't here. Ma, you saw him, how long ago? Just after Thanksgiving?" Old Mrs. Linehan nodded. "Whenever he's out this way, he stops. He and Ma like to talk about old times."

"We go way back," Mrs. Linehan yelled.

"How's he doing, Ma?"

"What?"

"How's he doing, she wants to know. How's Dean doing?"

"Fine, fine, doing fine."

Stacy reached over and tapped my arm. "Why don't you leave him a note, so the next time he stops—"

"I'll get you something to write on," Sherry said. Again she ducked into the kitchen, this time returning with a steno pad and pen.

"What should I say?" The question was more to myself, but Stacy answered it.

"That you're in Brackton on a spur-of-the-moment visit and tried to look him up. Give our address and phone. Tell him you're a manager at a bar—I don't know—what else do you think he'd like to hear?"

"That I won the jackpot at Vegas and am giving him half."

"What?" Mrs. Linehan shouted.

Sherry told her, "She's wondering what to write, Ma. She's leaving Dean a note, for when he visits." She lowered her voice to normal. "He's going to be here last week of January. John, Mary's husband, they're going to take Carmella's boys ice-fishing."

"Tell him you're healthy," Mrs. Linehan shouted. "First thing a parent wants to know. Tell him you're healthy."

I couldn't see writing 'I'm healthy.' Sherry must've figured the same thing. "Ma, you tell him that. You tell him you saw her, and she's looking great. Darn!" She snapped her fingers. "The camera. It's home. I could've taken a picture of you and your friend. He'd have loved that."

Hey, guess who was here while you yukked it up in the Sunshine State? I scribbled some more and flipped the page over. "How did that joke start, the one my uncle told about the pigeon? That's his kind of humor."

When I was done, I signed *Andy* and pulled the page off the spindle.

"Let me get you an envelope," Sherry said. "He'll get a kick out of a joke, when he's done being mad about missing you."

"I don't need an envelope. There's nothing in it I wouldn't want anybody to read. Unless they have a soft spot for pigeons."

"I'll put it right here on the mantel, under the trophy. That's where we put things nobody's supposed to touch. Remember, Ma. The note for Dean, up here on the mantel."

"What about pigeons?" Mrs. Linehan asked.

"It's just a joke for Dean," Sherry said.

Her mother cackled. "He likes jokes."

When we said our goodbyes, I leaned down and hugged Mrs. Linehan's plump shoulders. She smelled vaguely of lavender. "He's gonna be sorry he missed you. Shame 'bout the camera, Sherry."

"I know, Ma."

Dusk was starting to creep over the Meadows as we wound back to Old Country Road and turned towards Brackton. "How much spaghetti sauce is left?" Stacy asked. "Should we pick up something for dinner?"

You're gonna be mad when you find out who you missed. Andy. Yes, your daughter. Looking for you. That's right—she remembered us and this place. Before I forget, she wrote you a note. Where is it? I'll have to call Sherry. The mantel, check the mantel. He'd try to hide the sweep of his smile.

"Should we pick up something for dinner?" Stacy repeated.

"What do you think about going back to your father's now?" I said. "I've seen everybody I want to see. We could make it to Hastings by ten or eleven."

"Wouldn't it hurt Mathilde's feelings?"

"I'll say your dad called earlier and isn't feeling well."

Stacy didn't argue; her foot even pressed the accelerator harder.

Mathilde was napping in the recliner, the TV tuned to local news. She sat up as I tiptoed in and asked if we were hungry. I gestured towards Stacy. "Actually, we've got to hit the road. Her father called earlier, and he's not feeling great. She was trying to ignore it, but it's not working."

Mathilde looked alarmed. "What's wrong?"

Stacy shrugged and said she wasn't sure. I said he'd had a stroke a few months ago.

We took our stuff to the car, and while Stacy straightened the bedroom, I chatted a little extra with Mathilde. "I was hoping to stay longer—"

"I'm glad you came. Maybe you can come again—"

"For sure, without a zillion years in between. Hey, why don't you visit Chicago? Uncle Anthony, Lorraine, the three of you. We could put you up."

"Sissy can't even get me to go to bingo in Vineland."

"But we won't stack the odds so bad."

"She was glad to see you," Stacy said once we were on the road.

"Coming or going?"

"Admit it, you're glad you went."

"I admit it, but I'm also glad we left. Now the real vacation starts."

When we stopped for gas, Stacy phoned her father to say we'd be getting in late tonight. She reported back he didn't mention Tommy. "I told him not to wait up for us. Then I don't have to explain why Tommy isn't along."

"And the contingency plan, if he waits up anyway?"

"Tommy was restless from the ride and asked to be dropped off a few blocks away to walk the rest."

"In the cold and dark?"

Stacy's smile was as close to devil-may-care as I'd ever seen it.

We got to talking about things we wanted to do in New York, jobs Tommy might apply for back in Chicago, some woodworking projects I was considering. When we fell into our separate ruminations, mine were about Carmella. If Dean had taken her to meet the Linehans, she had to be a decent sort. And who was I to say what jobs folks should get if they have to support their kids?

The light above the front steps to the Grunner mansion was lit. Stacy went up the path and disappeared inside. A moment later, she walked briskly back. "Coast's clear. Dad's gone to bed."

I brought the bags in and locked the front door behind me. Chesterton slogged into the entryway, got himself petted, and slogged out again. While Stacy headed for the guest cottage, I climbed the spiral stairs.

Her room was in the modest disorder we'd left it. I cracked a window, sat on the window seat, and lit a cigarette, relaxing more than I had in days. A beer would be nice—maybe in a few minutes

I'd go down to the kitchen. And there was still plenty of single-malt. Thank God I didn't have to worry about Cherise coming up.

Was somebody coming up? *Cre-aaa-aak. Cre-aaa-aak. Cre-aaa-aak.* Did Stacy need something from the room? The whiskey, maybe. Awfully slow—could it be a burglar? No, the person wasn't trying to be especially quiet. And the *cre-aaa-aak, cre-aaa-aak* sounded like Stace, just slower. She was lugging her pack; that was it.

She came in holding only an envelope. Her chin was down almost to her breast-bone. "He's gone."

"Where to—the city? Is he taking the train back? Do they run this late?"

She handed me the envelope. It wasn't addressed to anybody.

I apologize for the manner of this communication, but it appears to be the only option. I have decided, for reasons too complicated to explain here, that I am at one of life's crossroads. I have fallen from my horse. Unfortunately, no vision has appeared. As you might say, "Where's a good epiphany when you need one?"

The "Chicago" episode of my life has concluded, and I must journey on. Where I shall tarry next, I don't know. But I shall always treasure the special time we spent together and wish you the best on your own personal journey.

It was unsigned. I had to give him two points for discretion.

"The bed and food were untouched."

All I could think of to say was "Shit." I repeated it every minute or so while she slowly paced the room. Eventually, the tears began. She plopped down on the bed and made harsh squealing noises into her hands.

"You want me to go hang out elsewhere?"

"No, stay."

For some minutes I simply listened to her weeping. But then I poured Scotch into two glasses and handed her one. She downed it and held the glass out for a refill. I obliged, and after gulping that, she lay face down on the bed. I said I was going to the kitchen to see if there was any beer.

At the bottom of the staircase I had two thoughts. First, to check out David's room, in case the note was Tommy's perverse idea of a joke. Second, to check out the guest cottage, in case Stacy missed a clue to some fate other than getting dumped.

I groped my way up the stairs to the East Wing. Neither Tommy nor his clothes nor his toiletries were in any of the rooms. I went back downstairs, putting on the hall lights as I walked the length of the house. The guest cottage was as Stacy'd said: untouched. He'd probably never even unpacked. Did he call a cab and make a beeline for the station? Which direction did he travel? I wouldn't try the Deep South if I were Tommy, but the worry-free life wasn't a priority for him.

When I got back to her room, Stacy was fast asleep, one arm hanging off the side of the bed, the fingertips grazing the floor. I gently unlaced her boots and gently tugged them off, then managed to get the blankets out from under her and pull them up.

Suddenly I was tired too. It had been a long day, a long trip, in time and miles and memory. I carefully slipped in beside my unhappy friend. Why I took such pains not to wake her, I couldn't have said, since she gorged on Nature's second course.

Chapter 24

"WHAT DO YOU mean, *grasshopper*? This is a real bar."

"She wants a grasshopper."

"Andy doesn't know how to make them."

"I know *how* to make them; just the smell's enough—"

"No one's paying you to *drink* it."

GinMar's was busier than hell after Sodom and Gomorrah got razed. We'd only been open a few weeks, but word had spread that the jukebox was even better, with great new dance numbers and some vintage Sixties. Stacy let me take the car to and from work, never going out herself; in fact, she took the two-to-ten shift at the bookstore, giving up on her classes.

"Don't stand in the doorway, don't block up the hall," I crooned to Table three, handing out the wines and steins, "for he that gets hurt will be he who is stalled."

"When did they start with the singing waitresses?"

"You call this singing?"

In late January, some cousin of Martha's got hired on and wanted as many weekend hours as I'd relinquish, so I started taking off either a Friday or Saturday night and going to Cleo's, a tiny new women's bar in the Near-Near North. It had a fun group, and I could go by IC and get as ripped as I wanted.

One wee hour I arrived home from some serious carousing to see Stacy sitting cross-legged on the couch in the dim light of a single lamp. She stared vacantly through the window into the dark. Both the TV and stereo were off. "Hey, kiddo, you worry me. Should I be calling a crisis line?"

About a year later, she said, "Don't worry. I would never consider suicide."

Her tone wasn't all that convincing. "Me neither. It would please too many people I can't stand."

"I'm trying to understand what I did wrong. Argue with him too much? I know I can be opinionated."

"And Tommy can't?"

"*When* did he decide to leave? In Chicago? Was that *why* he wanted to go East? Maybe I never sensed him slipping away because I never felt I truly *had* him."

"Hey, it wasn't *me* keeping him company in the Murphy bed."

"He was willing to go along with a relationship," she said softly, "but that's not the same as being in someone's thrall."

Only Grunner could use the word *thrall* during an I've-been-screwed-over sulk. But it was all mental morphine anyway. Some folks getting dumped took real morphine; others got drunk or stoned or chased anything that moved. The smarter ones threw themselves into work or a hobby. But each was a ploy to keep the mind distracted while Father Time got on with the actual work of healing. Stacy's method of coping with a relationship going south was to analyze it to death. Did I have a better idea?

"I have to keep reminding myself, this life is my *choice*. The bad with the good. You've heard Bess and me talk about my philosophical concept, my version of an Ivan's dream?"

"Vaguely."

"Do you want me to explain it?"

"Sure, yes." I perched on the chair arm.

"It's a fantasy more than a concept. Imagine before we're born we start out in a place like heaven. Not the way religions describe it; imagine a group of souls in some spiritual dimension. God periodically offers them—us—the chance to go to earth and inhabit a human being. An infant is about to be born and needs a soul. After the person dies, the soul returns to heaven."

"Like reincarnation?"

"You only get *one* turn, *one* experience on earth, so it's not based on how you behaved in a previous life. Another thing: God already knows what each life will be like—how long you'll live, where and when, what will happen to you. It's all predestined. God tells the souls these details before they choose."

"Seems only fair."

"So imagine a group of souls lining up to decide whether to inhabit a body at a given point in time. God describes the lives on the list of infants to be born that day, a summary of the good and bad they'll experience. If you don't want those experiences, you remain in heaven. The one catch for those who do choose a life on earth is that while you're here, you have no memory of the spiritual realm. You'll think your soul never existed before you were born."

She paused a moment, then continued, "Imagine I'm one of the souls in line. God says, 'I can offer you a boy who grows up in a fishing village in Italy; he'll get married, have seven kids, and die at fifty-five when his boat capsizes. Or a youth of privilege who'll grow up to be a member of the British Parliament and very wealthy, but his wife steals his money and runs off with a movie star. Or a Nigerian girl who will become a village matriarch, or a peasant girl in Thailand—'"

"Or a weirdo from Hastings-on-Hudson."

"Yes. God says, 'I've got this girl whose mother dies when she's a child, and she can't seem to stop missing her. She falls in love with this unusual woman and feels a happiness she's never known before. But the woman leaves her.' My soul would also hear how this girl would have a caring family, material comforts, freedom, a good education. She would love poetry, have an abundance of books, enjoy music and movies and have friends, *fantastic* friends."

"Hey, something to look forward to."

"My soul said it would take that girl. God reminded me that I'd miss Tommy as much as I missed my mother, but I said I was willing to go through that pain."

"'Tis better to have loved and lost."

"You see my point. I *would* have chosen this life. I *would* have chosen to have known and loved Tommy. I don't believe in God, but I *do* believe that being alive is a privilege. I can't lose sight of that. I need to remember, to be *grateful*."

I asked if this concept-fantasy thing was helping her to get over him. She gave a terse smile. "Not as much as I'd like. But tell me this: wouldn't you have chosen the interesting life of smart-ass Andy Gabe?"

"What other choices did I get? Shit, I'd have chosen the movie star who ran off with the rich English lady."

The only other time Stacy mentioned Tommy was, appropriately, April Fools Day. After flipping the kitchen-calendar page and doing her annual April-is-the-cruelest-month shtick, she asked if I thought he had been turned off by her love of poetry. Did it make her too flaky?

I said, "I don't think we ever really know why a relationship goes south. We might think it's one thing, it might *seem* to be that, but it could be something else entirely. The mind, in my humble opinion, is a crazily-wired, messed-up, nonsensical organ."

She laughed. "That's heresy in *his* book. The mind is the best organ we have, the consummation of evolution."

April showers brought May flowers. Blossoms blossomed, and bright green grass sprouted in parks and yards. Some days the temperature flirted with sixty. I traded in my parka for my jeans jacket, feeling like Earth had traded in her gravity allotment for the Moon's.

The political season was in full gear. Newspapers, TV, radio saturated us with talk about the presidential campaigns. Jimmy Carter led the pack on the Democratic side and Ford, on the Republican, yet the press couldn't get enough of Ronald Reagan, either because he'd once lived in Illinois or they were obsessed with Hollywood.

Carrying my cup of coffee into the living room, I found Stacy on the floor surrounded by scads of magazines. "You wouldn't think this many poetry journals would make enough money to survive," she said.

"Why not? They're running away with yours."

"This is from a collective that woman at the Lesbian Writers Conference told me about. I wrote to them."

"Cool."

Bess came in and riffled through the mail. Tearing into an envelope, she became a sight to behold: red hair flying, pink robe spinning, voice singing, "Ob-la-di, ob-la-da, life goes on, la-la how the life goes on." She halted, breathless. "McGill. Montreal. 'We are pleased to offer you a position' la-la-la-la-la-la-la." The singing trailed down the hall after her skipping form.

"I'm going to miss Her Royal Pinkness," I said.

"You ever think of leaving Chicago?" Stace asked.

"Not particularly. I'm not glued to it, but you know me: thinking about the future's against my religion."

"I'm twenty-eight," she said wistfully. "I feel stalled in neutral, like the future is passing me by."

"Shift to park, turn off the motor, lean back, and relax."

Later I wondered if she was regretting not sticking it out with school; she too could be looking forward to graduating in June and getting a post-doc. At least now she was *doing things.* Showing an interest in the outside world, other people, what they were writing. La la la la life goes on.

Unfortunately, my job didn't go on. Ginnie and Martha decided to sell the bar to somebody who would turn it into a straight place, and we'd fold up tent the end of May. My next trip to Cleo's, I asked about openings, and the owner said mid-July I could get twenty-five hours. Okay, I'd hit the bulletin board at Julesman to find something to tide me over.

But a funny thing happened on my way into work: I parked by a telephone pole with a sign saying *oferta de trabajo?* The following day I drove in early and instead of going directly to the bar paid a visit to Hernandez Produce. The supervisor was an asshole who kept staring at my breasts but explained that the job was for packing fresh fruit and vegetables in flats. Evidently stuff came in by truck in larger containers. You didn't get an hourly but were paid by the flat, the rate depending on whether it was lettuce or strawberries or something else. The warehouse opened at "five in morning" and closed "five at night," and I could work whatever hours I wanted. No, I didn't need to fill out "no forms"—they paid cash.

Hallie was tending when I came in, and I told her about Hernandez's, but she wasn't interested. Stacy was off today, it was sunny and warm, and I wanted to go home and gloat about my new job. It being midweek and slow, Hallie didn't mind my leaving early and in fact probably appreciated not having to split the tips. Ever since word had gotten out that we were closing, the bar had acquired the allure of fried manure.

Predictably, Stace was sprawled on the couch reading one of her poetry journals. The windows were open to the fresh air, and Joni Mitchell trilled through the speakers.

Night in the city looks pretty to me,
Night in the city looks fine.

The second she saw me, she got up and lowered the volume on Joni. "I've decided what I want to do with my life," she said with a smile. "I'm going to be a poet."

I staggered, holding my hands to my heart. "I'm shocked, shocked!"

"I mean it!"

"You already *are* a poet." I dropped my cigarette pack on the coffee table and took off my jeans jacket.

"I mean I'm going to center my *life* around it. Poetry will be my job, paying or not. I got another letter from the Berkeley collective. They use their house for readings and print a book of poems twice a year. It's not a lot, but they're getting their work out there. The collective, the poets, all live together."

"Cool." I imagined converting our apartment into a poetry collective when Bess left next month. Two women could share her room, and even if only one took it, we could still host readings. Coming home after work—at Cleo's or wherever—to a circle of women with notebooks—night in the city looked pretty to me.

Stacy grew more enthusiastic. "They have a vacancy in June, and the room is large enough to screen it off into two. Apparently bartender and waitress jobs aren't hard to come by. There are three guys and three women; we'd be housemates seven and eight."

"Whoa, Nellie. You're talking about moving to Berkeley?"

"What did you think?"

"I don't know—that you wanted to start a poetry collective here. Or in a larger apartment. In Hyde Park, or Chicago, at least. Why not? Heckuva lot easier than moving to the West Coast."

"Moving appeals to me; I don't know why. Maybe I'm at *my* crossroads. You wouldn't have to write poetry. I said you were into journals but not ready to publish—just to say something. They're not pushy."

"It's all kind of taking me by surprise."

She studied her cuticles. "You don't have to go. But I'd pay the first month's rent myself. With GinMar's closing, I thought you might be up for—"

"When would you—or we—head out?"

"I'd like to leave by the first week of June. Michael knows several people looking for apartments starting in July who'd be happy to take over our lease. Bess could sell the furniture and keep whatever she got for it. Unless you decide to stay and get new roommates."

The sadness in my voice was a surprise, to me at least. "No, I'm not going to stay, not in Hyde Park." I tried for an easygoing shrug. "Can I let you know tomorrow?"

"Sure. Want some coffee? I just put on a pot."

"If you're going that way, grab me a beer."

I braced myself to smile when Stacy returned. Getting hired at Hernandez's suddenly didn't seem so funny. Why *didn't* I just pack up and head out to Berkeley? We were good traveling buddies. I hadn't seen a speck of country west of the Mississippi—it could be cool to check out the Great Plains and Rockies and Pacific Ocean. This land is your land, this land is my land. The Bay area was a Mecca for gay folks, a laid-back place, flowers in your hair. Why not, Andy?

Granted, she'd checked on whether there was room for me at the collective before saying yes. But my saying no wouldn't matter; she was going anyway.

The phone rang but stopped abruptly. Stacy's voice ricocheted down the hall, followed by her laugh.

I was out of a real job, out of a home, out of a friend. When would Bess split—right after graduation? I didn't relish the idea of staying on alone. Picturing it bugged me more than the word crossroads.

I grabbed my jacket and went down to the Raven, which didn't have a jukebox or TV. The bartender was unfamiliar yet seemed willing to lend an ear once the place had emptied, which it did at the ridiculous hour of 10:30, but that was Hyde Park for you. No wonder nobody tried opening a gay bar here. I said I was in the dumps about a good friend moving to California to follow her dream of being a poet.

"Your drinking buddy?" he asked.

"Not really, not anymore."

"Eat your meals together?"

"On occasion."

"Go shopping, watch TV—"

"Not really."

"Work together?"

"No."

He squinted at me like I was crazy.

"Hey, I just like knowing she's around. We're roommates, she's the first friend I made when I came to Chicago back in '69, we've been best friends ever since. Tell each other anything and everything. I don't like the idea that I can't hang out with her if I want to."

"Your security blanket's leaving," he said.

I slid off my stool, scooped the change into my pocket, and left.

Stacy's light was off. I put the note by the coffee pot. *Stace—think I'll stay in Chicago awhile longer. Thanx for the offer, though.* She was following her dream, but I'd just be tagging along for the ride. Hell, there was no law against going to Berkeley later if something better didn't turn up.

I began putting in short stints at Hernandez's before showing up at GinMar's—the extra cash would come in handy. At least they paid every day at the end of your shift. It wasn't arduous work; the guys unloading the crates opened them with crowbars, so I just had to remove gallon or half-gallon containers of berries or pea pods or lettuce and repack them into flats. The weather was mild enough for working outdoors in the alley, and though I was the sole female and non-Hispanic, I didn't need to talk to anybody. I did have to figure out the bus route because Stacy needed her car, but Hallie gave me rides home, appreciating the company.

The remainder of May, Gabe and Grunner were ships not even passing in the night. She was putting in extra hours at the bookstore, and when I wasn't at GinMar's or Hernandez's or traveling to and fro, I went north to drown my sorrows.

Arriving home after my last day of work, I found a note from Stacy on my pillow saying I could still join her at the collective and though she didn't want to pressure me, if I did go with, she'd clean my pubic hairs out of the shower for a month. *Any longer than that might earn me sainthood and consign me to heaven, and I'd rather we be roommates in the Afterlife.* But in this one you didn't really give a damn. The note went on to say she was leaving in three days and did I want to go out for a beer tomorrow night.

The table at the Hangman we'd shared with Michael after *The Children's Hour* was taken, but we found an equally rickety one.

"Here's looking at you, kid," Stacy said, clanking her glass into mine, and I came back with here's-to-mud-in-your-eye, and she did bottoms-up, and we went on like that till the awkwardness was gone. Then we reminisced about everything from the early days at the Palace and biology not being destiny to Hecate Hore and the brawl at Vicki's. Stace even mentioned first seeing Tommy at Maxwell Street.

Two days later, we hugged goodbye.

With GinMar's now closed, I put in as many hours at Hernandez's as I could stomach. It wasn't just the humid heat that started getting to me but the men who walked by saying *meow*. One puckered his lips and made sucking sounds. If a dog strayed down the alley, they'd jab each other and shout, "You like dog? I like pussy." If anybody had tried laying a hand on me, I probably would've smashed his skull with a crowbar. I kept reminding myself that the second Cleo's gave me a starting date, Hernandez's was history.

Michael's friends got the landlady to agree to their taking over the lease July 1, and a woman at Cleo's wanted a house sitter for the summer, a backup plan if I couldn't find a place to live right away. Still, Stacy's absence was depressing. Lingering in her room, I'd recall where the bulletin board had been and the various clippings and photos over the years: the three civil rights workers, the four little girls, the Watergate target.

The chaos of Bess's imminent departure helped a little. Cartons cluttered the living room. Some, half-open, awaited more books, stuffed animals, or clothing; some, closed, were topped with address labels saying *Montreal, Canada*. As the cartons began disappearing, though, the furniture began to look lonely.

One afternoon, I happened to walk by Rockefeller Chapel when a graduation ceremony either was about to begin or had just ended.

Hundreds of students mingled with family and friends on the bright green lawns. Despite being draped in long black gowns and weighted down with mortarboards, the students smiled and laughed and posed for pictures. I scanned the crowd for Bess but didn't see her. Or anybody else I knew, for that matter.

On my big day, the mail brought a card from Matt containing ten dollars, one from Edward with a picture of Tony Curtis and Jack Lemmon in drag, and a postcard of the Golden Gate Bridge that said on the reverse: *Happy Birthday, tried calling, will write real letter soon if don't reach you by phone, housemates nice, busy as all get-out.*

The phone did ring, but I skulked past it; nothing would be cheering about Stacy's recounting her trip west, Berkeley, her new housemates. I considered going to Cleo's but didn't feel like springing for IC fare. I grabbed my jeans jacket and hit the Raven.

At least the regular bartender was on. "Hate to do this," he said, "but I have to card you. Graduation time, the cops are pests."

"Hey, no problem." I pulled out my wallet and handed him my license.

"It's your birthday. Your first one's on the house."

"Thanks."

Now I had to stay for a second to be polite, but that was okay; the lifelessness of the joint matched my mood. Bringing my refill, the bartender mused, "Wish I could remember twenty-four. That was over twenty-four years ago. Wasn't it George Bernard Shaw who said, 'Youth is wasted on the young'?"

The question jolted me like a cattle prod. I *was* young. More young than old—still south of the quarter-century mark. I had practically my whole life ahead of me. Why was I moping like it was over? And wasting time at Hernandez's? Why was I in *Chicago* even, with its 200 percent humidity and crime and pollution and meowing, hassling men? To hell with it. A simple phone call might be all the traction I needed to get out of my rut, get myself over the potential energy barrier.

I extracted the matchbook from my jacket pocket and carefully unfolded it. The handwriting was legible. Would she still be there? How long ago was that— October?

I walked across the room to the Raven's pay phone, my fingers flattening out the matchbook's creases.

Briiiing, briiing, briiing. Briiiing, briiing, briiing. Did they go to bed at sundown?

"Hello?"

"Is Laurie there?"

"Hold on."

The operator made me put in more coins, but then somebody said hello.

"Laurie?"

"Yes?"

"This is Andy Gabe. You might not remem—"

"Andy! Where are you?"

"In Chicago. But, hey, I was thinking about coming up to the farm you're at some time. You know, check it out, see what it's like. If the invite is still open."

"Yes! That would be terrific."

"When's a good time? In a few—"

"Now!"

I laughed. "Right this minute?"

"Yes."

"Need to pack my toothbrush. How about tomorrow? Where do I go? All you told me was Wisconsin. I'd be hitching, so—"

"Get close to Madison and call me."

After hanging up, this little piggy cried yay yay yay all the way home. *My* Chicago episode was ending.

Chapter 25

BACON SIZZLING IN lard couldn't have felt this greasy. The sun bore down without mercy, and the expressway shoulder, a stone's throw from O'Hare, was shadeless. Jets taking off and landing blasted my eardrums worse than the mammoth semis blasting their horns for fun. Diesel fumes swamped my face, infiltrated my nostrils. My armpits were soaking, and despite the Phillies cap pulled low, my forehead dripped stinging sweat into my eyes. If the bank lady hadn't taken forever closing out my account, maybe I would've been in Wisconsin already.

The backpack sat beside me on the glinting asphalt, ballooning with clothes, two towels, a carton of cigarettes, and the journal from high school. Also the Bacchus doubloon necklace from Mardi Gras. I'd left behind Lish's Bible, Gideon-like, for the new tenants.

Eventually a truck stopped and gave me a ride past the suburbs. I said no to a guy with a wild beard and to a car packed with teenage boys. Had I been this choosy hitching from Brackton to Chicago? It was dusk when I finally made it over the border into Wisconsin and twilight when I got dropped on a local road.

This time, Laurie answered the phone. I told her, "The gas station attendant says we're half a mile east of some motel called the Bus Stop."

"I'll be there in twenty minutes."

Stepping outside the phone booth, I mentally breathed a sigh of relief. No hitching in the dark in some godforsaken place—I was about to be met by somebody I knew, somebody who'd take me to a house with other women, *only* women.

After using the gas station restroom to wash up and change into a clean T-shirt, I bought a sandwich and can of soda and sat on a low wall beyond the pumps. The sky in the west was a blue-purple; to the east it was black. I watched the stars come out, a zillion stars.

Yet the Fates never let you stay comfortable for long. The trials and tribulations of hauling my body and belongings from Chicago to Wisconsin had spared me much thinking about what exactly I was jumping from the frying pan *into*; now I had nothing else to think about. What if Laurie wasn't as I remembered? What if she looked totally different, like a figure in a dream that one minute is young and dark-haired and the next is transformed into a matronly blonde with a beehive? Would her personality be different? Did I really *know* her personality? The first time we'd met was over a year ago, and the second, at GinMar's, we'd hardly exchanged ten words. Besides, how she acted at parties wasn't necessarily how she acted the rest of the time. True, she didn't know me either, not really, but she had the advantage of knowing everybody else on the farm. What about them—could some be former femmes de semaine? Vicki? Could I find a ride to Berkeley?

The vibes Laurie had given off last night were clear: she had a crush on me. An excitement seemed to pulse through the phone line. But was I really ready for a relationship? How could she expect me to jump right into one based on a few conversations? *I* hadn't acted like I had a crush. And I'd been careful to say I was interested in "the farm," not her. I was between jobs and homes so naturally wanted to check the place out.

Was it *wrong* of me to come here knowing our feelings were unequal? Was it taking advantage of her? The best moments I'd had all day were remembering how she'd laughed at my jokes. I wasn't *ruling out* a relationship, but I needed time, time to get settled into the new digs and to get to know her better. *You used to have no problem leaping before you looked.* But Chicago was different, Jiminy—I'd always had an escape hatch. In this vast, empty expanse, where the hell could I go? Was this how a mail-order bride felt, with cold— with *freezing*—feet? Why didn't I move to another city—even Madison—if I was bent on leaving Chicago? Some place with a ton of people, a ton of possibilities. Heck, Stacy had gone to the Bay Area not to find love but to try on a new way of life. Whether the poetry collective would fulfill her expectations, she didn't know, but she was right to move forward, take a chance. You *shouldn't* spend your life stalled in neutral. And I was moving forward by trying out a farm and commune. If Laurie was harboring greater expectations, wasn't that *her* problem?

A truck of some sort veered sharply off the road into a U-turn in the station lot, pulling up by the gas pumps. The driver's door sprang open, and a young woman jumped out and came towards me. "Andy?"

I strode to meet her, and the station light showed it was the Laurie I remembered, no blond beehive. And she was still really cute, with her dark hair and beautiful braless breasts under the T-shirt. But differences were apparent too. Farm life agreed with her. She radiated health; her arms were toned and tanned. And she moved with self-confidence, a giggly girl no more.

"We were starting to get nervous, when you didn't call. Bec hates me taking the truck out alone at night."

"Folks weren't all too keen on stopping, so it took a while."

"I've got to get gas, but it'll just be a minute."

I followed her to the truck and climbed up into the cab. It was a weather-beaten thing with tattered upholstery and the gear shift on the steering wheel. Through the small back window, I could make out that the bed was fenced but open on top, like something you might see hauling pigs. I watched Laurie's graceful lope towards the station, one hand reaching into a back pocket. Who was Bec?

When she got back in the cab, she flashed a brief smile, started the engine, and pulled onto the road. "I couldn't believe it when you called yesterday. What good timing—the berries are ripening."

"Mind if I smoke?"

"Go ahead, but it's not allowed in the house, not downstairs. Chloe doesn't even like it outside. She's the one who owns Geserenie. But I don't care, and Bec won't. Really."

I lit the cigarette and tossed the match out the window. "Maybe I shouldn't have come. Smoking's not something I'm ready to give up. Not yet, at least."

"No, it's okay, just not in common areas."

We passed a green neon *Bus Stop Motel—Weekly Rates, Kitchenettes.* If worst came to worst, I could go there till I figured out my next step.

"Who all lives at Jez—what did you call it?"

"G-E-S-E-R-E-N-I-E. Geserenie. The syllables are taken from the goddesses of earth, spring, and peace. Heather was a classics major and helped Chloe come up with the name. There's nine of us, not counting you. We're all lesbians, except we're not sure about Gertie. There used to be straight women. Chase used to be bi, and Heather was straight when she moved in, but they fell in love. Geserenie has that effect."

For a few minutes we rode in silence. Except for the stars and truck headlights, you couldn't see much—an occasional farmhouse with a lamp on inside, an occasional vehicle going the opposite direction. Streetlights were few and far between. Dark fields interspersed with woods and more dark fields interspersed with more woods. Eventually I mentioned I didn't have a ton of money, just a few hundred dollars, but hoped to find a job pretty quick. "It was kind of sudden—"

"Don't worry," Laurie said. "We can use the extra hands. You can work off most or all of your room and household expenses. That's what PJ, Chase, and Gertie do. Becca drives a bus in Madison and pays her share, though she works so hard on the farm, I always tell her she shouldn't have to pay." Laurie tapped the steering wheel. "Even takes Rubella into Madison for the shopping."

"Rubella?"

"Means measles. Sally suggested the name because of the rust spots, and Bec liked it."

I wasn't sure what to say, and besides, my throat felt dry. Maybe it was used to more pollution. Obviously Laurie was trying to let me know as kindly as she could that she and Becca were lovers. Hey, we hadn't promised each other anything. She was free to do what she wanted. They were a couple; that was cool. I was off the hook.

I mentioned that I'd done kitchen work in restaurants, but she said somebody named Wanda did all the group cooking. "The farm is vegetarian, but she makes *incredible* meals." A shyness crept into her voice. "I don't do as much as I should. The money my parents send covers my rent and household expenses. We're not self-sufficient like New Eden, but we don't care; that's not why Geserenie was formed. Chloe wants an all-woman, nurturing environment. The relationships we have with each other and the land is what's important. 'Friendships are our primary crop,' we say. The *men's* communes— there are women, but the men really run them—they're welcome to their rat-race mentality."

She continued on about this and that: somebody was a nurse; somebody did clerical at an old people's home; their last cow would be sold to the neighbors the Craybills the end of August; these chicken species were better layers than those; trading corn instead of ensiling it; something about nitrogen. Scorpio Rising, another commune, got hit with ergot and couldn't make the mortgage, but luckily Chloe's grandparents had paid off theirs before she'd inherited it.

I could see Laurie getting over me, the infatuation ending once she'd fallen for Becca, but why did she have to sound so enthusiastic over the phone? Why give off the same vibes she gave off last year *just last night.* I wasn't crazy to feel a little betrayed. She'd been *gushing,* said I should come *now.*

She slowed almost to a stop and made a left onto a dirt road, and we bounced along slowly. A jackrabbit or something darted across the headlight beams. A house came into view on the right, a large, Mama-Bates-style three-story. Only a single light was on, somewhere on the first floor. We turned right at the end of the house and went along the rear, passing some cars. Ahead I could just make out a barn and flat land on either side and trees in the distance.

Laurie turned off the engine and yanked the emergency brake. I climbed down from the cab to be greeted by sheer silence—silence and a glittering, starry sky with a sliver of crescent moon. Gradually my ears picked up the clicking clatter of crickets. The dippers were out and the North Star.

I followed Laurie up a couple of steps and into an entryway and through a second door. She flicked on an inside light in what was the kitchen. It was large and contained a long table with benches and a cast-iron stove covered with a gingham cloth. She asked if I was hungry, and I said no but did they have any beer. She opened the fridge, squatted, and reached into the bottom shelf. Her butt was nice and round.

I sat at the table, asking how many days I got to learn everybody's name. Bringing over two beers, she sat on the opposite bench and began to talk a blue streak, about who everybody was and where they were from, and rules like everybody washing their own breakfast and lunch dishes and what times we had to be out of the kitchen so Wanda could cook. Which would take longer, learning the names or the rules, I wondered.

Laurie looked off at the walls while she spoke, no doubt feeling guilty—and rightly so—for leading me on. She was disturbingly arousing, her body all gentle curves, as if the dark hair and dark brown eyes and long lashes weren't enough. Damn, I could've fallen for her. Maybe I should've gone with her when she'd first moved here. But that was blood under the bridge, as Miss August would've said.

After we were done with the beers, Laurie rinsed the bottles, and we went through a swinging door into the room with the lit lamp. Immediately to my left was a wide staircase. Laurie grabbed a flashlight from somewhere and started up. The second floor was a labyrinth. We quietly followed the flashlight beam along the wooden boards. "That's Heather and Chase's room," she whispered, "and those stairs go to the attic. Chloe moved her grandmother's four-poster and desk up. Gertie's bed's up there too."

So Chloe and Gertie were a couple? No, not if Gertie had her own bed. Down a different branch of the maze, Laurie pointed with the beam at another door. "PJ and Sally." The next turn took us into a cul-de-sac where the roof sloped. A mattress and orange crate were placed against the vertical wall. "This is our extra room. It's private because no one comes down this way."

"Reminds me of the alcove I had in Chicago. I'm used to a small cozy space."

We retraced our steps, and the light beam hit another door. "That's Becca and Wanda."

"Who?"

"Becca and Wanda."

Becca and *Wanda*. I followed Laurie through more turns, and we were back near the top of the stairs. She went in a doorway and switched on a lamp.

This room was also cozy. At the far end, a narrow window ran from just inches off the floor practically to the ceiling molding. The shade was up, and I walked over and peered into the darkness. Below to my left was the tree I'd seen by the kitchen door, and, beyond it, the barn roof.

"What direction is that?" I asked.

"West."

So Berkeley was out there some thousands of miles away. I turned around.

The double mattress on the floor was covered with a pale sheet, a thin blanket folded at the foot, and two pillows at the head. The room contained little else: a small rug, a wooden bureau with a hairbrush and ceramic bowl on top, a straight-backed chair, and a low table holding the lamp. Simplicity, not austerity. A maiden's room, not a nun's.

"Hey, this is pretty cool."

Laurie stood just inside the open door, avoiding eye contact. "I can give you sheets and a blanket for the extra room if you want."

I sauntered towards her. "And if I don't want?"

She didn't move. "You don't? It's the only empty bed."

"What if I don't want an empty bed?"

She tried to look at me but her neck stopped mid-swivel. That was okay: I saw the embarrassed smile. I touched her shoulder. Now she raised her face, with the long dark lashes, the gorgeous deep brown eyes. I kissed her lightly. She kissed back, also lightly. I was about to say something—I didn't know what—when she pressed her mouth firmly into mine. Electric charges shot every direction. Her arms grabbed me. When we caught our breaths, I reached back with my leg and closed the door.

Chapter 26

Pale daylight painted the walls eggshell white. The shade was half lowered, letting in fresh air through the screen. A sixth sense told me it was late morning. Lying on my back, I could make out Laurie sitting beside me, her knees raised. A sketch pad rested against her bare thighs, and the thick pencil in her hand shaded a tree limb. After a minute of soaking in the peace, I said, "Howdy, stranger," which came out like a frog's last croak.

She smiled. Her face was smooth and fresh, her eyes magnificent. "I thought you'd never wake up. I've already fed the chickens, had breakfast, and done my yoga." She placed the pad and pencil on the floor and lay on her side facing me, naked as a jaybird. Quelle jaybird.

"You fed the chickens like that?"

"I put on sandals."

"Jeez, you're beautiful. But you better tell me again where the bathroom is." I pulled on my jeans and T-shirt.

When I returned, I asked if I could smoke, and she said yes and gave me a shell to use as an ashtray. She went to the window and raised the shade more. Somebody outside caught her attention, and she waved.

Maybe if I'd been more awake, I'd have tried to hide my annoyance. "This a nudist colony?"

She tilted her head, puzzled, innocent. Lousy acting.

"Showing the world your birthday suit," I said.

"Not the world. Just Mr. Wiffle."

My face warmed. She'd said there were no men at Geserenie! What was this, some kinky bisexual cult compound? Any minute would guys—Charles Mansons, maybe—barge in and demand sex? I wanted to cry, I felt so duped.

"Mr. Wiffle loves me," she murmured, coming to the bed.

My hands shook as I lit a cigarette. "Who the hell is he?"

"Mr. Wiffle is our pig. I sometimes feed him."

Holding the inhale, I shook out the match, got up, and went to the window. Sure enough, in the fenced pasture across the path, a fat little pig on fat little legs peered up at me. Embarrassed, I blew smoke through the screen.

But the embarrassment quickly melted. Green pastures spread to the bordering trees, whose crowns formed an undulating green bunting as far as the eye could see. Closer in, haystacks blazed yellow in the sunlight. A breeze rippled gracefully through the stretch of uncut grass. Atop a barrel, a large white cat slept, and a small bird cocked her head on the branch just below the window. It was beautiful, serene and beautiful.

As soon as I finished my cigarette, Laurie gently tugged my arm till I followed her to the bed. Her eyes showed rueful apology. I let her lie on top of me and rhythmically push her hips into mine.

Since I needed coffee before meeting people, she dressed and fetched a cup from the kitchen. Sitting beside me on the bed, she hugged her legs and said, "I can't believe you really came."

"If I'd come any louder, I'd have woken the cat."

"To Geserenie, you silly goose. Tell me about your life—I want to know everything."

I hit the major milestones, giving a brief recap of childhood and Nina before moving on to Chicago. However, I edited out the femmes de semaine and gave Lish only passing mention. Then I said, "Your turn. I remember your telling me about coming out and a little about the jerks you were involved with—"

"Who said I was too clingy."

"—but not much about your family."

Laurie was from Boise and had four brothers. Only William, a hot-shot lawyer in L.A., kept in regular touch. "Except for him, my family would *die*—my parents especially—if they knew I was a lesbian. They think I'm on a church-owned farm." She let go of her knees and stretched her legs, and we watched her toes wiggle. "They expect to support me until I get married, but I wasn't spoiled the way Wanda was. I wish they'd pushed me to have a career. I feel like I should want one. Should I tell them to stop sending money? It would force me to look for a job."

I stroked her leg. "Leave things as they are, for now at least. I just got here."

"Your stomach's growling."

"Isn't it too late for breakfast?"

"Not your first day—Wanda won't mind. I brought up some mints. To hide the cigarette."

"I can take a hint. And a mint."

"It avoids arguments."

Descending the stairs, I got a good look at the large, airy living room. Sunlight streamed through the tall windows onto a comfortable mishmash of upholstered and beanbag chairs, rockers, hassocks, and square pillows big enough to sit on. The adjoining dining room also had tall windows, which looked out past the dirt driveway to fields and crops. The old table, which could easily seat a dozen or more, might've been English oak. The entire expansive area was cheerful without being in your face about it.

I followed Laurie through the swinging door, telling her I was fine with something simple like Cheerios. "We don't have processed cereal," she said. "Let me surprise you."

While she got busy with her concoction, I toured the kitchen, taking an instant liking to the hardwood floor and pine table, the cast-iron stove with its gingham cover, the blue-and-white checked curtains, the old-fashioned, homespun feel. Long metal hooks suspended from the ceiling beams dangled spatulas, ladles, some utensils I couldn't identify. Hooks on the far beam dangled copper bowls and colanders. A shelf of Mason jars held different pastas and dried beans, and the jars on the counter sprouted wooden spoons, chopsticks, skewers. The ancient yellow needlepoint on the wall said *Home Is Where the Heart Is.* Best of all was the clock, a white ceramic circle with a yellow mother hen nesting in the center. Surrounding her in the twelve hour-spots, little yellow chicks pouted. Maybe Mama wasn't serving dessert because they'd refused to finish their worms.

I grabbed a coffee refill and sat at the pine table. Laurie brought over a creamy, swirly thing that tasted great. I said, "You could be poisoning me for all I know, but hey, I'll die happy."

"The commercial stuff is the poison. That's yogurt, pecans, strawberries, granola, and raspberries."

Too much time working prep and using packaged stuff made me genuinely surprised that Laurie's combo tasted better than the secret recipes food companies came up with. We'd been brainwashed by the civilian-industrial complex to believe that natural ingredients needed doctoring.

After a few more spoonfuls, I said I was ready to start learning names. "You said Chloe owns the house, and Becca drives a bus, and Wanda—"

"I'm Wanda!" The swinging door swung open, and in floated Little Bo Peep, barefoot, with bobbing yellow ringlets and blue eyes. She wore a loose white sundress that seemed to hover without actually touching her body.

"Hi, I'm Andy."

"Welcome to Geserenie." Wanda threw Laurie a knowing smile on her way to the counter.

After we exchanged a few pleasantries about my ride up, Wanda began peeling onions, and she and Laurie got to talking about some meeting Chloe was at. Apparently Geserenie and the other communes in their co-op would spend the whole day arguing about who got priority for trading what crops. Everybody couldn't trade corn or zucchini, Laurie explained to me, but if one farm got totally screwed on priorities, they would quit, so every commune had to get some of the trades they asked for.

"Although it doesn't always work out," Wanda said, slicing an onion, "because Mother Nature and Father Weather have their own plans."

"New Eden's the biggest farm and always tries to get its own way." Laurie made an exaggerated frown.

"Their May Day festival is fun, though."

"Except when one of the guys tries to 'convert' us."

Wanda scraped the onion slices into a mammoth bowl. "Tim always lets PJ know when they have a cheese surplus. And Mitchell's brother is nice."

"The submariner?"

"Yes, Luke."

"It's brave of him to visit," Laurie told me. "New Eden is *so* anti-military." She looked at the Mother Hen clock. "I wonder if Gertie will be awake for supper. She keeps odd hours because she's working on her fear of people."

"I've heard of that," I said. "Agoraphobia?"

Laurie exchanged a brief look with Wanda. "No, Gertie ... has a special problem. I mean, *the world* has a problem. They *make* the problem. But she's stuck dealing with it."

The two of them acted so uncomfortable, I said they didn't need to tell me; I respected folks' privacy. "She wouldn't mind our telling," Laurie finally said. "You'll find out anyway. Gertie has really big breasts. *Really* big."

"Men are always leering," Wanda said. "Women and kids stare. Anyone would be self-conscious. She's been harassed since elementary school. That's all we know."

"She came in February but never goes anywhere. Geserenie is the first place she's felt safe since she was a kid. Just to walk around without people gawking." Laurie noticed I was done eating and took my bowl and spoon to the sink and quickly washed them, telling me, "Sally's a nurse, and she and PJ started pushing Gertie to get an operation to make them smaller."

"Became quite the bone of contention," Wanda said. "Chloe argued *Gertie* shouldn't have to change; it was the people who were mean who should change."

"Makes sense," I said.

Wanda shook her head, her ringlets bobbing. "But the world is *not* going to change. Does she want to spend the rest of her life feeling self-conscious?"

"Becca has a point too," Laurie said. "It's about being different. You can accept it and say fuck you to everyone who's a jerk. Look at the people who *can't* change, like midgets and—"

"Bec wasn't saying Gertie *should* or *shouldn't* get the operation. She was just listing all the pros and cons."

"Chloe says every one of us has a duty to resist conforming, because in every way that we remain different, we provide—what's her phrase?"

"Solace and strength," Wanda said.

"Yes, we provide solace and strength to other people who don't fit in."

"I can dig it," I said. I really could've digged a cigarette. "I guess every person's got to decide for herself how much bullshit she wants to put up with."

They both laughed. "That's what Becca says."

Laurie was itching to give me the grand tour, so I didn't dawdle over a third cup of coffee. We began outside with the beautiful old apple tree shading the kitchen steps, the one whose branches reached almost to her bedroom window. Little green balls hung like Christmas ornaments. "Those edible when they ripen?"

"Yes, it's a Jerseymac."

"Never heard of it, but I'm from Jersey, so they can't be all bad."

"We have McIntoshes in the front yard. We get so many, they're a priority for us for trading."

We walked along the fence that penned in lazy Mr. Wiffle and the broad pasture dotted with haystacks. Laurie wasn't kidding about the apples: an orchard, practically, filled the area between the front yard and what had to be the road. Retracing our steps, we reached the pantry, and Laurie grabbed two small buckets.

"I'll show you the crops. Almost everything is planted in the south field this year. The tomatoes take lots of water. Next year we may try sweet peppers." She led me across the dirt driveway and up and down paths of taller and smaller stalks and leaves of various shades of green, identifying zucchini, kale, carrots, cucumbers, corn. She picked as we wound through the raspberries and strawberries, so I took one of the buckets and picked the darker berries too. Was that Millie-the-Cow milling in the pasture? Mrs. Bumble Bee strafed my nose but kept her stinger tucked in the bomb bay. The only sounds were an occasional chirp and the faintest echo of traffic bouncing off the apple trees. Farming wouldn't be easy work, but I'd be in fresh air, surrounded by Nature, and among women, where seldom would be heard a discouraging word.

"You sure everybody will think there's enough for me to do that I won't have to get a job? I don't want their first impression to be that I'm some kind of freeloader."

"Helping with crops will be enough over the summer: watering, picking, cleaning, bundling, storing. Chase and PJ won't share composting or swilling out the gutters—that's cleaning the barn and coop—because they earn *so* many credits from that. Chloe does all the calculating, how much work is the same as contributing money. She supplies the house and does the administrative work, paying bills and taxes, and plans the crop rotations. She also helps harvest. I do too, so nothing goes to waste. You can learn to milk Millie for backup until the Craybills take her in September. She doesn't like me or Chase."

I helped rinse and store the berries and haul food scraps to the compost heap. We sat down to lunch in the kitchen, lunch being a humongous jumble of cold vegetables and chilled macaroni noodles

and a side of bread with nuts in it. After two bites I gave my enthusiastic compliments to the chef.

"The vegetables and herbs are all home grown," Wanda said.

Becca was working only a half-day and joined us midway
through the meal. Short with short reddish brown hair, she looked
to be 200 percent muscle. She showed Wanda a pamphlet titled
Workshop on Natural Pesticides from some women's center in Madison
called Artemiz—I got the impression it was a Palace kind-of-place.

After lunch, I got the indoor tour except for the attic, since
Gertie was meditating. Becca and Wanda's room was cool: they used
an old barrel for dirty laundry and a butter urn for clean socks. The
neatest thing, though, was this rectangular cabinet of cubbyholes.
Each cubbyhole was a different size from its neighbor, and each
held something different—a miniature carving, shells, or weird
stones. I could see someday making something like that for myself,
for me and Laurie.

On my next pass through the airy living room I noticed more
details, like the geometric red-and-black design on the rug, which
Laurie said was Navajo, and the batik cushions. The Georgia
O'Keeffe goat-skull poster looked familiar—Ms. Early February
might have had it.

I pointed to the ashtrays. "Thought there was no smoking."

"Those are for pot."

Now I pointed to the wall. "Hey, that's Becca, isn't it? And
Wanda. This a portrait gallery?" Even in charcoal, Wanda's ringlets looked blond. Laurie turned away, and remembering the sketch
pad, I put two and two together. "*You* did these. They're incredible.
Who's this?" The slightly thin face, framed by long straight hair, for
some reason made me think of a Sunday school teacher.

"Chloe. It was my first and not very good. This is the parlor."

Laurie flicked on a pink-tinted light, and we stepped off the Navajo reservation into the psychedelic Sixties, a room with multicolored lamps, bongs, and a Joan Baez calendar. Futon-type mattresses and bolsters lined three of the walls; a record case and stereo system took up the fourth. The rug was a purple shag—purple in the rosy light anyway.

"You can listen to music even at night because the tile's acoustic," Laurie said.

I flipped through the album covers: Roberta Flack, Judy and Joni, Carole King, Laura Nyro. "Just curious—any males?"

"Underneath."

Gordon Lightfoot, Simon and Garfunkel, Leonard Cohen—a decent if small assortment.

Laurie studied the Joan Baez calendar. "We'll have to hold our awareness meeting on the fifth if everyone's off. The first Sunday of every month, after the business meeting, we talk about interpersonal things. With so many people living under one roof, the nitpicky stuff builds up, so we put it out in the open. And when there's a new person, she'll tell about herself. Gertie hasn't done that yet, but I think she wants to in July. We'll have to do it Monday because Sunday's the fourth, when we host the carnival."

"Carnival? With fireworks?"

"The fireworks are elsewhere. Neighbors and some communes in the co-op bring the food, and we set up activities for the kids. This will be my first too."

We returned to the living room as a bright orange van shot by the windows. "It's PJ and Sally," Laurie said. A minute later, laughter filtered in from the kitchen, and the swinging door swung towards us. The two women entering were different enough that I was able to remember which was which when Laurie introduced us. PJ, the taller and broader, had a tangled mane of light brown hair; Sally, small and wiry, had dark curly hair. Laurie told PJ that I was willing to learn to milk Millie and be a backup the rest of the summer.

"I'll teach you in the morning," PJ said with a toothy grin. "In the afternoons, Millie's one stressed-out bitch."

I met Heather and Chase when we gathered in the dining room for supper. They reminded me of the hip younger women who used to order mixed drinks at Shay's. Chloe wouldn't be joining us, somebody said; she'd gone to a composting workshop at Artemiz after the co-op meeting. And Gertie wouldn't either—she wasn't hungry.

A few of the women hit me with questions, like where I was from, but nobody came on heavy, and everybody seemed in a good mood. The food was fantastic: different kinds of salad, a pot of stew with a zillion vegetables, bread, and plenty of beer and wine.

Laurie was especially cheerful and at one point stood and tapped her glass with a spoon to quiet us. "The Fourth of July's a Sunday," she said. "We could do the awareness meeting Monday since everyone's off."

"And Chloe said the business agenda is short."

"Andy must think we're nuts, using *agendas*."

"Hey, I'm not about to call anybody nuts. You don't know *me* yet."

"It's not *quite* Robert's Rules of Order."

"More like Robert's Rules of *Dis*order."

I said, "You should make it *Roberta's* Rules of Disorder."

"Yes! I move to amend Robert's Rules of Order—"

"Why don't they just say *mend*, since that's what it means?" Wanda called down the length of the table. "They *fix* them, *mend* them. Why add an A in front?"

"Amen."

I chanted rhythmically, "A-a-mend, a-a-mend, a-mend the rules, a-mend—"

"What was that movie? Sidney Poitier stayed in a house with nuns—"

"*Lilies of the Field.*"

Laurie quoted, "'Consider the lilies of the field, how they grow; they toil not, neither do they spin.'"

Wanda clapped her hands in time. "A-a-men, a-a-men—"

"A-women!" I sang out.

Like a firestorm, the room burst into, "A-women, a-women," our voices rising like an enraptured choir, "a-a-women, a-women a-women." We sang past Bec's second trip to the kitchen for beer and wine refills, past Chase falling on the floor laughing, past Sally racing to the bathroom, past our throats going hoarse, clear past the cows coming home, or Millie, at least. Finally, under PJ's fork-baton, exhausted and spent, we gasped our last *a-women.*

After cleanup, we hung out in the living room. Somebody rolled joints, and PJ strummed her guitar, and we sang "Roll on, Columbia," "Homeward Bound," "Five Hundred Miles," and some ballads I didn't know. Chloe had arrived home and gone upstairs while I was in the can, but I'd met enough new faces for one day.

Despite all the beer and pot, I didn't fall asleep as fast as Laurie. The air coming through the screen was pleasantly cool, and I lay gazing at the shadowed ceiling, marveling at the wholesale change in my life. Like Dorothy, I'd been abruptly transported to an un-imagined land. And a welcoming one, where I was accepted as just another munchkin. But *un*like Dorothy, I could see laying down roots. Had I ever felt that before?

An old argument between Stacy and Tommy came back to me, about the meaning of the adage *A rolling stone gathers no moss.* Tommy had said the adage *praised* a rolling stone; it was a good thing to move on and change, moss representing the decay of stagnation. Stacy had argued the opposite: the moss symbolized growth, and the adage criticized a rolling stone because it never acquired anything. Not just material possessions, amassing riches—it was that if you stuck with some pursuit, persevered at school or a job, say, you ended up acquiring experience and knowledge.

I came at it from a third angle, the Z axis. Like Grunner, Gabe had always thought that the moss symbolized something good and that being a rolling stone was bad. But I thought the *adage* had it wrong. A rolling stone didn't acquire things like possessions and knowledge, true, yet it had something equally precious if not better: freedom. Freedom to follow whatever whim or idea hit you, freedom to meet new people, experience new things, the freedom of possibilities. You could get mired down with the trappings of civilization—no accident, folks calling them *trappings*.

Freedom's just another word for nothing left to lose, Janis sang, and Gordon too. Yet when had I ever felt freer than I did now, having so *much* to lose? Laurie, a bunch of friendships in the making, a lesbian community to work and live in, and a clean, natural environment: talk about amassing riches! Freedom was just another word for a *lot* left to lose.

Sleep began to overtake my overtired brain, but the lobes cranked out one final thought. I wasn't homeward bound—I was home.

Chapter 27

"WHA?" MY SKULL was a lead block, a lead block in a deep dark cave. How could I lift it, so heavy, heavy?

"You wanted to milk Millie," Laurie whispered.

"In the middle of the night?"

"It's almost dawn. Wanda will have coffee ready when we return."

"Return? From where?"

"The barn, silly goose."

Wanda stood by the stove wearing a pale blue robe. She didn't look up, and Laurie gave no greeting as she went to the doorway, so I followed in silence. When in Romerenie.

Darkness lay over the pastures and distant hills. The cool, moist air tingled my bronchia as I tried to keep up with the flashlight beam. The wide barn door was ajar. Inside, a lantern hanging on a peg illuminated a circle of dirt floor strewn lightly with straw. Objects and walls began separating themselves from the deep recesses: a rake, buckets, jugs and containers of different sizes and shapes. Smells of resin and old wood mixed with smells of grass and dirt and animal. Eventually my eyes made out, in the far reaches, a ladder leaning against a loft. Below sat bales of hay.

PJ emerged from the dark. "Didn't think you'd make it."

"Left to my own devices, I wouldn't have."

Laurie said she was going to feed Wiffle and the chickens. PJ took the lantern off the hook, and I followed her to a long table with metal pails and containers, sponges, and towels. She washed her hands in the nearby sink. Then we went to a low table by the first stall. I could make out brown cow hindquarters.

"Good morning, Millie," PJ said softly. "How are you feeling? Get a good night's sleep? I've got Andy here to watch. She won't bite. She'll even feed you." PJ motioned for me to squeeze up to the front of the stall. "Give her some of that hay, so she'll like you. Don't worry, she can't bite hard. No top teeth, not in the front."

"Guess I won't stick my hand in far enough to find out."

"You're not wearing slippery rings or bracelets, anything that can come off? She's dumber than shit, will eat anything."

Millie yanked the hay from my hand, and I sidled out of the stall and sat beside PJ on the second stool. She withdrew a sponge from a wooden bucket and ran it gently all around the udder, which glowed a pale pink in the lantern light. Again and again, reaching under the belly, her arm twisted and turned like the udder was a maze, re-soaping the sponge from time to time. She repeated the movements with a second sponge and bucket, maybe the rinse cycle. The space over the rafters remained in shadow. The vaulted roof, the silence barely broken by Millie's quiet chewing, gave the barn a cathedral feel. I was an acolyte learning the ropes before services began.

PJ told me to bring the lantern, and I followed her to the sink. She did some futzing with a tall metal canister and a metal pail with a domed lid, which had a softball-sized hole in the top. She brought the pail with us back to the stall, and we sat again on the stools. Millie shifted her weight a few times, which I hoped wasn't the pre-lude to a crap. PJ stroked her udder, saying, "Your boobs look nice and big this morning. Let Andy see how much milk they can hold." She placed the pail midway between the opposite-side teats and, after a few more sweet-nothings, said, "Down to business."

Business was a two-handed affair. Reaching underneath, PJ took a far teat in each hand and pulled on one, downwards but slightly angled towards the top of the pail, and milk splashed into the opening. As she let up with that hand, the other descended, and a rhythm was established—tug, squirt, ease up, tug, squirt, ease up—alternating teat for teat. Tug, squirt, ease up; tug, squirt, ease up. She rested her forehead against Millie's flank, her arms and hands continuing their steady movements.

"Hey, fur-ball," I said to the cat brushing my leg.

"Is that Smoky? He's usually the first to show. Give him a good kick."

I gave him a gentle prod with my foot. PJ's rhythm never altered, and we sat in the quiet barn, the lantern lighting Millie's haunches and PJ's bowed form, her shoulders moving to and fro, her forehead against the hide.

When she finally rose and brought the pail to the table, I got up and stretched. Daylight had begun to filter through the barn roof and cracks along the sides. The stalls farther on and the loft, ladder, and bales of hay in the back became clearer.

"Ready?"

"For what?" I asked.

"The other two boobs."

We both washed hands and returned to the stall. PJ placed the pail under the two closest teats, motioning for me to sit. "Talk to her, let her know you're a friend."

"Hey, Ms. Cow, I'm Andy from South Jersey. They have cows there too, some even named Jersey, but I've never milked one. I'll try not to hurt you."

E. Adrian Dzahn

"Put your hands near the top. That's right."

I had to rest my forehead against her flank just to reach the *near* teats. They felt warm and spongy, like waterlogged, overcooked string beans.

"Start with one, and squeeze your index finger and thumb at the top and then your middle finger on down to your pinkie, pushing the milk as you direct it towards the pail."

My left hand worked better than my right, but neither knew what the hell it was doing. "Like this?"

"Yeah, but try to get it in the pail."

Eventually some squirts actually went in the hole in the domed cap. Millie was patient as all get-out, probably figuring passivity was her best hope for getting it over with quickly. I developed a rhythm too, if a bit jerkier than PJ's. As more daylight snuck in the barn, I could see foam collecting on the gauze inside the domed top, dispersed by each new squirt. I *was* getting the hang of it.

When the milking was done, PJ showed me how to release Millie from the stanchion and lead her out the side pasture door. The sky to the west was a soft blue-gray. The cow sauntered, her large haunches rising and falling, her emptied udder swaying. PJ tossed some hay after her and lowered the bolt into place. We cleaned up, and while I was wiping the counter, PJ opened the front barn door all the way and extinguished the lantern. "Later on I do the fun stuff," she said. "Sweeping Millie's manure into the gutter, straightening her stall." She picked up the milk canister and headed to the pantry.

I remained in the doorway. The sky to the east, beyond the Craybills' house, was brushed pink, as though beneath the horizon some giant painter stood on tiptoe with his giant brush to color a blue canvas. The hues deepened at intervals to raspberry, rose, magenta; he—why not she?—had dunked and dabbed again. Strawberry, scarlet, red, crimson. As Mythic Matissette progressed into the orange shades, tiny sounds gathered in the background like a warming-up orchestra. The lone percussion, a lingering cricket, made a small click-click, but in the reed section, Mother Bird chirped loudly at her lazy nestlings. A truck along the road sent a bass roar over the apple trees, and the Craybill rooster, finally hoisting up his feathery overalls, blew hard on his trumpet. Lo and behold, the paintbrush streaked yellow!

Bucket in hand, Laurie headed from the chicken coop to the water tap near the driveway. PJ brought the hose to the herbs. I stood idle and useless, but even the lilies of the field, right?

"Why don't you bolt the barn," PJ yelled over. Lily could do that. I closed the door and slid the wood bolt in place.

Minutes later, Laurie appeared beside me, as miraculous as the sky. "How did it go? Did you milk her?"

"Yep, and she didn't complain."

We trooped inside the house and hit the hand-wash sink. A stack of steaming pancakes and bowls of yogurt and berries and nuts and granola awaited us at the table. I poured myself coffee and sat with Laurie and PJ, joined minutes later by Becca and then Sally and Heather. Bec had on a bus driver's uniform, and Sally and Heather looked dressed for the real world. Nobody spoke till PJ said, "Wanda, this place would die without you." Grunts from full mouths seconded and passed the motion.

After breakfast, Laurie and I grabbed some baskets and a wide-brimmed straw hat apiece and went out to pick berries. Thankfully there was no rule against snacking while you worked. Crouching did a number on my legs, but bending would've been harder on the back. With practice, maybe I'd achieve Laurie's pace.

While we picked, she filled me in on the different communes in our co-op. New Eden was the only one entirely self-sufficient, but

Jedediah almost was and Moonsilver hoped to be by selling more of their clothes and fabrics—they had looms.

"How can New Eden really be self-sufficient?" I asked. "Don't they have to buy coffee and detergent and the same things we do?"

"It means no one works off-farm. They grow enough and make enough dairy to sell in farmers markets to pay for everything they buy. They're over seven times our size."

Later, PJ joined us picking. About the time Laurie and I took a break, Chase brought several huge baskets to the vegetable area. When we returned to the berries, nobody talked, the four of us being spread out. I made no complaint when Laurie tapped me on the shoulder and said we'd done enough. We rinsed the berries in the pantry sink and divided them between the trades containers and those for ourselves.

Again at supper the chairs at either end of the table were left vacant, but the one beside me had a place setting. PJ lit a joint and passed it around. Who paid for it? I wasn't about to look a gift toke in the mouth, but I'd ask Laurie later, not wanting to get surprised one day with a huge tab.

Becca, sitting closest to the stairs, must have heard a noise because she yelled, "Come on, Gertie, before it's all gone."

Thirty times, at least, I'd lectured myself not to look at Gertie's breasts when we met, to keep my eyes trained on her face. Luckily, she was watching Wanda as she descended the stairs because unluckily, her loose brown smock wasn't enough to stop me from staring. But when Laurie said, "Gertie, this is Andy," I was able to look directly in her eyes. Her hair was cut very short, Gertrude-Stein-like. Was Gertie an assumed name? She sat at my end. Her irises were a neat purplish gray.

"I hear you milked your first cow," she said softly.

"More or less. I think you'd have to ask Millie if it was technically milking or just yanking weirdly at her boobs. I mean, a bunch of the milk missed the container is what I mean."

"Where's Chloe?" somebody asked.

"Migraine."

"Did she say how the meeting went yesterday?"

Still softly, Gertie said, "The big fights were about dairy. We were able to keep priority for summer and winter squash." She said nothing else the remainder of the meal yet seemed attentive to the conversations around her. Right after we were done she went to the parlor.

The next day I asked Laurie who paid for the pot, and she said PJ was allowed to buy it with house-fund money because she shared it. "If you want your own private supply, you have to pay for it yourself and use it in private, but PJ would get it for you from her secret source. It's really good."

"The house fund pays for it even though Gertie didn't smoke any and Chloe wasn't there?"

"You can't keep track. People eat and drink different amounts too. We live like a family, without comparing."

"Never thought of it that way, but makes sense."

"Bec says she doesn't *want* to know how much tampax everyone uses."

"No kidding."

Anyway, I'd be the last to complain, thinking how much Stacy had shelled out for me over the years—my karma would be in the red for a long time to come. And what did she get for all her generosity? Not a whole helluva lot. Okay, Jiminy, I'll quit being mad at her for moving to Berkeley.

At the August meeting when they would vote me in or out, Chloe's vote would be the most important—she probably had unofficial veto power—so my anxiety over meeting her morphed into a wish to get it over with. From little things that Laurie and Wanda had let drop, I believed I'd scored with eight of the Geserenes, so I was optimistic about closing out the ninth and getting the win.

The final at-bat occurred in the living room after lunch, when we were heading out to tour the creek and chicken coops. Chloe stood with her back to us, her brown hair down to her waist. She was studying the trade deliveries schedule on the bulletin board, and one hand held a pencil; the other, a steno pad. The board also contained a picture of Emma Lazarus and Geserenie's *Declaration of Interdependence*, which I'd been meaning to read.

"Chloe, this is Andy."

Laurie's portrait had surprised me because the expression was deadpan almost to the point of unflattering, but when Chloe turned, I realized the sketch went easy on her. She shifted the pencil to the hand with the steno pad and shook my hand solemnly. "How do you do. What do you think of Geserenie so far?"

"It's great. Just the fresh air alone, not even counting the people and terrific food and all. It's great the way you can all live as a com—"

"We don't have every wrinkle ironed out, but we continue to make progress. You'll have to excuse me now because I need to phone New Eden, but I look forward to getting to know you better."

Once we got outside, I said to Laurie, "That didn't come across real friendly."

"She's always like that. She told me the responsibility of managing a farm weighs heavy on her."

The creek was beyond the bushes at the north end of the pastures. A path ran between the bushes and fence, and when it forked, one tine led down to the bank, the other continuing on to the woods forming Geserenie's western border. Pausing at the junction, I could now identify maples and oaks mixed in with the white-barked birches and shimmering-leaved aspens. Plenty of firs or spruce or whatever they were grew farther back, their higher branches visible from Laurie's window. The breeze carried traces of that minty needle aroma.

We descended the right tine to the creek. It looked to be about thirty feet wide at its widest, a bit narrower where it skirted a boulder on our side. The water was clear.

"They say it's warm enough for swimming in mid-July."

Our next stop was the coops. I'd imagined low ceilings and darkness, but we didn't even have to duck our heads entering, and plenty of sunlight poured through the windows. We stood on boards; on the floor was an ankle-deep dry stew of what looked like paper, sawdust, straw, and leaves, giving off a weird pungent smell. A row of little doors ran along the opposite wall. Laurie pointed out "roosts," horizontal poles jutting from one wall, and the cubbyhole nesting boxes.

"That an air conditioner?"

"Yes, and the coop is heated in winter. Now we just keep the windows open."

"Where is everybody? There's no one here but us non-chickens."

I followed her outside and around to where metal fences of various kinds—including chicken wire, of all things—cordoned off enclosures. Easily two dozen chickens pecked the ground within a fence contraption that was up on wheels. Every bird was round and fluffy, some were totally white, some had darker feathers at the neck, and some weren't white at all but shades of brown and gray. The wheels on the fence allowed you to move the chickens to different parts of the pasture, Laurie explained, and a grazing diet was better than grain. Geserenie believed all animals should be free-range. Imprisoning calves for veal was especially evil.

"No kidding," I said. "Who's this?"

"A Spanish White Face. And that's a Leghorn. Those two are Hamburgs, that's a Buttercup, behind is a Minorca, and that's an Andalusion." She pointed out the distinguishing features of each breed and described gathering the eggs. My only comment was that she had no reason to be down on herself for not having a career because she knew a ton about raising chickens and obviously had a career here. And I hoped the ugly brown hen trying to peck her own butt wasn't the Andy-lusion.

"Nineteen are still laying," Laurie said proudly.

"What do you do with the ones that aren't?"

"They live out their lives just the same."

"Cool." Why shouldn't our feathered friends have their lilies of the field too?

At my third supper, we were a full ten at the table, and Chloe asked who wanted to say grace. Heather volunteered. "Thank you, Mother Nature, for your bounty in food and friends." Folks chimed in with *A-woman*, surprising Chloe; I hoped she'd find out that the amendment—or mendment—was my doing.

Right away she was hit with questions about the co-op meeting. The communes argued for hours. Jedediah wanted a rule banning antibiotics in feed, and New Eden wanted a rule banning wood-burning stoves.

"We have only one stove!"

"I emphasized that," Chloe said.

When the discussion moved on to the Fourth of July carnival, she said—probably for my benefit—that we all had to remember that she wasn't ready to let the neighbors know we were lesbians.

Hadn't they figured us out, somebody asked, this being the third year?

Chloe kept her gaze on her water glass while answering. "You may have noticed this about human nature: when people *want* to like you, they ignore facets of your character or behaviors they would find objectionable. The neighbors loved my grandparents and so were prepared to like me and my tenants, which means thinking we are who they'd like us to be."

"Psychologists call that denial."

"They may believe I'm more comfortable with female tenants until I marry. That wouldn't be unusual."

After dinner, Bec took Laurie and me aside. "Be forewarned—some of the neighbors set up a grill and make hamburgers and hot dogs."

Laurie looked shocked, shocked. "Chloe *lets* them?"

"She wants to keep up the traditions her grandparents were known for. Says we have a better chance of changing attitudes through example."

Laurie had a long talk with Chloe about how much I should contribute to the farm, and the upshot was that during my trial period, I would pick fruits and vegetables a total of four hours a day, and Laurie and I would take over the supper dishes every night. I would also milk Millie if I awoke in time, nothing PJ banked on. I mentioned I wouldn't mind making trade deliveries, but Laurie said there was a rule you didn't lend out your car except in special circumstances. That way, none of the vehicle owners would feel pressured to lend it to somebody if they didn't trust their driving.

The existence of that rule, of so *many* rules at Geserenie, no longer rubbed me the wrong way. I appreciated how they permitted a large group to live harmoniously in a single house. And no rule sprang out of thin air. You could always see the problem it aimed to solve—in contrast to, say, laws against homosexuality. Maybe Adam and Eve needed such a law to jump-start the species, but by now, not having kids was doing the planet a favor.

On the third of July, Becca's bringing home a newspaper brought home to me how much the outside world had faded away. Although Heather subscribed to *Ms.* and *Mother Jones* and Chloe subscribed to a zillion seed and farm equipment catalogues and all sorts of "proxy" stuff, the goings-on of government, foreign nations, even baseball rarely infiltrated Geserenie. And the DJs on the college radio station Wanda listened to in the kitchen had the decency to use low-key voices, so I could ignore them without trying. If it weren't for the occasional sight of the Craybills working their fields, you could also forget men existed. Was it any wonder I had finally let my guard down enough to really fall in love?

Chapter 28

USED TO THE freedom of not having guys around, I wasn't looking forward to the carnival. And in addition to XYs entering Geserenie, I expected pious types—folks who would look down their noses at everything I said or did—Aunt Polly grafted onto Aunt Cherise. Plus, the carnival was forcing Gertie to stay indoors, and the day was already hot as hell.

Yet with breakfast and the morning picking done, I found myself excited by the idea of a little excitement. Rubella and the cars had been put in the garage and under the overhang to leave the driveway free for parking. Several of us waited for Chloe and Bec to finish hauling supplies from the basement, which yielded up card tables, benches, a washtub, boxes containing frisbees and yoyos and an honest-to-god softball and bat, finger-paints, and plastic bags with lanyard strips, beads, buttons, felt squares in a zillion colors, cotton remnants, glitter, and glue.

The neighboring farms were the first arrivals, Norman Rockwell white nuclear families consisting of a man, a woman, and bunches of no-necks. The littler kids scampered to the crafts tables, and the teenage boys found the frisbees, avoiding introductions. But to my surprise, the communes too were infested with children; one flatbed shot kids out the back like buckshot. An earth-mother type with a long braid and long peasant dress hugged Chloe and came over and introduced herself as Shenandoah. I said my name, but she didn't seem to hear, since she was busy pointing out the kids racing every which way.

"That's Sunshine, my oldest, and Jade—stop picking at that skeeter bite—and the tall boy is Absalom, and that's Virgil, and Oleander and Sage, and the baby—I don't mean you're a baby—that's Caleb." Two more ran by. "The twins—the one with the snotty nose, that's Cayenne, and her sister Cinnamon—not mine, thank heavens."

Laurie and Wanda were swarmed with little girls eager to finger-paint, and Sally was manning—make that woman-ing—the lanyards and sewing tables. PJ seemed to have the apple-bobbing under control; Bec was helping with the kites. Chloe, arms folded and hands for once denuded of pad and pencil, chatted with the neighbors, and Chase pulled the hayride cart with two little boys waving at everybody. The Moonsilver commune, which had looms, brought their own tables to display scarves and sweaters for sale along with jars of homemade herbal remedies.

I waltzed around announcing softball in the fallow pasture, and a bunch of kids took me up on it. The commune and neighbor kids mixed easily, so we had enough for six-person teams. Burlap sacks worked for bases, and I pitched for both sides.

During an inning change, I watched the smoke rise from the grill. It may have been hypocritical of me, a Joanie-come-lately to vegetarianism, but I considered cooking meat at Geserenie a stain on Paradise. The Bible had it wrong: eating our fellow animals, not an apple, was the original sin. Nature couldn't have intended for us to pollute the air with the smell of cooked cattle and pigs only a stone's throw from innocent Millie and innocuous Wiffle. On the other hand, why did God make those smells so goddamn

enticing? *Because Temptation wouldn't be Temptation if it didn't tempt you.*
Hey, Jiminy, who invited you?

By four, most everybody had left, except for some kid-less commune
folks. I joined Wanda, Chase, and Sally on a blanket in the shade of
the Jerseymac and got introduced to a guy named Rob and women
named Cam and Tina. Rob asked why nobody from New Eden had
showed, and Tina said they'd gone to an imitation Woodstock near
the Dells where, supposedly, naked women would be dancing.

"If I had known that would do the trick," Chase said, "I would
have told them that *last* year."

"You did all right at the trades meeting," Rob said. "Chloe
seemed happy."

"We don't ask for a lot."

"Clive says you don't produce worth a damn. *His* words, not
mine."

Sally and Chase arched an eyebrow each. "What did Chloe say?"

"Not in front of her. It's a running joke with them. They call
you—never mind."

"What?"

"Nah, never mind."

"Sticks and stones can break our bones, but names—"

"He calls you 'the pussy farm.'"

Chase stood abruptly. "We should call them 'the pricks farm.'"

"They have women too," the one named Cam said.

Sally said our goal wasn't producing the most crops but living
in a supportive community, and Rob asked why do it on a farm,
and she told him we wanted to be *partly* self-sustainable and close to
Nature. Tina took off her rose-tinted glasses and wiped them in the
folds of her skirt. "New Eden is sexually frustrated, all except the
two with girlfriends."

Chase said over her shoulder before walking off, "I worry about their sheep."

After the commune folks split, I combed Millie's pasture for trash that might've gotten blown there. Sol's late rays eyed the tops of the aspens and birches, which fluttered their leaves coquettishly. The sky to the east was beautifully turquoise. A hush, the presaging of dusk, fell over Geserenie, the hours of commotion making the quiet all the sweeter.

Laurie joined me just as Sally called from the kitchen steps, "Are you two going to the fireworks?"

I whispered to Laurie, "Was just getting into the quiet."

"Me too."

I called to Sally, "We're staying."

She went inside, and Laurie sidled closer. "Sometimes I feel Geserenie is the only world I need. But I *do* like going into Madison and Artemiz. Bec and Wanda will be making a trip in a few weeks for the farm shopping."

"Soon enough for the real—make that *un*real—world."

Chapter 29

LAURIE WAS RIGHT: Gertie was determined to tell us about herself at the awareness meeting. We arranged ourselves in a lumpy circumference in the living room, some on the couch, some on chairs and pillows, everybody facing the upholstered chair that Gertie preferred. Chloe took her straight-backed chair and leaned over to the shelf for her pad and pencil, nodding at Gertie to begin.

"Usually you talk about things we *all* have to face," Gertie said in her usual soft voice, "but I'm not going to do that. My life has been different from yours. Most of my life has been shame and embarrassment. I know it's not my fault, I've done nothing wrong, but that's what I feel. People don't react to *me*; they react to my breasts."

She raised her voice a little. "You already know I'm from Montana, my father works in the mines." After a quick rundown of her brothers and two sisters—she alone had such large breasts—she told about the teasing, which began when Gertie was nine. Cartoons and drawings were left on her desk or taped in the school hallway; she was touched, poked, and grabbed. That was grades four through six. By junior high, the misery had spread, her brothers coming home with bloody noses and torn clothing from fighting off insults.

"What did your parents do?"

Before Gertie could answer, Chloe said, "Her mother told her to pray for their souls."

A bunch of us mumbled and grumbled. Heather sat up straight and tossed her hair over her shoulders. "Why didn't she use the harassment as a *learning* tool?"

"Did you ever speak to a teacher, Gertie? Couldn't they see what was going on?"

"When the boy touched me during assembly, Mrs. Rogers said I should be happy—it meant he liked me."

No mumbling now: we yelled loud enough to wake the dead.

"Fuck a shit piss."

"He liked you—praise the Lord!"

"What more can a woman ask for than *male admiration*?"

"The measure of happiness."

"Hey, that and some change can get you a cup of coffee."

After about a year of cursing, we let Gertie continue. But when she described her youngest brother coming home with a shiner and her oldest sister saying the whole family could be living normal lives if it wasn't for her, we yelled again.

"Because of *you*? Because of the way people *treated* you!"

"How could she turn you into the villain? You were the *victim*!"

"If that's her idea of *normal*—"

A surprised Gertie murmured, "But it was true. Their lives *would* be different. That's when I started thinking about leaving."

"Why should *you* be the one to leave?"

"One of my brothers is allergic to peanuts," Laurie said, "and we worried a lot about him growing up but *never* wanted him to leave."

"Same with my cousin who has Down's."

"Every day I see patients' families hurting, but they'd never think of *abandoning* them."

"Didn't leaving seem more dangerous than staying?"

"She *started* to think of leaving," Chloe said. "Leaving was still years away." Gertie nodded solemnly. It was weird how different they were: Chloe with an almost-thin face draped by long brown hair, and Gertie with her wide, smooth cheeks, flat nose, the ultra-short cut.

Life only got worse during junior high and high school; Gertie was routinely groped and squeezed and once was almost raped by a visiting football team. She'd stopped going to church because her father complained that her self-consciousness made it hard for the rest of them. Even her mother was useless, just wanting to pray. "Their church believes prayer is the answer to everything," Chloe said.

"You've been through hell, Gertie."

"You're with friends now."

Tears ran down her cheeks. A picosecond later the rest of us were bawling. If some poor fool had happened to poke his head in, he'd have thought it was a wake. Unless, of course, he'd stared at Gertie's breasts, in which case it would have been his own funeral.

After the tissues had made the rounds, we took a short break for hitting the can and fridge. Resuming where she'd left off, Gertie described how a school counselor gave her the name of a psychologist in Kalispell, prompting Heather and Chase to shout in perfect unison, "You're not the one with the problem!"

"I *wanted* to go," Gertie said. "I wanted someone to help me. Dr. Asplund says life is a search for hidden treasures, and it's not easy to find self-confidence and friendship and peace, and I shouldn't expect to find every treasure right away."

"Living among people she was comfortable with was the first hidden treasure," Chloe said. "Dr. Asplund wrote to Artemiz asking if they knew of any place that would be a nurturing, all-women environment, and they put her in touch with us."

"Is it hard being away from your family?" Wanda asked.

Gertie shook her head uncertainly.

I said, "*Real* family is the folks who care about you. They don't have to be blood relations." Looking around at Laurie, Wanda, Bec, and everybody, I believed that now more than ever. These women—all nine of them—would go to bat for me, take on society and anybody messing with me in ways my blood relations never did. "Sisterhood is powerful."

"A-women!"

Becca, who hadn't spoken before, said, "I, for one, Gertie, don't give a damn about your breasts. They could be half or twice the size; you could have three, four, or a dozen, and it wouldn't matter a horse's ass to me." The rest of us laughed, and Gertie managed a grateful smile.

The awareness meeting worked wonders. Now usually awake by nine, Gertie became a fixture at lunch and occasionally threw her two cents into the conversation. She regularly quit Chloe's attic to hang out in the living room when PJ played guitar or we just shot the bull. In a formless cotton smock—dubbed "frock" in her special catalogue—she'd sit quietly in her favorite upholstered chair and absorb the goings-on. Gradually any remaining uneasiness I had around her disappeared. If she was poking at sprouts in the herb garden, I might wave. She'd wave back, making me feel my idiocy didn't faze her.

One day she tacked something onto the bulletin board, and I immediately went to read it.

Grant me the serenity to accept the things I cannot change,
The courage to change the things I can,

And the wisdom to know the difference.

"That's cool."

Moving over, I reread Geserenie's DECLARATION OF INTERDEPENDENCE:

We hold these truths to be self-evident: that all people are created equal and bound by common needs and endowed by Nature with certain inalienable rights, among them life, liberty, and the pursuit of happiness free from war, oppression, poverty, and discrimination.

No offense, Mr. Jefferson, but ours was a huge improvement.

Chapter 30

IN COOLER WEATHER Becca and Wanda did the farm shopping on their own, but when summer came, others would pile onto Rubella and go into Madison too. Today the weather was glorious. Sally, PJ, Laurie, and I stood in the front of the truck bed right behind the cab, our faces to the wind. Heather and Chase sat against one side, using large pillows and blankets for shock-absorbers. Feet apart and hugging the top slat with my elbows, I pushed back and forth to counter the sway left, right, left, right. Rubella took us over hill and dale, by farms and grazing horses and enough bucolic beauty to inspire every one of Stacy's favorite poets. Even when we hit the city outskirts and the scenery switched to gas stations and stores, I couldn't imagine sitting down and missing the sights.

For almost a week, folks had been compiling individual shopping lists separate from the farm one, which ran a mile long and included things like toilet paper, spices, coffee, tea, pastas, rice, olive oil, soil nutrients, and light bulbs. Laurie's list was short: scented candles and special charcoal pencils from the art supply store. Mine was even shorter—a carton of cigarettes. Becca had picked up my last carton which, amazingly, hadn't run out.

Madison proper seemed small and clean by Philly and Chicago standards. We were near the university, Laurie said, which explained the streets swarming with folks under the age of thirty and the abundance of small restaurants and bars. Becca pulled into a no-parking zone, and those of us in the back climbed down. We agreed on the time we'd all meet up again for the ride home.

Laurie's and my first stop was the candle place, which sold a whole lot more than candles. We browsed through counters of funky bracelets and neat stone rings and small pottery and cool shawls. Laurie tried on wacky hats and quilted jackets stitched with pictures of dragons. She insisted on buying me a new wallet as a belated birthday present, so I picked out one with a zebra etched into the leather.

On the street, I transferred the stuff from my old wallet into the new. I showed her the photos with Stacy taken in the booth at the Randolph Street IC station the night we trashed Vicki's, but she wanted to know about the credit card. "This?" I held up John Q. Public.

"It's not real."

"Not a real *credit* card but a real *shim* card. For picking locks. Want me to show you how? We could duck into this building, and—" Okay, not everybody thought shimming was a skill worth mastering.

We grabbed some pizza for lunch, hit the art supply store for pencils, and circled around to where Becca had dropped us. Now I noticed the house set back from the street and the sign on the door saying *Artemis Women's Center.*

It was an old house with high ceilings. Every room, it seemed, was crowded with women—young, old, middle-aged—milling about, talking quietly. The tables stacked with pamphlets and petitions reminded me of the Palace. In one room, women in white outfits were doing judo.

I moseyed over to the bulletin boards.

DOMESTIC VIOLENCE IS A CRIME! Wasn't that a self-evident truth?

A Milwaukee woman was stabbed to death by her husband last night ... Police had been called to the house twice in the past year. The first time, they escorted the woman to the hospital for stitches around her eye. The second time, she was treated for three broken ribs. In both instances the woman refused to press charges, saying her husband was truly sorry, so no arrest was made.

When Laurie joined me and read the article, she said Artemiz had a domestic violence hotline. I dropped some bucks in the donations box on the way out.

We headed to a women's bar, but along the way I spotted a newsstand advertising a decent price for cigarettes. Laurie waited on the corner while I went to wait in line. Naturally, one of the headlines on the stack of newspapers beside me was about a rape. But the next stack over made me grab a paper. *MYSTERIOUS ILLNESS IN PHILA*; *American Legion Convention-Goers Felled.* I almost forgot to buy the cigarettes.

"What's wrong?" Laurie asked.

"Some disease killed a bunch of guys in Philly at the Bellevue-Stratford Hotel."

"Food poisoning?"

"They don't know. They're calling it a 'mystery illness.'" I read out loud, "'Officials refuse to say whether there is an epidemic on their hands, cautioning the public to stay calm.' Hey, you mind if I phone Mathilde when we get back?"

"Are you worried she'll catch it?"

"Not her—she doesn't go up there anymore. But I could see my cousin Edward staying there if a friend came into Philly; the Bellevue-Stratford's a neat hotel."

Peg O' My Heart, a few blocks farther on, was pretty empty. A handful of women sat at the bar and two more were shooting pool.

We got a pitcher, and I lit a cigarette when we sat—if anybody from Geserenie came in and didn't like it, they could sit elsewhere.

"Everybody's focused on the American Legion guys at the convention," I said. "Nobody thinks about the working stiffs. How many of *them* have gotten sick—valets, chambermaids? They might not have the money to go running to the doctor or don't trust them and just figure they'll recover. And with a convention, the hotel probably hired extra kitchen help, caterers. Temps who could be in the thick of it but have no idea."

Laurie made a sympathetic face.

"Anyway, might not be a bad idea to let Mathilde know where I am."

"You haven't told her you moved here?"

"Hey, I'm getting around to it."

None of the other Geserenes showed at the bar, but at the appointed time, everybody gathered at the no-parking zone in front of Artemiz. When Becca and Wanda appeared in Rubella, we climbed in the back. Large cartons containing tissues, toilet paper, detergent, and other stuff were strapped down against the sides, and the blankets and cushions had been moved to right behind the cab. We sat on them during the ride home and recapped where we'd been.

Everybody had hit Artemiz at some point, and Chase said she'd run into "Miranda." Sally and Heather groaned.

"What's new with *them*?"

"She wanted to know if we're campaigning."

"For Carter?"

"And the Congressional races. They're also looking for new housemates."

"They're *always* looking for new housemates. They should try not shoving politics down people's throats."

E. Adrian Dzahn

"One of them knows Angela Davis."
"Bullshit."

I carried the phone into Laurie's room and sat on the floor by the window. Luckily Mathilde was home, and I told her I'd moved to a farm in Wisconsin with a bunch of friends. I was milking cows, feeding chickens, the whole nine yards. She asked if Stacy was there too, and I said no, she'd moved to California.

"Hey, we don't have a TV or get news all that often, and I was wondering: what's this disease hitting the American Legion folks in Philly?"

"Isn't it awful."

"Edward or anybody been up there lately?"

"Not that I know. He hasn't called."

Mr. Wiffle came out from behind the barn and was sauntering, one hip at a time, towards the fence. Laurie's voice drifted up. "Here, Wiffle, Wiffle; here, Wiffle, Wiffle."

"Don't know if you'd know, but was wondering if maybe Dean might be in Philly?"

"Funny you should ask. I just ran into Mary Linehan at the market." Mathilde gave a little laugh. "I forget her married name. She heard you stopped by her mother's."

"Yeah, right before we left, Stacy and I, last December."

"And Sherry told you Dean was dating a woman named Carlotta?"

"Thought it was Carmella."

"Carmella. And they'd gone down to Florida. Mary said as soon as they returned, Carmella went back to her husband. She got somebody to load her stuff in a U-Haul. Drove away, just like that. Mary, Sherry, *all* the Linehans were pretty mad. They'd met her. I guess your dad was pretty upset."

"Shoot."

"Mary said he's working at the Chowder House."

Laurie came in just after I'd put the phone back on the hallway stand. "Is everyone okay?" she asked.

"Yeah. Dean got dumped by his girlfriend is all."

"Do you want to go down to the creek? The others went, to cool off."

"Nah. I'll probably park in the can."

I really just wanted to be alone. Was that why he never wrote? Too much shit to shovel when they returned from Florida? I could empathize. And if he was working at the Chowder, then he likely wasn't also holding down a job in Philly.

Chapter 31

THE ANDY GABE Life Story wasn't scheduled to be narrated till the August meeting, but Laurie wanted everybody to hear it before they voted on Andy Gabe joining Geserenie—despite my insistence that to know me more was to like me less. And she said I couldn't omit the year and a half of being raped—what I had dubbed The Major Trauma.

I re-titled it The Trauma Drama, and it starred Roy, with me in the sole supporting role. "*My* preference," I told the Geserenes, "would've been a one-man show. I'd rather he'd gone and fucked himself."

They were sympathetic in spades, hearts, diamonds, and clubs. Reclining in one of the beanbags, my bare feet on a hassock, I basked in their cursing Roy to the high heavens and lower forty-eight. A shame he couldn't have heard it too.

Chloe asked if he had ever said anything to me about it. "Just the first time," I told her. "'Stop crying, you're not gonna bleed to death.'"

The narrative moved onto job shit—asshole bosses and the guy putting his hand up Bertha's skirt, all the crap that went with low-paying restaurant work. Chase told of a stint at a sawmill and PJ, of one as a janitor. Suddenly we were all trashing the capitalist system for not giving a damn about the folks at the bottom, the ones that made it run. I hauled out stories of Mathilde at the glass factory and Dean gypped out of sick days and vacation.

"But isn't Geserenie our answer?" Chloe asked rhetorically. "Each of us is worker *and* management. We pool our resources and decide by vote."

"One woman, one vote."

"A-woman!"

Laurie was no dummy. If Chloe had been a holdout on my joining Geserenie, her comments about Roy made it clear she considered me a munchkin. While the debate and vote were occurring, I was directed to give Millie fresh hay. On my way out of the barn, Laurie, Bec, and PJ doused me with a bucket of water. Laurie said I'd been voted in unanimously, and even though I wasn't surprised, it felt good when the results were now declared official.

Chloe did some calculations and negotiations that resulted in my doing pretty much what I had been doing—harvesting the ripened crops, washing the supper dishes—plus taking over some of Chloe and Gertie's weeding and irrigating chores. In the fall, I'd do other stuff, and in spring help with the tilling and planting.

Laurie's brother William, the Hollywood lawyer, was also a jerk, though not a violent, raping one. He loved phoning to brag about his movie star clients and then not tell Laurie their names. Once some famous actress had flown him to Catalina Island to finalize divorce papers, and another time he went hunting with an actor who'd won an Oscar. Every call ended with her being pissed at being kept in the dark and my being pissed at him.

"Besides, the secrecy about the actress is fake," I told her, "because all the folks at the hotel saw him and her together."

"But they don't know *why* he's there. It could be about a movie contract. He says he would lose his license to practice law if he gave away confidential information."

"So why does he tell you *any* of it?"

She didn't have an answer. The next time he called and said he'd gone hunting with the Oscar guy, she slammed down the phone. Sisterhood was powerful.

Summer flew by, Millie getting milked, Mr. Wiffle growing pinker and stouter. The corn ripened daily; we picked, we shucked, we ate. Little green berries turned blue, tomatoes swelled on the vine, and squashes thickened in their skins. Herbs and peas went forth and multiplied. The Jerseymacs morphed splotchy red, and the McIntoshes got big and juicy. If the sun hogged center stage too many days in a row, I watered; if he retired to the wings and allowed the rain clouds to perform, I applauded. When the heat lassoed us with lassitude, we swam in the creek or lay in the shade to estivate with the chipmunks and squirrels. And every morning that I managed to rise with Laurie and PJ and get my butt to the barn, I was rewarded with—to paraphrase Stace—a dawn coming up like thunder outer China crost the fields.

Although our days had a sweet sameness to them, Friday nights were different: Geserenie buzzed. Five days of working off-farm made Bec, Heather, and Sally ready to party, so we'd move the parlor speakers to the doorway and dance in the living room, acting every bit as boisterous as any happy hour crowd. If we happened to fall short, we gave it a second shot on Saturday.

Yet come Monday, Laurie and I welcomed the return of routine. After collecting the eggs, she'd join PJ, Chase, and me picking fruits and vegetables. Then PJ and Chase would divvy up the errands, like hitting Moonsilver and New Eden for trade deliveries, or PJ might hit her pot source. While Gertie sewed in the attic, Chloe would come down for her teapot and re-ascend to work on accounts and read about exciting things like pests and fertilizer. Wanda would put on the kitchen radio and start on supper, and at that point, the rest of the house and farm became ours.

Sometimes Laurie and I would just wander, purposefully purposeless, soaking in the stillness of the sun-drenched dining and living rooms, breathing in deeply summer's special fragrance. Other times we'd amble over to the pasture and nod at Millie chewing her cud, or stroll to the creek, maybe pointing out a ladybug or weird tendril or the way some birch ran a tall uninterrupted trunk higher than the others before bursting into branches. A songbird in the woods might practice her scales. *Our* Eden.

Yet by the time we'd finished the afternoon chores, we were ready for the group gathering at supper. My only real complaint was Laurie hanging my portrait in the living room. "Sure, you did a good job, but why inflict my mug on the whole group?" Verisimilitude wasn't always a virtue.

Of course, in any household of more than one person, friction was inevitable. As Laurie said, the key was to not let peeves fester. The awareness meetings were a help. And those who had to adhere to an off-farm job schedule didn't resent the rest of us dawdling over morning coffee, because *we* were beholden to Mother Nature. In the midst of a leisurely pot-and-beer fiesta, a thunderclap would send us charging outside to batten down the hatches. Once Becca broke up our raucous sing-along by announcing a family of raccoons digging by the coops, and Laurie and I had to scare off the masked marauders. She stood sentry and held the lantern while I filled in the dirt. Maybe if we'd been sober it wouldn't have taken so long, but that just added insult to injury.

In September we bid adieu to Millie as she was led to the Craybills' as part of some deal that got us cheap yogurt. We harvested the late summer vegetables and planted grasses as cover crops for the long Wisconsin winter. The weather cooled, windows were closed, and before the month ended, Wanda removed the gingham cloth that covered the cast-iron stove in the kitchen, and we began to burn wood. Chloe pried open the cedar chest and liberated woolen blankets, and PJ distributed down comforters.

October was a firestorm of color. The woods to our west and hills to the south and east burned gold, yellow, bronze, amber, ginger, scarlet, crimson, copper, orange, coral, tangerine, and shades that hadn't been named yet. When the leaves browned, winds and rain strewed them everywhere. We picked apples and more apples and more apples. The pumpkins were carved out for pies; Geserenie didn't celebrate Halloween because it reinforced a view of strong women as evil. I'd tried to promote Hecate Hore's view that witches were symbols of feminism, but in vain.

Carter won the election, and though the rest of us wanted him to win—the Republicans being anti every minority you could name except millionaires—Chloe, Heather, and Chase were the only ones voting. As PJ said, "It's just one rich WASP male or another."

Laurie's parents paid a short visit to Geserenie, and she did as Sally had done with hers: put them up at the Bus Stop Motel. When they came for a quick look at the farm, everybody but Wanda hid out, and we covered the Declaration of Interdependence with an Elvis photo.

Chapter 32

EVENTUALLY REAL COLD hit. Every morning the pastures lay covered in frost. PJ left the bottom spigot on the tap trickling all night so the pipe running under the driveway wouldn't freeze, and by daylight, the bucket catching the drops was frozen over except for a glossy silver-dollar puddle on top. Mr. Wiffle ate in the barn and huddled in his hay; only the chickens lived it up, in their heated coop. Of course, with the first snowfall we romped like little kids, hurling packed wads at fence posts, building a snowwoman, digging our names in the drifts.

Winter on the farm was a double-edged shovel. On the one blade side, even a blizzard didn't mean a day off; the animals still needed feeding and tending and their quarters cleaned. On the other side, the chickens were taking a break from laying, and it was too late for harvesting and too early for planting, so some idleness was actually forced upon us. Chloe and Bec carried a stack of board games up from the basement—Parcheesi, Sorry, and Clue—along with a backgammon set, decks of cards, and five or six jigsaw puzzles.

On Pearl Harbor Day, I got bombarded with what Sally called a "vicious rhinitis," but whether it came from rhinos or the Rhine River didn't much matter. It lasted ten days and indirectly led to Laurie's and my first real fight. Becca and Wanda had gone down to Oklahoma to visit Bec's mother for Christmas, and Chase and Heather had gone to Heather's folks, so PJ and Sally were taking their van, good old Flying Fritzie, into Madison for the shopping. I was eager to go with, having finally recovered from the rhinitis and now feeling cabin feverish. Laurie meanwhile had caught my bug and felt crappy. She whined she didn't want me to go—she had kept *me* company when *I* was sick.

"I slept most of the time," I said. "And I wouldn't have minded if you'd gone somewhere."

"Whenever you wanted soup or juice, I always went down and got it."

"I appreciated that."

"What would you do there?"

"Hit Artemiz, maybe Peg's for a game of pool."

She did the pout routine. Shoot, if I'd wanted a guilt trip, I could have called Mathilde. Suddenly she got all contrite and said she didn't mind if I went, she was just grumpy because of not feeling well. Her expression was so rueful, I didn't dare change my mind.

Sally and PJ dropped me in the usual spot, and we arranged to meet up later at Peg O's, since the sign on the front door of Artemiz said *Closed until January 3, 1977.* At first, it was weird being off-farm without Laurie. I wandered around taking in the sights and holiday decorations, but it was cold, so I hit Peg O's way early. The bar was dead and the TV not working; I split after only one beer. A straight bar had a football game on, so I went in and ordered a draft.

"Anything to eat?" the bartender asked.

"I'm thinking about it."

Right then a guy emerged from the kitchen yelling, "Bacon cheeseburger." He deposited a plate on the counter not ten feet away.

We eyed each other, the bacon cheeseburger and I. I thought of
Mr. Wiffle. I thought of Millie. I thought of a lot of things. While
my mind was busy thinking, my mouth opened, and out came, "I'll
have one of those."

"Bacon cheese? How you want it cooked?"

"Medium. And fries."

Mrs. Delucci had made Nina go to confession whenever she
wanted to borrow the car, so Nina adhered to the dogma that as
long as you were going to get the slate wiped clean, you might as
well mess it up pretty good beforehand. Did she confess to *our* do-
ings? Probably not. But I'm sure she confessed to sassing, because
that would have allowed her to parade all her mother's provoca-
tions. Still, the dogma had merit. I might as well savor every morsel,
since I was sinning anyway. It wasn't a hard row to hoe.

With time to kill before meeting PJ and Sally back at Peg O's, I
wandered along streets I hadn't been on before. Ahead lay Rudy's,
the restaurant everybody at Geserenie detested. I got closer and
could read the smaller neon: *Prime Rib and Veal.* The establishment
was good-sized, with a good-sized parking lot containing good-
sized gas guzzlers.

Unlike Heather and Chloe and everybody, I could tolerate a
restaurant serving veal, tolerate the fact that they profited from
hurting calves. Not that I *liked* the veal industry. But the world was
filled with things I didn't like—wars, rape, torture—so a place
serving veal wasn't on my 10 Most Wanted list. But Rudy's was different. Rudy's *went out of its way* to get folks to eat veal: veal specials,
veal advertised in neon lights. If I hadn't gotten a D in chemistry, I
might've considered fire-bombing the place. Instead, I wandered in
and used the can. On the way out, I grabbed a bunch of mints from
the dish by the register to hide my bacon and burger breath.

Geserenie didn't celebrate Halloween or Thanksgiving because they either put down women or sanctified European imperialism, so I wasn't surprised we didn't celebrate Christmas. But the afternoon of the 25th, I phoned Mathilde.

She sounded chipper. "Yes, we both have the day off and are having Christmas dinner on Christmas." I could hear laughter in the background. "Sissy wants to talk, but don't let her go on and on. You're paying for the call."

"Edward there?" I asked.

"Roy just took him home. His eye infection came back, so he didn't feel up for poker. Here she is."

"Merry Christmas, Andy." Lorraine sounded like a couple of grasshoppers had already hopped down the hatch. "I've got a story about that crazy father of yours."

"What?"

She laughed. "It's a real doozy. He got admitted to St. Joe's. Don't worry, not for long. That's what's so funny." She paused, maybe to catch her breath. "Last Thursday morning, I come in at nine, I was off Wednesday, and Darla, she says, 'Edith says your sister was married to a Dean Gabe.' Edith's in Records, and they're right next to us. I says, 'That's right,' and Darla says, 'He was admitted yesterday,' and I says, 'What for?' and she says, 'Ankle might be broken.' 'They don't admit you for a broken ankle,' I says, and she says, 'Maybe there's more, but they'll never know,' and I says, 'Why not?' and she says, 'Because he's gone—flew the coop.'"

Lorraine laughed for a good twenty seconds. The she-says/I-says bit meant she was pretty loaded, but it still was annoying that she was enjoying a joke without letting me in on the punch line, assuming there was one. "What do you mean 'flew the coop'?" I asked. She'd probably never seen a real coop in her life.

"You have to hear the whole thing. He comes in the ER just after lunch with a swollen ankle. Their writing's awful. Darla, she sees the chart when it comes back from X-ray, and all she can make out is 'tonic.' Guess he didn't want to fess up to the gin." Again the laugh. "After the X-rays, they admit him. Maybe a compound fracture, where you have to operate, and somebody was going to do it first thing in the morning. After the *tonic* wore off. They put him on Ortho. Third floor. Middle of the night, he escapes."

"How do you escape with a broken ankle?"

"And taped up! Maybe a compound fracture, something bad enough to get admitted. Manages to get his clothes on, even his *pants*—which means unwrapping the temporary bandage—or maybe he sawed off a cast! And nobody saw him go."

I did find myself chuckling. "Dean Houdini. You think he staged it like in the movies? You know, stuffing pillows under the blankets to make it look like he was asleep? Or leaving the bathroom light on and the sink running, so if the nurse comes in, she thinks he's in there?"

"It gets *better*," my aunt said. "The floor nurses weren't the only ones with egg on their face. His chart was supposed to be in Ortho, right? But somebody sent it to Neurology, up on *Five*. Then Records gets notes from Dr. Micklemeister to put in the file. He's *Chair* of Neurology. So why didn't they put them in the chart when it's up there?"

Her mouth went a-mile-a-minute. "The gals in Records were in a tizzy. They called Neuro, but they don't have it, and Ortho don't, and they track down the fellow with the cart, and *he* don't. The gals in Records are pulling their hair out. You can't lose a chart. That's worse—"

"Did they ever find it?"

"They find it. Want to know where? You sitting down?"

"Yes," I lied.

"It was with Dr. Wu. Now guess what department *he's* in, Dr. Wu?"

"Haven't the foggiest."

"What's the *last* place you'd think?"

I tried recalling discussions among Lish and her friends about various hospital departments. "Pediatrics?"

"OB," my aunt shrieked. "Obstetrics!"

"Obstetrics? You telling me Dean's *pregnant*?"

Both of us laughed hard enough to get hernias. When one of us stopped to catch a breath, the other would still be going, and that would start the first again. Screw the phone bill—this story was worth the price of admission.

At one point I calmed myself enough to ask, "Didn't you think he'd take precautions? Wait a sec, he had a vasectomy. Maybe a vasectomy only prevents somebody *else* from getting pregnant, not yourself."

Lorraine blew her nose. "Here, Sissy wants to talk."

Matt got on. "I meant to tell you, your friend Stacy called earlier. I gave her your address and phone number."

After hanging up and putting the phone back in the hallway, I returned to the bedroom and told Laurie the whole St. Joe's story. She listened without smiling and asked, "Why did he sneak out? They can't make you stay."

"He doesn't like to argue. Especially if the nurses are just trying to do their job. I'm guessing the doctors acted all patronizing, and he'd had enough. His *m.o.* is to hot-foot it, and no swollen ankle, even a compound fracture, is gonna change that." Laurie still didn't see the humor, but she didn't know Dean and wouldn't understand the kick *he* would have gotten from the stunt. "Micklemeister and

Wu sounds like some vaudeville act." I did a soft-shoe beside the rug.

"My name is Micklemeister,

"My name is Dr. Wu.

"Some say that I'm a shyster.

"Some say that I should shoo."

At *this* nonsense she smiled.

"Is that the phone again?" I ducked back into the hall.

"Is Andy Gabe there?"

"Mathilde said you'd called!"

"I thought it sounded like you." Stacy's voice hadn't changed one iota. "How's farm life?"

"We've got a pig, but he's no male chauvinist. Where are you, Hastings?"

"No, Berkeley."

I brought the phone back into the room, and we must've talked an hour. Midway through, Laurie brought me a beer and lingered in the doorway before getting bored and splitting.

Stacy was impressed I'd settled down, and I said I was surprised too but it felt good. I told her about the other folks at Geserenie and about Millie and Mr. Wiffle and the corn and berries, even Dean's latest, which elicited her acorn comment. She in turn told me about writing a lot of poetry, working in a bakery, and attending readings at some coffeehouse.

"Doing any reading yourself?" I asked. "Your own poems?"

"Not yet. I'm not sure they're good enough."

"And you used to give *me* a hard time about self-confidence!"

She laughed. "I'm happy just kibitzing."

When we finally hung up, I had to massage my face—my cheek muscles hadn't had such a workout since watching Charlie dine on his boot laces.

We dined much better—Wanda had left a dozen thick, delicious stews in the freezer for us while she and Bec were in Oklahoma. But with them and Chase and Heather gone, and no visiting kith, kin, or kibitzers at Geserenie, the week after Christmas was quiet.

When the travelers got back, the house recaptured the beehive feeling you needed in winter. I taught Laurie poker so with Bec, PJ, and Sally, we had enough for a game. To keep losses low, I limited the betting. However, PJ bet randomly, screwing up any chance the rest of us had to strategize; her left hand couldn't have known when her right was bluffing. And down only $2.80, Laurie ended the game sore at being, technically, the big loser. Okay, I'd run poker up the flagpole at Geserenie, and nobody'd saluted.

One evening while we were drying the last of the supper dishes, Laurie mentioned the snow had stopped and we should go for a walk. I said I'd been planning to hang out in the parlor and listen to records, something we hadn't had a chance to do with Becca and Wanda since their return. She said they were outside, so I said okay.

The air was windless; the sky, clear. The pasture fences bore a thick white trim, and to the north and west, the fields spread uninterrupted, a milky, luminous canvas framed by forest. To the south and east, a pale satin wave rolled to the Craybills' barn and miles beyond. Even our house was draped in white: the sloping roof, the top of the chimney. Only the areas under the eaves were dark. A dim light framed the attic window, and thin lines of light slipped through the gaps in the dining room shutters.

We followed Bec and Wanda's boot tracks northward. The fleece we now used as a curtain in our window mirrored the white pastures. The Jerseymac, *our* apple tree, cut a stubbled figure after Chase's pruning. The barn roof formed a perfect white rhombus, and white icing coated the fence planks in smooth bands. On the full pine branches, the snow lay heavily, but on the leafless deciduous, it seemed to hover and trace each branch like a white shadow. Every structure and object was white or dark topped by white. Only the western rim of the sky hinted at color, a bordering-on-black deep purple. The weather vane was capped by such a thin wafer of snow, a single gust would shake it loose, but the night was still, still and lucid. No sound jarred the liquid silence.

Ursa Major and Minor came out. All the stars sparkled like diamonds. Which constellation was that: Gemini? Every moment we remained, more bright flickers emerged. They couldn't be suns, even for planets in distant galaxies; the light they radiated was too cold, too crystalline. How many millions of miles between us? We were so tiny in this magnificence.

Becca and Wanda trudged over. The four of us gazed around at the white fields and barn and fences and trees and starry solar system. You could almost feel your soul float upwards. The universe was magical, mystical, wondrous.

I walked beside Becca to the kitchen steps. "By the way, been meaning to ask, how was your trip to Oklahoma?" She shrugged and went inside. I waited by the apple tree for Laurie and Wanda, who were talking softly. "Did I say something wrong? Asked how your vacation went."

Wanda threw Laurie a look and passed by and up the steps. When the kitchen door had closed, Laurie murmured, "Bec's mom is really, really sick."

"Shit." After one last lingering look at the starry canopy, I followed Laurie inside.

Chapter 33

STACY'S PRECIOUS T.S. Eliot was right: April was the cruelest month. Tilling just the herb garden was a deceptively punishing labor of bending and pressing and pulling with the hoe, followed by squatting to pick up the unearthed intruders. Stones, garbage, and vegetation had to be sorted into separate bags, only the vegetation headed for compost. My shoulders were sore; my thighs, hamstrings, and back ached. Fortunately, we were only doing the strips along the south and east sides of the house—Chloe had rented the Craybills' tractor for the main field and the grazing pastures. Weeds were worse than stones; you had to get the blade completely underneath to extract the entire root.

Planting was tiring too, but sowing and spreading the soil wasn't bad. How crows could memorize where every single seed lay buried I'd never know, but one of these days I'd write Grunner and say I finally knew what *real* fieldwork was. At least the smells of spring were a job perk, till the fertilizer was laid. I threatened to quit when the Craybills manured their entire west section. But by the end of the month, we'd planted everything that could withstand a late frost. And being outdoors at least dispelled some of the cabin fever that had made late winter such a drag.

New Eden threw a May Day party, and after all the hype, I expected to be disappointed, but it was definitely worth a Michelin detour. Easily two hundred old hippies, pseudo-hippies, and ersatz hippies plus their no-neck monsters swarmed around tables of food and booths of carnival games and even a mule ride. New Eden's barn was five times the size of ours, and their crops were planted as far as the eye could see. I got ripped on tequila sunrises in the first hour and spent most of the day in the shade sucking flavored ice.

By the time June busted out all over, the days were uniformly hot. There were moments picking berries when I could've sworn Joshua had made the sun stand still. For my birthday, Wanda baked me a cake, and Laurie gave me a stuffed aardvark because I said I liked words starting with A. My one-year-at-Geserenie anniversary coming the next day, along with my and Laurie's one-year anniversary, made me feel like I'd won the Triple Crown.

And we were arguing less. Other couples would argue as much, I maintained, if both halves worked on the farm. What I meant was that with Bec and Sally and Heather gone for thirty, forty hours each week, the time *available* for arguing was less. But Laurie initially took it to mean I wanted an off-farm job, which almost started its own fight.

At least the stuff pissing us off was minor. Her main complaint was my staying up late drinking and getting high with whomever else was in the mood, and mine was getting bugged about staying up late drinking and getting high with whomever else was in the mood.

"You know it makes it harder to find time to fool around," she once said.

"Hey, I tried waking you last night."

"It was two in the morning. And you were drunk."

"What's wrong with that? I can still do it; I'm not a guy."
"You should come to bed earlier."
"You should come to bed later."
"Then who would feed Mr. Wiffle and the chickens?"

The Fourth of July was upon us. New Eden told Chloe they couldn't make the carnival this year either, which was a relief because Gertie wanted to use it as her next step on the journey into self-confidence. Independence Day morning, she covered a long table near the outdoor tap with an old plastic cloth and placed three folding chairs on each side. The top was arranged with containers of finger-paint, jars of water for rinsing, a stack of blank paper weighted down with rocks, and clean rags. In her usual legs-apart stance, she surveyed the setup. Her large slate-blue smock fell loosely from her breasts, shading her sandals.

She remained indoors at first, when the neighbors and commune folks were arriving. Cayenne and Cinnamon paused at the finger-paints but ran towards the northwest pasture where Bec had the sprinkler going. The Andersons showed with their kites, younger kids got into freeze tag, and older girls gathered at the crafts table.

After some tearing around, the Spices screamed to the whole world, "Can we do finger-paints?" Shenandoah followed them to the table, where they unscrewed the caps with demonic speed. The kitchen door opened, and Gertie came down the steps, her face set in a shy smile—I was guessing she'd been waiting by the window. Usually she was plain Gertie to me, but now I was seeing her as the visitors might. *Change your mind—go back inside*, one of my brain lobes wailed.

Cayenne or Cinnamon was busy smearing red paint all over her hands when the other delivered a sharp elbow to the ribs. "Quit it," the smearer shrieked.

Everybody's attention was drawn first to the brats and then to the direction Brat number two was pointing. *All* the kids stopped what they were doing and stared. One Schmidt boy broke into a grin, another snickered, and one of the Anderson twerps, probably to impress an older brother, cupped his hands over his chest. If that weren't enough, Cinnamon—or whichever the fuck it was that got hit in the ribs—mimicked her sister and pointed a red hand, little Hitlerites with arms thrust forward and stupid mouths open a mile.

Heather had ESP and came running from around the side of the house. "I want to talk to each of you," she school-marmed, with broad arm gestures herding the kids to the finger-paints table. "Come with me right now. Yes, you too," she scolded the Schmidt and Anderson goon squad. They all went. The adults went too.

I followed Gertie up the kitchen steps saying, "Kids are ass-holes till somebody teaches them—"

"You did a courageous thing, Gertie," Laurie called out.

Gertie went through the swinging door and up the stairs. Sally followed Laurie and me into the dining room and went to the window. "Good, the parents are listening too."

I peered out. Yes, the adults looked somber as Heather lectured. The kids' expressions were all too familiar: *trying* to look contrite. The minute the grown-ups left, grins and laughter would erupt. I knew—I'd been young.

Chloe came inside and went upstairs. Laurie must've gone too, because a few minutes later she came down and said Gertie was okay, that Dr. Asplund had said the journeys that mattered were never easy.

I was wrong about the kids. There was no laughing, no snickering, no huddled giggles. Instead, the afternoon was draped in a pall. The wind had died completely, so kite-flying was out. Despite the heat, nobody went swimming in the creek or through the hose while Bec watered. I hauled the burlap to the fallow field for bases and fetched the bat and ball, but nobody came over to play. The apples sat untouched in the bucket by the bobbing basin. The girls at the crafts table fingered the beads and stones mindlessly, making nothing. When I announced that the water balloons were ready for tossing, nobody cared.

Once the Schmidts finished grilling the dogs and burgers, they packed up their gear and split. By three, everybody else had gone too, apologizing to Chloe on their way out for their kids' behavior. By 3:45, we'd lugged everything to the basement.

Despondency dogged us into the living room, where we bitterly recalled the excitement of the morning's preparations. "Why can't the world be a safe place for women?" somebody asked. "Why can't a person who has never harmed anyone walk the planet in peace?"

Yet Gertie suffered no obvious setback. She continued to hang out with us at sing-alongs and when we listened to records in the parlor. I overheard Chloe tell Heather, "She's proud of her ability to cope. I let her know that if the children *hadn't* reacted unkindly, it wouldn't have been a real test. She was *strong*."

"But I worry the pain is just buried inside."

"Dr. Asplund spent a great deal of time discussing suicidal thoughts. Gertie understands the world needs her; she's very keen on helping the blind. And she's proud of how her suffering has made her kindhearted towards all living creatures."

I couldn't say the same. I fantasized about using a mortar and pestle to crush Cinnamon and Cayenne.

My second summer at Geserenie pretty much mimicked the first, but in September, Heather and Chase hit us with the news they were jumping ship. Even worse, they were climbing on board Miranda's commune in Madison—with the excuse of wanting to "get political."

"We're trying to get the legislature to pass a rape-shield law," Heather said, already using "we."

As soon as they left, everybody trashed them pretty good. Chase hadn't worked as hard as she pretended; Heather was stuck-up and left her clothes everywhere. The rape-shield stuff had actually sounded okay to me till somebody explained that rape-shields weren't actual physical jobbies but some law about testimony at trials.

Gertie volunteered to draft a roommates-wanted ad. She read it out loud at supper, and Becca asked, "What's a 'true capital V' vegetarian?"

Gertie explained that meant we wanted somebody who wouldn't eat meat ever—even off-farm. Bec said she not only ate meat when she visited her mother but suspected the milkshakes she got in Madison contained animal lard. Chloe said as long as Bec didn't *order* meat when she had an option not to, it wasn't a problem—we lived in an imperfect society, so compromises were necessary. And no one was asking us to check ingredients on things like milkshakes.

But Bec said it was the principle of the thing, that what we did off-farm was nobody's business. Gertie surprised us all by jumping into the fray, telling Bec we wouldn't accept a roommate who *murdered* somebody off-farm. I was glad it started to rain so I had an excuse to hit the coops, telling Laurie to vote my proxy.

Whatever the ad ended up saying, nobody called. Chloe told us we could last till early spring without new roommates because she had gotten another distribution from her grandparents' trust. The distribution was large enough to even pay the Craybills to plant the cover crops.

Yet Heather and Chase's absence was felt. Winter approached, and a glumness settled over us, not helped by it being too cold to ride in the back of Rubella. PJ and Sally were rarely in the mood to go into Madison, so riding in Flying Fritzie wasn't an option.

New Year's Eve we drank ourselves silly, or at least I did, and I had just begun sawing my first log when Laurie sat up abruptly, whispering, "Who would phone so late?" We heard footsteps in the hall, but nobody knocked.

Getting up later to pee, I heard noises in the kitchen. I went downstairs and through the swinging door. Wanda was in her parka, and the cast-iron stove had been lit. Removing her baby-blue wool cap, she shook her ringlets. "Did I wake you?"

"No," I said, "Mother Nature did. Where have you been?"

"Bec's mom is in the hospital. I just took her to the airport."

"That the phone call last night? You should have told me. I could have gone with for company on the ride home."

The comment amused her. "It would be pretty cold in the back of the truck."

"You probably could have borrowed Flying Fritzie."

The door to the dining room swung in; it was Laurie. "What's going on?"

"Wanda just got back from the airport. Bec's mom's in the hospital." I glanced at Mother Hen and the chicks. "It's almost six. I got some winks while you were on the road—let me deal with breakfast for the early crew. You go to bed."

"You don't mind?" Wanda asked.

"Andy's right," Laurie said, "go to bed."

Wanda smiled gratefully and went out the swinging door.

Chapter 34

BECCA'S VISIT WITH her mom was stretching into February. With the household now reduced to seven, cabin fever flared with a vengeance, and I started seriously thinking about an off-farm job. Sally agreed to keep an eye on the hospital listings for cafeteria help, but her hospital was much smaller than St. Joe's and much, much smaller than Julesman's. I tried to get folks interested in another trip to Peg's—Fritzie had snow tires and did fine getting Sally to and from work and PJ to and from trades deliveries—but driving in the dark proved a deal-breaker.

"In a few weeks, the weather will be better," Laurie said to cheer me up. "Let's see if anyone wants to play games."

"We've already played the board games past boredom and gone through 'If you knew you'd be marooned on a desert island and could only have three foods, which would you pick?' *And* three beverages and three records and three famous people. Talk about being marooned!"

Eventually the temperature hit the forties for several days running, and Laurie and I went into Madison with Wanda, PJ, and Sally. I kept my eyes peeled for help-wanted signs, despite knowing a zillion university students were looking for work. In a kind of karmic insult, the only restaurant window that had one was Rudy's.

"Any more word on when Bec's coming back?" I asked, hitting the fridge for a beer before tackling the downstairs bathroom, which I'd agreed to clean now that we were short-staffed.

Wanda looked up from the cutting board. "She's not."

"What do you mean?"

Putting down the knife, she smiled meekly. "We broke up. We planned to—before her mom's relapse. But we hadn't decided who would stay and who would go. I suppose you could say her mom decided it for us." She turned and faced me. "We both felt the relationship had run its course. We're not mad at each other; it's not like that. The amazing thing is how mutual it is. She's still my best friend."

I was in shock. Wanda smiled again and said she had better go tell Chloe.

I went upstairs and told Laurie, who was really bummed too. The four of us used to hang out in the parlor a whole lot, just listening to records and bullshitting. Wanda and Bec were *our* best friends.

Nobody was happy at the news. According to Wanda, Chloe's first words were "How long have you kept this from me?"

"We didn't 'keep it' from you," Wanda had answered. "We were sorting things out, trying to decide who would stay."

"But you knew *one* of you would be leaving and that I would want advance notice so I could plan."

Chloe called a meeting for that very evening, and things got pretty heated over whether Wanda should have to contribute some cash to make up for Bec's contribution. Gertie was willing to take on half the cooking in exchange.

The following evening, Laurie and I sat on the bed watching the sun set, neither of us in the mood to ooh and aah.

"They're not asking her to pay the whole amount Bec did," Laurie said, "and she *should* do less cooking and let Gertie—"

"Wanda's supposed to get a job?"

"She has Rubella; she can drive. And savings. Why shouldn't she—"

"She's just broken up with her lover. Can't they cut her some slack?"

Laurie got quiet, and we resumed watching the sun die. More to herself than to me, she mumbled, "Too bad it was Bec who left. We could use the money—"

Not waiting to hear more, I grabbed my cigarettes and stormed out.

The sky was a dull violet. The brown fields lay empty. Hard to believe it was almost the spring equinox. I lit a cigarette and leaned on the fence. Longer days would be nice. Dean got excited by spring because it meant the track would open, and could baseball be far behind?

I walked along the side path to the north end of the pasture. By the time I retraced my steps, the sky had darkened. The light from our room threw the apple tree branches into shadow on the ground, a deformed skeleton.

When I got upstairs, Laurie was contrite. "I didn't mean it like it sounded. I was upset. Everything was perfect before."

The Lord taketh away, but She also giveth, and what She gaveth Geserenie was two new housemates. Newbie number one and Newbie number two took Chase and Heather's old room and worked like dogs during the tilling and planting. I still wasn't crazy about them, though. Maybe they were *too* agreeable, or I was too *dis*agreeable.

The May awareness meeting was the day before New Eden's festival. The business half didn't get started till late, which pissed me off because I'd given Wanda money to pick up a bottle of Southern Comfort and was anticipating a pleasant evening of listening to Janis. Probably from spite, I had a couple of shots in our room right before the meeting.

Luckily, the business agenda was short. During the break, I scooted upstairs for a cigarette and another shot—I'd forgotten how good it tasted.

When I got back down, they'd begun without me. Laurie pointed at the purple cushion beside her on the Navajo, beneath the portrait gallery. Yes, that was where I'd been sitting. I teetered over and sat, hearing my knees crack. I put the cushion against the wall and leaned back, legs extended. My stomach felt funny in that position, so I sat up and crossed my legs. That didn't help, so I uncrossed them and tried a different angle.

Gertie was speaking. "Like Sally said, we become absorbed in the difficulties of living in a group and forget that what brought us together was shared ideals. A peaceful, nurturing community of women who want to live *with* the earth and don't want to harm other creatures—"

"Except roaches," I said before Laurie could clap a hand over my mouth. I pushed it off. "I mean *cock*roaches. I mean all forms of cock." I hiccupped.

Chloe said, "Continue, Gertie." Wanda flashed me a peace sign.

"You heard me say this before: the reason I've survived is because of the spiritual support you sisters have given me. It's *saved* me."

Holy shit, Gertie meant it! Laurie, Wanda, Chloe, PJ, Sally, maybe even the newbies—*we* might have prevented a suicide. *I* might've played a role in keeping somebody alive.

The realization should have been sobering, but the room began to spin. I summoned the coordination to stand and serpentine through the bodies and make it to the downstairs bathroom. My aim was true, and I even got the seat up in time. After, I ran the fan and washed my face and smeared toothpaste over my teeth. The face in the mirror was sickly white but no longer sickly green. I too was a survivor.

Only Laurie paid me any mind when I returned. She squeezed my knee once I'd sat again. Sally looked like she'd been crying. PJ said, "We get so caught up in the little shit."

"It's become a habit, not something we do from *within*."

"I look at the labels, but I'm not in touch with the part of me that says, 'You're doing it to share the earth.'"

"It's become a *rule*," Chloe said, "not a *choice*."

My stomach was at peace, and I wanted my spirit to be at peace, to be part of this communal moment. But all I could think of to say was Stacy's old line, "The world is too much with us late and soon."

Yet Gertie appreciated it and nodded. "That's why the wish has to come from our hearts." She turned to Chloe, half-asking, "So it will be an *individual* choice."

"But a *group* commitment."

My stomach felt heaps better. "Count me in," I said.

A smile broke across Chloe's face. "Me too."

One by one around the room, folks said "me too." Then we held hands and sang "We Shall Overcome."

I hunched over on the bed and tried to tug off a sneaker without undoing the double-knot. Laurie knelt and untied it. "You know what you agreed to?"

"Please don't say an orgy."

"Never to eat meat." We got the one sneaker off, and she untied the other.

"What do you mean, *never*? Like if I go back to Jersey for a visit . . ."

She picked up the pair and put them by the wall. "The point is to follow our ideals everywhere. Otherwise, Geserenie is like Sunday School; we're just temporarily on our best behavior."

I pulled off my jeans and on my sweatpants and climbed under the comforter. "The idea that I can't *ever* do something rubs me the wrong way. Not like it did Bec—she was principled. But a rule saying 'never' really makes me want to break it."

"You can *never* have sex with me."

"That'll be next, you'll see."

New Eden's May Day festival was like the previous year's, with makeshift carnival booths and tables of food and crafts. By two the temps were in the upper 80s. Somebody named Tim greeted PJ and whispered in her ear, and she asked the rest of us if we wanted to try a really strong weed. I was the only other taker. Wanda grabbed Laurie's arm, saying they should look at the pottery, and they skipped off, both on a whim having worn peasant skirts. Sally and the newbies headed in the direction of Moonsilver's tables with their loom clothes.

Tim led PJ and me towards a small grove of trees some distance from the crowd, across a culvert stinking of manure. He took out a joint and handed it to PJ and flicked a lighter. She toked and handed it to me, and we passed it back and forth till Tim took out a roach clip and finished it. The two of them huddled a minute, and then we headed back towards the crowd. Tim angled away after crossing the culvert.

"What was that all about?" I asked.

"Don't you get it?"

"This where you buy your weed?"

"Me and a lot of other people." She grinned and nodded at the woods. "It's over there."

I imagined a clearing with rows of marijuana plants. "*That's* why they're so fucking self-sufficient!"

"Don't tell anyone—only Sally knows."

"*We* should become self-sufficient by blackmailing them."

The two of us started to laugh and then couldn't stop—we fell down in the grass, holding our bellies like imbeciles. Sure, the pot contributed, but New Eden's pious hypocrisy was hilarious in itself. Wasn't their self-sufficiency based on black-market prices?

Eventually we made it to the food tables and ate corndogs and fries and ice cream and wandered through the maze of booths. No way could I get the tennis ball into the plywood clown's mouth. We started our own contest of stupidest jokes and would've wasted the entire day if Laurie hadn't tapped me on the shoulder.

"Hey, lady, what you been up to?" I had an incredible urge to kiss her.

"Not much. You seem to be having fun."

I repeated some of our jokes, but she didn't find them funny. Sally and the newbies joined us, and we all agreed to split. Laurie said she'd go get Wanda. I stepped to the side to watch her walk in the skirt and spotted Wanda sitting with about a dozen folks in a circle on the grass. Cam and Rob were the only ones I recognized.

One of the newbies meanwhile shoved a wad of pamphlets in our faces. The top was titled *Your First Loom: A Beginner's Guide.*

"You're not leaving us for Moonsilver?"

"No, no! I want to get my own loom."

Chloe and Gertie were chopping vegetables when we filed in. Chloe stopped to take a look at the pamphlets and asked the newbie if she was going to buy a loom. She'd like to, the newbie said, but wasn't sure where to put it. I suggested the extra room, the area under the stairs.

"It's too small. I need space for a work table and shelves."

Wanda brought a pitcher of lemonade to the table, and I grabbed some glasses. Laurie joined us, and Wanda poured. The newbies studied the pamphlets, and Chloe resumed chopping.

After a minute, Chloe asked how New Eden was doing. Laurie said she didn't know—Luke was the only one sitting with them.

"Luke? Is he new?"

"No, he's Mitchell's little brother."

Chloe's knife hand paused midair. "He moved to New Eden? Wasn't he in the *navy*?"

"He's only visiting—I don't know for how long."

"Until October," Wanda said, studying her skirt hem. "His tour's done, and he's taking Spanish over the summer and helping harvest. Then he's going hiking in the Andes. When he returns the end of February, he'll work for his father in North Carolina."

"Straight people are lucky," Laurie groused. "They don't have to hide their lifestyle if they live near their parents."

"Thought you didn't *want* to go back to Idaho?" I said.

"But they have the choice."

Wanda finished her lemonade, washed the glass, and went into the living room. The instant the swinging door closed behind her, Chloe asked the newbie if Wanda's room was large enough for a work space.

"It might be. I would need to measure it."

"Come on in," Wanda called out to my knock.

"Just thought you should know: at some point what's-her-face is going to come in here and measure the dimensions. Maybe she's planning on telling you first—"

"To put the loom. And Chloe will ask me to move to the alcove, as you call it."

"You're okay with that?"

Wanda nodded. "Then I may get by without contributing cash. I might even *volunteer* the room."

Wanda did volunteer the room, and it was large enough, so Laurie and I helped carry her furniture to the alcove, including the cool cubbyhole cabinet. Figuring I'd only get in the way, I let everybody else deal with hauling the new loom upstairs when it arrived.

Chapter 35

FOR MY TWENTY-SIXTH birthday I got a card with a ten-dollar bill from Mathilde, a card from Edward, and a postcard from Stacy with a picture of an orca. *Isn't it time for you to pay the West Coast a visit? No problem putting you up, just putting up with you.* Laurie gave me a small hand-painted Incan bowl so we had matching ones to go with the matching aardvarks and matching picture frames with the photos of us Bec had taken.

Gertie again ventured outside at the Fourth of July carnival. I got the impression Chloe had made some phone calls beforehand, because Gertie greeted each child individually, handing them bags of raspberry cookies she'd baked herself, and they seemed to be expecting it. Later in the afternoon, Mr. Schmidt talked Gertie's ear off about all the trout fishing he'd done in Montana. Only Magic Dragon showed among the communes.

With our bumper berry crop, Gertie and the newbies became hell-bent on making preserves. Wanda suggested they do it the Saturday she was planning to go into Madison so she wouldn't need the kitchen, and having made preserves with her mother, Laurie agreed to help. I volunteered to keep Wanda company on the ride to town and assist with the shopping, but she said she wanted to clothes-shop first and it would be easier for her to do the farm shopping alone. I said I'd still go into Madison for the ride. No, I wouldn't get bored, honest; I could keep myself amused at Peg O's.

Strolling the city streets in summer was pleasant. I knocked about the university area, checked out Lake Mendota, bought pencils for Laurie, grabbed a veggie enchilada at a small Mexican restaurant, and spent the remainder of the afternoon at Peg O's watching baseball on TV. At 6:20, I split for the usual sidewalk spot in front of Artemiz.

When Rubella pulled to the curb and I climbed into the cab, Wanda asked if I still recognized her. She was wearing a pink-and-white checked blouse and a white skirt, and one arm sported a gold bracelet. Then she wanted to know if I thought everybody at Geserenie would flip out.

"No, they'll think *you* did."

"Don't you sometimes feel the need to do something *different*? You're in a rut and don't know what will help, so you try something just *different*?"

"Sure."

"I bought jeans and T-shirts too. But I felt like being a little crazy."

"Hey, it's not crazy."

About a mile shy of Geserenie, Wanda pulled Rubella onto the shoulder. "They'll give me such a hard time." She got out and climbed onto the truck bed and returned to the cab two minutes later wearing her old cut-offs. "Now they'll just tease me about the shirt."

But the kitchen crew was too absorbed in their work to notice Wanda. Laurie was doing yoga when I opened the bedroom door. "How did the preserving go?" I asked.

"Okay." She unwound her legs and rubbed them.

I gave a brief recap of my afternoon, and she asked what Wanda had done, and I said I thought she had gone to some mall for new jeans.

The trips to Madison became something of a fix for both Wanda and me. She went every Saturday, since the kitchen became off-limits while Gertie and the newbies made preserves and experimented with recipes. While the weather was warm, Laurie joined us—she got into baseball and would watch with me at the bar. But even before the fall equinox hit, taking turns riding in the truck bed was no longer an option. Laurie seemed to accept my going without her. Besides, the TV at Peg's croaked, and she didn't like to shoot pool.

One evening she pulled me into the bedroom and asked accusingly if Wanda had a secret job.

"Not that I know of," I said. "Wouldn't she tell us?"

"Not if she doesn't want us to ask her to contribute money. She was so flustered when I brought the laundry down and saw skirts hanging. She must need them for work."

"Bet you're right." I was sorry Wanda didn't trust us to keep her secret, but Laurie pointed out Wanda was protecting us—this way we couldn't get in trouble for hiding it.

"And it explains why she's never missed a Saturday," I said, "or wanted to head home before 6:30. If it were just shopping, the times would vary."

The following Saturday, Wanda was ready to go into town at her usual time, and Laurie smiled conspiratorially as she accompanied me to Rubella, sizing up Wanda's new yellow blouse. Her jeans were old, but she'd brought a bag of clothes, supposedly to be returned to some store. Or changed into at work? Spy versus Spy.

I spent most of the afternoon at Peg O's shooting pool and bullshitting with the bartender but decided to stretch my legs before heading back to Artemiz. I wandered around till it was my bladder that felt stretched. Should I duck into one of the straight bars? Rudy's was on the next block and had a nice bathroom.

The entryway was pretty dark; my eyes took a few seconds to adjust. Aromas set my salivary glands to churning, but right now other urges took a backseat to the toilet seat. I passed a wide doorway on the right, which opened into the dining room, and hurried down the hall to the left.

On my way out, again passing the wide doorway, I paused to see what the clientele was like. Most folks looked to be in their sixties and seventies. Booths ran along the windows, but the nearest was by a wall, and to compensate for the lack of daylight had its own lamp. My eyeballs practically shot from their sockets. Wanda sat there— Wanda sat in a booth at Rudy's. Holy Toledo. Holy Cincinnati and Akron and Cleveland. She gazed at her nails. Waiting for the check?

I smiled. Wanda had the guts to break Geserenie's rules. I stepped back from the doorway so she couldn't see me. Was she eating veal? Or just other meat? Maybe she worked at Rudy's and got an employee discount on food—that would explain everything. Poor Wanda, all by her lonesome, hiding out from her supposed friends. Should I join her? Assure her I didn't care? Order a steak to prove it?

A bunch of customers passed back and forth while my brain lobes debated. She must be getting ready to leave, to meet me by Artemiz. I peered in again.

A guy went to her table. Men could never leave a woman in peace, not if she were by herself—they assumed she just *had* to be hoping for their company. Jesus Christ, he even had the gall to sit down across from her! Wanda smiled. Wait a sec, where had I seen him before? The candle shop? Art supplies store? No. Like a two-by-four between the eyes, it hit me: New Eden's festival.

A waitress stopped at their booth, blocking my view. When she moved off, Wanda was laughing. Their hands clasped across the table top.

My brain did backflips and somersaults all the way to Artemiz. Wanda had a *beaut* of a secret—something a whole lot bigger than a job. And they probably went to Rudy's only because it was the last place on earth anybody from Geserenie would set foot. Rubella pulled to the curb some minutes later, and I hopped in. "Hey, how's it going?"

"Pretty good."

We rode for about fifteen minutes just listening to the radio. On a deserted stretch of road, I couldn't take it any longer. "Don't have an accident while I'm talking," I said. "I'm going to say something that might startle you. It's that I'm *happy* for you, that you're dating whoever that guy is. I saw you at Rudy's, and I mean it—I'm happy for you."

She said nothing, so I explained how I had ducked in to use the can. "Are you going to tell?" she asked. "They'll want me to leave. Right now I have nowhere—"

"Not even Laurie. For starters, it's none of my business, the way I see it." I felt proud saying that.

"I *plan* to leave. But not just yet."

"I don't want you to. Who else can I tell about the cheeseburger I ate for lunch?"

She smiled. "Partners in crime."

"Partners in crime." Damn, I *should've* had a cheeseburger for lunch. A *bacon* cheeseburger.

Wanda's hands relaxed on the wheel, and she gave me the full story. Luke and she hit it off "incredibly" at the May Day festival—he'd even remembered her from his visit before. They went out for drinks in Madison and had a great time, then began meeting here and there for an hour or two, plus all afternoon in Madison every Saturday. I was right: they usually wound up at Rudy's because she couldn't imagine anybody from Geserenie setting foot in there, plus it was close enough to the no-parking zone by Artemiz that the two of them could linger together till the last possible minute.

"You ever hang out at New Eden?" I asked.

"No. Only Mitchell knows. He doesn't trust them to keep it secret."

No kidding—they'd gloat they had converted one of us. "Why do you have to leave?" I asked. "I'm not going to tell anybody. Now that I know, I can even cover for you."

"It wouldn't be right away. He's going home next month and then to Peru and won't be back in Asheboro till the end of February." She shot a glance my direction. "He wants me to move there. He's going to work for his father. I told him I'd have to think about it."

"Seems fair. After all, he hasn't asked where *you* want to live."

My words didn't seem to register. "That was three weeks ago. Today, I told him I would. His grandmother has a carriage house in the back she'll rent me—he insists on paying for it—and we can see how things go. He's the nicest person I ever met except for Bec. And you."

"Hey, keep me out of it. I know my virtues, and niceness ain't one of them."

Wanda began to gush like a kid home from the circus: Luke had a wonderful smile, hated Brussels sprouts, loved fishing, didn't like his last stint on the sub. I let her go on without interruption. For as much as she needed to talk, *I* needed to listen. I needed reminding that exuberance existed. To recall that life was more than just the same routine day in, day out. Where was the electricity of meeting new people, doing new things? Despite the emptiness her departure would entail, Wanda's secret amounted to my biggest thrill in ages. Ergo, I was in a rut. Would Laurie be willing to move somewhere new? If I pushed it. But she loved Geserenie, maybe as much as Chloe did.

"You're thinking four months isn't a long time to know someone before deciding to move to be with them," Wanda said.

"Hey, Laurie and I didn't know each other two full days." Ergo what?

"I'll tell everyone in January that I'll move out the end of February. But not why, not at first."

"Andy, it's for you."

I picked up the phone. "Hello?"

"Andy?"

"Matt? Something wrong?"

"No. Did you watch the game?"

"Don't have a TV, and the radio's been idiotic."

"The Phillies won the division. We were sure you'd be watching. Lorr and Anthony are here."

Mathilde described the highlights, and then let Lorraine get on. My aunt was busting with excitement and told me which National and American League teams had made the play-offs and who was playing whom and how great Steve Carlton was. No question about it: if the Phillies went all the way to the World Series, I was springing for a TV.

A Friday night while doing the supper dishes, Laurie said that one of the newbies was hoping to go into Madison with Wanda on Saturday.

"Nobody mentioned it to me." I wasn't in the greatest of moods, since the Phillies had blown the pennant. Besides, I knew Wanda would want me riding shotgun so she could talk freely—Luke was leaving Sunday for North Carolina before heading down to Peru.

"What if PJ and Sally take Flying Fritzie," Laurie said. "We could *all* go."

"That's cool—the more the merrier."

A picosecond later, Laurie was rounding up a posse. She succeeded: PJ, Sally, Laurie, me, and a newbie would go in Flying Fritzie, and the other newbie would go in Rubella. I figured I'd find some excuse to ride in the truck on the way home. Wanda herself suggested meeting up outside Artemiz at 6:30 to take our shopping bags so we wouldn't be crammed like sardines in the van.

Chapter 36

THE SIDEWALKS NEAR the university were peopled with students, shoppers, and folks heading out for an evening's entertainment. All afternoon, rain had threatened, and the air's coolness warned of winter, yet with dusk approaching, Sol spilled yellow across the horizon. Lake Mendota was a deep jade. Along the shore, trees formed a motley crew, some already bare-branched, some with a full complement of bright leaves, some with a smattering of brown. The breeze couldn't decide whether to pinch cheeks or stroke them so did a little of both. Laurie and I hovered in some limbo land too. The usual haunts had been haunted, and whether we returned to Peg O's to dance or homed in on home didn't much matter.

Everybody but Wanda was already waiting by the no-parking zone when we showed up. I watched in the direction of Rudy's for the truck.

"Look!" Sally said, pointing.

I turned. Marching towards us was a smiling, waving Heather, a large cardboard sign tucked under her arm. A dozen or so sign-toting women marched in tow. Heather raised the cardboard so we could read *Veal=Torture*. "We want to shut down Rudy's," she shouted. Another woman held up a poster with a photo of a calf looking paralyzed with fear.

I was paralyzed with panic. We all exchanged cheerful hellos. Sally asked where Chase was, and Heather said, "She ran off with Miranda."

"To Taos," a woman with a bullhorn told Sally.

"I'm *long* over her," Heather said. "Too much meaningful work to be done."

"A-woman."

"Why don't you join us? We have extra signs."

While the Geserenie folks debated Heather's offer, I said I'd go case Rudy's and let everybody know if any cops were inside. I raced off without waiting for objections.

Footsteps tailed me. "I'll come with you," Laurie called.

"No, it's better one person."

"But—"

"No!"

I broke into a sprint. Maybe, just maybe, Wanda and Luke had decided *not* to end the day at Rudy's. Maybe they were at some motel.

Rubella wasn't in the lot, but Wanda had said she always parked on a side street. I entered the dark entryway and hurried past the register to the dining room. They were in the same booth as before and didn't notice me till I was practically in their laps. "Guys, there's a problem."

"Andy! Luke, this is An—"

"Heather and a bunch of others and maybe some of Geserenie are on their way here to picket!"

Luke was on his feet. He laid some bills on the check while Wanda rose and grabbed her coat, asking if there was a back door. I said I didn't know. "What about *you*?" she asked. "What will *you* tell them?"

"I already said I was coming in to case the joint."

While talking, we moved towards the entryway. Wanda tugged my jacket sleeve. "What if you say we ran into each other and you asked me to come with you to case it?"

"I can wait here," Luke added, "so they won't connect us."

"Let's say you just came in to use the restroom," I said, "and I saw you leaving."

Now we were at the door. They stepped off to the side and embraced. I had the etiquette to mosey back to the register. The hostess smiled graciously. Wanda and Luke must have been favorites among the staff. When she took off her glasses and blew on them, I swiped some mints.

After the dark entryway, the pale dusk made me squint. Heather's group had assembled on the corner, and Wanda and I walked rapidly over. The woman with the bullhorn began to chant, "Veal is vile; veal is vile." Passersby slowed to read the signs. *Vicious is not Delicious, Cruel Isn't Cool.*

I gave an exaggerated arm flourish. "Guess who was coming out of the restroom."

Wanda laughed nervously. "I couldn't hold it any longer."

I told Heather's friends that the dining room was less than a quarter full. While Wanda chatted with Heather, I crossed kitty-corner to where Laurie watched from beside a street lamp. Her dark eyes were large and sad.

"Hey, I just wanted to do it alone—thought it was safer."

"Wanda went too."

"She was using their restroom. We ran into each other."

"You're lying." Her lower lip jutted out.

What did she suspect? I looked over the buildings towards the sunset. The yellow had faded to a burnt orange. "You're right." I motioned for her to walk beside me. We went a block and crossed the next intersection. "*Swear* to keep it a secret?"

She nodded.

"Wanda doesn't want *anybody* to know. You have to swear."

Again the nod.

"She works at Rudy's."

Laurie halted.

"You were right about the job," I said. "She looked everywhere for something on Saturdays only, and Rudy's was all she found." I gave a true account of stopping to use the can some weeks back, true except for the part about what Wanda was doing.

I had come to know Laurie's face well, and she bought the story hook, line, and sinker. Why wouldn't she? Wanda having a job had been *her* idea, and it being at Rudy's made Wanda's and my secrecy all the more plausible. And it explained my determination to get to the restaurant quickly and alone. Spy versus Spy versus Spy. Was there something on the lesbian gene that made us wizards at deception? Or did social forces hone such skills?

More pro forma than sullen, Laurie asked, "Why didn't you tell me?"

"The secret wasn't mine to tell."

"You sound like my brother Will."

"Hey, no need to hurl insults—accuse me of sounding like a lawyer."

Sally and everybody wanted to skip both the demonstration and Peg O's, and we fifth-ed and sixth-ed the motion. I didn't try to find a reason to ride back in the truck, since Laurie might get suspicious all over again.

The conversation in Flying Fritzie on the way home was lively. Heather's reputation was reinstated to that of her pre-defection days, and Chase's relegated still further into the abyss. Nobody mentioned Wanda, which convinced me that only Laurie had followed me as far as the restaurant.

Rubella was already parked when we turned the driveway corner. Once we got out, I whispered to Laurie that I wanted to reassure Wanda nobody had seen her. I hurried inside the house, clambered up the stairs, and bolted down the hall. Stopping short of the cul-de-sac, I called out, "Hey, can I come around?"

"Andy?"

"By my lonesome."

Wanda's face was tear-streaked. I kept my voice low. "You guys didn't break up or—"

Her ringlets shook. "I'm going to miss him. I know it's silly, and he loves me, but the end of February is a long time."

"And I'm guessing there aren't too many phone booths up in the Andes. Look, I'm sorry, but I had to tell Laurie—no, not about him. She saw us come out of Rudy's and was suspicious, so I said you work there."

Wanda's forehead wrinkled. "What did she say?"

"She suspected you had a job, from the new clothes and going into Madison every Saturday. I said I'd run into you there once when I dropped in to use the can, and today I ran there to warn you. So it all hangs together. Don't think anybody else spotted you except Heather and company."

Her forehead smoothed. "You better tell her I quit. I won't be going anymore."

"That's right. I'll say you got too disgusted. That it wasn't worth the cash."

"Thanks so much, Andy."

"Hey, March will be here before you know it."

Wanda's eventual departure got me to thinking more about an off-farm job, but the outside world was proving such a downer, being holed up at Geserenie seemed preferable. For starters, in early November some cult leader persuaded hundreds of followers to move to a remote area in South America and then kill their kids and themselves by drinking poisoned punch.

Possibly rhetorically, Wanda asked at supper, "How can people do that to their own children?"

"They crave an authority figure," Chloe said, "someone telling them how to live."

And the month ended with some hetero male assassinating Harvey Milk and the Mayor of San Francisco. Sally brought home a *New York Times* from work, and I pored over the articles from start to finish, feeling guilty I hadn't known more about Milk when he was alive. I tried giving Stacy a call, figuring it'd be an even huger deal out there, but she wasn't home.

Every night, practically, I hit the parlor to listen to records, usually till one or two in the morning. It was the only time the house felt like it belonged to just me or me and the few folks I wanted to share it with. Laurie sometimes lasted till midnight. The newbies had added a bunch of good albums to the record collection, but that was about all I was ready to say on their behalf.

Wanda'd given me a heads-up to watch for a thin blue envelope when Laurie and I did our daily walk to the mailbox, and today I'd spotted one and managed to smuggle it into my coat pocket. Later, I ran it up to the alcove. Wanda grabbed it from my hand faster than you could say Pony Express.

It was almost midnight when Laurie bade her reluctant goodnight by the parlor door. Wanda surprised us both by slipping in behind her. "I can't sleep," was all she said, carrying her beer to a futon. I had to smile, figuring she was busting to talk about Luke's letter.

I was right—not a minute after Laurie had closed the parlor door, Wanda began telling me about his arrival in Peru. She went upstairs not long after, but I lay down and got wasted again with Jimmy Buffett. When Dylan started knock, knock, knocking on heaven's door, I accidentally knocked over my beer, spilling enough to soak through to my underwear. I took off my jeans and everything and lay back down, covering myself with blankets.

My clothes were still damp when I awoke and put them back on. Passing through the living room towards the stairs, I could see folks at the dining room table—was it lunchtime already?

"Laurie around?" I called over.

"She's up talking to Chloe," Gertie said.

Laurie *wasn't* in the attic; she was lying on her stomach in bed. She lifted her torso, turned, and looked over her shoulder when I came in. She'd been crying.

I closed the door. "What's the matter?"

She raised herself into a sitting position. The tissue box had been moved nearer, and she grabbed a tissue and blew her nose. But before she got a word out, Chloe burst in—without knocking. Ignoring me, she said to Laurie, "I can't go along; I can't keep the secret, not even for a day. That's what I am so mad about. Not at you—I understand why *you* kept it. And you. But her deceit, her dishonesty towards *everyone*, has to be shared. I'll call a meeting as soon as Sally gets home." She left as abruptly as she'd barged in.

"Hey, what's going on?"

Laurie picked up the crumpled tissues on the bed and dropped them in the basket. "Why should *I* be the one who has to leave," she said.

"Leave?"

"How *stupid* do you think I am?" Her eyes narrowed into slits.

"I mean it, I don't get—"

"*I'm* not going."

"Look, I *really, really* don't understand what you're talking about."

"You and Wanda," she hissed.

"Me and Wanda? Me and Wanda *what?*"

"Are lovers."

"What?"

"Are lovers."

"Jesus Christ!" I strode to the window and jerked up the bottom sash, letting in some mighty crisp December air. "You're nuts, you know that?" I grabbed my pack of cigarettes, took one out, and lit it. "What's wrong with you? How do you dream this stuff up? So now I've got to go tell Chloe I'm not having an affair with Wanda?"

"That's not what I said. Why were you sleeping there and your clothes off?"

I pointed to the good-sized stain on my pants. "Because I spilled my beer and was too drunk and tired to haul myself upstairs."

"I don't believe you."

Smoking furiously, I exhaled through the open window. When I crushed the butt out in the ashtray, I raised the window higher and fanned the air, then slammed the sash down. I went and sat on the chair. Hunching over, elbows on knees, watching the floor, I spoke so slowly I could hear my own words. "If you dare say anything to *anybody*—Chloe, Gertie, PJ, *anybody*—I'll be out of here so fucking fast, you won't know what—Wanda is leaving in February. She's going to North Carolina to be with Luke, the submarine guy. Mitchell's younger brother. When he gets back from Peru."

I looked up in time to catch Laurie sucking in a smile. An instant later, her eyes widened in horror like I was a corpse back from the dead. "I didn't know," she wailed, "I didn't know, I didn't know. I'm sorry, I'm sorry."

"I'm just saying if you ever *do* breathe a word—"

"I won't, I won't." Her face grew red and contorted; her eyes were little mud puddles. She hobbled forward on her knees, grabbed my shins, and burrowed her nose into my pants leg.

I un-gripped her arms. "It's okay. As long as—"

She sat back, her arms out to brace her body. "I told Chloe she worked at Rudy's."

"What—"

"I wanted her to go. I thought you were lovers. You *said* she worked—"

"So you wouldn't suspect about Luke!" It took all my strength to keep my voice low. "Rudy's is where they'd meet, the only safe place, where nobody'd see them. I happened to, like I said, going in to use the can. I knew they were there when Heather and everybody were going to picket, so I ran ahead to warn them."

"I believe you," she yowled and again threw herself down, sobbing, this time clutching my ankles.

I rose and shuffled free without kicking her. "Fat lot of good that'll do Wanda."

"I'll tell Chloe it was all a mistake."

"You better—"

A knock. Laurie quickly got to her feet. I opened the door.

This time Chloe had the decency to wait. Arms folded, she remained in the hall. "I thought you would be interested to know, Laurie, because I know how guilty you feel, that when I confronted Wanda and asked for an explanation, she said where she works is *her* business. I pointed out that the issue is not that Rudy's serves meat and veal in particular, but that she knew her housemates would feel betrayed. Her answer? None. *Not a single word of apology.* So don't cry over *her*. She hasn't been losing sleep over *you*." Chloe turned on her heel and left.

I shut the door. "Nobody had to know a thing—she could've hung on till February and parted friends. Now they're going to kick her—"

"I'll do anything, *anything*," Laurie wailed.

"Like what?" I stormed out.

The halls were empty. I went towards the cul-de-sac and knocked on the wall. "It's me, Andy."

"Okay," Wanda said.

An open suitcase lay on her bed. The shelves of the cool cubbyhole cabinet were empty. "Look, I need to explain. Laurie thought we—you and I—were shacking up, so she told Chloe what I'd said about you working at Rudy's, so you'd get kicked out."

Wanda craned her neck to peer over my shoulder. Laurie came forward, her chin lowered, saying, "I got paranoid and crazy and thought—" Her glance darted to the suitcase. She went over and picked up a stack of photos. "Is this him?"

"His confirmation."

"And this, in uniform, it must be recent."

Wanda nodded. At that moment you could have mistaken them for friends.

I spent the afternoon alone in the parlor listening to records and getting stoned—Laurie must've told everybody not to mess with me. She stuck her head in when Sally got home to say Chloe called a meeting before supper about Wanda.

"Couldn't they wait till later," I said. "Do something *fun* in the meantime. The desert island thing."

I finally slogged into the living room. Wanda wasn't there. Chloe said, "Now we can get started." Laurie scooted over on the couch to make more room for me. I sat beside her, not wanting to escalate the war. Silence loomed like a mushroom cloud.

"As everyone *now* knows," Chloe said, "Wanda worked at Rudy's. She has hid that fact ever since—"

"Hey, she quit."

"Why does it matter if she quit?" Gertie asked. I'd say this for Gertie, she was genuinely curious—no rhetorical questions in *her* bag of tricks.

"If that's not bad enough," Chloe continued, "she has only *grudgingly* given up her kitchen duties, only *grudgingly* allowed Gertie to cook. Her excuse has always been that she has no money—"

"Hey, she never hid the fact she has savings."

Laurie chimed in, "She just didn't want to use them because—"

"She didn't have to!" Chloe glared at both of us. "She was working at Rudy's!"

Sally said, "To think that every time she told us she was going shopping, she was lying to our faces."

"And going to *Rudy's*!"

"Does anyone want to make a motion?"

"I move Wanda be told to move out."

"Second."

"Any more discussion?"

I stood up. "Doesn't she get to defend herself? Roberta's rules—"

"She doesn't want to. That's why she drove into Madison: to look for a place."

"All in favor?" Chloe asked. "Against?" I raised my hand. "The motion passes."

"Do we give her a deadline?"

"I move we give her a deadline of two days."

"Second."

"You can't make her leave right away," I shouted. "She's got no place to stay."

"She's had ever since she started at Rudy's to find a place. She knew we'd ask her to leave if we found out. She can't expect *us* to wait because *she lied* for so long."

Heads were nodding. Barking, "I vote *no*," undoubtedly out of order, I strode into the kitchen, grabbed my parka, yanked on my boots, and went outside.

It was overcast, and the clouds to the north looked ominously like snow-haulers. I paced back and forth by the pasture fence to keep circulation in my toes. To the southwest, the sky brooded a dolorous purple. The fields were silent, birdless, cricketless. For the first time I could remember, the stillness brought no peace.

Headlights caught me—it was Rubella. Wanda parked and came around the back holding cardboard boxes.

"Any luck?" I asked.

"I called Mitchell. Did you meet Carolyn? She said I could share her room. We both thought—Mitchell and I—it would be nice to get to know each other better." She smiled wistfully. "Luke will be glad."

I dreaded mentioning the deadline. "When will they let you move in?"

"Tonight. I already filled the suitcases. These cartons should hold the rest."

"Look, I'm really sorry."

"It's okay."

"No, it's not."

I helped carry down the suitcases and cartons. Before you could say *Happy Trails*, Wanda was back up in the cab. "I hope things go well for all of you," she said.

"Don't know that I'll be here much longer myself. It's not the same."

"I thought Laurie would never leave."

"Doubt she will. Guess you could say we've run our course too."

Wanda started the engine. "I hope our paths cross again."

"Hey, if I'm ever in North Carolina, you can be sure I'll look you up. And tell that Luke of yours—he's one helluva lucky guy."

Wanda smiled. "Take care, Andy." Shifting into gear, she closed the door, made a U-turn, and was gone.

Chapter 37

FOR SEVERAL MINUTES I lay in bed motionless, listening, hearing only the creaks of an old house. When I did rise and go to the window, it was on tiptoe. Pushing aside the fleece, I saw no new snow had fallen. The fields lay inert in the morning mist. The bottoms of the boards along the north side of the barn were dark with dew. Goodbye, Mr. Wiffle, wherever you're lollygagging. Steer clear of the sausage factory, my good man.

I dressed in layers: T-shirt, flannel, sweater, two pairs of socks. I retrieved the dusty journal from the closet shelf and laid it on the bottom of the backpack. Somehow I managed to cram in the denim jacket, all my jeans, the Phillies cap, and most of my sweats, shirts, underwear, and socks. I wore the Bacchus necklace underneath the layers. The sneakers got tied together and hung through the strap. I half-hid the pack on the far side of the bureau.

Returning from the bathroom, I hooked back the fleece and cracked the window for a final smoke. Laurie must've heard the toilet flush, because now she cautiously opened the bedroom door. Her face had eager-to-please written all over it. "I put on fresh coffee," she said. "Chloe and Gertie are upstairs, and the others have gone to Moonsilver. But PJ could come home soon."

In other words, for now it was safe to go downstairs. Because they were pissed, or I was? "Thanks," I said. "Was thinking of taking some time to myself."

"I can do my yoga in the parlor. I'll—"

"Don't mean just for a few hours. A lot's been happening, and I need some space to pull it all together."

Her expression offered a fleeting glimpse of Chicago Laurie: young, sweet, open. "Do you want the alcove?" she asked. "No, I'll take it; you can have this."

That's right, the alcove was empty now. I blew smoke down towards the narrow window opening. "Was actually thinking more like a couple of days off-farm. Get some distance from everybody. Yesterday, well, there was a whole lot of anger …"

She did a decent job of reining in the panic. Maybe my tone warned that the more heated her reaction, the colder mine. Our relationship was teetering on the edge of a cliff, as she saw it, and one wrong move could push it over. She bit her lip, then burst out with, "The motel, the Bus Stop. You could stay there. I'll pay for it. They have kitchens. I'll pack a box of food. When PJ gets back, I'll ask if I can borrow Fritzie."

I pictured the low building with the neon *TV, Kitchenettes*, and, invariably, *Vacancy*. Had Wanda and Luke used it for trysts? It was near the gas station where Laurie had picked me up on my arrival in Wisconsin. Decades ago, that seemed. It now occurred to me they didn't name it the Bus Stop in honor of Marilyn Monroe or what's-his-name Inge.

"Not a bad idea," I said. "I could catch up on sleep. Things might calm down around here in the meantime."

Laurie nodded enthusiastically and took a bunch of bills from her wallet and placed them on the bureau top. Yes, she would lobby hard for them to excuse my behavior over Wanda's eviction.

"I should probably take a few days' worth of clothes," I said, "just in case. Don't want to shell out for laundry."

"I'll make sandwiches and pack milk and juice. And beer."

"Just a sandwich will be okay. I'll need some exercise and can walk down to the gas station."

"It's a rip-off."

"It'll just be for a day or two."

She went down to the kitchen, and while I was supposedly packing, I scanned the bedroom for anything I'd forgotten. The price of avoiding a scene was what I would leave behind: the bureau photos, the stuffed aardvark, the Inca bowl, her drawings of me. Maybe I wouldn't have taken them anyway.

Returning from the bathroom, toothbrush in hand, I heard Flying Fritzie's clanks. I waited in the bedroom till PJ's steps creaked on the stairs and along the hall.

When I went down, Laurie was sitting on a bench in the kitchen staring at the floor, Fritzie's key on the table near her hand. I placed the pack where she couldn't see it well. While I drank my coffee, my eyes did an inventory of the everyday details that would soon be relegated to memory: Mother Hen and her chicks, the cast-iron stove, the utensils and copper pots hanging from the beams, the glass jars of pasta. How charming a room could look before it became soiled by unkindness.

At the glass door marked *Main Entrance* Laurie shifted into neutral. "I'll wait to make sure they have a vacancy."

"The sign says."

"Just to be sure. You have enough money?"

"Yeah. Probably sleep most of the time. Besides, I'm only going to pay for one night to start."

"Give a wave if it's all right, if they have a room."

"Okay. See you Saturday or Sunday. I'll call."

As I entered the small lobby, a short man with glasses peered up. No Norman Bates, he. "Can I help you?"

"When's the next bus to Milwaukee?"

He glanced at the clock. "Twenty minutes. I'd go out in ten."

I waved out the window. Laurie waved back and slowly pulled the van onto the road. "Thanks."

I bought a postcard and stamp, not wanting Laurie to think the guy was lying when he said I took the bus; she could get the cops searching for my body in the fruit cellar. *Decided I needed to change where my life is headed. Going out west to see Stacy. Take care of yourself. Andy.* I stuck the postcard in my back pocket. Maybe I *would* go west.

The driver said to transfer in Monroe, and, having time to kill there, I mailed the postcard. Then I hit a store and bought a magic marker and wrote on a piece of cardboard *CHICAGO*. I got rides pretty easy—before the sun had even tagged the horizon, I was seeing familiar Windy City sights: the white church with the blue minaret, the double-antennaed John Hancock.

After getting dropped on Fullerton, I asked a couple of guys who looked gay if they knew of any women's bars. They told me about one off Halsted, and I walked in to McCartney singing *Jo Jo was a man who thought he was a loner.* Sitting at a table near the door, I nursed a beer, hoping a familiar and friendly face would show. No luck. But the bartender told me about a Y kind of place some blocks east.

It turned out they had a pretty cheap room on the ninth floor beside the elevator shaft. The window looked out on two high rises by the lake and a patch of water in the gap between.

The street below me was still. I spent a long time gazing into the night. Bit by bit the windows of the high rises went dark. The patch of water looked like an inky pool. Some kind of boat with a lone orange light drifted into the pool from behind one building, a small full moon haloed from below by its own reflection. I watched the round orange glow glide slowly behind the second building. Yes, there was a peacefulness in the wee-hours in the city too, the spans of silence interrupted by a bus braking or an engine starting. I tried to picture Laurie and everybody asleep at Geserenie, and Wanda at New Eden, and Stacy way out west. Mathilde and Lorraine and Anthony still in Brackton along with Edward and the Linehans. Where were you, Dean? Anywhere somebody could find you?

And where was *my* next move? Should I hit one or the other coast? Stay in Chicago? Anyway, for now it was enough—it sufficed—to be back, back to where I once belonged.

Chapter 38

"YOU *LIKE* INFLATION? You *enjoy* watching your retirement fund lose value? Andy, how about a refill?"

"It's not Carter's fault—he doesn't run OPEC."

"He doesn't run *any*thing. That's the problem."

"Why are you arguing politics? The election's almost two years away."

The regulars had been going at it most of the afternoon. Occasionally I'd join in the banter, but now I was thinking ahead to tomorrow, my first Sunday off, the day I'd picked to phone Stacy and rib her about how easily I'd gotten hired on at Grateful Fred's.

Fred was a burly guy in his fifties who reminded me of my uncle Anthony. He joked he'd found me in the nick of time, because business had been crazy. A blizzard in December and another in January dumped snow to break records and make the streets impassable, which meant folks were forced to party hard and in their own neighborhood joints. Fred's being just north of Old Town, we made out like bandits.

Finding an apartment near the bar had also been easy, thanks to Fred pestering his customers. And with the zillion hours of overtime during the snow craziness, I'd already repaid the advance he'd given me.

Now the city was returning to normal. Mounds of snow blocked the corners, and slush was everywhere, but buses and cars could navigate. It was amazing how much noise accompanied the resumption of movement, how much the snow had blanketed not just sight but sound. Chains rattled, motors rumbled, horns honked. Even the wailing sirens and screeching brakes were energizing. Headlines screamed about rioting and revolution in Iran, sure, but headlines had screamed bad news since Day One. *EVE BITES APPLE, USHERS IN FALL OF MAN.* Okay, it wasn't *technically* Day One—she wasn't around for most of the first week—but close enough.

"You *do* exist!" Stacy shouted so loud I had to move the receiver away from my ear. "Where are you? Who are you living with? What are you up to?"

"You want me to *answer* any questions or just keep firing them?" It was great hearing that old, familiar laugh. I brought her up-to-date on my move back to Chicago, though without all the whys and wherefores, which I didn't know myself.

"We won't be able to visit for a while," she said.

"Who's this *we*?"

"Long story."

"Then get started."

"It's a guy. I should say 'He's a guy,' but that's redundant."

"Quit the grammar shit. You pervert, hooking up with an XY!"

Again the laugh. The XY's name was Jerry, he was from Grinnell, Iowa, had gotten a doctorate in anthropology, and was waiting to hear about funding for research on some Pacific island. "Tropical populations, tropical botany and zoology, they're very popular among post-docs."

"So the poor penguins get ignored," I said. "Hey, you found somebody who does fieldwork. Just curious: he know your sordid history?"

"In general, but not about Tommy."

The two of us talked for about a year, and right before hanging up, Stacy said Jerry was taking her to a Giants game in April—he was a baseball fanatic. I said I'd be picking up a Cubs schedule one of these days and maybe go to a game when the Phillies came to town.

"Which team will you root for?" she asked.

"Maybe both. That make me bi too?"

Now the Three Mile Island reactor dominated the news, with radioactive fumes escaping and nobody knowing if Hershey's would start selling glow-in-the-dark chocolate. Naturally the regulars at Fred's argued non-stop about nuclear power.

When the TV mentioned evacuating folks, I went home on my lunch break and phoned Mathilde. Getting no answer, I tried my aunt.

"Hey, Lorraine, it's Andy. Just been hearing about evacuations from this Three Mile Island thing and wondering if you all are affected?"

"Good thing Pennsylvania has so many disasters or we'd never hear from you. Last time it was Legionnaires. You want to talk to your mother?"

"She's there?"

"Andy?"

"Hi, Matt. Tried reaching you."

"I've only got a minute—Roy's expecting me. How are you?"

"Fine. I moved back to Chicago. Was wondering if you all were downwind of this Three Mile Island thing."

"I don't think anybody's concerned. Give Sissy your address and phone, and I'll get it from her later."

"Quick, before you go, what's Edward's phone number?"

When Lorraine got back on, I asked if she'd heard of any more escapes from St. Joe's.

"No, but Edith, a gal in Records, her son—*he's* a wild one—he saw Dean at a bar. Didn't know him, just says there's a guy they call Dancing Dean. Always looks like he's dancing when he's had a few. Edith mentioned it because she knew Sissy was married to somebody named Dean. It's not that common—the name."

"*Was* it him?"

"I asked what he looked like, and she asked, and it matches."

Immediately after hanging up, I called Edward. "Hey, I just heard about Three Mile Island and was wondering if you're in your lead bathrobe."

He laughed. "I'm sure there's no radiation here—my apartment is freezing. How are you?"

"Pretty good. Not in Wisconsin anymore—back in Chicago."

"I can tell who you take after, moving around all the time."

"Heard anything from him lately?"

"About a month ago. He's working by the old fairgrounds at that steak—"

"Drake's?"

"Yes."

"As maitre d'?"

"Now I don't know about that."

"How did he sound?"

"Fine. We talked quite a while. He had questions about our mothers and their parents. Being ten years older, I remember more. That happens when you age, Andy; you become interested in the past. You'd be surprised what details come back, memories you'd thought were lost forever."

"The reason I ask is: Lorraine said he's been acting pretty wasted."

"Did she see him?"

"No, somebody told her—"

"At St. Joseph's? I would take it with a grain of salt. The department she's in is a rumor mill."

"You're right. I should take it with a *barrel* of salt. Hey, next time you talk to him, tell him I say hi. I don't suppose you happen to have his address and phone? I'll give you mine."

"Hold on a moment." Edward had a phone number, but I didn't have time for another call.

Back at Fred's, the TV was off, which meant the arguing had gotten too loud. I gave folks refills and began hand-drying glasses.

So Dean got smashed once in a while—what was the big deal? Besides, what's-her-face's son might have exaggerated, or his mother could have, or Lorraine could have, or all three. A variation on that kid's game Telephone, where the message the first person whispers gets ridiculously garbled by the time it reaches the last.

And sometimes an "always" sprang from a single incident. Laurie and I'd had plenty of fights where one of us accused the other of "always" or "never" doing something. When we talked it over, the "always" turned out to be twice, and the "never" boiled down to not-for-a-week-or-two. So the stupid name Dancing Dean could've arisen from a *single* incident.

"Another of the same, Andy."

"Sure enough, Vito."

Maybe his ankle had never healed properly, and he moved funny. "Look, Dean's dancing," somebody might've said, and with the alliteration, somebody else might've turned it into a Dancing Dean nickname. The same thing had happened here to Bellicose Bill and Teddy Kennedy Keller. Plus, Lorraine was wrong about the name being uncommon. And who said it was the guy's *first* name? Could've been the last, like with James Dean and John Dean and a zillion other Deans.

"Better make it a pint, Andy. I have to explain to Bill why you need class action lawsuits."

"I already know: so lawyers can get rich."

"You moron, they make more money handling separate cases. The point of a class action is to spare lots of people from having to prove the same thing over and over again. Once one person proves the car company screwed up, they prove it for everybody."

Vito chimed in, "Yeah, so you don't have to be a millionaire to take on the big corporations."

"That's why they have *contingency fee cases*," Bill drawled sarcastically. "The lawyer doesn't get paid unless you win. Class actions are a different ballgame."

"Both help the little guy," Vito said.

"The little whiners, you mean."

Even the physical description didn't mean much. Dean was five-ten or -eleven, a white male with blue eyes and light brown hair. A thousand men in Brackton fit that. What a load of crock my aunt could cook up.

I opened my recently purchased address book to G. A half-drunk beer and lit cigarette rested on the bedside table. Was the last time I'd seen him the field trip in seventh grade? He'd smiled the second he saw me. Came right over, didn't try ducking around the corner like some other kid's father might've. When he'd mussed my hair, he was genuinely beaming.

I dialed, but after three rings, my hand got cold feet and hung up. Later, another beer under my belt, I dialed again, letting it ring nine times. No answer. After the third no-answer, I decided the Fates were trying to tell me something.

All work and no play would've made Andy a dull girl, so she began hitting the women's bars. A Stacy-like friendship was the most she wanted—the mere *thought* of a sexual relationship set my teeth on edge. And set my Martin Luther King mantra going: *Free at last, free at last, thank God Almighty, I'm free at last.*

I found a few women to shoot pool with and some who liked movies, but the biggest find was two couples from Rogers Park who liked to play poker. Before you could say deuces wild, we had a regular Sunday afternoon game. It was friendly, not cutthroat, and each of us had our peculiarities. I took the longest to decide what to bet or whether to fold, and Katie took the shortest. Joan called lots of wild cards; Anna didn't call draw. And if she stayed in till after the last up-card in seven-card stud, Mary *never* folded, regardless of how crappy her hand. "There's only one more round of betting to go," she'd say, cheerfully tossing her coins in the pot, "so at least I'll know right away." Which killed any chance to bluff. But we were all identical in liking banter, beer, and take-out from their neighborhood Korean joint.

Naturally, the Phillies had to decide that now was a great year to stink, and the Cubs didn't make the play-offs either, so my baseball season ended in September.

In November, Iranian militants stormed the American Embassy in Tehran, and at Fred's our eyes became glued to the TV, watching mobs of angry men with dark beards yell "Death to America." The hostages were paraded blindfolded, looking terrified even with their faces half-covered.

"You can't blame the Iranians," Keller said. "The CIA installed the shahs, and their secret police have been torturing and killing people for decades."

"But the embassy people aren't the CIA."

After some weeks, a number of hostages were freed. At the start of my shift, I raised my cup of coffee in toast. Leaving his glass untouched, Bill said, "They just freed women and blacks. Sounds to me like *discrimination*."

Keller laughed. "*Finally*, Bill, you understand the concept."

"Half a loaf is better than none," Fred grumbled.

Stacy called with good news: she and Jerry were going to Iowa for the holidays, would be visiting some folks in Illinois, and would take the train up to Chicago right before New Year's.

"We'll only have a few hours, so could we meet you at this restaurant his cousin recommended near Union Station?"

"No problem."

"I'll warn you: Jerry will insist on treating. It's not because of male chauvinism—it's because he really wants to meet you."

"Don't care if it *is* male chauvinism—a free meal's a free meal."

Christmas Day, before heading to dinner and poker in Rogers Park, I phoned Mathilde. Edward got on at one point and said Dean had moved to Tennessee, of all places—some resort had offered him a plum job. "He'll let me know his address once he finds a place to live. I have to marvel how he's never lost his sense of adventure, has no trepidation about starting anew."

After hanging up, I wondered: would I be the same? Daughter was a rolling stone; wherever she laid her Phillies cap was her home.

Chapter 39

THE RESTAURANT NEAR Union Station looked like a ground-level rathskeller and was crowded and noisy, but the boisterous commotion was in a holiday-spirit sort of way, not like a rowdy Super Bowl party. Stacy hugged me so tight I almost needed CPR. When we got a good look at one another, I saw the same face—maybe a tad thinner—and the same length hair, though it managed to stay behind the ears better. Small silver studs in the lobes—that was new. The glasses were almost the same. The shit-eating grin hadn't changed one nanometer.

"Jerry Silkman, Andy Gabe. Andy, Jerry."

He was about my height and had dark, wiry hair and an open, friendly face. After being seated, we quickly conferred and agreed on a pitcher, and the waiter recommended one of the German lagers on tap. After shutting our menus, Stacy and I grinned at each other like embarrassed idiots.

Jerry put an end to the idiocy. "Whatever the pitcher's like, it won't be as good as Steve Carlton."

"Hey, she told you my bad habits."

"Thought the Phillies would make it to the Series this year," he said. "What happened?"

"Damned if I know. Three years in a row they win the division, and I have to be living somewhere without a TV. I move back to Chicago and get one, and they stink. Maybe it was for the best; I didn't need to get my hopes up only to be dashed."

The other kind of pitcher arrived, and the waiter took our orders. Though the menu listed prime rib, I went for something less expensive, figuring Jerry shouldn't have to pay for Stacy's past sins.

Before we had a beer each under our belts and some talk of the Giants, the ice had been broken, chopped, and darn near melted. Stacy and I did some reminiscing, and Jerry told me about his plans to do research on some obscure South Sea island.

I said, "She claims you anthropologists only study tropical stuff because you want to do your fieldwork in warm, scenic locations."

"She's right. Although I sometimes kick myself for not specializing in paleo. A friend of mine was part of the dig that discovered Lucy. East Africa's *arid*, not tropical."

"Lucy in the sky with diamonds?"

Stacy explained, "Paleo-anthropology is the study of our sub-human ancestors."

"She *was* named after the song," Jerry said. He talked fast when he got excited. "A young female Australopithecine skeleton—a partial skeleton." Using the back side of a cardboard coaster and a pen he pulled Tommy-like from his pocket, Jerry scribbled with un-Tommy-like speed. When he rotated the coaster, we read *Genus Australopithecus* and *species afarensis*. I said it was cool both names started with an A, and Stacy and I each practiced saying *Australopithecus afarensis* out loud, which wasn't any easier than *she sells seashells*.

After some more discussion of sub-human primates, I told them about several sub-human customers at Fred's, and Stacy talked about her poetry collective and some readings she'd done. By the time the Bavarian cream pie was demolished, I'd decided Tommy couldn't hold a candle to Jerry. Jerry's face lit up like a Christmas tree whenever he looked at Stacy. Or menorah, maybe—I wasn't sure. Whatever he was, it was beyond salvation.

Despite the great visit, we proved lousy at keeping in touch, talking on the phone only a couple of times. Stacy did call on my birthday, and I learned Jerry had gotten funding for his research, but she said breaking it to her father that they were moving to the South Pacific in January wouldn't be easy—not unless she and Jerry got married first.

"Then why don't you?" I asked.

"Grunner-Silkman sounds like a law firm. But if we do, would you come to Hastings for the ceremony?"

"Wild horses couldn't keep me from seeing you in bridal get-up."

"Jerry wants us to wear Hawaiian shirts."

Mathilde and Edward both sent birthday cards. His had a post-script. *Guess who's moved back to Brackton. He's been hired as a concierge of sorts at the country club where he used to wait tables. They remembered him from over 20 years ago.*

The conventions came and went. Reagan got the Republican nomination; Carter, the Democratic; and Anderson was running as an Independent. In September, Fred said he wanted to teach me the beer accounts. On the social front, Katie said a friend moving back to Chicago in December might like to join the poker game, and I said fine, suspecting they secretly wanted to fix the two of us up. My post-Laurie claustrophobia had finally dissipated, and even if the friend and I didn't hit it off romantically, six was a decent number for poker.

But work and play ceased to matter the day the Phillies edged into first place in the Eastern Division. I devoured every form of baseball news: in the paper, on the air and land and sea. Others babbled about Carter, Reagan, and Anderson; I babbled about Carlton, Schmidt, and Boone. If the Ayatollah could've struck out the side during an inning in relief, I'd have helped smuggle him into the country and onto the roster.

The TV was always off at Fred's now—till the election was over—though the minute I got home, I turned on my own. But it was through a phone call from my half-hysterical aunt as I walked into my apartment that I learned we'd finally clinched the division.

"Why don't you go back to New Jersey?" Keller asked. "Get tickets to the World Series."

"The Phillies might not be in it," I said. "First they have to win the pennant. And even if they do, if the pennant race goes to five games, with the Series starting only two days later, I wouldn't be able to give Fred more than one day's notice."

"Go back anyway. You've never taken a vacation."

He had a point. And say the Phillies did win the pennant and went to the World Series: even if I couldn't get a ticket to a game, it would be cool to watch on TV among fellow Phillies fans.

I asked Fred about vacation time and ended up taking two full weeks, starting the weekend before the Series started. That way, I could watch the last pennant games—if the race went to five games—in the privacy of my apartment totally tanked on beer. I bought a plane ticket for the following Monday, the Series starting on Tuesday. But if the Phillies lost the pennant race, I wouldn't blow my entire vacation at Mathilde's. Maybe I'd hit New York first and see some sights. She didn't have to know in advance I was coming East—I'd just show up, like I'd done with Stacy.

Vacation started off on the wrong foot, with Houston leading the pennant race two games to one. Maybe they'd clinch it Saturday, or maybe the Phillies would tie it, in which case Sunday would be winner-take-all.

While in the shower Saturday, my hair in a lather, I thought I heard the phone ring. Whoever it was would have to wait. After getting dressed, I phoned the Rogers Park crew, but it wasn't them. That meant either a wrong number or somebody at Fred's wanting me to sub. What if one of the other bartenders was faking being sick—why should I have to cover for them? It would be worse if it was Fred—he'd promise to keep the TV tuned to the game and pay overtime and tack on extra vacation, and how could I say no after all he'd done for me? I crossed my fingers he'd find another sub, but barely ten seconds later the phone started up again. I ignored it. The damn thing rang almost like clockwork till I unplugged the cord.

Game four was a nail-biter, cuticle-picker, and cheek-chomper, but we beat the Astros—the pennant battle would go the full five games. I plugged the phone in just long enough to call the Rogers Park foursome to say why didn't they come down Sunday to watch Game five and keep me from pulling my hairs out.

Sunday, after everybody showed up and dropped their coats on my bed, I told them to keep the bedroom door closed because I'd plugged the phone in again but didn't want to hear it ringing during the game. And under no circumstances should anybody answer it till the game was over.

Game five made yesterday's seem like a Sunday afternoon on the Island of Quaaludes. The teams leapfrogged over each other score-wise, and to make matters worse, ended the ninth tied. Who wanted extra innings? The Phillies managed to eke out a run in the top of the tenth, but we were so tense that when the Astros headed for the dugout, we couldn't budge from the TV. Katie wouldn't even go into the bedroom to grab a new pack of menthols from her coat, and she was a chain-smoker.

Then the Fates showered sisterly love on the City of Brotherly Love, letting the Phillies win. I hollered, "We're going to the Series; we're going to the Series!" and danced around the room. Joan grabbed a wooden spoon and saucepan and beat time to my shouts while Anna clanged two metal pot covers together like cymbals. Katie ran to get her cigarettes. Only Mary had the sense to take out the champagne.

A minute later, Katie emerged from the bedroom looking like an Astro's fan. I ran over and lifted her up. "If you're out of cigarettes, you can have a whole pack of mine. We're going to the Series; the Phillies did it!"

She didn't smile—she was trying to say something. With the clanging and banging, I couldn't hear, so I set her down and followed her back into the bedroom. She pointed to the bedside table, to the phone receiver on its side. "Aunt Lorraine?" she said.

I raced over. "Hey, Lorraine, we're going to the Series! Can you believe it? They did it! What? Hold on a sec, can't hear. Let me close the door."

Katie closed it for me on her way out. The dim room, the bed piled high with coats, felt too small to contain my exuberance. Connecting with folks back home was *perfect*.

"Andy?" Her voice sounded odd. Was it a bad connection? Instantly she came through clear. "Something terrible has happened. Dean had an accident."

I sat on the edge of the bed and started sliding off a slippery parka. I pushed it aside. "What kind of accident? Is he okay?"

"No, he's not. He died."

Chapter 40

"Sissy's been trying to reach you all weekend. She has to work today. Andy?"

"I'm here. What happened?"

Lorraine broke into her mile-a-minute. Had she been drinking? Probably, if she'd been watching the game. "Saturday, it was, around noon. He fell down the steps at the station. You know, off Bristol? The witnesses—people were on the overpass—they said he could've been meaning to just walk by or else wanted to catch a train. One man says he swayed and lost his balance, but another says he tripped. Happened so quick, nobody was paying attention."

I pictured the one-story brick structure at the bottom, by the cul-de-sac. The iron door handles. The old clock. "How far did he fall?"

"Don't know. Hit his head just right, the doctor said—I mean just wrong. He was unconscious, and the ambulance came, and they tried CPR and took him to St. Joe's, but he never—a freak accident is what it was, a freak accident. One *good* thing: he didn't feel much. The doctor says it was quick, being the head. We're so sorry."

I nodded at the wall.

"The funeral's Tuesday. Can you get home?"

"Yeah."

The bedroom door opened. Anna whispered, "We need to leave soon."

I raised my palm. "Let me call you back in just a sec." I hung up and heard myself say that Dean had died. That was all—I must've been too surprised to say more.

Others came in the room and talked, but the words didn't register, seemed to occur behind an invisible partition. Somebody brought a glass of water, and a lit cigarette was placed between my fingers. The partition came down, and Katie asked if they should call my aunt back. I gestured at the address book. It got handed to me, and I opened to Lorraine's number. Somebody dialed. "I'm a friend of Andy's. She has a reservation on a flight to Philadelphia tomorrow morning."

Who knew how long I sat smoking and sipping water. I pictured the station again but on a mild spring day. Dean had taken me along to pick up some elderly aunt. I'd just finished counting the steps as the train was pulling in. She was very frail, and he had me sit beside her on the bench while he brought the car around. What was her name? Great Aunt Somebody.

Katie said they'd drive me to the airport in the morning. Yes, I was okay. Shocked but not in shock.

The plane ride was a blur. When we landed, Uncle Anthony was waiting by the gate. We hugged, and he took my pack. "This all you have?"

The whole time we walked to his car and exited the airport and maneuvered through traffic, neither of us spoke, though my uncle was never much of a talker. After hitting the state road, I asked how Mathilde was taking it.

"All right. Told Lorr she said some of her goodbye at the divorce." He gestured with one hand. "Emotionally. And Roy—" he began but ran out of words.

"Roy couldn't care less. He living at home again?"

"No, has his own place."

We rode in silence another umpteen minutes, past towns and truck farms and vacant fields, the same old South Jersey. The sky was mildly overcast. Familiar sights and signs popped up: the state institution, the turnoffs to the glass factory and Old Country Road. A billboard showed an inverted hand with splayed fingers on top of an open Yellow Pages. *Let Your Fingers Do the Walking.*

Just walking. It shouldn't be like that—one false step and you're dead. Even if the stairs were ancient, they could've put in an extra railing. Or else something textured at the top to make it less slippery.

"Just curious," I said, "was Dean drunk when he fell?"

My uncle seemed surprised by the question. "Nobody said anything like that."

"Anybody ever suggest the stairs might be unsafe?"

Anthony shook his head.

"You wouldn't happen to know any lawyers?" I asked.

His brow furrowed. "Just the union."

"Think Lorraine might? If somebody's just moseying along the sidewalk, and they happen to slip on something, and there's no railing or anything to grab onto, and they fall down a whole bunch of steps, the city or railroad or *somebody* could be liable. It's not the money. Heck, Dean probably *owed* people money. But maybe it would force them to put in a railing so it wouldn't happen to anybody else."

"Thought there *were* railings."

"In the middle, I mean, not just on the sides."

Anthony pondered a bit. "He had that bad ankle. Lorr tell you—"

"Shoot, it shouldn't matter. Even if he twisted it again, and that made him trip, there should've been *something* to help a person break their fall. Especially if the steps are steep enough that you could hit your head hard enough for it to kill you."

He made no reply. I wracked my brains for what the guys at Fred's had said about lawyers taking cases for free. If you won, the lawyer got to keep some of your winnings; if you lost, that was tough luck all-around, but at least you hadn't shelled out anything. "On contingency," that was it.

"You can sometimes get lawyers on contingency," I said, "which means you don't have to pay them unless you win your case, and then they just get a cut of your winnings. Couldn't hurt for me to talk to one, see if it's worth a try. And if other folks have fallen at the station, you can have what's called a class action."

Anthony still said nothing. Would I need to look for a lawyer in Vineland? Brackton's court just did DWIs, misdemeanors, as best I could recall.

I asked my uncle if his union lawyer might know the name of somebody who did contingency fee cases. Instead of answering, he asked, "Ever hear of Huntington's Chorea?"

"Don't think so. Just North and South. That where Mathilde's working now, a Korean restaurant?" How many folks in Brackton liked kim chee?

"It's a disease. Can make you fall."

"Are you saying Dean had—what's it called—Huntington's Korea?"

"Might've."

Was it an Asian VD? Had he been dating a Korean woman? If she came to the funeral, what would I say?

"Is it pretty common in Korea or Asia in general?" I asked.

"Spelled with a C-H, not a K."

C-H-O-R-E-A. "Well, it's water under the bridge."

Three blocks later, Mathilde's house in sight, my voluble uncle said, "That's right."

Lorraine was the one to open the back door. Welcoming me with a sad face and big hug, she murmured, "So sorry." Asked if I wanted coffee.

"Please. Matt around?"

"In the bathroom, I think." She peered past me. "Where did you put the car?"

Anthony, still holding my pack, wiped his shoes over and over on the doormat. "I'm not blocking her."

"She wants to go to the mall," Lorraine said. "Andy, if there's anything you need, let Sissy know. For the funeral. I don't know what clothes you brought."

"Stuff I wear to work."

"Maybe she can pick up some nicer slacks." Lorraine took my parka and marched off to the coat closet.

I went to the counter and poured myself a cup of coffee, asking Anthony if he wanted any.

"No. I don't know what she wants me to do next."

Lorraine returned. "I heard the toilet flush, so maybe she's almost done."

I wandered into the dining room. The *Brackton Gazette* lay on the table. *PHILLIES TO THE SERIES!* They had a photo of the team whooping it up in the Astrodome after the final out. *Excitement has engulfed not only Philadelphia . . . .*

Lorraine was whispering in the kitchen.

"I *had* to," my uncle said.

"*Why?*"

Try as he might, Anthony's whispers were of the stage variety. "Just he *might* have."

I couldn't catch Lorraine's words, only a hissing sound.

"She's never heard of it," he said.

Another hiss.

"Was asking questions. Wants to sue the railroad because there's no railing. Asked the name of a lawyer."

"*After.* We'll explain *after* the funeral."

Poor Anthony, getting yelled at for nothing. Did they really think I cared how Dean had died? Say he was drunk, or had syphilis and leprosy and cancer and Huntington's Chorea all rolled into one: what difference would it make? Couldn't people get off your case even when you passed away?

The upstairs bathroom door creaked. I placed the newspaper back on the table, picked up my coffee, and headed for the stairs.

Matt's bedroom wasn't large yet didn't seem cramped, containing only a bed, end table, the cherry dresser with attached mirror, and a chair where Dean's bureau used to be. On a bleak day like this, the bedside lamp's soft glow and pale walls and light pink afghan made me think of a nursery at naptime.

Mathilde stood in front of the mirror gently brushing her hair. It hadn't gone gray, or enough was still blond to camouflage the gray. "Andy." She put down the brush and came towards me. We hugged, both of us mindful of my hand with the coffee. She stepped back and asked, "Are you doing okay?"

"Yeah. Don't think it's actually hit yet. How about you?"

"I guess the same." She went to the open closet door. "This your first time in an airplane? I've always wondered what it would be like. They say houses and cars look like ants." She spoke the way she always did, softly and with pauses between sentences.

"I had an aisle seat and couldn't really see."

The near end of the dresser contained the familiar cloth doily holding small cologne bottles—one was the *Chanel* from Stacy's family. Towards the center was a short stack of papers, what looked to be store receipts, maybe a newspaper clipping, an envelope or two. I moseyed over to the row of photographs at the far end. The newer, in color, were probably of Anthony Junior's tykes.

"So what's the plan?" I asked. "For the funeral and all?"

"The service starts at eleven. At Pirelli's. Same place as your grandmother's."

"I didn't go to hers."

"That's right." Mathilde brought a scarf to the dresser, telling my reflection in the mirror, "He felt you were too young. After the service, we drive to the cemetery." She turned to the real me. "I said people could come here after. For something to eat."

"Sure, why not?"

"Edward's place is small, and since you're staying here, it seemed—"

"What cemetery?"

"The national. He was a veteran."

In one of the photos, a grandkid had a smile just like Lorraine's. "Why is everybody so hush-hush about this Huntington's Chorea thing?" I asked.

Mathilde pivoted away and glanced dismally at the brush, maybe forgetting I could see her expression in the mirror. "You know Sissy. Anything to do with the hospital gets her going." One hand forlornly lifted the brush while the other plucked a hair from the bristles. It struck me then how much she'd aged. Maybe it was her still-slender shape that made her look younger than her chronological years. Or the air of calmness, of quiet imperturbability. Calmness had been her friend. If she'd never seemed to experience the excited highs the rest of us did, she also never crashed. Anger, severe or intense moods of any kind eluded her, giving the impression of a girl teetering on the cusp of adolescence but never quite making it over. How could the same parents have produced sisters as different as Lorraine and Matt, night and day?

"I'm going to the mall," she said. "Shelby's puts together trays—cheese and crackers, dips too. For tomorrow."

"With the Series starting, it'll be a zoo."

"Do you have anything to wear for the funeral? I could pick something up."

"I'll come along."

"No, you must be tired. What size are your blue jeans?"

"I brought black chinos."

"How about a button-down shirt and blazer?"

I took out my wallet. "Guess it wouldn't hurt for me to look presentable. Be awkward if Pirelli asked me to leave because I couldn't meet the dress code."

"Don't worry about the money."

"Well, let me know what it comes to. I'm working."

Mathilde handed me a news clipping from the pile of papers on her dresser. "I saved this for you."

Obituaries and Death Notices.

Gabe, Dean, 50, of Brackton, died unexpectedly October 11, 1980. Survived by his daughter, Andrea Gabe, and first cousin, Edward Cavanaugh. Services to be held Tuesday, Oct. 14, 11 o'clock a.m., Pirelli & Sons Funeral Home.

"Can I keep this?" I asked.

"Yes, I cut it out for you. Did you eat anything? I could make lunch before I go."

"I'll throw something together." I carefully folded the clipping and slipped it in my wallet beside the shim card.

Mathilde looked at her watch. "Roy might call. He's supposed to have an interview at the Rip Tide. They want somebody full-time. He's only working twenty-five."

"Job market tight?"

"If you want a living wage. Is that so wrong? If he calls, don't say anything. Especially in front of Sissy. Sore subject. She says he's too fussy."

Lorraine had already whipped up lunch for the four of us, so we sat at the kitchen table and ate. My aunt pestered me with questions about Fred's, and I said this and that and made up some stuff, like him putting me in charge of the beer accounts because he saw me as an investment.

When I asked what all went on at a funeral, Lorraine explained that I would sit in the front row, which was reserved for immediate family. She and Anthony, Matt, Roy, and Edward would be right behind. When the service was over, I'd be escorted out of the chapel and shown where to stand for the receiving line, and when everybody else came out, they'd stop and pay me their respects. Afterwards, we'd go to the cemetery. I'd ride in the limousine, as immediate family.

"Alone?" I asked.

"Yes, only immediate family."

The idea didn't appeal to me, so I said, "Seems like a waste of money. Hey, who's paying for this?"

"Edward," Mathilde said. "He's insisting."

"Shoot, if he's paying, forget the limo."

"It's part of the package," Lorraine said.

"We'll be right behind you," Mathilde added, "the third car."

"Who's in the first?"

"That's the hearse."

What's on second; I-don't-know's on third. Heck, returning to family was supposed to be comforting. But that presupposed your family shared your grief, and Mathilde's family wasn't grieving. Maybe I hadn't exactly started yet, but I knew sorrow was hovering in the wings. It wasn't that they wanted Dean gone, just that it was no big deal—he hadn't been a part of their daily lives for ages. With all due respect, Mr. Donne, the bell wasn't tolling for them. Maybe I should've stayed at the Linehans'.

Mathilde rose. "I better go. Anything else I should get? Besides the food trays and some things for you, Andy?"

"How are we fixed for beer?"

"Anthony will get it," Lorraine said. He rose too.

After they left, I cleared and scraped, and Lorraine washed. I put on a new pot of coffee. Eventually I broke the silence by asking how they'd first found out about the accident.

"Sissy gets a call from Edward Saturday afternoon. The hospital called *him*. Remember the admit with the ankle? He put Edward down in-case-of-emergency. They want somebody local. Edward called Sissy to drive him, to do the ID. Can't drive himself on account of his eye acting up. Big nuisance it is."

I pictured a white-tiled room, a body on a gurney, an old man in a white lab coat folding back the sheet, Matt reflexively averting her eyes. I'd seen way too many movies. Still, it was hardly a task Mathilde would've warmed to. "Why *her*?" I said. "Couldn't other folks have driven him? Or couldn't he have taken a cab?"

"Face might've been messed up worse than it was. Sissy might recognize a mole or remember his dentist. Anyways, she calls me to find out where to go, which entrance and all, once they get to St. Joe's. I says, 'It's easier if I pick you both up and we all go.'"

Lorraine *would* have warmed to the task. "Is that when they told you he might've had this Huntington's Chorea thing?"

She straightened the items on the counter—the salt and pepper, the hot plates, the rack with the mugs—and for a full five seconds said nothing. Then she was like a shaken soda can that, once opened, couldn't stop fizzing. "By coincidence, just by coincidence. Darla, she sees us when we come in and calls to come over and asks what I'm doing—it's not my shift and I'm with Sissy and Edward—and I tell her, and she gets me his chart. I just wanted a peek, see what they put as cause of death. But the ER form wasn't in it yet, so the papers from the ankle admit were on top. One listed the differential. The 'differential diagnosis.' It's not a real diagnosis— people don't understand that. Differential diagnosis is a list of all the diseases you *could* have, before they run the tests to find out which it really is. A list of the *possibilities*. And Huntington's Chorea was on the list and circled. Didn't mean he had it, just that he might. Also listed other things."

"Any of them circled?"

"No. Anyways, we had a long wait because Saturday's short staffed. I ask Darla who's on, and she shows me the schedule, and I see Dr. Wu and remember he's the one got sent the chart the time with the ankle. I borrow Darla's phone and call, and it's another coincidence: he's the one answering. I say I work in Admitting and explain we're there to do the ID, and I say, 'Could you tell me about this differential diagnosis and the Huntington's Chorea they circled?' And he was very, very nice—said if we'd wait, he'd come down and explain."

That *was* nice. Why should he bother, especially for a patient who'd run out on him? Or was he worried the family might sue? *That* was it: we might sue. Sue Wu. Could be a Motown refrain, *soo-oo woo*.

"What did he say?" I asked my now-quiet aunt.

She picked up a sponge and wiped the counter. "Just Huntington's Chorea might be why he fell. And why he hurt his ankle that time."

Made sense: they ran some blood tests, and the Huntington's thing showed up. Sally had said her hospital ran lab tests even on folks brought in unconscious. Which had royally ticked Chase off. *They have no right to run tests without the patient's consent.* But they had to, Sally'd argued, because certain medications in combination with drugs or alcohol could be deadly. *Informed consent* was Chase's phrase. Wasn't that Tommy's too, talking about Tuskegee?

"They ever try to get ahold of Dean?" I asked. "I mean after the ankle admit. Tell him maybe he should be on medicine for the Huntington's Chorea?"

Lorraine put down the sponge. "I don't think—"

"What I'm saying is—okay, maybe his ankle was weakened, even permanently, from the sprain or whatever, but at least he wouldn't have had the Huntington's Chorea on top of it to deal with. It was a double-whammy, the bad ankle and the untreated—"

"There's no treatment."

"Well maybe they could've shown him some exercises to strengthen the muscles or tendons or whatever it is that gets weak. I know somebody who has special shoes—what are they called—orthotics?"

"The disease, it's not like that." Lorraine picked up the sponge and resumed wiping the counter.

"Make you dizzy? If it makes you dizzy, maybe they should've told him to lay off the alcohol. And not walk near—"

"It's the nerves. The nerves don't work, can't control the muscles."

"All the more reason."

She put down the sponge, took the dish towel off the rack and folded it, and hung it on the rack again. "Dr. Wu can explain. He said you should call and make an appointment. Won't charge, he said, just to talk. Gave Sissy his card."

My poor aunt. In her self-important way, she didn't realize Dr. Wu was just being polite to a St. Joe's employee—he had no interest in talking to me. But was I coldhearted for not wanting to learn more details of the disease? Hell, Dean himself wouldn't have cared. *When the old nag limps in last, does it matter if it's hemorrhoids or a broken leg?*

"I don't need to take up his time," I said, "but I could call and thank him for the offer." And ask him if they'd tried to track Dean down to tell him he shouldn't walk near steep drop-offs.

"He said he wanted to talk in *person*."

She spoke with such sadness, I was a little ashamed for thinking she wasn't grieving. Why wouldn't she be? For about a dozen years Dean had been her brother-in-law. Sure, he and her sister had split up, but it wasn't a nasty divorce—Matt had never spoken of him with bitterness. Lorraine *was* sorry; it showed in her face and in her voice. Most of all, it showed in her reticence. The soda had run out of fizz.

I changed the subject slightly. "You happen to know if Dean left a will?"

Lorraine perked right up. "Yes. While we waited to do the ID, Edward says they'd gone to a lawyer. It was already all typed, and Edward just had to watch him sign. You were the only—the *sole*, he says—*sole beneficiary*. He's just executor, the one that files the court papers."

Take that, Carmella! Not that I expected a King Midas fortune—I'd be lucky if he left me enough to pay Edward back for the funeral. Did Dean have another paycheck coming? Life insurance? A bank account? A mattress stuffed with fifty-dollar bills? What about his apartment: was it a year lease? Would I be responsible for his debts? Maybe his lawyer could answer those questions. And ones about suing the train station and hospital.

"You don't happen to know if he was living alone?" I asked.

"Edward said he was."

What would it be like to wander through Dean's apartment, to see the objects that had formed his domestic landscape? Just everyday stuff like his coffee mug, slippers, toothbrush. Would he still have the old shaving bristle with the porcelain handle that had been his father's? What about the black-and-white photos—their wedding pictures, some of me as a baby? I couldn't imagine he put up decorations, considering how often he moved. Would I find, say, an old drawing of mine from kindergarten?

The coffee was done perking. I poured us each a cup. "How's Matt doing, her job and all?" I asked.

"Same. Gets tired. I keep telling her to look for something where she's not on her feet all day. Roy says if she's going to stick with waiting tables, do it someplace with better tips. Course, *he's* one to be giving advice." She rolled her eyes.

When Anthony returned with the beer, I stowed it in the fridge, and the two of them left. Despite all the caffeine, the second I lay on the couch, I fell fast asleep.

The phone woke me, and for a moment I thought I was back in Chicago. Then Mathilde's voice came in a murmur from the kitchen. I got up and went to retrieve my cigarettes.

"Will they keep your name on file? ... That's not stupid. ... Yes, this morning. Anthony got her." She heard me and turned. "Oh, you're awake. Want to say hi to Roy?"

I took the receiver. "Hey, Roy, what's happening?"

"Not much. Sorry about Dean."

"Yeah, well, such is, you know."

Matt took the receiver back. "Listen, I want to show Andy some things I bought for tomorrow. Just be there at ten. And wear your *nice* suit." Looking put-out, she hung up. Was Roy giving her a hard time about having to go to the funeral? Was he worried about missing the game? It wasn't starting till three-something. Shoot, let him stay home.

"You were right," Mathilde said on the stairs, "Shelby's was mobbed. Everybody getting ready for the Series." In her room, she handed me a shopping bag. "I can return anything you don't want."

The dark blazer—it was wool—had space for a sweater or three underneath, but it would do. The white shirt with a button-down collar was baggy enough for a T-shirt under. I offered to write Matt a check, but she said we could worry about it later.

"I also need to pay Edward back for the funeral," I said, "the limo and—"

"He won't let you."

"I'm next-of-kin, and besides, if I'm Dean's sole heir or what-ever, he might've left enough money—"

Mathilde shook her head. She wasn't arguing; she never ar-gued. "I know Edward feels he lost a relation *and* a friend. Maybe they weren't as close as me and Lorr. They were cousins, not broth-ers. And ten years difference. But they never lost touch. Both only-children, only sons. It was a bond."

"He'll come back here after the funeral, won't he?"

"Oh, yes. Before I forget: he wants to know if there's anything you want the minister to say. In particular. He picked somebody that knew your father. So he'll add his own memories. And Edward suggested things. Lorr and I did too. How at Christmas he used to help at the State institution and then the blind. That type of thing."

Presumably the minister had been a restaurant customer—you didn't see many clergy at bars or the track. Or had Dean become more than a Lukewarm?

I said, "Just that he loved being alive. And wanted other people to love it too, to be happy and enjoy themselves. He liked making folks laugh. Wanted friends, strangers, everybody to get a break from their worries."

Mathilde went to the closet and burrowed among the hangers, pulling out a dark skirt. One hand held it up to the light while the other picked off a piece of lint. "When the minister arrives tomorrow, you tell him."

Now a white card topped the pile of papers on the dresser.

Dr. Wayne Wu
St. Joseph's Hospital and Medical Center
Department of Obstetrics and Gynecology
Peri-natal and Genetics Counseling

"This the guy who told you about the Huntington's Chorea? Just Dean's luck, he gets treated by an obstetrician. Hey, you're not going to tell me he had some sort of sex-change operation?"

That coaxed a smile out. Mathilde shook her head.

"Or that he wasn't my—wasn't biologically or whatever you want to call it—the male parent?" The smile disappeared. Her anxious expression was making *me* anxious. Was there some family secret I wasn't clued into? Was Roy's father mine? No, that couldn't be—he'd died before Matt had even met Dean. Was I adopted? Fertilized by a sperm bank donation?

The sternness in my own voice surprised me. "I mean it. I'd rather know now if he wasn't biologically my father."

Mathilde leaned into the closet. "He was your father."

Falling asleep in Roy's room again was no big deal, maybe because the bed was against a different wall and the one I'd shared with Stacy, or maybe because of the catharsis at Geserenie. Before drowsiness completely overcame them, my brain lobes actually had me *looking forward* to the funeral. Not to the rigmarole and religion but to connecting with Dean, locating him, pinning him down. He'd be there, for sure. Unless, of course, he pulled another Houdini.

Chapter 41

PIRELLI & SONS Funeral Home was a short, gray structure in the middle of a block of empty lots. The building had no windows, and only the dark green awning with the name gave it away. Uncle Anthony let us out in front so we wouldn't get drenched in the downpour.

The father Pirelli and a replica son met us at the door. Both had their shiny jet black hair side-parted in a perfect line. Lorraine said, "Mr. Gabe," and we were led into an octagonal room, an atrium of sorts with a marble floor. I got to have my parka checked, evidently part of the package deal for immediate family. I told Mathilde and Lorraine that Edward should say he was immediate family and get his coat checked too. And I wanted him standing in the receiving line with me. The protocol could bend a little.

Three sets of wooden double doors—one ahead and one each to the left and right—were separated by corridors receding diagonally into who-knew-where, restrooms and offices, maybe. Pirelli-the-father pointed to the double doors on the left. Lorraine peered inside Door number one and motioned for us to follow. The room was actually a small chapel. Gray carpeting sloped down to the front, where a dark lectern faced the pews. Right behind it, a little off to the side and surrounded by flowers, a casket rested on a low

platform. The casket looked eerily small. Dean was around five-ten.
I wanted to pin him down but not in something like that.

We returned to the atrium, and Anthony came in. Roy showed
up wearing a decent suit and tie. The five of us stood together on
the marble floor and gazed unenthusiastically at the shiny paneled
walls, carpeted corridors, recessed shelves with vases containing
too-bright red flowers. Were they artificial? Mathilde kept her gray
raincoat on, holding the plastic hat so it wouldn't drip on her purse.
Anthony looked at his shoes; reflexively, I looked at my boots.
Should have polished them. At least they were black.

Roy asked if the casket would be open or closed, and Mathilde
said closed. Was that the custom or was his head too bruised? How
would we know it was really him inside? Could be some little old
lady. Or somebody's pet collie. Maybe the casket was their floor
model, a demo.

"I'm going out for a cigarette," Roy said.

"Not in front," Mathilde told him. "Don't smoke where people
are coming in."

"I don't want to get rained on." He walked down one of the
diagonal corridors.

My uncle said, "Rain's supposed to stop."

Lorraine nodded. "I heard Philly is dry."

"Only in the weather sense today."

Who else would show? If old Mrs. Linehan was still alive and
brought some of her brood, then with Anthony Junior and Sharon,
we could fill two rows. Would the staff at Drake's come? What about
other places Dean had worked? How many of them even knew?
Damn, I really didn't want the chapel to be empty, even though
Dean himself wasn't in a position to see.

Young Pirelli came down the corridor looking like he'd been to a
funeral. Roy came down the other corridor and immediately went to

him. Pirelli pointed over his shoulder, and Roy re-joined us saying, "There's a place out back with an awning, if you want to smoke."

Lorraine frowned—maybe she thought he was being disrespectful. Which made *him* frown. Shoot, formal ceremonies were hard enough without folks bickering. Since I wouldn't have minded a cigarette, I said I'd go with him if he waited a little while.

Roy seemed placated. He gestured at the polished wood doors and walls, marble floor, vases. "How'd you like to work in a place like this? Worse than a church."

"Reminds me of *Let's Make a Deal*," I said. "I want to know what's behind doors two and three."

He folded his arms and grinned. "Wonder what embalmers get paid. How much training they need. Guess how to inject—"

"What a thing to talk about!" Lorraine snapped.

"You happen to see a water fountain?" I asked Roy.

He pointed. "Past the restrooms."

I headed up the corridor. The emptiness of the place was getting to me. On-and-off since the airplane flight, I'd been imagining funeral scenarios—drawn from movies, TV, books—and each had its twin version in which none of Dean's friends showed up. Could I blame them? Most were probably just drinking buddies. Folks he owed money to and now wouldn't repay. With the World Series starting, they probably figured there was no point in getting mired down at some somber service. All the same, it pissed me off. So he wasn't perfect, and maybe he was a lot less perfect than a lot of other people. He wasn't a model husband or model anything. Still, he had a friendly smile for just about everybody. Not a mean bone in his body. They could come and pay their respects, get to the bar an hour late one lousy day of the year.

I returned to the octagonal room. Ah, his friends *were* showing up. A large group arrived at once, maybe a dozen or more, in dark coats, several of the women wearing scarves on their heads. Would it be in bad taste for me to go over and introduce myself? Should I wait till the receiving line to find out who they were, how they knew him? Pirelli Senior popped out from somewhere and shook hands. He walked over and opened Door number three; several of the women peered inside. Okay, not our party.

More people arrived, and the atrium lost its cavernous feel. Some folks carried umbrellas; others, raincoats and hats; all wore serious expressions. Amid the white faces, an occasional black or Hispanic or Asian appeared. There was no real dividing line, but I got the impression the majority of folks were heading into Chapel number three because they drifted towards a group with an elderly woman, yet a few nodded at Mathilde. Ours wouldn't be completely empty. I spotted a few kids here and there, the boys looking as uncomfortable in their little suit get-ups as I felt in my get-up.

Lorraine returned from her reconnaissance mission to report that Door number three was just a viewing. How many folks went to a viewing? Would it draw more than Dean's actual funeral? I hit the restroom.

When I came back to the atrium, Mathilde hurried over. "The minister was here, but I didn't see you. I told him what you said. About how he loved life and wanted to make other people feel it too. He'll be back in a little bit if you want to add more."

I told her that was pretty much it. Was that Edward? No, the hair was too dark. Some redheads congregated in the corner, but I wasn't sure they were Linehans. Where was I supposed to stand for the receiving line? That would be cool, people paying their respects. Maybe the ritual and rigmarole at funerals wasn't such a bad idea, even if you weren't crazy about ceremonies in general. The concept of setting aside time to mourn with other mourners, not at home but in public—yes, yes, that was it. Time was set aside for *public* remembrance. My brain lobes had been trying to pinpoint what I was hoping for, and now they'd succeeded. Getting visitors, flowers, cards would be nice, would bring some measure of comfort, but a public service provided something special. We would sit together and listen, as a *community*, to Dean's virtues spoken out loud. Sure, he didn't perform great acts, wasn't a war hero, but even the lilies of the field, right? Today I would sit among other people and hear described out loud his fun-loving, genial nature, his sense of humor, his optimism, and everybody—even if we didn't add up to a full dozen—would know the truth of it, would remember the human being that was Dean Gabe.

I stood a little taller. The itchy wool blazer and starchy shirt weren't as uncomfortable now—the uniform was part of the ritual. Each new person coming in set off a small burst of sympathy in me, whether they were here for Dean or the mystery corpse behind Door number three. Being Dean's *only* immediate family was an honor, a huge honor. I'd phone Stacy later because of all people she'd appreciate the irony of me eager for a minister's sermon. If the dude needed to throw some God and Jesus into the mix, so be it. I'd be getting the kind of solace *I* needed; let others get what *they* needed.

"Ready for a cigarette?" Roy asked.

"You better go now if you're going," Lorraine said.

I followed him down the corridor to a red Exit sign. He held the door open, and I stepped out onto a platform. An awning ran the entire thirty or so feet, protecting us from the rain, which was coming down hard. Closing the door behind us, Roy asked if I wanted some weed. I shook my head. This sense of belonging to the larger world, of wanting to pay proper respect, had lifted me to a higher plane. Let Roy have the family black sheep role all to himself.

I lit a cigarette and tossed the match down the three feet to the driveway. This must be a loading dock. Roy lit his joint and held it towards me, but I shook my head. The gutter at the end of the awning was spouting water vigorously onto the platform. I inched closer to the wall so my boots wouldn't get splattered.

"You don't get high anymore?" he asked.

"I do. Just don't feel like it now."

A minute later, the rain ceased abruptly, like a switch had been hit. Two crows landed in the street and picked at a cardboard burger box. They tried ripping it in half, one at each end. Could birds digest cardboard? Was it cardboard or styrofoam?

"How long you staying?"

"Not sure," I said. "Probably go to Dean's apartment tomorrow, check out his stuff. Maybe meet with the lawyer who wrote the will, tie up loose ends like that."

"He leave you a lot of money?"

"Doubt it. Doubt he had much money."

Roy made some chuckling sound. "What about life insurance?"

"Haven't a clue. Just hope he didn't leave behind debts, or left enough money to cover them." I inhaled and exhaled a smooth stream of smoke. "Need to pay Edward back for the funeral. And don't know if the ambulance folks or St. Joe's will send a bill."

"St. Joe's sure will." Roy, the Sage of South Jersey, nodded sagely. "They sent Dennis's family a whopper when his brother OD'd. Not just the hospital—doctors too. His mom was going to pawn her fucking wedding ring till Dennis got ahold of a lawyer. Threatened to sue the pants off. *That* shut 'em up."

One of the birds grabbed the box and flew up to the phone wire. Take that, Brother Crow!

"He charge much?" I asked. "The lawyer?"

"Hundred, I think." Roy drew deep on the joint.

What if Dean's lawyer wasn't the kind who sued people? Laurie's brother never did courtroom stuff. "Guess it wouldn't hurt for me to get his name," I said.

"But wasn't Dean DOA? Or you thinking of fighting the ambulance bill?"

"Not thinking of fighting *any* bill. Just seems to me St. Joe's should've made some effort to track Dean down and tell him about the Huntington's Chorea."

"They told you about that?" Roy sounded surprised. He hurled the roach into the puddle between us. The embers sizzled loudly. "Why'd they give me this big lecture not to say a *word*?"

"Who?"

"Ma and Lorraine."

Was it worth the effort to explain that not everybody wanted to hear the gory details of a close relation's death? Rhetorical question, Jiminy. "Beats me," I said.

Roy lit a cigarette. "You think he was lucky, dying that way?"

"*Lucky*? No, I don't think he was *lucky*." I flicked my ashes. The absconding crow returned with the box, and the two eyed it as if now it didn't seem so appealing. I should go in—Edward had probably arrived.

"I mean before the shaking and jerking and going insane. You might've been too young to remember."

Letting my cigarette fall onto the platform, I pressed it out with my boot and kicked it below. "Too young to remember what?"

"Dean's mother."

"*She* had Huntington's Chorea?"

"You said they told you."

"Not that *she* had it. She give it to him?"

Roy shrugged and inhaled on his cigarette.

"Is it some kind of infection?" Sally'd said they put drops in babies' eyes when they were born because the mother could transmit VD to them in the birth canal. Was Huntington's Chorea one of those? Back in '29, they might not have known about it, so Dean could've caught the infection when he was born. Did Grandma Margaret have VD? *That* would explain everybody's acting weird.

"Is it some kind of infection?" I repeated.

Roy scratched the back of his neck and took another long inhale on his cigarette. Then he exhaled extra slowly.

"Quit the bullshit, Roy. Is it an infection or isn't it?"

"No."

"Then how did Dean get it?"

"Inherited it."

Pirelli Junior appeared in the doorway. "The service is going to start."

Roy dropped his cigarette and walked towards him, calling over his shoulder, "It's only a 50 percent chance, not a hundred." He followed Pirelli inside.

Now it was Lorraine in the doorway. "Come, they're ready."

Reluctantly, with one final glance at the burger box, I went in.

The octagonal atrium was empty except for my aunt. Young Pirelli came through our chapel door, organ music rolling out with him and echoing off the marble. The instant the door closed, the music ceased.

"Hey, Lorraine, let me ask you something."

"Remember, you sit in front. Edward and us will be right behind you. Mr. Pirelli, he's going to escort you down."

"This disease," I said, "this Huntington's Chorea, Roy said it's inherited."

Lorraine glared fiercely at the chapel. "We'll talk later at Sissy's."

She started towards the doors, but I grabbed her arm. "Dean seemed all right when I was a kid. How could he suddenly get it, if it's inherited?"

She tried tugging free, but I held fast. "They don't show symptoms," she said, "till they're older."

"Can *I* get it?"

She nodded her head towards the chapel. "Back at Sissy's. I'll explain."

I clutched her arm tighter. "*Can I get it?*"

"Yes," she whispered. "But you might not. Half don't."

"How do I find out?"

"That's why Dr. Wu wants to talk."

"I don't know how much the test costs, but can they do it here, at St. Joe's, before I go back to Chicago?"

"There's no test."

"Then how do I find out?"

Lorraine looked away. "You have to wait."

"For what?"

"Symptoms."

"What do you mean? When would I get them?"

She shook her head at the wall. "They don't know. Might take twenty years."

My hand loosened its hold. Lorraine took a deep breath and now spoke in her normal, matter-of-fact voice. "There's no reason to think you're going to get it. Just as likely you won't. And besides, they might have a cure by then. Come, they want to get started."

Young Pirelli opened the chapel door, the organ played, and my aunt went in. He continued to hold the door for me and, not knowing what else to do, I approached. At the threshold, he held out a bent arm, and I linked mine limply through. Like a bride and her father, we proceeded slowly down the aisle. I glanced up from the carpet once midway and once when we reached the bottom. The first time, I saw the room was packed. Faces turned towards me—young, old, male, female, white, black, shades of tan. At the moment the suit arm unhooked from mine and guided me into the empty pew, my peripheral vision detected shapes and colors nearby: a swath of redheads and, closer, somebody with an eye patch. I sat alone in the front pew—me, the sole beneficiary.

When the organ stopped, the minister began to speak. God this and God that, verily this and verily that. I didn't pay much attention; I had my own book of revelations to contend with. Fifty percent says I won't—fifty percent says I will. No way to tell.

The crowd seemed to press forward, as though the minister tendered hope. "In our sorrow, we are reminded of the briefness of our sojourn here. 'Lord, make me to know mine end,' David says, 'and the measure of my days, what it is; that I may know how frail I am.'"

Frail—that was the least of it. I remembered hearing about my grandmother throwing things—her arms jerking. She drooled. Her eyes didn't focus. She couldn't walk. She got dementia. Was injuring the ankle Dean's *first* symptom, or were there earlier? Something to do with pruning shears. Dancing Dean: when was that?

"But what do the Psalms tell us further? 'Make a joyful noise unto the Lord, all ye lands. Serve the Lord with gladness; come before His presence with singing. Know ye that the Lord, He is God; it is He that made us.'"

"Amen," they chorused behind me. Easy for *them* to say—for them, the tragedy was over. It was catharsis-and-move-on time. *They* didn't have to worry about turning a corner and running smack into a monster: their own deteriorating selves.

I could feel their eyes on the back of my head, sense them wondering if inside my skull a genetic time bomb ticked. "Poor

Andy," they were thinking, "she could be next. A fate worse than death." I hated them, hated them all, not only Roy and Mathilde but everybody I'd ever known. Each object King Midas had touched had turned to gold; each person my thoughts touched turned to black bile. The Rogers Park group and Fred and the bar crowd and Stacy—Stacy, with her open-ended contentment.

"We are gathered here today … "

Keeping my eyes on the carpet, I rose. Take it slow—don't let them think the shaking has begun. At the end of the pew, I turned and carefully put one foot ahead of the other, pacing myself, eyes still lowered. The minister kept droning. When I reached the top of the aisle, somebody opened the door, and I stepped into the empty, marble-floored room. The door closed, cutting off the minister's voice. I went up the diagonal corridor to a red neon Exit.

Cold rain battered me. I walked quickly, arms clutched across my chest, hands tucked into armpits. A block down, a bus at the curb puffed smoke. I ran.

Car after car sped by, many decorated in red: red streamers tied to antennas, red dashboard junk, red paint sprayed on trunks and hoods. Drivers honked; passengers in red baseball caps smiled, waved, and gave the V sign.

Finally, an old pick-up signaled and pulled onto the shoulder. The window lowered, and an old man leaned out. "How far you going?" he asked. "I'm headed to the hinterlands in Maine, but Fritz here—" he patted the steering wheel—"can't move too fast."

"That's okay. Thanks." I ran around, climbed up into the cab, and shut the door.

Book Two

Chapter 42

"Move or I'll call the cops!" Seconds later the roaring lion purred, "Come in, ladies. We have a fresh shipment of Italian purses." High heels stepped around me. "I'll have you arrested!"

Rising and clutching my coat closer, I trudged to another store. This entryway was shallower, so the gusts got under my pants legs and froze my shins. The next was deeper but stank of piss. I braced for a blast and hurried past two with grates. Damn wind. The entrance to the liquor store went back four feet so I huddled there. It wasn't open yet. Candy wrappers, shreds of newspaper, plastic bags had blown in, but no decent-sized cardboard I could use for a cover. A magazine page advertised: *Lose Weight!* I'd learned how the hard way.

My hands plunged deeper into the coat pockets, an olive-green army issue I'd paid three bucks for at Goodwill by stealing the tag off a sweater. It had kept me warm the first weeks or however long. Now it was no better than a goddamn tissue.

Yet I wasn't going to any homeless shelter—no way was I falling asleep in a room full of strangers, half of whom might be crazy. Till all the guards had come to know me, I had managed to catch short stints at North and South Stations, and once I'd snuck on the Blue Line to the airport. The security at Logan let you be, figuring you were a passenger whose flight had gotten cancelled, but the food cost more and was harder to steal. The woman I traded sentry with at South had told me about a women's center in Cambridge, an Artemiz of sorts, it sounded. She'd never been, would "never cross the river." I was about ready to cross the Styx. Would the women's center tip me off to some Geserenie look-alike where I could crash?

Eventually I located the house with the *Cambridge Women's Resource Center* sign. Beneath it, a smaller sign said that they tried to allow visitors Mondays through Saturdays from noon to three, but sometimes the residents had to study. A tag hanging from the door knob said *Closed*.

It was nowheres near noon, but at least it wasn't a Sunday. You could always tell a Sunday in Boston, with all their stupid blue laws. Did the Lord really want Christians to take a day off from giving the poor a place to get in out of the cold? Guess us meek folks weren't supposed to rest on the Sabbath. But hey, *we'd* inherit the earth. I wasn't holding my breath. And who knew what we'd inherit in the meantime.

I hit some campus or other, hoping to find coffeehouses like at Julesman, or at least a building with classrooms, a place to get warm. My daily routine—scrounging for food, panhandling, getting drunk—had been confined mostly to the South End, Back Bay, and downtown. I'd tried checking out the universities south of the river but kept landing on Huntington Ave, and who needed that shit.

I panhandled as I walked, with no luck except for a cigarette. They expected you to light up right away, so you couldn't store any for later. I tried some buildings and found one with a large cafeteria. Enough students looked grungy, so I wouldn't stand out. I hit the can first, and it was a find too, having a large stall with its own sink. After sitting fully clothed to get warm, I took off my coat, blazer, sweater, shirt, and tee and washed my top half, including hair, using soap from the dispenser. Dunking my head under the tap wasn't easy, but I managed and matted it with paper towels. I put on the navy turtleneck I'd swiped and took off my boots, socks, underwear, and pants and did as good a bath as I could for my bottom half. I tossed the stinky tee.

The cafeteria was a treasure trove. Some students didn't bus their trays, so it was no big deal to slip into a chair and dig into leftover eggs or pancakes or hash browns. Somebody left a coffee cup, and refills apparently were free. And when the cashier went to get more cream, I was able to make off with a Danish, cramming it into the plastic bag I had ready in my pocket. That was one good thing about the coat: really deep pockets. Whoa—this was my lucky day: somebody dropped an orange ski hat.

Around noon I headed back to the Cambridge Women's whatever-it-was. The street was mostly brick townhouses—I'd seen nicer, I'd seen worse. The road itself was jagged cobblestone at the far end, and cars crammed into every inch of parking space.

Lights were on in both upstairs and downstairs windows, and the *Closed* tag had been removed. I went up the stairs and tried the door. It was locked, so I rang the bell.

A young woman with long dark hair answered. I could feel the warmth behind her.

"Hey, name's Andy. Somebody was saying you all might have a place I could crash? I just got into town, into Cambridge."

"I'm sorry, we don't rent rooms."

"Oh." I looked down and pushed at an imaginary pebble with my boot toe. "Don't really want to go home. Last time, he broke two ribs."

"My gosh. Come in a minute."

She said her name was Sophie and led me to this large room that might've once been a living room. Now it had desks against the walls and a big round table in the middle.

"Hitched all the way from Chicago," I said. "In Pennsylvania, this guy picks me up, but he takes an exit, says he needs gas. Starts getting weird on me, and basically I had to jump out. Couldn't risk reaching into the backseat for my suitcase, so all I've got is my old man's coat and the clothes on my back. Hoping to find a job and start over. Maybe change my name."

"Do you have any friends or family in this area?"

"Picked this area because I *don't*. He tracked me down before, in Milwaukee. Two ribs it cost me."

A phone on a desk rang, and Sophie answered it. Living on the street gave you an eagle's eye for the essentials—in the far corner, under a window, lay a mattress. I also noticed a jar labeled *Donations*, but it was empty.

"Yes, at one. ... No, her rotation ends in December." Hanging up, Sophie said she would make a few calls and see if she could find a shelter I could stay at.

"Really appreciate it. The thing is—I don't have the energy to go anywhere right this minute. Haven't slept for forty-eight hours. If I could just grab a quick nap, nothing much, just so I can see straight—"

"Why, sure," she said, looking unsure.

"What if I just crashed on that mattress?"

"We're having a meeting in here soon. Maybe we can move the mattress into another room. Let me get a blanket and pillow and see where we can put you."

I watched her start up the stairs. The phone rang again but stopped midway through the second ring. The mattress looked inviting anyway but with the radiator two feet away became damn irresistible. I went over and took off my boots, coat, and ratty blazer and folded the blazer into a makeshift pillow. Lying down, I pulled the coat up over my body and savored the warmth. For the first time in weeks, I stretched out.

A hand shook my shoulder. "The meeting's starting." I feigned sleep. The floorboards vibrated; I heard voices. I fell back asleep for who knew how long.

"According to our source, the Christmas season is when they make a third of their income. It's an assembly line, no-skills operation putting together holiday baskets. Most of the work force is immigrant Latinas. They lay everyone off for several weeks or a month before rehiring again. By keeping them temporary, they avoid having to offer benefits and can fire for any reason."

"Are the immigrants legal?"

"Do they want to organize?"

"Yes, they're legal. They want to organize but also need the paycheck."

"He hires a few Anglo men and assigns them to the back room. He might allow a *few* Anglo women on the lines because 'women don't make waves.'"

"It amazes me they find it cost-effective."

"Half are rehires—they don't even fill out new applications. The others are relatives of rehires. Ferguson's daughters spend a day doing the paperwork. It costs less than the benefits you have to give a permanent work force."

"But don't they shut down production for weeks at a time?"

"Tax write-off. They go on vacation."

"The point isn't why he does it. And he's very hard on the old and pregnant. No special consideration for how long they can stand."

"Do the organizers know when they'll do the Christmas hiring?"

"Monday. They'll start the factory up Tuesday."

"And fire everyone when?"

"Right before Christmas."

"What do they want from us?"

"Extra hands picketing on Monday."

The next time I awoke, the room was dark and empty, the house completely still. I found the bathroom; the clock said 4:30. I tiptoed to the kitchen. The streetlight shone through the blinds enough for me to find some cereal and a bowl and spoon. I wolfed down two huge helpings of cereal, rinsed the bowl and spoon under a trickle, and returned them to the drying rack before tiptoeing back to the mattress.

The phone woke me. Daylight came in the windows. I didn't get up immediately, needing to formulate a plan. The long, warm sleep had taught me something huge: I didn't want to live on the street again. And if it was unavoidable, I would at least try to wrangle one more night here. I pulled on my boots, laced them, and put on my blazer and coat. I walked softly to the kitchen.

This Sophie had blond hair. I thanked her for letting me crash. She said her name was Kathleen or Katherine or something and they could give me a list of women's shelters, and I said I was hoping to find work and maybe a room in an apartment. Did she know of any place that might have help- and roommate-wanted notices? Yes, she said, a place on campus, and she'd draw me a map how to get there. While she went to fetch a pencil and paper, I swiped some granola bars from a drawer. I thanked her for the map and list of shelters and split.

Again I hit the student cafeteria and grabbed food from the trays people hadn't bused. At the university bulletin board, I copied down help-wanteds for housecleaning and yard work, figuring I wouldn't have to dress nice. Plus I wouldn't have to talk to anybody. The card saying *Carpenter wanted* also said *Must supply own tradesman's tools*, so the hell with that.

When Blond Sophie answered the door, I acted like it was the most natural thing in the world I'd return. Showing her the list, I asked to use their phone to call the places, and she said yes.

Half the numbers didn't answer or had a busy signal. The other half expected you to have your own equipment or a truck to haul stuff. At some point Blond Sophie came in the room and sat at another desk, so I redialed a no-answer and spoke to the ringing.

"I'm calling about the ad for somebody to do housecleaning? ... In half an hour? ... Sure. ... That'd be great." Hanging up, I said, "Got an interview in half an hour. Know where this is?"

I showed her the address and handed her back the map, and she wrote in the street where it was. I also asked about the other addresses I had written down. She could see from my notations that some were for folks needing roommates. I could see the donations jar contained bills.

The house with the supposed interview was a three-story brick with a Japanese maple in the front yard. While I stood by the wrought-iron gate debating whether to actually go ring the bell, the front door opened, and a woman stepped out and reached in the mailbox. I swung back the gate and started up the path.

Seeing me, she asked, "May I help you?"

"Just saw the ad for somebody to clean." I held out the piece of paper like it was evidence. "This being on my way home—"

From her expression, you would've thought I had scorpions clinging to my nose. "It's already filled." She practically slammed the door. I spat in her Japanese maple.

Brunette Sophie let me in, and Blond Sophie came downstairs asking how it went.

"She wants me to start on Tuesday," I said. "It's only one day's work a week, but her sister's looking for somebody too. The bigger problem is a place to live. I have enough cash for the first month's rent but not a security deposit, which they all want."

"You may have to look outside Cambridge—somewhere less expensive."

"Don't know other places." I interlaced my fingers and kneaded my hands together. "Do you think—never mind."

"What?"

"Having trouble shaking this guilty feeling. That I should have given him one more chance. He really does love me."

Brunette Sophie's eyes looked ready to pop from their sockets. "Listen," she said, "it's frightening being on your own in a strange city, but if you take it one step at a time, you can make a new—and *safe*—life for yourself."

"And the T goes everywhere," Blond Sophie said. "Don't get discouraged. We'll put you in touch with a social services—"

"But don't you think he's learned his lesson? Hey, would it be okay if I used the bathroom real quick?"

"Of course."

I sat on the can several minutes trying to decide whether to fake being sick to my stomach. When I came out, one of them said, "We have to ask Maureen and Evie, but you may be able to stay here through the weekend. That would give you a few days to find a place. And we have the number of a social services agency that can help you apply for benefits and a church that runs a shelter and provides food donations."

I chewed my lip but said nothing.

"Men like him don't change," they said. "Your leaving him was very brave. You should be proud of yourself."

I said I figured it wouldn't hurt for me to go back to the big bulletin board on campus and check out more ads.

After panhandling in Central Square I hit a liquor store and bought a pint of cheap Scotch and shoplifted a sandwich from a grocery. Back at the Center, I told the Sophies I had *another* cleaning gig and maybe a room in a house starting in another week, and they in turn told me I could stay till Monday in Evie's room, which was right at the top of the stairs. They'd left a key on her dresser and asked only that I not call long distance. I said unless I decided to go back to my old man, there was no point in anybody knowing where I was.

Evie's drawers contained only sweatshirts and a box of tampax. The closet had summer dresses and sneakers; the shelves, only books. Nothing worth pawning. No wonder she didn't mind a stranger crashing.

The next morning, I left early so I wouldn't get on the Sophies' nerves. Plus I wanted them to think I was busy scoping out jobs and apartments. I panhandled enough to get a burger at a fast-food place and went looking for a bar with cheap draft. I had stumbled upon a women's bar shortly after arriving in Boston but quickly learned their clientele wasn't fussy about the price of a pint.

Not far from Central Square I found a quiet hole-in-the-wall— didn't notice the name, but the customers called the bartender Simon. Sitting at a table with my back to the TV, I tried to figure out my next step. I needed to buy more time—I didn't want the Sophies to ask me to leave on Monday. Two of them were going to the factory picket that day, and if the third Sophie would be at class, I'd have the house to myself—something they might not like.

Maybe they were right about Cambridge being too expensive. I had ridden most of the T lines my first days in Boston to keep warm and had learned some of the city layout. Dorchester was where I'd spotted the church with the *Free Hot Meal Thanksgiving* sign. Maybe I should check out that area.

Again I waited till late to return to the Center. The windows were dark.

Dear Sophie, Kathleen, and Maureen: I've rented a room in an apartment starting Dec. 1st doing some grounds work to cover a chunk of the rent. My first cleaning gig is Tuesday and I have another Thursday, and Wednesday I have another interview. Just want to say I <u>really</u> appreciate your giving me temporary shelter. You saved my life, and that's no exaggeration. Not sure how to repay you but would feel better about myself if I could do some giving too, so if it's OK with you, I'd like to join the picket tomorrow. Andy

Rereading my little epistle, I almost smiled. After *they* had read it, how could they possibly ask me to leave before the end of November? Rhetorical question, Jiminy.

Chapter 43

THE SCHOOL BUS left Cambridge and passed through all sorts of neighborhoods. This one looked rundown. Grant, the leader of the picketers, told the driver to park near the T stop so the company would think we'd taken the train.

Altogether we numbered around twenty, half Hispanic—or Latino, as they said in Cambridge—the rest, Anglo. The signs were mostly in Spanish, but a few said *It Pays To Organize* and *Demand Fairness*. There weren't enough for everybody, so I gladly went without, stuffing my hands in my pockets. It was cold and damp. I wore the orange knitted hat. The Sophies' friend Sven had one just like it but in navy. He wore his so low, you couldn't tell he had red hair, and the sunglasses hid the piercing blue eyes.

"Did the mole quit or get laid off?" somebody asked Grant.

"Quit. No one wants to work at Ferguson's long."

"But you trust his information?"

"He told Sven they plan the hiring day well in advance."

I hung back so I wouldn't have to talk to anybody. On the walk from the Women's Center to the church, the Sophies had tried including me in their conversation, which was about Reagan getting elected and what that might mean for Roe versus Wade. They asked my opinion, and I said I didn't know about politics, just that my old man liked Reagan, so I figured he must mean trouble. Neither mentioned my note.

"We'll be in front by the parking lot, where they set up the tables," Grant was saying. "There's a back door where people might go to fill out applications, but let's see if that happens before we position anyone there. Our hope is the company's not expecting us and won't have enough goons for the back door. And remember, stay on the sidewalk—don't put even a *toe* on Ferguson property."

The factory was a three- or four-story brick fortress and, together with the parking lot, took up a whole block. Several cars were parked at the far end. Three Anglo women in parkas and hats sat behind two long tables set up in the middle of the lot. Some Anglo guys lingered nearby, and five or six Latino women stood in a line. When they saw our approach, the Latino women turned their backs to us.

We started marching in a loop. A guy with a bullhorn chanted, "Unionize when? Unionize now!" Brunette Sophie's sign said *JUSTICIA*, and one of the Latino men's said *Sindicato Sí*. Maybe we were supporting the Mafia. After the unionize bit, they shouted in Spanish. The Latino women by the tables huddled closer together. I wasn't sure what they were waiting for, till a tall, broad-shouldered Anglo came strutting out the front door with a pile of papers. He didn't even glance our way but went directly to the Anglo women. They arranged the papers in stacks on the tables, and the Latino women stepped forward, bent over, and began to write.

After a long time walking and chanting, somebody said, "The fuzz," and a squad car pulled to the curb. A cop got out, went to the guy with the bullhorn, talked for thirty seconds, and returned to his car, where no doubt he and his partner stayed warm and filled themselves with doughnuts and hot coffee on the taxpayers' dole. Good work if you could get it.

A large group of men and women arrived on foot, and Ferguson's Anglos had them form separate lines in front of each of the Ferguson women. Grant and some other picketers left our loop and went to meet the stragglers before they stepped onto factory property. A few hesitated and talked amongst themselves, but most continued on.

I would definitely need to shoplift a parka soon. The trench coat was big enough for me to wear lots of layers underneath, but a down parka would be warmer. What if I got nailed? The first cold night after running out of money, I'd debated going into a restaurant, ordering a porterhouse, stiffing them, and waiting while they called the cops. Then I might get to spend the night in a warm cell. But I could've been jailed for days, and even one day without alcohol scared me. Going dry was too steep a price to pay for a warm, safe place to sleep. The way I saw it: I could be warm or drunk but not both. Imagine not having to pick between them.

More folks showed up to fill out applications. Grant left the line and stood frowning. I went over and told him I saw some folks going towards the back and did he want me to stand there and see if I could talk anybody out of applying? I'd stay on the sidewalk, on public property. He nodded, abstracted.

I told Blond Sophie, "Grant thinks it makes sense for me to go around back."

She smiled and shouted, "Unionize when? Unionize now!"

Midway along the rear of the factory, a sign on a gate said *Keep Out: No Trespassing.* The gate was padlocked. On the other side, a short path ran to a back door. I loitered there smoking.

"Can't you read? No trespassing." It was the tall dude.

I dropped my cigarette on the ground. "Just wondering if you got any openings? Any shift?"

He waved his hand. "I've seen you out there."

"I came with them, but, like, could use the cash. They said they'd pay me to hold a sign but got enough people doing it for free."

He looked down the street both directions. "You want to fill out an application?" He unlocked the padlock and opened the gate, locking it behind me. I followed him inside. Around a corner, he halted at a metal desk and pulled a paper from a folder. "Got ID?"

I took out my wallet and handed him my license.

"Illinois. What are you doing here?"

"Looking for work."

"No jobs in Chicago?" He copied some stuff onto a piece of paper and handed the license back.

"I kind of had to leave."

"Trouble with the law?"

"No. More a personal thing."

He gave me a form, and I filled it out on the desk top, using my real social security number because there might have been a way they could check. But other than that and my name, everything was bogus. When I finished, he read it over.

"I'll tell you what, Andrea. You show up for the seven a.m. shift tomorrow, and we'll see if we've got a spot for you." He smiled, not as a come-on but in triumph.

After he padlocked the gate behind me, I went for a walk down some side streets. What would I say if one of the picketers had seen me go in? That I had gotten myself hired on and could be a mole?

Eventually I wound my way back. I had another cigarette by the rear door, then bit the bullet and headed around front.

Nobody was there—not the Ferguson family, Anglo goons, folks filling out applications, picketers. Even the tables and cars were gone. It was like a movie studio had finished shooting a scene and packed up every last thing and left. I hoofed it to where the church bus had let us off. It was gone. I hit the station and nabbed an inbound.

Panhandling in Central Square, I got enough to buy an alarm clock and some bread, peanut butter, and jelly. When twilight descended, I returned to the Women's Center. The kitchen light was on.

"Andy, what *happened?*" Brunette Sophie looked genuinely worried. "Grant went to the back but didn't see you, and we waited over ten minutes."

"I needed to find a restroom."

She gave an I'm-sorry smile. "It was great of you to join us. We think we kept the applications too low for them to run the lines." She held up two crossed fingers.

"Cool. Going again tomorrow?"

"No one has the time."

"Because I'll be cleaning this one place in the morning, and there's a coffee shop that might hire me to do prep on weekends."

"Great!" She still said nothing about my note.

The house was dark and silent Monday morning when I tiptoed downstairs, grabbed some cereal, and snuck out. In Central Square, I got cheap coffee and waited for the train. Dawn arrived before I got off, so I found my way to the factory easily. The picketing had been useless—the parking lot swarmed with hires.

At the entrance, we slowed almost to a halt. The only language I heard sounded like Spanish. Stepping over the threshold, I couldn't hear anything, just the roar and squeal of machinery. We were funneled into a line that barely inched forward. I could make out a wide aisle running crosswise, maybe the full length of the building, with iron columns at twenty-, thirty-foot intervals. Young men—some Anglo, some Latino—went by carrying cartons. When I got to the muscular Anglo holding a clipboard, he barked over the clanking and rumbling, "Name?"

"Gabe. Andy. G-A-B-E."

He scanned the sheet on his clipboard. "Andrea? Belt five, to the left. Name?" he barked over my shoulder.

I went left down the wide aisle to where the fluorescent light fixture said five and waited. Two Latino women joined me. A scowling guy hurried over and directed me to a spot by a long counter running perpendicular to the aisle. My right-side neighbor at the counter, a young Latino woman, turned just long enough to appraise me. I was soon joined on my left by a few more Latino women. There looked to be ten or eleven of us on Belt five in total. The belt itself was a black rubbery-looking thing about a foot-and-a-half wide and running the counter's entire length.

The rest of the factory wasn't much. The upper reaches were empty, letting daylight in the high marbly windows. Pipes and ducts ran along the walls. The pipes had to be for something other than heat, since the place was freezing—everybody kept their coats on. Steel shelves running along the walls were filled with cartons. I counted six speakers attached to steel beams and nine identical two-foot glossies of Jesus taped on the iron columns. At least the pictures were of him as a smiling young man, not on the cross dripping blood.

The machines on the other side of the front door finally stopped making their ungodly noise. The PA system crackled. "Okay," a voice blasted through the speakers, "Listen up." It spoke in Spanish before reverting back to English and explaining what we'd be doing. The finished product was a gold plastic basket holding fake straw, a pink plastic Baby Jesus, white lamb, and some other junk. The women at the start of the line put a small box with tissue paper and the gold basket on the belt, the rest of us added the straw or lamb or whatever was in the cartons stored beside us, and the two women at the end closed and taped the box. I peered in my carton. Wow, I got Baby Jesus. The young woman on my right got the fake hay, and the one on my left, the lamb.

Motors started, and a bell rang. Some seconds later, the belts started moving. I already had a couple of pink Jesuses ready in my right hand. When the first basket got to me, I placed one of him— Him?—in the middle, realizing afterwards that I should've put Our Savior closer to the end to make room for the lamb. I got the second Savior right.

The hum the belt machinery gave off was quiet enough that the women on either side of me had no trouble chatting with their neighbors. Extend, flex, extend, flex. Another clump of hay, another pink baby Jesus. Yellow clump, pink baby. Extend, flex, extend, flex. Did one company supply everything? Brother or Son of Ferguson?

The belts sped up—it wasn't my imagination. Not Charlie Chaplin fast, just enough to keep you alert. The others on the line barely seemed to notice. Maybe they'd all done it before, with Easter bunnies or Pilgrims. Probably at some point— after our break—I'd switch hands. Count your lucky stars, Andy, working here, something you won't be able to do if you get Huntington's.

The next time the PA cackled, it was followed by music.

When I was just a lad of ten
My father said to me,
Come here and learn a lesson
From the lovely lemon tree.

It wasn't a singer I knew, and his sugary accent made Trini Lopez sound Anglo in comparison. Did Ferguson think the Latinos would be grateful for "their" music? Pick up Jesus, place in basket. Pick up Jesus, place in basket.

Lemon tree very pretty
And the lemon flower is sweet,
But the fruit of the poor lemon
Is impossible to eat.

Pick up Jesus, place in basket. Pick up Jesus, place in basket. Jesus, basket, Jesus, basket, Jesus, basket, Jesus. When my carton got down to its last layer, a young guy placed a new one beside me containing a fresh supply. He did the same with the others on the line and then returned and grabbed the empties. Extend, flex, extend, flex.

Somebody screwed up the tape, because again it played *When I was just a lad of ten* and the whole *lemon tree* crap. Nobody else seemed to notice. The third time through, the song really got on my nerves. It wasn't that great to begin with, but three times in a row could kill even "Honky Tonk Women." Was the lemon flower actually sweet? The smell in this place wasn't—more like a musty cellar. Whoever had coined the word olfactory obviously had never worked in one. *But the fruit* Jesus basket *is impossible* Jesus *eat.*

When the bell rang for morning break, the belt stopped. Craving a cigarette, I rode the crowd outdoors, which was everybody not going to the restrooms. Folks stood idly in the parking lot smoking, talking. Some Anglo dudes positioned themselves along the perimeter of the property like prison guards. Would they shoot us if we tried to escape? Or were they keeping the rest of the world out? Factory very pretty, but the work sucked.

A bell rang, and the PA said, "Two minutes. You must be back at your station when the belts begin." That was quick. Following the other folks funneling through the doors, I had to stop in the jam before the main aisle split. I realized they'd divided us—the left was for women; the right, for men.

A brand new carton of pink baby Jesuses awaited me. The bell rang, the belt started, the gold basket approached, the Son of God gazed down from the walls, my arm began its extend, flex, extend, flex. Jesus basket Jesus *a lad of ten* basket Jesus *said to me.*

The next time the bell rang, I made my way through the exiting crowds to the restroom. A huge line had already formed. When I got past the sinks, I saw three stalls *total.* For what—a hundred women? With ten-minute breaks? I asked another Anglo if there was another restroom. "Just portables outside."

After my turn, I went out to the parking lot and ate my PB & J. The prices the silver truck was charging for sandwiches and tacos and everything were ridiculous. I found a recessed doorway of a boarded-up store and drank some Scotch.

The afternoon shifts were as monotonous as the morning. Lemon Lover kept singing, the belt kept rolling, my arm kept thrusting, and my legs and feet kept aching. When the final bell rang, it was already dusk, and by the time I got to Cambridge, it was dark. I managed to sneak in the house and kitchen unobserved, scoot up to Evie's room, make a bunch of sandwiches, drink, hit the can, and fall fast asleep.

Wednesday morning we entered the factory quicker, and the bouncer seemed surprised when I asked my belt number. "Same as yesterday." It was also the same pink Jesus, same lemon tree, same gray daylight, same gray walls. Again I ate my lunch and drank my Scotch in the recessed doorway. Thursday was a repeat of Wednesday except that it rained, and Friday, the same. As we headed inside after lunch, I asked an Anglo woman if she knew when we got our paychecks. The end of the day, she said.

"Any place near here to cash it?"

"The truck that hands them out."

"That's cool."

"Charge a dollar fifty."

Nobody said Ferguson was stupid.

At the final bell, I bit the bullet and cashed my check at the truck, forking over almost an hour of Baby Jesus time. Moments later, I couldn't care less about the gouging; my pockets had money—money for booze, cigarettes, and hot meals somewhere cheap.

Back in Cambridge, I hit the liquor store and bought a few pints of Scotch and a bottle of wine they were practically giving away. I left the wine on the kitchen counter at the Women's Center weighing down a note. *I've found three part-time jobs! The woman moving out of the room I'll be renting sold me her furniture, so I'll be standing on my own two feet soon. This wine is to thank you for being so supportive. Andy.* Far be it from me to bite the hand that fed me. I'd slobber all over it.

I hung out at the student cafeteria and Simon's bar all weekend to make myself scarce. By now the Sophies certainly had to wish me gone, and I was banking on their being afraid to ask me to leave if they had to do it in writing. By doing it in person, they could gauge my reaction, pile on heaps of encouragement, cajole me into staying at a shelter—maybe give me a small amount of cash to help pay for a Y. If they simply left a note, I might return to my old man. For even with their sympathy exhausted, I was guessing they wouldn't want to be hypocrites and responsible for pushing an abused woman back into the arms of her abuser. I sure as hell wasn't going to make it easy for them to tell me in person.

The second week at Ferguson's was no different from the first. When one arm got tired, I switched to the other. When one leg or hip ached, I shifted my weight to the other.

Friday night, Simon's was practically empty—a few guys sat in the back. The old guy with the straggly beard was hunched on his usual stool. I took my pint to the table where the window met the wall. Depending on my mood, I could stare at the sidewalk or the cheap paneling.

When I headed for the can, Simon was coming through the back door, maybe after dumping the garbage. Just to be friendly, I pointed to the old couch against the wall. "That for folks too drunk to get home?" He smiled, acknowledging the joke, or at least my intent.

I returned to the table while he was in the act of setting down a fresh pint. "Hey, not sure I can pay for that."

He nodded towards the old guy. "It's on Noah."

Shoot, who'd refuse? I raised the new stein in toast and said, "Thanks." Noah didn't acknowledge my thanks, if he even heard it.

It began to rain and soon was raining heavily, long darts of water hitting the window, street, and sidewalk. Large puddles formed where the pavement dipped. Men in trench coats ran by, some holding briefcases over their heads. Wasn't a fit night out, but for now, I was in. And I had my immediate needs met: I was warm, getting a little buzzed, and sitting on enough dough to cover beer, food, and cigarettes. When the 30th rolled around, I could tell the Sophies the woman had to delay moving out by two weeks. I couldn't see them asking me to leave anyway.

My peripheral vision took in the old guy splitting. He slouched past the window, eyes on the pavement, his hat brim barely deflecting the downpour. With his grizzled gray beard, he *looked* like Noah. Maybe he was going to build himself an ark.

I should go soon too. I peeled the wrapper off a candy bar I'd grabbed at a newsstand. Suddenly there was Simon, again placing a pint on the table. "Noah left money so you could have one more."

"Shoot, what did he do, win the lottery?"

"He's a regular. Likes to see new faces come in."

Maybe Noah was afraid his favorite haunt would go broke and close.

I leaned back, smiling at my amber fortune. Sure, the Sophies were generous—I wasn't knocking it. But what they gave wasn't at much of a sacrifice. They still had their material comforts and yellow brick road to the future. But old Noah, he couldn't have had much, not if he picked this seamy little joint to get drunk in every night. His generosity was at a real cost. The poor lent a hand to one of their own though they were the ones least able to afford it. In my book, that was a truer generosity.

Saturday morning the front bell rang like crazy. I cracked open Evie's door and listened. A big meeting was starting. Great, the Sophies would be too busy to bug me; I could hang out in the house awhile.

After a bit, I crept down to the kitchen and stole some coffee. Back in the room, I did a more thorough job scouring the dresser drawers. No, Evie hadn't squirreled away any money or jewelry. I left alone the Susan B. Anthony silver dollar encased in plastic hanging from a nail—a Sophie glancing in might notice it missing.

I perused the books. So Evie took chemistry, physics, microbiology. The bottom shelf was all heavy hardcovers with words on their spines like physiology, anatomy. *Neurology*.

The Table of Contents was confusing. I flipped to the index. It got its own chapter.

Huntington's Disease, also called Huntington's Chorea, is an inherited disorder of the nervous system. The gene responsible for Huntington's Disease is dominant; hence, offspring receiving the abnormal gene from only one parent acquire the disease. ... Scientists believe the Huntington's Disease gene does not reside on the sex chromosomes, but its exact location is unknown. The disease is rare, occurring in only one out of ... .

So the abnormal gene Dean had gotten from his mother was what had given him the disease. He could have gotten a normal gene from his father, *probably* got a normal gene from Grandpa Pat, since the disease was so rare.

Each child of a parent with the Huntington's gene has a one in two chance of inheriting the abnormal gene and, therefore, the disease.

That made sense. After meiosis or mitosis or whatever the hell Stacy said, half of Dean's sperm got the good gene passed down from Grandpa Pat and half, the bad gene passed down from Grandma Margaret. Which type of sperm fertilized Mathilde's egg? The $64,000 question.

The following signs and symptoms ... typically first appear between the ages of thirty-five and fifty ... . All patients undergo physical deterioration leading to death ... within ten to twenty years.

Uncoordinated hand and foot movements
Large-scale, dancing-like gait
Staggering as if drunk
Arm flailing
Brief, repetitive jerking of arms and legs
Writhing
Noticeable grimace
Sinuous twisting of the trunk
Abrupt and rapid movements starting in one part of the body and unpredictably jumping to another

How come you never saw people writhing or sinuously twisting? Were they all institutionalized? Or did embarrassment keep them from going out in public?

Loss of inhibitions
Mood changes

Loss of cognitive abilities
Unexplained anger
Psychosis
Dementia

Were they for real: *unexplained* anger? The chapter ended with a footnote saying the famous folksinger Woody Guthrie had had Huntington's.

Chapter 44

SINCE HE WAS closing both Thursday and Friday for Thanksgiving, Ferguson paid us the Wednesday right before. On the train back into Cambridge Wednesday evening, I finalized my plan to stay longer at the Women's Center. Before splitting for Ferguson's next Monday, I would leave a note saying the woman whose room I was supposed to move into couldn't leave till December 10th but I *insisted* on paying them for the extra days in Evie's room. I would paperclip a twenty-dollar bill to the note *as a start*. With any luck, the Sophies would return the dough, but if they didn't, I'd just be a little bolder with the donations jar.

Thanksgiving morning, I split before any of them were awake. By the time I got to the free-dinner church in Dorchester, though, a line had already formed. Most of us looked like we needed a free meal, our pants and coats tattered and dirty. And Ferguson's was a spring bouquet compared to the smells here, liquor-breath and dried urine.

Once inside, we were guided into a huge cafeteria that was part of an adjoining school. Except for a crucifix on one wall, it wasn't all that different from the lunchroom at Brackton High, with rows and rows of long tables and benches. We didn't need herding—we went straight to the stacks of trays by the counter and got on the food line.

My tray full, I began looking for a place to sit. The bench ends were occupied, but plenty of spaces remained in the middles, some larger than others, usually around a guy who looked filthier than the rest of us. Slowly I strolled towards the back, hoping for a spot by a woman. A group of black women glared at me. Here was a possibility, a white woman around my own age. Part of the space beside her was taken up with a rumpled coat—maybe she was saving somebody's seat. Across from her were two ancient Asian women.

"Excuse me, that seat taken?" She didn't seem to hear, so I called louder. She peered up. I gestured towards the coat. She pulled it closer, making some room but not a lot. I sidled past the men and put my tray down.

For an instant she looked at me and I, at her. Her eyes were pitch black. Not dark brown, not a glossy ebony, but pure, opaque black. Her hair, cut jagged in the front and chopped unevenly at the shoulder, was also black. Something about her made me nervous, like I had awakened a tiger from a deep sleep. Was she thinking: *Try to sit here and I'll kill you?* Maybe the opposite was true: her deadpan expression didn't mask *any* emotion.

Proving me wrong on both counts, her voice came out normal. "Never sees you here before."

"First time I've been here. Name's Andy."

"Jackie."

Too intent on eating, I didn't look at her again. I dipped the fork into the mashed potatoes and dunked the glob into the pool of gravy. Even lukewarm, it tasted good; in no time I'd finished everything. Some food remained on Jackie's plate, but she lit a cigarette. I glanced around, and not seeing any *No Smoking* signs, took out one of my own. She flicked her lighter for me. After inhaling and exhaling, I said, "Thanks."

"Live around here?"

"Cambridge, but it's just temporary."

One dark eyebrow arched. "How much you paying?" Her cheekbones were pronounced, like in gaunt or starving people, yet she wasn't particularly thin. I explained it was a student women's center of sorts and they were letting me use somebody's room for free while she was away.

"How you find out about this place?" she asked.

"Trucked around a bit when I first got to Boston, looking for warm places to spend the night. Saw the sign. It's nice they do this."

"Christmas dinner's better. Where you from?"

"Chicago." I wasn't sure how much to tell her. Yet a belly that actually felt full and the company of somebody else who knew what it was like to need a free meal made me want to let my guard down a little. I said I needed to get out of Chicago and ended up in Boston because that's where my last ride was going. "Though now I'm thinking I should've headed south, someplace warm. Hey, you mind watching my tray while I get some coffee? Want some too?"

She shook her head. I got myself a cup from the table with the urns, and when I returned she asked, "You watches baseball?" Sometimes, I said, and she asked what I thought of the Red Sox season.

"Didn't follow it—just the National League."

"Gots money coming in?" Jackie sure changed topics fast. Was she psycho?

"No. Barely come up with enough for beer and cigarettes."

"Want to buy some hash? Don't have any but knows someones that might."

"Love to, but can't see coming into that much dough any time soon. What does it go for around here?"

"Depend. Can get half lid for ten. *Good* hash."

"If I ever see a ten, I might take you up on it."

"Shit," she whispered, lowering her head.

"What's wrong?"

"Curly hair, black jacket." She bent like she was picking something up off the floor. "What he doing?"

"Went out."

She sat up. "Cop."

"I wondered why he didn't grab a tray."

"See guy with the beard? Dro say he used to be rich. Wife catch him cheating. Get a divorce, take everything: mansions, cars. Imagine living on the street when used to have *millions*?"

It wasn't all that great for the rest of us. "Who's Dro?" I asked.

Her dead-black eyes scanned the tables. "My old man. *Damn.*" The undercover cop had come back in. "Do me a favor? If he follow me, cough, acts like you choking. Just for a minute."

Before I could answer, she'd risen, grabbed her coat, climbed out from between the bench and table and, with her back to the cop, edged her way to the aisle. She threw her coat over her shoulders like a cape and strode to the exit sign. The cop didn't notice—he was busy watching some young black guy. I picked over Jackie's tray, the untouched cranberry sauce and string beans, the burnt muffin piece.

Nobody was at the Center when I got back. The donations jar had a lot of singles, so I swiped two and some coins. I lay low all weekend, hanging out at the student cafeteria and Simon's. Monday morning I clipped twenty dollars to a note saying I couldn't move into the new place right away on account of the woman there not moving out till the 12th.

Other than getting assigned to Belt eight and putting plastic St. Nicks beside teams of reindeer, the week at Ferguson's went pretty much like the previous. Friday morning, though, the pipes in the women's restroom leaked—maybe they had frozen the night before—and Belts seven to ten got herded to the middle of the plant while repairs were going on. The older women sidled up to the columns for something to lean on while the rest of us just stared at the gray walls, pipes, valves, and grimy machines. A group of Anglo men, maybe the restock crew, stood idle too.

While my mind wandered, I got the weird sensation of being watched. The Latino women around me were absorbed in conversation. Lackadaisically I scanned the faces of the Anglo men by the metal shelves. They looked bored, their eyes glazed over. Except for one face. Two keen blue eyes. I lowered my gaze fast, hoping Sven might forget he saw me. Was he a scab? Mole?

"Lines seven through ten, take your places," the PA barked.

Back on the line, with the lemon tree in the background and plastic St. Nick in the foreground, I tried convincing myself that Sven wasn't a mole—that he, like me, needed the money. Yet his stare was bold, accusatory. Or was that my guilty conscience? What conscience! Jiminy had gone, gone with the wind. Could Sven be a *Ferguson* mole, infiltrating the community group? But one of the Sophies had said they'd been friends since freshman year. Then why wouldn't he be worried I'd blow *his* cover? Maybe he *was* worried; *that* was the reason he looked accusatory: to scare me out of ratting on him. *I'll make you a deal: you shut up about me, and I'll shut up about you.*

No, he didn't look scared. The opposite: he stood in plain view, purposely letting me see he had me in his sights. Could he think I

was a mole too? Maybe his stare was a signal, one resistance com-
rade to another. *Allons enfants de la patrie, and the lemon flower is sweet.*
And pigs would fly. When would he tell the Sophies? Maybe they'd
never learn, or not before the end of December, when I probably needed to move anyway. Even if he had seen me arrive at the
school bus with them, the three of us could have just met up the
block before—why would he know I was staying with them?

I continued to make myself scarce at the Center, and on the ride to
Ferguson's Monday morning, I debated what to say if Sven was lying
in wait at the factory door. Would he believe a line that I had decided on my own to become a mole? Maybe he thought I'd chicken out
and not show. Well, he could go fuck himself if he thought I gave a
damn. Or pay me to stay away, if he cared so damn much.

"Shit!" The parking lot was empty. I walked across the deserted asphalt, kicking at pebbles. My peripheral vision picked up
two others—middle-aged Latino women—approaching from the
side. We met at the front door.

CLOSED UNTIL 1981
FELIZ NAVIDAD
We exchanged brief smiles. They said something in Spanish.

I arrived back in Central Square during the morning rush hour.
Avoiding the store where I'd swiped the backpack, I found one selling knitted hats for a buck apiece. I bought a black and a brown, it
pissing me off to shell out for anything without another paycheck
coming in. But I needed the camouflage—not only security guards
but Sven and possibly Grant might be on the lookout for a five-five
towhead in bright orange.

With the black one pulled down to my forehead, I hit the student cafeteria. Would it close during Christmas vacation? Would all

the Sophies go away? Should I offer to house-sit or drop by to take in their mail? When would Evie actually return?

After eating, I hit the bulletin board and copied down some phone numbers of folks looking for sitters and people to clean, then headed back to the Women's Center. Even if the Sophies were around, they wouldn't mind my calling about jobs. If the house was empty, I'd see what their bedrooms had to offer.

Our block was pretty quiet, all residential and not much traffic. A taxi came around the corner at the cobblestone end, but I had plenty of time to cross. I took out my key. The lights were off both downstairs and up. I climbed the steps and inserted the key in the lock. Brakes screeched.

Reflexively, I turned. Blond Sophie stood between two parked cars, the taxi stopped beside her. She waved it past. After crossing, she looked up at me.

"Kathleen!" somebody shouted. I turned towards the voice.

Trotting towards us, a big smile plastered across his face, was Sven. His look bounced from her at the bottom of the steps to me at the top. The smile vanished.

I had two choices: stand there or go inside. Without extracting the key, I went in and tore up to Evie's room, imagining the conversation below.

Why does she have a key to your house?

She's staying with us.

A friend of yours?

No, she's on the run from an abusive husband.

Do you know where she works?

She has some part-time jobs housecleaning.

That's what she told you?

Once they realized I'd lied about the jobs, they would figure I was lying about being a battered woman and everything else.

Things that had puzzled them, like missing cash and food, would fall into place. They were trusting, but not idiots.

While these thoughts raced through my brain, my hands raced to cram my clothes and food into the pack, along with two of Evie's sweatshirts, a pair of sneakers, and her box of tampax. Was there anything else worth taking? I grabbed the Susan B. Anthony dollar off the wall. Cracking open the bedroom door, I listened. Hearing nothing, I crept downstairs.

The front door was closed and the hallway, empty. Were they still outside? Now I heard voices, low, hushed, coming from the kitchen. Slowly I pried open the front door. Nobody on the steps or sidewalk. I went out, closed the door quietly behind me, hit the street, and ran like hell.

I hoofed it to the bridge and over the Charles. Cambridge was Injun Territory now. Cars zipped by fast. The air was cold; the wind, colder. The dark water was depressing.

Downtown was teeming with people, people who couldn't spare a quarter. Sometimes I spared a fuck-you. One street with offices and banks looked familiar. In October, I had panhandled here and stumbled upon Pinky's, a women's bar. I hadn't known that was what it was. Just attracted by the darkness, I'd gone in and sat at a back table, ignoring the well-dressed business types, men and women, who looked like they'd come from work. The bartender looked a little butch but didn't pay me any mind. Around seven o'clock, she dimmed the lights further, and bit by bit the remaining customers left. I had a second beer. Around eight, also bit by bit, obvious dykes started arriving. Just like GinMar's, catering to straight clientele in the daytime and lesbians at night. Had Ginnie and Martha moved here? I hadn't stuck around to find out, not wanting to see anybody I knew.

The misery of those first weeks came back in full force: alternating nights at North and South Station, catching what sleep I could while sinuously twisting on weirdly molded plastic seats or curled in the fetal position on hardwood benches. Occasionally riding the T. Panhandling and lurking near trash bins in parks and the Common in hopes of somebody tossing something fresh. Now I had to live like that again, and it was colder.

From the outside, Pinky's looked the same. Maybe I'd go later and see if it was run by Ginnie and Martha and try to get hired. Or try to get picked up, see how long I could parlay my company into a room-and-meal ticket. Bite the bullet and deal with people.

Finding a bar with free nachos, I went in and downed a shot of Scotch, nursed a beer, and made a dozen trips to the counter for stale chips soaked in warm cheese. But just when I was starting to actually mellow, the sonofabitch said I had to order another drink if I wanted to stay. Slinging my pack over my shoulder I barked, "You just saved me from leaving a tip, asshole." He couldn't see me scoop up the singles on the empty table near the door on my way out.

It was almost eight, and the sidewalk traffic had thinned. I got to Pinky's and took the same small table as the last time. The bar was a one-room deal but big enough for a dozen or so tables semicircling a dance floor.

The conversion occurred shortly after I arrived, and the newcomers cruised me, but I barely met their glances. Yet I was glad to be in a women's bar, and the jukebox was playing lively stuff, which helped distract me from all the shit coming down. Gloria Gaynor got a crowd on the dance floor. "I Will Survive" was the national anthem, practically, at the Chicago bars. Of course, survival to them just meant getting over a lover dumping you.

By eleven, the place had pretty much cleared out, hardly unusual for a Monday night, but around midnight, women started arriving in twos and threes. Did a lot of Boston lesbians work three to eleven shifts like Lish and her hospital friends? Somebody asked if they could borrow the extra chairs at my table, and I said sure. That way nobody could sit down and bug me.

At some point Rod Stewart came on the jukebox.

Tonight's the night

It's gonna be all right.

It was a decent song. More and more women came in.

The second time through the chorus, Rod got as far as *gonna be all right* before getting cut off. The bartender had opened the machine and was replacing records.

Imagine there's no heaven,

It's easy if you try—

Jeez, if you were going to yank a record mid-song, at least put on something good, not old Beatles slop. But nobody else looked pissed. In fact, they all flocked to the dance floor. They didn't dance, though—they stood in a circle, arms around each other, swaying and singing. Some were crying.

Imagine there's no countries—

A woman came over. "Join us."

"Sorry, not into dancing."

"You could stand, out of respect." Her face was earnest.

I'd had enough of earnest women. "For what?"

"Didn't you hear? John Lennon was shot."

That explained it. I sipped my beer. "Imagine."

"What?" She bent closer. The droning had gotten pretty loud.

"How did it happen?" I asked.

"He was going home with Yoko, walking into their building, and this guy shot him." Her eyes widened. *Must've been the biggest fucking event of her life.*

Sharing all the world.

I drained my glass and stood. "There are worse ways to go."

Again the bulging eyes. "You're messed up."

"Tell me about it." I grabbed my pack and left. *Fuck that shit. At least at Simon's I could drink in peace.*

Trucking over the bridge to Cambridge, ready to whack would-be rapists and muggers with my pack, I debated the best place to spend the night. If the guy on duty at North Station was the one who had tried to nab me when I'd stolen the cookies, he would probably trump up something if he saw me again. *Didn't Cambridge have shelters? Maybe Simon would know. Simon says do this; Simon says do that.*

The bar was sleepy. Noah nodded at me, and I nodded back. When Simon grabbed a stein from the shelf and came over, I asked, "You know any places to crash nearby, like for folks on the street? I just got kicked out of my apartment and—"

"A shelter?"

"Yeah."

He pushed back the spigot handle and watched the beer flow into the glass. "You might ask down at the Sisters."

"The church place? They still open?"

"Doubt it. It's past one." When the glass was filled, he set it down and leaned forward, saying in a low voice, "Tell you what. I don't usually do this. We could lose our license." He motioned with his head towards the back. "You can crash there until I open tomorrow."

I looked over at the dark hallway, remembering the couch. "Thanks. Guess I'll take you up on it."

"When I call closing, look like you're getting ready to go but need to use the ladies' room. Wait a few minutes till they leave."

"Thanks, I really appreci—"

He walked to the end of the bar to wait on Noah. I took my stein and pack to a table.

When Simon called, "Closing," I did like he said and went into the can and waited. When I emerged a few minutes later, the lights were off, but the street lamp shed enough illumination for me to make out most of the room. Simon and Noah stood by the door.

Simon came over, his voice low and confiding. "I wonder if you could do me a little favor. Noah's not a young guy. He's pretty lonely, living in a room by himself. No family or friends."

Was Noah low on cash? I didn't have much myself but would spare a buck or two—I hadn't forgotten the beers.

Simon continued, "He's on a pension, has a little saved. Thirty dollars on him right now."

I breathed a mental sigh of relief, not really wanting to part with any dough.

"Do you think," Simon said, "for the thirty he has on him, you'd let him lay you? On that couch?"

My throat tightened, my heart pounded, I could feel my armpits flooding. What are you so scared of, Andy? Being screwed? Obviously Simon thought it was no big deal, wasn't too much to ask.

Eventually words emerged, short-circuiting my frozen brain. "Yeah, sure."

"Let me pour you a shot of something. Scotch? Gin?"

"Scotch," I mumbled.

He went behind the bar and took down a bottle. I kept staring at the floor even while he put the glass in my hand. "He's too old to be rough on you. I'll tell him to warm it up first." I swallowed the shot in one gulp.

Simon stayed near the front, tilting the side window blinds to block out most of the street light. The couch area was completely dark except for a pencil of light under the women's restroom door. I took off my boots and pants and lay down. Noah came over and lay on top of me. I was damn glad he didn't try to kiss me, just buried his beard in my hair while he buried his dick in my crotch. Maybe he half-supported his body with his elbows because I felt none of that crushing pain on my ribs—either that or he was all skin and bones. Even the thrusting didn't really hurt.

After, he got up and walked away, and I heard the front door close. I grabbed my pants and went into the bathroom and peed. Wiping, I saw blood mixed in with Noah's scum. So that was why it didn't hurt. Would he think he'd screwed a virgin? Good thing I had Evie's tampax.

There was enough light for me to make out my empty shot glass on the counter, weighing down three ten-dollar bills. I pocketed them and waited for my eyes to adjust, then found a bottle of Jack Daniel's and took it to a table. The light from the street lamp coming in the edges of the blinds made shadows on the floor, turning parts of tables and chairs into black geometric shapes, half circles, rectangles, triangles. The shelves behind the bar were hidden by the darkness; only the rim of the old wooden counter caught the lamp's glow, taking on a sheen it had never had in daylight.

Tommy's question came back to me, the one he recited from the Passover Seder: *Why is this night different from all other nights?*

Yes, for me too a sea had parted, and I had passed from one side to the other. To the Promised Land? Hell no, not for thirty dollars, it wasn't.

Chapter 45

I HAD TO have been waiting hours. The sidewalk was cold—you could feel it in your feet. The Sisters had said this shelter didn't fill as fast as some others, maybe because it was out in nowhere. The young woman directly ahead of me apparently knew them all and while furiously chewing gum gave me a rundown. Some had cots; some, you got a pad on the floor, "not even a mattress." This one had wire-spring beds, "and any funny business from the mentals, they're gone." For an extra dollar, you could use the shower.

Inside, I had to stand in another long line, but at least the hall was heated. Nearer the front, I got a glimpse of a woman behind a metal desk and a large man, arms folded, standing behind her. "These are *our* rules," she was telling a woman in a dark green poncho. "Doors locked at nine, lights out at ten." A sign on the wall said *Absolutely NO Alcohol, Illegal Drugs, or Weapons.* Would they search our bags? Was a warm place to stay worth giving up the bottles of Scotch I'd swiped from Simon's? I could always leave.

When it was my turn, the lady asked my name. Nobody ahead of me had shown ID, so I said, "Andy Fritz." She wrote it in a ledger and told me to take a blanket from the pile.

The "dorm" resembled the army barracks you saw in movies, with rows of metal-spring beds and thin, dark-striped mattresses.

Children ran up and down the aisles, which made me feel safer. I found an unclaimed bed not too close to the can. I unfolded the blanket and tucked it in at the foot.

In the restroom, I hung my coat on the stall hook and sat on the toilet fully clothed. Somebody went into the adjacent stall, so I waited and listened to her pee, fart, yank toilet paper, flush, and turn on the sink. Right after she left, I opened the pint, took some swigs, and ate part of the shoplifted Danish.

Most of the beds in the dorm now had blankets. About twenty women and children hung around, only a handful engaged in conversation, at least with somebody in the real world. Some read magazines; the gum chewer applied nail polish; an older one knitted.

I scoped out the bulletin board. *At the following locations you can receive help applying for public assistance and public housing.* A sheet listed phone numbers and addresses for job training, educational programs, AA, day care.

Not being used to a room full of people and doubting the sanity of several, I had trouble falling asleep. But suddenly somebody was yelling, "Rise and shine."

The line at the place helping you apply for public assistance ran around the corner. The wind shot through my coat like ice-rays. Somehow I would have to get a parka.

"Jeez, can't they let us wait inside?"

"People *are* waiting inside, ahead of us."

"Fuck this shit." I walked away, walked fast to stay warm. A greasy spoon had a *Help Wanted* in the window. It also had my reflection. Besides, it was a joke to think I could be pleasant to customers, much less stay sober.

When the buildings got seedier, I saw a group of black women in ridiculously short skirts. Hell, hookers had to eat like everybody else. This must be Roxbury, which meant I would have to pony up for the T. It was Chicago all over again—you took your life in your hands being in a neighborhood where your skin color didn't match the locals'.

I got off at Park and ducked into the side entrance of some fancy hotel. Across the lobby, broad, red-carpeted stairs led to a mezzanine. The valets were busy loading luggage onto chrome racks while people swarmed to the reception desks, so I strode across to the carpeted stairs like I had important business. Nobody stopped me.

The mezzanine was King Solomon's mines—six or seven tables had been laid out with a buffet. Not a soul in sight. I briefly peered through the door panes of the adjoining rooms. In one, a man was giving a lecture, and in another a slideshow was going.

I moved fast, scooping into my coat pockets sandwiches, muffins, cookies, a can of soda. When the pockets couldn't hold any more, I ran to an exit sign and down an enclosed staircase. The door at the bottom opened into the alley.

No, I wouldn't spring for a parka after all—the layers of shirts and one of Evie's sweatshirts under my long coat would have to do. The huge pockets were my tradesman's tools.

The next day I hit the same hotel again, but the mezzanine was empty. I took the elevator up, and my timing was perfect: the busboys hadn't collected the room-service trays. Zigzagging the corridors, I wolfed down leftover portions of sausage, pancake, omelette. At the same time I was rolling pastries and biscuits in napkins and storing them in my coat for later. Some fool even left a two-dollar tip.

In the stairwell, I transferred everything in my pockets to my pack. And the pack did double-duty as camouflage: Boston teemed with grungy backpack-toting students. Probably half were Kennedys.

To play it safe, I alternated among different hotels and varied my hat, and some days I stuck to panhandling. The fast-food joints let you stay for hours as long as you bought *something*—burger, milk, coffee—and they gave you free rein pillaging the tray remnants other customers left behind, especially if you dumped the trays afterwards.

In the evenings, I'd hit a shelter. They didn't care how zoned out you were when you arrived as long as you didn't drink on the premises or cause trouble. I got loaded beforehand and never caused trouble.

Not that I slept great. Three nights in a row, I had practically the same dream. Like Superman with X-ray vision, I would hover over the glass factory watching Mathilde at work. Her fingers and wrists were scratched like I remembered from childhood, but she was putting white plastic lambs in baskets, not glass beakers in cartons. The big hand on the factory clock jerked spasmodically, and occasionally she would glance up to check the time. Was she imagining me arriving home from school? Playing with my miniature cars? Doing homework? Some homework. Dick *in* Jane.

The first night, the dream ended there, but the next two, I flew from the factory home. I could see into Roy's room, from above his bed see him lying on top of me, see the back of his shirt, his greasy, mustard-colored hair. And I could read his thoughts. *I know I'm a sonofabitch for doing this, but you can't stop me, and your knowing it's unfair only makes it better.*

Christmas Eve, I hit the shelter near the T line that went to the church giving out the free meal. It wasn't my favorite shelter—you only got a thin mat on the floor—but by now I knew "Beggars can't be choosers" wasn't just an adage.

In the morning, after the rise-and-shine and Merry Christmas bullshit, some lady told us she had an important announcement.

"A *bitter cold has descended*! Overnight, the temperature dropped to *below zero*. We will stay open all day, and you may remain here until tomorrow without having to go out. But it will get very crowded. Extra mats are being delivered. We hope not to turn anyone away."

The church with the free meal also bent the rules, letting us wait indoors. After filling up my tray, I started down the cafeteria aisle looking for a place to sit. Somebody waved—it was Jackie. Like before, she was using her coat to block off more than her fair share.

She scooted over, saying, "Wondered if you'd show up."

"Hey, if some place else serves free hot meals, I haven't found it."

"Take off your coat, leave it on mine."

"Maybe if I warm up."

"Got three layers under." She pinched her kelly green pullover. Her hair was shorter, cut even with her jaw, accenting the sharp cheekbones. The eyes were blacker than coal.

I dug into my ham and potatoes, letting her do the talking. Her expression remained deadpan, but her voice was upbeat. "Dro woke me. 'Merry Christmas,' he say. Didn't know the phone was turned on, but he say better be; paids the bill. Heards on the radio we had bad cold. I say, 'That great. You in Florida where it eighty.' He say, 'Yeah, might have to take a swim.'" She laughed.

I tried to sound interested. "What's he doing there?"

"Business. Guess who he saw at a store? Yaz. Know who he is?"

"Yastrzemski? Heard of him, but—"

"Used to watch all the games till Dro busted the TV. Pitcher walked in a run, made him mad. Glass everywhere, smoke. Had to open the window, borrow Mark's vacuum."

I finished the glazed ham and began on the potatoes.

"Can't believe that sonofabitch is here."

"The cop?"

"No, Cowboy. Owes *big*. Only had half the money—*swore* he get the rest. He a regular, so will. But get me nervous. If Dro show early, I'll have to pay."

Who knew canned peaches tasted so good. "How much will you have to pay?"

She rolled up her sleeve and showed me a greenish bruise the size of a baseball. "This how I pays." She examined it like Yaz had signed it.

"Just wondering," I said, "you going to eat your peas and peaches?"

"Have 'em."

When I'd consumed her leftovers and every last crumb of roll and cookie, I took out my cigarettes, offering her one.

"No, gives it up. Never did much. Social smoker, Dro say. How's your place in Cambridge?"

"Moved out a while ago. Staying at shelters." I pulled up my sleeve to lick glaze off my wrist.

"What's that?"

"Tried to slit my wrist when I was a kid. Chickened out."

"Me, I'll OD. But won't have to—Dro's get me first."

I lit the cigarette and exhaled. "Ever think of leaving him?"

"Finds me soon enough."

"Or calling the cops?"

"His brother's a cop. Uncle's a cop. Half his cousins is cops. Be out on bail in five minutes and kill me." Her tone was matter-of-fact.

"What about moving far away, like California?"

She seemed to mull that idea over. "Thought 'bout Vegas once. But it's my fate. Knows it the minute I lays eyes on him." The sides of her mouth curved up. "Dro and me, we each other's fate."

Jackie wasn't the first drama queen I'd run into, not by a long shot, and if believing he was her fate got her through the day, who was I to suggest leaving him? I could give her the Women's Center address. *I was referred here by Andy.*

"How you getting by?" Jackie asked.

"Shoplifting, panhandling."

"When you sits near me Thanksgiving, thought you was a narc. Going to a shelter tonight?"

"Yeah. They're getting extra mats so nobody will be turned away." I pressed my cigarette out in the peaches dish. "Want any coffee?"

She shook her head. "Come to our place. Plenty of room."

Without answering, I strolled to the table with the urns and cups. Dro-the-maniac was in Florida, but did she have other roommates? How long would she let me crash for?

When I sat again and asked, she said she didn't have any other roommates, and Dro wouldn't be back till February or March. "Business take him all over." She lowered her voice to a whisper. "Ever do skag?"

"What's that?"

"Smack, horse."

I lowered mine too. "Heroin? No. Got enough problems without addiction."

"Snorting don't addict. It's how come I does it. Weed nothing to me now, nothing."

Not wanting to argue, I just said I had to stick to vices I could afford.

Suddenly her spine straightened. I tracked the direction of her stare. A white guy in a dirty blue parka came towards us. "Thought you might be here," he said.

"Got my Christmas present?" She sounded coy.

"*Two* presents. I missed your birthday."

"In a minute." She tossed a glance at my coffee. "C'mon. You can have the guest room. Best radiator in whole 'partment."

She quickly put on her coat and grabbed a large black handbag from under the table. The two of them headed for the rear exit. I grabbed my pack and followed.

We walked a block and down an alley. The guy took out a thin bundle of bills and peeled off some. Jackie pocketed the money with one hand while unzipping her coat with the other and producing small, shiny, light green envelopes. Within seconds, the guy was history.

"Let's go," she said. On the main drag, she pointed to a bus. "We can takes that." I hurried after her. They weren't kidding; a bitter cold had descended.

Chapter 46

ON THE BUS, Jackie bragged about charging Mac less when he was a new customer. "You got to feed the need, I tell Dro. Now he a regular and pay my rates." She smiled at her reflection in the window. "Women's better at sales."

We got off in a dingy neighborhood, and I followed her up a wide dirt alley between three-story brick apartment buildings. All the buildings had back staircases and long yards, some bordered by chain-link or decaying picket fences. In the alley itself, metal trash bins kept company with cannibalized cars, tires, discarded furniture. But the space felt airy, maybe on account of the combination of wide lane, long back yards, and low buildings. You could almost imagine that instead of a city you were in a small town, a small forlorn town.

Jackie flipped the latch on a weather-beaten wooden gate and went up a cracked cement path. I closed the latch behind me and followed. We climbed old wooden stairs past the boarded windows of the first-floor apartment. She paused briefly on the second landing and knocked twice on the door before continuing to the top, where plywood covered the window in the door and a metal grille covered the curtained window.

Once inside, she turned on an overhead. Dozens of cockroaches dove under the fridge, and several ran into cracks in the wall plaster. Jackie went down a hall on the left that appeared to go towards the front of the apartment, but since she didn't tell me to follow, I remained by the formica table, resting my pack against one of the rust-spotted legs.

The table top, a faded pink, was bare except for a saucer with some used matches. The chairs had worn plastic cushions, also a faded pink. The cupboard doors were dirty; so was the fridge. The stove was the worst: brown grease smeared the top and down the front. An aluminum kettle and small saucepan sat on the back burners. The counter had nothing—not a toaster, not canisters of flour or sugar, not even salt and pepper.

Jackie came in without her coat and handed me a small pipe. "Saids you like weed. This old, but you might gets something."

"Thanks. Wish I could pay you but barely have enough for my next pack—"

"Don't matter. Like I said, weed don't do nothing for me." She pulled out a chair and sat. A second pipe materialized, along with a blue bic lighter and small tin box. "Want some opium?"

"Never had it."

"Like smoking skag, you don't get hooked. Skag better, give a rush. But I gots to slow myself." Abruptly Jackie rose and went to the hall. "Better go to the john. Opium shut you down. You can after." She motioned with her hand. "C'mon, gives you a tour."

The first doorway, on the left side of the hall, was a bedroom containing only a double mattress on the floor and some blankets. "This yours," she said. She hadn't lied about the radiator: the room was toasty.

The next room was on the right, the bathroom. Cracked paint, old porcelain tub, old sink and toilet. The third room, on the left, was "storage." It stored a metal ironing board, empty beer cans, cardboard boxes, a broom and dustpan. We continued on till the hall made a right turn into pitch blackness. Jackie flicked on another overhead. The front door, straight ahead, had wood planks nailed across it vertically, horizontally, and diagonally.

"Guess nobody goes in and out that way," I joked.

"Dro taking no chances on the Feds."

Was there some law against them using the back door? Maybe Dro was a drama *king*.

"This our bedroom. Supposed to be the living room."

A single uncovered bulb in the center of the ceiling provided the only light—the windows opposite, which must have faced the street, were completely blocked with heavy maroon drapes. The floor was littered with clothes, magazines, wine bottles, soda cans. The sole piece of furniture besides a bureau was a double-bed mattress and box spring. A clock radio and phone sat nearby on the floor. The walls were bare. A cockroach dove behind a knee-high black leather boot lying on its side.

I gestured at the large ax in the corner. "That to bust out in case of fire?"

"Dro used to be a fireman. Stole it from the station."

While Jackie was in the can, I brought my pack to the room she was letting me use. The same type of heavy maroon drapes she had in her bedroom covered the windows here. I pushed one aside and looked down onto a narrow walkway between the buildings. The windows opposite had their shades lowered. I let the drape fall back into place and opened the closet door. The hooks and shelf were empty—not even any hangers.

Though the room was a poor cousin to Evie's, I was welcome here. Jackie *wanted* me to stay—I didn't have to come up with lies to stall for time. And yet I didn't trust her completely. Why not? Maybe the problem wasn't her but me: I'd stopped trusting anybody, period. *Pot calling kettle, pot calling kettle.* You still around, Jiminy?

After scouring the room for hiding places, I pushed the drapes aside and found a gap where the window sash had separated from the wall. I took out my wallet and removed my driver's license and my last two twenties. I wrapped the license tightly in the bills, making a thin packet. The packet slid easily into the gap. Only the very edge showed between the plaster and wood, and if you didn't know any better, it looked like part of the wall. I let the drapes fall back into place over the entire sash. From now on, I was Andy Fritz.

What else was in this zebra-etched relic of Madison besides some singles? My shim card. I could be John Q. Public. The obituary. The photos of Stacy and me taken at the booth in the Randolph Street IC Station. I went to the kitchen and used Jackie's lighter to burn the photos over the sink, dousing the ashes with tap water. The obituary was so shredded, I just tossed it.

The fridge didn't have much: beer, cheap-brand cola, bottles of rosé, two cents' worth of orange juice. The freezer, however, was packed solid, mostly with pot pies and TV dinners. I squished a cockroach with my boot and took the Scotch from my pack and drank some and had a cigarette by the side window. A middle-aged woman in a heavy coat hauled a shopping bag to the alley, inverted the bag over an open garbage can, and dumped in a pile of magazines. Husband's *Playboy* collection? The sheer ordinariness of a person taking out the trash was somehow comforting.

Jackie came in. "You can gets in the bathroom now."

"Here's some Scotch if you want."

"I like my wine; that's alls I drink. 'Cept when Mark makes his specials. Do number two if you can." She pointed to the tin box on the table. "Shut your gut down."

The only object in the bathroom besides the bar of soap in the tub holder and the dirty towel on the rack was a mirror lying flat on the toilet tank. I sat on the toilet a while, staring at the small hexagonal tiles. Maybe tomorrow I would relax enough to take a dump.

While the toilet was flushing, I opened the medicine cabinet. The bottom shelf contained a stack of razor blades, box of tampax, one of Q-tips, bottles of rubbing alcohol and aspirin, and a bag of cotton balls. The upper shelves contained a metal spoon, tube of toothpaste, two toothbrushes, a box of wooden matches, some bobby pins, and a translucent yellow prescription vial. *Droghan Moore. Three times daily.*

I returned to the kitchen. Jackie handed me a cold soda, saying, "Don't drinks liquor with ope."

We sat at the table, and I watched her clean her pipe. "Can't believes you never does it before. Babe in the woods. Do's your weed first."

"Dropped acid when I was younger, a little MDA," I said. "Speed and 'ludes in high school. Last few years I've stuck to weed. And beer."

"They's your weakness. What's your flaw?"

"Flaw, singular? Don't have just one." I held the bic to the pipe and tried inhaling.

"Your 'Destiny Flaw.' Everybody's gots one flaw that's special, that control their life. Mine is trusting people. Guys that takes me in when I gets here, easy pussy all they want. 'Cept Dro. But he was the one that gots me." She made a fake cackle.

"How long you two been together?"

"Three years. First six months, didn't touch me, not once. Told me: stay here, do what him and Mark say. Mostly deliveries. This place nice then." She glanced around at the bare walls, flaking plaster. "One night, we drinking, he asks do I want to be his girl. 'What takes you so long?' I say. When he start going away, Baltimore,

Florida, Mark, he gives me money if I'm broke. Keep an eye out. Pay bills, sometimes shop. He know a store where a junkie at the register. Mark take care of my needs. 'Cept one. Mark don't take care of one." So she wasn't cheating on Droghan. But didn't she wonder if Droghan was cheating on her? He could have another girlfriend—a wife and kids—down in Florida or just about anywhere. Maybe she was right: her special flaw was trusting.

"I helps him back. Eileen got appendicitis, I cook for Rachel. Going to have another in the spring. Hope a boy."

Jackie seemed to forget about the opium, talking a blue streak, mostly about different kinds of heroin. She used names like Sky High, Persian-this, Pakistani-that, Angel White, Black Beauty. It reminded me of the chicken breed names Laurie had rattled off at Geserenie.

"The vein shooters say smoking don't gives the rush, but they're used to the fastest. Skin popping's just under the skin, and muscling, I don't likes them; can gets infected. Smoking, second and third toke gives a rush. But mainline too easy get hooked."

"How many times does it take to get hooked?"

"No two people same. You—might take seven, eight. Space it out, might *never.*"

Amazingly, I had finally gotten the damn plug to light and even managed to inhale some. If it was pot, it was staler than shit.

"Dro say it genes. Know what they are? Your hereditary, what your parents gives you. Like hair color and skin. You Swedish?"

"Don't know."

"I'm Apache, white, Black-Irish. People thinks Italian, but it Apache."

To be polite, I offered her the pot. She shook her head. I pretended to continue toking, but there was nothing to toke.

"I mixes. Some days, just wine. Some days, uppers. Some, this baby. Tells you what: have my coke every day, if I could. Coke, that my flaw. But Dro don't lets me."

Jackie pried the lid off the small tin. Inside was a dark powder that she pinched between her thumb and index finger. I expected it to flake, but it was gunky. She put it in the pipe and tamped gently, first with her pinky, then with the butt of the bic. She used the bic to light it and sucked on the stem till the black gunk glowed. She handed the pipe across the table to me, and I inhaled cautiously, then more strongly. The opium gave a thick, warm smoke, fuller than weed but not unpleasant, not like the cheap cigars Roy used to bring home. We passed the pipe back and forth, Jackie relighting and reloading from time to time. Neither of us spoke.

I heard sizzling. My neck turned slowly. Radiator. Did a good job. Warmer than the shelter. *Gimme shelter. Gimme, gimme shelter.*

"Nice?" Jackie's coal black eyes ... almost had ... glint.

"Yes."

She smiled ... watching shadow ... on the wall. ... Did she ... grow up ... on a reservation? ... Maybe ... one pico ... Apache ... Droghan Moore ... hard G? ... F like tough? ... rough ... Moore ... Sir Thomas More ... one O ... no more ... A joke ... more and moor ... homonyms ... not synonyms ... Homo ... not syn ... homo not sin ... also joke ... Othello ... different kind ... of Moor ... not like moors ... in England ... *Wuthering Heights* ... Nina liked ... Heathcliff ... Nina nano nun ... nano ... chance ... Nina ... nun. ... No munchies ... gut stopped ... Sally's word? ... Peristalsis ... not ... Perry Mason ... Three ... jokes ... yes ... Merry Christmas ... Lump ... of opium ... beat ... lump ... of coal.

Could ... opium ... cure ... Huntington's? ... Arm ... can't ... fling ... Body ... can't ... writhe ... No energy ... for ... large ... prancing ... gait ... How ... could ... I ... sinuously ... twist ... or ...

grimace? ... Can't ... smile ... either ... but ... smile ... is ... what ... I ... feel.

Bright light. Kitchen overhead. Jackie standing. "You in dark all this time?"

The words came slowly. "Guess so." My lips felt heavy.

"What you think?"

My arm reached. Hand touched. Grasped. Pack of cigarettes. "Opium? ... Nice."

She handed me another soda. "Stay off liquor tills tomorrow."

The warm fog, a little-cat-feet fog, began to lift. ... Somehow, sometime ... I popped the soda can top. ... Sipped. ... Lit a cigarette. ... Jackie in hall saying, "I'm going to bed."

My room. Turned on light. Closed door. Swung back open ... few inches. Tried again. ... Latch wouldn't click. Maybe in morning ... would ... figure it out. ... Pulled blankets flat. Took off sweatshirt. Made pillow. Took off boots ... pants. Turned off light. Lay down. Pulled blankets up. Warm. Warmer than shelter. I'm gonna fade away.

Chapter 47

"'Stop it, Cindy,' I said, 'you'll scratch the skin off.'" The voice was a man's.

Jackie's: "Nam?"

"No, rum. The last day, Joey was a grasshopper." The guy sounded amused.

"Complain?"

"You bet. 'What's so great?' He blew the shot."

"Know who OD in Somerville?"

"Harley."

"Harley!" Jackie sounded annoyed. "He one of ours."

"Not anyone's anymore."

"Serve him right. Where he get his dough? Dumber than a dog."

"Hustling. Boy bars."

I pulled on my pants and boots, grabbed my cigarettes, and tiptoed to the can. When I was done, I walked normally into the kitchen.

"Here she is," Jackie said.

A clean-shaven guy about thirty-five, give or take, was sitting beside her. His smile was friendly but not too friendly—no up-and-down bullshit. He wore a nice blue sweater.

"This Mark, from downstairs. Bring our mail."

We nodded at each other. He had a cigarette going and a mug in front of him. Jackie had a mug too. She saw me eyeing it. "Kettle still hot."

I saw the jar of instant by the stove. I found a mug in the cupboard and poured myself a cup and joined them at the table.

"He telling 'bout Dro's package," Jackie said.

"Two ODs," Mark said.

"Second pull through?" she asked.

"Not sure." He patted his ash into the saucer. His eyes were sharp; he seemed smart.

"Bumpkin *really* cry?"

"Like a baby," Mark said. "Remembering your last batch."

"Don't overcuts that."

"Droghan taught you well." He pronounced it with a hard G.

"Last time, Barbell puke *second* I walks by."

Mark grinned at me. "Not because of Jackie's looks. Some junkies can't contain the anticipation of their next fix and puke right before."

Carly Simon's song started running through my head. *Anticipation, anticipation is making me late, is keeping me waiting.*

"Woman from Beverly comes?" Jackie asked. "Yellow raincoat?"

"She's not from Beverly."

"Say so."

"Worcester."

"Why comes *here*? Dro say there plenty—"

"All the cops know her since that bust. Kiss of death, everyone scatters. She should get a different raincoat." Mark leaned the chair back on two legs. "I'm waiting for the day they try to kick in *your* door."

Jackie seemed to enjoy picturing it. "Dro say shin bones split if they tries. You know, Andy like weed."

Mark brought the front legs of the chair back down. "Do you?
I can get—"

"Need to drum up some money first," I said.

"Tell you what." He reached under his nice blue sweater and
pulled out a baggie. "You can owe me ten."

I kneaded the baggie gently. "Just not sure when I'll have a
chance—"

"You and Jackie will have to stay put until this arctic blast
leaves. If worst comes to worst, later you can sell a few lids."

I nodded, hoping he didn't mean heroin.

While the two of them continued talking, I cleaned the pipe,
put in some weed, and lit it. Nice draw. Nobody else wanted any, so
I nursed that baby all by myself.

"Whens you gots to be at work?"

Mark rose and put his cigarettes in his pants pocket. "Not till
three. Promised Eileen I'd do a grocery run. Need anything? Better
stock up."

"Juice, wine, coffee, soda, bread. Andy, what you like?"

"Guess just beer. I'm used to scrounging around for free stuff.
Like I said, don't have much cash."

"Nothing out there to scrounge but frostbite," Mark said. "How
about milk, Jackie? You have a hundred boxes of Wheaties."

"Dro like it. Eat cereal? Okay, gets her milk."

As soon as Mark left, she bolted the door and asked if I played
board games. I said a few, and she went down the hall and returned
with a box. "Know Sorry? What colors you wants?"

"Don't care."

"I likes red."

As we played, Jackie went on again about drug dealing. I learned
that somebody OD'ing on your heroin was great for business—"good
advertising." You didn't want them to croak, just go by ambulance

to the ER and have word spread. And you would sell only a little the first day so its "rep-tation" would get around, and days two and three you could charge more, not to mention lace it with quinine or powder.

"November, him send stuff so good I could mix and gets full price. Couldn't stop dipping. Took extra two, three times. That my flaw—no willpower. He come back December—FBI, ATF, somebody nosing. The cops, he don't worry. Pays them off. Feds, can pay *some*, not all."

I asked if that was when she got the bruise on her arm, and Jackie's nostrils flared. "Should've seen time he breaks my wrist."

Her head jerked; we heard a noise. She said nothing, waiting. Somebody knocked Morse-code style. "It Mark." She rose and undid the bolt.

While the cold temperatures lasted, Jackie and I stayed indoors and played countless games of Sorry and gin rummy. She moved her clock radio into the kitchen and tuned it to an AM Top Forty, but at least folks had pretty much gotten over Lennon's death, so I wasn't stuck listening to his words of wisdom nonstop. If Jackie took a nap or went to bed first, I sat at the table with my beer, pot, and cigarettes and played solitaire. I might get lucky even when she was awake if she brought out her stickers and loose-leaf paper. Dozens of sheets of colored stars, kittens, puppies, little girls with parasols would litter the table, and one at a time, she'd peel a sticker off and carefully press it onto the paper.

Once while she was in the can, I swiveled the page 180 for a better look. True, none of the animals or figures were upside down or sideways, but they weren't arranged in any order either: not in rows, columns, or some kind of scene. Even the spacing was random, meaningless. Not that solitaire was all that meaningful.

What was more disturbing, though, was how one minute she would add an *s* to a word and the next minute, drop it. Or might add or drop an article like *a* or *the*. Or mix singular and plural. The rest of us jumped back-and-forth between slang and so-called proper speech, but Jackie's inconsistencies made you feel she had suffered some terrible injury so early in childhood it had messed with the brain's basic gears.

When the weather warmed a little, she left the apartment for short periods in the middle of the day. Mark continued to play Santa, bringing up beer, wine, pot, and food. One day he brought us an old TV somebody was chucking. It only got three channels but none with sports, so it might survive Droghan's next visit. If Mark stayed for a cup of coffee or beer, his and Jackie's conversation invariably centered on drug deals. He used *horse* and *skag* and *smack* but also *jenny* and a bunch of other terms.

A food bank nearby apparently distributed groceries two mornings a week. Jackie said she wouldn't go because "There's people I can't lets see me," but I was happy to contribute to the cause, even if it meant standing in line in the cold. She would wait for me in the kitchen, and the moment I stepped over the threshold would grab my pack and dive in for the stuff she liked. Still, she rewarded my efforts with a back-door key. The implication that I wouldn't have to live on the street again any time soon made me immensely grateful.

It was in February, I was guessing, that Mark came upstairs with twenty bags of weed he wanted me to sell. "Jackie will show you what to do. Don't worry about the cops—they don't like busting small-fry."

"She not worried. Tells 'bout the hotels and restaurants."

Mark's eyebrows rose. "Hotels and restaurants? Did you stick them up?"

I couldn't keep from laughing. "No. Just figured out some ways to get free food." I described a few jaunts, pretending to have taken only untouched things.

"I would worry more about getting busted for stealing than selling," he said. I could sell all twenty lids or keep one for myself as my pay; they went for ten each.

My first time, Jackie took me. The park was only a few T stops away, and we strolled the perimeter slowly, then wandered along the inner paths. Every few minutes, some guy would come up and pretend to be bumming or lighting a cigarette or asking the time. Bills would be exchanged for bags, and we'd all mosey on. *I'm no prophet. I don't know Nature's way.* Actually, Nature had a pretty easy way, and we were on the train not half an hour later.

Other than to sell, hit the food bank, and go with Jackie to the grocery, I saw little point in leaving the apartment. All the commercial stretch nearby had was a Chinese take-out, laundromat, and shoe repair shop with a picture of President Kennedy in the window.

I got introduced to Eileen on one trip back from the grocery; she happened to be sweeping the landing. In response to my hi, she nodded curtly. I had imagined Mark's wife would be less frumpy, not that sweeping was anything to get dolled up for.

"Wake up. You's got to come with."

I raised my arm to block out the glare of the ceiling light. "Where?"

"Gots to do a drop-off."

We took a bus to a neighborhood way seedier than ours. This one street we walked down was so narrow, anybody driving would have to go at a crawl to avoid scraping the parked cars, though they looked pretty wrecked anyway. Buildings were fire-gutted or boarded up. Old metal garbage cans lined the sidewalk, not that anybody used them. A dead rodent of some kind lay on the curb amid the cigarette butts and wrappers and dog shit.

Midway down the block, people loitered in doorways or on stoops. One guy had the leathery skin you saw on the Delaware Bay fishermen. A few resembled the commuters at North and South Stations, nice coats dangling open over suits and ties. One woman in heels could have been a secretary. The very last guy, sitting on a stoop, stared vacantly as we went past like we were ghosts.

Actually, I would have preferred being invisible, since Jackie was making me wear a bright yellow stocking cap. Not so her—she carried herself like a model: confident, her eyes focused on some object straight ahead. But you could tell her peripheral vision detected everybody. No comments, no catcalls, no whistles—nobody hassled us.

We came to an intersection with a wide, busy avenue, and Jackie pointed to a bench opposite. "Sits there. You're lookout. If somebody comes down this street, takes off your hat. After they gone, puts it back on, 'less somebody new coming."

"Where will you be?"

"Back there."

"On the sidewalk?"

"Inside." Her coal black eyes darted everywhere.

"How will you see me if I take off—"

"Others sees you. They lets me know."

"What if it's a car?"

"Same thing. Just keeps the hat's off till nobody coming."

"What if traffic backs up from the light, and a truck blocks my view and nobody can see if my hat's on or off?"

"There's peoples can. Why's you so nervous? *You* clean."

She started back down the narrow street, and I crossed the avenue and sat on the bench. The loiterers seemed to come to attention as Jackie passed; the vacant-faced guy on the stoop stood. To my right, a young guy with a shopping bag approached. I was afraid he'd block my view, but he crossed at the light. When he headed up the narrow street, I pulled off my hat. Feeling stupid, I scratched my head just to look like I had some reason for removing it. Hopefully scratching wasn't a signal for snipers on the roofs to open fire. The guy with the shopping bag seemed to pause at everybody he met. I waited till he had gone around the far corner before putting the hat back on.

Jackie emerged from a doorway, and the loiterers flocked to it. She came towards me, crossed the street, and passed by, muttering, "Follows in a minute." I met up with her at the T. When the train came, she walked to the rear.

"That was quick," I said, sitting beside her.

"This time I just drops off."

"I only had to take off my hat once. This guy with a shopping—"

"Jay sell syringes, needles. His works okay. Only sells new."

"Who'd buy used?"

She smiled in her superior way. "Packages *looks* new. Till they sticks the needle in, can't tell. Sometimes till they pushes the plunger, if it don't go smooth. But too late—infection already start. Jay work at the hospital, so his always new. You see guy in the purple jacket? Doctor, before loses his license."

I looked across the aisle. On the back of the seat ahead somebody had scrawled *eat shit and die.*

"Why would anybody subject themselves to a craving so strong they'll risk anything to satisfy it?"

Jackie laughed. "Babe in the woods, what you is. The *high.*"

"Guess I'm okay with beer and weed."

"Chip like me. Don't sees me addicted. Twice a week."
Did she have a calendar to keep track?

Droghan got "delayed," and we had to quit dealing for a week—I
didn't know if the two events were related—but in what was probably April, we were selling hand-over-fist. Mark told me I could keep
two lids per twenty, so he must've figured I'd paid him back for all
the food and beer he'd bought during the big freeze. He continued
to supply me with cigarettes by the carton, saying he got them for
practically nothing. Maybe he was lying—all I knew was he didn't
want me to shoplift.

Except for the mornings I hit the food bank and the afternoons
I hit the park, the hours blurred together. Usually when I awoke,
Jackie would be gone, so I'd have my coffee and cereal in quiet tran-
quility and bask in the scenic surroundings. Off to starboard was
the lovely back door, plywood across its pane, grating across the
adjacent window. To port was the stove, its grease stains like trickling maple syrup. The ceiling and walls were vistas of cracked and
peeling paint. And glory be to God for the dappled fridge. Finally,
the counter, adorned with crumbs, spills, and cheerful indigenous
roaches.

When Jackie came home, the TV went on, tuned to soap operas,
talk shows, or reruns of crap not worth watching the first go-round.

At some point she said I needed to bring in cash "for utilities."
I tried explaining that panhandling worked best when folks were
leaving work or after they'd had some drinks, but it didn't penetrate,
so I'd have to split in the middle of the day. She never failed to
hear me come up the back steps, and I'd hand her money like I was
stopped at a toll booth. Less than a week into that bullshit, I quit the
hope-this-helps-with-the-utilities. But I hid the bulk of my earnings
in my sneakers during the day and under the mattress at night.

From then on, I only hung out with her in the kitchen when she specifically asked. We would sit opposite at the table, me with my beer, cigarettes, and pot, and her with her wine. She'd talk a blue streak: So-and-so puked; So-and-so scratched like a monkey; So-and-so couldn't stop yawning. X had pupils the size of a baseball; Y had no pupils; Afro Joe liked to shebang; Molly had no veins and had to skin-pop. I couldn't always tell if she was describing folks *after* they'd shot up or while waiting to buy, not that it mattered.

To stay on Mark's good side—though I never saw his bad—I loaded up on fresh vegetables at the food bank and dropped them off with Eileen. The one time I kept a zucchini for myself, the first bite flooded my brain with memories of Geserenie, and who needed that shit. Yet despite the freebies, Eileen never grew friendly. She would open the back door to my knock, take the tomatoes, cukes or whatever, thank me brusquely, and close it. Once I glimpsed Rachel, a young girl with braids, sitting at a table with an open book, but none of us said anything.

Chapter 48

EILEEN OPENED HER back door while Jackie and I were trudging upstairs with groceries and surprised me by telling Jackie, "I baked you cookies." Without saying thanks, Jackie continued on up to the apartment.

While I stored the perishables in the fridge, Jackie took a small square pan covered with foil out of the oven. Lifting a corner of the foil, she removed several large chocolate chip cookies. To me they looked store-bought.

She smiled. "You's ready for going somewheres?"

"We just got back. Was hoping to sit, relax, have a beer."

"Not outside. Going to heaven. We's going to smoke jenny." She showed me the small, translucent green envelopes—what she called "glassines"—in the bottom of the pan.

"No need to waste it on me. Keep them for yourself."

She practically snapped my head off. "How's I knows you's not a narc?"

"Getting high every day? Selling weed?"

"Not havings no roommate who don't even smokes it."

"Can I have a beer first?"

"If you wants to waste your beer."

I followed her to the bathroom, and she gestured for me to sit on the tub ledge. Maybe I wouldn't toke deeply. She arranged things along the side of the sink: a glassine, box of wooden matches, small sheet of foil, glass tube the size of a cigarette, wooden-handled metal spoon. She patted down every square inch of sink basin with toilet paper and molded a small square of foil over the drain, smoothing the edges. We used two bobby pins apiece to pin our hair back. She rolled up her sleeves to above the elbows and told me to do the same. "Keeps your arms bare so's you can wash 'em after. Dogs can smells a speck."

"You're going first, right?"

"We don't do's all at once. Waits in between. I likes seconds and thirds best." She sat on the closed toilet lid and again smiled. "Ready to chase a dragon?"

"Hope my lungs are ready." I studied the dirty white hexagons on the floor. So many old buildings had the same kind, buildings in Philly and Chicago too. Were they still manufactured? Must've been hell to lay, being so small. Did they use grout?

"Lights me a match." She leaned one elbow on the sink, her hand holding the spoon over the basin. In the spoon was a small mound of sand-colored powder. After the flame finished bursting, she took the match from me. "Quick, picks up the tube and puts it in a nostril. Pinch the other and inhales the smoke." I wanted to protest *she* was supposed to go first, but with the spoon in one hand and lit match in the other, she obviously couldn't. "Watches me so you's learn. We cooks it *real* slow." Her black eyes crossed when they focused on the flame, which stretched to an inch or two below the metal. Smoke began rising from the spoon. I leaned over and inhaled through the tube.

"Keeps going till it's done and blows it outs to the side when you can't holds it. Then takes the spoon and match so I go."

After my turn, I did my best to mimic her and let the heroin burn slowly. She kept inhaling till the smoke stopped. I couldn't tell if anything was happening. Then it did. Warmth, sunshine, joy flowed through my arteries and veins, through my organs and skin and probably hairs. Exuberance, a luxurious exuberance. Why on earth had I been *glum* for so long? Why couldn't I see that life was good, *really* good. I felt radiant; I *was* radiant, supremely and serenely radiant.

A few minutes later we smoked again, and a few minutes after that, once more. Jackie was right: each rush came on stronger. Power and vitality and peace and a delicious serenity filled body and soul alike. I was King of the Mountain, Queen of Sheba, Jack of All Trades, and Master too. Aloha, arrivederci, willkommen, bienvenue, shalom. Yippie-i-ay. I'll stay right here 'cause these are the good old days.

The next morning, Jackie barged in my room and said I needed to come up with thirty-five dollars. She wouldn't leave till I got out of bed, which pissed me off royally.

I had some luck panhandling on Arlington and grabbed some bills from some guy's violin case. That night she stayed holed up in the front room, so I had to settle for beer and pot.

Often in the next few days I reminisced about the high, but she was right—the sharp appetite passed. You *could* chip and not get addicted.

Mark began getting weed in larger quantities and now brought it upstairs to be divided. Jackie dug out a set of scales, and I did my own measuring. The storage room became my lab, and the ironing board, my lab counter. Should I short the customers, maybe lace with oregano? Wouldn't that demonstrate initiative, get Mark to see me as a long-term investment? Maybe I could work my way up to being in charge of the pot accounts. But he never pressured me to sell skag.

Shouting startled me awake; I sat up immediately. A man's voice, loud but not angry. I yanked on my jeans and tiptoed to the door, open its usual inch.

"Tell him at five." The voice came from the left. The toilet flushed. I remained in darkness, my foot positioned against the door bottom so it wouldn't swing open more. The daylight in the hall suggested late morning. Now the speaker moved into my inch-wide field of vision but halted, turning to face the front of the apartment. He was early thirties, about five-eight, clean-shaven, with a pug nose and brown hair curling out from under a red baseball cap. I could read above the visor *Sox*.

"Anything else?" he shouted.

"Wine," Jackie called from farther down.

He turned and continued past. I heard the back door shut and waited a minute before hitting the can. The seat was up, and I lowered it and sat. Jackie came in seconds later, clutching a large green robe against her chest. She wore pink fuzzy slippers I'd never seen before. Her eyelids drooped. "Can't you stays somewhere—that hotel by the gas station? Dro be here all week, maybe next."

"Don't they charge five a night?"

She reached in the robe pocket and pulled out a wad of bills. "This help. Go now, 'fores he get back." She re-pocketed the money and shuffled to the kitchen.

I crammed most of my stuff into my pack, leaving behind only the boots and heavy sweatshirts. Waiting by the back door, Jackie peeled three twenties from her wad. "Okay?"

"Could I have one more?"

Her mouth lazily curved upward. "Sure." She handed me a fourth, and immediately I regretted not asking for an even hundred. "Now go's."

"Let me grab a beer for the road."

She wandered down the hall. I grabbed three bottles and hurried out.

Droghan hadn't locked the door, so I didn't either. From the landing I could see both directions along the wide alley. Nobody in sight, not below or on the other landings. I hurried downstairs and went the roundabout way.

I wasn't completely sorry to be staying at the hotel, but the interrupted sleep—every noise woke me—made me crazy. The third evening I got good and tanked, hoping that would knock me out for the night. The men loitering in the halls looked as friendly as jackals. Jackie and Jackals. Imagine not having to pick between them. What a fucking mess, a fucking fucking mess. There must be some way out of here, said the joker to the thief.

I went downstairs and into the phone booth. I dialed the operator and plunked in some coins and listened to ringing.

"It's me, Andy."

Mathilde gasped audibly. "Andy! Where are you?"

"Boston."

"Boston. We didn't know what happened."

"Sorry about that. Guess a lot was coming down all at once."

"You had us so *worried*."

"I'm really sorry."

"Are you working? Do you need money?"

"Got a little coming in."

"We didn't know what happened," she repeated.

"Like I said, with everything at once, Dean and the Huntington's—"

"You won't get it."

"What do you mean? Why not?"

"Because."

"Because why?"

"Hold on, the water's boiling."

Did Dr. Wu decide for some reason that Dean *hadn't* had Huntington's? He could have remembered that Lorraine worked in Admitting and tracked her down and told her. And if Dean had had some *other* disease, maybe it wasn't genetic. Or maybe Dean did have Huntington's, but now they realized the odds were way less than fifty-fifty for, say, girls inheriting it from fathers. Odds were never exactly what they said—didn't some families churn out five sons in a row or only daughters?

Mathilde got back on, apologizing.

"Anyway, you said I wouldn't get Huntington's. Why not?"

"Not everybody does."

"But the odds, are they 50 percent? Lorraine said they were. Or do they now think—?"

"Sissy's not a doctor."

"But that's what Dr. Wu said. And other doctors say the same thing." I remembered Evie's textbook chart.

"Even so, you're just as likely *not* to. Why think the worst? It could all be for nothing. Honestly, I wouldn't worry about it. You'll be fine."

I hung up.

Some days later, Mark knocked on my hotel room door. "Droghan's leaving early tomorrow morning if you want to come back."

"Guess so," I said.

"I'll tell Jackie to expect you."

The wide alley was mostly unchanged—the broken tricycle still sat by the dumpster, along with the car tires. Eileen must've just swept the back steps, because up to their landing was clear. The staircase up to Jackie's, like in one of those before-and-after advertisements, was caked with dirt, leaves, bits of foil and waxed paper that probably came from her lifesaver wrappers, and a still-damp spill—probably soda. I knocked on the back door, feeling funny about using my key. She let me in with a smile.

My bedroom appeared untouched. I dumped my pack and checked the fridge. "Mind if I have one of the beers?"

"Haves 'em all. Dro gone down to Florida."

I picked up where I left off, selling weed, hitting the food bank, getting drunk and high. When Jackie was home, I tried not to be; when she wasn't, I played solitaire. Some evenings Mark came up to play hearts or three-handed rummy, especially after the second kid was born. When his nosebleeds were bad, he'd make us all gin and tonics.

Now and again Jackie and I chased the dragon. Pot and beer helped my mind wander away, but skag allowed it to alight anywhere, dwell for any length of time on any thought, because nothing had the power to hurt. Mathilde, Roy, Laurie, everybody floated by like cartoon clouds, and all guilt, anger, and fear became fairy dust: mythical, insubstantial. You too, Disease, be not proud, though some have called thee mighty and dreadful, for thou are not so.

Seasons came and went. Droghan surfaced now and again, usually late at night, and Jackie would shoo me out at dawn. The only change in that routine was in his Red Sox cap, which he often left on the kitchen table; each visit the X was more lopsided and at one visit had fallen off completely. Maybe Yaz had autographed the visor so he didn't want to part with it.

"Shit, shit, shit!" Jackie sat slumped in a chair. A somber Mark stood by the kitchen door.

"What's going on?" I asked.

"Droghan's been arrested," Mark said. "In Miami."

"What do we do?"

"Dump, sell everything."

"Should I try to find customers now?"

"No, go your usual time."

I grabbed a beer from the fridge. "Can he make bail?"

"Yes and he has a lawyer. Discount all you have and get rid of it. I'm sending Eileen to her parents. I may join her." He paused, deliberating. "Andy, the hard part is going to be you and Jackie losing your steady income."

"Hey, we'll manage. I know places to get food and drum up spare—"

"I know you'll manage. You are two resourceful ladies."

For a while things went okay. It being summer, my appetite shrank, and I could walk places or hitch instead of hopping a T. Without dope to sell, Jackie hung around mornings, but I kept to my old hours and went scavenging in the afternoon. The days I showered, I would try the hotels, at least where I wasn't recognized.

At some point, though, the food bank ran low on handouts, and hunger made us bitchy.

"Wear this," Jackie said one evening, tossing me her red blouse.

We walked a good dozen blocks in the sticky humidity to a seedy lounge. She held open the door, but I didn't go in, saying I didn't want to waste money buying beer by the glass. She continued holding the door and said, "You can'ts get cheapers than zero."

It was nicely air-conditioned, and when the waiter came to our booth, Jackie said we were "waiting on our friends." I asked what friends, and she smiled a fake smile. A few minutes later, two middle-aged men in suits came over. Jackie scooted down on her seat to allow one of them to sit. The other didn't wait for me to move and shoved me with his hip. Jackie ordered mai tais for both of us and a nachos platter.

For the next hour, she flirted up a storm with both men while I gobbled the nachos, which I didn't have to do, since they also ordered onion rings and fries and barbecued pork. When I went to use the can, she followed, but before I opened the ladies room door, she shoved me forward, hissing, "Run!" We bolted out the fire exit and ran several blocks and caught the T, which she paid for from a wad of singles.

Chapter 49

"WASH YOUR HAIR and wears that." This time she flung her purple blouse at me.

"What for?" I said.

"You wants to eat, don'ts you?"

"What's that?"

"Skirt."

"I'm not wearing—"

"Do's like I say." Her black eyes drilled into me like large-bore bits. She herself wore a black skirt and ugly brown cardigan buttoned to the top.

I showered and put on her ridiculous purple blouse and brown fake-leather skirt. The skirt was too loose at the waist and rested on my hips, which was okay, since then the hem hit below the knee.

She gaped at my legs. "You didn't shaves."

"Guess not. Hey, if I've got to wear this outfit, I deserve a decent-sized meal."

"*Ten* meals. Wears those."

"High heels? You got to be kid—"

"Hurry, will's you."

We took an inbound and walked a few blocks, me trying not to break my neck in the stupid shoes. Jackie stopped at a mailbox. "Sticks your tits out," she said.

"What?"

"To gets them interested."

"You didn't say we were going to trick."

"What you think?"

"That we were going to do like last time."

"They knows me now. You's tricked before—said so."

"A long time ago. And not on the street."

She shrugged her shoulders.

"Don't even know—what do I say?"

"Say your man make you asks for twenty-five. So they thinks he watching." She pulled off her ugly brown sweater and tied it around her waist. All she had on underneath was a tight black V-neck sleeveless shirt. Goose bumps arose on her arms. "Watch and learns." She rested an elbow on the mailbox.

A minute later, a powder blue Cadillac pulled up. She opened the passenger door and leaned her head inside. Then she climbed in, and it drove off. Was I supposed to do the same thing: get in a damn car and ride somewhere with some asshole to get fucked?

I lit a cigarette—I was down to my last half pack. Should I go back to the T? How could I—I had no money. I kicked an empty soda can, or what had looked empty; dark brown liquid drooled out. Hell, they were *her* shoes.

Screeching tires made me turn. The Cadillac had pulled up to the same spot, and Jackie got out. Striding towards me, she flashed a smile. "There's thirty dollars I didn't have five minutes ago. Let's do's a couple and gets somethings to eat."

The mention of food practically killed me. And I didn't want to appear chickenshit, so when another car pulled to the curb, I walked over. A young guy reached across the front seat and opened the door. I quickly mumbled, "Got to ask for twenty-five my man says."

"I only have twenty. That's all I have."

Not knowing what else to do, I got in. He drove to the corner, turned right twice, and went slowly up an alley, bumping along the rough pavement. Midway, he turned off the engine, unzipped his fly, and pulled out his penis. "Suck me."

Taking a deep breath to stifle the nausea, I leaned over and placed one hand low on the prick—more to steady myself than anything—and the other on his thigh. My mouth went on the gross, warm thing. He stroked my hair while jerking, and salty foul scum squirted over the insides of my cheeks. I rose off him, frantically fumbling with the door handle, and once outside, spat and spat. When I started to walk away, he shouted, "Wait." His arm stretched across the empty seat, his hand holding two tens. I reached in and took them and shut the door. As he drove off, I spat again and again.

"How'd it go?"

"He only had twenty, but I figured—"

Jackie walked to the curb—a green car had pulled up. I went around the corner and vomited on a pile of moldy leaves. Down the street was a liquor store. I went in and bought two dollar-bottles of Scotch. I drank one right away.

This time she marched towards me shouting, "Sixty! I asked for sixty, and he gave it. What's the matter?"

"I think mine's semen was some kind of raw sewage."

She gestured at the receding green. "He was a *tank*. A sixty-dollar *tank*. Let's eat."

We hit a nearby diner, and I ordered the Breakfast Super Special.

"What's wrongs with you?"

"Think I have a fever."

"I takes you to the VD clinic. It free."

The gray one-story prefab kind of building had a small and crowded waiting room. They gave me a number instead of asking my name and told me to have a seat, which was a joke: this was standing-room-only. When they called my number, a nice woman checked my temperature and blood pressure, and another "took a culture" and said come back Friday for the results.

I won the trifecta: Friday my fever was gone, the culture was negative, and Mark brought up two pounds of pot and a carton of cigarettes. Eileen and the kids moved back the following week. Their presence downstairs was a mixed blessing, though. I didn't like Jackie and me being the only tenants in the building, but kids shouldn't have had to live near us.

Weed had its boom periods as well as its busts. Once I made enough to buy some brown. We chased the dragon three days running and might've done more except that Mark came up to tell us Droghan had called from Providence, and I had to grab my stuff and split.

When Jackie showed at the hotel some days later, she played the Grand Inquisitor all the way home. "Gets sick? Ever throws up? Fever? Don't wants to eat? Cramps: ever gets muscles cramps?"

"Nope. Did you?"

"Tears in your eye? Goosebumps? Legs kicks at night? Trouble sleeping?"

"I always have trouble sleeping there." Poor Jackie. Andy hadn't become addicted to her jenny.

The next time Droghan visited, it was Mark who fetched me, saying Jackie wasn't feeling well. Her face was purple and swollen.

"Dro don't likes me chipping," she said. I actually felt sorry for her.

My shoulder was poked, waking me. "Mark and Eileen's gone," Jackie said. "Feds sniffing. You's got to brings in money for rent and food. Hundred a week."

I rolled so my back was to her. "Like hell."

"You cans tricks three, four times."

"That's just to pay *you*. What about the stuff I've got to buy for *me*?"

"I brings johns here. You don't haves to go out."

"Am I supposed to say thanks?"

"Don't cares what you say. Don't likes it, leave."

Maybe I *would*, damn her.

Most days I hitched downtown to panhandle and scavenge the hotels. I had to space out the hotels, since the staff everywhere recognized me, and one place even called the cops.

With no pot around, I relied on beer to alter my consciousness, and it became my main source of calories. But I didn't develop a beer belly; if anything, my jeans got looser. I thought about food morning, noon, and night. Even my dreams were about food— stews and roasts I could practically taste. The pain was always worst on waking; my stomach felt like I'd swallowed nails.

The only silver lining was I didn't have to spring for tampax. My periods had stopped a while back, and when I had asked at the clinic if I could be pregnant, they had me tested. Luckily, it came back negative, and the nurse said I'd probably stopped menstruating because I had too little body fat. Jackie didn't seem to lose weight. Some evenings she went out in her hooker get-up, so she probably ate enough.

Even those days the panhandling went well and I forked over twenty-plus, she continued to nag me for more dough. Today wasn't looking to be one of the good days. I was starting to emerge from an alley recess after peeing when some guy in an apron farther down rested a large garbage bag on top of a dumpster. The second he walked away, I ran over and pulled the bag to the ground and stretched apart the string. A still-warm turkey carcass! Shreds of meat remained on the breast bone and thigh. My fingers moved faster than my brain; they had a life of their own, pulling at warm chunks and shoving them in my mouth. I chewed and swallowed, chewed and swallowed. Hallelujah, a drumstick. My teeth tore into the juicy skin.

"What the—" The apron guy was back, holding another bag. I ran, drumstick clutched in my hand, not knowing why. Who called the cops on somebody stealing garbage? A few blocks later, I got to the Common and finished gnawing the thing to the bone.

"Here she is." Jackie held the door wide open. A guy with a bushy mustache, about forty, stood by the kitchen table. Jackie locked the door. "What you say?"

His eyes zeroed in on my crotch. He nodded.

"Lou's a friend. I got my period."

Heat flooded my face. I strode to the fridge and yanked it open, grabbed the half bottle of Riesling, popped the cork, and guzzled, not giving a shit what Jackie thought. The taste was sickeningly sweet, but who gave a damn.

Regularly, now, she brought johns to the apartment. If I left without doing one, when I got back she would be sitting at the kitchen table eating pizza or a burger. Naturally she didn't offer me any, and at first I wouldn't give her the satisfaction of thinking I cared—I'd sit and drink, maybe play a game of solitaire. But the smells would start my belly growling, and I'd have to go to my room. I hated her, and she knew it.

When summer came for real, I decided to leave. I didn't tell her, but she would put two-and-two together once she saw my stuff gone.

Some nights I managed to stay awake at one of the stations and in the morning would crash on the lawn of a well-peopled park. Other nights, I'd hit a shelter. Food was becoming more of a hassle, since I didn't have the energy to trek down to the food bank and couldn't even get *near* the hotels—security seemed to descend out of thin air. Mostly I rifled through garbage. Once I lucked onto a white cardboard box with beef strips, pea pods, and water chestnuts floating in a brown sauce, still warm. But that evening, on my way to the shelter, I had to retch something awful. For the next two days, I was forever ducking into fast-food restaurants to use the can. Somebody must've complained at one because the instant I came out, the manager threatened to arrest me if I ever returned. Even when I was better, they tossed me from some lousy taco joint because a woman with a bunch of kids bitched. Where the hell was I supposed to shower?

Franklin Park became my favorite place to sit and watch the day happen to other people. I was calmly brooding now, on a sunny spot not too far from the zoo. I had just finished a joint some guy had given me for the privilege of touching my crotch while he jacked off in the bushes. The downside of smoking a joint was the appetite that came with. But a dumpster nearby often had stuff, even pizza boxes with lots of crusts.

"Do you need a place to crash?" He wore a clean shirt, and his hair and short dark beard looked trimmed. "Do you know about the St. Aloysius Mission?" Squatting, he handed me a white card. "We have a van and can drive you there. You would get your own bed, something to eat, a place to wash up. It's safe. The only rule is no drugs or alcohol on the premises."

I tried handing the card back. "I'm not Catholic."

"We're not actually affiliated with the church, and you don't have to belong to any religion. It's starting to get colder. You don't want to be on the street—"

"Don't live on the street."

"You have a warm place to stay? Good." He paused, his index finger stroking the beard. "We offer counseling free of charge, and when there's space, we can get people into a treatment program."

Obviously he wasn't going to go away easily, so I thrust the card closer to his hand. "I like my drugs and alcohol."

He quickly stood. "No, you keep it. We're always there." At least he didn't say *God loves you.*

Yet God did love me, because when I started towards my favorite dumpster, the alley was blocked by a beer truck. The driver wheeled a dolly inside the building, and I checked the back doors, which were unlatched. In a nanosecond I was able to make off with an entire case and trade it to some old dudes in the park for enough cash to buy a pint. The Scotch tamped my hunger most of the day, and in the evening, I found a deserted alley with a doorway recessed enough to hide in. I curled up on my pack, using newspaper as a blanket.

I wasn't sure which had awoken me, the dawn breaking or the rat sniffing the paper, but I raised myself to a sitting position. My head throbbed. The beady-eyed thing wasn't scared off, and we engaged in a mutual staring contest. He caved first and ran.

My neck ached, and my skull felt like lead. I pushed myself into a standing position. Not six feet away was a gigantic mound of shit; the dog must've been the size of a horse. I went down to a dumpster and rested my pack on top. Bracing my back against the brick wall, I lowered my jeans and assumed a sitting position. The pee went quickly from a trickle to full force, splashing onto the pavement and streaming between my sneakers.

"What the hell you doing?" His voice was deep, and he was large, but I couldn't stop. The sonofabitch ran over and grabbed my arm while I was still peeing and yanked me forward, the final drops landing on my jeans as I pulled them up one-handed. "In a public place, you no good junkie. I should—"

He forced me to turn by twisting my arm behind my back. I was directly in front of him, facing the brick wall. Where I summoned the energy, I didn't know, but I kicked my leg back sharply at the knee, ramming my sneaker heel into his shin. His grip loosened, and he let go completely when I kicked again. Grabbing my pack, I ran.

"Damn bitch," he yelled, "junkie bitch." Like I had the money to be a junkie.

I was bound to surrender—Jackie had only to wait for cooler weather. I returned to the apartment and put out for the guys she brought up the back stairs. Some were new; some were repeats wanting the same thing; some were repeats wanting something different. They were young, middle-aged, and old; they were black, white, Asian, mixed. I was an equal opportunity employer. No matter how dirty or drunk I was, some guy was willing to shell out ten or fifteen bucks for the one-minute thrill of putting his prick in me. Tommy had used to say the human brain was the pinnacle of evolution, but for plenty of men, it was cunt.

Some days when I hadn't put out, I still woke wearing less clothing than I had gone to bed with. When I peed, all sorts of scum came onto the toilet paper. "Seems to me I got fucked last night," I complained. "Where's my money?"

Jackie's opaque black eyes would look up momentarily from the kitchen table, where her stickers lay scattered. "Don't knows any-things 'bout it. I sacks out too." She knew I knew she was lying, but who gave a fuck. Apparently I did.

Chapter 50

THE SEASONS STOPPED mattering; they started and they ended. But all good things must come to an end, they say, and eventually Mark, Eileen, and the kids moved back in downstairs. There was pot to sell, and I made it to the park in rain, sleet, snow, like a goddamn postman.

Mark did ask us to cool it when he thought he was being tailed. The last time was for a week, but he came up this morning and said just wait till the weekend to be safe. He was his same clean-cut self, the gray around the temples making him look distinguished. He sat with Jackie at the kitchen table.

"How comes you sad?" she asked me as I poured myself coffee. "Just have to waits few days—thens you can sell."

"I miss tricking."

"You's grumpy. You needs a change of scene."

"Sure," I said. "Trip to Disneyland, Tahiti. Who's paying?"

Mark laughed.

"Don't means it that way," Jackie said. "Means your head. Tries mainlining."

"Just one more need to feed. Hard enough paying for cigarettes and beer. Besides, chasing the dragon's okay." I took my cup to the side window. The sky looked like it was clearing.

"*Okay* not that perfect happiness mainlining's is," she said.

"Perfect happiness, my ass."

Jackie smiled dreamily. "That what they say. When hits the vein is perfect happiness."

"For how long? Most junkies spend six hours in heaven and eighteen in hell."

Mark tilted his chair back and grinned. Let the two broads go at it, verbal mud-wrestling.

"If it so bad, why they comes back for more?"

"Addiction," I said. "Ever hear of it?"

Jackie gave her babe-in-the-woods look. "Addiction *doctor* word. Happiness, love, all in one."

"Don't see *you* doing it, or you."

Mark smiled. "I hate needles."

Jackie grew serious, her black eyes, pistol holes. "Dro kills me. No other reason in whole wides world. Smokin', snortin', s'like weed to me now. One bigs nothing."

I drained my cup and placed it in the sink. "Life's one big nothing." I went to my room for my pint and coat and headed for the back door.

"People need to be loose," Mark was saying. "Relaxed. Stoned."

"That's right," I said. "Everybody must get stoned."

"Or drunk, right?" He looked at me like we shared some private joke. "I ran into my old buddy Eddie. Eddie has a case of Seagram's gin in his trunk."

"Lucky Eddie."

"He can't drink a case by himself."

I opened the door part way. A drop or two fell from the gutter pipe. I pulled up my collar. "Sure he can, if you give him enough time."

"He doesn't want to. Wants to share it."

"Thanks, but not much of a gin drinker."

"You've had my gin and tonics."

"Yeah," Jackie said. "They's something else."

You're something else. I closed the door behind me.

The air was misty, but the rain had stopped. I went down to the alley and strolled towards the main drag. Weeds and tufts of grass had begun to sprout in the yards and along the borders of the mud. Back landings, steps, paths, the whole broad area was deserted except for one guy picking through garbage. Maybe his wife had come across his *Playboy* collection.

I needed cash to get me through the next few days. What was this Eddie business—did they want me to trick with him? Screw that.

I hitched downtown and spent the day panhandling, sifting through garbage cans, and hanging out at a new fast-food place. It took forever for somebody to stop and give me a ride back south, but finally a middle-aged white guy pulled over. "As close to Dorchester as you're going," I said, closing the door.

He looked surprised. "You're a woman."

"What did you think?"

"That you were a boy."

"I can blow just as well and charge only twenty-five."

"No, you can't." He motioned for me to get out.

"Twenty?"

"Get out."

"You won't even give me a ride?"

"No. I thought you were a boy."

"Well fuck you."

The pint was almost empty by the time somebody else stopped, but he drove me to within a block of the alley. A guy loitering near the telephone pole approached, and I stepped off the curb in case he was some kind of mugger, but he walked quickly past without making eye contact. Had our neighborhood become a gay rendezvous? It figured: AIDS Grand Central. I tossed the empty pint in a pothole.

"Andy's home!" Jackie sang out like Santa himself had waltzed in.

Mark pointed to the guy sitting next to Jackie. "This is Eddie." Eddie nodded. "We were just getting ready for my special gin and tonics. Take off your coat and stay awhile."

What the hell else did I have to do? I sat in the empty chair between Mark and Jackie, across from Eddie. Jackie brought four glasses to the table, then the Seagram's and tonic and ice tray. Mark poured a healthy dose of gin into the first glass, added a little tonic, and pushed it to me. They must have wanted me to fuck this guy really bad. Did he like something kinky nobody else would put up with? One john had tried my ass but quit when I hollered bloody murder.

When all four glasses had been filled, Mark raised his in toast. "To friendship." They clanked theirs, but I just drank. I'd show them—all the gin on top of the Scotch might be enough to make me puke. I could make puking noises in the bathroom anyway. If Eddie wasn't turned off, that meant he was crazy, and I'd get the hell out.

I tuned in and out of their conversation. Apparently he lived on Nantucket and had a kid who was autistic. When Mark refilled my glass, he became stingy with the gin. Maybe Eddie didn't like his hookers stewed. Too late, Eddie—I was already there.

At some point I went to the can, and when I returned, Eddie and Mark were standing by the back door. "Eddie has to catch the ferry." Waving to Jackie and me, Eddie left.

Mark sat down and motioned for me to sit too. When I did, he said, "You know, Andy, we did a lot of talking this afternoon, Jackie and me." He leaned forward. "About how we never get close, you and me and Jackie. We play some cards, chew the fat, but never *really talk*, never *open up* to each other. You know what I mean?"

I lit a cigarette.

His voice was soothing. "Eddie was telling us about a lot of pain he's been through with his kid. And Eileen, I don't know if she told you, but her sister was in a car accident. Thirty-three years old and may never walk the same again. You can imagine how that's left the family feeling."

"Life sucks," I said.

"But we brush our problems underneath; we don't share them. It's easy to see *your* life has taken some hits. But you keep it bottled up inside, don't you? You don't let anyone know."

I flicked ash into the saucer.

"Did somebody dumps you?" Jackie asked. "Somebody's you loved?" She too sounded sad.

I shook my head.

Mark put down his glass. "No, Jackie, it's worse than that. I can tell. Andy, someone died, didn't they?"

I fought the pooling in my eyes. "That's only part of it."

He leaned closer. "Didn't catch that."

"And *why* they died," I said. "A disease. I might have it."

Jackie jerked her chair back. Mark didn't budge; I could sense him watching me. "Did the VD clinic tell you?" he asked.

I shook my head. "Not an infection. Genetic. Might have inherited it."

"You don't knows if you haves it?" Jackie asked.

"Won't know unless I get the symptoms."

Mark touched my sleeve lightly—*very* lightly. "What are the symptoms? Are they painful?" He looked sadder than I had ever seen him.

"You lose control," I said. "Of everything. All your muscles. You drop things, fall down. Then go crazy."

"Poor Andy," he whispered. "Poor Andy."

Tears ran down my face. Snot came out too; I wiped my nose on my sleeve. The silence stretched. When I stole a look at one or the other, their eyes were downcast. They didn't offer stupid reassurances. Maybe they understood. Their own lives hadn't been smooth. Jackie's childhood was brutal; Droghan was brutal. What did she have going for *her*? And Mark, wasn't he a coke addict? His life a complicated web, never knowing if some guy in the alley was a nobody or a narc—never able to shed his paranoia, no matter how well he hid it.

"You're carrying a huge weight," he said.

"Wanted to do a bunch of things," I told him. "Maybe some woodworking."

Jackie pointed to my empty glass. Mark shook his head, murmuring, "I wish we had known. All these years you've been carrying a huge burden inside you, and Jackie and me, we had no idea. Jackie, can you grab some tissues?"

She returned to the table with a roll of toilet paper. I tore off some and wiped my nose.

"I'll be honest with you, Andy," Mark said. "There were times I thought you were a cold person, without feelings. Now I realize the *opposite* is true; you feel too deeply. I'm sorry I misjudged you, really sorry."

Eileen must have seen it in him, his kids too: he had a heart. I was wrong about them wanting me to trick with Eddie and was probably wrong about a lot of things. Maybe they had tried to be friends, but I was so damn suspicious and closed-up. When did I have a kind word for *anybody*?

I told them about Huntington's and Dean dying and his mother having dementia. Jackie was silent, but Mark kept shaking his head, saying, "Poor, poor Andy," which made me cry even more. We sat listening to the rain on the roof, pit-pat, pit-pat, pit-pat. Mark put on the kettle and made him and me coffee.

Sitting again, he cradled his cup between his strong hands. "You know, Andy, I'm thinking about how much pain you have, and how alcohol and pot and smoking skag doesn't do shit to ease it. You're still hurting. So it occurs to me you might find relief from shooting up a bit. Not a whole dose, no, just a half. But I'm having second thoughts and think it's actually a bad idea. You're in a very fragile state. You should wait. In a few months, a year, you might be strong enough to experience the kind of beauty and warmth and wonder of mainlining. Sitting here, watching you cry, I'm convinced you're not ready."

I sipped some coffee.

"What are you thinking?" he asked softly.

"About this furniture place in Chicago. The woods, oaks especially, were beautiful. I would have liked to work with them, sand them, turn them into something."

"I wish I could appreciate beauty the way you do. Jackie, I don't mean to offend you, but I think that skag, shooting it, would be wasted on you, like it would on me. The people who deserve it are those with a certain kind of soul, an *artist's* soul, with a beauty inside that the skag brings out." Mark looked at me again. "I just wish there was some way. I really, really do. It's a beauty that *you*, of all people, could appreciate. But wait until you're stronger."

Abruptly, he was on his feet. At the door. "I'll see you guys next week."

Why did he have to go? This was the first the kitchen had felt like a home, like I was among friends. The feeling would disappear if it were just me and Jackie. I heard myself asking, whining, almost, "Why do—"

"I'm sorry, Andy, I am." He shook his head. The bolt knob clicked loudly. "The intensity of the joy would overwhelm you. You're not ready. It takes an artist's soul, which you have, but I worry you can't *handle* that much happiness." His eyes looked so sadly into mine, I had to drop my gaze. "I *really*, *really* wish you could. Suffering but so capable of appreciating pure beauty. Be honest with me. Can you handle it?"

I didn't know what to say.

His hand turned the bolt closed. His voice got soft again. "I'll tell you what. If you are going to try mainlining, it should be with us. I would rather you do it in a *safe* place, among friends. People who care for you and can take care of you. Who make sure it goes right and you get the most out of it. You deserve nothing less. Is that all right? That we watch over you? Please?"

I nodded. He turned to Jackie. "Why don't you." She got up and left the room. "Sensitive people like you, Andy, suffer so much more than the rest of us, but you appreciate beauty so much more. I'll be interested to hear you describe it. Will you describe it for me? Please?"

I nodded. After a moment, he tapped my chair back. "Let's go." He went down the hall. I uncapped the gin and guzzled a whole bunch before standing.

From the bathroom doorway Mark smiled kindly and gestured for me to go in. Though the sadness in his eyes remained, the disappointment didn't.

The side of the sink held a glassine, syringe, wide metal cap maybe from a mayonnaise jar, other stuff. I sat on the closed toilet lid. For some reason I didn't want to watch the preparations, so I stared at the hexagonal floor tiles. They seemed to veer off in every direction like little space ships. I fought the nausea. What was that song: "I Fought the Law, and the Law Won"? The last thing I wanted was to waste Mark's dope. I fought the nausea, and I won. I sensed them working methodically.

"Jackie," Mark murmured, "you do the tourniquet."

She wrapped a black cord around my arm above the elbow. "Great veins," she said admiringly.

Hopefully I hadn't drunk too much to enjoy the rush. The little floor tiles jumbled together. It was too late to say no—Mark had already mixed the stuff. Somebody held my hand. I looked up, surprised. It was Jackie, and she rubbed alcohol on the vein. They were taking care of me.

"*Wonderful* veins," Mark said.

The floor tiles moved some more. I closed my eyes, waiting for the jab. That made me dizzier, so I opened them and focused as best I could on a spot on the wall. My head was pounding bad enough that it seemed like things were crashing all around. Was it the gin? The skag? Had he injected already, and I hadn't felt the needle? No, he was looking away, still holding the syringe in the air. Noises *were* coming from outside. Jackie yanked the bathroom door shut. Mark squirted the syringe into the sink and knocked the tap on full blast. Why was he frantically filling the syringe with tap water and pumping it into the basin? Jackie flattened herself against the shower wall. My skull pounded like war drums. Was I having a bad trip? The door swung open. Guns pointed right at me. The room spun. My arm hurt bad; the cord was severing it.

"Police! Don't move." It was too late. I could feel myself moving, falling.

Chapter 51

"ANDY FRITZ, ANDY Fritz!"

I raised my hand from the bench but couldn't lift my head to see who was shouting. Seemed like years since they'd done the right-to-remain-silent bit and asked a million questions and flashbulbs fired. I'd had to put on some weird jumpsuit and was led to a room with other women wearing the same thing. Found a bench to curl up on and fell asleep.

Most of the other women were gone now. I got myself to sit, my head throbbing bad, and eventually was able to stand and trudge across to a young guy in a dark suit holding a clipboard. He gave some name and said he was my lawyer. A uniformed guard opened a door, and we stepped into a courtroom like in Perry Mason. Nobody was sitting on the witness stand or in the judge's seat, but at a desk below where the judge would be a guy sat typing. About a dozen people in suits loitered around, talking in hushed voices.

A table with paper cups had a pitcher of water, and the lawyer let me drink some. Then we sat on a bench out of earshot of everybody else. He gave a long spiel and said everything I told him would be "completely confidential." Like Laurie's brother. I was about to be arraigned, and they would charge me with possession of a controlled substance, heroin, with intent to sell.

"Hey, I wasn't selling."

"Were you using it?"

"Jackie and Mark wanted me to try mainlining. It was my first time. Or would've been."

"Jackie and Mark—they're the people you were arrested with?"

I nodded. God, my head hurt.

"Do *they* sell it? The reason I ask is that the prosecutor may offer you a deal. She doesn't seem as interested in prosecuting you as in prosecuting them. If you would agree to testify against them."

I looked around the courtroom. Maybe Jackie and Mark had been arraigned in the morning while I was sleeping off the fucking Seagram's. In a low voice, I said, "No way. They know folks who might not let me live."

The guy looked nervous and picked up his clipboard. "Let me ask you a few background questions. Are you employed?"

"No."

"How long have you known them, Jackie and Mark?"

"Not sure. What day is it? Actually, don't even know the month."

"It's April twelfth."

"Thanks. Guess I should ask the year."

"1988."

"Jesus. Sorry. It's just that—well, I didn't realize how much— it's *1988*?"

An older guy came over, and the younger said he was also my lawyer and told him what I had said about Jackie and Mark. The older asked if I had any addictions or "personal or medical circumstances" that might make the judge sympathetic. I told him I was probably an alcoholic. Did I have any priors? The younger said that meant prior convictions. I said no. The older said I should be able to plead to possession and maybe St. Aloysius had room. He walked off like he had better things to do, which he probably did.

"Would you be willing to go to a residential recovery facility?" the younger asked. "If they have room? You would live there. They have counselors—"

"Would that be instead of jail?"

"Yes. I would need to get the prosecutor to agree. If they'll drop the intent-to-sell, they should. But you *would* have to plead guilty to possession. You would have a criminal record. And you wouldn't be able to leave the facility for the entire period—"

"What if I don't plead—what happens?"

"If you want to contest the charges, the judge will set your case for trial. We can discuss possible defenses. They had a warrant, but perhaps it wasn't properly obtained or executed. Can you post bail in the meantime? Is there someone—"

"If I agree to this St. Aloysius thing, I definitely won't go to jail?"

"No, you wouldn't go to jail. You would plead guilty to possession and get probation conditioned on your completing their program. If you didn't complete it, however, your probation would be revoked and then you *could* go to jail if—"

"How long did you say it was for? The program?"

"I believe twelve weeks. I have to check the details. To be honest, this is my first case where—"

"It's my first too. I'll plead to what you said, possession, but not selling."

"You don't have children or someone else who relies on you for support or—"

"Nope. Or place to stay, really."

The guy did his best to look like he'd had a hundred clients like me.

While he talked to the prosecutor, I waited back in holding. Over *seven years. Seven years.* Like a broken mirror. How old was I?

Eighty-eight minus fifty-two. In a couple of months, I'd turn thirty-six. Holy shit, everybody must think I was dead.

When I was brought back into the courtroom, a lady in a skirt suit introduced as an assistant-something asked me a bunch of questions about Jackie and Mark and acted bored by all my I-don't-knows. The judge eventually showed, and my lawyer and the lady talked in front of him, and the judge fired off a series of questions at me: Did I realize I was waiving this right? That one? That one? I did what the lawyer had told me to do and said yes to everything.

I was taken to a restroom to change into my clothes. The gaunt face in the mirror had a forehead bruise the size of a softball. Somebody escorted me to a desk where Andrea Fritz signed a bunch of papers. Andrea Fritz was handed a plastic bag containing the couple of bucks that had been on her. Would I sign this receipt? Sure.

A woman about my age with large glasses and a larger smile introduced herself as Megan, and we got in a van that said *St. Aloysius Mission* on the side. We stopped at a two-story brick building and got out. Nobody stood guard. On the way to the door, Megan asked if I needed to phone anybody to say where I was. Nope.

Somebody named Brenda did "check in." My head was killing me. I eyed the red neon *Exit*. It would be easy to split—neither woman looked the type to chase after. I needed a drink bad. What if they called the cops and I got carted off to jail? I didn't know this neighborhood. Maybe I should wait till I could figure out how to split without anybody realizing right away.

Brenda wrote in a ledger that I had given her a couple of bucks for the safe, and she had me fill out forms. Megan gave me a card listing the symptoms of recovery so I wouldn't be "caught off-guard." It said I would feel anger, anxiety, and a bunch of physical symptoms. She rattled off rules like no alcohol or non-prescription drugs or smoking in the bedrooms, when mealtimes were, something about group therapy and individual therapy.

St. Aloysius had one *good* rule: we were to be supplied with cigarettes and candy and soda for free. I asked for cigarettes and a soda. But I wanted a real drink. It would be nothing to run out the door. No, wait till you've gotten the lay of the land, maybe a decent meal in your stomach. Hold off just a few more hours. They took all your cash, remember.

I was examined by some nurse—the whole temperature, blood-pressure bit. Then I took a shower and put on the clean sweats they gave me. At supper I got introduced to the other residents, some of whom were friendly, some of whom weren't, and I signed on to the unfriendly contingent. I gobbled the meatloaf and potatoes too fast to taste them.

All evening, the dumbest things ran interference with my plan to escape. Like the lounge fridge being stocked with cold sodas. Bowls of popcorn and pretzels on the lounge counter. Nobody hassling me. Even taking a dump in a clean bathroom. Eventually my right brain lobe convinced the wrong one that a good night's sleep would let them both think clearly in the morning and figure out what to rip off when I did split. Maybe I could locate the petty cash. A term obviously coined by somebody who'd never lived on the street.

I was put in a bedroom with three other women and given sheets and blankets to make up the vacant top bunk. Clean sheets, clean pillowcase, clean blankets, and no johns. Like Janis used to sing, *get it while you can.*

In the middle of the night I was startled awake. All was dark and quiet. Where was I? Don't you remember: the recovery place. After the courthouse, they brought you here. I rolled onto my stomach.

The curtains didn't quite meet, but I could only see black sky. Should I escape now? Did they have alarms on the doors? Guards? My body was too heavy. Just go back to sleep, Andy, go back to sleep. Okay, okay.

Now the sky between the curtains was slate blue. Did the window face east? Was it cloudy or just early dawn? The woman below snored mildly. How could seven years have come and gone? Wasted—years wasted being wasted. What had happened in the rest of the world? Who was president? Was the Women's Movement still around? Gay Liberation? Or had everybody crammed back in the closet?

"Time to get up, everyone!"

I hadn't realized I'd fallen back asleep. My head felt worse. Should I see if they would let me use the phone? Mark would have gotten Droghan or somebody to bail him and Jackie out—maybe they could help me escape. They wouldn't have cordoned off her apartment as a crime scene, would they? I was glad nobody spoke to me as I got washed and dressed. What was making me so angry? Nothing—I was angry for anger's sake. Art for art's sake. Another big Stacy-Tommy argument.

A hot breakfast helped a little. After clean-up, my "team" was escorted down the corridor connecting the Mission to some "halfway" for a job skills class. At least I could smoke, and all I had to do was fill out a questionnaire about my job experience and interests. I left off the dealing and tricking.

When we got back to the Mission side, I went to the rec room and pounded the punching bag. Probably should've checked first to see if they had gloves. I debated splitting right after lunch, during "nap time," but got so stuffed on the stroganoff, I needed the sleep.

Right after nap was Group Therapy. I got introduced to six or seven other women, and we all sat in a circle. The counselor or whoever said we were supposed to talk about AA's Twelve Steps. She handed me a sheet of paper listing them.

Came to believe that a Power greater than ourselves could restore us to sanity. But didn't Stacy or Tommy quote something about religion being the opiate of the masses? Here AA was saying religion was the anti-opiate—religion would *save us* from drugs and alcohol.

Made a searching and fearless moral inventory of ourselves. If I'd already made the moral inventory, did I have to go through the searching? Couldn't there be a shortcut for those of us willing to plead guilty to everything?

Except for saying my first name at the beginning, I wasn't forced to speak, so I passed the hour inventorying items to rip off. One woman had a watch; I'd have to find out when she showered. The sugar packets, candy bars, and gum might be parlayed into a joint. Maybe petty cash was a pretty stash, wherever it was. Too bad my shim card had disappeared ages ago. Maybe they'd give out new John Q. Publics in the job skills class.

For "individual therapy" I got assigned somebody named Roberta. Would she come up with some helpful rules of order? She chain-smoked worse than I did, and I liked that she dressed in plain clothes like Megan and Brenda, even though the diploma on the wall said *Doctor of Clinical Psychology.*

I was eligible for the St. Aloysius halfway when my probation ended, she told me, because I wasn't in withdrawal. Why *wasn't* I in withdrawal, I asked. Why didn't I have the DTs, given my history? She explained that marijuana and alcohol were different from the opiates, and some people didn't become physiologically dependent, possibly because of genetics. Then she started with the shrink bit and wanted to know how I landed in the criminal justice system. I gave a quick rundown of my glory days since Dean's funeral and all the Huntington's shit. She listened without saying *poor, poor Andy.*

For both laundry detail and cleaning, our required chores, we had to wear yellow plastic gloves like the nurses at the VD clinic. I wasn't crazy about the vacuuming, but mopping bathrooms was worse— the disinfectant gave me a splitting headache. Yet I stuck to the routine for an entire week because I was having trouble formulating an escape plan. The actual leaving wasn't the hard part, but what to do next.

The time of day I dreaded most was going to bed. No mind-altering substances carted me quickly off to sleep, and, stripped of the insulation of pot and booze, I was face-to-face with memories. Memories of strangers touching me, sweating and panting all over me, hurting me. Nightmares were a constant, and sometimes my shouts felt so real, I couldn't believe the other women hadn't awoken.

Chapter 52

"I've spoken to a neurologist at Mass General about Huntington's," Roberta said at my second session, gesturing for me to sit in my usual chair. "They've made significant progress in their own labs locating the gene mutation that causes the disease, *and* they offer counseling services specific to Huntington's." She handed me a pink message-pad note. "That's the number to set up an appointment. I believe they might not charge for the first visit, and you may be able to work something out for subsequent visits."

"I'm okay bouncing stuff off of you."

"It's not that. They essentially told me I'm out of my league. I *shouldn't* be counseling you—not about Huntington's."

I tucked the note in my back pocket. "I'll think on it."

I did think on it. I even dialed the number a few times, almost letting it ring twice. What was I so afraid of? That they'd say because of some new discovery, my odds were even worse? *Do you hate Brussels sprouts? Then you've got the bad gene.* Staying dry was hard enough, from waking to sleeping my temper at a hair-trigger. Maybe a few months down the line I'd make an appointment.

But I didn't mind talking to Roberta about stuff other than Huntington's. Describing—*remembering*—the hunger and tricking was rough going, but I did feel better afterwards. And despite having believed Geserenie had given me all the catharsis I needed for the Roy crap, I found myself talking about the rapes and other family shit again.

The only tussle we got into was on the subject of my strained relations with Mathilde. Roberta thought my guilt over what I called "my disappearing act" would lessen if Mathilde understood Roy's role in it. To be fair, Roberta wasn't pushing for me to tell Mathilde he had raped me, just that he had done something awful enough to make his presence—and her home—uninviting.

Of course I maintained that the only way to convince Mathilde he bore any fault at all for my disappearing was if I dropped the A bomb. "Or the R bomb, to be precise. And if I did that, then I would have something *new* to feel guilty about: cluing her in that her son's a rapist." But Roberta was always cool about moving on to other subjects when I wanted.

Some days, it seemed as if *twenty*, not seven, years had passed. Leaning on the counter, Andy Van Winkle would watch as Brenda typed and the words appeared on a separate screen resembling a small TV. A "computer," she said, "so you don't need carbon paper." Another machine answered the phone and let the person calling leave a taped message you could listen to later. And the aerobics instructor used a gizmo that played a miniature record smaller than a forty-five—a CD, she called it—that held an entire LP's worth of songs. Not that I did the aerobics; just watching it exhausted me.

Amazingly, the job skills list I had to write actually paid off. In late May, St. Aloysius needed somebody for breakfast and lunch prep, and they offered me the job. I dropped in on Roberta with the news and a quick question: didn't she have to keep everything I told her confidential?

"Yes, unless you plan to commit a crime."

The opposite, I said: I was trying to come clean. My last name wasn't really Fritz, and I wanted to revert to my real name but didn't want to tell the court. "What if we tell personnel I'm just going back to my maiden name," I said. "It's technically true."

She was cool but said St. Al's would have to run another background check. I was cool with that.

The job was a godsend—I could keep myself distracted for almost the whole day. Working like a maniac, I not only did prep but also ran down to the basement to fetch supplies, refilled the condiments and salt and peppers, cleaned the counters, and started on the supper prep. It wasn't to brown-nose, just that every task helped distract me from craving alcohol.

And the job probably helped me to land a bed in the halfway next door when my twelve weeks was up. The way I figured it: St. Al's worried that if they made me move out, I wouldn't keep the job, and who else could they find to put in eleven-hour shifts for eight hours' worth of pay? Plus, they didn't have to fork over as much cash, since they could dock a chunk of my wages for room and board.

For me, another plus was that as paid staff, I wouldn't be forced to move out of the halfway at six months like the other residents. In fact, the only downside to my twelve weeks at the Mission ending was my sessions with Roberta ending. Still, a roof over my head, a safe place to fall asleep, sufficed.

Seasons passed, but I kept track of them. Sometimes an obvious dyke would move into the halfway and seek me out for companionship, but knowing she'd be leaving in six months, I didn't see the point of getting beyond the casual interactions I had with everybody else. I did venture outdoors more and by my second year learned to withstand the allure of bars. My beer yearnings hadn't disappeared, but they had contracted into yens. Maybe that was why the following year I summoned the courage to go to Mass General.

Wanting to start with a lay of the land, I hit the Neurology clinic without an appointment. The folks in the waiting area looked no more sad or bored than those in other waiting areas. I asked the receptionist if she had any free literature on Huntington's Disease, and she sort of freaked out, which freaked me out, but then she explained she was just temping during lunch hour and didn't know where they kept things. She managed to scrounge up a hodgepodge of brochures, news clippings, and articles xeroxed from magazines, which I took back to St. Al's to read.

One brochure described symptoms I hadn't come across or else had blocked out, like *difficulty eating and swallowing, inability to focus the eyes, worm-like movements.* What parts of your body moved like a worm? Didn't an inability to focus your eyes basically make you blind?

A fold-out jobbie said *If you have no Huntington's symptoms, you should continue all regular activities, such as driving, swimming, and bicycling.* Hard to remember regular activities.

Another brochure was titled *Family Therapy for the Diagnosed and Undiagnosed.* Hell, being cooped up in some therapist's office with Mathilde and Roy would be worse than moving like a worm.

The most recent brochure—with a 1990 date—was titled *If Your Parent Has Huntington's Disease (HD).* I skimmed to "How can I tell if I have HD?"

There are two ways to tell if a person has HD. The first is through clinical examination by a physician trained in recognizing HD signs and symptoms, usually aided by family history. The second is through predictive testing in the laboratory using genetic linked markers.

So Lorraine was wrong—they *could* do a test. Or maybe they hadn't known how back in '80.

"My mother died from HD. My sister and I are her only surviving relations. I want predictive testing, but my sister refuses, so my doctor won't test me. Why not?" Predictive Testing is not highly accurate, and if it is performed on a sample from only one individual in a family, the results are not meaningful.

So much for that.

Unfortunately, the materials said nothing about pills, capsules, injections, any kind of therapy except family.

Maybe it was the lounge TV showing *Casablanca*, or the calendar being on the cruelest month, or just a whiff of spring air, but something made me dial Information and get Mr. Grunner's phone number. He answered and happily talked my ear off, whether he remembered me or not. Stacy and Jerry were on some island in the Pacific—their third trip, if I could imagine. But they would return next January. "Whitman, he calls me Grampy. To hear him pronounce it. He's only three! And Dylan, he's ready for first grade."

In a way, it was the best of all possible worlds—getting news about Stacy without talking to her. For even over the phone, she'd know something was wrong. And I didn't want to burden her with the Huntington's shit. What could she do about it? Not to mention she obviously had her hands full.

After the success of one phone call, I tried a second. Mathilde sounded guarded, like she was hesitant to get excited about somebody who disappeared for years on end. "How are you?" she asked.

"Okay. How about you?"

"Okay. You still in Boston?"

"Yeah. Doing prep at a small restaurant. You still at the diner?"

"Yes. Edward passed away."

"Jeez. When?"

"November. Pneumonia. He left you ten thousand dollars. A little for me and Roy. Hold on. Let me look for his number, the lawyer."

Poor Edward. And if he left me that much money, he couldn't have had a lover. I wished he had. Shit.

"The lawyer's last name is Greenstreet." Mathilde read off a phone number. "You have to call him, so they don't think—if they don't know you're alive, then your part goes to charity. Something to do with AIDS. Andy, are you still there?"

"Yeah. Just wasn't expecting this. So how have *you* been? Did you say you're still at the diner?"

"Yes. You like where you're working?"

"It's okay."

"Ever think about moving home?"

"Sometimes," I lied.

"Roy's working the desk at The Bungalow. Motel near the Wilmington turnoff. Taking a class too. Hotel-Motel Management." She paused. "Lots of jobs advertising around here. I mean restaurants."

"It's just that right now—"

"Families take care of each other."

Anger flared up, but I quickly tamped it down. Just an ember, just an ember.

"What's so special about Boston? That you want to stay there?"

"Nothing's so special; I'm not even crazy about the place. It's just that I have a decent job, my rent's not bad—"

"You wouldn't have to pay rent if you lived here."

I wouldn't have to pay for a long-distance guilt-trip either.

"You could have either room," she went on. "Your old or Roy's. And his apartment's only five minutes away. Don't know what I'd do if I couldn't call on him. When something goes wrong. Or Lorr and Anthony. Like I said, families take care of each other."

This flare was no ember. I silently repeated the things Roberta had suggested for tougher moments: that I couldn't control external events and other people, but I had some say in how I reacted to them. Like Gertie's Serenity Prayer. And if all else failed, count to ten, or twenty. One, two, three, four—

"I don't mean I'd put you to work," Mathilde said, "making you do chores for me. I just meant—"

"I know."

"And after I'm gone, Roy would be there—"

"I've got friends here." I lit a second cigarette off the first.

"Friends aren't the same as family. You could always count on Roy if you needed help with anything."

One, two, three, four. "No offense, but I wouldn't … he's not somebody I would call on if I needed help."

"He's your *brother*." She sounded genuinely surprised.

"That doesn't mean we get along that great."

"You've hardly seen or spoken to him these—how many years?"

One angel screamed, *Don't let her pile on the guilt!* Another screamed, *Go easy.* The one operating my mouth said, "Like I said, I've got friends—"

"Friends come and go. Roy would always—"

"Like I said, he's not somebody I would go to for help. You didn't know it, but he was pretty nasty to me growing up."

Her tone acquired an edge. "You can't still hold a grudge. About what he did as a child? Not after all these years." We were silent a moment, and when she spoke again, the edge was gone. "He's here when I need him."

"That's not the point. And just for the record: he wasn't a child; he was a teenager."

"Teens have their ups-and-downs. You did too. And brothers and sisters fight. You think Lorr was always Sweet Big Sis? I told you about the birthday party. When she put bubble gum in my hair?"

"I'm not talking about pranks. I mean *really* nasty—"

"Gum in my hair wasn't nasty? And brothers are worse than sisters. *Everybody* says. Anthony Junior, he took his younger brothers' brand new skates and—"

"Not typical older-sibling shit—*really* nasty."

"He's not nasty now. Why, if you knew—"

"I'm not saying *now*."

This silence lasted an eon. The R bomb hadn't been on my mind at all when I had dialed. Just the opposite: I'd been hoping for a reconciliation. Should I change the subject? To what?

Mathilde knew where *she* wanted the conversation to go. "Roy would be the *last* to pretend he was well-behaved when he was young. But that was so long ago. How old are you both? He's forty-four, and you'll be forty in another year. How can you still be mad—"

"It's not about being *mad*. Just about *recognizing*—"

"And look how *well* you turned out. Nobody has a better sense of humor. Roy *himself* says that. 'Andy, she could be a comedian.'"

I rested the receiver in its cradle.

Did Edward pick the lawyer because of Sydney? I phoned, and Mr. Greenstreet's assistant said once probate was "concluded," they'd mail me a check, though it could take over a year. I asked if instead they could keep the money in Brackton because I might move in the meantime, and she said yes. What did I want done with the "papers" Mr. Cavanaugh had left me? They would hold onto them if I preferred. That would be great, I said.

The might-move line wasn't a lie; rumors were flying that St. Aloysius might go belly-up. What were the papers? Edward had had a wall of photos of famous actors and actresses, some autographed—could be those. Whatever it was, I ESP'd a thank you, which didn't stop me from feeling guilty for not having stayed in touch. Sure, most people didn't maintain a lot of contact with second cousins thirty years their senior, but we were the last of the Mohicans.

Over the next bunch of seasons, I kept on the dry and narrow. Every six months or so I would drop by Mass General for more literature. The latest was a page saying *scientists are hopeful that, with the genetic mutation narrowed down to a segment on Chromosome 4, it is only a matter of time before they are successful in their hunt for the gene.* Only a matter of time. *Everything* was only a matter of time. If enough time passed, we'd all be dead. Roy was right—I could've been a comedian.

Eventually, the rumors came true; St. Aloysius was closing. My sanctuary these last few years was kicking me out, and I was scared shitless. But the staff helped me find a prep position at an old people's home in the South End and a furnished room in a boarding house. Good thing the rent was cheap, since the Halcyon didn't pay shit, not enough for me to even bother opening a bank account. I kept my paltry savings in an envelope tucked in the bed slats. It wasn't like the landlady bent down to vacuum.

Still, the changes might've been the kick in the pants I needed to start thinking about leaving Boston. Somebody had said the winters on Martha's Vineyard weren't such a bitch. But why stay in Massachusetts, Andy—you have the whole country to choose from. *This land is your land.* Yes, I would leave Massachusetts. For where? Not the Midwest; I wanted to be near the ocean. The Atlantic was a whole lot closer than the Pacific. Farther north was out; so was the Bible Belt. South Jersey was too close to family. What about the

Delaware side of the Delaware Bay, where Dean used to go fishing with the Linehans? That would work.

Unfortunately, moving would have to be over a year away, because I wanted to accumulate enough savings so I wouldn't have to dip into Edward's legacy for living expenses. Ten thou was a hefty rainy-day fund, sure, but some of it would eventually go for a used car once I found an apartment and a job. I'd also have to use some for furniture, insurance, utilities. And who knew how long it would take me to find a job? It wasn't like I'd forgotten what being penniless could lead to. Anyway, just knowing I would be moving was a mood booster.

Not long after the Ides of March, I ventured out to the forum for cigarettes, stopping at a newsstand. My eyes locked in on the headline before my brain lobes knew what was what. *Team Pinpoints Genetic Cause of Huntington's. 10-Year Quest Produces Key to Brain Disease.*

I paid for a paper and must have literally flown back to my room.

After 10 backbreaking years in a research purgatory of false leads ... an international team of scientists says it has discovered the most coveted treasure in molecular biology, the gene behind Huntington's disease. If it was such a coveted treasure, how come most people had never heard of Huntington's? ... *researchers say they can begin making headway in understanding the disorder, a neurodegenerative illness that usually strikes a person in the 30's or 40's, insidiously destroys body and sanity alike, and kills within 10 to 20 years.* Making headway. Making headway! ... *molecular genetics ... mutation ... tiny segment of the gene ... abnormally ... repeated over and over ... .*

Sentences raced by, meaningless and confusing. I reread a few paragraphs slowly and comprehended a little more. They had identified the gene—the genetic mutation—causing Huntington's; they knew where it was located on the chromosome and what it looked like. The bad gene had a sequence of molecules called CAG that kept getting repeated like a broken record: CAG, CAG, CAG.

Researchers emphasized today that much work needed to be done before they could use the mutation as any sort of precise prognostic tool. In plain English: there would be no improved test right away. But there would be someday! *Nor does the finding the gene mean that a treatment for the disease is imminent.* Nor does it mean it isn't. Didn't some medical breakthroughs occur suddenly, sometimes by accident? Like what's-his-face—Fleming—with penicillin. And if a treatment was, say, three or four years away, then maybe it didn't matter if I had the bad gene.

I tried reconstructing the various conversations with Edward and Lorraine about Dean's symptoms. The stories jumbled together—the Dancing Dean nickname, the spilled drink, the unsteadiness on his feet. And would I follow in his footsteps—or stumbles—if I lost the coin toss? He was showing symptoms by his late forties, for sure. Did the funny movements begin earlier, in his mid-forties? Or *at* forty? June was on the horizon—I would be forty-one. Could my *lack* of shaking mean I was home free?

One paragraph almost made me smile. *The disorder sometimes begins in childhood or adolescence but more often is silent until well into adulthood, at which point the symptoms begin: random, uncontrollable movements in every part of the body, psychiatric disorders, mental deterioration and death. Researchers now suspect that some of the Salem witches may have suffered from Huntington's.* And Hecate Hore said they were *strong* women!

I stuck it out at the Halcyon for another year-plus, at the end of every month counting the money I'd saved and vacation time I'd accrued. To keep my emotions on an even keel, I shied away from baseball news, even after the Phillies clinched the division. Maybe the memories of them going to the Series when I was in Chicago made me uncomfortable, like their success was a jinx. Anyway, my refusal to get swept up in the excitement paid off because they ended up losing to Toronto.

My forty-second birthday arrived with my body still symptom-free. My savings reached the goal I had set, so in late July, I gave the Halcyon two weeks' notice and swung by Mass General one last time.

The single new piece of literature explained the CAG "stutter." A normal gene, one without the Huntington's mutation, contained a stretch of DNA where the CAG sequence repeated between eleven and thirty-four times. The abnormal Huntington's gene repeated the CAG sequence anywhere from forty-two to eighty-six times. If you landed in the middle, with thirty-five or forty repeats, say, then reply hazy—try again later.

Still, it wasn't all hazy. If you had fewer than thirty-five CAG repeats, you were home free. And if you had forty-two or more, the news was grim.

We will soon have a more accurate predictive test. The bottom of the page said *Summer 1993.* A year had passed. Could they have the more accurate predictive test now? Wilmington would have a decent hospital; I'd ask there.

Chapter 53

THE AFTERNOON BEFORE my departure from Boston, I went for a farewell—or maybe good riddance—walk. It was hot and humid; car exhaust hung in the air like dust bunnies. Every newspaper headline, it seemed, screamed about the baseball players' strike, and everywhere you went you heard people arguing who was greedier, the players or club owners. I couldn't get worked up either way, since none of them were likely to be living on the street any time soon. Besides, my own plans preoccupied me.

Tomorrow's itinerary was set: a bus to New York City and one to Philly. The following day, I would probably head to Wilmington and talk with the locals about towns near the bay. But postponing Wilmington and first swinging by Brackton remained a possibility. Brackton offered a chance to hit Greenstreet's and the bank.

My brain lobes had been debating it for weeks. The pro-Brackton lobe said it would be helpful to have Edward's money in a checking account and some checks on me before I went to Delaware. The anti-Brackton lobe said I should first get settled in a home and job so I would be mentally fortified to deal with Mathilde and everybody.

Pro-Brackton Lobe: But you need Edward's money to buy a car. And you could hit Greenstreet's and the bank without Mathilde or Lorraine seeing you.

Anti-Brackton Lobe: How can you guarantee that? And besides, you'll need to get some sort of ID, like a Delaware license, so the bank knows who you are—they're not going to hand you ten thousand dollars just because you *say* you're Andy Gabe.

But won't I need an ID to get a Delaware license? Whatever happened to my Illinois license? It had disappeared ages ago, before I even went to St. Al's. I remembered handing it to the guy at that factory, Ferguson's. Did I have it at Jackie's? Shit, yes—my first day there, I'd hidden it in a gap in the wall, folded up in two twenties. Did the cops find it after the bust? Doubtful—then they would've booked me under my real name. Was it worth forty dollars to return to hell to find out? Orpheus had pursued a much worthier prize. Maybe somebody else lived there. Would some stranger let me in? I could offer them the forty bucks—or at least twenty—if they'd let me look. But it could all be gone—the *building* could be gone. Anyway, the license would've expired.

Maybe Edward's papers included something that would work as ID. Holy cow—why hadn't it occurred to me before? Edward's papers might have originally come from *Dean*. Things *he* had left me, left *for* me. Maybe I should give Mathilde a call, see if we could patch things up enough for a short stopover. She might even have a copy of my birth certificate.

The guy in the blessedly air-conditioned dry cleaners said there was a pay phone five or six blocks past the gas station, "if the junkies haven't busted it." He was nice enough, letting me change a couple of dollars.

The phone had a dial tone, so I arranged my pocketful of nickels, dimes, and quarters in stacks on the metal ledge beside the peeling *oycott lettu* sticker.

"The number you have reached is no longer in service. If you think you may have reached this recording in error—"

I hung up and dialed again. Same recording. Had Mathilde moved? Or just had trouble paying the phone bill? Where was helpful Roy? I dialed my aunt.

"Hello?"

"Aunt Lorraine?"

"Who is this?"

"Andy."

"My goodness."

"Sorry for the shock. I tried Mathilde—"

"She passed away January."

My lobes went into paralysis. Eventually my mouth eked out, "What happened?"

"Stroke's what they think. Went to bed one night and didn't wake up. The Lord was merciful about that."

I started picking at the *oycott*. "Poor Matt."

"Where are you?"

"Boston."

"Roy's married. Moved to Enid, Oklahoma. Lawyer doing the probate says don't expect to hear for eighteen months. So he took the job. Nice gal, Donna. From Waterloo, Nebraska. Near Omaha." Lorraine rattled on about the funeral, where Mathilde was buried, what the house had fetched, that I got half of everything. She and Anthony had both retired; two of the grandkids were at Rutgers.

I finished peeling the *oycott* and started on the *lettu*. "Did Matt ever say anything about talking to me?"

"Not for a couple of years. Last time, said you weren't on long."

"She seem mad?"

Lorraine spoke slowly, as if her mind actually controlled her jaw. "Said you had cross words."

"That's all?" Then maybe she didn't leave Earth hating me.

"She said more, but it didn't make sense. Talking to you now it does." She was silent a moment. "Isn't that funny? Sissy must've meant it as a message, in case she died before telling you herself. Yes, she wanted me to pass along a message in case she never saw you again."

"What did she say?"

"I'll have to tell Anthony. At the time, I was so bothered. I says to him, 'Sissy says the strangest thing. And the *way* she says it.'"

A little more insistently, I repeated, "What did she say?"

"She said it's hard explaining to somebody that doesn't have children, meaning explaining to *you*."

"Explaining what?"

"She didn't want you feeling bad about the cross words; that's what it was. She says, 'No matter what they say or do, a mother never stops loving her children.'"

The recording came on again and told me to deposit more coins. I told my aunt I was out of money and hung up. Stashing the remaining nickels and dimes in my pocket, I left the phone booth and lit a cigarette.

The miserable August clamminess clung to every pore of skin. I smoked down to the filter and dropped the butt on the pavement, pressing it with the ball of my sneaker. A dark-haired woman in a long-sleeved blouse crossed the street towards me, clutching a huge shoulder bag under her arm. I stepped over to the curb to allow her room to pass, but she stopped. Her face broke into a smile.

I squinted. "Jackie?" An older, wrinkled Jackie. Her hair was laced with gray, her cheekbones gaunter. But the lusterless coal black eyes hadn't changed. *Apache eyes*, she'd once said—*I's parts Apache.* Almost imperceptibly, her head jerked. Did *she* have Huntington's? Just my luck, I'd spend my final days in a ward with Jackie.

"Saids that's you. Alls the ways from there." She pointed to a black guy on a stoop near the corner. "Darrin and me's watching you. 'Gots to be Andy,' I says. 'Nobodys but Casper that white.'" She tilted her head towards the phone. "Trying to score?"

"Talking to my aunt. Just found out my mother died."

"No kidding? Sorry. So what's you doing? Where's you living?" She grinned like we were kissing cousins at the family reunion.

"Leaving town tomorrow."

"For wheres?"

"Not sure. Still absorbing the shock. About my mother."

"Tells you what, I can gets you something to takes the edge off."

I'm sure you can. "That's okay."

"Gots your own stuff?"

"No. Gave it all up." Not everybody has your one-track mind. Ah, *that's* why the long sleeves in this miserable heat.

"'Nother week, Dro's be back. Boatload of White Virgin coming in."

"You two still together?" You two still not locked up?

Smiling, Jackie glanced back at the dude on the stoop. "Yep, it our fate."

"So who's Darrin?"

"Help me out when Dro gone."

"Like Mark."

"No, Dro's don't wants me hanging with black—" She stopped mid-sentence. A cream-colored monstrosity—maybe a Cadillac—was pulling to the curb beside Darrin. The top of his head appeared over the car roof; he must have gone to the passenger side. Seconds later, the car drove off, and Darrin strolled leisurely towards us.

"Mark, Eileen, they's moved to Lynn. Three kids. Third a boy." Darrin waved; Jackie waved back. "He gots it. Needs to make up before Dro back. Know anybody like black tar, Turkish Taffy? Sends you alls the way to Turkey." She drilled me with her eyes.

"Your mother leaves you money?"

"Don't know. Probate—I guess it takes a year or two. Anyway, she was pretty much living hand-to-mouth—"

"Owneds her house, car?"

"Yeah."

"Shit, gal, you's rich." Jackie was mighty pleased for me.

"Doubt it. My half brother gets half. And—"

We watched Darrin approach. "Look," Jackie said, tapping my arm, "I's going home, makes my packages. You can haves one, free."

"That's okay."

"Come by tomorrow, gots beer, soda. Likes old times. Same place. Mark's empty—nobody living there."

"Jackie," Darrin called out, "I got to go." She went and hugged him. It didn't take binoculars to see the paper bag fall into her purse. Darrin walked off.

"Comes in the morning. The afternoon I selling." Before walking away she threw me the widest, friendliest smile in her whole damn repertoire. Geronimo right before the charge.

I bought a pint of Scotch on my way back to the boarding house. The shock of Mathilde's death hadn't worn off, and I wanted painkiller handy when it did. But the Fates must have been watching over me, because I fell asleep without having to break the seal on the bottle.

Chapter 54

IN THE MORNING, I started for the station, my backpack over my shoulder. With Mathilde's death and Roy's move to Oklahoma, the pro-Brackton lobe handily won the debate about whether to stop there before heading to Delaware. I would crash at my aunt and uncle's a few days and deal with Greenstreet and the bank. Should I consider *living* in Brackton? The biggest con was it being such an armpit of a town. But it had some pros. For one, it would be kind of cool to run into one of the Linehans and maybe some other folks who had known Dean. The Veterans Cemetery was just past the city limits.

Would I need to prove who I was? Was there a birth certificate among Mathilde's things—or did Roy toss everything? Should I drop by Jackie's to see if the old license was still in the wall? Yes, I might luck out, I just might—the gap in the wall was close enough to the sill to not be noticeable even with the drape pushed away. You had to *suspect* something was hidden there, had to think to look. And the cops were searching for dope, not paper. Nobody hiding skag would use such a tight spot and risk the glassine tearing.

Jackie's alley hadn't changed much. The three-story buildings with their zigzagging wooden staircases looked as dilapidated as ever.

The wide dirt lane and overgrown grass yards still gave the feeling of some place half rural. The metal trash cans stank of rotten food, and in the humidity, the dank vegetation gave off a fetid smell all its own. Somebody had gotten rid of a maroon couch that had to have been hideous even in its heyday. A baby carriage by the dumpster was minus the rear axle. In the distance brakes squealed, but here all was silent, inert. No birds chirped—the only sounds were my sneakers crunching bits of gravel.

The yard was a jungle of weeds and garbage. No Eileen to make little efforts at tidying. I mounted the old, weather-beaten staircase. At what used to be Mark's landing, I paused to peer in. The kitchen was dark and empty. The steps up to Jackie's had traces of squished strawberries, the dark, overripe kind I used to unpack at Hernandez's. Her kitchen curtains were closed as always. I knocked loudly and waited. I knocked again. Waited some more. No sound of footsteps, no sound at all.

I glanced around to see if anybody was watching. Jeepers creepers, somebody was. Directly opposite, also on a third-floor landing, an old woman sat in a rocker and appeared to be looking right at me, though for all I knew, her eyes were closed. A little kid played at her feet.

I knocked more insistently. To my surprise, the door gave, but only a tad, not like somebody opening it. Was Droghan back and gone to the store? I felt stupid with the woman watching, so I stepped inside.

Music faintly floated down the hall from the front. Jackie must be in her room with the radio on. I called, "Jackie, it's me, Andy." No response. I closed the kitchen door and tiptoed to my old bedroom, went in, and turned on the light.

Only trash—beer cans, mostly—remained, no mattress. I strode to the window, pushed aside the drape, and squatted. They were there! Carefully, very carefully, I closed my thumb and index finger like pincers on the outer edges of the money and pressed tightly. A light tug and another. A wiggle and another wiggle. Out came the two twenties and my Illinois license. Hip-hip-hooray! I tucked them in the back pocket of my jeans, knocked the light, and went into the hall.

Should I just split? What if Droghan came in while I was leaving? He might think I was a thief. I could explain I was a friend of Jackie's, but he might haul me down to their bedroom for confirmation, and what would I tell her? I sure didn't want to piss her off, not with him there.

Okay, I'd just poke my head in, say I was dropping by but had to get to the station pronto to catch my bus. I called, "Jackie, it's me, Andy." Still no response. I walked towards the front of the apartment, each step making a sound like paper ripping. Cleaning had never been her thing; I could be stepping in soda spilled five years ago. The door to the storage room—my old work room—was open, but the drapes must've been pulled because I couldn't see in. What was that odor?

"Jackie? It's me, Andy." I went around the corner. Light from her bedroom slanted across the far end of the hallway. The front door was still boarded up, but the planks looked different. The music stopped. "Jackie, it's me, Andy."

An announcer came on and said something about the baseball strike. You'd think the rest of the world no longer existed. Was she fast asleep? The stink was really strong here, making me queasy. Something familiar. Not a chemical, but not food either.

"Jackie, it's me, Andy. You said to come by in the morning." I reached the archway and peered in the room.

The overhead light glared harshly. The place was harsh, a mess, a mess. Cranberry spatters on the wall. Black beads dotting the ceiling. Not paint, but blood—blood was what I smelled. Blood was everywhere. And not just blood—chunks of purple and green and yellow, scattered as though flung from a paintbrush. The sheets were soaked, dark pools surrounding the box spring. A hump on the mattress, *two* humps. The neck bent unnaturally. Near the pillow, unconnected to any arm, lay a palm with curled fingers. Some cottage-cheese-like thing perched on a shoe where you might expect a tassel. The stench crowded out the air—I couldn't breathe.

I turned, and the pack swinging almost made me lose my balance. I ran and ran. Down the foul sticky hall, through the foul kitchen, out the door, down the steps, avoiding the dark spots but trying not to slow, a landing, more steps, through the yard, the gate, into the alley, away from the walls and smells and sickening mess. Was that me screaming? Squatting by a rut, I retched and retched.

For who knew how long, the sole sound was my retching and spitting. Then people asked what was wrong. All I could do was point. I heard shouting. More people, more shouting. I moved some distance from the puke and sat on a tire and tried not to faint. Sirens wailed. Brakes screeched, lights flashed. "Take the kids away," a man yelled.

A woman squatted beside me, touched my shoulder. "You all right?" I was handed a water bottle and drank. I was offered a cigarette and took it. A small flame shot up. Menthol. That was okay, a different smell. I toked deeply. A folding chair materialized. I sat. People around me talked in urgent voices. Somebody asked my name. I used Gabe, thinking of my license. More questions—some different, some repeated two, three, four times. Jackie—not sure of the last. Smith, maybe. Hadn't seen her in years, not till yesterday. She'd invited me to drop by for a visit.

A cop inspected my hands. I did too. No blood. Would I mind if they examined my sneakers? I didn't want the sneakers; they could have them. She wore yellow plastic gloves. Took the socks too. Good riddance. I put on my boots barefoot. Somebody mentioned Miranda. Another voice said, "She left footprints going *in*."

"Whoever did this has to be covered in it."

"The witness saw her enter the apartment only a minute or two before running out. Wouldn't have had time to wash off—"

"How long she been out there?"

"The witness? Half hour, she guesses."

"See anybody else go in or out?"

"No."

"Somebody strong, the way they wielded that axe."

"Manson with muscles."

A shoulder tap. "Recognize this?"

I looked up. Four white male cops, in a half circle, watched me. "Seen lots of Red Sox caps," I said.

"Without the X?"

"Don't think so."

Could they look in my pack? Yes. The voices debated whether I should be taken to the ER, whether I was in shock. I was led to a squad car, and we rode. They led me into a building and to some office with people typing. A bunch more times I had to repeat how I'd gone in and found her. Yes, the back door was unlocked. Always used the back door. Just went into one other room, the first on the left. Because I'd stayed there long ago and was curious. Peered out the window, that was all. Did I know what Jackie did for a living? Have any enemies? How about a boyfriend? One cop must've asked twenty times, "You *sure* you have no idea who might have done this?"

"No idea," I repeated twenty times.

Eventually they said I was free to go but they might want to get in touch. I gave them the boarding house number, address.

"You want to avoid reporters?" somebody said. "I'll show you a side exit."

The bus to New York wasn't crowded. I got the two rear seats to myself, drank some Scotch, and fell asleep. Yet images of maroon streaks and spatters and viscous gobs kept jerking me awake. Worst of all, the stench, the god-awful stench, clinging as if blood were up my nostrils.

At Port Authority, I went to the women's restroom and had the dry heaves. Later, I ate some crackers and in Philly managed a sandwich. I caught some sleep in the waiting area and got a ticket on the afternoon bus to Brackton. My alcohol tolerance had gone down, so I didn't need another pint for the ride.

Small ugly towns and stretches of coarse countryside went past. Ugly and bleak, everything was ugly and bleak. Where did I get the idea that leaving Boston would make a difference? The miles were merely geographical, not mental. There was no escaping the stink. And it wasn't from Jackie, Jackie's body and body parts—it was from me, my own self. I was lousy with rot. Of no use to myself, much less to anybody else. I had certainly been of no use to my mother. Roy, that raping sonofabitch, at least he had helped take care of her.

Even the wretched physical conditions of my life for so many years were nothing compared to my wretched cowardice. Using the fear of Huntington's to justify despair, to justify addiction to alcohol and weed, to justify submitting to repugnant acts. People all over the world were dying prematurely and horribly from war, famine, AIDS, diseases too numerous to count. And axes. Self-pity was my true addiction.

Night descended. My drunken brain didn't have the wherewithal to identify landmarks in the dark or to figure out anything besides postponing calling my aunt and uncle till I had sobered up.

Chapter 55

THIS END OF Main was a carved-out shell totally at odds with the busy commercial street of my childhood. A five-and-ten once took up half the block, and across had been a kid's shoe store and Hiram's Haberdashery with the large *H*s. Now the signs were gone and the bus depot the only lit building—everything else had been razed or boarded up.

I hung a left on Front Street. If this neon skid row was the front of Brackton, you could only imagine the back. Spacy Tracy looked as good a place as any to get a cold beer and ask about cheap motels.

The bar was quiet, funky, not biker or hard-hat. The two shooting pool gave me the once-over and resumed their game. I ordered a pint, and the bartender told me about a motel back on Main. I took my glass to a small table in the back. The cold beer felt good, at least going down. Who knew how my stomach would react after all the Scotch.

"Andy, right?" A skinny guy holding a beer stood across from me. "Dennis. Used to hang out with Roy."

I nodded.

He pulled out a chair and sat. "Somebody said he got married and moved to Okla*ho*ma." Dennis swigged his beer, his Adam's apple pulsating like an imprisoned frog.

"Heard that too."

We bullshitted awhile. At some point he asked if I was interested in any meth. He pulled out a small peppermint candies tin and pried it open. "No charge for your first."

If I took some speed, I could wait till morning to spring for a motel and have an extra day to clean up my act before calling Lorraine. I said thanks and washed a pill down with beer. Dennis put the tin back in his pocket and started talking about kids from high school, kids he and Roy had hung out with. Not really caring, I barely listened. One died in Vietnam. One was in prison. Some girl moved to—

Knives jabbed my ears, slashed my face. Somebody grabbed my throat, choked me. Searing pain split my skull. A high-pitched tinny noise. The knives again, my ears, my face. Air sucked from my lungs. Ants, thousands of them, army ants, burrowed into my brain. Get them off of me! Blood spurted everywhere. Fish slithered down my neck, all over my chest. I'm too dizzy. Ouch, my arm. Stop, stop this spinning. Were my eyes open or shut? I couldn't see. My hands, did I have my hands?

Cold, freezing cold. Block of ice, I was inside a block of ice. Tried to yell, but no sound came out. Or was I deaf? Blind and deaf. And cold, in a dark ice tunnel. Noises far, far away. Tapping, thumping, pounding. Tomtoms? Getting closer, fading, closer, fading. A war dance? On fire, I was on fire. Not flame, a pool of molten wax, bubbling wax, oozing across my back, wrapping my body like a jacket of fire.

Are those birds? No, it was buzzing. Bees, flies, mosquitoes. Buzzing, buzzing, they won't stop buzzing. Pricking my cheeks, my chin. I can't move to whack them. The flames, I'm on fire again. I scream, and sound comes out. I scream again. Voices, many voices, loud, stern.

All is quiet. A peaceful lake, and the grass so green and fresh. Mathilde sitting at a picnic table, wearing a straw hat and red-checked dress. "Andy, come taste the berries." I look down at my bare feet. Black ants, they're everywhere, on my toes, ankles. I scream.

Listening carefully, I could hear a bud-dip, bud-dip, bud-dip. I was in a bed. I could see cupboards. A sink against the wall. A pale plastic bag hanging from a chrome stand. An IV, that's what it was. I must be in a hospital.

A noise woke me. Had I fallen back asleep? "Where am I?"

Hands midair, she stopped to turn. "Four West." She wore a pink smock.

"Where? This a hospital, right?"

"Yes, St. Joseph's."

"St. Jo—in Brackton?"

"Yes."

A younger woman, this one in yellow, poked her head in. "You're awake?"

"Guess so."

The one in yellow was a nurse. She told me I'd been at St. Joe's almost two weeks. EMTs had brought me into the ER, and I'd spent some days in the ICU and then the CSU, whatever that was. I'd been tested for HIV, STDs, TB, and hepatitis A, B, and C—the whole alphabet, practically. Everything had come out normal, to my amazement more than hers. Yes, they would remove the catheter, after she checked my vitals. And see if anybody had given the EMT crew a backpack. When I was discharged, any money and possessions that had been on me would be returned.

"When will that be, that I'll be discharged?"

"Probably tomorrow or the day after, if you're stable."

I drifted off to sleep and awoke in the dark needing to pee. The thing in my crotch was gone; so was the IV. I was dizzy standing but slowly made it to the can.

"Tell me what's wrong. Are you hurt?"

"Is she okay?"

"I think it's just her period."

They helped me to the bed, and a lady said she'd be giving me a pelvic exam. I willed my mind into the darkness beyond the window.

"Press the call button when you want to change your pad," somebody said. I fell asleep imagining Lish tending me, being soft and gentle.

In the morning, I asked the nurse if she knew of any halfway houses for recovering alcoholics. The social worker did—would I like to speak to him? If I could. How was I feeling? Still a little dizzy.

They actually had him come to my room. He said that the halfways had waiting lists a mile long. The sole exception wasn't technically a halfway but something midway between a rehab and true halfway, and that was at St. Joe's itself, their annex. The residents were "past needing medical interventions," yet the program required them to stay on-site for six months minimum anyway. "Instead of having a job and earning money like at a traditional halfway, you would share the chores that run it." Plus, you couldn't have visitors or leave the premises except to be escorted to and from psychiatrist appointments at the hospital.

He sounded apologetic. "The rules were set out in the foundation grant that pays for the program. To be honest, the residents call it the Prison. Most leave before they can be transitioned to a traditional halfway."

"Does it cost anything?"

"No, it's entirely funded through the foundation."

Halfway to a halfway house: a Zeno house.

The Annex was a one-story building across St. Joe's rear parking lot. There were about twenty of us, and the rules and routines weren't all that different from the Mission's—chores, group therapy, individual therapy—except that smoking wasn't allowed. Dr. Wilder would be my psychiatrist, and my sessions would start next week when she returned from vacation. Any relation to Billy or Gene? She should have a sense of humor. But apparently not—two of the residents called her Adolf, and some ex-resident had hurled a book at her. It wasn't like St. Joe's would draw the cream of the crop anyway. Not that it mattered. My plan was to stay only a few weeks, then see if my aunt would let me crash at her place while I looked for a job and apartment.

"Prison" was no exaggeration: people were always in your face. My years in Boston had demanded little personal interacting, but here we had to cook and clean in teams and sit together at meals. And the staff was always popping up asking how we were *feeling*. At group therapy, I had to hear about the Twelve Steps for the twelve hundredth time. They spent an entire session arguing about whether "one day at a time" was a better or worse mantra than "Just today, Lord, just today." Ironically, group therapy was the one time I *wasn't* forced to speak; I could be Andy Garbo.

Maybe I shouldn't have expected another Roberta. Dr. Wilder was small and delicate with dark hair in a perfect pageboy. Her cashmere sweater matched her gray skirt perfectly. She languidly shook my hand and motioned for me to sit in one of the padded mahogany armchairs by the large mahogany desk. I was relieved she took the chair behind the desk, not the one next to mine—this coiffed mannequin was nobody I could open up to.

As my eyes adjusted to the dim lighting—she used lamps, not an overhead—I noticed a huge painting on the wall to my right, a portrait of a bearded, somber-faced dude. I didn't like him either. The desk was nice, with leaves carved into the corners. Her own, no doubt—I couldn't see St. Joe's supplying it. Or the grandfather clock. The carpet was a deep purple, almost burgundy.

"You went through a tumultuous few weeks at the hospital. How do you feel now?" Her voice was super-smooth.

I shrugged.

She pursed her lips briefly. "We—you and I—will meet once a week for fifty minutes."

How did she end up working in Brackton anyway? Why not some nice suburb where she could listen to the problems of women who stayed home all day playing bridge? Did she get her perfect pageboy at Mrs. Delucci's? Doubtful—Mrs. D's customers weren't all that particular.

"Are you listening?" she asked.

"Sorry."

"I would like to make the most of our time. I asked when you first began using drugs or alcohol."

"High school."

"Was it for fun then? Or were there painful circumstances?"

"It was fun."

She continued to hit me with questions, and I gave rote answers. I didn't want her as my shrink any more than she wanted me as her patient. Yet *she* got paid to be annoyed for fifty minutes; I merely got to keep my options open.

When she asked what had led to the drugs and alcohol in my system the evening I was admitted, I said that the day before, I'd gone to visit a friend who had just been murdered, and I was the one to find the body.

"Hacked up pretty good, with a fire axe."

Applying this phony pained expression, she asked the details, and I got some satisfaction from giving them: the sticky hallway, the blood beaded on the ceiling and pooled by the bed, the gobs, the severed hand. Knowing I was grossing her out made it into a game, like describing not reality but a creepy horror flick to somebody who freaked easily.

"Were you very close?" she asked, nodding in this knowing way like she was expecting me to say Jackie was my lover and she was cool with stuff like that.

"No, didn't even much like her. But chopped up body parts can get to you anyway."

At another session, Dr. Wilder asked how the group therapy was going, and again I didn't mince words, saying it was stupid. She asked in what way, and I said, "The point of AA is to get you to apologize for all the things you did wrong in your life, but it seems to me it was the wrong things that got done *to* you that made you an alcoholic or addict in the first place."

"You're absolutely right. The program is geared to the present and future, not the problems of the past. It targets the habit, not its root cause." She wound her watch. "It doesn't replace individual therapy."

Good thing—otherwise she'd be out of a job.

Predictably, she asked what I thought the causes were for my alcoholism. I didn't mention Huntington's—the folks at Mass General had told Roberta that counseling about the disease was out of *her* league, and that had to go double for Wilder. I went the easy route and retold the Roy saga, just to give her a bone to chew on. Which was a mistake.

"Why didn't you tell your mother?" she wanted to know.

I shrugged.

"Was it because you felt *you* were in the wrong, somehow?"

Where had I heard this bull before? Some pamphlet at Artemiz. Crap sure made the rounds. In the afternoon light, the carpet looked more maroon than purple. Had to be Wilder's, not St. Joe's.

"I don't mean you *should* feel you did something wrong," she said. "Quite the contrary—it *wasn't* your fault. Yet it's a very common and natural response for rape victims to feel ashamed and guilty, in essence to turn the anger inward."

My cuticles were a mess—that was what giving up smoking did for you. But who really used to do a number on her cuticles was Nina. Good old Nina.

Chapter 56

WILDER GAZED UP at the dark portrait on the wall. Mr. Beard didn't seem pleased to be there either. For the millionth time, we were talking about—what else?—Roy. My lobes had already agreed that I would call my aunt and uncle by the end of the week so I wouldn't have to endure this woman any longer.

"Why did you never confront him when you were older and no longer afraid of him?" Broken-Record asked.

"Like I said: he'd changed. Wasn't violent—not to people. Might kick a chair was all. And he didn't live at home much."

"And he never apologized. Did you ever *ask* for an apology?"

"What was that going to get me? With two bucks, a cup of coffee."

"You ate dinner with someone who had *raped* you. You watched TV together, played cards, talked about baseball. Why?"

"Was just keeping the peace."

She pursed and un-pursed her lips. "*Whose* peace?"

"Everybody's."

She plucked a piece of lint off her sweater. "I would like to return to earlier, the period when the rapes were occurring. You said you knew Roy wanted to keep them a secret because otherwise he would get in trouble."

"Obviously."

"But if you knew he would get in trouble, why didn't you say something?"

"You tell me; I ain't the shrink."

"What was your thought process *at the time*? Why you didn't tell Mathilde?"

I laced my fingers together and looked at the ceiling, almost expecting to hear, *The answer's not written up there, young lady.* "Like I *said*, she had enough to deal with."

"What in particular?"

"Working long hours. At a factory, not some cushy office. Had to put in overtime whenever they wanted. Take two buses each way if the car was in the shop. Raising two kids. Going through the divorce. Even if you're the one wanting it, that doesn't make it easy. Especially back then—*nobody* got divorced. And always having to worry about money. It's not like we were living on Easy Street."

Wilder tilted her head forward without speaking. Her damn hair moved without mussing.

"Add to it the fact that Roy was a pain in the ass," I said, "mouthing off, flunking classes, drinking, leaving everybody wondering if he'd total the car. She was *tired*; she was tired by breakfast. I got my own cereal. Made my own lunch, got myself to school. How the hell was she going to deal with one more hassle? Especially *that*?"

"Wasn't it her *responsibility* to deal with it?"

"Like at ten years old I'm thinking about whose responsibility it is? Didn't they make you take child psych courses? How many ten-year-olds get all analytical?"

The pageboy rested back against the leather headrest. "Did you go to her when you got hurt? Fell and skinned a knee?"

"I assume so. Don't remember anything specific."

"Do you think you would have gone to her if a *stranger* had raped you?"

"Maybe—I don't know."

"What about when Roy did things brothers typically do, like teasing or taking your toys: did you go to your mother then?"

"Don't remember. Might've."

"But not when he raped you."

"That was different." Damned if I was going to spell it out any plainer. If she was too dense to see how different raping was, then how could these sessions possibly help me? I had a better grip on human psychology than she did. And if she just wanted to sit in silence, hell, I could match her minute for minute.

But she didn't want to sit in silence. "Was the difference that your mother didn't *want* you to tell her?"

"That's ridiculous. She had no idea what was going on."

"I am not saying she did. I am only saying that you believed she wouldn't want to know."

"What mother would? Name one who'd want to think her own son—besides, I'm sure she couldn't imagine that."

"It's not that she did or didn't want to know, necessarily. It's that she behaved in a way that told *you* not to tell her if Roy did something that awful."

"Just because I didn't want to tell her doesn't mean she told me not to."

Wilder glanced briefly, maybe unconsciously, at the dude on the wall. I had finally gotten to her; she realized there was more to life than what they wrote in books.

"Why would she suspect?" I said. "I was back in my room before she punched out of work. You don't know how it was. She was young, a teenager, when she'd had Roy. He was always trouble: yelling, breaking things. *Dean* could handle him. He'd look him in the eye and say—very quiet—'Pick up the chair you threw, Roy.' The quieter Dean said it, the quicker Roy'd do it. But Mathilde hadn't a clue. And she wasn't strong. Couldn't have weighed one-twenty. She'd had enough to do to keep the place together, food on the table. Roy out of jail."

"*Should* she have kept Roy out of jail?"

"Dump on her all you want for the stuff she did wrong but not the stuff she did right."

"He was a criminal."

"All she knew about was petty shit: shoplifting, joyriding. You don't turn in your son for those."

"Breaking things?"

"They were *her* things. She could've let it slide."

The way the sunlight hit the glass cover of the grandfather clock obscured the hands. How many more minutes of crap?

"Raping her daughter was a serious crime."

I rolled my eyes. "She didn't know."

"She didn't *want* to know."

"How do *you* know?"

"*You* knew she didn't want to know. That's why you didn't tell her."

"I didn't tell her because I was ten."

"Why didn't you tell her after that? When you were twenty or thirty?"

"There was no point. It was over, *long* over. Let sleeping dogs lie. You're trying to make her into an ogre, like she didn't care about me. That's bullshit. If she'd known what he was doing, she would have stopped it."

Wilder leaned forward, her dark eyes glistening. "Yet you didn't tell her! You hear what you just said? *If she had known what he was doing, she would have stopped it.* Yet you didn't tell her."

No, I didn't, I didn't tell her. Why not? It wasn't logical. But since when were kids logical—especially kids who were raped? Once something that far outside reality happened, logic disappeared from the universe.

"I didn't think it through," I said. "But that was *my* stupidity, not Mathilde's meanness."

Wilder leaned way back, as if to put her feet up on the desk. "You must have realized she loved him far more."

"Says who?"

"It's what *you* think."

"Just because I didn't want to hurt her? That's nuts."

"If *you* had done something awful to Roy, *he* would have told."

"That's because of who *he* is."

"You would have considered it his right, to tell on you."

"So?"

"What did you think she would have done if you had told her? Called the police? Sent him away, or at least ordered him out of the house? Tell me what you think she would have done."

"Cried a lot."

"Would she have believed you?"

"Wouldn't have wanted to."

"But *would* she have?"

"Yes. In fact, that's why I didn't tell her: I knew I'd be sticking her with some really bad news."

"Would she have turned him into the police?"

"Doubt it."

"Sent him away? Done anything to protect you?"

"Like I said, never sorted through it, didn't think in that much detail."

"But she would have done *something* to protect you? To make sure you were never alone with him?"

"Probably."

"But you didn't want that? Why didn't you want that?"

I *did* want that. How to explain?

Wilder explained. "You knew it would break her heart."

"Yeah."

"Is that what you thought, even if you didn't put it into words?"

"Yeah." Suddenly I was dog tired.

"She would still love him, despite what he had done to you."

"He was her son." A mother never stops loving her children.

For a while neither of us spoke. The sun had shifted enough for me to make out the clock hands. Only a few more minutes.

Wilder said softly, "So Mathilde preferred having him rape you to learning about it."

"I never said that."

"But that's what you felt."

"No. Just that she wouldn't have wanted to know."

"That her daughter was being raped."

"That her son was a rapist."

It came back to me how she smiled wistfully whenever I said something amusing, as though she'd wished for the energy to laugh out loud. *Thank you*, the smile said, *thank you for lightening my load.* Even now, so many years later, I could relive that tingle of pride and pleasure. "She wasn't a tough, together person," I said. "Still a kid in some ways."

"Once she became a mother, Andy, she gave up the luxury of being a child. Like it or not, she was a parent."

"You don't change overnight."

"She wasn't a teenager when you were ten; she was in her thirties. She had a responsibility to protect you."

"Like I said: she didn't know."

"Your thoughts at the time were: 'I would be ruining Mathilde's life if I squealed on her son. Roy matters to her more than I do.'"

"I didn't think it through."

"Andy would be *selfish* if she told on Roy, thinking only of her *own* comfort. Wanting to disrupt the household, disturb the peace. Bad enough that Dean had left, or was so careless about money that Mathilde had had to ask him to leave. Now along comes mean little Andy, the *squealer*. She wants to make poor, tired, unhappy Mathilde even unhappier."

"She didn't *know*." This bitch was really pissing me off. "What the fuck is going to get that through your thick skull? She was at the glass factory. Every. Single. Time."

"Her crime wasn't in *knowing*. Her crime was in letting *you* know not to tell her if Roy *did* hurt you. She gave that message loud and clear: she was not to be made sad over him, no matter what. Even if he raped you *over* and *over* and *over*. You should *let* him!"

I was on my feet. "That's not what she thought!"

"She was supposed to love you."

"She *did* love me. *I* was the one who split. As soon as I could, going to Chicago, hardly ever—"

"Better you should be raped than that she should know the truth."

"That's not what she thought!"

"She can't hear you, Andy. Mathilde can't hear you."

"But I could've been—I was wrong!"

The clock face glowed a pale pink. Was time really a fourth dimension? Stacy had said if you traveled at the speed of light, time slowed down. Joshua had made the sun stand still. I stood still. I was a statue. Niobe? What had made her turn to stone? Or was it salt? No, that was Lot's wife. For turning around? Orpheus—I was confused; the stories muddled together. But *somebody* had turned to stone, not just me.

"Mathilde can't hear you, Andy. It's not going to hurt her, whatever you say, whatever you accuse her of."

No, Mathilde couldn't hear me, not from a cemetery plot. But what if there were an afterlife? Dr. Wilder seemed to read my thoughts. "And if she *could* hear you, she would understand. Accuse her *aloud*. Accuse her of not loving you enough. Of not caring if you were raped, if the rapist was Roy."

I paced the dark purple carpet. Surroundings disappeared. The clock, the portrait, all the objects in the room, Dr. Wilder herself disappeared. Only the purple oval path I trod and Mathilde were there, Mathilde and me. And in the pacing my voice was born. Indeed, my voice was born. An accusing voice, like Dr. Wilder wanted, an angry, venomous voice.

"Maybe you felt guilty for marrying Dean," I spat out, "though Dean *tried* to be nice to him. But even if you wanted to make it up to Roy, *I* didn't deserve to be punished, to be raped."

From my room, I would listen for the heavy footsteps. The door would swing in. His bulk would block the hall window, block the daylight. I might be sitting on the floor fingering some toy, but which toy wasn't important, since I wasn't playing, only listening. He never had to speak, just loom there. I could either stand and go willingly or have him yank me, jerk me along. The faster I moved, the less brutal. He never bothered closing his own door. So he could hear her car? I listened for footsteps on the stairs, footsteps that never came.

I cried some, and Dr. Wilder pushed the tissue box closer, but the accusations didn't slow. "You let me know, as plain as if you'd said it, that you couldn't bear to hear anything bad about him. Yes, *Mother*, you preferred to have him rape me than to punish him, maybe send him away. *His* feelings mattered, and *your* feelings mattered. *My* feelings didn't amount to shit." She could rot. My fucking mother could go fucking rot.

I ranted till my voice grew hoarse. At one point Dr. Wilder made a short phone call but otherwise remained still, except for occasionally pursing her lips. Twilight came and then darkness. When I limply sat again, Dr. Wilder made another call and turned on another lamp, which shed a soft glow. A tray with sandwiches and juice was brought in. We ate and drank.

Her voice, always quiet, now had a conversational lilt to it. "You know as well as anyone, recovery doesn't happen overnight. But you have begun. Anger towards your mother—and hate—are justified, are appropriate, healthy emotions for what you were put through. Do not try to stem them. Let them out, *indulge* them."

I rose and fingered the leaves carved into the desk corner. "I know my session is more than over—I've probably used up ten. You're usually home by now. I just have one last question. If I let myself hate Mathilde, can I hate Roy too?"

She smiled—Dr. Wilder smiled.

Chapter 57

INDULGE I DID. Anger and hatred came out of the closet and into the streets. From sunrise past sunset, I recalled and denounced Mathilde's crimes, hurled my judgments into her imagined face. The first of her two capital offenses was in letting *me* know her peace of mind hung on Roy; the second was in letting *him* know. His meanness was no secret. Hell, before I was even in kindergarten, everybody could see he was no kind, caring older brother, no Bert Bobbsey. *Boys will be boys*: was that your excuse? Why didn't you show that little girl a love that would have led her to seek your protection? *I* wasn't spared the rod, not his.

Fuming gave way not just to fury but to fumigating, to prying into mental recesses where affection for my mother might be lurking. When I found any, I flushed it out. No memory of her would be free from the taint of her selfishness; everything she had ever said or done was another manifestation of her manipulative victimhood, of *her* need for equanimity taking precedence over mine. "Vocalize it," Dr. Wilder repeatedly urged, and I did, once a week in her office and, on occasion, in the group therapy sessions. I said my piece and un-kept the peace.

By Lincoln's birthday, I felt emancipated. If my language sometimes startled Dr. Wilder and her pageboy mussed, I didn't worry;

each hair would resume its rightful place in short order. But I did ask if hate would become just another addiction.

"It will ebb naturally," she said, "and when that happens, see if you can let it go."

If nothing else, hate began losing out to other interests. Dr. Wilder gave me her vote of confidence for moving to a traditional halfway and getting a job, and the Annex counselors assisted me in the transition, finding a place not far from Drake's that had an opening in early April. It was near a bus stop, so I could put off springing for a car right away. Mr. Greenstreet's office would be mailing me a check for a little over ten thousand dollars and said I could arrange at some point to come by and pick up the papers they were holding. And best of all: the judge was expected to rule on the baseball players' strike, so there could be a '95 season.

The end of March marked my last session with Dr. Wilder. Was there anything in particular I wanted to discuss, she asked. "One subject you have barely touched upon is your relationship with Dean."

I leaned back in the chair. "Maybe because we always got along. Can't say for sure that would have continued if I'd seen him much after the divorce. I guess I was upset that he was gone, but it quickly got crowded out by Roy."

Fair or not, I couldn't see a meltdown about Dean similar to the one about Mathilde. True, he hadn't been there to protect me, but I was sure he wouldn't have moved out unless Mathilde had asked him to. And he had never led me to think he wouldn't have wanted to know about the rapes—he *would* have wanted to know. And not just because Roy wasn't his son, but because Dean hated seeing me unhappy. Mathilde adapted just fine.

"I believe you said he fell down the station steps?" Dr. Wilder asked. "What a tragic accident."

"He'd injured his ankle a few years before, so it might have been weak. And ever hear of Huntington's Chorea?"

"The neurological disease?"

"Dean had it. I have a 50 percent chance of inheriting it."

In all my sessions, this was the first Dr. Wilder was at a loss for words. After about a year, she managed an "Are you sure? That he had it?"

"That's what everybody told me. He was seen here at St. Joe's. Would have been in '76, '77, thereabouts."

She jotted on a notepad. "Listen, I'll talk to someone in Neurology, put you in touch with someone there. To have *this* to deal with on top of everything else." She shook her head, some hairs falling out of place. "Tell me what you learned."

The baseball strike ended! The prospect of going to a Phillies game over the summer put me in such a good mood, I adopted one of the group mantras, *Just today, Lord, just today*, which might've actually helped tamp down beer and cigarette cravings a few times. Counting to ten might've worked equally well, but I wasn't about to look a gift horse in the mouth. I hit the hospital gift shop and bought myself a nice bright red Phillies cap.

The Neurology receptionist, an older lady with an ID tag saying *Doris*, had me fill out some forms. For *Purpose of your appointment* I wrote *Discuss maybe having Huntington's Disease.* A young dyed-blond nurse in make-up thick as a pancake called my name. She led me to a room with an examining table, a small desk containing a huge book, some uncomfortable-looking plastic chairs, and a table loaded with magazines. After doing the temperature and pulse stuff, she said to just have a seat—unfortunately Dr. Robbins had gotten delayed. The magazines were your usual *Time* and *National Geographic* assortment. I leafed through several without really reading. When the doctor finally showed, he gave me the once-over, sat on the rolling stool, and consulted his watch. He read the forms I had filled out, now clipped to a folder, then proceeded to delve into the huge book. I got restless. The plastic chair was designed for a baboon butt.

"Any peculiar movements?"

I almost looked around to see if he was talking to someone else, it had been so quiet. "Not that I've noticed."

"Why do you think you might have Huntington's?"

"They said Dean had it."

"Who's Dean, your father?" He looked off at the wall, as though it were the more interesting company.

"Yeah."

"Who diagnosed him?"

"Not sure. Somebody here, though, at St. Joe's."

"He told you that?" Again he looked at his watch.

"No, he never knew he had it. He died in '80, and they diagnosed him in '76, '77. It's a long story, but they never got around to actually *telling* him he had it, and I only found out when—"

"How old was he then?"

I loved it when doctors cut you off. Like what you were going to say was, at best, irrelevant and, at worst, a pack of lies. "He was born in '29, so in '76 would have been around forty-seven. Died in '80, just shy of fifty-one."

"When did he first become symptomatic, begin to show motor control problems? Odd gait, twisting, jerking?" Dr. Jerk took to writing in the folder.

"Not sure. I wasn't living near him, hadn't seen him for a bunch of years."

"When could he no longer take care of himself?"

"Don't think he ever reached that point. Had an apartment when he died."

"With family?"

"Not according to my cousin, who was alive at the time. Lived by himself."

"You must mean an assisted living facility, not an apartment."

"No, a regular apartment."

"Did he have someone come in to help him?"

"Don't know. He was working at—"

"He was *working*? He was still employed at *fifty*?" Jerk turned full-face, the face full of disbelief. My eyes took in the red embroidery across his breast pocket. *Dr. Monroe*. Still Dr. Jerk to me. "Then why did they think he had Huntington's?" He stared like I was trying to sell him snake oil, like I had nothing better to do than come here and make up bullshit.

"Somebody—Wu—that was his name. In '76, '77, Dean got admitted because of hurting his ankle, and this Dr. Wu—"

Monroe rose and removed some black cylindrical thing off the wall and flicked on a small light in the end piece. "Your father was a very lucky man."

"Ex*cuse* me?"

He came at me holding the black gizmo. "If he didn't present with symptoms until his late forties, if at fifty he was employed and living on his own and working, then he was very, very lucky."

My fist shot out. I didn't hear a crack, so for all his wailing, I knew I hadn't broken anything. Maybe if I'd had a clue ahead of time of what it planned, my fist would have landed harder, but I was as surprised as Jerk-face. He was very very lucky he didn't keel over.

I quickly sat back down, not wanting him to think I was going to do it again. He held his jaw with one hand and with the other picked up the phone. "Doris, can you hear me? Call security." As he was speaking, the dyed-blond came in. He hung up.

She batted her goopy lashes at him. "Is something wrong?"

I grabbed a magazine and spread it open across both knees. Some *National Geographic* article about—wouldn't you know it—baboons.

"She hit me."

Meeting her glance, I stared like it was the first I'd heard of it too.

She turned back to him and purred, "Are you okay?"

"No, I'm not okay! Yes, I'm okay, but she *did* hit me."

The nurse looked back and forth from him to me to him to me like we were playing Wimbledon. That pissed him off more. "In the face!"

She removed his hand and examined his jaw up close. "It does look a little red."

"You don't believe me?"

I thought he might hit *her*, but the door opening again distracted us. I awaited the uniform with a patch on the sleeve, awaited the escort to the hospital dungeon. I was sorry for disappointing Dr. Wilder.

But it wasn't security—just another white-coated doctor. Late-thirties, I was guessing. Tall, dark hair, dark eyes—I'd wager a lot more handsome to straight women than I'm-so-wounded Jerk Monroe.

"Am I interrupting?" the new doctor asked.

"The patient struck me in the face while I was taking a history."

The new guy cocked his head. Had he heard correctly?

"Her father had Huntington's," Monroe said. "I simply pointed out how very lucky he was to be essentially asymptomatic at fifty, and she *hit* me."

The new guy glanced my way for barely a nanosecond and nodded thoughtfully. "Ginger, would you mind accompanying Dr. Monroe to Ortho. They might want an X-ray."

The nurse grabbed the jerk's arm. "Come, let's get that examined."

Following Ginger out, Monroe glared at me, warning over his shoulder, "Don't be alone with her."

Once the door closed, the new guy held out his hand. "How do you do. I'm Dr. Robbins. So your father was diagnosed with Huntington's? Was it here?"

"Yeah. It's kind of a weird story. Maybe you heard it? A guy with an injured ankle escaping?"

He shook his head but smiled, curious, his eyes twinkling.

"He got admitted with a swollen ankle," I said, "maybe broken, which I guess they don't always do—sometimes they send you home? I heard this from my aunt, who used to work in Admitting. I was living in Wisconsin at the time. Anyway, for some reason they put him in a room."

I paused for a cue I was rambling, but all he said was, "It's possible they had concerns and wanted to keep him overnight." He nodded for me to continue.

"So here his ankle's in bandages, but he manages to get his clothes on, probably sneaks down some stairwell, and splits. My aunt said everybody was flabbergasted—people who didn't know him, that is."

Dr. Robbins looked a tad flabbergasted. "Did he think he would be forced to remain against his will?"

"Don't know *what* he thought. Might not have wanted to make a fuss, get folks upset. Maybe he was afraid the nurses would try to stop him. Like I said, it didn't surprise anybody who knew him. Anyway, a few years later, he fell down the station steps at the

Bristol Street overpass. The way he landed killed him pretty much instantaneously. When my mother and aunt came to identify him, one of the doctors said he'd had Huntington's. They weren't sure if that's why he fell, but it might've been."

Dr. Robbins nodded thoughtfully. "Do you have any children?"

"No."

"Brothers or sisters?"

"Half brother. Not related to Dean."

He folded his arms. "When did you say he died?"

"October of '80."

"Any blood relations on his side still living? Grandparents, aunts, uncles, cousins?"

"No."

"You're the only one?"

"Yep."

"Were any of them diagnosed with Huntington's?"

"Not that I know of. My grandmother, Dean's mother, might've had it." I told him what I remembered hearing of her symptoms and being put in the institution. "I'm pretty sure it got affiliated with St. Joe's at some point."

"Yes, we send residents there for training. Have you been having any unusual movements? In your arms and legs, for example, or your hands?" He didn't stop making eye contact to see for himself.

"Not that I've noticed."

"You haven't found yourself dropping, spilling things? Accidentally grazing a wall or piece of furniture? General clumsiness?"

"No more than I've had all my life."

He squinted to see if I was joking. "No one at the Annex or elsewhere has mentioned anything?"

"No."

"We *will* want to schedule a neurological exam. Tell me, did Dr. Monroe—the fellow who alleged you hit him—did he discuss the course of the disease? And your chances of getting it?"

"No, but I've read some stuff about the symptoms. And I know my chances are fifty-fifty. And there might be a test someday that could tell me for sure."

"There is a test now. We have identified the mutation and can say with virtual certainty whether you'll develop the disease or not. We don't recommend having the test *or not* having it; that's a decision to be made carefully by each individual after a great deal of deliberation." The sparkle left his eyes. "It's a hard thing to face. If the news is good, that's one thing. In any event, we can provide you with information—not just me, but others on our staff—about the disease and some perspectives and experiences of other patients. We're here to answer questions. If you decide sometime down the line you may be interested in getting tested for the gene, we'll provide a fair amount of counseling to see if that is truly the right course to pursue."

"If I do have it, is there anything to take—any medicine?"

"No. But research is going on all over the world, and we hope that before too long, some lab will report a breakthrough leading to a treatment." He frowned at the blood pressure gauge on the wall. "Do you know the age at which your father *first* showed signs, any unusual arm or leg movements?"

"Not really. I wasn't living in Jersey, didn't actually see him. People told me he was acting drunk or else like he'd had the DTs. *Either* could've been true, theoretically. I'm guessing he was definitely having problems in '76, '77, around the time he came in with the ankle. He would have been forty-seven, forty-eight."

The door opened—it was pancake-face Ginger. "Do you need me for anything?"

"Since you're here, ask Doris for a Huntington's packet for Ms. Gabe."

"Informed consent?"

"Not yet." He absentmindedly pushed the medical book to his right.

"Ken's in the library," she said before closing the door.

"Why don't I get the informed consent?" I asked. Were they planning to pull some sort of Tuskegee?

"I don't want to jump the gun. Whether or not to get tested is a big decision, not something you rush into. There are many issues besides whether you have the mutation. Granted, some aren't relevant in your situation—how family members could be affected, for instance. But your ability to obtain medical insurance in the future *is* relevant. If you tested positive, you could be considered to have what's called a 'pre-existing condition,' which could prevent you from buying insurance. And there are employment issues. If you decide later to explore the pre-test counseling, we will of course have you review and sign the informed consent."

"So I can't start the counseling now?"

"When are you done with the Annex program?"

"About ten days. I'll be staying in Brackton though."

"Do you have someone nearby, a close friend or relative, who could accompany you to the counseling?"

No way could I see talking about this stuff with Lorraine, Anthony, or Anthony Junior. "Not really. Haven't lived around here for over twenty years."

"Hmm. Our protocols generally require patients to bring someone with them. Not just for emotional support but to be sure there are no misunderstandings. We don't always hear emotionally charged information clearly."

Ginger came in and handed me a manila envelope. Again she threw Dr. Robbins a smile before leaving, but he was looking at his loafers.

"We'll meet after your neurological exam and explore this further," he said, looking up. "Do me a favor. When you go out, take a right and use the far set of elevators. That way, you'll avoid the library."

Chapter 58

I WAS RELIEVED the doctor doing the neurological exam wasn't Monroe, though she looked equally young. She shone a light in my eyes, banged my knees with a rubber mallet, made me push my hands against hers, hop on each foot, and practically beg, roll over, and fetch. I didn't have the courage to ask the results. I did ask Doris when I'd get them, and she said at my next appointment with Dr. Robbins.

Most of the materials in the manila envelope repeated things I had read at Mass General. One booklet was quite old, the St. Joseph's Hospital masthead printed in an ornate font you didn't see nowadays.

Because it usually progresses slowly, Huntington's Chorea is frequently mistaken for other illnesses. General practitioners, in particular, often ascribe its symptoms to drunkenness, insanity, or syphilis.

That was what'd happened to Grandma Margaret. Maybe she did drink a lot, but to *cope* with the symptoms—the drinking didn't *cause* them.

At the next group therapy, Andy Garbo became Andy Gabby and told everybody about maybe having Huntington's. When I said there was no cure, one woman asked was I supposed to just give up. Another suggested I take wheat germ to strengthen my immune system. I must've looked skeptical because she added, "You can *always* do things to strengthen your resistance. That's what we've been learning *here*. If anyone had said there was *nothing we could do*, we wouldn't be in recovery."

"Andy, you said you *might* get it. You aren't sure?"

"I have a 50 percent chance. If I want to find out, I can take a genetic test."

They all pressed to know: why didn't I take the test. I explained that after the special counseling, some folks apparently decided not to.

"*I'd* take it," one of them said, "and if I had the disease, I would snort coke again. Why not?"

"And if it tells you you're not going to get the disease, you wouldn't waste the rest of your life worrying about it."

That was pretty much what I'd been thinking too, I said—not having to worry.

"Your neurological exam was fine," Dr. Robbins said right off the bat. "Nothing abnormal."

"Guess that's good news."

I looked around for a place to sit. His office was a cluttered mess and about as different from Dr. Wilder's as night and day. The overhead was fluorescent, the windows had blinds, and the visible floor was linoleum. Most of the floor was *in*visible, covered by stacks of books, papers, medical magazines, videotapes, loose-leaf binders, even computer disks. Ditto the desk and file cabinet. On the shelf above the desk, children's faces in small picture frames presided merrily over the chaos. More children's photos filled the windowsill, along with photos of a woman and one of a minister clutching a Bible. The minister looked like he could be Dr. Robbins' brother.

Motioning for me to sit in the now-cleared chair by the file cabinet, Dr. Robbins began clearing off the desk chair for himself. The top page of the paper mound beside me said *Respondent St. Joseph's Hospital and Medical Center et al's Motion for Summary Judgment Dismissal of Plaintiff's Claims for Malpractice, Negligence—*

"Have you had a chance to review the information packet?" he asked.

"Most of it."

"Did anything puzzle you? Leave you with questions?" He remained standing by the bookcase, despite the cleared chair.

"How come the gene doesn't give you symptoms till middle age?"

"To use a little medical jargon, when a gene codes for a certain trait, that trait is not always 'expressed.' Sometimes genes tell a cell to behave in a certain way, and sometimes the genes sit idle. Science hasn't advanced to the point of understanding the why or how. The Huntington's gene is present since birth—since fertilization—but except in Juvenile Huntington's, doesn't get expressed for decades."

"Like a dormant volcano?"

"In a sense."

"If I stay sober, would it make any difference? Not in having the gene—I don't mean that—but in how soon it would get expressed?"

"There's no evidence of that. Which isn't to say you shouldn't stay sober." He crossed his arms, studying me.

I studied my hangnails. "If I have it, will I get symptoms the same age as Dean got them?"

"Mid- to late-forties? What are you now?"

"I'll turn forty-three in June."

"We know in some families—*not* all—symptoms appear at roughly the same age. But when they *don't* appear at the same age, they can be off by as many as fifteen years. So you shouldn't rely on the course the disease took in him to predict how it would go in you, *if* you should happen to have the mutation."

"How come it would be different, if I inherited it from him?"

"Let's back up. The mutation in the gene has to do with what's called a trinucleotide sequence, a sequence of three genetic building blocks."

"That the CAG?"

"Yes, abbreviated CAG. Think of a beaded necklace where the beads are supposed to alternate red-orange-yellow-green-blue, red-orange-yellow-green-blue but at one particular spot they repeat red-orange-yellow, red-orange-yellow fifty extra times. The Huntington's mutation is like that: excessive repetitions. We use the abbreviation CAG, not—as in my example—"

"ROY. But if I inherited the extra repeats from Dean, why wouldn't I have the same number?"

"We don't know the reason, but sometimes a child has a different number of extra repeats."

"Does the number of repeats say when the symptoms will start?"

"Not for certain. *Some* of the data suggests that the greater the number of extra repeats, the earlier the onset of symptoms, but it is by no means a perfect correlation. These are all excellent questions."

I looked out the window at the blue sky. In the distance, a plane soared, leaving a long contrail. Strange, how almost two decades ago, Dean might have been in a room near here looking at the same patch of sky, seeing planes fly by, maybe contrails too. All the while harboring a secret that brought me to this office today.

"So the gene test," I said, "it counts the repeats?"

"Yes, the number of CAG repeats. Which tells us, in most cases, whether or not the disease is present."

"*Most* cases? You said it was accurate."

"It *is* accurate. All I mean is that below a certain number of repeats, it's clear a person *doesn't* have the mutation, and above a certain number—around forty-two—it's clear he or she *does*. But there's a small range in between—in the vicinity of thirty-five or forty repeats—where we don't know."

"That would be just my luck: for my results to be in limbo."

Dr. Robbins moved to the window and peered into the street. "Having a definitive test isn't necessarily a good thing. If a crystal ball could tell us when and in what manner we would die, how many of us would really want to know? But for those who do, a definitive test is vastly preferable to a percentage estimate, which was all the old test could provide."

"How come, if you can *find* the extra repeats, you can't go in and zap them?" The instant the question left my mouth, I realized how stupid it sounded. "I mean with a drug, not a blowtorch."

"We don't have that ability, not yet. But people are working on ways to interfere with gene expression or interrupt—there are *many* avenues to explore for attacking the disease process. I can't stress that enough."

My eyes fell on a stack of brochures on the radiator cover. *What You Don't Know About Hypertension Can Kill You.* You could say that about a lot of things. What Dean didn't know might have killed *him*. I turned and saw Dr. Robbins watching me. Embarrassed, I asked, "Is hypertension a neurologic disease?"

"No. My wife wants those for the Women's Clinic."

I slowly rose. "Guess those are my only questions for now. If I end up having the gene, I'm sure I'll have a whole lot more."

He waved for me to sit. "Andy, the question of whether you should get tested is *not* something you can decide now or even in a week or two. You need a series of counseling sessions over an extended period, plenty of time to think about it. Among other things, we would need to discuss how you would handle a negative outcome."

"You mean a positive test?" I sat again and rested my elbows on my knees, my hands dangling.

"Yes, if you tested positive for the mutated gene."

"The positive outcome is a negative test, and a negative outcome is a positive test. Why do I feel like I'm in a Marx Brothers movie?"

He too sat, but no sooner had he done so when a knock on the door made him rise. "Oh, hello, Susie. I'm with a patient. Could we meet at 4:30?"

"Yes. We're going to miss you, Dr. Robbins. But have fun in New Haven."

"I'll miss you all too." He gently closed the door.

"You're moving?" I asked.

"In June. I applied for the position, so I can't complain. But I'll have to learn to cram more appointments into my day. And I wish I had more time before I go to mend some fences."

"Can't imagine you pissing people off."

"No?" He sat again. "Do you have any idea how you would react to testing positive for the gene?"

"Wouldn't be too happy. But I'm not happy wondering, either."

"What would be your next step? How would you plan to deal with it?"

"My immediate next step would probably be to pound my fist into something. Could you send Dr. Monroe around?"

"Let's put aside the issue of testing for a moment. What's your next step after leaving the Annex?"

"They've lined up a spot for me at a halfway house near the old fairgrounds. Restaurants are always looking for help, so hopefully I'll find something pretty quick. I have savings and an inheritance a cousin left me to live on in the meantime."

"Perhaps you should plan to get your feet on the ground first. Establish friendships at the halfway house and at work. After six months, a year, if you are still interested in finding out if you have the gene, come back to the clinic."

Six months, a year—he made it sound like no big deal. What if I only had three or four healthy years left? Or not even?

"Seems to me that *I* should get to decide if I want to learn about the mutation with a companion or alone. It's *my* information; it's about *me*."

He looked surprised. "But I have a responsibility—"

"To help me make medical decisions, to inform me so I can give informed consent. How can I consent to getting tested, or *not* getting tested, if I'm not allowed to go through what you said—the protocols?"

If nothing else, he dropped the paternalistic tone. "I'm all for you—for *all* my patients—making informed decisions. But I need to be certain you will consider the information in a rational, non-emotional way."

"Who's non-emotional about Huntington's? And why do *you* get to decide what I can and can't handle?"

"Look, you've only recently given up alcohol or drugs. It's wonderful that you have, but you need more time on your feet. Just like we have the Hippocratic Oath, we physicians have a set of principles, medical ethics, we are obligated to follow—"

"It's *my* body. I can get abortion counseling by myself and an abortion too. With Huntington's, there's not even this separate embryo whose rights you might need to think about."

He looked annoyed. "There are other concerns. I mentioned problems with obtaining medical insurance. Employment issues. As I said, I have a responsibility—"

"To cover your ass?"

"Cover my ass." He laughed. "The hospital lawyers wish I had done more of that." Abruptly, he became serious again. "You yourself will admit you're in a somewhat vulnerable state. Getting terrible news, if that's what—"

"But what if one of the reasons I'm messed up is the uncertainty? I can't get better emotionally unless I take the test, but I can't take the test unless I get better emotionally. Talk about a Catch—"

"I'm not trying to create an obstacle course for you, Andy; I'm trying to navigate between what you call *your* rights as a patient—which I don't dispute—and *my* obligations as a physician. And I don't mean 'my obligations' as defined by any damn lawyers. I mean my obligation to do you no harm. You have to admit that for the people who are going to hear bad news—hopefully you won't be one of them—for the people who are going to hear bad news, there can't be a worse situation than to be alone, without family or friends."

I looked away, at the photo of the minister dude.

Dr. Robbins picked up the phone. "Would you like a soda?" He punched a button and asked somebody to bring in snacks.

We sat in silence. Why was I pushing so hard for the test, since I wasn't absolutely sure I wanted it? It was the principle of the thing. I didn't like the idea that somebody could keep me from knowing facts about my own body. Our bodies, our selves.

Doris brought in a tray with sodas and doughnuts, and Dr. Robbins let me pick first, so I chose the one with the most sprinkle repeats. We polished off two each, and he crammed the paper plates into the already full wastebasket, saying he wasn't used to patients arguing their own case so well.

"Look, could I get tested and not find out the results?" I asked.

"You mean, what if you get tested and change your mind? Certainly. No one is going to force you—"

"Because what I'm thinking is: what if I get tested but don't find out? Then once I get a job and medical insurance, if they ask if I have any—what did you call them?—pre-existing diseases, I can say no, not to my knowledge. Some time later, if I ever wanted to and felt ready, I could start the counseling protocols, bring a new friend along, and eventually get the results."

"But why not just wait to have the test?"

"The woman who gave me orientation at the Annex said I have all my medical stuff paid for, and some restaurants don't give you insurance, or not right away, and sometimes it doesn't cover much. I don't know what the test costs—"

"Let me double-check the funding. The foundation is paying for our appointments; I know that. It's something to consider. But you would still have to go through counseling before learning the results."

I nodded.

"One last point," Dr. Robbins said, "and this bears repeating. If it turns out you do have the mutation, that doesn't mean you'll develop the full set of symptoms. Research is going on for a cure. You can never discount a sudden breakthrough. One minute, a disease is terminal; the next, it can be nothing. Yes, that sudden. Look at penicillin. What used to be fatal infections are now cured in a matter of days. And the many new antibiotics after penicillin. Juvenile diabetes is a manageable, if difficult, chronic disease. But throughout history, going back to the ancient Greeks, it was known to be terminal. Children simply wasted away. Then insulin is discovered and—a colleague down the hall just turned sixty-six."

The session left me feeling better. I didn't discount the possibility it was the doughnuts. As for Dr. Robbins' spiel about a sudden breakthrough and cure, it seemed half BS, half possible. Every damn thing was a sure maybe.

Chapter 59

ONE STEP AT a time, I got my ducks in a row. I opened a bank account and deposited both the check Mr. Greenstreet had mailed me and the money I'd had on me when I was brought to the ER. Whether or not the whole ATM and PIN secret-number business made sense, I liked having a decent shim card again. Plus, it was cool that the bank was a national, so if I was in Philly and on the spur-of-the-moment decided to see a game, I could get extra cash.

I also called the court and got the name of the lawyer handling Mathilde's estate. He said it would be a while before probate was concluded, so I promised to update him each time I moved.

Finally, I did something that had been brewing quietly in my brain lobes. I drafted two letters, essentially duplicates. One was to the FBI; one, to the Boston Police Department. Each contained the handful of facts I knew about Droghan that might relate to Jackie's murder.

But I chickened out on signing and mailing them. Maybe Dr. Wilder could ease me over my anxiety when I went to see her—she was leaving for a weeklong conference and asked me to stop in beforehand to say goodbye.

Arriving for my next appointment with Dr. Robbins, I hesitated in the hallway because he was on the phone, but he motioned for me to come in and sit. "Neither of us *has* to be there," he was saying. "There won't be witnesses taking the stand, only lawyers arguing. ... That's right; he has our depositions. ... Yes, a colossal waste, the drive alone. But they want the judge to have faces to go with the CVs. ... I *read* you the excerpt. They imply any physician working at St. Joe's couldn't possibly get hired somewhere prestigious. We are *by definition* incompetent. ... Yes, I'll be home. I promised them sloppy joes. Better not say it too loud; their lawyers will use it against me."

Hanging up, Dr. Robbins told me he had checked on the foundation insurance plan, and it covered the gene test. "If you still want to do it, we will send the sample to an outside lab, and they will mail us the results. Bear in mind that Doris, me—*everyone*—will keep the envelope sealed. No one will have the slightest idea what the report says, so you won't be able to read anything into my behavior—or anyone else's—if you start the counseling."

"Fair enough."

He set a notebook on his desk. "Usually I have no patience with bureaucratic protocols, but these serve a very legitimate purpose. You leave when?"

"Wednesday morning."

"That soon? Let me see if Ginger's free now. It's just a simple blood draw. I'll get you an informed consent."

When he left, I picked up the copy of the *Gazette* on the windowsill, but before I had a chance to check the Phillies' schedule Ginger scurried in. "Ready for a little poke?" she chirped. The tourniquet was a blue band that looked nothing like the cord Jackie had used.

Doris came in as Ginger went out and handed me a piece of paper with maroon letterhead. I informed St. Joseph's Hospital and Medical Center that I consented to their drawing my blood and submitting a sample for genetic analysis for the Huntington's gene. When she left, Dr. Robbins strode in, his hands in his pockets.

"Andy, you know the speech I am about to give."

My spine locked. They knew. They had some instant test, one of those dipstick things you dunk in a beaker, and the color had changed and given the answer. Judging from his face, it wasn't something I wanted to hear.

He tried pacing in the three feet of clear floor space. "Promise me," he said. "Promise me that you will seek counseling if circumstances leave you in despair. And when I say 'circumstances,' I don't mean only if you decide to find out the test results and they're bad— I mean *any* problem. Promise me you will not act rashly."

I nodded, my eyes jumping to the stack of hypertension pamphlets. Sure hoped his wife didn't need them in a hurry.

"What I am most concerned about," he went on, "is—well, first, obviously, that you will turn out to have the mutation. Mind you, I have *no reason* to believe you do; your neurological exam showed no abnormalities. But if you *do* have the mutation, my fear is you will do something terrible. As I said, a cure may be just around the corner."

"Like penicillin and insulin."

"Yes. Drugs can halt a disease in its tracks and often reverse the damage already done. You understand me?" His brown eyes demanded a reply.

"Yes," I said. "You don't give up hope."

"Exactly. You don't give up hope."

"Doubt I'll actually want to know any time soon. Rather have a year or two of stability under my belt." I had begun to believe it.

"Excellent idea. By then you will have people to celebrate with when the news is good."

"If the news is good, the whole damn town will be celebrating. I'll be singing from the rooftops."

"I like that. Singing from the rooftops."

"Only because you've never heard me sing."

"Another point, and I can't stress this enough either: don't assume that any unusual movements you may develop are from Huntington's. Other diseases and conditions can mimic Huntington's, diseases that are treatable, that are *already* treatable. Have the symptoms checked out. You leave Wednesday morning? I'll be up in Trenton Monday. Can you drop by Tuesday for a quick good-bye? How about right at noon?"

Dr. Wilder read over the letters to the FBI and Boston PD.

"The thing is," I said, "he's got relatives in the police department and probably drug gangs, and I'm afraid they'll come after me."

She pursed her lips a moment. "What if you leave them unsigned, and I mail them when I go to Pittsburgh? The detectives will be able to question him, and perhaps his DNA is on the Red Sox cap. You are not really a witness to anything—you are just furnishing a tip to focus their investigation."

"That would be cool—if you wouldn't mind doing that." I then thanked her for helping me with the whole Roy-Mathilde business. She said I'd done all the hard work, a blatant lie.

At my last group therapy, I was given the standard graduation gift: a booklet containing the Twelve Steps, some sappy aphorisms, and empty pages for me to drip in sap of my own. I wore my Phillies cap, which started everybody talking baseball. The wheat-germ woman bragged how her grandfather had worked at Yankee Stadium and met all the greats: Babe Ruth, Lou Gehrig, Joe DiMaggio. Still, it was hard not to get excited about the season starting.

Spring was definitely in the air, and the scent of cherry blossoms accompanied me across the parking lot to the hospital on my way to say goodbye to Dr. Robbins. Even South Jersey had natural beauty, in its flowers and gardens and meadows, its deciduous and evergreen trees, and the famous Pine Barrens. The Brackton High field had a weeping willow behind the backstop. And of course there was the shore an hour away and the bay, even less.

Babe Ruth, Di Maggio, Lou Gehrig: no question they were among the greatest. Lou Gehrig's disease was pretty gruesome, the little I knew. What was its official name? Had to be called something else, at least when he was diagnosed—the doctors didn't say "What a coincidence, Mr. Gehrig, you have Lou Gehrig's disease."

The creative writing teacher had taught us some word for temporal screw-ups, for a work of fiction containing a fact that didn't exist at the time of the story, like if Macbeth had used a telephone. What was it? *Anachronism.* I could hear Miss Z's voice like it was yesterday. *From chronos, the Greek word for time.*

Wait a minute! How could they have diagnosed Dean in 1976 or '77 if the first test didn't come out till the *'80s*? It made no sense; it was an anachronism. Dr. Robbins and I had overlooked that obvious fact. Dean *couldn't* have been definitively diagnosed because the definitive test didn't exist. All they could've figured out back then was a vague *percentage estimate.* No, not even that: the *first* gene test, the percentage-estimate test, didn't get invented till around '83. So Dr. Wu had only meant that they *suspected* Huntington's, that it was part of the differential diagnosis. Dr. Wu couldn't have known for sure because in 1980 there was no *way* to know for sure!

God, You better exist, if for no other reason than to have a good laugh at how stupid we mortals are. What a fantastic joke. I couldn't wait to see Dr. Robbins. No, you couldn't have a definitive diagnosis without a definitive diagnostic test.

Doris told me Dr. Robbins had said to go on down. I feigned shock entering his office. "Jeez, what happened? It almost looks clean." "A lawsuit against us—a *frivolous* lawsuit—was thrown out." He gestured at the sodas on the sill.

I grabbed a can and opened it. The cold carbonation felt good; I licked it off my lip.

"So," he said smiling, "excited about your departure tomorrow?"

"Yes, but I have a question for you. You said the first test came out in the mid-'80s?"

He also grabbed a soda, the can making a tinny popping sound when he opened it. "That's right. In '83. They narrowed the location on chromosome—"

"And that was just the *first* test, not even the *definitive* one, right?"

He sat in the desk chair, leaned back, and crossed his leg so the ankle rested on the knee. "There was *no* genetic test before '83, not even a less accurate one. Doctors had to rely on—"

"Dean died in '80. So how could they have diagnosed him *definitively?*"

Dr. Robbins didn't look surprised, only puzzled. Was he embarrassed at having missed the obvious? My trap couldn't shut; the words spilled out. "He was seen here in '76 or '77. Dr. Wu, the doctor who talked to Mathilde when she came to identify him, he had to have said Dean *might* have had Huntington's—it was part of the differential diagnosis—but he couldn't have said Dean *definitely* had it, since he couldn't have known for sure. There was no test!"

Dr. Robbins shook his head. "The clinical signs were well-known long before the '80s. They had been described in the literature back in the eighteen *hundreds*."

"But they couldn't *confirm* it. The literature also said—the stuff you gave me—that lots of times doctors mistook Huntington's for other diseases and vice versa. You *yourself* said that other diseases mimic Huntington's, have the same symptoms. So, sure, they would have put it in the differential diagnosis, but—"

"When Dean injured his ankle, he was still walking around? Yes, he walked out of the hospital. There are certain aspects of the gait in Huntington's—"

"He couldn't have been walking normal with a hurt ankle!"

Dr. Robbins took another sip of soda. "He may have been presenting arm and hand, facial movements. And with a family history, your grandmother—"

"But she hadn't been diagnosed. They all thought it was from drinking."

"You said he was seen here in Neurology?"

"I'm not sure where. His chart was sent all over the place. I seem to remember a weird name—Nickle-something?"

"Micklemeister?"

"That's it, Micklemeister." My soft-shoe in Laurie's room, Micklemeister and Wu.

"Micklemeister was a well-known neurologist," Dr. Robbins said. "Suspected Huntington's patients from all over were sent to him for evaluation."

"Wu was in Obstetrics."

Dr. Robbins looked like I was pulling his leg.

"I'm serious," I said. "I remember my aunt saying nobody could figure it out, why Dean's chart got sent there. We joked about him being pregnant. And Wu was the one who had mentioned the Huntington's when they came to identify him."

Dr. Robbins rose and turned to the desk, putting his soda can down and moving the stapler from one spot to another like a chess piece. "No, it makes sense. At that time, genetics counseling could have been done in Obstetrics. Not anymore—the neurological diseases are handled separately." He faced me again. "But you have answered your own question. Dean was referred to Dr. Wu for genetics counseling."

"So?"

"Dr. Micklemeister referred him because he had made a clinical diagnosis of Huntington's."

"But without the definitive test, it was just an educated guess."

"No—to him, Dean's movements would have been unambiguous. And learning that his mother had shown the same abnormal movements, and their progression, would have erased all doubt. Dr. Micklemeister wouldn't have referred Dean to genetics counseling unless he was confident of the diagnosis."

Seemed like a good idea at the time. "Well, if nothing else," I said, "at least he never knew, Dean never knew he had it."

Dr. Robbins looked surprised. "Huntington's? Of course he did. They would have told him."

"No, don't you remember: he escaped *before* the appointment with Dr. Wu."

"Dr. Micklemeister would have told him." Robbins sounded amazingly sure of himself, given he hadn't been there.

"What would've been the point of meeting with Dr. Wu?" I said. "That's *why* they wanted Dean to meet with him. To *get* the counseling."

"The *reason* Dean was referred to genetics counseling was the Huntington's diagnosis. He was a father and could still father more children."

"Actually, he couldn't; he'd had a vasectomy."

Dr. Robbins looked puzzled, so I added, "Wasn't done here. He might not have mentioned it to anybody."

"Consequently, they referred him to Dr. Wu."

"But Dean didn't know why."

"They would have told him."

Dr. Robbins sounded so smug, I had to stifle a laugh. "You weren't there," I said. "Look, I'll admit Dr. Micklemeister knew he had Huntington's, but he wanted Dr. *Wu* to do the counseling. I'm not blaming him; it was Dean's own fault he didn't stick around to find out the diagnosis."

It was incredible how many times Dr. Robbins was shaking his head—talk about extra repeats. He said, "Dr. Micklemeister, *any* of the neurologists would have explained why they were making the referral. The purpose, as I indicated, was for Dr. Wu to talk about family planning issues."

"All these *protocols*, these hoops you make us jump through to find out *anything*, and now you're saying that without making Dean jump through a *single* hoop, Micklemeister would've told him he had Huntington's? Give me a break."

"Post-symptomatic cases are treated—"

"And who's to say he had a *companion* for the counseling? You're making *me* wait. Why wouldn't they have made *him* wait?"

"I'm trying to explain—"

"Sure, they had figured it out amongst themselves, they're all thinking: he's got Huntington's, so we'll send him to Dr. Wu. But the idea was for Dr. *Wu* to handle the long, drawn-out shit—your *weeks* or *months*."

"They wouldn't have handled it that way because—"

"—the doctors at St. Joe's are all so damn competent?"

Dr. Robbins' mouth dropped open. Nothing came out.

"Hey, I'm not saying they *weren't* competent. I'm not going to sue you guys. I've already *said* it was Dean's fault he didn't stick around to get the diagnosis. And I never said all the protocols are stupid. I understand why you have them. The only reason I'm arguing—"

"*Dean was diagnosed based on clinical signs!*" Dr. Robbins quickly lowered his voice. "Based on findings from a physical exam, a neurological exam, like you had. But *un*like you, Dean was symptomatic. In fact, he manifested enough signs of Huntington's to suggest to whoever saw him for the *ankle* that he should be given a neurological work-up."

"That's not what I'm saying! I'm not saying they didn't diagnose him. All I'm saying is: they figured it out and planned to tell him the next day, during the appointment with Dr. Wu, and in the meantime he escapes. Why is that so impossible?" Robbins was *trying* to miss the point. Men just couldn't stand women being right. Especially when you were this super-duper specialist and she was just a patient. Well fuck all that sexist, chauvinist bullshit, even coming from him.

He shoved some papers around on his desk without speaking. Shoot—I didn't want to leave on bad terms. My voice came out quieter. "All I'm saying is: he left before finding out. Maybe they started to explain—told him the name and some of the symptoms—but that's as far as it went."

Taking a deep breath, Dr. Robbins also spoke softly. "Whoever examined him, Andy, either Dr. Micklemeister or another neurologist, would have questioned him about his own parents, as I said. And in explaining how he got the disease, they would be explaining how he could pass it on. That's standard practice. Even back then—"

"You're wrong. They never mentioned the hereditary part, the 50 percent."

"How do you know?"

"Because he would've *told* me!"

Dr. Robbins darted a glance at the pictures on the shelf. "But who knows what was going through his—"

I shouted, "You would've told *your* kids, once they were grown up. You wouldn't have made them find out from somebody else." I strode to the door and swung it open.

"Do you have an appointment with Dr. Wilder this afternoon?"

"Right after lunch. She'll get an earful."

"Andy, remember your promise."

I phoned the halfway to say I had decided to move out of state. Right before leaving the Annex, I dropped the Phillies cap in the lost-and-found box.

Where on the West Coast I was headed I didn't know; all I knew for certain was that I would put thousands of miles between me and the Veterans Cemetery. I didn't forgive Dean for not telling me about Huntington's, and I wouldn't. But I was quitting him for another reason too.

In the time between Lorraine's phone call to Chicago to say he'd died and the funeral, one particular fear had dogged me. I feared learning that Dean's last months on earth had been spent alone and unloved. Anger at Carmella had resurfaced—I blamed her for abandoning him, regardless of the reasons. Even during the hopeful moments in the marble-floored atrium when I'd pictured many mourners joined in tribute, this fear haunted me, this image of Dean alone and unloved.

But the walk down the aisle to the front pew showed me he hadn't been alone. He'd had friends, plenty, some even from childhood. Friends who had cared enough to make time for him at his death. That could only mean one thing: that he'd made time for them. When had he made time for me? Not once since I was ten— not once. Dean had said, in essence: the hell with Andy. So Andy was saying the hell with Dean.

Book Three

Chapter 60

CHICAGO LOOKED PRETTY much the same, plus or minus some buildings. I hit a bookstore and bought a travel guide for the West Coast that had decent maps. And being on my own pseudo-odyssey, I picked up a prose version of Homer's *Odyssey*. Certain episodes had stuck with me since high school, like Circe turning the men into swine. A lot started out that way, in my opinion. Had the lab test been run yet?

Back at the bus station, I studied the routes west, nixing the ones passing through Madison. Switching my mantra to "one leg at a time," I bought a ticket to St. Louis, figuring the arch would be a cool symbolic gateway to my new life.

It was evening when we arrived, and I took advantage of a motel's two-night deal to give the body a full day of non-rolling. Both nights I fell asleep debating whether to start the counseling sooner rather than later once I settled in somewhere. I would send for the results *eventually* no matter what, because if I got symptoms, I'd want to know if they were from Huntington's, and if I didn't get any, the confirmation I was home free would be too sweet to pass up.

My next leg was to Kansas City, and during the trip across the Show-Me State, I narrowed my destination possibilities to Oregon and Washington because I wanted seasonal change. I also narrowed the list of possible towns to a dozen or so along the coast that were large enough for anonymity and yet not too large. Grandma Margaret had had only one kid, and he'd had the bad luck to inherit the bad gene, so if *he* had only one kid, didn't the odds favor *that* kid *not* inheriting it? Fifty-fifty, right: one got it for every one who didn't? Dean had rolled tails; I rolled heads.

In Kansas City, after booking a room in a small hotel, I went out for a stroll, my brain lobes craving a break from the twin debates over where to live and when to start Huntington's counseling. The air was pleasantly warm; April was holding back the showers. Yellow, purple, and white flowers cropped up in rows along the sidewalk—crocuses, maybe. A park across the street was filled with bright red tulips—hard to believe a flower could be any redder. Or the grass any greener, for that matter. Walking felt good—so did the afternoon sunshine on my arms and face.

The concierge had recommended a spot along the river for nice scenery, so I headed that direction. This stretch was shops and restaurants. The aromas by the blue neon *Jane's Barbecue Ribs* practically killed me. Maybe later—

"Andy!"

I turned just as he yelled again, practically in my ear, he had bounded up so close. I took in the brown leather cowboy boots with pointed, jab-you toes, the denim shirt with the fake-pearl snaps barely containing the beer belly, the yellow-green eyes.

"Hey, Roy."

He grinned like a pig in mud. "Thought you were in Boston—didn't expect to see you here." The grin vanished. "You know Ma died?"

"Lorraine told me."

He positioned his boots apart, resting his weight evenly, arms folded. "Did a double-take across the street."

"Heard you were in Oklahoma. Got married—"

"Donna's terrific. Have to meet her. Just visited her folks up in Waterloo, in Nebraska." He gestured with his thumb at an ugly turquoise awning. "That's where we're staying. Get a special rate, part of this hotel-motel association. Not a franchise, just an industry thing. I call it 'the brotherhood,' like the Mafia." He laughed. "You know, I don't drink anymore."

"Me neither."

"Went to AA. Still go once in a while. Donna says I should go more, be an example. If *I* can quit drinking, anybody can." Again he laughed. "Clean twenty-two months."

"Great."

"So what you doing here?"

"Just passing through, actually. Moving but not sure where yet."

"You know you got money coming? From the house and car, other stuff. In an account back home, over thirty thou. I'll give you the lawyer's name—"

"Lorraine did. I've been in touch with his office."

Roy looked at his watch, a shiny monstrosity. "Donna's expecting me. But join us for dinner, on me. We found an all-you-can-eat buffet. King Henry's. No alcohol in the main dining room. At 7:30 the dinner crowd starts clearing out. That way, past the hotel, not too far. Big flag, medieval kind of thing." After one more big smile, he bounded towards the turquoise awning.

By the time I had set foot in my hotel room, the first layer of shock had worn off. Roy looked pretty much an older version of his old self. I was surprised he was on the wagon; no doubt he was surprised *I* was. Of course I wouldn't join them for dinner. Even if staying sober had morphed him into somebody decent, there remained enough bad blood between us to transfuse

a woolly mammoth. Of all the sidewalks in all the towns in all
the world.

And yet I couldn't deny that there was *something* reassuring about
running into a familiar face. The feeling of being a stranger in a
strange land and on strange roads eased a little. And he was somebody I had known for more than a handful of weeks or months,
somebody I had known for years. Despite all the shit, we shared
some decent history. When I was in high school and he used to come
back on leave or visited from Vineland, maybe all we'd do was watch
TV or sit across the table at poker, but we'd had some laughs. He
immediately told me about the money—if I never claimed it, then
presumably it would all go to him. And Lorraine had said Donna
was nice. It was all-you-can-eat, and I'd practically skipped lunch.

I picked up Homer but stuck with it only till Odysseus made it
past the Sirens. What would I do if I had the mutation? Wouldn't my
resolve to stay off liquor and weed crumble? But say I had the mutation and *didn't* send for the results? I could still have some time left,
healthy time. Dean's symptoms might not have begun till he was
forty-six, forty-seven, and Dr. Robbins had said the disease might
take a different course in me—maybe I would have *eight or ten* good
years. What if I had the bad gene but didn't send for the results, and
instead of getting symptoms, say, at forty-eight—if that was what
lay in store—what if the Fates sent a car to run me over at forty-
seven? Wouldn't I have been better off *not* knowing?

The little fridge in the corner began to hum. Keep on humming, little buddy; I ain't opening your door.

It wasn't a flag but a green and yellow banner stretching across the
entrance: *Welcome to King Henry's Buffet.* The dining area was huge and
done up like everybody's idea of a medieval banquet hall, with scores
of wooden tables and some long boards seating ten or twelve apiece.

The ceiling was a good sixty feet up, and poles jutting out horizontally from the walls suspended brightly colored flags with zigzag hems. The guys busing wore shiny gray shirts and pants with markings some idiot must have thought gave the effect of chain mail. The waitresses had it worse, sewn into some peasant-maid costume. And the place was packed. Kids ran loose, knocking into every body and thing.

Roy waved from beside a booth. Just one meal, Lord, just one meal.

"Andy, this is Donna." He gestured at the plumpish woman with dark hair sitting against the wall wearing no facial expression whatsoever. I smiled and said hi and sat opposite. She mustered a hi, which I decided to take as shyness rather than sheer hatred.

"Which King Henry is it?" I asked Roy. "I like my head attached at the neck."

"The food's supposed to be good. And it's all-you-can-eat. On me, I told you. But I don't have to tip because you're your own waitress."

A waitress did come by. "Three?" She wrote out the check and placed it face down beside Roy. He took a peek, pushed it aside, and pointed to the spread. "Let's go."

I heaped my plate full and made it back to the booth without any food landing on the rioting no-necks.

"Is that all?" Roy asked, his plate piled higher than a haystack.

"Saving room for pie," I said.

If Roy had a talent, it was eating and talking at the same time without too much food shooting from his mouth. He told me about his job as assistant manager of a seventy-room motel, how he was making good money, bought a '94 Buick Riviera that had only two thousand miles. The job was rough at first because he worked graveyard, but the new guy had that now. "Looks like Norman Bates." Roy turned to Donna. "Ever see *Psycho*?"

She shook her head. I told her, "You live with Psycho; who needs to see the movie?"

"Tell me about it," she said.

"Andy's seen 'em all." Roy bit into a drumstick. "Didn't you see 'em with Edward? What's his name, the bald guy?"

"Alfred Hitchcock. Saw a lot. Not all."

He put down the drumstick and smeared his hand across his leg. Maybe he'd placed a napkin there. "See the one—what was it called? This town gets taken over by birds, and they attack everybody, poking their eyeballs out. Dennis and I got stoned, and on the way home, every damn pigeon made us jump fifty feet. Remember Dennis?"

Whatever had possessed me to do this? "Yeah."

"It's called *The Birds*," Donna said.

I said, "Roy mentioned you were visiting your parents."

"Yes. They live in Waterloo."

Roy scooped corn into his mouth, at least using a fork. "Our hotel's pretty fancy. There's a Jacuzzi—"

"Hot tub," Donna corrected him.

"Thought you said it was a Jacuzzi?" He turned back to me. "You said you're dry too. How long's it been?"

"Since August."

"Go to AA?"

"Yeah."

He speared a meatball. "Don't know where you're moving?"

"Think I'll try some new part of the country. Seems to be working for you."

"Yep, working for me. But she's the reason." He nudged Donna with his elbow. I was about to ask if they had kids—could I be *Aunt Andy?*—when he grew serious. "Somebody else too."

Jeez, was he going to drop a mistress bomb?

"Jesus," Roy said. "You find Him? Must've, if you've gone to AA."

I ran my index finger through a droplet on the outside of the water glass. "Not exactly. I guess we all think about the higher power differently."

"Who's yours?" Donna asked, point-blank.

Heck, if she was going to be blunt, I'd be blunt too. "Don't really believe in God. It's more a sense of letting things be." There will be an answer, let it be, let it be. Did I owe John Lennon amends?

"You don't accept Jesus?" she asked.

"I accept who he was as a person. He probably was a pretty decent guy and all, but—"

Roy leaned forward, his elbows on the table. "I know exactly where you're—"

I stood. "If this conversation is going to get heavy duty, mind if I grab some pie? Then I can be all ears."

"Go ahead." He leaned back against the booth cushion and nodded sagely to Donna.

I had no intention of enduring a sermon without my—or his—money's worth of dessert. I took slices of blueberry and apple and dumped vanilla ice cream on both.

They were whispering when I returned. "Aren't you having dessert?" I said. "I got all this for myself."

Roy rose and let Donna out. "She's getting coffee. Want a cup?"

"No, thanks; I'll stick to water." When she was out of earshot, I said, "Didn't mean to piss her off, but I'm past pretending—"

"Forget it. When we started dating, I wasn't born-again either."

Some folks weren't sure he'd been born the first time—more like excreted.

"You know, it doesn't matter that you don't call him Jesus," Roy said, "not at first, as long as you're open to Him entering your soul.

You see, He's a *forgiver.* He was given to us to forgive our sins, and He *does*, if we let Him. Just be open to Him, let Him come into you."

This dinner wasn't going to end well. "Like I—"

Roy raised his palm. "I'm just going to tell you about *me.* Judge for yourself."

Donna arrived with two cups of coffee balanced in saucers. Roy slid over to make room. "Andy, I fought like crazy—Donna will back me up on this—fought like crazy to keep Jesus away. Why? I had too many sins. I told her, 'I've got *hundreds.*' Know what she said? 'Jesus has a hundred hearts. He can forgive every sin.'" He turned to her. "Isn't that right?"

She sipped her coffee. I ate apple pie.

"That's what's so great about Jesus," Roy went on. "Why people all over the world, all different countries, love Him. His forgiveness has no limits."

Should I take issue with "all over the world"? Draw a replica of Tommy's map and show him where other religions ruled the roost? Explain how 99 percent of every generation just followed the religion they were taught, by people who followed the religion *they* were taught, who followed the religion *they* were taught. Or had shoved down their throats, depending on how you looked at it.

But Roy was on a roll, and not the two he'd already eaten. "He *wants* to forgive us. He *knows* we've sinned. Our sins were destined since Adam and Eve. The point is to wash them off. That's what Jesus offers. He's offering it to *you, now*, sitting there. He's waiting for you; He won't quit. Just wants you to bring Him your sins and be free of them."

"Your sorrows too," Donna said.

"That's right!" Roy practically shouted.

What was the point of arguing? If Jesus helped them through the day, more power to him. I had my little mantra; the Hindus had theirs; the Muslims, theirs. But I was hoping Roy would stop the sermon soon because I'd eaten enough pie and ice cream to pack my belly solid, and a walk would help the peri-what's-his-face.

We sat a few moments in silence, them sipping their coffees, me chipping away at crust with my fork. I mustered an "I'll think it over. Appreciate your sharing it all with me. And thanks for the dinner."

"You want to see our room?" Roy leaned to one side to get his wallet from his back pocket. "Rooms, I mean. It's a suite."

"Not tonight. I'm pretty behind on sleep."

"We'll be here until the day after tomorrow," Donna said. "You're welcome to come to our afternoon prayer service."

Would it be in the hot tub? "I'll have to figure out my plans," I said. "Sure you don't want me to throw some money in?"

Roy dropped a bunch of tens on the table. "No, I got it. Let me borrow your pen." Donna opened her purse and took out a pen. He scribbled on a clean napkin and handed it to me. "Remember the blue awning? Room 414."

I tucked some bucks under the rim of my plate, and we headed towards the main entrance, me in the lead. I decided not to mention leaving Kansas City in the morning—let them think we would meet up again. Maybe they'd actually be relieved at avoiding a long, drawn-out good-bye. In any case, the problems of three little people didn't amount to a hill of beans.

The doorway was mayhem and bedlam. Waitresses and busboys rushed around, sidestepping customers coming and going, everybody trying not to trip over the wild no-necks. The hostess pointed to a spill on the carpet, so I sashayed to the side, behind a tiny old man hunched over a cane. I didn't judge his speed right—his *lack* of speed—or else he had stopped abruptly. Being brought up short, I had to teeter on my toes so as not to topple him. Regaining my balance, I turned to warn Roy and Donna, but they had already halted. Their eyes bulged like balloons. Was my face etched with swastikas? Were the rafters lined with crows? No, only cheap, phony tournament flags.

"Just trying not to run that guy over," I said.

As we exited, Donna mumbled something.

"What did she say?" I asked Roy.

"Come to Jesus."

Harsh pavement, not yellow brick road, led towards my hotel. Once I was free of them, my blood began to boil. It wasn't the religious bullshit itself but Roy so sure he had been saved. If that was how God, Jesus, and the Holy Ghost were running the show, the whole team could fry in hell. Crunching the napkin in my clenched fist, I bee-lined for the trash bin on the corner.

Slow down, one of my lobes called out. Why should *you* be the angry one? I stopped and watched the light turn yellow and then red. Good question: why should *I* be the angry one? Why not him, why not Roy? Wasn't it high time *he* was on the receiving end and *I*, on the dishing out? Should I storm up to his hotel room—his *suite*? I wouldn't deck him—no, that would let him off too easy. I would ask what made him so *sure* God thought a couple of nights of whining about forgiveness were enough to undo a year and a half of raping a child. Let Donna hear the whole thing. I would make him suffer through knowing that *she* knew, would *always* know. She had a right to, it seemed to me.

Isn't that hitting below the belt? Hey, Jiminy, he fucked a little girl below the belt. Dr. Wilder said I shouldn't pull my punches. Roy's peace of mind and my warring mind—was that justice? Was I supposed to turn the other cheek? I'd already had them turned too often.

Maybe Donna already knew. A B-movie rolled in my brain. The two of them in the dark, on a bed, kissing. Her murmuring how wonderful he is jostles something loose, and he pulls away. "No, I'm *not* wonderful." She listens patiently, lovingly, as he makes his confession, and whatever horror she feels passes like a hiccup. *You were just a boy. Didn't you join the army for your country and become a man? And Jesus forgives all, and that means you too, already, because Jesus understands your sin.* Moments later they pick up where they left off.

Actually, this wasn't the best time to confront him. Better I should be a cool, calm customer, able to choose my words and tone carefully. Show him I had my life in order, better than he had his, even if he was married and had a good job. *I* didn't need to cower behind some phony God-forgives-me crap; *I* wasn't afraid to let my sins chasten me. Not that Roy would ever understand that in a million years.

Chapter 61

THE LOBBY PHONES were off to one side of the tiny-mosaic-tiles floor. The turquoise drapes were open, letting sunshine pour in the windows. Everybody going to and from the front desk and in and out the glass doors looked middle class or comfortable working class. Roy and Donna wouldn't stick out, not like I did, in jeans and sneakers and with a backpack leaning against my leg.

My bus was slated to leave in an hour, allowing ample time for what I had to do. I punched 4-1-4. Roy answered.

"It's me, Andy. I want to stop up for a bit."

"Now?"

"Yes. I'm in the lobby."

"I was going to take a shower. How about forty, forty-five minutes?"

"No, I'm leaving Kansas City soon."

"Sorry to hear that. Hoped we could meet before the prayer service, talk some more. Or take in some sights. Well, you don't have to come all the way up just to say good-bye. Donna said she liked meeting you, and—"

"No, I want to come up. There's something I'd like to discuss in person." My heart pounded like a tom-tom. Say it, Andy, say it. "You talked about forgiveness for your sins, and I want to discuss them, your sins. The ones against me."

"That's fine, but I've got to get in the shower now because we prom—"

"It won't take long." I hung up and lifted the heavy pack onto my shoulder. I hadn't settled on the exact words yet, but what was the point? My mouth would do its own thing anyway.

The elevator made its *boing* sound at four. My shoes sank into the thick beige carpet. Hey, Donna, with all the stories Roy told you about growing up, did he mention that when I was ten and eleven, he used to drag me into his room and rape me? For over a year, a scared little girl and this big prick forcing its way into her small, very sore vagina. Isn't that how it was, Big Bro? Sure hope Donna doesn't think of that when you're putting it in *her.*

The door with a chrome *414* gave my rap a deep sound. I pictured his yellow teeth when he smiled, imagined him gesturing widely for me to enter, tour their fabulous digs. So I was startled when the door finally opened. Roy's face, which in the restaurant had been ruddy and robust, now looked ashen.

Donna came into view at the far end of the room, wearing a coral-colored blouse and slacks. The tilt of her head seemed to ask *Why are you blocking the doorway, Roy, and not inviting your sister in?* She said something, and he turned her direction. What was *her* story? A mother always picking on her to lose weight? A sister she could never compete with, pretty and popular and doted on: could that explain the vulnerability in Donna's eyes?

Roy faced me again. Quietly, I said, "You raped me." He instantly looked down to where the jamb met the carpet. "You raped me," I repeated. "Again and again and again." A coral blur entered my peripheral vision. Switching to a normal voice, I said past his shoulder, "Catching a bus soon and wanted to say good-bye." I turned back to him and whispered, "Raped me. Remember?"

Roy didn't look up, *couldn't* look up. I lingered for a good year and a half. Then, Will Kane style, I pivoted on my heel, the badge in the dust, and sauntered slowly down the corridor to the elevator. Never had my pack felt so light.

Odysseus had made it past Scylla and Charybdis—what next? Central Kansas, flat as cardboard. We crossed vast expanses of plowed earth, planted earth, grazed earth, farmhouses and silos, cattle, hay piled in stacks and hay rolled in bundles. I would travel cowboy-style, riding by day and resting by night.

In Salina I mastered the ATM. Western Kansas too was vast stretches of pasture and prairie. The air coming through the bus ventilation system smelled of horses and hay and manure.

By the time we reached the Colorado border, I had picked my destination. Plan A should *start* with an A, shouldn't it? And A stood for Andy and anonymity. Of the towns in Washington and Oregon close to the coast, the first alphabetically was Aberdeen. It sat on the eastern edge of a bay called Gray's Harbor which, according to the travel guide, was named for a Captain Robert Gray, the dude who supposedly discovered it. But with places nearby named Queets and Quileute, I suspected Native Americans were there first. Like with Columbus, though, you had to be white for it to count as a discovery. In any case, I would start my new life in Washington State, named for the first president of a new nation, in the town of alphabetically-first Aberdeen.

With one of the two questions haunting me settled, I was able to enjoy the Rockies, the magnificent views of jagged peaks, blue-green forests, streams shining platinum in the light. Now smells of mint invaded the air vents. As we climbed through the pines, I saw squirrels and chipmunks running free and little birds darting along branches and spreading their wings in the bluest blue sky.

The folks boarding in Laramie looked grim. Passengers on both sides of the aisle talked in hushed, urgent voices. Had another bus plunged down a ravine? I finally asked the guy next to me if something bad had happened.

"Didn't you hear? They blew up the federal building in Oklahoma City."

Across the aisle, another guy said, "Arabs."

As details spread from passenger to passenger, I learned that the explosion had killed hundreds. Many of the victims were children in the daycare on the first floor. Others were just ordinary folks going to work or running some errand.

"Why would anyone *do* that?" The woman's question hung like a dangling girder. The views lost their wonder.

I took the Annex booklet from my pack and opened to a blank page. I would resolve the second question: whether after nailing down a job and place to live, I should find a doctor and start the counseling and ask them to send for the test results. Or should I just try to forget about Huntington's and let the chips fall where they may.

The alphabet wasn't any help on this one, but I could still be systematic. For starters, I would assume my CAG repeats weren't in that reply-hazy land between thirty-five and forty-two—though that would be just my luck. If I'd get a clear positive or negative result, then I was looking at four possible scenarios. First, I could find out the lab results soon and turn out to have the good gene. Second, I could find out the results but have the bad gene. Third, I could *not* find out the results and have the good. And lastly, I could not find out and have the bad. I wrote down the four possibilities, leaving spaces on the page between them.

What followed from each scenario? Under the first, the best-case scenario—learning the test results and having the good gene—I would sing from the rooftops. After the singing, I would just keep on keeping on—work hard, live my life.

What about the second scenario, finding out I had the bad gene? No time for delusions: the odds were *huge* I'd start drinking again. Why not? Even if I didn't start drinking immediately—if hope for a cure helped me stave off *total* despair—the hope wouldn't outlast the temptation to drink once some symptoms kicked in. Or imagined symptoms.

What if I *didn't* learn the results and got the good gene? I'd keep on keeping on, work and live. Maybe at fifty I would send for the results as icing on the cake.

What about the fourth scenario, not learning the results but getting the bad gene? Same thing at first: I'd keep on keeping on. That would last till symptoms started. Maybe in a month, maybe a year, maybe five or ten years.

I looked at the page and the four possibilities. Three said 'Keep on keeping on.' The *only* one sending me straight into despair was the second: sending for the results and having the bad gene. One in four. The other three had me living *some* period of time hopeful.

Heck, I'd been to the track often enough to know where the smart money lay. If the payout was time to live a hopeful life, then I should not find out the test results. Sure, the *biggest* payout, the jackpot, was in finding out the results if they were good. But I was guaranteed *some* future, no matter how short, if I stayed in the dark. That meant coping with uncertainty, but I was learning to. And wasn't uncertainty the reality for everybody? Who could predict the next Oklahoma City? Yes, I would live with uncertainty; I was done playing the long odds.

I dozed off, waking when the driver stopped for gas. We had twenty minutes to stretch our legs, he said. I left the booklet on my seat and went for a walk.

The arrow-shaped sign up the road said *Continental Divide*. A memory returned of a day not unlike this: sunny, the air both crisp and mild. The landscape, however, couldn't have been more different from this beautiful vista of mountains and endless blue sky: the streets of Hyde Park. A lazy Sunday afternoon, Stacy and I ambled along with no place we had to be, waiting only for our boot heels to be wandering. In luxuriant freeness, we lived *in* the present and *for* the present. Now, a quarter century later, I was going to try to live in and for the present again.

We traversed Western Wyoming, Utah and Salt Lake City, then snaked along the Snake River in Idaho up into Oregon. I got to talking with a woman boarding at the Dalles who was from Ocean Shores, a town at the far end of Gray's Harbor. She said her husband would be meeting the bus in Portland, and would I like a ride into Aberdeen? I gratefully accepted her offer. We rolled on with the Columbia.

Her husband, it turned out, knew of an inexpensive motel in Aberdeen where he could drop me. So A also stood for Auspicious Arrival.

Twilight had deepened when the first *Aberdeen* sign popped up. I had traveled almost 3,000 miles, across a continent, to the Pacific Ocean. Andy Balboa. We slowed at a curve, and a lone street lamp lit a lone tree, its masterful, tawny branches reaching out in bold relief against the night.

That's when it happened, *my* epiphany. I understood—understood with an immediacy that felt spiritual—the real reason why I shouldn't learn the test results. The reason was that the knowledge of death should never poison the sweet gift of life. Wisdom lay in being thankful for the gift, and I would be. I would be thankful for every sunrise and sunset, for the slashing winds of winter as much as the gentle breezes of summer, for the days my team won and the days we got slaughtered, I would be thankful for it all. The todays I had left would not merely suffice; they would *gladden*.

Chapter 62

MY FIRST DAY of exploring Aberdeen was under a dreary sky—the air had the consistency of fog. I found the bay with little trouble. No false advertising here: the water of Gray's Harbor was a murky gray. The surrounding area was an industrial spread of vats, steel rigs, storage tanks, and loading equipment. Freight ships skulked slowly, and the barges stacked with logs seemed not to move at all. Seagulls speckled the piers and muddy flats. Maybe I should have worked backwards from Z.

I wandered through a lot of residential neighborhoods. Most looked working class but not untidy. Churches were plentiful— every other block, it seemed. Along with your standard Catholic, Presbyterian, and Lutheran denominations, you saw names like Nazarene-this and Pentecostal-that and some Lamb dish. Maybe Aberdeen was its own Bible Belt. One sermon board read *Hate the Sin, Love the Sinner.* Why did I think the sin they meant wasn't gluttony? I returned to the motel and studied the want ads and the *Aberdeen and Vicinity* street map.

For the next week, in rain or shine—but mostly a dank mist— I hoofed or bused it to different areas within the city and to the conjoined-twin town of Hoquiam, which the locals pronounced *ho-kwee-um*, and to the inaptly named Cosmopolis. At every large and small restaurant and fast-food place, I asked if they needed somebody to do prep or wait tables. A few establishments had me fill out applications, but nobody called. Or if they did, when they heard the front desk say the name of the motel, hung up. I didn't venture out to Ocean Shores because I was told all their establishments served liquor. Not knowing what else to do, I sprang for another week at the motel.

The second week of job hunting wasn't going any better than the first. At least I found some restaurants I hadn't hit before. This place, a diner, was pretty empty, which didn't bode well, but 10:30 in the morning could be slow anywhere. The register was unmanned, and the lone waitress was so intent on wiping the counter, she didn't see me come in. I would have put her age at close to mine. She was a few inches taller and had medium-short, sandy brown hair.

Though her face was averted, she must have sensed my approach because she turned and tossed her head back to get the bangs out of her eyes. "You can sit anywhere," she said. The name tag read *Jeanette*.

"Actually, I was just stopping in to see whether you might need somebody to wait tables or do prep."

"Oh." The hand without the dishrag had a diamond engagement ring and gold wedding band. She turned away and hung the rag over the faucet. They let you wear pants. When she turned back, her expression seemed almost angry. "Have you waitressed before?"

"Done pretty much everything, restaurant-wise, except the books. Prep, griddle, grill, waiting tables. Even tended bar and was the supervisor, but I don't want to do that again. Been dry eight months and don't need to surround myself with it." My big trap wouldn't shut, she made me so nervous.

"We don't serve alcohol. Where else have you worked?"

I described a bunch of Chicago jobs and pretended I'd waited tables at St. Aloysius and the Halcyon. While she fiddled with the sugar canister, a small cross on a gold chain slid into view above the V of her blouse, which was buttoned almost to the top.

"You haven't worked anywhere around here?" she asked.

"No."

"Where do you live?"

"Right now I'm staying at a motel about fifteen, twenty blocks yonder. Hope to find an apartment or something soon. I just moved to Washington, just last week."

She stared—or maybe glared. Her eyes were hazel. "Why?"

"Long story. Basically, I just need to start over."

"Were you in trouble?"

"Not with the law, if that's what you mean. Like I said, I'm an alcoholic in recovery. The psychiatrist I was seeing thought it made sense for me to move far away from all the things that hold bad memories." Why was I spewing this crap?

"And what if you don't like it here?"

"Guess I'll move elsewhere. But I'm planning on giving it a year. You can't tell right away if a place is going to agree with you. I'm not looking for a whole lot. A job, an okay apartment, staying dry. Not in the rain sense."

She didn't see the humor. Could I blame her? Here somebody comes in looking for work, takes up her time, and admits to being an alcoholic transient with a shrink. Should I also mention having smoked heroin? Being busted by the cops? Hell, why not go the whole nine yards and say I might have a terminal disease and in a year or two could be throwing dishware at the customers.

She fiddled with her rings. "Tell me the things you liked best about the places you worked."

"Guess where the staff acted like a team. In this business you get a lot of folks who don't really care about doing the job well. Don't suppose I have to tell _you_ that. Anyway, guess the places I liked best were the ones where morale was good." I finally shut up.

She pondered the pepper shaker, her little cross glittering. Give me a debauched woman over a prude any day. The Mae Wests of the world, for all their women-as-sex-objects shtick, had warm hearts; it was the Carrie Nations you had to watch out for. Would she ask if I was a Christian?

"We left it on the table, Jeanette," an old lady said, passing behind me. "You give Philip a big hug for us." The man following nodded gravely.

"Thank you." She sent a warm smile towards their departing backs, a smile that vanished once she looked at me. "What hours could you work?"

"Pretty much any."

She turned towards the doors, but nobody was coming or going. After a zillion years, her eyes still on the doors, she said, "Ross may kill me for not checking references, but you seem honest. You said things most people wouldn't when they apply for a job. I like that. I like honesty more than almost _anything_. If you want to start now, we could use some help during lunch. You'd be on probation three months."

"Sure."

She came out from behind the counter and tossed me an apron and headed towards the kitchen. "I'll introduce you to Willie, the daytime cook. His assistant comes in to help from eleven to two. And you'll have to fill out some forms." She halted. "What did you say your name was?"

"Andy."

She called through the horizontal opening at the end of the wall, "Willie, we got a new hire. Her name's Andy. She's starting now."

A young black guy on the other side of the ledge waved a spatula. "The special's meatloaf with mashed potatoes. Sub fries and slaw but bakers add a dollar. Soup's minestrone." He left off the final E. I would have to learn a new way of talking.

"I'll give you those four booths to start," Jeanette said, "since they're closest, five, six, seven and eight. Put your slips on the right. I'll help out if you get overwhelmed. Pay at the register."

I met Adam, the sullen teen who bused, and John, the dishwasher, and five minutes later, after completing just the top few lines of the job application, waited on my first customer. Before the clock hit 11:40, the place was three-quarters full; by noon, a small line wound into the vestibule. But I was glad, not only on account of the tips but because I could show Jeanette she wouldn't regret having taken a chance on me.

At two, the diner had pretty much cleared out. Jeanette gestured for me to sit at eight. "What would you like? Willie will throw something on. No charge."

"What's easy?"

"There's still some meatloaf and mashed potatoes."

"Sounds great."

"Willie, give Andy loaf and tates." She turned back to me. "Can you come on tomorrow morning at seven?" While I was nodding, she called again through the ledge opening, "I'll be back at four; the coach is giving him a ride home. Merri's on." Striding towards the doors, Jeanette undid her apron, tossed it somewhere behind the register, grabbed a purse from below, unhooked a raincoat from the rack, and split—pretty much all in one motion. It only hit me after she'd left that I hadn't asked the hourly.

I went in the kitchen, and Willie, his apron spattered with grease, handed me a plate with the special. He asked how it had gone, and I said I was out of practice, but nobody had thrown food at me. "The only guy who acted annoyed—"

"You forgot Mr. Cooper's tartar sauce. He puts it on everything. He puts tartar sauce on his tartar sauce."

Chapter 63

WHEN I SHOWED up at the diner the next morning, a burly guy in his late forties with the expression of a marine sergeant stood at the register. He learned I was Andy; I learned he was Ross. Merri was on, but Judy had called in sick, and Jeanette had had to take her son to the doctor. Could I handle all the booths till she came in? I'd try.

Again 11:30 was the witching hour. Despite her making me nervous, Jeanette's arrival was a relief, both physically and mentally. She could juggle plates and glasses at the same time she dropped off checks and refilled coffee and smiled at everybody, except me.

Aberdeen not being prime real-estate territory, I found an apartment pretty quick. By mid-May, less than a month after bidding good riddance to the Eastern side of the Continental Divide, I had acquired a regular weekday breakfast-and-lunch schedule at Ross's and the basics in terms of furniture and household stuff. Wanting to buy a used car at some point, I studied the rules-of-the-road booklet from the Motor Vehicle place and managed to pass the written test; I aced the eye exam. Plan A was working acceptably and adequately.

My relations with Merri, Judy, and the other waitresses were friendly, and we often took our breaks in Booth eight, Willie and the assistant cook and prep folks occasionally joining us. I chalked up Jeanette's relative aloofness to her trying to convince herself I wasn't one of those sinners, since Willie had mentioned she belonged to some offshoot of the Nazarenes. I remembered Chloe saying that when people wanted to like you or at least not *dis*like you, they gave you the benefit of the doubt on traits they found objectionable—it was her explanation for why Geserenie's neighbors had assumed we weren't lesbians. The diner had been desperate for somebody who would accept Ross's skimpy hourly rate, so Jeanette likewise was giving me the benefit of the doubt. Of course you could argue I wasn't the only one benefitting.

She was aloof with *everybody* if the discussion turned political. The Pacific Northwest had its own political issues, I was learning, having to do with the environment and Indian treaty rights. Merri and Willie sided with the spotted owl and Native Americans, a position that put them in the minority in Aberdeen. Yet I couldn't tell for certain where they stood on gay rights, nor was I about to ask.

Among the customers, my most regular regulars were two retirees from the fisheries, both named James—or so they teased me. We had a running argument over the American League's use of a designated hitter. I of course championed the National League rule that the pitcher had to bat like everybody else—not that I had anything against Edgar Martinez, the Seattle Mariners' DH. But like I told James and James, hitting wasn't as important to me as playing good defense. Take Ken Griffey, Junior, the Mariners' centerfielder: he could hit home runs *plus* rob the opposing team of them with his amazing leaping catches. Unfortunately, one of his amazing leaping catches broke his wrist, so he was probably out for the rest of the season.

Ross had asked me to sub on the Sunday before Memorial Day, and lunch had been a madhouse. During the lull afterwards Willie joined me at Booth eight, and we got to talking carpentry. I told him about the project I had in mind—basically a smaller version of Becca and Wanda's cubbyhole cabinet. When Jeanette sat beside him—only the second or third time she sat in eight while I was there—he changed the subject, asking her how Philip was.

"The boy's parents haven't called," she said. "And he was looking forward to the sleepover." She glanced across at me. "I don't know if Willie told you, but Phil—he used to have nightmares and—I don't know—nervous breakdowns?"

"He's been through a lot," Willie said.

Jeanette poked at her potato salad with a fork. "I shouldn't throw a damper on your break."

"Hey, I don't mind whatever you want to talk about."

She tossed her bangs out of her eyes, but they fell back when she looked down at her plate. "I'll give you the short version. After Roger—my husband—died, Phil had a hard time bouncing back. I didn't expect it to be quick, but you hope your kid will bounce back quicker than *you* do." She turned to Willie and smiled. "I bounced back *so* quick, didn't I?"

"You have your days."

She rose abruptly. I turned. Two old ladies had come in.

"Hey, I'll get them."

"No, it's Shirley and Edith—they just want tea and pie." She hurried down the aisle.

The puzzle had been solved. I had wondered why Jeanette never flirted with any customers. Usually straight waitresses did—those under fifty, at least. Not all the time, and not with all guys, but with some of the people some of the time. Especially when a guy made it obvious he was pleased to have her waiting on him, she would smile or use feminine mannerisms or act embarrassed or excited. Not Jeanette. Because she was a widow.

"How did he die?" I asked Willie.

"Cancer. It was bad. She was doing everything: the IVs, baths, driving him to the radiation. *And* raising a kid and half-shifts here."

"They didn't have family, friends—?"

"Her church did shopping, cleaning, things like that. Roger's parents came up from Oregon just before he died. They're pretty old. Hers, they're in Florida."

"When did this happen?"

Willie looked at the ceiling. "Be three years October. I started in August, and she stopped working in September. Nick of time—I owe my job to her. Ross interviewed me, said he would call. I knew what *that* meant: needed a day to come up with an excuse. Can't say, 'No dice; you're black.' That's illegal."

Jeanette returned and sat beside him. Willie continued, "She tells him don't be prejudiced, give me a chance."

"Don't make me sound saintly," Jeanette said. "I told Ross he was stupid because the cook we had was smoking marijuana before coming in and getting the orders mixed, and we had advertised three weeks and gotten only two calls, both from people with no experience."

"You also said—"

"I was a walking dragon because of Roger."

Willie laughed. "That part's right. He was scared you'd quit on him."

Jeanette speared a cold potato chunk. "I didn't mean to interrupt."

"I was telling her about the lumberyard. She's going to build a cabinet."

"Nothing big," I said. "More school-project size. Do they sell tools too?"

"You can borrow ours," Jeanette said, "what I have left. The ones at Roger's shop went when the business was sold, but I have some I use for repairs and in case Phil takes an interest. Come over Friday evening if you're free and see what you want."

You could've knocked me over with a tack cloth.

I was in Hyde Park, standing on the lush green lawn beside Rockefeller Chapel. A large crowd of students in dark robes and mortarboards stood nearby among families and friends. It was sunny, almost hot. Jeanette, Willie, and Merri were there, huddled in conversation. As I approached, Jeanette turned my direction. Her eyes were slits. Nobody said anything, but I knew, through the hypno-osmosis of dreams, that she had learned I was gay. Somehow that was a betrayal; somehow I had deceived her. Willie and Merri and everybody stood nodding solemnly as if they too considered me Judas Iscariot. Wanda, dressed in black fishnet stockings, high heels, and a shiny sapphire-blue dress, sashayed over to them and said the service was about to start. They followed her into the chapel as the carillon rang, leaving me alone on the lawn.

I slammed off the clock radio. No need for Dr. Wilder's help interpreting *this*. But jeez: when had I ever told Jeanette I was straight? Was it a lie just because it was one of the few things I *didn't* blab about during the interview?

She lived less than a mile away, so it was no big deal to walk. Her street was relatively tidy, and a few of the front yard gardens looked well-tended. Jeanette's could've used a mowing. The one next door could've used a goat. I went up the porch steps and rang the bell. The door opened, and a huge, shaggy, dirty-white carpet of a sheepdog tried to land in my arms.

"Bardey, get down. Phil, get him down."

"Hey, buddy, at least let me in before we dance." Once inside, I patted the tangled head. "Let's sit this one out and wait for a polka. What's his name, Barney?"

A boy of about eleven was holding the dog's collar. His hair—auburn, not his mother's light brown—was just long enough to form a cowlick. When his eyes, a greenish hazel, met mine, they brimmed with emotion. Hate? Defiance? Cheer up, chum; if your God really does rule the roost, we won't be neighbors in the afterlife.

"Bar-*dee*," he said.

"With a D, not an N," Jeanette said. "Roger had an album of songs from the 1920s, and when Phil was little he loved 'Barney Google,' but he pronounced it Bardey. So that's what he named him."

I joked, "Doesn't have *any* eyes, seems to me, googly or not."

"Phil, I told you—I'm going to let Andy look over the tools and borrow what she needs to make her cabinet. Why don't you take Bardey to the park."

"You said I could have ice cream."

"After you walk him and shower. Why are you taking your shoes off?"

"For the shower."

"You were going to walk him first."

"I don't want to."

While they sparred, I took in the combo living room/dining room. The dining room table was beech and badly in need of refinishing. A brown and a beige recliner framed the fireplace, and the mantel held knickknacks and a small American flag. The couch, which faced the TV, was a brown-and-white plaid and had a green blanket folded over the top.

Phil crossed the room to the hall and disappeared around the corner. Jeanette asked if I wanted some coffee—she was putting a pot on for herself. I said okay and followed her into the kitchen. While she ran the tap, I moseyed to the wall calendar by the back door. The picture on top was of Jesus in a white robe talking to a group of cross-legged children listening eagerly at his sandaled feet. *Flock of the Merciful Nazarene +++ June 1995.* I peered through the back-door pane into the yard, which had a large leafy tree.

"Here are the tools," Jeanette said, opening a bottom drawer. "See if you need any of these, and check that drawer too."

I sorted through hammers and screwdrivers and wrenches while she chatted about this and that. Phil was trying sleep-away camp in August, they were going down to Southern Oregon over the Fourth of July to visit her in-laws, her car and house insurance both came due next month. She dished ice cream into three bowls and said we would eat in the dining room.

Phil came in wearing a green sweatshirt with an iguana on the front, his hair shiny wet. His expression was more merciless than merciful. The Flock of the Nazi-rene. We ate in silence.

"The coffee must be done," Jeanette said, rising.

Phil rose too and got the leash from the wall hook. The dog squealed and pressed his nose into Phil's knee. "Hold on, Bard." He linked the leash to the collar ring.

"Be back before it gets dark," Jeanette called from the kitchen.

I thought he was going, but he stood eyeing me. "Can I ask you something?"

My left hand, holding the spoon of vanilla, stopped midair. "Sure. Can't promise I'll know the answer, but go ahead." I put the spoon in my mouth.

"Are you a lesbian?"

Ice cream surged forward through my teeth, but my lips sealed fast enough to block the escape. Jeanette's voice boomed like a jet breaking the sound barrier. "Phil!" Her body charged in after the voice. "You don't ask—"

"Hey, it's okay. I told him he could."

He ignored his mother's bulging eyes and scarlet cheeks. "Well are you?"

"Guess so."

He opened the door. Bardey bounded in front of him, and quicker than you could say Sodom and Gomorrah, boy and dog were gone.

"Sorry to spring that on you," I said. "Wasn't expecting to be asked."

She was scowling at the floor. "It's okay. I thought you were." She lifted her hands palms up. "I might be too."

Chapter 64

"LET ME GET the coffee. Why don't we sit there." Jeanette motioned towards the couch.

I took one of the recliners, and while she was in the kitchen, my brain cells tried to reassemble themselves into their accustomed lobes and locations. Damn, I could've used a drink, a real drink. She made several trips from the kitchen, bringing a hot plate, two mugs, and the coffee pot. When she finally sat and I poured, the booze and cigarette cravings were almost subsiding.

Her eyes remained on the floor as if she were reading from it. "Roger was in the Air Force when we started dating. It felt like he was here one minute and gone the next. I was still living at home, in Klamath Falls. Not far from his parents." She blew across the top of her cup.

"When he finished his last tour, we got married. He was offered a great job in construction up here, so we moved. After a few years, he was able to go out on his own, a general contractor." She smiled at the mantel. "He loved that, being his own boss." The smile disappeared. "We wanted a child, badly, and our friends were having children, but I wasn't getting pregnant. Still, our faith kept us going. We looked into adoption, and suddenly I was pregnant. We talked about

adoption for a second child—Phil had just started kindergarten—but
Roger got sick."

She ran through the details of his illness quickly: the vomiting day and night, the pain and withering and dying. "We were in
the dumps for a long time. I took Phil to a psychologist because
he wasn't bouncing back at all. That helped. On the drive down to
Klamath Falls for the Fourth of July, he asked if his grandparents—
Roger's parents—would be mad at him if he wasn't still sad. I said,
'No, and what do you think *Dad* wants, when he looks down from
heaven? All of us being sad or happy?' 'Being happy,' he said. 'That's
what I think too.'" Jeanette paused. "Am I boring you?"

"No way."

"Things kept improving. He was made a forward on the soccer
team. Everyone at work was great to me, and I had my friends at
church. My parents had moved to Florida, near Orlando, but spring
break we visited and went to Disneyworld and SeaWorld. He was so
excited to see real iguanas, and he loved the whales. Once in a while
I went out on a date, but nothing clicked. I didn't care. Phil and I,
we had our routines. Until Kiki."

Jeanette's gaze remained on the floor, but her fingers laced in
her lap. "Kiki lived across from the field where his team practiced.
She was always outside tinkering with her Harley and riding up and
down the street. She's not like *anyone*. Carrot red hair in a cute spiky
cut. A black leather jacket twice her size. Only five-three, but wiry,
athletic, always on the move. They loved her joining their practice;
she could out-dribble, out-kick the best of them.

"She could out-talk any human being under the sun, sell you
the Space Needle promising to wrap it up with ribbon. She could
whistle with two fingers in her mouth, drink two pints of beer and
act stone sober. The boys *worshipped* her."

A noise outside made us turn. Just a car starting.

"The house she was living in was sold, and she asked if anyone knew where she might rent a room for a few months, until she went down to her job in Costa Rica. Phil *begged* me to let her stay with us, in the extra room. I said okay. He was in a tizzy; his teammates were so jealous." Jeanette looked at me. "Oh, I liked her too. She was constant fun. But I thought she would be gone at the end of the summer, and in the meantime, we would have an interesting houseguest. And seeing Phil excited again—" She poured more coffee in her cup; I covered mine with my hand.

"Kiki had us coming and going, kayaking and white-water rafting. *Sky*diving. Well, we watched. One evening after Phil had gone to bed, we were on the sofa, and she offered me a shot of Wild Turkey. She always had a bottle in the house, *one-oh-one*, she called it. I was used to wine but said okay, and we were laughing, I don't remember about what, and then she says she has something awful to tell me. I panic—all I can think of is cancer."

Jeanette inhaled deeply and exhaled slowly. "She says I'm beautiful, charming, all these wonderful things. And she's in love with me. And then, just like that," Jeanette snapped her fingers, "she says she has to go. I asked why, and she said, 'Because you don't feel the same.' She was going to her aunt in Chehalis and would come back in a week for her stuff. She went out, and I heard the Harley start, and she drove off in the middle of the night!"

The look Jeanette threw me was like I should share her surprise. I said nothing, and she went on, "I didn't know what to think. My life had been very sheltered. The next morning, I told Phil she had gone to visit her aunt. He didn't care, not at first—Kiki was always doing things on the spur of the moment. That week was sheer torture. All I thought about was her, the things we had done together, the things she had said, telling me she loved me. It had been so long—" Jeanette stopped and stared off at the fireplace. Her voice became softer. "I was afraid she would come back while I was at work and grab her things and be gone. So I left an envelope on her bed with a note saying, 'I've done a lot of soul-searching. Please hear what I have to say.' I *had* done a lot of soul-searching. You don't grow up in a church like mine and decide in an instant to do what they say is a very bad sin. And there was Phil—how would he feel? Would it disgust him? Would he fear for my soul?

"She finally came back—*eight* days later. Well, to be blunt: we, we, we became a couple."

In perfect synchrony, the two of us turned to the window. Dusk had gathered; the sky was a deep blue. Barely enough time for a last round of hide-and-seek. "It's nice it stays light so late," Jeanette said. "Bardey gets a good, long outing. To finish: I felt I couldn't stay in the church. They were condemning Kiki to hell, and I would go with her unless I repented. And that's not what I believe. Jesus wants us to love each other, to care for each other. He isn't fussy about the details, what sex you are, what race or religion, even. He doesn't want us to find reasons *not* to love." She looked at me questioningly. "The word *lesbian*—we never used it. Does that seem strange? But our love wasn't like anyone else's, not to us. We weren't lesbian or homosexual or bisexual or anything, just Kiki and Jeanette."

She rose and turned on some lamps and the porch light. "I told Phil that Kiki loved us and wanted to be part of the family. I said not to tell other people because they wouldn't approve. It would be like he had two moms, and they weren't used to that. He didn't really understand. He thought it was natural for *me* to love her because *he* did. I didn't use the word sex, just love and caring."

"So Ross and everybody—they don't know?"

"*No one* does. Ross would be horrified. I'm not sure what *Willie* would think, though he's easygoing. I told people her job in Costa Rica had fallen through and she was looking for something else. I keep trying to make this long story short. Kiki stayed here, got Phil off to school and soccer practice, and I went back to full shifts. She traded in the Harley for a pick-up that could seat three. It was an exciting time. We had gone from feeling the universe had abandoned us to feeling it revolved around us. Around *her*, and us because we were near her.

"One day Ross tells me I have a phone call and the woman says it's important. It's Kiki. She's in Anacortes, about to board the ferry. She's with some other woman, someone she *really needs to be with*, and she's sorry. She knows some day I'll understand. And hangs up!

"I walked out of Ross's office not knowing whether to laugh or cry. Could it be one of her pranks? Was Phil in on it? I stopped by home before picking him up from practice, and the truck and all her things were gone. Clothes, sleeping bag, everything. But that's not all. *My* TV. *My* camera—Roger's last gift to me, she knew that—and any jewelry worth anything."

"Fucking bitch," I said. "Excuse my French."

Jeanette glanced at her hand. "Except my rings. I still wore my rings, so people wouldn't suspect. And the binoculars, which were in the car. She took the emergency cash in the tea tin and—"

I spoke more French.

"Did she have an aunt in Chehalis?" Jeanette asked. "Another woman? Instead of Anacortes, she could have been on her way to Las Vegas or California. It puzzled me, why she phoned to say goodbye. But then I realized she didn't want me to think we had been burglarized and call the police."

"You *should've* called the police. She stole your stuff."

"I couldn't do that to Phil—have her arrested. Leaving was bad enough. I told him as much of the truth as I thought he could handle: she had left and stolen some of my things. I didn't pretend to understand it. I said she could have been a drug addict." Jeanette smiled harshly at the floor. "She must not have known what Roger's painkillers were or she would have taken them too, to sell."

For a good minute longer she stared at the floor. Then she spoke in a low, sad voice. "You know what I blame myself for the most? Not what the church thinks I should. I blame myself for being blinded by flattery."

"Hey, you said she could out-talk anybody."

"Phil should have had me watching out for him. He didn't suffer as badly as he had with Roger, but then at least he had known what was coming. And we could rejoice that Roger was freed from pain. With Kiki, Phil has to wonder if she ever cared about him at all."

Darkness hovered at the side windows and tinged the living room with melancholy—only the porch window glowed. The brown plaid couch looked old and forlorn; the rug, more gray than green.

"So I'm not sure if I'm a lesbian or heterosexual or bisexual," Jeanette said, her right hand rotating the rings again. "I've been in love twice, if it was love with Kiki. A man and a woman. But it's not important. I won't be getting involved with anyone until Phil is grown."

"Now I understand his reaction to me. He thinks all lesbians are slimes."

"You are nothing like her. She says the right thing to get what she wants. You are honest, you—"

"I'm curious: are you back at your old church? Do you think being gay, being lesbian, is a sin?"

Jeanette smiled to herself, almost Stacy-like. "Phil and I had a long talk about that. He was hearing things at school about lesbians and asked if that's what Kiki and I were. I tried explaining—not about sex but about loving someone as a companion, a special companion. He seemed to understand, to agree that love is love, and it shouldn't matter who. Yes, I'm back at my old church. They're my friends, my community. I guess I could look for another—God spreads joy everywhere—but Phil has friends there too, and he's okay with not agreeing with everything they say. He asked me what Dad—Roger—thought about lesbians, and I said I didn't think he knew any, and Phil said, 'I bet he wouldn't care.' I said, 'You're right. He was always saying people should mind their own business.'"

She tossed her bangs to the side. "I told Phil it was the grief over his dad that made me emotional around Kiki, that she represented an escape from sadness, not true love. He understood, he *identified* with that. In some ways, he's so much older than twelve."

We sat in silence a bit. "I do hope to fall in love again," Jeanette murmured. "But only after he graduates high school and is more on his own. It's not fair to put him through something like that again. *Stability* is what he needs, we *both* need."

"Hey, I hear you."

She tilted her head. "I had that impression, when you first came into the diner and said you wanted to start over. You're struggling with alcoholism, I know. Are there other things?"

"Guess I'm not quite ready to get into it all." I hoped it didn't come out rude. Again we sat in silence, till definitely hearing noises. Barking, happy barking.

First Jeanette had been aloof; now I worried she would be too confiding, that her personal life would spill over into our interactions at the diner. My fears were quickly put to rest, however; the busyness of business, if nothing else, returned us to our old groove.

And that wasn't a bad place to be. Certain people have an intuitive synchrony. Probably trapeze artists have fellow artists they prefer over others, folks who give them more confidence of being in the right place at the right time. You definitely saw it in certain shortstop/second base pairings. Say there's a man on first and less than two outs. If the batter hits a sharp grounder towards left field and the shortstop has to lunge to nab it, he can toss the ball without turning to look, knowing exactly where second will have positioned himself for the catch. And second would be there, anticipating when and where the ball would arrive, and be poised to shoot a bullet to first for the double play. Jeanette and I had that intuitive synchrony. When the diner was a madhouse, I preferred handling it with just her and not Merri or Judy or another waitress getting in the way.

My birthday showed up at its usual time, and I gave myself a present in the form of a navy-blue Mariners cap. Heck, if Phil could belong to a church and not agree with all its rules, I could root for an American League team and not agree with all *its* rules. The Fates gave me a birthday present too: starting my forty-fourth year symptom-free.

Lunch was winding down, and while rinsing the pie knife, I heard Jeanette whisper, "You know about the Gay Pride Parade?"

I turned off the tap and whispered back, "Aberdeen has one?"

"No, Seattle—next Sunday. Phil will be at a round-robin tournament in Shelton all weekend. I wondered if you might like to go. I know it can feel isolated here."

Was that a Kiki complaint? *Isolation gets a bad rap*, I was tempted to say.

Scooping out the drain garbage, she added, "I've been feeling guilty telling you all my difficulties. Now you think being around me means being around misery."

"I don't think—"

"I *do* have other sides. Not a happy-go-lucky side like you, and I don't make jokes, but I enjoy them. I could show you some of the sights on the drive up, like the state capital and the Nisqually Wildlife Refuge." She washed her hands and switched the water to cold as I grabbed the pitcher. "Unless it's cloudy, you can see Rainier."

I held the pitcher under the tap. "When's it not cloudy?"

"Summer *will* come. To Seattle before Aberdeen."

"Sold."

Chapter 65

THE DRIVE TO Seattle took several hours, but the scenery was pleasant, at least starting out. A few towns and residential areas cropped up, but mostly we passed vegetation in some form: pastures and wildflowers, bushes high and low, trees, ferns, the ubiquitous ivy. Compared to South Jersey, at least, Southwestern Washington was unspoiled.

"What the heck are those?" I asked. No need to point; two enormous gray concrete structures stuck up in the middle of nowhere like giant salt and pepper shakers.

"Cooling towers," Jeanette said. "It was going to be a nuclear power station, but they ran out of money. People call them 'woops.' It stands for something."

So Washington had its half-finished projects too. I fiddled with the radio. "Whoa! Didn't expect to hear *this* around here." It was one of Stacy's—and my—favorites.

We are stardust, we are golden,
We are billion year old carbon,
And we got to get ourselves
Back to the gar-ar-den.

"I don't recognize it," Jeanette said.

"An old sixties song." Had she and Roger hated the anti-war movement? He had been in the Air Force, and both of them had grown up in Southern Oregon, probably as conservative a place as Aberdeen. Loved the protester, hated the protest?

Jeanette pointed out some mountains, the light-stone government buildings in Olympia, and the tidal flats and marshes of the Nisqually Wildlife Refuge. Mt. Rainier loomed to the east, a towering white pyramid.

About the time we came even with SeaTac Airport, Seattle appeared in the distance with enough tall buildings to qualify as a metropolis. On the left, a herd of loading cranes gathered at the harbor's edge as if to drink. Jeanette pointed out the Kingdome, and I said it was an ugly mother-of-a-stadium and I couldn't imagine watching baseball indoors anyway.

It took about a year to find a parking space, but no map was needed to find the parade route—scores of obvious dykes and gay men trooped in one direction, joined by plenty of straight couples and nuclear families with their orbiting children. The clouds had thinned, and people tied their sweaters and sweatshirts around their waists and put on sunglasses, optimism abounding.

Finding a spot near the curb was hopeless, but I noticed some room beside three women and guided Jeanette in their direction. The one with fashionable short brown hair reminded me of Chase. The other with dark hair was talking animatedly to the blonde, who glanced at us briefly when we scrunched in beside them.

"Isn't it expensive," the blonde asked the two brunettes, "an apartment here and house there? Why don't you move to Seattle?"

"Fran likes the people she works with," Longer Hair said.

Shorter Hair, presumably Fran, said, "We'll stay here during the kitchen remodel."

Blondie looked appalled. "You'll *commute* down there?"

"No, I'll take vacation time."

Blondie stood on tiptoe. "I've got to find them before the parade starts." She looked disappointed she couldn't rain on theirs.

"When the remodel's done," Longer Hair said, "you're welcome to visit, if you and your friends want free lodging when you go to Ocean Shores."

Blondie gave a ta-ta and disappeared into the crowd. Jeanette and I exchanged surprised looks. "Excuse me," I said, "but we couldn't help overhear somebody say 'Ocean Shores.' You from there? We live in Aberdeen."

"*We* live in Aberdeen!"

The four of us acted like a couple of Texas cowboys running into Colorado ranchers atop the Eiffel Tower. In no time we traded info on who worked and lived where. Fran was an ex-cop who had thrown her back out and now was employed as a claims adjuster in Hoquiam. Debby was a lawyer at a Seattle firm and stayed in their Seattle apartment during the week but went down to Aberdeen Thursday evenings and worked from home on Fridays. Jeanette said that she and her husband had moved from Klamath Falls when he'd gotten a job in Aberdeen, and she hadn't wanted to move back after he'd died because her son had lots of friends at school.

"We know two gay men in Aberdeen who have a son in middle school," Debby said.

"Fran! Debby!"

Five or six women descended on us, all apparently from Seattle. Fran asked if anybody wanted to go with her to the ice cream cart, which sparked a debate over veganism versus vegetarianism versus carnivorism. If there was a chromosome for lesbianism, it also had to carry the gene for fighting over what you could eat. Actually, I would've preferred that folks had kept arguing about food instead of the next topic, which had to do with some brief Debby was writing about "the right to die with dignity." Stuff about respirators and intractable pain and pulling the plug were tossed around as if none of us had actually watched somebody succumb to cancer.

I was the only taker on ice cream, and Fran and I wended our way through the mass of bodies to the cart. While waiting in line, she asked how long Jeanette and I had been together. We weren't, I said—just friends and co-workers.

"Really? Debby loves fixing people up. We know quite a few single women—although most live in Seattle."

"Thanks, but I'm not looking for a relationship right now."

"Is Jeanette straight?"

"I don't know how much she wants this broadcast, so if you could keep it to yourselves: she's not sure."

"But she came to the parade."

"As a favor to me."

Faint strains of horns—trumpets or trombones, maybe—filtered through the general commotion. The crowds on both sides of the street turned expectantly in the direction of the music. Debby popped up at Fran's elbow saying she'd changed her mind and to get her a scoop of strawberry. "And I just met more women from Aberdeen! One's named Cheryl and one, Samantha—"

"By the way," Fran said, "Andy and Jeanette aren't a couple, just friends."

Debby's eyebrows shot up. "You're not a couple? I'll fix you up. I *love* matchmaking; I'm a regular yenta. If it gets serious, I can draw up a partnership agreement to make everything community property."

"That's her area of expertise," Fran said. "Community property, trusts, wills—"

"*Estate-planning*, in lawyer lingo. Family arrangements, inheritances. Let me go tell Cheryl you're not a couple—she was asking about Jeanette."

After Debby disappeared into the crowd, Fran said that one of the grossest things she'd had to do as a cop involved somebody named Cheryl. "We got an anonymous tip about a body in a river, and it turned out it was this Cheryl person. She had OD'd, and her boyfriend, who was running a meth lab, panicked and dumped her. I was on the crew hunting the body. We found her floating. Know why?"

"It was near where he dumped her?"

"No, why she was *floating*. When you die, bacteria in your body produce gas, so you bloat. Bloat and float. Then the skin pops, and the gases escape. The guys christened me 'Tough Gut Fran' because I was the only one who didn't toss their cookies."

I was glad Jeanette missed out on the story.

The parade was in full swing when we finally got our cones and made it back to the others. I was introduced to a non-bloated Cheryl, Jeanette saying, "She lives in Aberdeen and wants to sell her '87 hatchback. Just needs some body work."

"Hey, don't we all," I said.

Actually Cheryl didn't. She wore a burgundy tank top practically molded to her body, which was of the lithe, athletic variety. Not my type, but a popular one. Just to make Jeanette happy, or not unhappy, I gave Cheryl my phone number and took down hers.

Cheryl and the other women wanted to move closer to the curb, but Jeanette and I stayed in our spot with Fran and Debby. The four of us cheered on local politicians, beauty queens, musclemen, floats, this union and that, and various organizations keen on saving the whales, preserving the old-growth forests, fighting AIDS, and keeping abortion safe and legal. When we had to head home so

Jeanette could pick up Phil at his friend's, Debby and Fran said to keep in touch, and we third-ed and fourth-ed the motion.

After getting us past the worst of the traffic, Jeanette made some comment about them reminding her of her parents, the way they squabbled. "Happily married, but—what was Debby's word— *kvetching*? I don't remember that with Roger, little fights. Maybe I've forgotten."

I thought of the fights with Laurie over my going into Madison and getting a job off-farm. From the distance of years, I could see they were about deeper issues, insecurity and jealousy on her part, claustrophobia and maybe other stuff on mine. Out of the blue, just like the jet rising overhead, I found myself wishing her well, hoping she'd found true love, and at Geserenie.

Equally out of the blue, Jeanette asked if the discussion about Debby's right-to-die case upset me. "*Me*?" I said, surprised. "I was the one cracking the jokes."

"They seemed—you know—forced?"

"Sorry I'm not Bob Hope or—"

"It wasn't that. I thought you were trying to change the subject."

"I *was* trying to change the subject. Figured it might be bringing back memories of what Roger went through."

Jeanette smiled at the road. "You're a good person, Andy Gabe, a really good person."

"I wouldn't bet the ranch on it. I wouldn't bet a bottle of ranch dressing."

"I didn't think about those issues when he was sick. I was so caught up in making him comfortable, trying to remember the doctors' instructions, the different medications. The last few weeks, I knew the morphine was shortening the time he would be awake, but what was the point? He was in excruciating pain." She was silent some minutes. "I understand what Debby was saying about people having the right to make their own decision about when to die. But I also feel that people who are sick should never feel like a burden. Couldn't that happen, if everyone around you decided to take their life when they got a terminal disease? Wouldn't that make you feel guilty if you didn't want to take your life?"

Good god—I should tell her about Huntington's! She would empathize, would understand—

Stop, stop, that's the Bad Angel talking! Think what would happen if you told her. The atmosphere at work would be poisoned faster than you can say CAG.

Yes, Good Angel was right. Jeanette would grow alert to what other folks were talking about just as I had today. And how could she keep from spying on me, watching for odd movements, a change in gait, a frown that might be an HD grimace?

But was it wrong of me to want a friendship, a friendship like I'd had with Stacy, where you told each other everything? Dr. Wilder, Dr. Robbins, everybody had urged me to make new friends. And to find someone to take with me to the counseling.

Towns and woods went by. You would never know it was almost six, with all the daylight. We cruised beneath an overpass, and as the road curved, the Nisqually Delta opened up on our right, its tidal flats and reeds yellow in the slanted rays. The water in the lagoons and inlet beyond the reeds was a cobalt blue. Jeanette said otters and muskrats lived in the marshes. And wrens and thrushes and all sorts of other critters.

No, I wouldn't tell her about the Huntington's. Yet why did it feel like lying? Did every secret, practically by definition, carry with it a sense of guilt? That was Dr. Wilder's message. It was also the message we'd preached in the glory days of Gay Liberation: concealing something important about yourself fostered feelings of sinfulness. Which was why coming out of the closet was as much a personal liberation as a political act. But telling Jeanette would stick *her* in the position of concealing something—from Ross. It wouldn't be fair to saddle her with that.

Besides, if you thought about it: how could it be dishonest for me to not mention an uncertainty? Or to conceal something that was as likely *un*true as true? You couldn't lie by concealing a falsehood, could you? This beat Zeno's: how could it be dishonest if all you omitted mentioning was that you didn't know something?

As we passed the nuclear cooling towers, Jeanette asked if Debby and Fran thought we were a couple. "No, I said you didn't consider yourself gay; you had brought me to the parade as a favor."

"I'm glad I went. It did me good to see so many lesbians that aren't like Kiki. And they seem so—what's the word—freer? They don't fuss about foo-foo." She laughed, her wrist dangling over the top of the steering wheel. "That's what Roger called it. The women at church fret about the silliest things—whether someone's nail polish is right for her complexion or she should wear a different kind of sweater—like it's *important*."

"I guess if society's already telling you you're a deviant, it gives you the freedom to chuck a bunch of other conventions while you're at it."

"*Unconventional*, that's the word—lesbians are free to be unconventional." She smiled again at the road. "And now I know a lawyer if I need one. What was Fran saying about matchmaking?"

"Debby likes to pair people up. If we want to start dating, we should let her know. Guess she would weed out the vegans."

"That's six years away for me."

A-woman.

Chapter 66

Since Roger's mother had allergies, Bardey couldn't accompany them to Klamath Falls for the Fourth of July weekend. I agreed to walk him in the evenings—their neighbor Christine was taking the mornings. Jeanette invited me to supper Friday so she could show me where everything was.

When I arrived, she suggested I go into the backyard to start getting the dog used to me. I went out the kitchen screen door and down the steps. Bardey sat beneath the tree gazing up at the branches. Phil whacked a stick at the overgrown grass like he was wielding a scythe.

"Has he trapped something?" I asked.

"A squirrel."

"How often does he catch one?"

"Never. Something's wrong with his legs." Phil's legs took him back into the house. Noticing his audience had diminished, Bardey came over wagging his tail, and I petted him.

While we ate, Jeanette filled me in on details like taking in the mail and how much dry food Bardey got. Phil sat glumly silent, and the instant he finished, grabbed Bardey's leash and took the dog to the park. I then got the grand tour.

Two things about Phil's room would have struck anybody. The first was the giant poster of a giant green iguana. Its skin was shiny and wrinkly and froglike with weird little humps and lumps, and its expression was nasty, the eyes glowing like radioactive emeralds. "He *likes* looking at that thing?" I asked.

Jeanette pointed to the bookcase. Except for the framed photo of Bardey on top, it contained only toy animals. I stepped closer and could see each and every one was an iguana. Some were plastic; some, glass or fabric.

The second unusual thing about the room was the orderliness. The bed was made, and the floor was clear except for a small blue rug. Six or seven pens and pencils were lined up in a row beside the stapler, which was perfectly parallel to the Scotch tape, scissors, and ruler.

"No wonder he was sulky," I said. "You made him clean his room."

"No, he keeps it this way."

I started to peer at some of the pictures on the walls—there were rows and rows of magazine cutouts—but Jeanette turned off the light and went back in the hall. I followed, the iguana's eyes glaring after me.

"I'll show you the dining room lamp to leave on at night; it sheds light into the kitchen too. If you need to change a bulb, they're in here." She opened a closet door and pointed to the cardboard boxes on the top shelf. "Those bottles in the back are Roger's pain-killers. They stock you up because they don't know how long it will be. I can't believe Kiki never noticed them." She closed the door. "Let me show you the park they always go to."

Saturday evening after Bardey's walk, I wandered through the house as softly as a ghost. Jeanette's bedroom looked the same—no signs of pre-trip packing disorder. I examined the pictures on her dresser. In the first, Roger had a shy smile that seemed to say he'd put up with being photographed if it didn't last too long. His expression in the second, where he was in uniform, was harder to read. In the wedding shot, Jeanette was practically unrecognizable. The white lace gown made her look slender, and she had long hair, but it was the unrestrained smile that really took me by surprise. Would her next relationship be with a man or woman? Anybody's guess.

I followed Bardey into Phil's room. The pictures on the wall at the head of the bed were family photos. One row of magazine cutouts along the side of the bed was soccer players, men caught mid-kick or knocking the ball with their heads. The caption under the last said *Pelé Performs Magic*. Other rows had pictures of mountains, cars, polar bears sniffing at an ice floe. Whales dominated the bottom row, some long and gray, some black-and-white.

Suddenly it hit me: each picture was aligned with or symmetrical to some other, colors balancing, shapes and sizes in counterpoint. The room *itself* was a work of art, the result of planning and organizing. Did Phil's aesthetic sense foretell his being gay? Of course that was a stereotype—not all gay men were artistic, not all artistic men were gay, and Socrates wasn't all gay artistic men. But it would be kind of cool if Phil turned out to be gay.

At the front door, I gave the dining area and living room a last scan. The brown-and-white couch with the green blanket, the brown and beige recliners, the picture of Canadian geese by the sideboard, and the photo of Mt. Rainier by the telephone table all together gave the space a log-cabin coziness. A comfortable place to hang your hat and leash.

After they returned, Jeanette let me borrow her car for practicing and then taking the driving test. I passed, even without offering the

examiner a joint. My ATM card got a new wallet mate—bye-bye, Illinois; hello, Washington.

I called Cheryl and arranged to check out her car. It drove fine and was blue, not bright red or some other color likely to attract cops' attention. I dipped into Edward's legacy and wrote her a check.

Handing me the keys, she said, "Debby says you and Jeanette are just friends, not a couple."

"That's right."

"Is she seeing anyone?"

"No. Doesn't want to till her son graduates high school and is living on his own. Plus, she—"

"How old is he?"

"Twelve."

Cheryl snorted, or maybe oinked. "Twelve is old enough to deal with Mommy in a relationship."

"Well, good luck."

Chapter 67

"DID I WAKE you?"

"Not really," I croaked. "Where you calling from?"

"Home," Jeanette said.

"Shit, am I supposed to be on? I thought *you* wanted Merri's—"

"Phil's sick. Threw up his breakfast."

I clambered out of bed. "Call Ross and say I'll be there in twenty minutes."

"I hate to ask this. You've helped me out with walking Bardey and—"

"I don't mind."

"It's not that. I need the money. The insurance is coming due. Would you be willing to come over and stay with Phil? Until five? I know you would be giving up a day off, but I'll trade you in August and cook a batch of meals you can freeze and—"

"Don't worry about it. The Mariners are playing—in Baltimore or Detroit, I forget. The game will come on at some point."

"You don't know how much I appreciate this."

Jeanette was out the door the second I turned off the engine. "I left Bardey in the yard so he won't be a nuisance. He's been walked.

There's a fresh pot of coffee. Thanks so much. I *will* return the favor."

"It's nothing," I lied. A day with a surly kid wasn't my idea of fun. Maybe he would sleep the whole time.

The bedroom door was ajar, and Phil lay on his side facing the wall. I tiptoed back into the living room and perused the TV listings. Good, there would be a game on.

Hearing something, I rose and hurried to the hall in time to see him go into the bathroom. With the door still open, the sounds of retching carried. I walked softly to where the bathroom light made a shiny rhombus on the hallway floor. The face in profile leaning over the toilet bowl looked younger than twelve. His stomach wasn't done; his narrow shoulders thrust forward repeatedly. I stepped away from the door, listening. When the toilet flushed, I ducked back into the living room.

After a minute, I went to his room and asked if he was okay. Lying on his side again, he grunted. I lingered a few minutes scoping out the iguanas. His breathing became slow and rhythmic.

Shortly before eleven, Jeanette phoned and asked if he had a fever. "Don't know," I said. "He's still sleeping." Did she really think he would let me take his temperature, even in the armpit?

"If he does, give him Children's Tylenol, not aspirin."

Another hour passed before I heard the patter of feet, a door slam, and the toilet flush. A few seconds later Phil came into the living room. He was barefoot and in pajamas with a sailboat design. He slumped onto the couch.

"Your mom called. Wondered if you had a temperature."

He lifted one palm to his forehead and shook his head uncertainly. I took a step, reached over, and rested the back of my hand against the smooth skin. He didn't flinch or duck away. "Feels okay to me," I said.

"I'm hungry."

"No wonder—you gave back your entire breakfast and maybe last night's supper. Think you can keep something down? I could toss a piece of bread in the toaster."

"I want a hamburger."

I couldn't help laughing. "Why don't you pick a food that will go easier on the stomach. You spent the morning exercising it and now you want to drop a burger in? How about fries and a milkshake too? I'd love to see *that* coming up for air. Maybe cherry pie?"

He gave a girlish giggle. "Apple. With chocolate ice cream on top."

"Tell you what: start with a piece of toast, and if you keep that down, I'll fry you up a burger if there's any in the fridge. Your mom's going to kill me if she finds out." A smile crept across his face. "You're going to tell her, aren't you? Just to watch her kill me?" I paused in the kitchen doorway long enough to see the nod.

While the toaster was doing its thing, I brought in a can of soda, swirling it to get the bubbles out. "Sip just a little at a time—see what your belly has to say."

"I can have soda?"

"Easier on your stomach than milk or juice."

He sipped a little and let out an enormous belch.

"If all you're sending up is air, you're probably on the mend."

He nibbled on the toast and half an hour later still wanted a hamburger, so I fried us each small ones. Being sick could mellow a person—it would be interesting to see if his dislike returned when his health did. After lunch, he yawned, but I told him he couldn't lie down for an hour; the food needed time to work its way to the intestines. We put on some western. Again he didn't flinch when I felt his forehead.

While he slept, I did the dishes, kept Bardey company in the yard, and settled on the couch to watch the game. I still wasn't a fan of the designated-hitter rule, but Edgar Martinez—or "Gar," as some fans called him—could certainly hit.

In the fifth inning, Phil reappeared saying he was thirsty, so I fetched him another soda.

Sitting on the opposite end of the couch, he asked, "Will Griffey play again?"

"Don't know. A broken wrist is pretty bad. If he comes back next year, maybe we'll have a shot at something. The infield seems pretty good." I shouted at the home-plate umpire, "You're blind as a bat."

"Do you swear?"

"Sometimes."

"Kiki swore."

"Kiki did a lot of things. A bunch weren't so nice."

"She's a lesbian too."

"She's also a jerk, from what I hear. Just because we have a couple of things in common doesn't mean I'm like her. I've never ridden a motorcycle or gone skydiving."

"You think the Mariners will ever win the World Series?"

"Sure. Have they ever won the pennant? No? Won the division? Hey, they're a young team. The Yankees, they go back probably eighty, ninety years, maybe more. And Randy's an ace pitcher, and the way everybody's been hitting—"

"Do you like my mom?"

"Course I do. She's a neat lady. If you mean as a special companion, then no. I'm not interested in *anybody* as a special companion and don't expect to be for many moons to come. I've got a ton of personal issues to deal with first."

"What?"

"What what?" I craned my neck to make out who was in the batter's box.

"What personal issues?"

"You must be feeling better, to get so darn inquisitive. Alcoholism, mainly. I've managed to quit drinking, but staying dry is a daily effort."

"Who taught you about baseball, your dad?"

"Dean, yeah."

"Where does he live?"

"Doesn't—he died about fifteen years ago."

"Are you still sad?"

"Actually, we weren't close. He divorced my mother when I was ten and totally abandoned me, so I can't say I feel much of anything."

By the bottom of the eighth, Phil had nodded off. I lowered the TV volume. He didn't flicker an eyelid when I draped the blanket over him, even as I tugged it up to his shoulder. Sleep had knitted up the raveled sleeve of care.

When Jeanette came home, I reported on the patient's progress and also said she had given birth to an artist, the way he had arranged all the pictures in his bedroom. She beamed in that proud-parent way.

A moment later, her face went south. "You don't think there's something wrong with him? Christine once mentioned—I think she called it 'obsessive-compulsive disease.' He used to spend *hours* lining up the backing, the construction paper, rearranging it, changing the colors. He kept the door closed—maybe to block out the sound of Roger vomiting. Truthfully, it was a relief he could keep himself busy."

"I can think of worse ways to cope with stress than doing something artistic. I've *done* worse ways."

Jeanette seemed to mull it over. "I hadn't thought of that. A way of coping. A *good* way."

"You don't want him bottling it up. And of all the ways for it to come out, fixing up his room—"

"You are so wise, Andy, even though you say you're not. Can I make you some supper? I have—"

"Not tonight. Got to do laundry."

"You could have brought it over."

"I'm too wise to have thought of that."

Chapter 68

DEBBY AND FRAN invited us to dinner a couple of times, and we took them out to eat in return; a restaurant we all liked ran two-for-one coupons in the paper pretty often. When they stayed up in Seattle during their kitchen remodel, I took in their mail and watered their plants—another advantage to having a car.

Helping them—helping *anybody*—made me feel like I was erasing some of the red ink on the Great Ledger, considering the stealing I had done and all the help I had gotten from St. Aloysius and St. Joe's, not to mention food banks and the Cambridge Women's Center and a zillion other places. And now that Phil didn't see me as some species of Kiki, I could do little favors for Jeanette, like dropping off an extra box of laundry detergent or bundle of paper towels I had found at some too-good-to-pass-up price. A few times I even picked Phil up from practice, though it took only once to learn to not bring Bardey, who liked the creek near the field.

And with a car, I could go exploring. Everybody raved about the Olympic Peninsula and especially the Hoh Rain Forest. I calculated that with an early start, I could drive up the coast to the Hoh for a short hike, hit a beach on the way back to actually dip my toes in the Pacific, and get home before dark.

When I mentioned my plan at work, Jeanette volunteered her tent, sleeping bag, and other gear if I wanted to camp overnight. I said I had never done it, and before you could say Andy Boone, she had convinced Ross to let us trade with the weekend waitresses and take two days off during the week. We'd go when Phil was at sleep-away camp. Christine agreed to walk Bardey, the crazy mutt having forfeited his camping privileges years ago by baying all night at some owl—spotted or unspotted, nobody knew. We ended up taking Jeanette's car, which was bigger, plus she kept a bunch of nature books and hiking guides in the backseat.

The trees themselves weren't what was so astonishing; we'd seen gigantic spruce, fir, and cedar lining the road to the Visitors Center. Nor was it the wealth of vegetation in a mostly sun-shielded woods. What made the Hoh Rain Forest so fairy-tale-like was the moss. It hung indiscriminately, fringing the limbs of bigleaf maples, folding over alders, dangling from burls, unfurling from knobby knots. Delicate strands hung across slim branches like lace curtains screening a lady's parlor. On the large branches, the moss hung as heavy as drapes or quilts on a clothesline. It caped stalks like shawls on a coat rack. Atop boulders and rocks it looked like toupees. It toweled trees and stumps and logs.

Ferns too grew everywhere. Some clusters were waist-high; others were squat and drooped their long fronds a good three feet. Andy-in-Wonderland saw cattails, vines slithering along the ground, dark ivies and light ivies, lichen, reeds, and toadstools large as pies.

Walking was easy, our steps cushioned by pine needles, leaves, and spongy twigs. The softness only added to the Hoh's strange upholstered feel. At intervals the mossy woods gave way to grassy clearings filled with purple and yellow wildflowers emitting a sour smell. The mountain views were impressive, the rock zigzagging above the tree line. Jeanette scanned the sky with her binoculars hoping to spot a bald eagle.

We returned from the hike at once tired and invigorated. After supper, we sat with our cocoa at the picnic table. Figuring Jeanette was entitled to some of my personal history, I gave her a short bio, omitting the Huntington's. The years at Jackie's were summarized in a single sentence: I had done a lot of things I wasn't proud of. But she got a little of Lish and Laurie plus the Roy Trauma Drama and my sessions with Dr. Wilder and running into Roy in Kansas City. She sat silent throughout but commented at the end that she wouldn't have been comfortable with Phil's therapist riling him the way Dr. Wilder had riled me, "even if it was the right thing to do."

"Desperate minds call for desperate measures," I said.

"And as much as I love Phil, I can't imagine loving a daughter less."

The woods had grown dark; the trees had merged together into a formless black cloak, allowing in only a patch of night sky. Lanterns and angled flashlight beams moved along the paths. The campfire flames danced.

"My mother just got dealt a lousy hand," I said. "And had no earthly clue how to play it."

The first beach we stopped at on the way home had too many people. The map in one guidebook showed a stretch farther south off the main road, and Jeanette insisted on taking over the driving so I could enjoy the views. When we got stuck crawling behind an RV, I grabbed her marine animal book.

"Hey, where do folks get off saying Nature intended *females* to do all the child rearing? Listen to this." I read out loud, "'The gafftopsail catfish father incubates the eggs in his mouth for six to eight weeks. When the eggs hatch, the babies swim into the water, but the father does not leave them. Lingering nearby, he allows the young to return to the safety of his mouth if they feel threatened.'" I closed the book. "Had to be a guy who named it the *gaff*topsail, figuring any species where the male has childcare duties is an evolutionary gaffe. A woman would've named it the about-time catfish."

Jeanette slowed at a dirt turnoff and pointed. "Is that it?" A broken sign with an arrow said *Ocean Vie*.

"Not sure. This might take us up along the bluff."

"Let's find out."

We drove past a washed-out wooden shed and up to a dirt parking lot. Jeanette brought the car to rest beside a log, and we got out. The place was deserted. Gulls called to one another overhead.

We climbed a small knoll to a promontory with a wooden railing at the cliff's edge. The drop had to be a good hundred feet. To our left, the cliff fell away and curved out again, forming a small cove. To our right the ground sloped down towards a beach. A row of houses with broad windows facing west sat back from the beach where the land rose.

I walked along the bluff in the direction of the beach and could see in front of the nearest house a path leading to a dock. Two rowboats and a small yacht with a cabin bobbed in the water.

Jeanette joined me and peered through her binoculars. "I wonder if it's the Coast Guard. Can't read the insignia."

We returned to the promontory. In the distance, the ocean was covered in fog. Now I noticed slab-like rocks standing upright by the cove's entrance. "Looks like a fish cemetery," I said.

"We always called them sea stacks. The water eroded the sandstone. I think what's left is basalt."

"Hey, otters." A half-dozen shiny, rotund creatures—some dark, some gray—lay on boulders along the cove's interior. One rolled itself into the water, making a splash.

"Those are harbor seals."

The wind picked up, and Jeanette made several attempts to hold the bangs out of her face before saying she was going to the car to get her hat. I offered her my Mariners cap, and she pulled it down over her bangs, pushing them to the side.

Shrill shrieks—non-avian—pierced the air behind us. A thousand no-necks tumbled out of a minivan and ran to the railing, jumping and screaming. Scowling, Jeanette gestured with her hand—the seals had slipped into the water and were swimming out past the sea stacks. A minute later the adults herded the kids back in the van and drove off.

Hoping there might be a way to get inside the cove, we took a switchback down on the beach side of the bluff. At the bottom, a line of boulders fringed the cliff all the way to its westernmost edge. Piles of smaller rocks—but still good-sized—jutted out midway to form a jetty protecting the dock. We stepped along carefully on the wet surfaces past the jetty. At the end, I could see the boulders continued along the cliff's outer rim almost to the sea stacks. I kept going.

Our gamble paid off in spades, hearts, diamonds, and clubs: the boulders formed decent stepping stones all the way to the cove's innermost curve. Making it onto the beach, I paraded back and forth as exultant as any explorer discovering a hidden paradise, though old charcoal bits in a makeshift pit said Kilroy had been there. Jeanette too surveyed our solitary domain with pleasure. The sea stacks protected us from the full brunt of the winds and tide but were narrow enough to allow a good view of the western horizon. And the sun began smiting the fog.

For close to an hour, we poked around on our little crescent of sand, finding mussels, snails, coral-colored cockles, driftwood, colored stones, and all sorts of seaweed. Jeanette identified shiner perch, gunnels, and a bunch of birds: cormorants, puffins, terns, and sandpipers. I was sure some of the imprints in the cliff were fossils.

"Hurry!" She was standing close to the cove's entrance, peering through the binoculars out at the ocean, waving impatiently with her free hand.

I made my way over and stood where the boulder sloped up, so our shoulders were even. Sunlight reflected off the waves in tiny bits as if off shattered glass. Forming a visor with my hand, I squinted. In the distance, a gray mass began to emerge. The prow of a ship? A rising sub? "What is it?" I asked. In answer, she handed me the binoculars. "Holy moly. What *are* they?"

"Gray whales."

Some dove below the surface, their tails flying upward; some spouted like geysers. But others moved solemnly and steadily, the ocean no more substantial than air. Though their heads and tails curved downward, giving their backs a broad-arch shape, the impression was of blocks. It was a majestic procession, regal and dignified. Another and another and another and another.

"Must be fifteen, twenty," I said.

"Some flotillas are in the hundreds, though this is really late for a migration. Boy, he's going to be jealous."

"Bring him next summer. His crazy mutt will bark himself hoarse."

For the remainder of the ride along the coast we talked only of the whales. When we hit Queets and the Quinault Reservation, the topic somehow switched to if-*I*-ran-the-zoo, the zoo being the diner. Jeanette said she would offer more local seafood—fresh, not frozen—and salads made entirely from local produce. I got into catchy names, with brilliant suggestions like *J and A's Fillets*, *No Finer Diner*, *The Queasy Spoon*, and *Itchless Crabs*.

Chapter 69

DEFYING THE ODDS, Griffey returned to the lineup. Not only that, he was swinging the bat and hitting home runs. By September the little team that couldn't was showing it could. The mere *possibility* of the Mariners playing in the postseason infected every Washingtonian with acute baseballitis. The State's unofficial mottos became *Refuse to Lose* and *You Gotta Believe*.

We had just won another game, so when I brought over a large pizza, taking advantage of a coupon deal, I expected them to be in a great mood. But Phil sat at the dining room table glowering at an open textbook. On her way back to the kitchen, Jeanette said, "I'm finishing the salad, but we can't eat until Phil is done studying for his test. He's just wasting time."

"Hey, you gotta study. You want to go to college, don't you?"

"No."

"Of course you do. You've got to learn—"

Jeanette strode in briskly. "You need to study, and that's the end of it. Andy, why don't you visit with me in the kitchen so he can concentrate."

"I can concentrate with her here. It's just stupid memorizing." Phil pushed the book to the center of the table. A map of Europe and the Middle East spread across both pages.

"What do you have to memorize?" I asked, sitting opposite.
"I'll quiz you."

"The capitals."

"What's the capital of Italy?"

"That's easy, Rome. It's the ones here."

I turned the text 180 and shielded it with my hands. "Okay, what's the capital of Jordan?"

"I don't know."

"What's Michael Jordan?"

"A basketball player."

"A woman basketball player?"

"No."

"Then what?"

He looked at me like I was nuts. "A man," he mumbled.

"That's right. Amman, Jordan." I removed my hands and briefly turned the book so he could read where I pointed. "It's got two Ms."

"A-man, Jordan," Phil said. "Do the others." Jeanette hovered like a cop unsure if something fishy was going down.

"You know about conjugating verbs?" I said. "I run, you run, they run? I-ran, they-ran. Only it's spelled and pronounced differently. Tay-ran."

Again he looked to where I pointed on the map. He mouthed to himself *Iran* and *Tehran*.

"Now if your mom will leave, I'll teach you Syria." Still distrustful, Jeanette sidled into the kitchen. I whispered, "Syria is three bad words in a row: damn, ass, cuss. Damascus."

He looked at the map and, loud enough for the Babylonians to hear, hollered, "Damn, ass, cuss. Damn, ass, cuss."

"Phil!" Jeanette shouted.

"It's the capital of Syria," he shouted back.

"Hey, just be sure to spell it right."

When the Mariners became Western Division champions for the first time in history, Aberdeen went completely nuts, so Seattle must've been in rubber-room mode. Everywhere you looked was a Mariners bumper sticker, baseball cap, or jersey. But we were up against the Yankees in the first round of play-offs and promptly lost the first two games. The Division Series was three-out-of-five, so we would be eliminated if we lost one more. At least the remaining game or games would be played in the Kingdome, so we wouldn't lose in front of the jeering crowds at Yankee Stadium.

I was glad Ross had scheduled me for both lunch *and* supper during Game three and the possible Game four—who really wanted to watch the agony? Jeanette was also on during Game three. By the coffee machine, she whispered that Debby had called, and if Seattle won both games and tied the Division Series at two games apiece, she and Fran were throwing a bash for winner-take-all Game five. "The two men with the boy Phil's age are invited."

I gnawed my cheek while cleaning the decaf filter. "Wouldn't your introducing him to a bunch of gays and lesbians suggest you think you're a lesbian, and wouldn't that send the message you're looking for another relationship?"

Jeanette gnawed *her* cheek. "But he feels a little freakish because he was so fond of her. It would help if he knew another boy who cared about gay people and accepted homosexuality. And he knows we've been to Debby and Fran's house and go out to dinner with them."

"It will be moot anyway—the Yankees will slaughter us today or tomorrow."

Once the game started, every time a side was retired, Willie emerged from the kitchen to announce the score. I imagined the same scene playing out across the state, everybody everywhere tuned to a radio or TV. Surgeons probably had TVs wheeled into their operating rooms so they could watch while removing gallbladders. No doubt cops and the state patrol had turned off dispatch and were listening. I could use my break to rob a bank.

When the bottom of the eighth ended, the Mariners were ahead, so how could I keep from hoping? Cleaning the countertop, I practically scrubbed off the formica.

In the top of the ninth, Willie shouted through the ledge each Yankee out.

"One more to go," I told the lady in six, who was dressed more for a French restaurant than for Ross's.

"I would like a cup of coffee," she said.

"No problema."

As I headed behind the counter, Willie shouted that we'd won. Jeanette came over and high-fived me.

"Hey, we didn't get swept," I said. "Tomorrow we can lose with dignity."

"Refuse to lose!" she scolded.

"Excuse me, but I asked for coffee."

"Oops, sorry. Got caught up in the excitement."

Six's frown told me she hadn't. Okay, not everybody was into baseball. I poured a cup and returned to her table wearing the most apologetic expression I could muster under the circumstances. Setting down both cup and saucer, I squeaked, "Sorry about the delay. No charge for the coffee."

She looked down at the cup and then up at me. The frown etched deeper. Shoot, what else did I forget? The sugar and substitutes were in the bowl, and I had filled the cream pitchers five minutes ago. She slowly enunciated each word like I was a complete imbecile. "The. Saucer. Is. Full. Of. Coffee."

Sure enough, the cup seemed to float in a dark moat. "Jeez, I'm sorry. Guess the excitement was more than I realized."

Holding the saucer in one hand, the cup in the other directly beneath it, I made my way back behind the counter and deposited them in the sink. I hurried to the register, where Jeanette was refilling toothpicks.

"Hey, cover for me a couple of minutes—I need to use the can. Six needs a fresh cup of coffee. Be sure to tell her no charge." I gave Jeanette my order pad and split down the hall.

The air in the alley was cold. I held both arms straight in front of me. They seemed to stay still, two parallel limbs with mirror-image fingers, hands, and wrists. No shaking. Besides, didn't the literature talk about arms *flailing* or *jerking*? Not trembling. Grandma Margaret had *tossed* the glass, not spilled it.

I kicked at a pile of leaves. But wasn't *trembling* the word Edward had used, or *shaking*? Maybe Dean had had the DTs along with the Huntington's. Dr. Robbins had warned against this—assuming every odd movement was a signpost. *Was* sloshing a little bit of coffee into a saucer a signpost? No. Anybody could do it, especially in the excitement of the play-offs. It wasn't as if I had dropped the cup or tossed—*flailed*—it. At worst, I wasn't paying attention. Even Jeanette must have sloshed drinks now and then. Shit, Andy, don't make a federal case out of it. I strolled up and down the alley till I was able to shake the anxiety.

Booth six had been cleaned and reset. Jeanette was ferrying dishes to her tables. "She didn't leave you anything."

"Was probably a Yankees fan."

"Phil says I *have* to get tickets to the World Series."

"Who says we're *going* to the World Series? I wouldn't be chilling the champagne just yet, if I were you. The Yankees have two more chances to clean our clock, and if they don't, the winner of Cleveland and Boston can."

Jeanette threw me a smile. "You gotta believe!"

The cook on Saturday didn't keep us up-to-date in Game four the way Willie had in Game three, so I ducked into the kitchen now and again and played messenger. It was a batter's game, especially Edgar's bat, and we won 11 to 8. Now I *did* believe: I believed in the designated-hitter rule.

Back in my apartment, I did some Charleston and cha-cha and hitchhike and twist. How could I have Huntington's and still do these steps at the ripe old age of forty-three? I grabbed a soda from the fridge and popped the tab. Every muscle, large and small, moved the way I intended it to. My large-motor coordination was fine, and my fine-motor coordination was fine. Forgive me, God, for changing my mantra. Refuse to lose, Lord, refuse to lose!

Chapter 70

DEBBY AND FRAN'S party began an hour before the first pitch. Fran answered the door, and faster than you could shout "safe!" I saw they had invited all of Aberdeen, Hoquiam, Cosmopolis, and Ocean Shores.

"Hey, I'm leaving if there's any Yankees fans here."

"They wouldn't *want* to be here."

She took my bag of chips and sodas and led me into the dining room. It turned out they had invited a bunch of folks from their jobs as well as their gay friends. I couldn't tell who was gay and who was straight; distinguishing male from female was taxing enough, and I might've been wrong on some of those. But as long as a person rooted for the Mariners, I wasn't prejudiced. A few faces were familiar from the parade, and we nodded if our glances met. Cheryl was talking intently to a taller version of Sally. The smell of beer was everywhere.

Fran said I had my choice of three TVs, one downstairs in the rec room and one each in the living and dining rooms. The dining room table had been moved against a wall and smothered in food platters.

Phil bobbed beside me. "What took you so long?" Jeanette floated in his wake holding a glass of white wine. They both wore their new navy blue Mariners caps, making the family resemblance all the more obvious.

"Where's Peter?" she asked him.

"Bathroom."

I said it was incredible how many people they knew in the area, and Jeanette said that one of the departments at Debby's law firm was having a retreat at Westport this weekend, so they all came. A little wistfully, she added, "It's nice they aren't afraid to mix friends and co-workers."

No doubt she was comparing them to the Nazarenes, who were a bit more homogeneous, if less homosexual. Though this crowd was pretty white. One barrier at a time, Lord?

Debby tapped my shoulder. "Don't turn around, but Samantha asked me to invite you and her over for dinner some evening. To fix you up, essentially."

"I'm beyond fixing."

"Who's Samantha?" Jeanette whispered.

"Lavender shirt," Debby said. "She was at the parade."

Jeanette scanned the room. "I remember her. Pretty."

"She's very interesting. Librarian by day and translates Greek poems by night."

"Well, like I said," I told Debby, "I'm not looking for a relationship now and don't plan to be for another four, five years."

Debby smiled at us like you would at impish children. "When you two *do* go back into circulation, let me know." After she glided off, Jeanette looked about to speak, but somebody yelled the game was starting.

Having two TV sets to watch upstairs let me pace between them. I had mumbled *Just today, Lord* so many times, She must have turned off the phone. But I wasn't alone in being miserable; nobody was happy. Actually, the Fates were, leaving the teams tied at the bottom of the ninth. The tenth was like being awake for gallbladder surgery. And neither side scored. How long would the torture continue?

Not long, evidently: the Yankees scored a run in the top of the eleventh. As the Mariners headed for the dugout, I said, "Hey, at least we put up a fight."

"It's not over," Jeanette said cheerfully. "We can score too."

"And pigs can fly."

"If baseball was that predictable, there wouldn't be any fun to it."

"You call this fun?"

"Joey's on," Peter shouted.

Peter was farther along into puberty, with a real Adam's apple. Yet remembering how frail Phil's shoulders had been when he had retched in the bathroom and comparing that to now, I could see he would be following his new friend in pretty short order.

"Steal," somebody yelled at the screen.

"No, don't," somebody else yelled.

"Junior's up!"

The room went silent. Griffey could homer or just as easily hit into a double play. A homer would win the game; a double play would come close to losing it.

He didn't do either. Junior got a single, and speedy Joey made it to third. I grabbed a cold soda.

Edgar positioned himself in the batter's box. Yesterday was Edgar's good day, and even with a good batting average, the odds said today would be a bad.

But it wasn't. He lined one past third. In a picosecond, Joey scored, tying the game! Who was up next?

No, wait—holy shit—here comes Griffey pedaling around the bases like a goddamn Keystone Kop. He raced along the third base line and scored too. The room erupted. We won, we *won*! We won the Division Series! The Mariners' dugout emptied, a zillion uniformed guys piling on top of poor Junior and Edgar. The Kingdome roared. We roared too. Shouting, laughing, high-fiving one another, everybody at Fran and Debby's was in motion. Some woman did a little jig; folks clinked glasses and toasted who-knew-what, since you couldn't hear anything in all the mayhem and bedlam. A cork popped, followed by Debby yelling, "Champagne!" Another cork popped and another.

With folks swarming to the table, I was able to get close to the TV. A reporter outside the stadium was talking into his mike, but everything he said was drowned out at our end, maybe at his too. Young guys behind him made V signs and idiotic faces at the camera. Young, old, fat, thin, male, female, white, black, Asian, shades of tan, everybody leaving the Kingdome grinned ear to ear. Maybe the Yankees fans had located an underground exit. A young woman held up a piece of cardboard with the scrawl *Marry me, Edgar.*

The chairs in front of the set were moved, and Phil and Peter began a war dance, shouting, "We won, we won." In the general celebratory chaos, they fit right in.

My eyes scanned the room for Jeanette. There she was, standing in a doorway at the quiet end, watching Phil. Her right shoulder leaned against the jamb, her weight mostly on her right leg; the left bent slightly, the knee cozying up to its partner. Her cap was pushed back a little, and her bangs lay across her forehead. The relaxed smile and casual angle of her body stoked a memory from the past, but I couldn't remember of whom or where or when. An amalgam of people, probably. The smile—far merrier than Mona Lisa's—I had seen on Laurie, on Stacy when she was with Tommy, on many women on many occasions. Taller than me by a few inches, with fuller hips and breasts, more mature by a couple of decades, experienced in both motherhood and widowhood, Jeanette had never radiated *youth*. Modesty, artlessness, yes. Enthusiasm? In a subdued way. But never youth. Yet now, leaning against the jamb, her cheeks flushed from wine, amused by her son's antics, she looked downright girlish.

Chapter 71

THE EUPHORIA OF winning the first round of play-offs lasted far longer than it had any right to. Longer than it took Cleveland to mop us up in the pennant battle and go on to the World Series. We were so isolated in the top left-hand corner of the contiguous continental U.S. of A. that nobody got word to us to quit being happy. We relived that Game five against the Yankees like Miss Havisham relived the wedding rehearsal, only enjoying ourselves a whole lot more.

October and early November passed without a spilled-coffee or spilled-anything episode, though Jeanette came into the diner one Friday looking like the sky had spilled half an ocean on her. "I walked from the mechanic's," she said, taking off her coat. "The muffler was dragging. Luckily, he's open Saturday and says he'll have it ready."

"I can give you a ride to pick it up."

She put on her apron. "Could you give us a ride to the library instead? Phil put off writing his Civil War report, and all the books at school are checked out. It's two blocks from the shop."

Saturday was gloomy, the low dark clouds rushing across the sky like they had a train to catch. Watching Phil climb into the backseat, I could have sworn he'd sprouted ten new hairs over his lip. I gave a cheery hello, Jeanette gave a we-appreciate-your-doing-this, and Phil grunted. Their own civil war erupted.

"Is this how you thank someone for doing you a favor?" she asked.

He gave a double grunt.

"Hey, it's an ugly day, and he's stuck writing a paper. That wouldn't exactly make *me* chipper."

"But on your day off, you're going to the trouble—"

"It's okay, I've been meaning to get a library card anyway."

"Thanks," Phil mumbled.

When we got there, he followed some gray-haired lady to the history stacks. Jeanette and I filled out forms for library cards, and she said I didn't have to wait around, but I pointed out it was pouring.

We wandered to a table with a globe, and I lightly spun it west to east. If anybody were ruing the breakup of the Soviet Union, it had to be the kids taking geography tests.

"Andy?" The woman in lavender—though no longer in lavender—from Debby and Fran's bounced towards us, practically singing, "I'm Samantha." I had no choice but to shake the extended hand. She smiled almost as energetically at Jeanette and offered her the hand too. "I'm sorry, I forget your name."

"Jeanette."

"That's right. What brings you here?"

I gestured at Phil, who on cue had emerged from the stacks with a couple of heavy books and an even heavier scowl.

"Would you like to check those out? I can help you." Samantha bounced off to the counter, and Phil followed. I spun the globe. *Myanmar,* neé Burma. On the road to Mandalay.

"Why don't you go out with her?" Jeanette asked. "She seems nice."

"Not up for a relationship."

After watching me put the earth through a few more rotations, she said, "It can't be easy staying off alcohol. Someone caring for you could make it easier."

"Like I said, not up for a relationship. Even if I was—"

"You make it sound like a *bad* thing instead of a comfort."

"Look who's talking!" I swatted Corsica.

"Only because of Phil."

"Whatever the reason. A person might come along you'd fall head over heels for at a different time and place, but right now your mind is elsewhere."

She turned towards the windows. "I suppose."

"You *suppose*? If you *have* fallen for somebody, shouldn't you let the lucky guy know? He might be more than willing to wait if he knows how you feel."

"Why do you assume—" She looked over at the counter. I looked too. Phil had his back to us and was writing. "You can't ask someone to wait five years."

"Isn't that their decision?"

"Roger and I didn't ask each other to wait even two. Our feelings just didn't change. But they could have."

No more Southern Rhodesia. Had there ever been a *Northern*? Eastern or Western? What about a Lower Volta?

Phil headed towards us, the books tucked under one arm.

"We work well together," Jeanette murmured. "I hope at least *that* doesn't change."

"Nothing will change."

Willie directed me to a nearby lumberyard, and I had them saw some nice English oak into two-foot pieces. I set up a couple of horses near my living room window and did the remaining sawing myself. Now I began the loving task of sanding what would become the exterior sides of my cubbyhole cabinet.

Jeanette and Phil went down to Roger's parents for Thanksgiving, and I accepted an invitation to join Debby and Fran and a cast of thousands for turkey dinner. At the last minute, I faked a cold and treated myself to a quiet day at home sanding, my sole obligation feeding and walking Bardey.

Again I wandered ghost-like through the silent rooms. Phil's looked as tidy as ever. Bardey nosed insistently under the bed, so I prodded him away and reached beneath the frame. What a haul— three pizza crusts and a stack of magazines. So Phil snuck food into his room! Whoa, *these* magazines wouldn't supply cutouts for his walls. Like *Playboy* but with fewer articles. I pushed them back under the bed.

As I disposed of the crusts in the kitchen, my mind conjured up Phil at sixteen, seventeen. I pictured an outdoor high school graduation ceremony like mine in Brackton: hundreds of parents in nice clothes sitting on folding chairs, "Pomp and Circumstance" booming from the band, the students walking down the side aisle to the stage. The black gown would sway from his shoulders, and when he went up the stairs and walked across the stage to take his diploma, Jeanette would spring from her seat to snap a photo. She would have to own a new camera by then. I knocked the kitchen overhead and went out.

December was the cruelest month. Jeanette phoned to say Bardey had gotten hit by a truck. It didn't kill him, which might have been a shame because his vertebrae were so messed up, they had to put him to sleep. Phil wasn't taking it well, but who was?

Roger's parents were arriving Christmas Eve, so I brought over Chinese take-out the evening before for our own little gift exchange.

A small fir where one of the recliners had been was decorated with ornaments and lights. The mantel held a miniature crèche scene and red candles in the candlesticks. I added my little stack of wrapped packages to the ones under the tree. The room still felt sad. You kept expecting the crazy mutt to saunter in.

While we ate, I gave Jeanette and Phil the latest off-season news: which Mariners Seattle was holding onto for sure, which might or would leave, and any rumored trades. "And besides those under the tree, I got one more present for you," I told Phil, "but I can't buy it till March, probably. Tickets to a game."

He finally perked up. "At the Kingdome?"

"Yep. You'll have to tell me which team you want to see us demolish."

After supper, we unwrapped the presents. Jeanette gave me a spanking new drill set, and I gave her a camera shop gift certificate. I had found a really nice glove for Phil, along with a Mariners T-shirt with *Griffey* on the back, a fake ice cube with a fly in it, and plastic vomit. The second box for me, with the tag *To Andy, From Phil and Jeanette* in her handwriting, contained a Mariners keychain. I was always fishing for my keys.

I marked the holidays in only one other way—shooting off a card to Mr. Grunner in Hastings-on-Hudson, asking for Stacy's address and phone number and enclosing my own. Maybe he had moved or even passed away, but hey, nothing ventured, nothing gained.

With the New Year, my new mantra became "one board at a time." I went through sandpaper the way I used to go through cigarettes. The smell of sawdust permeated the apartment no matter how often I vacuumed, but I wasn't complaining.

In February Mathilde's lawyer sent a check for my share of the inheritance. I was a nervous wreck till I got it safely to the bank.

Then I called Debby and asked if I could hire her to make my will. Yes, she would draft it, she said, but no, I couldn't pay her—she would do it for free. At least it will be simple, I said—I was leaving everything to Jeanette.

She laughed. "We knew you were a couple!"

"Actually, we're not. She's just the person I feel closest to. And I don't want my half brother to get a dime." In fact, I explained, it was our *not* being a couple that made me want to keep the will secret from Jeanette. "The idea of being my beneficiary might bother her." Debby was cool and said she had to keep what I told her confidential anyway.

The draft will she sent me was no one- or two-page jobbie but an encyclopedia, practically; it even had an *Addendum*. The cover letter instructed me to fill in the blanks and call with any questions.

A lot of the heft, it turned out, was from phrases like *In the event that* and *Provided, however* and *Notwithstanding any of the foregoing* and *Except as set forth in paragraph such and such above in this Document*. I filled in Jeanette's name as beneficiary, and where it asked who would get my *Estate* if she *preceded* me in death, I wrote in Phil's. You would think that would have put an end to it, but on the next page it wanted to know who should get my stuff if *both* of them preceded me in death. How long would this go on—through beneficiaries C, D, E, and F all the way to Z? Did Zeno ever have to write a will? I put that if Jeanette and Phil preceded me, the *Estate* should be split evenly among Anthony Junior and his brothers. I phoned Debby with my questions, and she said I needed a trustee for Phil since he was a minor. I used some cousin of Roger's they liked.

Though she wouldn't take any money, Debby did allow me to treat her and Fran to dinner the next time the four of us went out. Phil was at a birthday party that night, and when I drove Jeanette home, she asked me to go by way of the park to pick him up.

After I turned off the engine, she gazed for a moment at the fields, murmuring, "He hasn't been back here since Bardey."

"When are you getting the new puppy?"

"Not until after spring break, when we return from Florida."

She had barely gone inside the birthday boy's house when she was out again—alone. "Can you hurry?" she said, slamming the car door. "They went outside to throw glow-in-the-dark frisbees, and someone walked by with a dog that looked like Bardey, and Phil left suddenly. They just *guessed* he went home."

"Does he have a key?"

"Yes."

I peeled away from the curb.

Except for the porch light, her house was dark. Jeanette was inside in a flash, and I wasn't far behind. The lamp by the kitchen shed little glow into the dining room/living-room area—maybe one of the bulbs had burned out. Jeanette raced towards the hall, reaching for the living room overhead switch, missing it, her body not stopping. I hit the switch and followed. The hall was dark, but a gold thread ran under Phil's closed door. Phew—he'd made it home. I waited while she knocked, first softly, then harder. She rotated the knob and pushed the door open. I was about to return to the living room when her face, in the full light of his bedroom, gaped in horror.

I ran. Why wasn't she rushing in, rushing to save him? Was it too late? I must have shouted, because she moved aside and said, "He's not here."

A cyclone had hit. Almost nothing remained on the walls, not the posters, the pictures, the construction-paper background. Just fragments: Pelé's shin and shoe, a giraffe head, a dark-lettered *to Lose!* The floor was a mass of shredded paper, hundreds of colored scraps, plus clothes, toy iguanas, notebooks, everything. The desktop and bookcase were bare. Darth Iguana had been reduced to two thin stripes.

My stupefaction lasted only a second; I charged in and swung open the closet door further. It was a mess too, but a personless mess. I stepped back into the paper scraps and toys, trying not to break the plastic iguanas or crush the stuffed one from his grandparents. Only the family and Bardey wall photos had been left untouched. The framed picture and dog collar lay on the pillow.

"Phil," Jeanette shrieked, running down the hall.

I ran too, to her room, flicking on the light, checking the closet, under the bed. As I came out, she was going into the guest room. I took the kitchen. The back-door bolt was undone. I ran over and hit the switch to the outside bulb. It illuminated enough. "He's here," I hollered. "He's okay."

I went down the steps into the yard. Phil sat huddled over on a log under the tree, wearing a red-and-blue-striped rugby shirt, no jacket. He didn't look up as I approached. A few feet away, I stopped. The screen door squeaking made me turn; Jeanette's form was framed by the jamb. I turned back to Phil, who still stared at the ground. Leaves rustled. The breeze was cold. A yellow tennis ball lay by the fence.

I spoke quietly. "He was the friendliest, happiest dog that ever lived." The overgrown grass, the hedge, the vines ensnaring the fence were all reminders. "Remember the time he treed that squirrel and it leapt clear across—"

"He didn't see and kept barking." Phil's voice sounded congested.

"All that hair in his face," I said.

"But sometimes he could smell like a bloodhound."

"He could smell, all right. I remember how he smelled when he came out of the creek."

Phil's head rotated slightly my direction. "He shook himself out all over you."

"Like I can forget?"

He turned away. The undersides of the tree's lower branches caught some of the back-steps light, but the tops merged into darkness. Though I knew buds had formed, I couldn't see them. For a few moments, the air was still. Then the breeze blew again and stopped again. Phil wiped a cheek with the back of one wrist and made the same motion with the other. Stepping closer, I squeezed his shoulder briefly, saying, "He really was the nicest darn dog I ever knew."

I started back towards the house, slowly plodding through the long grass, watching Jeanette through the screen door. She was scooping coffee from the can into the filter, her movements short and brisk. Would she want to go outside once I came in? I could finish putting on the pot.

Abruptly I was arrested. Arms came from behind, one on each side, and clasped me and pinned my own arms to my ribs. A cheek pressed hard between my shoulder blades. Equally abruptly, I was released. Phil loped past and went up the back steps and into the kitchen. The screen door banged.

Nothing will change, I'd said. Everything had.

Chapter 72

MY TABLES DIDN'T want anything. I gathered all the counter place settings and condiments and stored them beside the pie rack. Starting at the end closest to the kitchen, I began scrubbing the counter down, back and forth, back and forth.

So much for deliberations, debates, vows, for analyzing best-case scenarios and worst-case scenarios, for weighing odds. So much for resolutions, for living one day at a time, keeping my shoulder to the wheel and eyes on the road and nose to the grindstone, patiently working and saving and organizing the hours. My great epiphany—that each day was a gift to be savored—was evil temptation. Or if not evil, then self-deluded temptation. I needed to know what the future held. I would climb the tree of knowledge and wrest the apple from the serpent's mouth. I would learn if I had the gene.

"Check, please."

"Here you go. More coffee?"

"No, thanks."

I went back to the counter and began arranging the silverware. But if things panned out, couldn't this be the *best* of all possible worlds? Of the four possibilities I had written in the book during my trip west, why couldn't the first be true: I would learn the results of the gene test and not have the mutation? Murphy's Law wasn't the only law in the universe, any more than Murphy's Bed the only bed. Maybe it was time for *un*happiness to get shut up into a wall.

The receptionist at the first neurology doctor I phoned said she didn't know if he did Huntington's disease counseling but would I please hold. My shirt was a wet rag by the time she got back on. I should call some hospital in Seattle, she said. She read off the number.

Jeez, it was hard enough going through this rigmarole without having to schlep a hundred miles. Wait a sec—maybe that wasn't a bad idea. Aberdeen's doctors' offices might be like St. Joe's, confidentiality-wise. The nurses or receptionists could belong to the Flock of the Nazarenes, or know Willie, and what was to stop gossip about the skinny patient with the really light hair?

I phoned the Seattle hospital and got transferred to Neurology. The receptionist gave me a three o'clock appointment the following Thursday with Leah Somebody. I asked Ross for the day off, saying I had a cousin passing through.

Not wanting to drive both ways, and the bus schedules stinking, I decided to pull a Zeno and drive halfway. In Olympia I would catch a bus. Even then, my options stank; I could arrive in Seattle either a zillion hours early or barely on time. My lobes unanimously voted for the latter, later option. Who wanted to fret anxiously in a city with as many real bars as espresso? Doctors were never ready to see you anyway. Sure hoped Monroe hadn't moved out here.

Thursday took forever to arrive. At least the drive to Olympia, past the woops nuclear reactors, was simple enough. So was catching the bus to Seattle. Once there, however, the local bus to the hospital got stuck in traffic.

It was going on 3:45 when I finally found the Neurology clinic. The receptionist, an older lady, didn't look up right away; the phone was ringing off the hook. "Can you hold," she told the millionth caller and looked at me apologetically. I gave my name.

"I'm *so* sorry," she said. "Leah thought you weren't coming and left for the day."

I tried to sound whiny, not annoyed. "The bus got stuck in traffic. I came all the way from Aberdeen."

"Oh my, from Aberdeen."

"Is there somebody else I could talk to? Even if I only got a few questions answered, the whole trip wouldn't be a waste."

"Have you been seen here before? No? Well, fill these out, and I'll see if someone can squeeze you in. Dan can't, but if one of the doctors has a few minutes." She punched a button and picked up the receiver. "Thank you for holding."

Under *Reason for your visit*, I wrote *to find out the results of my genetics test for Huntington's*. When I handed back the forms, the lady said, "But if this is your first visit, you haven't *had* the test."

"I had genetics counseling at St. Joseph's Hospital, in Brackton, New Jersey, and had the test done, the sample taken. But I moved out to Aberdeen before they got the results. They said they would send them here."

"When did they send them?"

"They haven't, not yet, but I was told somebody here could ask for them to be sent. That's why I made the appointment."

"I'm still waiting to hear if someone can see you."

The phone continued to ring like crazy, which would have driven *me* crazy, but not everybody was cut out for restaurant work either. I moseyed over to the rack of brochures and took the one saying *Huntington's Disease (Chorea)*.

Like a lightning bolt, a young blond woman in satiny gold pants strode to the counter, hands in her bright white lab-coat pockets. Hanging up, the receptionist asked what was the matter.

Gold Pants exploded, "Did you see the article?"

"Yes. The picture came out lovely."

"Did you *read* it?"

"I haven't had a chance. The phones—"

"I spoke to that idiot for *half an hour.* Explained serotonin uptake, gave him *drawings.* Oh, what's the use. Basic research is boring." She snapped her fingers above her head. "I want a cure, presto! Otherwise, don't bother me."

Again the phone rang. Eyeing the receiver, the receptionist asked, "Do you need something?"

"No. Let me know when my 4:15 shows. *Another* reporter. This is the last time I agree to do PR." Her heels made a clicking sound down the tiled corridor.

The receptionist motioned to me after hanging up. "Dr. Williamson has a few minutes."

Dr. Williamson remained expressionless during my brief recap of Dean's diagnosis, Grandma Margaret's deterioration, and my sessions with Dr. Robbins, but he perked up once he realized I was just asking him to ask St. Joe's to send the lab results. "You will need to fill out a 'Consent to Release Medical Records' form," he said, "and set up a counseling appointment with Dan or Leah."

He ushered me back to the receptionist and had her give me the medical records form. When I was done filling it out, I asked if I could set up the next appointment. Figuring the fewer lies about my trips to Seattle, the better, I wanted one the week Jeanette and Phil would be in Orlando.

The receptionist put two more calls on hold, turned the calendar page, and again made her woeful face. "Dan and Leah don't have anything that week."

"What about there?" I pointed to the time slot beneath a large X.

"That's after the departmental seminar. Leah doesn't schedule appointments then because the seminar often runs late."

"I wouldn't mind waiting if it does. I put her through waiting for *me*. It's the only week I know for sure I can take a day off."

"All right, I'll put you down for Thursday at three, and if she doesn't want to have an appointment after the seminar, we'll call you. Oh, but that's what you had today. Would you be able to arrive on time, in case the seminar *doesn't* run late?"

"Yes, I'll take the earlier bus."

Again the phone rang, and she answered it and jotted on a message pad. Was she done with me? I lingered a moment to make sure. Had to be—she wasn't looking up. Oops, almost walked off with her pen.

"Are you from the paper?"

I turned to see Gold Pants staring accusingly. The dementia must have already begun, because I said, "Yes."

She led me down a corridor to her office and motioned for me to sit in a small upright chair, relaxing herself into the leather-padded swivel. Abruptly she raised herself and craned her neck to peer at the brochure in my lap. "Huntington's? I thought this was about SSRIs." Before I could answer, the phone rang. Shit—the real reporter had shown, and the jig was up. Would they kick me out, refuse to have me as a patient? Gold Pants reached over and punched a button harshly. The ringing stopped.

I said, "We're very interested in Huntington's too. Are you familiar with it?"

Her tone was icy. "Yes, but my time is not unlimited. Which do you want to talk about?"

"I guess Huntington's, because I know there's been some big discovery recently having to do with where the gene's located on the chromosome."

"The gene has been identified, yes—"

"That has to do with things repeating too many times?"

"Is that what you want to hear about? I don't want to discuss Huntington's genetics if all you're interested in is whether we have a cure."

"The thing is, I'll need both. We can't start the reader off with the technical. We *get* to that, we do want them to understand the basic genetics, but we have to draw them in gradually. So I need a short paragraph, just an introductory kind of thing, about cures on the horizon. Then, if you wouldn't mind describing the trinucleotides."

My mention of trinucleotides smoothed away her frown. "There are no cures," she said. "No real treatments, nothing significant. But with the discovery of the mutation, we can now study the gene at the molecular level." She paused to drink from a water bottle, watching me suspiciously. Was it because I wasn't taking notes like a real reporter?

"Now these CAG repeats," I said while she swallowed, "the number is significant, right? If a person has, say, more than forty repeats, then it's a pretty open-and-shut case they have the disease?"

"Forty-two, yes." She seemed placated and began rattling on about base pairs.

I scribbled gibberish on the blank page of the brochure till she took another water break, when I said, "I realize this is a crazy question, but our readers are always asking, so we like to, you know, throw them a bone when we can: do you think there could be an amazing breakthrough that could lead to a cure in, I don't know, three or four years? Like penicillin? And other antibiotics?"

"Unlikely. Finding a new antibiotic just requires finding a substance that poisons a foreign infectious agent without seriously harming the host. With genetic diseases like Huntington's, you need to interfere with the body's *own* processes, complex processes of protein formation."

"So a drug—"

"Even if we had a candidate," she said, "the entire process from a drug that shows promise *in vitro* to one that can be prescribed *in vivo* is a protracted one. Many, many years."

"You need trials with control groups, right?"

"Before the clinical trials you do toxicity screening. The clinical trials themselves require a minimum of three phases."

"Three," I said, writing *3*.

"Phase one establishes safety. Can people tolerate the drug? Are there unexpected side effects? These studies are not completed overnight."

I wrote *not overnight*.

"Phase two is to test for efficacy: is the drug *effective* in treating the disease? Usually you have to enroll a large number of subjects so differences in outcome between those getting the drug and those getting a placebo will be statistically significant. And preferably a sufficient number at different *stages* of the disease—some presymptomatic, some with early symptoms, some, advanced. Phase two may take *years* to complete."

I wrote *years*.

"Phase three typically takes even longer. You need *hundreds* of patients if not thousands. These are the randomized, double-blind trials that can last five, ten years."

The next time she paused to drink, I said, "What about something like insulin? Diabetes isn't an infection, right? Yet they came up with a cure—"

"Insulin-dependent diabetes, although *technically* an autoimmune disorder, is a simple deficiency problem. The immune system attacks and destroys the cells in the pancreas that produce insulin. Conceptually, treating diabetes with insulin is no more complicated than giving a vitamin pill for a vitamin deficiency. As I said, Huntington's involves a complex process of protein formation."

She continued on about DNA, but my ears stopped listening and my hand stopped writing. She had made her point. So much for betting on a cure. I would have to place all my money on the Normal Gene filly.

"Oh, my." Gold Pants glanced in mock horror at her watch, so I quickly rose and said thanks. As we stepped into the corridor, I pointed the opposite direction from the waiting room. "Can I get out that way?"

"Yes, I'll show you the elevators. I'm going there too."

We passed a bunch of door placards with *M.D.* after the names, then a *Daniel Mc*Somebody, *Leah* Somebody*ovich*, and folks named *Custodian Closet* and *Supplies*. Gold Pants decided on the stairs while I waited at the elevator bank.

Unbelievably, when I stepped outside the hospital, the sun was shining. The actual golden orb in the sky. Everybody in these parts beamed when that happened; you had to wonder if it were biologically possible *not* to. I joined in the grinning, despite the grim news about a cure. Maybe I was just relieved to get out before my cover was blown. Or buoyed by the simple fact that what had been hidden for so long was on its way to becoming known. I had set in motion the wheels and levers and gears that, in weeks' or months' time, would produce certainty. Theoretically, my CAGs could fall in that no-man's-land between the clearly healthy and clearly diseased, but I put *those* odds as small.

Mary from the Rogers Park poker crew had had the annoying habit of refusing to fold after a certain point in the game even if her hand was pure crap. If she stayed in past the second-to-last round of betting in seven-card stud, say, she would figure: why not stay in one more round? Even if everybody else showed four cards from a flush, she would toss those final nickels or dimes in the pot, telling us, "At least I'll know right away." The suspense would soon be over; knowledge was imminent. Her strategy royally screwed anybody bluffing.

Now, with the appointment card tucked in my back pocket, I understood her perspective. For despite my conscious mind being caught up in the details of daily living, my unconscious mind was always watching, waiting, worrying. Cheer up, Unconscious, maybe you'll know by summer.

Seattle's rush hour was in full swing, the sidewalks overrun with people. At the bottom of the hill, Elliott Bay sparkled. A ferry pulled away from the pier. Due west and in the distance, the Olympic Mountains formed a jagged phalanx, white on their peaks, a dusky blue below.

My gaze shifted inland, to a row of high-rises. If the lab report brought good news, which rooftop should I sing from? That one looked like it could use a better railing. I imagined the headline: ELATED TO BE DISEASE-FREE, WOMAN DIES IN FALL.

No, even if the news was good, there would be no singing from the rooftops. Not that I wouldn't be glad. But by the laws of probability, if I made it to the winner's circle, somebody else slogged off to the stables. I was no saint—hell, no. The bells tolling for strangers did *not* toll for me. Still, I would do my rejoicing quietly, privately. When the cure came, *then* I'd celebrate.

While the bus back to Olympia maneuvered its way to the interstate, I thought ahead to my next appointment. Should I plead with Leah to let me do the counseling solo? Argue like I had with Dr. Robbins? But I didn't want to appear emotional. I could run a personal in the paper: *Wanted: companion for visits to doctor. Must be discreet. No inmates.* What about Fran, Tough-gut Fran? Debby? Yes, Debby! She *had* to keep it a secret; she was my lawyer. And she would already be up in Seattle, so it wouldn't be as big a hassle.

I rested my head against the seat cushion, enjoying the rhythms of the highway. It amused me to realize I *wanted* Leah to insist on my bringing a companion. I *wanted* to tell somebody, to be justified in letting a friend in on the Huntington's.

Chapter 73

MY MAILBOX CONTAINED an honest-to-god letter, not just bills and advertising junk. *Mr. Alvin Grunner* and *Dobbs Ferry, N.Y.* were on the return label. The handwriting was squiggly. *I am living in a lovely apartment seven blocks from Pamela. Stacy and her family return from London in June.* He had sent her my address and phone number and now included hers, all zillion digits of the phone.

So Jerry had traded in tropical isles for London fog. What time was it now in the Bonnie Empire—could I call? And who was "her family"? Were there others besides Dylan and Whitman? Emily Dickinson Grunner-Silkman, Elizabeth Barrett Browning Grunner-Silkman? They would run out of room on their driver's licenses. Or maybe Jerry got to name some. Lucy Grunner-Silkman, Australopithecus Grunner-Silkman.

Friday evening I brought pizza over to Jeanette's as a bon voyage gift; they were leaving for Orlando Saturday morning. "By the way," I said, scooping a slice onto her plate, "I still have your key."

"Hold onto it. We may need you to walk the puppy the next time we go away." She smiled at Phil. "We get him in two weeks."

"Have a name picked out yet?"

"Pelé," Phil said. As he drank his milk, his Adam's apple bobbed—Adam's *pine*apple.

"Not Edgar?"

"You said we'd go to a game."

"Yes, when you get back, we'll take a look at the schedule."

When he went to the kitchen for a drink refill, I quickly whispered, "His voice drop an octave?"

Jeanette whispered back, "He asked a girl to the May Day dance."

Thursday morning I was on the road at a ridiculously early hour, taking no chances on being late to the hospital. Whatever hovered above—cirrus, cumulus, stratus—they sure were copious. Wordsworth obviously had never set foot in Western Washington. Our clouds were never lonely.

I arrived in Seattle with plenty of time to kill but headed directly to the hospital, being in no mood for the sights and sounds of the city. I strolled along the perimeter a few times and stopped at an espresso for a decaf. Somebody had left behind a newspaper, but I couldn't concentrate on the movie listings or even the comics. I did a few more circuits around the hospital and went inside and up to Neurology.

The waiting area was completely empty. The wall clock said 2:20. Forty more minutes. I told the receptionist that I wanted to check in now just in case Leah could see me early.

"She's at the departmental seminar. You can wait downstairs in the cafeteria if you want."

I moseyed to the elevator banks. What was the point of going down to the cafeteria, with my stomach in knots? This was the same set of elevators Gold Pants had escorted me to. I peered down the hall with the Neurology offices. Did one of them contain the lab report? It could be only a hundred, only fifty feet away—the information I sought, the information I had come all the way to Seattle and this hospital for. Within spitting distance, practically. Yet I would be returning to Aberdeen this evening without having seen it. Who knew when they would let me, how long they would make me wait?

Why should I have to? Why couldn't I see it now? It was *my* information, mine more than anybody else's. Of all the people on the planet, wasn't *I* the one with the most riding on it? And how many people had *already* seen it, already knew if I had the mutation? For starters, the lab folks who had run the test. The secretary who sent it to St. Joe's. Maybe whoever opened the mail there. Three or four people in Jersey might have known for a year. But what did they care? They went home every evening and relaxed, lingered over pot roast with family and friends, watched sitcoms, read a book, no doubt enjoyed a good night's sleep. *They* could take it easy—*their* lives weren't on hold. Like I had argued to Dr. Robbins, the data on my chromosomes belonged to *me*, was *my* information, so *I* had a right to it. Yet I was supposed to twiddle my thumbs for months till they—whoever *they* were—decided I was emotionally ready to learn it. Of all the crock of shit.

Bite the bullet, Jiminy said, *and wait. You have to.*

Maybe I do, Jiminy. And maybe I don't.

I read the placards one by one, hoping to see something like *File Room*. No luck. I knocked on Leah's door. No answer. I knocked louder. Still no answer. I pressed the handle, not really expecting it to give. It didn't. Some people walked past the intersection but didn't stop. It was your typical institutional lock.

I strolled back to the main corridor, took out my wallet, and examined the cards. The ATM looked the strongest. I returned to Leah's door. After a quick glance both directions, I slipped the card between the door and jamb at a spot even with the knob. The plastic met resistance. I placed my shoulder against the door panel and pressed while turning the knob. I kept on pressing with my shoulder and pushing the card harder, praying the plastic wouldn't break. *Click.*

The room was empty, the lights, off. I quickly stepped inside and closed the door. Would the people in the offices across the alley wonder about seeing somebody here besides Leah? How many rooms would I have time to rifle before the seminar ended? Or had it already ended? Leah could leave early to get ready for her three o'clock appointment.

Shelves took up an entire wall, but they were filled with books and what looked like journals. The only other furniture besides chairs was a desk with a computer. The computer was off. A plastic gizmo to the left held six or seven lime green file folders. I quickly thumbed through them. *Gabe, A.* Damn—all it contained was a xerox of the forms I had filled out my last visit. No, what was this? St. Joseph's letterhead, a grayish photocopy. *In the sealed envelope accompanying this letter are the laboratory results we received ... .* Nowhere did the letter say what the results were. Where was the fucking sealed envelope?

I opened the desk drawers. The top contained little pink and yellow note pads, boxes of pens, Scotch tape, paper clips. The middle had files. *Privacy Policy, Requisition*—just general crap. The bottom held a pair of running shoes, a package of nylon stockings, and a red collapsible umbrella. The desk clock said 2:28.

The hall was still people-less. I knocked on Dan's door. No answer. Without bothering to knock a second time, I shimmed my way in.

This room was a lot larger, seemed designed for visitors. Dan was tidy—no papers, books, or soda cans littered the radiator top, the windowsill, or floor. No journals were piled on chairs or resting at skewed angles on shelves. Dr. Robbins had never slept here.

An unassuming desk abutted the far wall. Beside it was a file cabinet. The middle of the room was taken up with a shiny, round rosewood table and four rosewood armchairs, each cushioned in a burgundy fabric. The table top was bare except for a box of tissues. How many did they go through in a week? A framed needlepoint on the wall said *Hope Is Where the Heart Is.* The wooden bookcase had books on the bottom shelves and small ornaments on the top—glass and china vases and porcelain figurines in kimonos. The gentle, deferential postures of the figurines enhanced the aura of repose.

I wasn't in repose. I checked out the desk but found nothing. I tried the top drawer of the file cabinet, which was labeled *Forms.* It had nothing except the same general crap that was in Leah's office. The middle drawer said *Reprints* and looked like it only had copies of articles. The bottom had no label. Was it empty? Contain running shoes and a collapsible umbrella?

No, the bottom drawer was filled with files arranged alphabetically. *Gabe, Andrea* was immediately behind the G tab. I pulled it out and flipped it open. The letter that had been copied and placed in Leah's file was here in all its maroon-embossed, St. Joseph's insignia glory. Behind was an envelope with some laboratory name in the return-address corner.

Chapter 74

I GOT A window seat on the west side of the bus, and within minutes of our leaving the station, the gray, behemoth Kingdome came into view. How long ago that seemed, at Fran and Debby's, watching on TV the cheering crowds pouring from the stadium exits, everybody in navy and white, in their caps and team shirts. *Ebullient*, Miss Z would have said. Ebullient and jubilant. One young woman had held up a hastily scrawled sign: *Marry me, Edgar.* Young men had mugged for the camera, making Vs with their fingers. The TV re-played Edgar's swing, Joey's and Junior's steps across home plate. I remembered our own cheering, the crowd at Debby and Fran's. Phil in a war dance. Jeanette leaning against the jamb.

Once we fell into a highway rhythm, the words on the labora-tory form did their own replay: *Patient tested positive for Huntington's Disease. Patient tested positive for Huntington's Disease. Patient tested positive.* My eyes had shot all over the page, to the top where my name and social security number were printed, to the *repeated CAG sequences well above the normal range* near the bottom. And the middle again. *Patient tested positive.*

The bus rolled through industrial areas and at Tukwila took the S-curve, which was wider than the S-curve along Lake Shore Drive. We exited at SeaTac and picked up folks at the airport. Jeanette and

Phil would be arriving Sunday afternoon; her car must be parked somewhere nearby. The elderly lady taking the adjacent seat smiled a little *how-do-you-do*. I tried returning it, my brain recycling endlessly, like a gene sequence run amok: patient tested positive, patient tested positive.

Back on the highway, trucks, cars, vans barreled past, keen on their destinations. The town names—Highline, Federal Way, Auburn—were just so many words; I hadn't been here long enough to endow them with memories. Was the town of Milton named for the poet? Willie had told me about some scenic spot on Mt. Rainier called Paradise.

You were worried I would do something rash, Dr. Robbins. But I'm not. My plan is as methodical and orderly as your protocols. Not an impulsive bone in this diseased body.

Would you have me make *my* problem *her* problem? How can you or God or Jiminy Cricket honestly claim that they deserve another long, drawn-out losing battle with death? Maybe there's a heavenly reason, but there's no earthly reason. No earthly reason why they should spend the next five or ten years watching me rot till I'm put in an institution. Not when so much of Phil's childhood has already been plowed over by a sickbed.

Skip the martyrdom sermon, guys. A martyr sacrifices her own happiness for others' happiness. What happiness am I sacrificing? Watching my own decay and watching Jeanette watch too?

But people with terminal diseases shouldn't feel they're a burden. Roger didn't commit suicide. I'm not speaking for other people, Jiminy—this is my *own* yardstick. Besides, I'm not in the same boat. These other people have family and friends already on board, kith and kin they have known and voyaged with for decades. With us, it's different. I haven't embarked yet. I'm barely on the gangplank. Suitcase in hand, I've got one foot poised in the air, one hand reaching for the banister, but my weight is still on shore. Yes, the two passengers on deck will be disappointed if I don't continue up; they want me to accompany them. But we haven't known each other a full year.

Strip malls and army barracks and woods glided past. We went down to the Nisqually Delta and up again, exiting in Olympia. It was actually a relief to have driving to concentrate on.

Traffic was lighter than on the trip back from the Gay Pride Parade. How upbeat we had been at the prospect of Fran and Debby calling. They would help in any way they could. She should straddle both worlds so when the time came she would have community in each. In five years. She would be ready in five years.

Now the epiphany stretch, the broad-trunked, leafy tree, its branches offering wide embrace. Where I had vowed to cherish each day as a precious gift. Seemed like a good idea at the time.

The red light on my phone machine was blinking. *You have two new messages.* "Hi, it's me, Jeanette. Nothing important. Wanted to see how the week's going, whether anyone called in sick and you're stuck working triple shifts." *End of message. Next message.* "It's Debby. I'll be bringing back the final version of your will. Let's arrange a time for you to come over and sign it." *End of message.*

It was too late East Coast time to call Jeanette back. I called Debby, and we picked noon on Saturday for me to go over and sign the thing.

James and James wanted to know if I'd seen the last game. "No, but I read about it in the paper."

"Bah," James said, turning his coffee cup right side up. "You can't see a double play in the paper. Ham and Swiss on Kaiser."

James turned his cup over too. "Denver, two bacon. Bases loaded, one out. He hardly touches the ball. Not a real catch, more a handoff, like the relays. Spec*ta*cular."

When lunch should have been winding down, cyclists training for some long-distance ride swarmed in. I hoped they were done for the day, since they were ordering burger baskets with fries. I paused to marvel at Willie flipping easily ten patties in quick succession. After the last, he looked up and smiled. Had I ever seen the Charlie Chaplin movie with the assembly line, he asked.

"*Modern Times*? Yeah. Didn't know you were a Chaplin fan."

He stepped away from the fan whirr. "Only other I saw was the blizzard, where he cooks and eats his boot."

"Is that what inspired you to become a cook?"

"No. I had to learn at home because my mom put too much salt on everything. Put salt on her salt."

The better of the new waitresses said she would be happy to sub for me Monday and Tuesday. I took home several empty cartons and dumped them in the living room and went out to make extra sets of keys and get packing supplies, paper, envelopes, and more cartons.

Fran ushered me through to the dining room. The will was on the table, and I read through it and signed where I was supposed to. As I was leaving, I asked if they were going to be around Sunday, and they said yes.

I poked the doormat with my sneaker. "I might buy a chair I saw at a yard sale. It's bulky, so if I do, I'll need help unloading it and getting it up the stairs."

"Just give a buzz," Fran said.

E. Adrian Dzahn

"Which reminds me." I reached in my pocket and took out one of the extra sets of keys. "I want to leave you these in case I ever lock myself out of my apartment."

On the way home, I stopped at a store selling used camping goods and bought an old sleeping bag and tarp. Back in the apartment, I phoned Orlando. An older woman answered and said she'd get Jeanette.

"You didn't need to call; we'll be home tomorrow." She sounded upbeat. "I was just wondering if the diner was a madhouse, if people were calling in sick."

"Nope. How's it going?"

"Fine. Phil and my dad have been playing checkers morning, noon, and night. And talking baseball."

"Gone to Disney, SeaWorld? Seen any iguanas?"

"It's orcas now. Mom bought him a wooden one with an enormous jaw and all those teeth."

"Cool."

"How have you been? You sound tired."

"I do?"

"Is something wrong?"

"Nope." I tried clearing my throat. "Just keeping an eye on the chili cooking."

"I should let you go, since you're paying for the call."

"Okay."

"See you Monday!"

"Yep."

By late afternoon, I'd packed most of my clothes, sheets, towels, dishware, glasses, and silverware. The remainder of the kitchen stuff didn't take long. Wanda would have gone nuts with my limited inventory of spices—she needed curries and chili and coriander and cardamom and cumin and cloves and a bunch of other Cs, not to mention marjoram, mace, mustard, parsley, sage, rosemary and thyme. I got by with nine, and that included salt and pepper. For whatever reason, I didn't put on the TV or radio while I worked.

"Hi, it's me, Andy. ... I took another look at the chair and decided to buy it. The thing is: it will probably take all three of us to get it up the stairs. The two guys selling it will help me haul it to the car and get it in the trunk. Could you and Debby come by around eleven tomorrow morning? ... Bring the keys I gave you, in case it takes us longer than I think to load it; that way you can wait in the comfort—relatively speaking—of my apartment. ... Thanks, thanks a ton." And forgive me my trespasses.

By the time Sol had hunkered down in Orlando, Chicago, and Geserenie, most of my personal possessions were hunkered down in ten cardboard cartons stacked against the wall. Some people might've accused me of living sparely, Spartanly, but it struck me how much simpler animals had it, just wandering off into the brush. Our ape and chimp cousins didn't pack up pallets of possessions. Nor did our Australopithecine aunts and uncles—each new sun-up they scouted out that day's food and that night's lodging. No need to amass and store. Even the early hunting societies got by with only those spears, clubs, and arrows they could carry—*they* knew how to live one day at a time. Supposedly Homo sapiens was a higher life form. Definitely higher maintenance.

I took the tarp and sleeping bag down to the car. The moment I stepped inside the apartment, the phone rang. The hospital? We're so sorry you missed the appointment with Leah, but it turns out for the best. St. Joseph's called Friday; they made a terrible mistake. The lab report they sent was incorrect.

I didn't answer but waited for the machine to do its thing. At first the voice wasn't familiar, but by the time she called me an "evasive, elusive eel," I knew who it was. "We're still in the UK but return in June." She listed the best times to reach her. "It's great hearing your voice, even on a machine."

Ditto, Stace, ditto.

I set three envelopes in the far left corner of the table. In the center, a pen. On the right, a stack of blank paper. The first drafts wouldn't necessarily come out the way I wanted.

To whom it may concern. This letter explained where to find my body. So as not to get some poor wandering hobo in trouble, I spelled out that I had *committed suicide because of bad medical news.* The phrase "taken my own life" didn't seem right—I wasn't taking anything; I was giving up, dispersing, dispelling whatever that elusive eel was. I included Fran's name, address, and phone number, saying she could identify the body, and added that her roommate was my lawyer and had my will and that they both might be at my apartment.

I put the letter into an envelope and wrote across the front *Attention: Law Enforcement: Please Open Immediately.* I inserted the envelope in a clear plastic bag and left it on the chair with my jacket.

The second letter was to Fran and Debby, explaining everything and apologizing for ensnaring them in the dirty work. I hoped they would understand, and not only was I sorry for what I was dumping on them, but it was a lousy exchange for the pleasure of their friendship. *Jeanette and Phil land at SeaTac around 3:00 p.m. They won't know any of this till they get home.*

This letter would remain here on the kitchen table. I wrote *Fran and Debby* in large letters on the envelope and also enclosed the lab report.

Before beginning on the heart of the third letter, I drafted an addendum with Aunt Lorraine and Uncle Anthony's address and phone number, Stacy and Jerry's UK info, and a bunch of details about my bank account, the lease, and utilities.

Jeanette:

You might already know when you read this, but in case things don't go according to plan, I need to warn you that what you read next isn't going to be pretty. Steel yourself for some very bad news. I found out I'm dying. So I'm taking a shortcut. Before you return from Florida, I'll have committed suicide. The cops and Fran and Debby should know before you do, but there's a chance they won't. I'm leaving them an explanation at my apartment.

I spent a couple of paragraphs describing the slow deterioration of Huntington's.

I agree with you that everyone deserves being cared for, but I can't go that route. For too many years I lived off the charity of good Samaritans at shelters, food banks, hospitals, halfway houses, other places when I had no right to, when I was young and healthy. So I've forfeited my right to be at the receiving end of more charity.

The next umpteen paragraphs were a breeze to write: I told her what she meant to me. Praise would ring in her ears. Then I said she should give a special good-bye to Willie, the two Jameses, and anybody else she thought might want one.

The final paragraph was hard. I didn't want Phil to believe that he too played a role; kids snarfed up guilt faster than Mr. Wiffle snarfed up slop. So I just wrote that she should tell him what a wonderful young man he was, he'd given me a ton of happiness the past year, if I'd had kids of my own I would have wanted them to be just like him, and he had better keep rooting for the Mariners.

Instead of signing the bottom, I grabbed my jacket and went for a walk.

It was dark but not too cold, and flower fragrances hung in the air. Streetlights flung shadows across sidewalks and yards. A porch light glazed a plant pot tangerine, changing it to peach as I went by. In some homes, lamps glowed behind drawn curtains. In others, you could see a lit television screen or people gathered around a table.

Bardey's park smelled of just-mown grass. Jeanette liked the roses that grew near the playground, roses that could startle you with petals in mid-October.

All these years I had thought nothing could be worse than dying alone and unloved. Dying loved was a whole lot worse. At least their grief would be fleeting. If I'd been granted a final wish, it was this: the certainty that Jeanette and Phil would rebound. My death sentence wasn't theirs.

You had no such comfort, did you, Dean? You didn't know if the disease devastating your mother might devastate you and then me. A wracking of body and soul not left to your imagination. Not muted by words in a pamphlet. You'd seen it up close. Seen it in somebody you loved. Could you have borne the fear better, more nobly, if you hadn't loved me?

I sat at the table and composed an additional paragraph to the letter to Jeanette, the new final paragraph. It went on a separate piece of paper so I could cross out and revise, get the language as close to perfect as time and wakefulness allowed. I copied the final version onto a fresh sheet, signed it, and folded and placed the letter and addendum in the third envelope. I wrote *Jeanette* across the front. This would be left with the extra keys on her dining room table early tomorrow morning. I went to bed with the final paragraph committed to memory more indelibly than patient tested positive.

Chapter 75

THE *OCEAN VIE* sign still marked the turnoff. The dirt road wound past the dilapidated shed, and I brought the car to a stop at the same log where Jeanette had parked. Not likely any van crammed with kids would show today; clouds smothered the sky. I placed the plastic-enclosed envelope, the one addressed to Law Enforcement, under a wiper. I removed the sleeping bag and tarp from the backseat.

I descended the switchback. Two rowboats lay inverted on the beach. The houses on the higher ground looked dark, but smoke came from one chimney. Good, somebody was around to notice the car. If they chanced to look out the window now, they'd take me for one of those crazy any-weather Nature lovers the Pacific Northwest spawned in abundance.

I followed the boulders past the jetty and around into the cove. I stepped along where the harbor seals had frolicked. I rested a moment where Jeanette had stood pointing to the gray whales. A few boulders more and I was on the crescent of sand. I deposited the tarp and sleeping bag near the cliff.

The water is a slate blue. Brown-tinged foam floods the pebbles, leaving behind twigs and seaweed. I remember Jeanette's marine animal guide, its chapter on caring for the young. The gafftopsail catfish father protects his offspring long after they've hatched, fearing the day they will have to voyage alone into strange, rough waters.

Questions come back, questions about what he was told, felt, maybe regretted. *Had* he left me a letter? Could it be among the items Edward had saved? A gull shrieks overhead. Dallying is not an option.

I unroll the tarp and place large stones at the corners. What more is there to do? Doubters don't have Last Rites. Tommy had been a true atheist, believing that the concept of death was so agonizing that the species had evolved to have spiritual experiences and believe in an afterlife. Something to keep us keeping on each time we stumbled and fell into some foxhole. Was he right?

I lay out the sleeping bag. I empty my pockets of the keys, wallet, doughnut, soda, Roger's painkillers—both the pills and the liquid version. Stacy seems present somehow, the old Stace. Is she floating in the clouds to ask whether I would have chosen this life? A gust of wind lifts up one flap of the tarp. I push the rock farther towards the corner. A wave breaks, and water nears the base of the crescent, darkening the pebbles just yards away. It recedes, returns, and now taps lightly, like a child hesitant to wake its mother.

I sit on the bottom half of the sleeping bag and pull the quilted top over my lap. I pop open the can. I eat part of the doughnut and wash it down with soda. I open the container with the pills and pour them into my palm. I swallow a bunch. My stomach is accepting. I recite to myself the final paragraph of my letter.

There is one more fact about heredity you need to appreciate. You've seen in me a love of life, what you call my "happy-go-lucky side." It too had a parentage. I inherited it, as surely as I inherited the Huntington's, and it too came from Dean. It came from my Dad. Whenever you remember it, he'll live, my Dad will live.

The remaining pills wash down easily, and I drink the liquid version. I lie on my side facing west, my head resting on my arm. The horizon is not a line but a blur where sky melts into sea. Gently I welcome the tide.

>⟡ ⟡<

Acknowledgments

I AM INDEBTED first and foremost to Ruth Pettis for her detailed and insightful critique of the manuscript. I am also indebted to Nancy J. Jones for her eminently helpful comments. I thank: Robin McQuinn for advice in many forms; Don McQuinn and Ilana McQuinn Miller for editorial advice; and Caitlin McQuinn for helping to untangle the tangled skein of self-publishing. I am indebted to Frances Woods for editorial assistance and to Steve Leiner for information about medical issues, information I may have misused or misconstrued through no fault of his. Last but hardly least, I thank my spouse, Dave, for his unflagging patience and support.

Made in the USA
San Bernardino, CA
15 October 2017